PENGUIN

T0200832

THE FEMALE

CHARLOTTE LENNOX (c. 1729–1804) was probably born in Gibraltar, where her father, James Ramsay, a captain-lieutenant in the 14th Foot Regiment, was posted at the time. In 1739 the Ramsay family moved to New York province; shortly after her father's death in 1742, Charlotte returned to England. Although she spent only a few years in America, she is sometimes called 'the first American novelist' in recognition of the American settings of her first novel *The Life of Harriot Stuart* (1750) and her last *Euphemia* (1790). She began her literary career as a poet, publishing her *Poems on Several Occasions* in 1747. Her most successful publication was her second novel, *The Female Quixote* (1752). Her influential patrons Samuel Johnson and Samuel Richardson both gave advice on the novel, and their continuing patronage underlined Lennox's literary respectability in an era which regarded women novelists with some suspicion. *The Female Quixote* received positive reviews from Johnson and Henry Fielding. It influenced a number of subsequent texts, most notably *Female Quixotism* by Tabitha Tenney (1801).

Lennox confirmed her status as a professional writer by working in a range of genres. She wrote three plays: *Philander: A Dramatic Pastoral* (1757), *The Sister* (1769) and *Old City Manners* (1775), and she worked with Johnson and John Boyle to produce *Shakespear Illustrated* (published in 1753). Her third novel, *Henrietta*, appeared in 1758. Between 1755 and 1775 most of her literary work was translation. In addition, she edited and wrote for the *Lady's Museum* (1760–61), which included her translations and serial publication of one of her novels. In her last years, she depended on financial assistance from the Royal Literary Fund and died in penury in Westminster on 4 January 1804.

AMANDA GILROY is Lecturer in the departments of English and American Studies at the University of Groningen, and was Visiting Associate Professor in the Department of English at Brown University, RI (2001–2; 2002–3). She has edited *Epistolary Histories: Letters, Fiction, Culture* (with Wil Verhoeven; 1999); *Joanna Baillie: Selected Plays and Poems* (with Keith Hanley; 2002);

Romantic Geographies: Discourses of Travel, 1775–1844 (2000); and Jane West's *A Tale of the Times* (2005).

WIL VERHOEVEN is Professor of American culture and cultural theory at the University of Groningen. In 2002–3 he held the Charles H. Watts chair in the history of the book and historical bibliography at Brown University, RI. He has edited *Epistolary Histories: Letters, Fiction, Culture* (with Amanda Gilroy; 1999); and *Revolutionary Histories: Transatlantic Cultural Nationalism, 1775–1815* (2000). He has also published modern editions of Gilbert Imlay's *The Emigrants* (with Amanda Gilroy; 1998) and George Walker's *The Vagabond* (2004), and is General Editor of the 10-volume series *Anti-Jacobin Novels* (2005).

CHARLOTTE LENNOX

The Female Quixote

Edited with Notes by AMANDA GILROY *and* WIL VERHOEVEN
with an Introduction by AMANDA GILROY

PENGUIN BOOKS

PENGUIN BOOKS

Published by the Penguin Group
Penguin Books Ltd, 80 Strand, London WC2R ORL, England
Penguin Group (USA) Inc., 375 Hudson Street, New York, New York 10014, USA
Penguin Group (Canada), 90 Eglinton Avenue East, Suite 700, Toronto, Ontario, Canada M4P 2Y3
(a division of Pearson Penguin Canada Inc.)
Penguin Ireland, 25 St Stephen's Green, Dublin 2, Ireland (a division of Penguin Books Ltd)
Penguin Group (Australia), 250 Camberwell Road, Camberwell, Victoria 3124, Australia
(a division of Pearson Australia Group Pty Ltd)
Penguin Books India Pvt Ltd, 11 Community Centre, Panchsheel Park, New Delhi – 110 017, India
Penguin Group (NZ), cnr Airborne and Rosedale Roads, Albany, Auckland 1310, New Zealand
(a division of Pearson New Zealand Ltd)
Penguin Books (South Africa) (Pty) Ltd, 24 Sturdee Avenue, Rosebank, Johannesburg 2196, South Africa

Penguin Books Ltd, Registered Offices: 80 Strand, London WC2R ORL, England

www.penguin.com

The Female Quixote first published 1752
Published in Penguin Classics 2006

014

Editorial material © Amanda Gilroy and Wil Verhoeven, 2006
All rights reserved

The moral right of the editors has been asserted

Set in 10.25/12.25 pt PostScript Adobe Sabon
Typeset by Rowland Phototypesetting Ltd, Bury St Edmunds, Suffolk
Printed and bound in Great Britain by Clays Ltd, Elcograf S.p.A.

ISBN-13: 978-0-140-43987-8

www.greenpenguin.co.uk

Contents

Contents

Chronology

1727 Charlotte Lennox's father, James Ramsay, captain-
lieutenant of Clayton's Regiment (14th Foot), posted with
his regiment to Gibraltar.

1729 James Ramsay transfers to the Coldstream Guards.

c. 1729 Birth of Charlotte Lennox, probably in Gibraltar.

1739 Family moves to New York province after James Ramsay
appointed Captain of an Independent Company of Foot.

1742 Death of James Ramsay.

1742–6 Charlotte returns to England, writes poetry and obtains
aristocratic patrons (Lady Cecilia Isabella Finch and the
Countess of Rockingham).

1747 Marries Alexander Lennox in London, where she lives
for the rest of her life. *Poems on Several Occasions. Written
by a Young Lady.*

1748–50 Works as an actress; becomes friends with Samuel
Johnson.

1750 *The Life of Harriot Stuart, Written by Herself* (novel),
2 vols.

1751 Translation work. Writes most of *The Female Quixote*.
Meets and is advised by Samuel Richardson.

1752 *13 March, The Female Quixote; or, The Adventures of
Arabella* published in 2 vols., having been advertised in the
Covent-Garden Journal nos. 18, 20, 22 and 24. Probably
translates Voltaire's *The Age of Louis XIV*. Begins work on
Shakespear Illustrated, in collaboration with Johnson and
the Earl of Orrery. Proposals for a new edition of her poems.

1753 *Shakespear Illustrated, or The Novels and Histories, on
which the Plays of Shakespear are founded, Collected and*

Translated from the Original Authors with Critical Remarks, Vols. I and II, dedication by Johnson. Vol. III published in 1754.

1755 *Memoirs of Maximilian de Bethune, Duke of Sully* (translation), 3 vols., dedication by Johnson.

1756 *The Memoirs of the Countess of Berci* (translation), 2 vols.

1757 *Memoirs for the History of Madame de Maintenon and of the Last Age* (translation), 5 vols; *Philander: A Dramatic Pastoral*, dedication by Johnson. David Garrick, manager of the Drury Lane Theatre, refuses to stage the play.

1758 *Henrietta* (novel), 2 vols.

1759–61 Illness, probably caused by overwork. Receives financial assistance from the Duchess of Newcastle. Assisted by Johnson, Orrery and others, translates *The Greek Theatre of Father Brumoy*, 3 vols (1760). Her periodical the *Lady's Museum* runs from March 1760 to February 1761, and includes serialization of a new novel, *The History of Harriot and Sophia*.

1762 *The History of Harriot and Sophia* republished separately as *Sophia* in 2 vols.

1765 Birth of her daughter Harriot Holles.

1766 Probably wrote the novel *The History of Eliza*.

1769 *The Sister* (a comedy based on *Henrietta*; one performance at Covent Garden on 18 February).

1771 Birth of her son George Louis.

c. **1773–4** Unsuccessful attempt to publish an illustrated edition of *The Female Quixote* by subscription.

1774 *Meditations and Penitential Prayers, written by the celebrated Dutchess De La Valliere, Mistress of Lewis the Fourteenth of France* (translation).

1775 Unsuccessful attempt to publish an edition of her collected works by subscription (proposals written by Johnson). *Old City Manners* (a comedy adapted from *Eastward Hoe* by Jonson, Chapman and Marston; several performances at Drury Lane).

c. **1783–4** Death of Harriot Holles. George Louis gains a literary reputation after the periodical publication of poems and prose fiction.

1790 *Euphemia* (novel), 4 vols.

1792 Begins to receive financial assistance from the Royal Literary Fund, which continues until her death. Separates from Alexander Lennox at some point prior to this date.

1793 George Louis forced to leave England; emigrates to America.

1793–7 Further unsuccessful attempts to publish by subscription, including a revised edition of *Shakespear Illustrated*.

1797 *The History of Sir George Warrington; or, The Political Quixote*, by the Purbeck sisters, erroneously ascribed to Lennox in the first edition.

1804 4 January dies penniless in Dean's Yard, Westminster.

Introduction

On its publication in 1752, Charlotte Lennox's *The Female Quixote* was immediately in vogue, and its heroine, Arabella, captivated the imagination of the novel's first readers. One of the leading 'Bluestockings' of the age, the poet Elizabeth Carter,[1] who must have had a copy of *The Female Quixote* hot off the press, wrote to Catherine Talbot: 'I have been reading a book which promises some laughing amusement, "The Female Quixote"; the few chapters I read to my mother last night while we were undressing were whimsical enough and not at all low.' Writing later to the same correspondent, she claims that 'Arabella, as a little book, is highly diverting, and much in fashion'. Another Bluestocking, Mary Delany, wrote to one of her friends: 'We have begun the Female Quixote. I like the design, and am glad to get into good company again.'[2] The author Samuel Richardson, writing to one of his regular female correspondents, observed: 'The Female Quixote is written by a woman, a favourite of the author of the *Rambler* [Samuel Johnson] . . . Do you not think, however her heroine overacts her part, that Arabella is amiable and innocent?'[3] This heroine quickly became part of eighteenth-century cultural vocabulary, as a letter from poet and artist Susanna Highmore to Bluestocking poet and essayist Hester Mulso Chapone suggests: 'I had some very odd adventures since I saw you, not unworthy of a Lady Arabella, which happily I may relate, when we have the pleasure of meeting again, when in return, I shall, questionless, claim your history.'[4]

These comments illustrate something of the novel's cultural success in 1752–3; they also share an uncanny emphasis on performance and fashion, themes that are connected with ideas about female authorship and readership. In the case of Highmore, we find a woman reader performing *as* Arabella, imitating her style for her female correspondent – Arabella is always demanding the 'history' of women she encounters, and 'questionless' is something of a linguistic fashion statement for her – but in doing so the writer also asserts her interest in and identification with other women, both within the novel itself and beyond its pages. Though the novel was later reprinted in Anna Barbauld's heterodox collection *The British Novelists* (1810) – the only novel written by a woman of the seven pre-1755 novels that Barbauld includes – *The Female Quixote* disappeared from subsequent similar collections, such as Sir Walter Scott's *Ballantyne's Novelist's Library* (1821–4), and from canonical twentieth-century histories of the novel, notably Ian Watt's *The Rise of the Novel* (1957). It has only in the last two decades been accorded a significant place in the history of the rise of the novel. Revisionist readings of this history have focused especially on issues of gender, that is, the role of women writers and readers in the rise of the novel, and relatedly, on the realist novel's efforts to distinguish itself from other types of writing such as the romance. In what follows, *The Female Quixote*'s place in the life and career of Charlotte Lennox is explored, as well as its complex status within the history of the novel genre. Just as Arabella's earliest readers write about her as though she were a familiar friend and absorb her into their lives, so does the novel itself engage with contemporary debates about realism and romance, history and scandal, absorbing, though not necessarily resolving, conflicting narratives into its plot, characterization and the texture of its prose. Arabella's persistent identification with other women means that we never lose sight of the way gender is intimately related to the novel's formal, commercial and ethical concerns.

Charlotte Lennox's history

Any account of the novel in these terms needs to begin with the history of its author. Charlotte Ramsay was born around 1729, probably in Gibraltar. There has been much debate about her exact date of birth, but there seems no reason not to accept Samuel Richardson's claim that in 1753 Lennox was 'hardly twenty-four'.[5] Between 1738 and 1742, she lived in Albany, New York, where her father was stationed as Captain of an Independent Company of Foot (when she arrived in England she would 'promote' him to the rank of colonel, and claim he was the Governor of New York, perhaps in an attempt to increase her chances of success in London society and, later in life, her chances of receiving financial aid from the Royal Literary Fund). She travelled to England shortly after her father's death in 1742. There is no contemporary biographical information about her mother, nor about the existence of any siblings.[6] Although she spent only a few years in America, she is sometimes called 'the first American novelist' in recognition of the American settings of her first and last novels, *The Life of Harriot Stuart* (1750) and *Euphemia* (1790).[7] In England she found two aristocratic female patrons, Lady Isabella Finch and the Countess of Rockingham, but she was disappointed in the favours she hoped to receive from them.

In 1747, Charlotte Ramsay married Alexander Lennox, a shiftless Scot who worked for the London printer William Strahan. Their apparently unhappy marriage was fraught with financial problems and disagreements about the upbringing of their children, a daughter, Harriot Holles, born in 1765, and a son, George Louis, in 1771. Charlotte received financial assistance from the Duchess of Newcastle in 1760 during a period of illness probably caused by overwork. When she recovered, she worked for a time as a governess. In the later 1760s, she lived in Somerset House, which had the reputation of being a sort of aristocratic almshouse.[8] From 1773 to 1782, Alexander Lennox worked for the Customs service and the family enjoyed, probably for the first time, the stability of a regular income. Their daughter died around 1783–4 and the Lennoxes probably separated some time in the early 1790s. For a period in 1793, Charlotte Lennox lived with Frances Reynolds, sister of Sir Joshua Reynolds, perhaps as a housekeeper and certainly in conditions of financial hardship, being obliged to support herself and her son on an income of £40 per year (this sum places Lennox on the very margins of gentility and would necessitate an extremely frugal lifestyle).[9] In the last decade of her life, she made a number of appeals to the Royal Literary Fund for financial aid, and the Fund subsidized her regularly, including 13 guineas in 1793 which enabled Lennox to send her son to America in order to extricate him from some unspecified 'dreadful circumstances' in which he was embroiled.[10] She died in penury in Westminster on 4 January 1804.[11]

Charlotte Lennox began her literary career as a poet, publishing her *Poems on Several Occasions. Written by a Young Lady* in November 1747, the month after her marriage to Alexander Lennox. This volume included what became her best-known poem, 'The Art of Coquetry', which was subsequently republished in the *Gentleman's Magazine* (1750). The poem advises young women to practise feminine 'wiles' in order to enslave men to 'their empire', it reminds them that women's 'wit' must consolidate what their beauty initially gains, and that female 'liberty' depends upon them not falling in love themselves. The poems embrace the tradition of the erotic writing associated with the seductive 'Astrea' (poet, playwright and novelist Aphra Behn, 1640–89) rather than the modest subjects of the chaste 'Orinda' (Welsh poet and dramatist Katherine Philips, 1632–64). Because women writers continued to be judged by the morality of their subjects, Lennox's reputation was tainted by her perceived allegiance to 'Astrea'. The *Gentleman's Magazine* printed a number of adulatory, and ardent, poetic responses, which praised her 'melting lays' and claimed her as the 'British Sappho'. However, women writers, who would later succumb to the charms of *The Female Quixote*, took a moral stance against Lennox's early poems, being 'scandalized' at a group reading of 'The Art of Coquetry' and preferring 'an edifying essay proper to be put into the hands of the Muses'.[12] Attempts to republish *Poems* by subscription[13] two years after the first edition were unsuccessful.

Lennox's first novel, *The Life of Harriot Stuart, Written by Herself*, was published in December 1750, and the reception of this novel, as well as her *Poems*, provides a useful context for reading *The Female Quixote* itself. Harriot Stuart is a young orphaned aristocratic girl who travels from America to England in search of a rich aunt, but finds herself unprotected in London. She is an inveterate coquette – claiming her first conquest at the age of eleven – and a poet whose works (which include some of Lennox's own previously published poems) earn her the title 'Sappho'. Various members of the aristocracy promise her patronage but then abandon her. She goes on to experience some sensational adventures, including an episode of Indian captivity, a drama at sea during which she stabs a villainous English captain who attempts to rape her, and a kidnapping, after which she is incarcerated in a French convent. She finally marries the man she loves, with a former suitor selflessly assisting at the ceremony.

The novel received mixed reviews. The *Gentleman's Magazine* declared it was 'penn'd with the purity of a *Clarissa*', while aristocratic readers like Lady Mary Wortley Montagu were hostile to Lennox's lightly disguised attack on her former patron Lady Isabella Finch, who appears as the despicable Lady Cecelia.[14] The *Magazine of Magazines* somewhat eccentrically classed the novel along with John Cleland's pornographic *Fanny Hill* (1748–9) as a book likely to debauch young men.[15] The *Monthly Review* recognized it as the graceful 'produce of a female pen' but thought it was not likely to 'improve the morals of the reader'.[16] Lennox seems to have allowed people to believe that the novel was autobiographical, but this attempt to add some glamour to her history gave substance to speculations about her own sexual reputation.

As a woman writer in the mid eighteenth century, Lennox's success was crucially dependent on her literary and aristocratic patrons. Samuel Johnson reputedly celebrated the publication of *Harriot Stuart* with an all-night party at a tavern, complete with an apple pie stuck with bay leaves and a laurel crown

for Lennox. He introduced Lennox to the men who would
subsequently publish her work, such as John Payne and Andrew
Millar, or collaborate with her, like John Boyle, Earl of Cork
and of Orrery. He reviewed many of her works favourably,
persuaded Edward Cave to promote her work in the *Gentleman's Magazine* throughout the 1750s and wrote a number of
the dedications to her literary efforts. Johnson also introduced
Lennox to Samuel Richardson, who offered criticism on her
second novel, *The Female Quixote* (1752), helped her find a
publisher for it, printed the first edition, may have printed
her third novel *Henrietta* (1758) and recommended her to the
publisher Roger Dodsley for translation work. Lennox's friendships with Johnson and Richardson helped her to maintain a
reputation as a respectable literary figure but she sometimes
had to accept the conservative advice of her more famous
mentors over her own literary wishes.

Lennox's most successful work, *The Female Quixote*, was
published by Millar in March 1752, with a dedication to the
Earl of Middlesex written by Johnson. Both Johnson and
Richardson had given advice on the novel, and their input is
discussed in more detail below. Positive reviews from Johnson
in the *Gentleman's Magazine* and Henry Fielding in the *Covent-
Garden Journal* promoted *The Female Quixote* as it entered
the literary marketplace. A second edition, corrected by the
author, appeared in July 1752, and editions appeared in Dublin
in 1752 and 1753. In 1783 it was reproduced in the *Novelist's
Magazine* and in 1810 in Barbauld's *British Novelists*, which
was reprinted in 1820. It was translated into German in 1754,
Dutch in 1762, French in 1773 and Spanish in 1808. Although
Lennox's name did not appear on the title page of the novel
until 1783, her authorship was generally known, and as noted
above, the characters, style and vocabulary of the novel
captured the imagination of the reading public.

After the success of *The Female Quixote*, Lennox continued
writing novels, but she also turned her hand to a number of
different genres in order to establish herself as a professional
writer. She wrote three plays with some success: *Philander: A
Dramatic Pastoral* (1757), *The Sister* (1769) and *Old City*

Manners (1775), and she worked with Samuel Johnson and John Boyle to produce *Shakespear Illustrated*, published in 1753–4, in which she claims that the Bard sometimes 'mangled and defaced' his source material, as well as criticizing his representation of women. Between 1755 and 1775, the bulk of her literary work was translation from French, which she seems to have learnt as a child, and Italian, which she acquired for the purposes of translation. Much of this was hack work, and Lennox had no qualms about recycling her work under different titles or using contributions from other writers. She certainly wrote as much out of economic necessity as from any sense of vocation, and we should remember that during this time her husband's income was erratic, and that she had two young children to support. Her translations also kept Lennox's name in the public eye and helped to foster her reputation for literary gentility. However, even her historical translations provoked her admirers to produce semi-voyeuristic poems about her; thus, an anonymous writer, 'who happened to see her riding on horse back in Windsor Forest in the dress of a country Girl', sent Lennox a poem in which she appears as the 'coy' Clio (the muse of history) disguised in an alluring 'rustic gown'.[17] Lennox also edited and provided much of the material for the magazine the *Lady's Museum* (1760–61), which included her translations and serial publication of one of her novels. The magazine also featured poems as well as essays on history, geography and philosophy for ladies, with topics ranging from the vestal virgins of Rome to the natural history of butterflies, but it had to compete against many similar publications and was discontinued after eleven issues.

What emerges from this brief history of Charlotte Lennox's life and literary career is a picture of a successful woman writer, savvy about the marketplace, 'networking' with skill and genre-crossing with panache. In Richard Samuel's engraving of 1778 (the basis for a painting exhibited in 1779), she appears as one of 'The Nine Living Muses of Great Britain', along with the likes of Anna Barbauld, Angelica Kauffman, Hannah More and Catherine Macaulay.

Romancing the novel: the literary context

The Female Quixote, subtitled 'The Adventures of Arabella', focuses on a young heiress whose sheltered life, remote from mainstream society, is dominated by her reading of seventeenth-century French romances. Arabella's ideas and behaviour are modelled on the heroines she encounters in these romances. Like the deluded hero of Miguel de Cervantes' novel *Don Quixote* (1605/1615) she makes all sorts of mistakes in her reading of the world. In the course of the novel, Arabella supposes a young gardener to be a disguised nobleman with designs upon her when his real object is to steal fish from the estate; she suspects her uncle, the father of her long-suffering suitor Glanville, of an incestuous passion for her; she rushes to rescue a cross-dressed prostitute from her rowdy companions in Vauxhall Gardens, imagining her to be a disguised noblewoman about to be 'ravished'. Finally, after she suffers a severe illness as a result of jumping into a river to escape imaginary pursuers, a clergyman 'cures' Arabella of her dependence on romances, and she marries the faithful suitor who has been waiting for her to come to her senses.

A simple summary would seem to suggest that Lennox's primary concern was to adapt Cervantes' ridicule of chivalric romances, substituting heroic romances and exposing their dangers for female readers. But such a reading fails to do justice to Lennox's self-conscious engagement with the controversies about fiction that took place in mid-eighteenth-century England (as well as oversimplifying Cervantes' great novel). In order to understand the significance of Lennox's representation of her heroine, of women writers (including herself) and of other female figures, we need first to understand something of this literary and cultural context. In particular, we first need to ask, why is 'Lady *Bella's* Foible' (I.VI)[18] her indulgence in French romances? These books of the early to mid seventeenth century, such as Madeleine de Scudéry's *Artamène, ou le grand Cyrus* (1649–53) and *Clélie, histoire romaine* (1654–60), had been translated into English, like those in Arabella's collection, during the second half of the seventeenth century. Arabella's representation of these romances is quite accurate: in them, 'Love was the ruling Principle of the World' (I.I), and the heroes spend years performing heroic deeds to gain the favour of imperious heroines; they were also extremely long, multi-volume products – thus Glanville is understandably dismayed when Arabella's servant returns from the library, 'sinking under the Weight' of only four 'voluminous Romances' (I.XII). However, as even Lennox's earliest critics pointed out, while such romances were read in the eighteenth century, they were not fashionable by 1752.[19] Indeed, even parodies of the French romances were already historically quite distant – de Subligny's *La Fausse Clélie* (1670) was translated into English in 1678 with the running title 'Mock-*Clelia*, or Madam *Quixote*'. Henry Fielding's review of Lennox's novel argued that 'the Humour of Romance, which is principally ridiculed in this Work, be not at present greatly in fashion in this Kingdom'.[20] Clara Reeve, in 1785, claimed that

> the Satire of the *Female Quixote* seems in great measure to have lost its aim, because at the time it first appeared, the taste for those Romances was extinct, and the books exploded ... [T]his book came some thirty or fourty years too late ... Romances at this time were quite out of fashion, and the press groaned under the weight of Novels, which sprung up like Mushrooms every year.[21]

It is worth noting that the romances Arabella reads are a legacy from her dead mother, who 'had purchased these Books to soften a Solitude which she found very disagreeable' (I.I), and, of course, such romances were and are traditionally associated with women writers and readers. So, from the beginning, Arabella identifies with a female tradition, but one which is apparently disavowed through parody.

For all the emphasis on romance, the 'naughty novels' of Aphra Behn, Delarivièr Manley and the early work of Eliza Haywood were more immediate for many readers,[22] as were the memoirs of writers like Laetitia Pilkington and Constantia Philips, whose amorous autobiographies scandalized, and fascinated, readers in the 1740s. Lennox was already identified with Behn's poetry, and like Manley she seems to have exploited the reading public's tendency to view women's texts as autobiographical, including in *Harriot Stuart* material from her own life. Bestsellers in the amorous intrigue tradition include: Behn's *Love Letters between a Nobleman and his Sister* (1684–7), Manley's *Secret Memoirs and Manners of several Persons of Quality of both Sexes. From the New Atalantis, an Island in the Mediterranean* (1709) and Haywood's *Love in Excess* (1719–20). To the early eighteenth-century reading public, such narratives appeared sexually immoral, exotic or foreign, imitating scandalous chronicles published in France, and they were either notoriously factual or spectacularly fantastic. Behn and Manley used sex as a cover for writing political allegories – *The New Atalantis*, for example, is Manley's criticism of the Whigs dominating the court of Queen Anne, and early eighteenth-century readers (like twenty-first century ones) displayed an insatiable interest in the sex lives of the rich and famous. Haywood turned the novels of amorous intrigue into formulaic fiction, that is, plot-driven fiction with simplified characters, standard motifs and didactic messages. Her fiction celebrates upper-class licentiousness, promotes heterosexuality and always ends by rewarding the good characters and punishing the bad. In the Dedication to *Lasselia* (1723), Haywood defended the characteristic erotic scenes of her novels by insisting that the explicit representation of vice functions as a practical warning to the unwary reader (though how the heroine's erotic dreams would fit within this pedagogic project is not clear). As William Warner points out, it was not only the sexy content, but 'the sheer quantity of Haywood's production in this period [1720s and 30s], and the unprecedented popularity it enjoys, which helps give the bad name to novels throughout the century'.[23] Unlike romances, scandalous fictions and memoirs are not mentioned by name in *The Female Quixote*, but as this Introduction will argue, this does not mean that they are absent, and they constitute the second significant literary context for Lennox's novel.

The third important context for reading *The Female Quixote* is the mid-century debate about fiction that polarized around Richardson's and Fielding's 'competing claims to generic novelty'.[24] Both men claimed to be the progenitors of 'a new species of writing'.[25] They shaped the terms by which their culture, as well as subsequent literary history, defined the genre of the novel. The 'new' novel 'exhibit[ed] life in its true state' (in Johnson's words),[26] and its realism was claimed to be morally improving. There were many differences between the work of Richardson and Fielding – Richardson's focus is on domestic life, serious plots and psychologically realistic and complex characters, while Fielding's novels feature typical characters, amusing incidents and plots which turn on surprise and coincidence (Fielding even burlesques the domestic morality of Richardson's *Pamela* in *Shamela* and *Joseph Andrews*). However, despite these differences and the instabilities surrounding definitions of the new genre, the new species of writing was taxonomically distinguished from the excesses of romance– romance was the negative example for the novel, everything that the realist, masculine, morally respectable English novel was not. Lennox acknowledges her debt to both Richardson and Fielding, and takes part in the literary controversy of her day.[27] Like *Joseph Andrews*, *The Female Quixote* makes clear its borrowing from Cervantes' novel, and like Fielding, Lennox has an ironic narrator and playful chapter titles that constantly remind us of the text's fictionality and materiality (for example, through comments on the 'shortness' of a particular chapter). *The Female Quixote* also contains many allusions to Richardson's novel *Clarissa*; in addition to the clergyman's explicit recommendation at the end of the novel, there are many parallels of plot and character. If Arabella does 'not remember to have read of any Heroine that voluntarily left her Father's House, however persecuted she might be' (I.IX), contemporary readers certainly would have caught the allusion to Clarissa's flight from paternal oppression into the hands of the rake Lovelace. In leaving her father's house, Clarissa does something more improbable than any romance heroine, while the romance-fixated Arabella is 'more irreproachable than even the eighteenth-century paragon of novelistic virtue'.[28]

Thus, Lennox mocks domestic realism as much as she mocks romances. Indeed, the narrator observes that in examining the heart of the heroine, she 'follow[s] the Custom of the Romance and Novel-Writers' (V.I), implicitly eliding the boundaries between the two forms. Even in Richardson's and Fielding's early attempts at generic clarification, novels and romances often seem interchangeable: in *Tom Jones*, Fielding dismisses both 'foolish Novels' and 'monstrous Romances' and he caricatures Eliza Haywood as 'Mrs Novel'.[29] Lennox draws on what must have been her own wide reading of romance for the novel's situations and language, and she borrows from the very sources that she is ostensibly criticizing. Despite the praise heaped on Arabella's *un*romantic discourse (Glanville 'was charmed to hear her talk so rationally', VII.VI), her sensible speeches often depend on her romance reading. The most extended of these is her observations on raillery, drawn from de Scudéry's *Artamenes*, and critic Margaret Dalziel has speculated that the original versions of Arabella's disquisitions on glory, indifference and suicide may be found in romances.[30] Within the novel itself, Sir George comments on the recycling of romance plots and characters in new novels, and it could certainly be argued that the decision of Arabella's father to live in a remote castle, far from the intrigues of political life, constitutes a movement from realism to romance (or, from real life to a fantasy of power that has similarities to Arabella's own empowering fantasies). Thus, *The Female Quixote* incorporates romance in a way that undercuts claims for the new realist genre's 'novelty' and cultural purity. The Spanish critic José Ortega y Gasset offers a useful way of thinking about this generic mingling (interestingly, his narrative theories devolved from his reading of *Don Quixote*); he writes that, although 'the realistic novel was born in opposition to the so-called novel of fantasy, it carries adventure enclosed within its body' and thus 'it is not only that [*Don*] *Quixote* was written against the books of chivalry, and as a result bears them within it, but that the novel as a literary genre consists essentially of such an absorption.'[31] It is worth noting that in his review of *The Female Quixote*, Fielding praises its *realism* (according to him, it was more probable that romances would have a subversive effect on a young woman than on an elderly gentleman).[32] As discussed below, Lennox plays with different levels of representation (drawn from romance, the realist novel, scandal and contemporary history) and offers her readers different perspectives from which to view Arabella's actions.

In spite of the satire against Arabella, and the romances with which she is identified, she is undoubtedly a heroine, whom we are meant to admire and with whom we are encouraged to empathize. If romantic heroines were unbelievably beautiful, then so is Arabella. Everyone who meets her is impressed by her looks; even her prosaic uncle Sir Charles is 'struck with an extreme Surprize at her Beauty' (II.III), while an unknown gentleman, whom she accosts during her flight from the gardener, is 'astonished' at her 'Beauty . . . Her Stature; her Shape, her inimitable Complexion; the Lustre of her fine Eyes, and the thousand Charms that adorned her whole Person' (II.XI). Arabella laments that her beauty, like that of her favourite romance heroines, 'has produced very deplorable Effects' (IV.IX); while she imagines such things as the death of her lovers and the disintegration of family ties, her 'Charms' do in fact have tangible effects. The unknown gentleman is, at least momentarily, deprived of speech, while the assembly at Bath, prepared to ridicule her, 'found themselves aw'd to Respect by that irresistable Charm in the Person of *Arabella*, which commanded Reverence and Love from all who beheld her'. The narrator continues, 'Her noble Air, the native Dignity in her Looks, the inexpressible Grace which accompany'd all her Motions, and the consummate Loveliness of her Form, drew the Admiration of the whole Assembly' (VII.VII). It is impossible to read Arabella purely as a mock-heroine, however much we are invited to laugh at her 'foible' of imagining herself as a romance heroine and constructing, or misreading, the world around her to suit this fantasy. She frequently comes off best in her forays into the fashionable world. At Bath, she unintentionally deceives the pedantic Mr Selvin, whose affectation of historical knowledge is demolished by Arabella's confident disquisition on ancient Greece derived from her reading of historical romances. When Mr Tinsel indulges in malicious gossip instead of recounting the type of histories that Arabella hoped would 'improve and delight me . . . excite my Admiration, engage my Esteem, or influence my Practice', she speaks out against the practice of satire in Johnsonian-inspired language (VII.VIII).[33]

While the text appears to mock the absurdity of romances, it also attempts to rescue or regenerate certain aspects of the genre, notably the ethical values of romance, which include not only romantic heroism but also the more down-to-earth and life-enhancing values of generosity, fidelity, compassion, disinterestedness and sympathy of imagination.[34] Arabella's combination of learning and sensibility is in marked contrast to the self-interest that motivates most of the characters in the novel. Arabella's frivolous and petty cousin Charlotte often serves as a foil that reveals Arabella's moral superiority. If Arabella uses the language of power and command shared by the romance heroine and the coquette (she 'commands' sick would-be lovers to get well and 'banishes' those who infringe upon her notions of propriety), it is Charlotte who displays the feminine wiles of the inveterate coquette. Charlotte spends a good deal of time perfecting her image, and practising her repertoire of smiles, blushes and sighs. She is dismayed at the negligence of Arabella's toilette, not least because it confirms her cousin's beauty as natural not contrived. Her relationship to Arabella, and other women, is competitive: she thinks that the attention Arabella receives, especially from Sir George, diminishes what is due to her; hoping that Arabella 'would be chagrined to see her [Charlotte] looking so well', she mistrusts Arabella's lavish compliments on her beauty, not thinking 'it possible, one Woman could praise another with any Sincerity' (II.IX). In the encounters between them, the reader is often first encouraged to find Arabella ridiculous but then prompted to revise this opinion as she displays her superior intelligence and generosity. For example, when Arabella maintains that Miss Groves's writing master was really a nobleman in disguise, Charlotte laughs: 'you may as well persuade me, the Moon is made of a Cream Cheese'. Arabella then launches into a pedantic discussion of 'the second glorious Luminary of the Heavens', taking literally

Charlotte's use of a traditional figure of speech. But we are soon taken aback by the astronomically challenged Charlotte who refuses to countenance 'such whimsical Notions' as that the 'same Moon, which don't appear broader than your Gardener's Face, is not much less than the whole World' (IV.I). Arabella changes the subject rather than continue to expose Charlotte's ignorance.

The two women have very different notions about female propriety, and again the target of the satire shifts from Arabella to Charlotte. Taking her romance heroines as models for her own behaviour, Arabella risks transgressing mid-eighteenth-century codes of conduct, as when, following the example of 'the fair *Amalazontha*' who condescended to visit a rejected lover who was 'dying for Love of her', she plans to visit the supposedly suicidal 'unhappy Bellmour' (Sir George) in his bedchamber and she defends her position against Charlotte's criticism of such social indiscretion. However, Charlotte's view of the world turns out to be more limited than Arabella's romantic vision, for she casually dismisses 'Foreigners' as potential of models of conduct.[35] Moreover, while Charlotte rejects Arabella's charge that she grants 'criminal Favours' to her male companions, she does admit to granting kisses, thus exposing the liberties that modish manners would sanction (V.I). The most damning indictment of Charlotte is that she epitomizes Arabella's disappointment with self-interested female society: instead of romance heroines, Arabella 'found only Miss *Glanville*'s among all she knew' (IX.III). According to Arabella, the thoughtless women who spend their days dressing, dancing and wandering the walks at Vauxhall and Ranelagh Gardens can have no time for 'high and noble Adventures' while the men are emasculated by their participation in fashionable amusements (VII.IX). In contrast to the anti-romantic tenor of 'real life', Arabella's books and solitude seem even more appealing.

'Singularity of Dress': the ethics of romance fashions

Throughout the novel, much attention is given to Arabella's idiosyncratic way of dressing. Lennox uses Arabella's attachment to the fashions of antiquity as a technique of character revelation, and also as a means of criticizing the excesses of contemporary female fashion and the way in which dress marked class and social status, even signifying moral respectability. It is notable that Arabella's desire to emulate the heroines of her favourite romances results in outfits that are striking in their simplicity, in sharp contrast to the styles of the emerging bourgeoisie, which encouraged women to encase themselves in steel or bone stays and wear enormous hooped skirts. There was much contemporary commentary on the epic proportions of female dress, especially hoops so wide that two ladies could barely pass each other in a room without raising their petticoats immodestly, and which impeded their access to carriages; one satirical poem descants on 'monstrous petticoats, bouncing hoop'd petticoats' and refers to 'towers of powdered hair'.[36] By 1754, a writer for the *Connoisseur* could claim that 'The hoop has lost much of its credit with the female world, and has suffered greatly from the introduction of sacks and negligees. Men will agree that next to no clothing, there is nothing more ravishing than an easy dishabille. Our ladies, for that reason perhaps, come into public places as though they were just out of bed.'[37] These comments expose the absurdity of mid-century fashion, as well as the way women were seen as sexual objects who deliberately dress to attract men.

Arabella seems uninterested in attracting the male gaze, and is oblivious to the conspicuous consumption that dominated English society of the period. In Book VII, Chapter VII, Arabella wants a robe like that of Princess Julia (a character in Gauthier de Costes de la Calprenède's *Cleopatra* (*Cléopâtre*; 1674)) to wear to a public ball in Bath. The modish Mantua-maker who is ordered to construct the gown, lacking Arabella's repertoire of historical romance, claims that 'that Taste was quite out'. When she realizes that Arabella is speaking of a 2000-year-old fashion, the dressmaker exclaims, 'Lord help us Trades-people,

if they did not alter a thousand Times in as many Days! I
thought your Ladyship was speaking of the last Month's Taste;
which, as I said before, is quite out now.' The dress, which is
ultimately made by one of Arabella's own female servants, has
'no Hoop, and the Blue and Silver Stuff of her Robe, was only
kept by its own Richness, from hanging close about her. It . . .
descended in a sweeping Train on the Ground'; the headdress
consists of only 'Jewels and Ribbons . . . dispos'd to the greatest
Advantage'. On the one hand, we are invited to be amused by
Arabella here (and Lennox may be indulging in a literary joke,
for there is no description of Princess Julia's dress in *Cleopatra*
that could form a pattern for Arabella's gown); on the other
hand, once again the satire against her is deflected – Arabella's
'Singularity of Dress', which Miss Glanville had assumed would
occasion ridicule, turns out to be 'singularly becoming': 'A
respectful Silence succeeded [the whispers that first greet
Arabella], and the Astonishment her Beauty occasion'd, left
them no Room to descant on the Absurdity of her Dress'
(VII.VII).

More is going on with Arabella's singular dressing than
meets the eye. Apart from the obvious satire directed against
contemporary fashion victims, Arabella's dress places its wearer
within a network of historical and cultural references, especially
in its allusion to the era of classical antiquity that was valorized
by eighteenth-century historians, philosophers and literary
critics. Arabella's costume also connects her – symbolically and
emotionally – to the Princess Julia, and her dressing-up is thus
an act of historical solidarity. Arabella offers a defiant rebuttal
of Mr Selvin's description of Julia as 'the most abandon'd
Prostitute in *Rome*' (VII.VII); she defends Julia's 'chaste'
character on the basis of romance 'Anecdotes', thereby
undermining 'the known Facts in History' and the truth claims
of history writing in general (VII.VIII). Earlier, she had cleared
up 'Mistakes' about the poet Sappho:

But for *Scudery* [the romance writer], we had still thought the
inimitable Poetess *Sappho* to be a loose Wanton, whose Verses
breathed nothing but unchaste and irregular Fires: On the

contrary, she was so remarkably chaste, that she would never even consent to marry. (II.III)

In re-imagining Sappho's reputation, Arabella might also be seen to vindicate Lennox herself ('the British Sappho') and implicitly to defend the heroine of Lennox's first novel, Harriot Stuart, whose Sapphic poems incite abduction and the threat of seduction. Arabella offers the type of 'protection and regard' that Jane Austen, in her famous defence of the novel genre in *Northanger Abbey*,[38] thinks 'the heroine of one novel' might expect from 'the heroine of another'; like Austen, Lennox links women writers, women readers and female characters, implying that these groups should not desert each other. In addition, Lennox may also be gesturing to alternative relationships between women, for Sappho's resistance to marriage has been seen in terms of her attraction to women.

Even when not actually dressing up in full historical costume, Arabella still incorporates some elements of historical fashion in her outfits. She is especially fond of veils, in defiance of contemporary fashion conventions. Before entering the Pump Room at Bath, for example, she pulls the black gauze veil in which she is swathed 'quite over her Face, following therein the Custom of the Ladies in *Clelia*, and *Artamenes*, who, in mixed Companies, always hid their Faces with great Care'. Arabella's veil creates 'great Disturbance' among the spectators (VII.IV), not least because they cannot immediately define its meaning or settle upon the identity it conceals:

> Some of the wiser Sort took her for a Foreigner; others, of still more Sagacity, supposed her a *Scots* Lady, covered with her Plaid; and a third Sort, infinitely wiser than either, concluded she was a *Spanish* Nun, that had escaped from a Convent, and had not yet quitted her Veil. (VII.IV)

Arabella's self-representation challenges labels of nationality (is she Scottish? Spanish? Or simply foreign). During this period, the veil also had imperial connotations, evoking orientalist fantasies of the exotic 'other' woman of the East.[39] Even Arabella's gender identity is metaphorically 'veiled' in the novel so that it becomes something mobile and hybrid. Arabella has all the attributes of the new ultra-feminine heroine of sensibility (she faints readily and is fashionably fatigued by a short walk), but she also imitates the 'Amazonian' Thalestris, whom Miss Glanville dismisses as 'a very masculine Sort of Creature' (III.VI); she is thoroughly immersed in retelling the tales of women in command – of men and of armies; Sir Charles speculates that 'if she had been a Man, she would have made a great Figure in Parliament, and ... her Speeches might have come perhaps to be printed in time' (VIII.II), and, of course, she draws constantly on the work of de Scudéry, the romance author who published disguised as a male writer and to whom Arabella attaches a masculine pronoun. Arabella's dressing-up and her identification with and defence of romance heroines functions within the novel as a mode of empowerment and self-fashioning – Arabella may make all sorts of mistakes in her reading of the world, but her investment in romances also prevents other characters, as well as the reader, from making straightforward judgements about her, as we see quite literally in the episodes when her veiling generates speculation about her identity. Of course, Arabella cannot completely control the ways in which she is 'read' by others – ironically, though she veils herself when she seems to be attracting too much attention (for example, when she goes to church in Book I, Chapter II), the veil itself makes her an object of curiosity and erotic speculation.

'Put yourself into my Protection, and acquaint me with the History of your Misfortunes': Arabella and other women

Arabella's fondness for romance heroines and historical figures finds an analogue in her empathetic relations with a number of women in the novel. On one level, Arabella's understanding of the likes of Miss Groves (whom she encounters at church early in the novel), the prostitute in Vauxhall Gardens and the actress/ Princess of Gaul in Richmond Park is part of her fantasy world, and the novel appeals to readers to read it with a realist perspective and thus to smile at Arabella's misperceptions. But on another level, Arabella's romantic misreadings offer alternative histories of these women which raise important ethical questions about the representation and naming of socially marginalized figures. Arabella immediately sees the magnificently dressed and physically alluring Miss Groves as the reincarnation of 'the beautiful *Candace*', and she observes 'a great Appearance of Melancholy in her Eyes'. She interprets Miss Groves's silence as the product of suffering, but the novel's ironic narrator explains that the latter's fashionable but superficial manners disqualify her from Arabella's refined conversation. In classic romance fashion, Arabella turns to Miss Groves's waiting woman, Mrs Morris, for the 'History' of 'the fair Stranger' and she is reduced to tears by the ensuing narrative of illicit sexuality and illegitimate children (II.IV). Mrs Morris gets nothing for her betrayal of her mistress's 'Secrets', for Arabella 'seemed so little sensible of the Pleasure of Scandal, as to be wholly ignorant of its Nature; and not to know when it was told her' (II.VI); as the narrator's sly observation makes clear, contemporary readers would certainly have recognized scandal when it was told them. The references to the Court of King George II, including Lennox's derogatory allusion to the King's fat German mistresses, his attentions to Miss Groves and Miss Groves's affair with an earl's brother, are the very stuff of scandal fiction and memoirs, and indeed provoked Lennox's publisher Andrew Millar to ask for alterations; she writes to Richardson that 'he assures me that the History of Miss Groves / in the first Vol. will not be printed'.[40] Arabella, however, finds precedents in romance for what she interprets as character defamation, and in doing so prompts us to rethink familiar trajectories of the fallen woman. Miss Groves, after apparent dalliances with a sportsman and her writing master, is abandoned by her dysfunctional family to fend for herself in London, where she is 'ruined' by the rakish Mr L—. During her second pregnancy she is abandoned by him, and she subsequently contracts a secret marriage with a country gentleman. Miss Groves may not be an especially appealing character, but

Arabella's sympathy is so contagious that the reader becomes less critical of Miss Groves's offences against propriety and more critical of the cultural and legal institutions that collude with Mr L—'s abduction of Miss Groves's daughter and his refusal to tell her what he has done with the child.

Towards the end of the novel, Arabella meets a tearful creature who recounts the history of her abandonment by someone called Ariamenes, who turns out to be Glanville; it transpires that this young woman, 'Cynecia', is an actress bribed and coached by Sir George to impersonate a Princess forsaken by Glanville as part of his plot to separate the cousins. Arabella is imposed upon, and we laugh at her credulity, but once again, her 'foible' is precisely what allows her to have the adventure of meeting someone with whom she would not otherwise have been able to associate. Moreover, though Arabella's discovery of Glanville's apparent infidelity provokes an 'Extacy of Grief' (clearly she is in love with him), she refuses to triumph over her new-found friend, thus putting her loyalty to the 'other woman' above her attachment to a man (IX.V).

The most dramatic and culturally significant encounter between Arabella and another woman takes places at Vauxhall Gardens, where Arabella tries to console an intoxicated, cross-dressed prostitute after a young man, 'pretending to be affronted at something she said, drew his Sword upon the disguis'd Fair One' (IX.I). It is important to note that prostitution was not a remote or abstract issue for writers in mid-century London; indeed, Lennox's mentors Johnson and Richardson were publicly involved in prostitution reform, while Johnson's friend and biographer, James Boswell, famously recorded his more intimate encounters with prostitutes.[41] In order to provide a context for Lennox's representation of prostitution (and of related modes of female sexuality), it is necessary first to sketch the two dominant models of the eighteenth-century prostitute. The first version has its roots in libertine and pornographic literature and anti-female satire; the prostitute is seen as monstrous, sexually voracious and often diseased, using her treacherous arts to entice men and to recruit other women into the ranks of prostitution. Prostitution is often depicted as criminal

as well as scandalous, and much attention is given to transgressive sexual practices (such as bestiality or sodomy). Memorable
examples include the prostitute in Robert Gould's satirical
poem *Love Given O're* (1682) who beguiles women into prostitution when her own body has become 'one putrid Sore', and
Richardson's monstrous brothel-keeper Madam Sinclair and
the unruly harlots over whom she presides in *Clarissa*. Ideas
about wanton women also extended to certain types of women's
writing as the product of 'a wanton Muse': John Duncombe's
1754 poem *The Feminiad* indites 'the bold unblushing mien'
of writers such as Manley and Behn, as well as scandalous
memoirists like Pilkington.[42] Social concerns about the moral
effects of fiction also focused on the figure of the prostitute:
after exempting Richardson's productions from his critique,
James Fordyce's *Sermons to Young Women* (1766) railed
against the impropriety of the mass of novels that 'are in their
nature so shameful, in their tendency so pestiferous, and contain
such rank treason against the royalty of Virtue, such horrible
violation of all decorum, that she who can bear to peruse them
must be in her soul a prostitute, let her reputation in life be
what it will'.[43] Here, female readers are warned to stay within
the boundaries of generic propriety if they do not wish to be
tarnished by association with prostitution.

The other dominant view of prostitution recasts the women
as victims – they are represented as sentimental, tearfully
repentant subjects worthy of relief. In 'The History of Misella
debauched by her Relation' (1750–52), Johnson portrays 'a
band of these miserable females, covered with rags, shivering
with cold, and pining with hunger'.[44] Richardson's Sir Charles
Grandison advocates 'An Hospital for Female Penitents', for
those innocent victims of male perfidy, 'who are eminently
entitled to our pity',[45] a plan that came to fruition with the
opening of the Magdalen House for Penitent Prostitutes in
1758. The Reverend William Dodd's sermons preached at the
Magdalen Hospital rejected the stereotype of the 'pestilent Prostitute', instead urging compassion for such 'ruined' women,
and especially for anguished maternal figures.[46] The Magdalen
Hospital's Sunday services became a popular attraction, open

to the public by ticket and patronized by fashionable bourgeois society. These occasions were famous for theatrical scenes of sentimental suffering displayed by the penitent prostitutes. Richardson encouraged Millar and Robert Dodsley to publish (and was himself the printer of) Lady Barbara Montagu's novel-length collection of Magdalen biographies entitled *The Histories of Some of the Penitents in the Magdalen-House* (1760); these narratives of women seduced into prostitution helped to transform society's view of the prostitute into a suffering individual who could be resocialized.

If we return to Lennox's scene of prostitution, we can see that she engages with these representations but she also reconfigures them. The transvestite mistress reminds Arabella of 'the beautiful *Aspasia*' and 'the beautiful *Candace*' (IX.I); for the reader, the prostitute recapitulates all the cross-historical dressing and rhetorical cross-dressing that punctuates the novel. In the almost obligatory confrontation between the innocent and the fallen woman in eighteenth-century novels, the innocent woman is usually terrified that people will identify her with the fallen one, as in the heroine's anxious encounter with the whores in Marylebone Gardens in Frances Burney's *Evelina*; in that episode, the two prostitutes are characterized by their boldness and callousness towards Evelina, while Evelina experiences only 'humiliating' 'mortifications' from their proximity. Like Arabella, Evelina also goes to Vauxhall Gardens, where she is accosted by a party of men in the 'dark walks', whereupon the distraught Evelina exclaims, '"I am no actress."'[47] The unruly prostitute in *The Female Quixote* conjures up the ghost of the racy sexual narratives of Behn, Manley and Haywood, precisely the literary heritage that was least acceptable for a mid-century woman writer with aspirations of respectability. When an audience gathers to enjoy the spectacle of her mock-lover kneeling at her feet and addressing her in mock-heroic verse, the prostitute is recognizable as an example of what Duncombe would call 'the wanton Muse'. But Lennox's representation also invokes contemporary reformist literature that casts prostitutes as victims and prefigures the ways in which the Magdalen narratives humanize and individualize the prostitute.

The young woman's face is pale with terror and woe, she is drawn to Arabella and though she finds the other woman's words strange, she responds to their 'affecting Earnestness' and thanks her in a quiet and dignified way. Arabella wants to hear the prostitute's story, 'the History of your Misfortunes', as a prelude to helping her 're-establish the Repose' of her life. We never learn if the prostitute would have become a reformed character under the protection of Arabella, for the naval officer, with whom she came to the gardens, wakes up from his alcoholic daze and brandishes his sword; Arabella gets Miss Glanville away from the scene, leaving Mr Glanville 'to take Care of the distress'd Lady', a command he ignores. Of course, Arabella does not even recognize the prostitute *as* a prostitute – culturally recognized sexual identities do not register with her, and in terms of the novel's anti-romance vision, this is simply comic. But this realist interpretation is qualified by the spectacle of these two women, holding hands in front of a crowd of spectators and sharing a predilection for exotic costuming. Mr Glanville is driven 'almost mad with Vexation' at the spectacle Arabella makes of herself: 'Are you mad, Madam, said he in a Whisper, to make all this Rout about a Prostitute? Do you see how every Body stares at you? What will they think' (IX.I). Arabella does not 'expose' herself so much as Glanville's hysteria reveals his own fears and prejudices. Arabella's fantasy has a significant ethical purpose; her sympathetic intimacy with the prostitute challenges the rigid separation of virtuous and vicious women that prevailed in conduct books and novels, and offers readers a vision of social coherence beyond such polarized distinctions.

Arabella's investment in romances is an escape from reality, but also a comment on it. While she believes in romances, and models her behaviour on romance heroines, she is empowered to have adventures, to meet women who inhabit the sexual shadowlands of mid-eighteenth-century English society and to fashion both them and herself in unconventional ways. These encounters also show how Arabella moves seamlessly between the past and the present, the fantastic and the plausible, the real and the imagined, as does Lennox herself in shaping the narrative. *The Female Quixote* alludes to the heroines of ancient history and seventeenth-century French romances; it features characters that are recognizably novelistic (Charlotte Glanville) and those that seem to have migrated from scandal narratives (Miss Groves), as well as refugees from the literature of prostitution. There are also references to real contemporary figures, notably a brief but revealing discussion of Lennox's contemporaries, Maria and Elizabeth Gunning.[48] This is a key episode in understanding how Arabella's – and Lennox's – investment in historical fiction is also a concern with the relation between fiction and history and with the way society privileges certain representations of 'reality' over others. The question at issue here is, who has the authority to legitimate representation? The Gunning girls came over from Ireland with their family in 1750, and their good looks and Irish charms made them celebrated figures. In 1752, Elizabeth married the Duke of Hamilton and Maria the Earl of Coventry.[49] They appear in the novel in a discussion between Glanville and Sir George about 'the Two celebrated Beauties' (in the first edition more explicitly described as 'the Two Sister Beauties'), who are attended by a 'Crowd of Beaux . . . to all Places of polite Diversion in Town'. Glanville pities the men enslaved by these women, for they must ignore the great actor Garrick in order to gaze on the sisters' charms and listen to their trifling conversation. Glanville and Sir George reveal the fear that men are disabled in their subjugation to beauty which compromises masculine rationality and self-possession. As we might expect, Arabella interrupts their conversation to defend these 'Town Beauties',[50] and once again she appeals to her repertoire of romance 'Beauties' and heroes for genealogical precedents that support her interpretation (IV.III).

There are significant links between Arabella and the Gunnings. Maria Gunning, in particular, seems to have liked to defy fashion conventions. Thus, Mary Delany (whom, we should recall, was reading *The Female Quixote* in April 1752, and writing to her friends about it) wrote to a correspondent about Maria:

Yesterday after chapel the Duchess brought home Lady Coventry to feast me, and *a feast she was!* She is a fine figure and vastly handsome ... she has a thousand airs, but with a sort of inno-cence that diverts one! Her dress was a black silk sack, made for a large hoop, which she wore without any, and it trailed a yard on the ground.[51]

Even her shoes could draw a crowd, with one shoemaker capitalizing on this fetishistic desire by charging a penny for a sight of the shoes he was making for Maria Gunning. The greatest similarity between the three women is in terms of the 'noise' they generate: Arabella is certain that she must make a great 'Noise and Bustle' in the world in order to rule within the Empire of Love (III.VI), and contemporary commentary on the Gunnings emphasizes the 'noise' (Walpole's word) that marked their conquest of the fashionable world.[52] Like the other women with whom Arabella empathizes, the sisters' public visibility placed them in close proximity, at least figuratively, to other 'public' women, such as prostitutes and actresses, and they actually considered joining the morally dubious acting profession, which again links the Gunnings both with the actress Arabella encounters and with Lennox herself, who worked as an actress, though a 'deplorable' one, according to Horace Walpole.

Arabella speaks up for the Gunnings, in her defence of the maligned beauties, and she identifies with them. In the midst of competing views of the Gunnings, which mostly judged them as guilty of inciting folly in their admirers, Lennox lends her support to the atypical account purveyed in a famous poem about Elizabeth and Maria Gunning, *The Charms of Beauty*, which casts their beauty as the transparent clothing for their chastity and sees their admirers 'chastiz'd' into respect.[53] In defending, befriending and even identifying with actresses, prostitutes and the Gunning sisters, Arabella contests dominant views about female publicity. To this list, we might add the female author herself, whose public identity frames the novel's ideological position: thus, Lennox implicitly chastizes those readers who had read 'The Art of Coquetry' and *Harriot Stuart* as adverts for her own sexual availability. Arabella's noisy, theatrical, cross-class and cross-historical acts of empathy startle the more conventional characters in the novel, but they must also have startled conventional realist readers, who may have become increasingly uncertain of their value judgements about genres as well as about gender.

Arabella's cures: 'my Heart yields to the Force of Truth'

Arabella's identification with a series of culturally suspect female figures and her social imagination depend on her investment in reading romance as historical reality, a true account of events that really happened. How then are we to read the ending of the novel in which Arabella is 'cured' of her romantic delusions? Near the end of *The Female Quixote*, Arabella develops a dangerous fever after she has thrown herself into the Thames to escape imaginary ravishers, thus preserving her 'immortal Glory' (IX.IX). Thinking she is going to die, Arabella requests the assistance of 'some worthy Divine' to help her prepare for death. While Arabella's 'delicate Constitution' slowly recovers, the Divine is more concerned with the health of her mind which he laments has been ruined by her 'ridiculous Study' of romances (IX.X).

In fact, it is worth noting that Arabella encounters *two* figures who offer revisionary and contrasting accounts of romance and templates for her own behaviour: the penultimate Book of Volume II introduces a divine countess and the final Book introduces the sententious divine. We first meet the countess at an assembly in Bath, when she rescues the absent Arabella from 'the ill-natur'd Raillery of her Sex', repeating as she does so Arabella's defence of maligned women throughout the novel. The ladies' jealousy of Arabella's beauty manifests itself as sarcasm and 'contemptuous Jests', fuelled by Miss Glanville's disclosure of Arabella's obsession for romance reading and the 'Extravagancies' it had led her into. Part of the countess's defence of Arabella against her defamers is that though herself a model of wit, learning and sensibility, she had also 'when very young, been deep read in Romances', as her subsequent detailed literary conversations with Arabella indicate (VIII.V). If the countess's compassion is grounded in their shared history of romance reading, her cure does not reject romance but rather insists on its proper historical context.[54] She argues that romance is culturally and historically specific, that is, that though the romance values of 'Glory, Virtue, Courage, Generosity, and Honour' endure, the way in which these ideals are expressed varies according to different historical moments and geographical locations. For example, Oroondates, that touchstone of romantic virtue, would be judged 'impious and base' according to contemporary Christian doctrine; likewise, if feminine merit was established in ancient times through multiple abductions, 'a Beauty in this [age] could not pass thro' the Hands of several different Ravishers, without bringing an Imputation on her Chastity' (VIII.VII). The problem then is not with romance per se, which clearly does help to create generous and virtuous subjects like Arabella herself, but with an unhistoricized reading of romance that leads to the delusion that mid-eighteenth-century English society is governed according to romance conventions.

The countess is whisked away suddenly to care for her sick mother before her therapeutic conversations can take effect. But if Arabella had followed the countess's instructions to put romance behind her in order to find a legitimate role for herself within the reality of her social context, we should ask, what would her autobiography look like? The countess's attenuated description of 'all the material Passages of my Life' (birth, education, happy parentally condoned marriage) suggests that the ideal virtuous female subject has no story to tell because any story about a woman inevitably becomes a sexual history: 'the History of a Woman of Honour' does not figure within history itself (VIII.VII). Her view of femininity is so extreme as to seem almost parodic. The countess equates female virtue with non-narratable female subjectivity, in other words, in accordance with conservative domestic ideology, the virtuous woman leads a profoundly uneventful life that differs very little from that of other sensible women of the same rank. All this contrasts oddly with Arabella's 'adventures' which enable her to meet people outside her social class and to bypass the conventions of female propriety, without compromising her virtue. The novel in which Arabella appears, which so delighted eighteenth-century readers, would itself not have been possible if Arabella's life resembled that of the countess.

After the countess disappears from the narrative, the 'Pious and Learned Doctor' takes over Arabella's cure following her potentially fatal dip in the Thames (IX.X). For many years critics suspected that Johnson wrote all or part of the text's penultimate chapter (which features the clergyman's sententious disquisitions on reason and reading, and which literally quotes Johnson's well-known praise of Richardson[55]), but the chapter may simply be Lennox's laudatory mimicry of Johnson, her strategic imitation of a male voice (alternatively, we might think of Johnson performing as a female author, as he did in the Dedication). Richardson seems to have encouraged the novel's hasty conclusion, advising Lennox that two volumes would do more for her future reputation than three (odd advice perhaps from the author of the longest novel in English). In an earlier draft, Lennox had intended that *Clarissa* play a more pivotal role in Arabella's cure but was discouraged by Richardson himself. As critics have pointed out, though Arabella must relinquish her romances, she does not have to relinquish fiction in favour of real life – rather, she must reject romances and embrace novel reading.[56] According to the clergyman, 'Truth is not always injured by Fiction' – what matters is that the fiction is realistic and ethical: 'Books ought to supply an Antidote' to the wickedness of real life. In his formulation, *Clarissa* 'convey[s] the most solid Instructions, the noblest Sentiments, and the most exalted Piety, in the pleasing Dress of a Novel' (IX.XI). But the clergyman's recommendation of truthful, didactic fictions recapitulates Arabella's persistent description of her romances as historical documents that encourage their readers to emulate the virtuous and heroic behaviour they represent. This similarity underlines the tendency for the novel and the romance to be confused throughout *The Female Quixote*.

What remains most troubling about the clergyman's cure is its rejection of romances as 'senseless Fictions' full of 'philo-

sophical Absurdities'. According to him, romances can only
teach 'the Arts of Intrigue', and he claims that

> It is impossible to read these Tales without lessening part of that
> Humility, which by preserving in us a Sense of our Alliance with
> all Human Nature, keeps us awake to Tenderness and Sympathy,
> or without impairing that Compassion which is implanted in us
> as an Incentive to Acts of Kindness. (IX.XI)

As we have seen, the character most alive to tenderness, sympathy and compassion is the inveterate romance reader
Arabella; like Arabella, the Countess seems uninjured by her
dangerous reading, being a model of 'Candour . . . Sweetness
. . . Modesty and Benevolence' (VIII.V). Ungenerous behaviour
proliferates among the novel's non-romance-reading characters, such as Selvin, Tinsel and Hervey, while Charlotte Glanville seems to have learnt the arts of intrigue without the help
of romances.

Many readers think that Arabella and the novel itself come
to a bad end: the novel is concluded abruptly and Arabella
dwindles into a wife. The feisty heroine, whose retreat from
reality was a form of empowerment and self-fashioning, ends
up with a consciousness of her own imperfections, seemingly
ready to take up a conventional role in the private sphere and
relinquish all her pretensions to public life. Barbauld was one
of the first critics to find the novel 'not very well wound up'.[57]
And yet the narrator offers the possibility of an ironic reading of
the conservative conclusion – indeed, the penultimate chapter's
title, 'Being in the Author's Opinion, the best Chapter in this
History', implicitly acknowledges alternative opinions. Kate
Levin argues that the ending had commercial implications for
Lennox herself; it was a marketing strategy that confirmed her
work as acceptable female reading matter and salvaged the
reputation that was tainted by her poems and by *Harriot Stuart*.
The Divine's 'cure' of Arabella's mind prefigures Lennox's post-
Quixote 'proper' novels.[58] It is worth returning here to the fact
that there are *two* cures for Arabella's addiction to romance,
and thinking about the meaning of this double solution. As

critics have suggested, Arabella is asked to historicize *or* to reject romance, and ultimately to embrace the novel. But these options screen the novel's scandalous history; especially, they occlude the relationship of mid-eighteenth-century female-authored fiction to its sexy predecessors. By the time she wrote *Henrietta*, Lennox seemed to have put these alternative histories behind her in a canny decision to promote her own and her novel's public respectability: Henrietta throws away Manley's 'secret memoirs', *The New Atalantis*, and rejects her landlady-cum-madam's recommendation of Haywood's novels, preferring to reread Fielding's *Joseph Andrews*. This preference for the new form of the (masculine) novel functions to ratify the heroine's virtue. But scandal narratives abound in *The Female Quixote*. Each time Arabella demands a lady's 'history' or her 'adventures', she thinks of romance while all those around her think of transgressive sexuality. She encounters prostitutes and actresses who are disguised as aristocrats or cross-dressed, recalling the disguises, substitutions and erotic intrigues that dominate Behn's and Haywood's narratives. Mr Tinsel's snapshots of fashionable figures are rejected by Arabella as 'detatched Pieces of Satire on particular Persons' (VII.VIII), but at the same time they would have reminded the eighteenth-century reader of Manley's distinctive style. Ostensibly parodying romance and disavowing scandal, Lennox reintroduces both into the history of the novel, while Arabella's sympathetic cross-class and cross-historical identification with other women complicates the dominant mid-eighteenth-century model of female domesticity.

Arabella's afterlives

Arabella's adventures do seem to come to an end with her marriage to Glanville, but unlike Richardson's sequel to *Pamela*, which shows the heroine constrained by marriage and suffering her husband's attentions to another woman, we remain free to speculate beyond this novel's conventional closure. Certainly, Arabella has an interesting afterlife in the sense that the novel continued to be read throughout the eighteenth and early nineteenth centuries, generated translations across Europe and significantly influenced a number of subsequent literary texts. Miriam Rossiter Small documents a range of texts indebted to *The Female Quixote*,[59] including a play entitled *Angelica; or Quixote in Petticoats* (1758), whose heroine, like Arabella, insists on her absolute power over her lovers and who quotes from Mandara and Statira. George Colman's farce *Polly Honeycombe* (produced at Drury Lane in 1760) features a heroine corrupted by reading the sentimental novels available at circulating libraries and who, like Arabella, mistakes servants for gentlemen; Colman's Preface cites three of Lennox's titles (*Harriot Stuart, Henrietta* and *The Memoirs of the Countess of Berci*) in an extract from a circulating library catalogue. Many novels, such as *The Spiritual Quixote* (1773), focus on quixotic behaviour, but are as much indebted to Cervantes and Fielding as to Lennox. Elizabeth, Margaret and Jane Purbeck's novel *The History of Sir George Warrington; or, the Political Quixote* (1797) was erroneously attributed to Lennox on the title page of the first edition; the novel includes a character called Charlotte Thornton, who elopes with her father's servant because her head is full of false ideas derived from French romances, and the novel's quixotic hero, George Warrington, almost dies because of his misplaced belief in democratic political theories, recovering as precipitously as Arabella when he learns that republicans are atheists.

Significantly, Jane Austen read Lennox's most famous novel more than once, and in 1807 she wrote to her sister Cassandra that reading it 'now makes our evening amusement; to me a very high one, as I find the work quite equal to what I remembered it.'[60] *Northanger Abbey* is, in many way, a tribute to and updating of *The Female Quixote*; Austen substitutes Gothic novels for French romances as the reading that misleads her young heroine, Catherine Morland, and like Lennox she qualifies her satire of 'horrid novels': Catherine's misreading of real life is, to some extent, validated by General Tilney's behaviour – she comes to believe that he did not kill his wife, but her 'terror' in his presence is well founded. General Tilney's tyranny exposes the gothic qualities within the home, so that the

English midland counties in the 1790s seem quite as terrifying as Ann Radcliffe's historical romances set in southern Europe. Just as Lennox reclaimed romance, Austen reclaims gothic conventions to make a political comment on paternal power. Like her predecessor, she also undermines the conventional novelistic closure of marriage, self-consciously observing that her readers 'will see in the tell-tale compression of the pages before them, that we are all hastening together to perfect felicity'.[61]

The novel that most obviously alludes to Lennox's appeared on the other side of the Atlantic in 1801 (which suggests something of the transatlantic culture of novels during this period; *The Female Quixote* was certainly available in America). Tabitha Tenney's *Female Quixotism: Exhibited in the Romantic Opinions and Extravagant Adventures of Dorcasina Sheldon* was reprinted several times between 1801 and 1841. Tenney's novel shares many features with Lennox's: Dorcasina, like Arabella, loses her mother at an early age and is raised by her father in seclusion; each heroine has a faithful female servant; both have genuine suitors as well as impostors, and both fantasize that servants are gentlemen in disguise; both dress eccentrically. The two novels function as both nationalist and anti-romance warnings, with Arabella obsessed by seventeenth-century French romances and Dorcasina by mid-eighteenth-century English novels, especially the sentimental fiction of Richardson. But *Female Quixotism* is more resolutely didactic and anti-romantic than its predecessor: notably it does not conclude with the marriage of the heroine (or her sentimental death, the other dominant plot option), rather, we follow the heroine to unmarried, lonely old age, bereft of all her romantic delusions. Through its mockery of the effects of fashionable reading, the novel registers a conservative protest against the new, mobile social relations of Jeffersonian America.[62]

After Elizabeth Gunning's second marriage to the Duke of Argyll, Walpole exclaimed in a letter: 'I would not venture to marry either of them [the two sisters] these thirty years, for fear of being shuffled out of the world *prematurely*, to make room for the rest of their adventures.'[63] Literary history did make room for Arabella's continuing adventures, but most nineteenth- and twentieth-century creators of novelistic canons, from Sir Walter Scott to Ian Watt, ignored or marginalized them. However, recent literary and cultural critics have restored them and the sophisticated, speculative and ethical fiction in which they occur to their rightful place at the centre of debates about the novel in the mid eighteenth century. We trust that new readers, despite the intervening two and half centuries, will be as absorbed by Arabella as were Elizabeth Carter, Susanna Highmore and Samuel Richardson.

NOTES

I would like to thank our former editor at Penguin, Laura Barber, for her useful and graceful comments on earlier versions of this Introduction.

Quotations from the text are referenced by Book and Chapter number.

1. Elizabeth Carter (1717–1806), poet, linguist and correspondent, was part of a group of intellectual woman – the Bluestocking Circle – which flourished in London in the second half of the eighteenth century; other members included Hannah More, Hester Chapone, Mary Delany and Elizabeth Montagu (the 'Queen of the Blues'). Carter, like Lennox, produced translations from French and Italian and contributed to Samuel Johnson's *Rambler* (1750–52).

2. Quotations from Carter's and Delany's letters are from Miriam Rossiter Small, *Charlotte Ramsay Lennox: An Eighteenth Century Lady of Letters* (New Haven/London: Yale University Press/ Oxford University Press, 1935), p. 85. Despite some inaccuracies, Small's study is a useful source of biographical and contextual information. See also Duncan Isles's invaluable annotations to Lennox's correspondence in 'The Lennox Collection', *Harvard Library Bulletin* 18.4 (1970), pp. 317–44; 19.1 (1971), pp. 36–60; 19.2, pp. 165–86; 19.4, pp. 416–35.

3. *Selected Letters of Samuel Richardson*, ed. John Carroll (Oxford: Clarendon Press, 1964), p. 223 (letter to Lady Bradshaigh).

4. Both Susanna Highmore (1725–1812) and Hester Chapone (1727–1801) were members of Richardson's circle; Highmore

married John Duncombe, author of *The Feminiad. A Poem* (1754), which celebrates the work of morally virtuous women writers; Chapone was friends with Bluestockings Carter and Montagu, wrote poems and essays and contributed fictional epistles to the *Rambler. Letters on the Improvement of the Mind, addressed to a Young Lady* (1773) is her most important work. Highmore is quoted in Small, *Lennox*, p. 86.

5. Richardson, *Selected Letters*, ed. Carroll, p. 223.

6. Small quotes from a late-nineteenth-century American biographical encyclopaedia that Lennox's mother had died some time before her departure for England (*Lennox*, p. 4).

7. See Gustavus Howard Maynadier, *The First American Novelist?* (Cambridge, Mass.: Harvard University Press, 1940).

8. See Isles, 'The Lennox Collection', *Harvard Library Bulletin* 19.1 (1971), p. 60, n. 121.

9. As Edward Copeland notes, £25 a year was the income of the labouring poor, while a single man living in London on £50 a year in 1767 had to practise a bitter economy (*Women Writing about Money: Women's Fiction in England, 1790–1820* (Cambridge: Cambridge University Press, 1995), pp. 24–7.

10. Letter to the Royal Literary Fund, dated 22 August 1793; reprinted in Small, *Lennox*, p. 59. She received £20 in 1802 to alleviate 'urgent distress', followed by a further 7 guineas in the same year, and a weekly allowance of one guinea established in 1803.

11. Ibid., pp. 57–8.

12. Ibid., pp. 8–10, for all quotations.

13. Subscription was a traditional mode of publication in the eighteenth century, whereby a list of subscribers, usually headed by an aristocratic or other influential patron, paid a small sum of money to defray publication costs; they would receive a copy of the book in question, in which their names would be listed.

14. See Small, *Lennox*, p. 126.

15. Reprinted in *Henry Fielding: The Critical Heritage*, ed. Ronald Paulson (London: Routledge, 1969), p. 271.

16. Quoted in Small, *Lennox*, p. 126.

17. Quoted in Isles, 'The Lennox Collection', *Harvard Library Bulletin* 19.4 (1971), p. 430.

18. The term 'foible' is used throughout the novel to describe Arabella's apparently misguided reading of French romances as real history and as guides for her conduct. The term makes her failing seem trivial, amusing and feminine.

19. The editor of Lady Mary Wortley Montagu's letters, published in 1861, notes in his Preface that Lady Mary 'possessed, and left after her, the whole library of Mrs Lennox's Female Quixote – Cleopatra, Cassandra, Clelia, Cyrus ... etc., all, like the Lady Arabella's collection, "Englished", mostly by persons of honour'; quoted in Small, *Lennox*, pp. 87–8.

20. 'The Covent Garden Journal, Numb. 24, Tuesday, March 24, 1752', in Henry Fielding, *The Covent-Garden Journal and A Plan of the Universal Register-Office*, ed. Bertrand A. Goldgar (Oxford: Clarendon Press, 1988), p. 161.

21. Clare Reeve, *The Progress of Romance through Times, Countries, and Manners*, 2 vols. (1785; New York: Garland Publishing, 1970), vol. 2, pp. 6–7.

22. Janet Todd, *The Sign of Angellica: Women, Writing and Fiction, 1660–1800* (London: Virago, 1989), p. 153.

23. William B. Warner, *Licensing Entertainment: The Elevation of Novel Reading in Britain, 1684–1750* (Berkeley and Los Angeles: University of California Press, 1998), p. 112. Warner provides a useful and entertaining account of this early tradition in fiction as 'media culture' (see, especially, pp. 45–127).

24. Mary Patricia Martin, ' "High and Noble Adventures": Reading the Novel in *The Female Quixote*', *Novel: A Forum on Fiction* 31.1 (1997), p. 45. Martin is concerned with 'the gendered rhetoric central to accounts of the new fiction', particularly Lennox's claiming of the novel as 'women's writing' (p. 46).

25. Quoted in Martin, ' "High and Noble Adventures" ', p. 47.

26. Samuel Johnson, *The Rambler* No. 4, 17th edn, 3 vols. (London: Rivington et al., 1816), vol. 1, p. 18.

27. Lennox's debt to Richardson is explicit and the clergyman's recommendation of *Clarissa* as acceptable and improving reading is unambiguous, but her implicit championing of Fielding is found throughout the novel. Lennox's divided allegiance is interesting because it complicates a dominant model of literary history which links the success of female novelists to an increasing emphasis on domestic femininity, and which thus locates women novelists within the tradition of Richardson (the domesticity argument is most influentially made by Nancy Armstrong in her *Desire and Domestic Fiction: A Political History of the Novel* (New York: Oxford University Press, 1987)).

28. Kate Levin, ' "The Cure of Arabella's Mind": Charlotte Lennox and the Disciplining of the Female Reader', *Women's Writing: The Elizabethan to Victorian Period* 2.3 (1995), p. 276. Joseph

F. Bartolomeo offers a detailed discussion of the intertextual relationship in 'Female Quixotism v. "Feminine" Tragedy: Lennox's Comic Revision of *Clarissa*', in *New Essays on Samuel Richardson*, ed. Albert J. Rivero (New York: St Martin's Press, 1996), pp. 163–75.

29. Henry Fielding, *The History of Tom Jones, A Foundling* (1749), Book IX, Ch. 5.

30. *The Female Quixote*, ed. Margaret Dalziel (London: Oxford University Press, 1970), p. 414, note.

31. José Ortega y Gasset, '*From* Meditations on Quixote', in *Theory of the Novel: A Historical Approach*, ed. Michael McKeon (Baltimore and London: Johns Hopkins University Press, 2000), pp. 282, 283.

32. 'The Covent Garden Journal' (see note 20), p. 160. See also endnote 1, Book I.

33. See endnote 36, Book IX.

34. Scott Paul Gordon discusses Lennox's regeneration of 'romance values' in 'The Space of Romance in Lennox's *Female Quixote*', *Studies in English Literature* 38.3 (1998), pp. 500, 502ff.

35. See Martin on Charlotte's 'parochial sensibility', '"High and Noble Adventures"', p. 56.

36. Quoted in Norah Waugh, *Corsets and Crinolines* (1954; New York: Theatre Arts Books, 1981), p. 62.

37. Ibid.

38. Jane Austen, *Northanger Abbey* (1818); Vol. I, ch. 5. Of course, *Northanger Abbey* itself pays tribute to *The Female Quixote*, replaying Arabella's romance-induced 'delusions' through Catherine Morland's gothic-induced ones.

39. On the imperial connotations of Arabella's veil, see Felicity Nussbaum, *Torrid Zones: Maternity, Sexuality, and Empire in Eighteenth-Century English Narratives* (Baltimore and London: Johns Hopkins University Press, 1995), pp. 114–26.

40. Isles, 'The Lennox Collection', *Harvard Library Bulletin* 18.4 (1970), p. 339.

41. See Markman Ellis, *The Politics of Sensibility: Race, Gender and Commerce in the Sentimental Novel* (Cambridge: Cambridge University Press, 1996), p. 160.

42. See excerpt in Vivien Jones, ed., *Women in the Eighteenth Century: Constructions of Femininity* (London and New York: Routledge, 1990), pp. 170–74.

43. Ibid., p. 176.

44. Quoted in Ellis, *Politics of Sensibility*, p. 165.

45. Samuel Richardson, *The History of Sir Charles Grandison* (1753–4), Vol. IV, Letter XXII.

46. Lennox may have known Dodd; in a letter to Johnson, she hopes for 'a reprieve for poor Dr Dodd', who had been convicted of forgery, and who was hanged in June 1777 (Small, *Lennox*, p. 51).

47. Frances Burney, *Evelina* (1778), Vol. II, Letters XXII and XV.

48. Reynolds's portrait of Elizabeth Gunning appears on the cover of this edition. Lennox herself sat for Reynolds in 1761; according to Small, two engravings exist of this portrait (*Lennox*, pp. 33–4; the 1813 Cook engraving produced for the memoir of Lennox in the *Lady's Monthly Magazine* appears in Small's biography).

49. It is worth noting that the circumstances of Elizabeth's marriage are the stuff of romance: the debauched Duke of Hamilton fell in love with her at a masquerade and six weeks later coerced a parson to marry them late at night in an impromptu ceremony at Mayfair Chapel, using a ring from the bed curtain as a wedding ring; after the death of her first husband, Elizabeth married the Duke of Argyll.

50. 'Woman of the town' was a common term for a prostitute.

51. Mrs Delany to Mrs Dewes, 10 November 1754, *Autobiography and Correspondence of Mrs Delany*, revised from Lady Llanover's edition, ed. Sarah Chauncey Woolsey, 2 vols. (Boston: Roberts Brothers, 1880), vol. 1, p. 453.

52. *The Letters of Horace Walpole, Fourth Earl of Oxford*, ed. Mrs Paget Toynbee, 16 vols. (Oxford: Clarendon Press, 1905), vol. 3, pp. 68–104; vol. 4, pp. 241, 245.

53. *The Charms of Beauty; or, the Grand Contest between the Fair Hibernians, and the English Toasts, A Poem* . . . (London: J. Gifford, 1752).

54. On the Countess's historicization of romance, see note 34 above and Christine Roulston, 'Histories of Nothing: Romance and Femininity in Charlotte Lennox's *The Female Quixote*', *Women's Writing: The Elizabethan to Victorian Period* 2.1 (1995), p. 36.

55. Johnson's praise of Richardson appeared in the opening lines of *Rambler* 97 (19 February 1751). See also endnote 36, Book IX.

56. See Martin, ' "High and Noble Adventures" ', p. 45.

57. Quoted by Dalziel (ed.), Introduction to Lennox, *Female Quixote*, p. xviii.

58. See Kate Levin, "The Cure of Arabella's Mind": Charlotte Len-

nox and the disciplining of the female reader', *Women's Writing* 2.3 (1995), p. 278.

59. See Small, *Lennox*, pp. 99–117.

60. Letter to Cassandra Austen, 7 January 1807, *Jane Austen's Letters*, ed. R. W. Chapman, 2nd corrected edition (London: Oxford University Press, 1959), p. 173.

61. Austen, *Northanger Abbey*, Vol. II, ch. 31.

62. It should be noted also that in transmuting her material for a new cultural context, Tabitha Tenny produces a more boisterously farcical version of her heroine's escapades in *Female Quixotism*, ed. Jean Nienkamp and Andrea Collins (New York and Oxford: Oxford University Press, 1992).

63. *Letters of Walpole*, ed. Toynbee, vol. 4, p. 232.

Further Reading

Bartolomeo, Joseph F., 'Female Quixotism V. "Feminine" Tragedy: Lennox's Comic Revision of *Clarissa*', in *New Essays on Samuel Richardson*, ed. Albert J. Rivero (New York: St Martin's Press, 1996), pp. 163–75.

Craft, Catherine A., 'Reworking Male Models: Aphra Behn's *Fair Vow-Breaker*, Eliza Haywood's *Fantomina*, and Charlotte Lennox's *Female Quixote*', *Modern Language Review* 86.4 (1991), pp. 821–38.

Gallagher, Catherine, *Nobody's Story: The Vanishing Acts of Women Writers in the Marketplace, 1670–1820* (Berkeley and Los Angeles: University of California Press, 1994), pp. 145–202.

Gardiner, Ellen, 'Writing Men Reading in Charlotte Lennox's *The Female Quixote*', *Studies in the Novel* 28.1 (1996), pp. 1–11.

Gordon, Scott Paul, 'The Space of Romance in Lennox's *Female Quixote*', *Studies in English Literature* 38.3 (1998), pp. 499–516.

Isles, Duncan, 'The Lennox Collection', *Harvard Library Bulletin* 18.4 (1970), pp. 317–44; 19.1 (1971), pp. 36–60; 19.2, pp. 165–86; 19.4, pp. 416–35.

Langbauer, Laurie, *Women and Romance: The Consolations of Gender in the English Novel* (Ithaca and London: Cornell University Press, 1989), pp. 62–92.

Levin, Kate, ' "The Cure of Arabella's Mind": Charlotte Lennox and the Disciplining of the Female Reader', *Women's Writing: The Elizabethan to Victorian Period* 2.3 (1995), pp. 271–90.

Lynch, James J., 'Romance and Realism in Charlotte Lennox's
The Female Quixote', *Essays in Literature* 14.1 (1987),
pp. 51–63.

Malina, Debra, 'Rereading the Patriarchal Text: *The Female
Quixote, Northanger Abbey*, and the Trace of the Absent
Mother', *Eighteenth-Century Fiction* 8.2 (1996), pp. 271–92.

Marshall, David, 'Writing Masters and "Masculine Exercises"
in *The Female Quixote*', *Eighteenth-Century Fiction* 5.2
(1993), pp. 105–35.

Martin, Mary Patricia, ' "High and Noble Adventures": Reading the Novel in *The Female Quixote*', *Novel: A Forum on
Fiction* 31.1 (1997), pp. 45–62.

Motooka, Wendy, 'Coming to a Bad End: Sentimentalism, Her-
meneutics, and *The Female Quixote*', *Eighteenth-Century
Fiction* 8.2 (1996), pp. 251–70.

Nussbaum, Felicity, *Torrid Zones: Maternity, Sexuality, and
Empire in Eighteenth-Century English Narratives* (Baltimore
and London: Johns Hopkins University Press, 1995),
pp. 114–34.

Ross, Deborah, 'Mirror, Mirror: The Didactic Dilemma of *The
Female Quixote*', *Studies in English Literature* 27 (1987),
pp. 455–73.

Roulston, Christine, 'Histories of Nothing: Romance and Femininity in Charlotte Lennox's *The Female Quixote*', *Women's
Writing: The Elizabethan to Victorian Period* 2.1 (1995),
pp. 25–42.

Small, Miriam Rossiter, *Charlotte Ramsay Lennox: An Eighteenth Century Lady of Letters* (New Haven/London: Yale
University Press/Oxford University Press, 1935).

Spacks, Patricia Meyer, 'The Subtle Sophistry of Desire: Dr
Johnson and *The Female Quixote*', *Modern Philology* 85.4
(1988), pp. 532–42.

A Note on the Text

This edition of *The Female Quixote* reprints the second edition of the novel ('*Revised* and *Corrected*'), which appeared in London in two volumes duodecimo. The copy used for the setting-copy here is in the Library of Congress, Washington, DC (PR3541 L27A66 1752).

The second edition corrected many of the printing errors that occurred in the first edition, but it also introduced new ones. The revisions also included substantive alterations, altered phrases and words, as well as changes in grammar, spelling, punctuation and typography. Among the substantive changes are expansions of the critique of the romance genre, additional descriptive details of places and scenes and some elucidation of obscure language. These alterations can confidently be attributed to the author.

Until the middle of the eighteenth century, there was still considerable variation in English spelling (and grammar). The publication in 1755 of Samuel Johnson's influential *Dictionary of the English Language* was the first major contribution to the standardization of English spelling. Predating Johnson's *Dictionary, The Female Quixote* (1752) reflects the relative instability of English spelling. It has been the aim of the editors to present Lennox's text in a format which is accessible to a modern audience, but which at the same time respects and retains the distinctive linguistic flavour and appearance of the novel as it was originally published.

Following the principle of minimal editorial interference, emendation is light. Thus, the editors have changed as little as possible of the text's original spelling, punctuation, accentuation or capitalization, even where these are inconsistent or idiosyncratic (as, for instance, in the case of foreign words and names). Among the inconsistencies that have been retained are these:

acknowlege/acknowledge (Acknowlegement/Acknowledgement, unacknowleging/unacknowledging, Knowlege/knowledge); confidant/confident; heroic/heroick; remembred/remembered; Style/Stile; Surprise/Surprize; to-Night/to Night/Tonight.

Among the eighteenth-century spellings (consistently used in these forms) that have been retained are the following (the modern spelling is given in brackets):

antient (ancient); Antients (Ancients); atchiev'd (achieved); chose (choose); Cloaths (clothes); couragiously (courageously); dazling (dazzling); encrease (increase); Falshood (falsehood); fansied (fancied); forborn (forborne); Gawse (gauze); Headach (headache); inconsoleable (inconsolable); meer (mere); threatned (threatened).

Obvious typographical errors, inconsistencies, as well as any spelling, punctuation or other usage that would otherwise obscure the meaning of the text, have been silently emended (where possible and appropriate against the first edition of the novel). Thus, the editors have corrected the misleading 'swiming' to 'swimming' and the inconsistent '*Harvey*' to '*Hervey*'. The present text follows current usage for quotations (using a single set of opening and closing quotation marks), and the eighteenth-century long *s* has been replaced by the modern *s*. Dashes have been made regular using em and 2-em rules.

Unfamiliar word usage, literary allusion and historical and biographical references are explained in the Notes, which also identify quotations and supply relevant information concerning sources, archaisms and foreign words. Full names and dates of persons appearing in Notes are given for the first citation only. The Notes are numbered per Book.

THE

Female QUIXOTE;

OR, THE
ADVENTURES
OF

ARABELLA.

In TWO VOLUMES

VOL. I.

The SECOND EDITION:
Revised and Corrected.

LONDON:

Printed for A. MILLAR, over-againſt
Catharine-ſtreet in the *Strand.*

M.DCC.LII.

Earl of MIDDLESEX.[1]

My LORD,

Such is the Power of Interest over almost every Mind, that no one is long without Arguments to prove any Position which is ardently wished to be true, or to justify any Measures which are dictated by Inclination.

By this subtil Sophistry of Desire, I have been persuaded to hope, that this Book may, without Impropriety, be inscribed to Your Lordship; but am not certain, that my Reasons will have the same Force upon other Understandings.

The Dread which a Writer feels of the public Censure; the still greater Dread of Neglect; and the eager Wish for Support and Protection, which is impressed by the Consciousness of Imbecillity; are unknown to those who have never adventured into the World; and I am afraid, my Lord, equally unknown to those, who have always found the World ready to applaud them.

'Tis, therefore, not unlikely, that the Design of this Address may be mistaken, and the Effects of my Fear imputed to my Vanity: They who see Your Lordship's Name prefixed to my Performance, will rather condemn my Presumption, than compassionate my Anxiety.

But, whatever be supposed my Motive, the Praise of Judgment cannot be denied me; for to whom can Timidity so properly fly for Shelter, as to him who has been so long distinguished for Candour and Humanity? How can Vanity be so completely gratified, as by the allowed Patronage of him whose Judgment has so long given a Standard to the National Taste? Or by what other means could I so powerfully suppress all Opposition, but that of Envy, as by declaring myself,

> *My* LORD,
> > *Your* LORDSHIP'S
> > > *Obliged and most Obedient*
> > > *Humble Servant,*

The AUTHOR?

Contents

VOLUME I

BOOK I

BOOK II

BOOK IV

VOLUME II

BOOK V

BOOK VI

BOOK VIII

BOOK I

CHAPTER I

*Contains a Turn at Court, neither new nor surprising.
— Some useless Additions to a fine Lady's Education. —
The bad Effects of a whimsical Study, which some will
say is borrowed from Cervantes.*[1]

The Marquis of —— for a long Series of Years, was the first
and most distinguished Favourite at Court: He held the most
honourable Employments under the Crown, disposed of all
Places of Profit as he pleased, presided at the Council,[2] and in
a manner governed the whole Kingdom.

This extensive Authority could not fail of making him many
Enemies: He fell at last a Sacrifice to the Plots they were continually forming against him; and was not only removed from all
his Employments, but banished the Court for ever.

The Pain his undeserved Disgrace gave him, he was enabled
to conceal by the natural Haughtiness of his Temper; and,
behaving rather like a Man who had resigned, than been dismissed from his Posts, he imagined he triumphed sufficiently
over the Malice of his Enemies, while he seemed to be wholly
insensible of the Effects it produced. His secret Discontent,
however, was so much augmented by the Opportunity he now
had of observing the Baseness and Ingratitude of Mankind,
which in some Degree he experienced every Day, that he
resolved to quit all Society whatever, and devote the rest of his
Life to Solitude and Privacy. For the Place of his Retreat he
pitched upon a Castle he had in a very remote Province of the

Kingdom, in the Neighbourhood of a small Village, and several
Miles distant from any Town. The vast Extent of Ground which
surrounded this noble Building, he had caused to be laid out in
a Manner peculiar to his Taste: The most laborious Endeavours
of Art had been used to make it appear like the beautiful
Product of wild, uncultivated Nature. But if this Epitome of
Arcadia[3] could boast of only artless and simple Beauties, the
Inside of the Castle was adorned with a Magnificence suitable
to the Dignity and immense Riches of the Owner.

While Things were preparing at the Castle for his Reception,
the Marquis, though now advanced in Years, cast his Eyes on
a young Lady, greatly inferior to himself in Quality, but whose
Beauty and good Sense promised him an agreeable Companion.
After a very short Courtship, he married her, and in a few
Weeks carried his new Bride into the Country, from whence he
absolutely resolved never to return.

The Marquis, following the Plan of Life he had laid down,
divided his Time between the Company of his Lady, his Library,
which was large and well furnished, and his Gardens. Sometimes he took the Diversion of Hunting, but never admitted any
Company whatever; his Pride and extreme Reserve rendered
him so wholly inaccessible to the Country Gentry about him,
that none ever presumed to solicit his Acquaintance.

In the second Year of his Retirement, the Marchioness
brought him a Daughter, and died in Three Days after her
Delivery. The Marquis, who had tenderly loved her, was extremely afflicted at her Death; but Time having produced its
usual Effects, his great Fondness for the little *Arabella*[4] intirely
engrossed his Attention, and made up all the Happiness of his
Life. At Four Years of Age he took her from under the Direction
of the Nurses and Women appointed to attend her, and permitted her to receive no Part of her Education from another,
which he was capable of giving her himself. He taught her to
read and write in a very few Months; and, as she grew older,
finding in her an uncommon Quickness of Apprehension, and
an Understanding capable of great Improvements, he resolved
to cultivate so promising a Genius with the utmost Care; and,
as he frequently, in the Rapture of paternal Fondness, expressed

himself, render her Mind as beautiful as her Person was lovely.

Nature had indeed given her a most charming Face, a Shape easy and delicate, a sweet and insinuating Voice, and an Air so full of Dignity and Grace, as drew the Admiration of all that saw her. These native Charms were improved with all the Heightenings of Art; her Dress was perfectly magnificent; the best Masters of Music and Dancing were sent for from *London* to attend her. She soon became a perfect Mistress of the *French* and *Italian* Languages,[5] under the Care of her Father; and it is not to be doubted, but she would have made a great Proficiency in all useful Knowlege, had not her whole Time been taken up by another Study.

From her earliest Youth she had discovered a Fondness for Reading, which extremely delighted the Marquis; he permitted her therefore the Use of his Library, in which, unfortunately for her, were great Store of Romances, and, what was still more unfortunate, not in the original *French*, but very bad Translations.[6]

The deceased Marchioness had purchased these Books to soften a Solitude which she found very disagreeable; and, after her Death, the Marquis removed them from her Closet into his Library, where *Arabella* found them.

The surprising Adventures with which they were filled, proved a most pleasing Entertainment to a young Lady, who was wholly secluded from the World; who had no other Diversion, but ranging like a Nymph through Gardens, or, to say better, the Woods and Lawns in which she was inclosed; and who had no other Conversation but that of a grave and melancholy Father, or her own Attendants.

Her Ideas, from the Manner of her Life, and the Objects around her, had taken a romantic Turn; and, supposing Romances were real Pictures of Life, from them she drew all her Notions and Expectations. By them she was taught to believe, that Love was the ruling Principle of the World; that every other Passion was subordinate to this; and that it caused all the Happiness and Miseries of Life. Her Glass, which she often consulted, always shewed her a Form so extremely lovely, that, not finding herself engaged in such Adventures as were common to the Heroines in the Romances she read, she often complained of the Insensibility of Mankind, upon whom her Charms seemed to have so little Influence.

The perfect Retirement she lived in, afforded indeed no Opportunities of making the Conquests she desired; but she could not comprehend, how any Solitude could be obscure enough to conceal a Beauty like hers from Notice; and thought the Reputation of her Charms sufficient to bring a Croud of Adorers to demand her of her Father. Her Mind being wholly filled with the most extravagant Expectations, she was alarmed by every trifling Incident; and kept in a continual Anxiety by a Vicissitude of Hopes, Fears, Wishes, and Disappointments.

CHAPTER II

Contains a Description of a Lady's Dress, in Fashion not much above Two thousand Years ago. — The Beginning of an Adventure which seems to promise a great deal.

Arabella had now entered into her Seventeenth Year with the Regret of seeing herself the Object of Admiration to a few Rustics only, who happened to see her; when, one *Sunday*, making use of the Permission the Marquis sometimes allowed her, to attend Divine Service at the Church belonging to the Village near which they lived, her Vanity was flattered with an Adorer not altogether unworthy of her Notice.

This Gentleman was young, gay, handsome, and very elegantly dressed; he was just come from *London* with an Intention to pass some Weeks with a Friend in that Part of the Country; and at the time *Arabella* entered the Church, his Eyes, which had wandered from one rural Fair to another, were in an Instant fixed upon her Face. She blushed with a very becoming Modesty; and, pleased with the unusual Appearance of so fine a Gentleman, and the particular Notice he took of her, passed on to her Seat thro' a double Row of Country People; who, with a Profusion of aukward Bows and Courtesies, expressed their Respect.

Mr. *Hervey*, for that was the Stranger's Name, was no less surprised at her Beauty, than the Singularity of her Dress;[7] and the odd Whim of being followed into the Church by three Women-Attendants, who, as soon as she was seated, took their Places behind her.[8]

Her Dress, though singular, was far from being unbecoming. All the Beauties of her Neck and Shape were set off to the greatest Advantage by the Fashion of her Gown, which, in the Manner of a Robe, was made to sit tight to her Body; and fastened on the Breast with a Knot of Diamonds. Her fine black Hair hung upon her Neck in Curls, which had so much the Appearance of being artless, that all but her Maid, whose Employment it was to give them that Form, imagined they were so. Her Head-dress was only a few Knots advantageously disposed, over which she wore a white Sarsenet Hood, somewhat in the Form of a Veil,[9] with which she sometimes wholly covered her fair Face, when she saw herself beheld with too much Attention.

This Veil had never appeared to her so necessary before. Mr. *Hervey*'s eager Glances threw her into so much Confusion, that, pulling it over her Face as much as she was able, she remained invisible to him all the time they afterwards stayed in the Church. This Action, by which she would have had him understand, that she was displeased at his gazing on her with so little Respect, only increased his Curiosity to know who she was.

When the Congregation was dismissed, he hastened to the Door, with an Intention to offer her his Hand to help her to her Coach; but seeing the magnificent Equipage that waited for her, and the Number of Servants that attended it, he conceived a much higher Idea of her Quality than he had at first; and, changing his Design, contented himself with only bowing to her as she passed; and as soon as her Coach drove away, inquired of some Persons nearest him, who she was?

These Rustics, highly delighted with the Opportunity of talking to the gay *Londoner*, whom they looked upon as a very extraordinary Person, gave him all the Intelligence they were able, concerning the Lady he inquired after; and filled him

with an inconceivable Surprize at the strange Humour of the
Marquis, who buried so beautiful a Creature in Obscurity.

At his Return home he expressed his Admiration of her in
Terms that persuaded his Friend, she had made some Impression on his Heart; and, after raillying him a little upon this
Suspicion, he assumed a more serious Air, and told him, If he
really liked Lady *Bella*, he thought it not impossible but he
might obtain her. The poor Girl, added he, has been kept in
Confinement so long, that I believe it would not be difficult to
persuade her to free herself by Marriage. She never had a Lover
in her Life; and therefore the first Person who addresses her has
the fairest Chance for succeeding.

Mr. *Hervey*, tho' he could not persuade himself his Cousin
was in Earnest when he advised him to court the only Daughter
of a Man of the Marquis's Quality, and Heiress to his vast
Estates; yet relished the Scheme, and resolved to make some
Attempt upon her before he left the Country. However, he
concealed his Design from his Cousin, not being willing to
expose himself to be ridiculed, if he did not succeed; and,
turning the Advice he had given him into a Jest, left him in the
Opinion, that he thought no more of it.

CHAPTER III

In which the Adventure goes on after the accustomed Manner.

Arabella, in the mean time, was wholly taken up with the
Adventure, as she called it, at Church: The Person and Dress of
the Gentleman who had so particularly gazed on her there, was
so different from what she had been accustomed to see, that
she immediately concluded, he was of some distinguished Rank.
It was past a Doubt, she thought, that he was excessively in
Love with her; and as she soon expected to have some very
extraordinary Proofs of his Passion, her Thoughts were wholly
employed on the Manner in which she should receive them.

As soon as she came home, and had paid her Duty to the Marquis, she hurried to her Chamber, to be at Liberty to indulge her agreeable Reflections; and, after the Example of her Heroines, when any thing extraordinary happened to them, called her favourite Woman; or, to use her own Language, her, "in whom she confided her most secret Thoughts."[10]

Well, *Lucy*, said she, did you observe that Stranger who ey'd *us** so heedfully To-day at Church?

This Girl, notwithstanding her Country-Simplicity, knew a Compliment was expected from her on this Occasion; and therefore replied, "That she did not wonder at the Gentleman's staring at her; for she was sure he had never seen any body so handsome as her Ladyship before."

I have not all the Beauty you attribute to me, said *Arabella*, smiling a little: And, with a very moderate Share of it, I might well fix the Attention of a Person who seemed not to be over-much pleased with the Objects about him: However, pursued she, assuming a more serious Air, if this Stranger be weak enough to entertain any Sentiments more than indifferent for me; I charge you, upon Pain of my Displeasure, do not be accessary to the Conveying his presumptuous Thoughts to me either by Letters or Messages; nor suffer him to corrupt your Fidelity with the Presents he will very probably offer you.

Lucy, to whom this Speech first gave a Hint of what she ought to expect from her Lady's Lovers, finding herself of more Importance than she imagined, was so pleased at the Prospect which opened to her, that it was with some Hesitation she promised to obey her Orders.

Arabella, however, was satisfied with her Assurances of observing her Directions; and dismissed her from her Presence, not without an Apprehension of being too well obeyed.

A whole Week being elapsed without meeting with the Importunities she expected, she could hardly conceal her Sur-prize at so mortifying a Disappointment; and frequently interro-gated *Lucy*, concerning any Attempts the Stranger had made on her Fidelity; but the Answers she received, only increased

---

* The Heroines always speak of themselves in the Plural Number.

her Discontent, as they convinced her, her Charms had not had the Effect she imagined.

Mr. *Hervey*, however, had been all this time employed in thinking of some Means to get acquainted with the Marquis; for, being possessed with an extraordinary Opinion of his Wit, and personal Accomplishments, he did not fear making some Impression on the Heart of the young Lady; provided he could have an Opportunity of conversing with her.

His Cousin's Advice was continually in his Mind, and flattered his Vanity with the most agreeable Hopes: But the Marquis's Fondness for Solitude, and that Haughtiness which was natural to him, rendered him so difficult of Access, that *Hervey*, from the Intelligence he received of his Humour, despaired of being able to prosecute his Scheme; when, meeting with a young Farmer in one of his Evening-Walks, and entering into Conversation with him upon several Country Subjects, the Discourse at last turned upon the Marquis of —— whose fine House and Gardens were within their View; upon which the young Fellow informed him, he was Brother to a young Woman that attended the Lady *Arabella*; and, being fond of lengthening out the Conversation with so fine a Gentleman, gave him, without being desired, the domestic History of the whole Family, as he had received it from *Lucy*, who was the Sister he mentioned.

Hervey, excessively delighted at this accidental Meeting with a Person so capable of serving his Design, affected a great Desire of being better acquainted with him; and, under Pretence of acquiring some Knowledge in rural Affairs, accustomed himself to call so often at *William*'s Farm, that, at last, he met with the Person whom the Hopes of seeing had so often carried him thither.

Lucy, the Moment she saw him enter, knowing him again, blushed at the Remembrance of the Discourse which had passed between her Lady and herself concerning him; and was not at all surprised at the Endeavours he used to speak to her apart: But, as soon as he began a Conversation concerning *Arabella*, she interrupted him by saying, I know, Sir, that you are *distractedly* in Love with my Lady; but she has forbid me to receive any Letters or Messages from you; and therefore I beg you will not offer to bribe me; for I dare not disobey her.

Mr. *Hervey* was at first so astonished at her Speech, that he knew not what to think of it; but, after a little Reflection, attributing to an Excess of aukward Cunning what, in Reality, was an Effect of her Simplicity, he resolved to make use of the Hint she had given him; and, presenting her with a couple of Guineas,[11] intreated her to venture displeasing her Lady, by bearing a Letter from him; promising to reward her better, if she succeeded.

Lucy made some Difficulty to comply; but, not being able absolutely to refuse the first Bribe that ever was offered to her, she, after some Intreaties, consented to take the Letter; and, receiving the Money he presented her, left him at Liberty to write, after she had got her Brother to furnish him with Materials for that Purpose.

CHAPTER IV

A Mistake, which produces no great Consequences — An extraordinary Comment upon a Behaviour natural enough — An Instance of a Lady's Compassion for her Lover, which the Reader may possibly think not very compassionate.

Hervey, who was Master of no great Elegance in Letter-writing,[12] was at first at some Loss, how to address a Lady of her Quality, to whom he was an absolute Stranger, upon the Subject of Love; but, conceiving there was no great Occasion for much Ceremony in declaring himself to one who had been educated in the Country, and who, he believed, could not be displeased with a Lover of his Figure, he therefore, in plain Terms, told her, how *deeply* he was enamoured of her; and conjured her to afford him some Opportunity of paying his Respects to her.

Lucy received this Letter from him with a worse Grace than she did the Gold; and, tho' she promised him to deliver it to her Lady immediately, yet she kept it a Day or two before she had the Courage to attempt it: At last, drawing it out of her Pocket, with a bashful Air, she presented it to her Lady, telling her it came from the fine Gentleman whom she saw at Church.

Arabella blushed at the Sight of the Letter; and tho', in Reality, she was not displeased, yet, being a strict Observer of romantic Forms, she chid her Woman severely for taking it. Carry it back, added she, to the presumptuous Writer of it; and let him know how greatly his Insolence has offended me.

Lucy, however, suffered the Letter to remain on the Toilet,[13] expecting some Change in her Lady's Mind; for she traversed the Chamber in great seeming Irresolution, often stealing a Glance to the Letter, which she had a strong Inclination to open; but, searching the Records of her Memory for a Precedent, and not finding, that any Lady ever opened a Letter from an unknown Lover, she reiterated her Commands to *Lucy* to carry it back, with a Look and Accent so very severe, that the Girl, extremely apprehensive of having offended her, put the Letter again in her Pocket, resolving to return it the first Opportunity.

Mr. *Hervey*, who had his Thoughts wholly taken up with the flattering Prospect of Success, no sooner saw *Lucy*, who gave him his Letter without speaking a Word, than, supposing it had been the Answer he expected, he eagerly snatched it out of her Hand, and, kissing it first in a Rapture of Joy, broke it open; but his Surprize and Confusion, when he saw it was his own Letter returned, was inexpressible. For some Moments he kept his Eyes fastened upon the tender Billet, as if he was really reading it. His Disappointment, and the ridiculous Figure he knew he must make in the Eyes of his Messenger, filled him with so much Confusion, that he did not dare to look up; but, recovering himself at last, he affected to turn it into a Jest; and, laughing first himself, gave *Lucy* the Liberty of laughing also, who had, with much Difficulty, been able to prevent doing it before.

The Curiosity he felt to hear how she had acquitted herself of the Trust he had reposed in her, made him oblige her to give a Truce to her Mirth, in order to satisfy him; and *Lucy*, who was extremely exact in her Relations, told him all that had passed, without omitting the smallest Circumstance.

Though it was impossible to draw any favourable Omen from what he heard, yet he determined to make another Effort, before he set out for *London*; and, taking Leave of his Confident, after he had appointed her to meet him again the next Day, at her Brother's, he went home to consider upon Means to effect his Designs, which the ill Success of his first Attempt had not forced him to abandon.

Arabella, who expected to hear, that the Return of his Letter would make her Lover commit some very extravagant Actions; and having impatiently waited for an Account of them from *Lucy*; finding she seemed to have no Intention to begin a Discourse concerning him; asked her, at last, If she had executed her Commission, and returned the Letter to the insolent Unknown?

The Girl answered, Yes.

Which not being all that her Lady expected, And how did he receive it? resumed she, peevishly.

Why, Madam, replied *Lucy*, I believe he thought your Ladyship had sent him an Answer; for he kissed the Letter several times.

Foolish Wench! replied *Arabella*, How can you imagine he had the Temerity to think I should answer his Letter? A Favour, which, though he had spent Years in my Service, would have been infinitely greater than he could have expected. No, *Lucy*, he kissed the Letter, either because he thought it had been touched at least by my Hands, or to shew the perfect Submission with which he received my Commands; and it is not to be doubted but his Despair will force him to commit some desperate Outrage against himself, which I do not hate him enough to wish, though he has mortally offended me.

Arabella was possessed of great Sensibility and Softness; and, being really persuaded, that her Lover would entertain some fatal Design, seemed so much affected with the Thoughts of what might happen, that *Lucy*, who tenderly loved her, begged her not to be so much concerned for the Gentleman: There is no Fear, added she, that he will do himself a Mischief; for when he discovered his Mistake, he laughed heartily, as well as myself.

How! replied *Arabella*, extremely surprised, Did he laugh?

Which *Lucy* confirming, Doubtless, resumed she, having taken a little Time to consider of so strange a Phænomenon, he laughed, because his Reason was disturbed at the sudden Shock he received: Unhappy Man! his Presumption will be severely enough punished, though I do not add Anger to the Scorn which I have expressed for him: Therefore, *Lucy*, you may tell him, if you please, that, notwithstanding the Offence he has been guilty of, I am not cruel enough to wish his Death, and that I command him to live, if he can live without Hope.

CHAPTER V

In which one would imagine the Adventure concluded, but for a Promise that something else is to come.

Lucy now began to think there was something more, than she imagined, in this Affair. Mr. *Hervey* indeed, in her Opinion, had seemed to be very far from having any Design to attempt his own Life; but her Lady, she thought, could not possibly be mistaken; and therefore she resolved to carry her Message to him immediately, though it was then late in the Evening.

Accordingly she went to her Brother's, where she had some Hope of meeting with him; but not finding him there, she obliged him to go to the House where he lived, and tell him she desired to speak with him.

William, being let into the Secret of his Sister's frequent Meetings with Mr. *Hervey*, imagined she had some agreeable News to acquaint him with; and therefore ran immediately to his Relation's House, which was but at a small Distance; but he was told Mr. *Hervey* was in Bed, very much indisposed, and could not be seen.

This News put *Lucy* in a terrible Fright: She told her Apprehensions to her Brother; which being such as her Lady had put into her Head, and were now confirmed by Mr. *Hervey*'s Illness, the young Farmer stood amazed, not being able to comprehend her Meaning; and she, without staying to explain herself any further, went home to the Castle, and told her Lady, That what she feared was come to pass; the Gentleman would certainly die; for he was very ill in Bed.

This being no more than what *Arabella* expected, she discovered no Surprize; but only asked *Lucy*, If she had delivered her Message to him?

Would you have me, Madam, replied she, go to his House? I am afraid the Marquis will hear of it.

My Father, replied *Arabella*, can never be offended with me for doing a charitable Action.

Ah! Madam, interrupted *Lucy*, let me go then immediately, for fear the poor Gentleman should grow worse.

If he be sick almost to Death, resumed *Arabella*, he will recover, if I command him to do so: When did you hear of a Lover dying through Despair, when his Mistress let him know it was her Pleasure he should live? But as it will not be altogether so proper for you to go to his House, as it may be suspected you come from me; I'll write a few Lines, which you shall copy, and your Brother may carry them to him To-morrow, and I'll engage he shall be well in a few Hours.

Saying this, she went into her Closet,[14] and, having written a short Note, made *Lucy* write it over again. It was as follows:

Lucy, *To the Unfortunate Lover of her Lady.*

My Lady, who is the most generous Person in the World, has commanded me to tell you, that, presumptuous as you are, she does not desire your Death; nay more, she commands you to live, and permits you, in case you obey her, to hope for her Pardon, provided you keep within the Bounds she prescribes to you.

Adieu.

This Letter *Lucy* copied, and, *Arabella*, examining it again, thought it rather too kind; and, seeming desirous of making some Alteration in it, *Lucy*, who was extremely anxious for Mr. *Hervey*'s Life, fearing lest she should alter it in such a manner, that the Gentleman might be at Liberty to die, if he chose it, conjured her Lady in such pressing Terms to let it remain as it was, that *Arabella* suffered herself to be prevailed upon by her Intreaties; and, remembring that it was not uncommon for the Ladies in Romances to relax a little in their Severity through the Remonstrances of their Women, told her, with an inchanting Smile, that she would grant her Desire; and went to Bed with that pleasing Satisfaction, which every generous Mind experiences at the Consciousness of having done some very benevolent Action.

In the Morning, this life-restoring Billet was dispatched by *Lucy* to her Brother, inclosed in one to him, charging him to carry it to the sick Gentleman immediately.

William, having a strong Curiosity to see what his Sister had written, ventured to open it; and, not being able to imagine Lady *Bella* had really given her Orders to write what appeared to him the most unintelligible Stuff in the World, resolved to suppress this Letter till he had questioned her a little concerning it.

A few Hours after, Mr. *Hervey*, who expected to meet *Lucy* at her Brother's, came in. His Illness having been only a violent Headach, to which he was subject, being now quite off, he remembred the Appointment he had made; but, having waited some time, and she not coming, he returned again to his Cousin's, leaving Word for her, that he would see her the next Day.

Scarce was he gone out, when *Lucy*, who longed to know what Effect her Letter had produced in his Health, came in; and eagerly inquiring of her Brother how Mr. *Hervey* was, received for Answer, that he had been there a Moment before she came.

Well, cried she, clasping her Hands together, with Surprize, my Lady said, her Letter would cure him, if he was ever so sick; but I did not imagine he would have been well enough to come abroad so soon.

Your Lady! interrupted *William*; why was it not yourself that wrote the Letter you gave to me?

No, truly, Brother, resumed she: How was it possible I should write so fine a Letter? My Lady *made* every Word of it, and I only wrote it after her.

William, hearing this, would not own the Indiscretion he now thought he had been guilty of, in keeping the Letter; but suffered his Sister to return to her Lady, in the Belief that he had delivered it, resolving, when he saw her next, to say he had lost it; for he knew not what Excuse to make to Mr. *Hervey* for not giving it him when he saw him.

Arabella received the Account of her Lover's Recovery as a Thing she was absolutely sure of before; and thinking she had now done all that could be expected from her Compassion, resumed her usual Severity, and commanded *Lucy* to mention him no more. If he loves me with that Purity he ought to do, pursued she, he will cease to importune me any further: And though his Passion be ever so violent, his Respect and Submission to my Commands will oblige him to Silence. The Obedience he has already shewn, in recovering at the first Intimation I gave, that it was my Will he should do so, convinces me, I need not apprehend he will renew his Follies to displease me.

Lucy, who found by this Discourse of her Lady's, that her Commission was at an End with regard to Mr. *Hervey*, followed her Directions so exactly, that she not only spoke no more of him to her, but also, in order to avoid him, neglected to go to her Brother's.

His Impatience at not seeing her made him prevail upon her Brother to go to the Castle, and intreat her to give him another Interview: But *Lucy* positively refused; and, to make a Merit with her Lady of her Obedience, informed her what he had requested.

Arabella, resenting a Boldness which argued so little Respect to her Commands, began now to repent of the Compassion she had shewn him; and, commending *Lucy* for what she had done, bid her tell the insolent Unknown, if he ever sent to her again, that she was resolved never to pardon the Contempt he had shewn for her Orders.

Mr. *Hervey*, finding himself deserted by *Lucy*, resolved to give over his Attempts, congratulating himself for his Discretion in not acquainting his Cousin with what he had already done:

His Heart not being very much engaged, he found no great
Difficulty in consoling himself for his bad Success. In a few
Days he thought of Lady *Bella* no more, than if he had never
seen her; but an Accident bringing her again in his Way, he
could not resist the Inclination he felt to speak to her; and by
that means drew upon himself a very sensible Mortification.

CHAPTER VI

*In which the Adventure is really concluded; tho',
possibly, not as the Reader expected.*

The Marquis sometimes permitting his Daughter to ride out,
and this being the only Diversion she was allowed,[15] or ever
experienced, she did not fail to take it as often as she could.

She was returning from one of these Airings one Day,
attended by two Servants, when Mr. *Hervey*, who happened to
be at some Distance, observing a Lady on Horseback, who
made a very graceful Figure, he rode up to her, in order to have
a nearer View; and, knowing Lady *Bella* again, resolved to
speak to her: But while he was considering how he should
accost her, *Arabella* suddenly seeing him, and observing he was
making up to her, her Imagination immediately suggested to
her, that this insolent Lover had a Design to seize her Person; and
this Thought terrifying her extremely, she gave a loud Shriek;
which Mr. *Hervey* hearing, rode eagerly up to her to inquire the
Reason of it, at the same time that her two Attendants, as much
amazed as himself, came galloping up also.

Arabella, upon his coming close to her, redoubled her Cries.
If you have any Valour, said she to her Servants, defend your
unfortunate Mistress, and rescue her from this unworthy Man.

The Servants, believing him to be an Highwayman, by this
Exclamation, and dreading lest he should present his Pistol at
their Heads, if they offered to make any Resistance, recoiled a
few Paces back, expecting he would demand their Purses when
he had robbed their Lady: But the extreme Surprize he was in,

keeping him motionless, the Fellows not seeing any Pistols in his Hand, and animated by *Arabella*'s Cries, who, calling them Cowards and Traitors, urged them to deliver her; they both, in a Moment, laid hold of Mr. *Hervey*, and forced him to alight; which they did also themselves, still keeping fast hold of him, whom Surprize, Shame, and Rage, had hitherto kept silent.

Rascals! cried he, when he was able to speak, what do you mean by using me in this manner? Do you suppose I had any Intention to hurt the Lady? — What do you take me for?

For a Ravisher, interrupted *Arabella*, an impious Ravisher, who, contrary to all Laws both human and divine, endeavour to possess yourself by Force of a Person whom you are not worthy to serve; and whose Charity and Compassion you have returned with the utmost Ingratitude.

Upon my Word, Madam, said Mr. *Hervey*, I don't understand one Word you say: You either mistake me for some other Person, or are pleased to divert yourself with the Surprize I am in: But I beseech you carry the Jest no farther, and order your Servants to let me go; or, by Heaven — cried he struggling to get loose, if I can but free one of my Hands, I'll stab the Scoundrels before your Face.

It is not with Threats like these, resumed *Arabella* with great Calmness, that I can be moved. A little more Submission and Respect would become you better; you are now wholly in my Power; I may, if I please, carry you to my Father, and have you severely punished for your Attempt: But to shew you, that I am as generous as you are base and designing, I'll give you Freedom, provided you promise me never to appear before me again: But, in order to secure my own Safety, you must deliver up your Arms to my Servants, that I may be assured you will not have it in your Power to make a second Attempt upon my Liberty.

Mr. *Hervey*, whose Astonishment was increased by every Word she spoke, began now to be apprehensive, that this might prove a very serious Affair, since she seemed resolved to believe he had a Design to carry her off; and, knowing that an Attempt of that Nature upon an Heiress might have dangerous Consequences, he resolved to accept the Conditions she offered him:

But while he delivered his Hanger[16] to the Servant, he assured her in the strongest Terms, that he had no other Design in riding up to her, but to have a nearer View of her Person.

Add not Falshood, said *Arabella* sternly, to a Crime already black enough; for tho', by an Effect of my Generosity, I have resolved not to deliver you up to the Resentment of my Father, yet nothing shall ever be able to make me pardon this Outrage. Go then, pursued she, go, base Man, unworthy of the Care I took of thy Safety; go to some distant Country, where I may never hear of thee more; and suffer me, if possible, to lose the Remembrance of thy Crimes.

Saying this, she ordered her Servants, who had got the Hanger in their Possession, to set him at Liberty, and mount their Horses; which they did immediately, and followed their Lady, who rode with all imaginable Speed to the Castle.

Mr. *Hervey*, not yet recovered from his Surprize, stood some Moments considering the strange Scene he had been Witness to; and in which he had, much against his Will, appeared the principal Character. As he was not acquainted with Lady *Bella*'s Foible, he concluded her Fears of him were occasioned by her Simplicity, and some Misrepresentations that had been made her by *Lucy*, who, he thought, had betrayed him; and, fearing this ridiculous Adventure would be soon made public, and himself exposed to the Sneers of his Country Acquaintance, he resolved to go back to *London* as soon as possible.

The next Day, pretending he had received a Letter which obliged him to set out immediately, he took Leave of his Cousin, heartily glad at the Escape he should make from his Raillery; for he did not doubt but the Story would very soon be known, and told greatly to his Disadvantage.

But *Arabella*, in order to be completely generous, a Quality for which all the Heroines are famous, laid a Command upon her two Attendants not to mention what had passed, giving them, at the same time, Money to secure their Secrecy; and threatening them with her Displeasure, if they disobeyed.

Arabella, as soon as she had an Opportunity, did not fail to acquaint her faithful *Lucy* with the Danger from which she had so happily escaped, thanking Heaven at the same time with great Devotion, for having preserved her from the Hands of the Ravisher.

Two or three Months rolled away, after this Accident, without offering any new Adventure to our fair Visionary; when her Imagination, always prepossessed with the same fantastic Ideas, made her stumble upon another Mistake, equally absurd and ridiculous.

CHAPTER VII

In which some Contradictions are very happily reconciled.

The Marquis's head Gardener had received a young Fellow into his Master's Service, who had lived in several Families of Distinction. He had a good Face; was tolerably genteel; and, having an Understanding something above his Condition, join'd to a great deal of *second-hand* Politeness, which he had contracted while he lived at *London*, he appeared a very extraordinary Person among the Rustics who were his Fellow-Servants.

Arabella, when she walked in the Garden, had frequent Opportunities of seeing this young Man, whom she observed with a very particular Attention. His Person and Air had something, she thought, very distinguishing. When she condescended to speak to him about any Business he was employed in, she took Notice, that his Answers were framed in a Language vastly superior to his Condition; and the Respect he paid her had quite another Air from that of the aukward Civility of the other Servants.

Having discerned so many Marks of a Birth far from being mean, she easily passed from an Opinion, that he was a Gentleman, to a Belief that he was something more; and every new Sight of him adding Strength to her Suspicions, she remained, in a little time, perfectly convinced that he was some Person of Quality, who, disguised in the Habit of a Gardener, had introduced himself into her Father's Service in order to have an Opportunity of declaring a Passion to her, which must certainly be very great, since it had forced him to assume an Appearance so unworthy of his noble Extraction.

Wholly possessed with this Thought, she set herself to observe him more narrowly; and soon found out, that he went very aukwardly about his Work; that he sought Opportunities of being alone; that he threw himself in her Way as often as he could, and gazed on her very attentively: She sometimes fansied she saw him endeavour to smother a Sigh when he answered her any Question about his Work; once saw him leaning against a Tree with his Hands crossed upon his Breast; and, having lost a String of small Pearls, which she remembered he had seen her threading as she sat in one of the Arbours, was persuaded he had taken it up, and kept it for the Object of his secret Adoration.

She often wondered, indeed, that she did not find her Name carved on the Trees, with some mysterious Expressions of Love; that he was never discovered lying along the Side of one of the little Rivulets, increasing the Stream with his Tears; nor, for three Months that he had lived there, had ever been sick of a Fever caused by his Grief, and the Constraint he put upon himself in not declaring his Passion: But she considered again, that his Fear of being discovered kept him from amusing himself with making the Trees bear the Records of his secret Thoughts, or of indulging his Melancholy in any Manner expressive of the Condition of his Soul; and, as for his not being sick, his Youth, and the Strength of his Constitution, might, even for a longer time, bear him up against the Assaults of a Fever: But he appeared much thinner and paler than he used to be; and she concluded, therefore, that he must in time sink under the Violence of his Passion, or else be forced to declare it to her; which she considered as a very great Misfortune; for, not finding in herself any Disposition to approve his Love, she must necessarily banish him from her Presence, for fear he should have the Presumption to hope, that Time might do any thing in his Favour: And it was possible also, that the Sentence she would be obliged to pronounce, might either cause his Death, or force him to commit some extravagant Action, which would discover him to her Father, who would, perhaps, think her guilty of holding a secret Correspondence with him.

These Thoughts perplexed her so much, that, hoping to find some Relief by unburdening her Mind to *Lucy*, she told her all her Uneasiness. Ah! said she to her, looking upon *Edward*, who had just passed them, how unfortunate do I think myself in being the Cause of that Passion which makes this illustrious Unknown wear away his Days in so shameful an Obscurity! Yes, *Lucy*, pursued she, that *Edward*, whom you regard as one of my Father's menial Servants, is a Person of *Sublime Quality*, who submits to this Disguise only to have an Opportunity of seeing me every Day. But why do you seem so surprised? Is it possible, that you have not suspected him to be what he is? Has he never unwittingly made any Discovery of himself? Have you not surprised him in Discourse with his faithful 'Squire, who, certainly, lurks here abouts to receive his Commands, and is haply the Confident of his Passion? Has he never entertained you with any Conversation about me? Or have you never seen any valuable Jewels in his Possession by which you suspected him to be not what he appears?

Truly, Madam, replied *Lucy*, I never took him for any body else but a simple Gardener; but now you open my Eyes, methinks I can find I have been strangely mistaken; for he does not look like a Man of low Degree; and he talks quite in another Manner from our Servants. I never heard him indeed speak of your Ladyship, but once; and that was, when he first saw you walking in the Garden, he asked our *John*, If you was not the Marquis's Daughter? And he said, You was as beautiful as an Angel. As for fine Jewels, I never saw any; and I believe he has none; but he has a Watch, and that looks as if he was something, Madam: Nor do I remember to have seen him talk with any Stranger that looked like a 'Squire.

Lucy having thus, with her usual Punctuality,[17] answered every Question her Lady put to her, proceeded to ask her, What she should say, if he should beg her to give her a Letter, as the other Gentleman had done?

You must by no means take it, replied *Arabella*: My

Compassion had before like to have been fatal to me. If he discovers his Quality to me, I shall know in what manner to treat him.

They were in this Part of their Discourse, when a Noise they heard at some Distance, made *Arabella* bend her Steps to the Place from whence it proceeded; and, to her infinite Amazement, saw the head Gardener, with a Stick he had in his Hand, give several Blows to the concealed Hero, who suffered the Indignity with admirable Patience.

Shocked at seeing a Person of sublime Quality treated so unworthily, she called out to the Gardener to hold his Hand; who immediately obeyed; and *Edward*, seeing the young Lady advance, sneaked off, with an Air very different from an *Oroondates*.[18]

For what Crime, pray, said *Arabella*, with a stern Aspect, did you treat the Person I saw with you so cruelly? He whom you take such unbecoming Liberties with, may possibly — But again I ask you, What has he done? You should make some Allowance for his want of Skill in the abject Employment he is in at present.

It is not for his want of Skill, Madam, said the Gardener, that I corrected him; he knows his Business very well, if he would mind it; but, Madam, I have discovered him —

Discovered him, do you say? interrupted *Arabella*: And has the Knowledge of his Condition not been able to prevent such Usage? or rather, Has it been the Occasion of his receiving it?

His Conditions are very bad, Madam, returned the Gardener; and I am afraid are such as will one Day prove the Ruin of Body and Soul too. I have for some time suspected he had evil Designs in his Head; and just now watched him to the Fish-pond, and prevented him from —

O dear! interrupted *Lucy*, looking pitifully on her Lady, whose fair Bosom heaved with Compassion, I warrant he was going to make away with himself.

No, resumed the Gardener, smiling at the Mistake, he was only going to make away with some of the Carp,[19] which the Rogue had caught, and intended, I suppose, to sell; but I threw them into the Water again; and if your Ladyship had not forbid me, I would have drubbed him soundly for his Pains.

Fye! fye! interrupted *Arabella*, out of Breath with Shame and
Vexation, tell me no more of these idle Tales.

Then, hastily walking on to hide the Blushes which this
strange Accusation of her illustrious Lover had raised in her
Face, she continued for some time in the greatest Perplexity
imaginable.

Lucy, who followed her, and could not possibly reconcile
what her Lady had been telling her concerning *Edward*, with
the Circumstance of his stealing the Carp, ardently wished to
hear her Opinion of this Matter; but, seeing her deeply engaged
with her own Thoughts, she would not venture to disturb her.

Arabella indeed had been in such a terrible Consternation,
that it was some Time before she even reconciled Appearances
to herself; but, as she had a most happy Facility in accommodating every Incident to her own Wishes and Conceptions, she
examined this Matter so many different Ways, drew so many
Conclusions, and fansied so many Mysteries in the most indifferent Actions of the supposed noble Unknown, that she
remained, at last, more than ever confirmed in the Opinion,
that he was some great Personage, whom her Beauty had forced
to assume an Appearance unworthy of himself: When *Lucy*, no
longer able to keep Silence, drew off her Attention from those
pleasing Images, by speaking of the Carp-stealing Affair again.

Arabella, whose Confusion returned at that disagreeable
Sound, charged her, in an angry Tone, never to mention so
injurious a Suspicion any more: For, in fine, said she to her, do
you imagine a Person of his Rank could be guilty of stealing
Carp? Alas! pursued she, sighing, he had, indeed, some fatal
Design; and, doubtless, would have executed it, had not this
Fellow so luckily prevented him.

But Mr. *Woodbind*, Madam, said *Lucy*, saw the Carp in his
Hand: I wonder what he was going to do with them.

Still, resumed *Arabella*, extremely chagrined, still will you
wound my Ears with that horrid Sound? I tell you, obstinate
and foolish Wench, that this unhappy Man went thither to die;
and if he really caught the Fish, it was to conceal his Design
from *Woodbind*: His great Mind could not suggest to him,
that it was possible he might be suspected of a Baseness like

that this ignorant Fellow accused him of; therefore he took
no Care about it, being wholly possessed by his despairing
Thoughts.

However, Madam, said *Lucy*, your Ladyship may prevent
his going to the Fish-pond again, by laying your Commands
upon him to live.

I shall do all that I ought, answered *Arabella*; but my Care
for the Safety of other Persons must not make me forget what
I owe to my own.

As she had always imputed Mr. *Hervey*'s fansied attempt to
carry her away, to the Letter she had written to him, upon
which he had probably founded his Hopes of being pardoned
for it, she resolved to be more cautious for the future in giving
such Instances of her Compassion; and was at a great Loss in
what manner to comfort her despairing Lover, without raising
Expectations she had no Inclination to confirm: But she was
delivered from her Perplexity a few Days after, by the News of
his having left the Marquis's Service; which she attributed to
some new Design he had formed to obtain her; and *Lucy*, who
always thought as her Lady did, was of the same Opinion;
tho' it was talked among the Servants, that *Edward* feared a
Discovery of more Tricks, and resolved not to stay till he was
disgracefully dismissed.

CHAPTER VIII

In which a Mistake, in point of Ceremony, is rectified.

Arabella had scarce done thinking of this last Adventure, when
the Marquis communicated a Piece of Intelligence to her, which
opened a Prospect of an infinite Number of new ones.

His Nephew, having just returned from his Travels, was
preparing to come and pay him a Visit in his Retreat; and, as
he always designed to marry *Arabella* to this Youth, of whom
he was extremely fond, he told his Daughter of the intended
Visit of her Cousin, whom she had not seen since she was eight

Years old; and, for the first time, insinuated his Design of giving him to her for an Husband.

Arabella, whose Delicacy was extremely shocked at this abrupt Declaration of her Father, could hardly hide her Chagrin; for, tho' she always intended to marry some time or other, as all the Heroines had done, yet she thought such an Event ought to be brought about with an infinite deal of Trouble; and that it was necessary she should pass to this State thro' a great Number of Cares, Disappointments, and Distresses of various Kinds, like them; that her Lover should purchase her with his Sword from a Croud of Rivals; and arrive to the Possession of her Heart by many Years of Services and Fidelity.

The Impropriety of receiving a Lover of a Father's recommending appeared in its strongest Light. What Lady in Romance ever married the Man that was chose for her? In those Cases the Remonstrances of a Parent are called Persecutions; obstinate Resistance, Constancy and Courage; and an Aptitude to dislike the Person proposed to them, a noble Freedom of Mind which disdains to love or hate by the Caprice of others.

Arabella, strengthening her own Resolutions by those Examples of heroic Disobedience, told her Father, with great Solemnity of Accent, that she would always obey him in all just and reasonable Things; and, being persuaded that he would never attempt to lay any Force upon her Inclinations, she would endeavour to make them conformable to his, and receive her Cousin with that Civility and Friendship due to so near a Relation, and a Person whom he honoured with his Esteem.

The Marquis, having had frequent Occasions of admiring his Daughter's Eloquence, did not draw any unpleasing Conclusion from the nice Distinctions she made; and, being perfectly assured of her Consent whenever he demanded it, expected the Arrival of his Nephew with great Impatience.

Arabella, whose Thoughts had been fully employed since this Conversation with her Father, was indulging her Meditations in one of the most retired Walks in the Garden; when she was informed by *Lucy*, that her Cousin was come, and that the Marquis had brought him into the Garden to look for her.

That Instant they both entered the Walk, when *Arabella*,

prepossessed, as she was, against any favourable Thoughts of the young *Glanville*, could not help betraying some Surprize at the Gracefulness of his Figure.

It must be confessed, said she to her Attendant, with a Smile, that this Lover my Father has brought us, is no contemptible Person: Nevertheless I feel an invincible Repugnance in myself against receiving him in that Character.

As she finished these Words, the Marquis came up, and presented Mr. *Glanville* to her; who, saluting[20] her with the Freedom of a Relation, gave her a Disgust that shewed itself immediately in her fair Face, which was overspread with such a Gloom, that the Marquis was quite astonished at it. Indeed *Arabella*, who expected he would hardly have presumed to kiss her Hand, was so surprised at his Freedom, in attempting her Lips, that she not only expressed her Indignation by Frowns, but gave him to understand he had mortally offended her.

Mr. *Glanville*, however, was neither surprised nor angry at her Resentment; but, imputing it to her Country Education, endeavoured to rally her out of her ill Humour; and the Marquis, being glad to find a Behaviour, which he thought proceeded from her Dislike of her Cousin, was only an Effect of an over-scrupulous Modesty, told her that Mr. *Glanville* had committed no Offence by saluting her, since that was a Civility which was granted to all Strangers at the first Interview, and therefore could not be refused to a Relation.

Since the World is so degenerate in its Customs from what it was formerly, said *Arabella*, with a Smile full of Contempt upon her Cousin, I am extremely happy in having lived in a Solitude which has not yet exposed me to the Mortification of being a Witness to Manners I cannot approve; for if every Person I shall meet with for the future be so deficient in their Respects to Ladies, as my Cousin is, I shall not care how much I am secluded from Society.

But, dear Lady *Bella*, interrupted Mr. *Glanville* gaily, tell me, I beseech you, how I must behave to please you; for I should be extremely glad to be honoured with your good Opinion.

The Person, resumed she, whom I must teach how to acquire my good Opinion, will, I am afraid, hardly recompense me by his Docility in learning, for the Pains I should be at in instructing him.

But, resumed *Glanville*, that I may avoid any more Occasions of offending you, only let me know how you would be approached for the future.

Since, answered she, there is no Necessity to renew the Ceremony of introducing you again to me, I have not a second Affront of that kind to apprehend; but I pray tell me, If all Cavaliers[21] are as presuming as yourself; and if a Relation of your Sex does not think a modest Embrace from a Lady a Welcome sufficiently tender*?

Nay, Cousin, cried *Glanville* eagerly, I am now persuaded you are in the Right; an Embrace is certainly to be preferred to a cold Salute. What would I give, that the Marquis would introduce me a second time, that I might be received with so delightful a Welcome?

The Vivacity with which he spoke this was so extremely disagreeable to *Arabella*, that she turned from him abruptly, and, striking into another Walk, ordered *Lucy* to tell him she commanded him not to follow her.

Mr. *Glanville*, however, who had no Notion of the exact Obedience which was expected from him, would have gone after her, notwithstanding this Prohibition, which *Lucy* delivered in a most peremptory Manner, after her Lady's Example: But the Marquis, who had left the two young People at Liberty to discourse, and had walked on, that he might not interrupt them, turning about, and seeing *Glanville* alone, called him to have some private Discourse with him; and, for that time, spared *Arabella* the Mortification of seeing her Commands disobeyed.

---

* The Heroines, tho' they think a Kiss of the Hand a great Condescension to a Lover, and never grant it without Blushes and Confusion; yet make no Scruple to embrace him upon every short Absence.[22]

CHAPTER IX

In which a Lover is severely punished for Faults which the Reader never would have discovered, if he had not been told.

The Marquis, tho' he had resolved to give *Arabella* to his Nephew, was desirous he should first receive some Impressions of Tenderness for her, before he absolutely declared his Resolution; and ardently wished he might be able to overcome that Reluctance which she seemed to have for Marriage: But, tho' *Glanville* in a very few Days became passionately in Love with his charming Cousin, yet she discovered so strong a Dislike to him, that the Marquis feared it would be difficult to make her receive him for an Husband: He observed she took all Opportunities of avoiding his Conversation; and seemed always out of Temper when he addressed any thing to her; but was well enough pleased, when he discoursed with him; and would listen to the long Conversations they had together with great Attention.

The Truth is, she had too much Discernment not to see Mr. *Glanville* had a great deal of Merit; his Person was perfectly handsome; he possessed a great Share of Understanding, an easy Temper, and a Vivacity which charmed every one, but the insensible *Arabella*.

She often wondered, that a Man, who, as she told her Confident, was Master of so many fine Qualities, should have a Disposition so little capable of feeling the Passion of Love, with the Delicacy and Fervour she expected to inspire; or, that he, whose Conversation was so pleasing on every other Subject, should make so poor a Figure when he entertained her with Matters of Gallantry. However, added she, I should be to blame to desire to be beloved by Mr. *Glanville*; for I am persuaded that Passion would cause no Reformation in the Coarseness of his Manners to Ladies, which makes him so disagreeable to me, and might possibly increase my Aversion.

The Marquis, having studied his Nephew's Looks for several

Days, thought he saw Inclination enough in them for *Arabella*, to make him receive the Knowledge of his Intention with Joy: He, therefore, called him into his Closet, and told him in few Words, that, if his Heart was not pre-engaged, and his Daughter capable of making him happy, he resolved to bestow her upon him, together with all his Estates.

Mr. *Glanville* received this agreeable News with the strongest Expressions of Gratitude; assuring his Uncle, that Lady *Bella*, of all the Women he had ever seen, was most agreeable to his Taste; and that he felt for her all the Tenderness and Affection his Soul was capable of.

I am glad of it, my dear Nephew, said the Marquis, embracing him: I will allow you, added he smiling, but a few Weeks to court her: Gain her Heart as soon as you can, and when you bring me her Consent, your Marriage shall be solemnized immediately.

Mr. *Glanville* needed not a Repetition of so agreeable a Command: He left his Uncle's Closet, with his Heart filled with the Expectation of his approaching Happiness; and, understanding *Arabella* was in the Garden, he went to her with a Resolution to acquaint her with the Permission her Father had given him to make his Addresses to her.

He found his fair Cousin, as usual, accompanied with her Women; and, seeing that, not-withstanding his Approach, they still continued to walk with her, and impatient of the Restraint they laid him under, I beseech you, Cousin, said he, let me have the Pleasure of walking with you alone: What Necessity is there for always having so many Witnesses of our Conversation? You may retire, said he, speaking to *Lucy*, and the other Woman; I have something to say to your Lady in private.

Stay, I command you, said *Arabella*, blushing at an Insolence so uncommon, and take Orders from no one but myself. —I pray you, Sir, pursued she frowning, What Intercourse of Secrets is there between you and me, that you expect I should favour you with a private Conversation? An Advantage which none of your Sex ever boasted to have gained from me; and which, haply, you should be the last upon whom I should bestow it.

You have the strangest Notions, answered *Glanville*, smiling at the pretty Anger she discovered: Certainly you may hold a private Conversation with any Gentleman, without giving Offence to Decorum; and I may plead a Right to this Happiness, above any other, since I have the Honour to be your Relation.

It is not at all surprising, resumed *Arabella* gravely, that you and I should differ in Opinion upon this Occasion: I don't remember that ever we agreed in any thing; and, I am apt to believe, we never shall.

Ah! don't say so, Lady *Bella*, interrupted he: What a Prospect of Misery you lay before me! For, if we are always to be opposite to each other, it is necessary you must hate me as much as I admire and love you.

These Words, which he accompanied with a gentle Pressure of her Hand, threw the astonished *Arabella* into such an Excess of Anger and Shame, that, for a few Moments, she was unable to utter a Word.

What a horrid Violation this, of all the Laws of Gallantry and Respect, which decree a Lover to suffer whole Years in Silence before he declares his Flame to the divine Object that causes it; and then with awful Tremblings and submissive Prostrations at the Feet of the offended Fair!

Arabella could hardly believe her Senses when she heard a Declaration, not only made without the usual Forms, but also, that the presumptuous Criminal waited for an Answer, without seeming to have any Apprehension of the Punishment to which he was to be doomed; and that, instead of deprecating her Wrath, he looked with a smiling Wonder upon her Eyes, as if he did not fear their Lightnings would strike him dead.

Indeed, it was scarce possible for him to help smiling, and wondering too, at the extraordinary Action of *Arabella*; for, as soon as he had pronounced those fatal Words, she started back two or three Steps; cast a Look at him full of the highest Indignation; and, lifting up her fine Eyes to Heaven, seemed, in the Language of Romance, to accuse the Gods for subjecting her to so cruel an Indignity.

The Tumult of her Thoughts being a little settled, she turned again towards *Glanville*, whose Countenance expressing nothing of that Confusion and Anxiety common to an Adorer in so critical a Circumstance, her Rage returned with greater Violence than ever.

If I do not express all the Resentment your Insolence has filled me with, said she to him, affecting more Scorn than Anger, 'tis because I hold you too mean for my Resentment; but never hope for my Pardon for your presumptuous Confession of a Passion I could almost despise myself for inspiring. If it be true that you love me, go and find your Punishment in that Absence to which I doom you; and never hope I will suffer a Person in my Presence, who has affronted me in the manner you have done.

Saying this, she walked away, making a Sign to him not to follow her.

Mr. *Glanville*, who was at first disposed to laugh at the strange Manner in which she received his Expressions of Esteem for her, found something, so extremely haughty and contemptuous in the Speech she had made, that he was almost mad with Vexation.

As he had no Notion of his Cousin's heroic Sentiments, and had never read Romances, he was quite ignorant of the Nature of his Offence; and, supposing the Scorn she had expressed for him was founded upon the Difference of their Rank and Fortune, his Pride was so sensibly mortified at that Thought, and at her so insolently forbidding him her Presence, that he was once inclined to shew his Resentment of such ungenteel Usage, by quitting the Castle without taking Leave even of the Marquis, who, he thought, could not be ignorant of the Reception he was likely to meet with from his Daughter; and ought to have guarded him against it, if he really meant him so well as he seemed to do.

As he was extremely violent and hasty in his Resolutions, and nicely sensible of the least Affront, he was not in a Condition to reason justly upon the Marquis's Conduct in this Affair; and while he was fluctuating with a thousand different Resolutions, *Lucy* came to him with a Billet[23] from her Lady, which she delivered without staying till he opened it; and was superscribed in this Manner:

Arabella, *To the most presumptuous Man in the World* ——

You seem to acknowledge so little Respect and Deference for the
Commands of a Lady, that I am afraid it will be but too necessary
to reiterate that, which, at parting, I laid upon you: Know then,
that I absolutely insist upon your repairing, in the only manner
you are able, the Affront you have put upon me; which is, by
never appearing before me again. If you think proper to confine
me to my Chamber, by continuing here any longer, you will add
Disobedience to the Crime by which you have already mortally
offended

Arabella.

The Superscription of this Letter, and the uncommon Style
of it, persuaded Mr. *Glanville*, that what he had been foolish
enough to resent as an Affront, was designed as a Jest, and meant
to divert him as well as herself: He examined her Behaviour
again, and wondered at his Stupidity in not discovering it
before. His Resentment vanishing immediately, he returned to
the House; and went, without Ceremony, to *Arabella*'s Apartment, which he entered before she perceived him, being in a
profound Musing at one of the Windows: The Noise he made,
in approaching her, obliged her at last to look up; when, starting, as if she had seen a Basilisk,[24] she flew to her Closet, and,
shutting the Door with great Violence, commanded him to
leave her Chamber immediately.

Mr. *Glanville*, still supposing her in Jest, intreated her to
open the Door; but, finding she continued obstinate, Well, said
he, going away, I shall be revenged on you some time hence,
and make you repent the Tricks you play me now.

Arabella not being able to imagine any thing, by these Words
he spoke in Raillery, but that he really, in the Spite and Anguish
of his Heart, threatened her with executing some terrible
Enterprize; she did not doubt, but he either intended to carry
her away; or, thinking her Aversion to him proceeded from his
having a Rival happy enough to be esteemed by her, those
mysterious Words he had uttered related to his Design of killing
him; so that as she knew, he could discover no Rival to wreak

his Revenge upon, she feared, that, at once to satisfy that Passion as well as his Love, he would make himself Master of her Liberty: For, in fine, said she to *Lucy*, to whom she communicated all her Thoughts, have I not every thing to apprehend from a Man, who knows so little how to treat my Sex with the Respect which is our Due; and who, after having, contrary to the timorous Nature of that Passion, insulted me with a free Declaration of Love, treated my Commands with the utmost Contempt by appearing before me again; and even threatens me with the Revenge he is meditating at this Moment?

Had Mr. *Glanville* been present, and heard the terrible Misfortunes which she presaged from the few Words he had jestingly spoke, he would certainly have made her quite furious, by the Diversion her Mistake would have afforded him. But the more she reflected on his Words, the more she was persuaded of the terrible Purpose of them.

'Twas in vain to acquaint her Father with the Reasons she had for disliking his Choice: His Resolution was fixed, and if she did not voluntarily conform to it, she exposed herself to the Attempts of a violent and unjust Lover, who would either prevail upon the Marquis to lay a Force upon her Inclinations, or make himself Master of her Person, and never cease persecuting her, till he had obliged her to give him her Hand.

Having reasoned herself into a perfect Conviction that all these things must necessarily happen, she thought it both just and reasonable to provide for her own Security, by a speedy Flight: The Want of a Precedent, indeed, for an Action of this Nature, held her a few Moments in Suspense; for she did not remember to have read of any Heroine that voluntarily left her Father's House, however persecuted she might be;[25] but she considered, that there was not any of the Ladies in Romances, in the same Circumstances with herself who was without a favoured Lover, for whose sake it might have been believed she had made an Elopement, which would have been highly prejudicial to her Glory; and, as there was no Foundation for any Suspicion of that Kind in her Case, she thought there was nothing to hinder her from withdrawing from a tyrannical Exertion of parental Authority, and the secret Machinations of

a Lover, whose Aim was to take away her Liberty, either by
obliging her to marry him, or by making her a Prisoner.

CHAPTER X

*Contains several Incidents, in which the Reader is
expected to be extremely interested.*

Arabella had spent some Hours in her Closet, revolving a thousand different Stratagems to escape from the Misfortune that
threatened her, when she was interrupted by *Lucy*, who, after
desiring Admittance, informed her, that the Marquis, having
rode out to take the Air that Evening, had fallen from his Horse
and received some Hurt; that he was gone to Bed, and desired
to see her.

Arabella, hearing her Father was indisposed, ran to him,
excessively alarmed; and reflecting on the Resolution she had
just before taken, of leaving him, which aggravated her Concern, she came to his Bedside with her Eyes swimming in Tears.
Mr. *Glanville* was sitting near him; but, rising at her Appearance to give her his Chair, which she accepted without taking
any Notice of him, he stood at some Distance contemplating
her Face, to which Sorrow had given so many Charms, that he
gazed on her with an Eagerness and Delight that could not
escape her Observation.

She blushed excessively at the passionate Looks he gave
her; and, finding the Marquis's Indisposition not considerable
enough to oblige her to a constant Attendance at his Bed-side,
she took the first Opportunity of returning to her Chamber;
but, as she was going out, *Glanville* presented his Hand to lead
her up Stairs: Which she scornfully refusing;

Sure, Cousin, said he, a little piqued, you are not disposed
to carry on your ill-natured Jest any further?

If you imagined I jested with you, said *Arabella*, I am rather
to accuse the Slowness of your Understanding, for your persisting in treating me thus freely, than the Insolence I first imputed

it to: But, whatever is the Cause of it, I now tell you again, that you have extremely offended me; and, if my Father's Illness did not set Bounds to my Resentment at present, I would make you know, that I would not suffer the Injury you do me, so patiently.

Since you would have me to believe you are serious, replied *Glanville*, be pleased to let me know what Offence it is you complain of; for I protest I am quite at a Loss to understand you.

Was it not enough, resumed *Arabella*, to affront me with an insolent Declaration of your Passion, but you must also, in Contempt of my Commands to the contrary, appear before me again, pursue me to my Chamber, and use the most brutal Menaces to me?

Hold, pray, Madam, interrupted *Glanville*, and suffer me to ask you, If it is my Presumption, in declaring myself your Admirer that you are so extremely offended at?

Doubtless it is, Sir, answered *Arabella*; and such a Presumption, as, without the aggravating Circumstances you have since added to it, is sufficient to make me always your Enemy.

I beg Pardon, returned Mr. *Glanville* gravely, for that Offence; and also, for staying any longer in a House, which you have, so genteelly, turned me out of.

My Pardon, Mr. *Glanville*, resumed she, is not so easily gained: Time, and your Repentance, may, indeed, do much towards obtaining it.

Saying this, she made a Sign to him to retire; for he had walked up with her to her Chamber: But, finding he did not obey her, for really he was quite unacquainted with these Sorts of dumb Commands, she hastily retired to her Closet, lest he should attempt to move her Pity, by any Expressions of Despair for the cruel Banishment she had doomed him to.

Mr. *Glanville*, seeing she had shut herself up in her Closet, left her Chamber, and retired to his own, more confounded than ever at the Behaviour of his Cousin.

Her bidding him so peremptorily to leave the House, would have equally persuaded him of her Ignorance and Ill-breeding, had not the Elegance of her Manners, in every other respect, proved the contrary: Nor was it possible to doubt she had a great Share of Understanding; since her Conversation, singular as some of her Sentiments seemed to him, was far superior to most other Ladies. Therefore, he concluded, the Affront he had received proceeded from her Disdain to admit the Addresses of any Person, whose Quality was inferior to her's; which, probably, was increased by some particular Dislike she had to his Person.

His Honour would not permit him to make Use of that Advantage her Father's Authority could give him; and, wholly engrossed by his Resentment of the Usage he had received from her, he resolved to set out for *London* the next Day without seeing the Marquis, from whom he was apprehensive of some Endeavours to detain him.

Having taken this Resolution, he ordered his Servant to have the Horses ready early in the Morning; and, without taking any Notice of his Intention, he left the Castle, riding, as fast as possible, to the next Stage, from whence he wrote to his Uncle; and, dispatching a Messenger with his Letter, held on his Way to *London*.

The Marquis, being pretty well recovered from his Indisposition by a good Night's Rest, sent for Mr. *Glanville* in the Morning, to walk with him, as was his Custom, in the Garden; but, hearing he had rode out, tho' he imagined it was only to take the Air, yet he could not help accusing him, in his own Thoughts, of a little Neglect; for which he resolved to chide him, when he returned: But his long Stay filling him with some Surprize, he was beginning to express his Fears that something had befallen him, to *Arabella*, who was then with him; when a Servant presented him the Letter, which Mr. *Glanville*'s Messenger had that Moment brought.

The Marquis casting his Eyes on the Direction, and knowing his Nephew's Hand, Bless me, cried he, extremely surprised, What can this mean? *Bella*, added he, here's a Letter from your Cousin.

Arabella, at these Words, started up; and, preventing her Father, with a respectful Action, from opening it, I beseech you, my Lord, said she, before you read this Letter, suffer me to assure you, that, if it contains any thing fatal, I am not at all accessary to it: 'Tis true I have banished my Cousin, as a

Punishment for the Offence he was guilty of towards me; but, Heaven is my Witness, I did not desire his Death; and if he has taken any violent Resolution against himself, he has greatly exceeded my Commands.

The Marquis, whose Surprise was considerably increased by these Words, hastily broke open the Letter, which she perceiving, hurried out of the Room; and, locking herself up in her Closet, began to bewail the Effect of her Charms, as if she was perfectly assured of her Cousin's Death.

The Marquis, however, who, from Lady *Bella*'s Exclamation, had prepared himself for the Knowledge of some very extraordinary Accident, was less surprised, than he would otherwise have been, at the Contents; which were as follow:

My Lord,

As my leaving your House so abruptly will certainly make me appear guilty of a most unpardonable Rudeness, I cannot dispense with myself from acquainting your Lordship with the Cause; though, to spare the Reproaches Lady *Bella* will probably cast on me for doing so, I could wish you knew it by any other Means.

But, my Lord, I value your Esteem too much to hazard the Loss of it by suffering you to imagine, that I am capable of doing any thing to displease you. Lady *Bella* was pleased to order me to stay no longer in the House; and menaced me with some very terrible Usage, if I disobeyed her: She used so many other contemptuous Expressions to me, that, I am persuaded, I shall never be so happy as to possess the Honour you designed for,

> My Lord
> Your most obedient, &c.
> *Charles Glanville.*

When the Marquis had read this Letter, he went to his Daughter's Apartment with an Intention to chide her severely for her Usage of his Nephew; but, seeing her come to meet him with her Eyes bathed in Tears, he insensibly lost some Part of his Resentment.

Alas! my Lord, said she, I know you come prepared to load me with Reproaches, upon my Cousin's Account; but, I beseech your Lordship, do not aggravate my Sorrows: Tho' I banished Mr. *Glanville*, I did not desire his Death; and, questionless, if he knew how I *resent*[26] it, his Ghost would be satisfied with the Sacrifice I make him.

The Marquis, not being able to help smiling at this Conceit, which he saw had so strongly possessed her Imagination, that she had no sort of Doubt but that her Cousin was dead, asked her, If she really believed Mr. *Glanville* loved her well enough to die with Grief at her ill Usage of him?

If, said she, he loves me not well enough to die for me, he certainly loves me but little; and I am the less obliged to him.

But I desire to know, interrupted the Marquis, For what Crime it was you took the Liberty to banish him from my House?

I banished him, my Lord, resumed she, for his Presumption in telling me he loved me.

That Presumption, as you call it, tho' I know not for what Reason, said the Marquis, was authorized by me: Therefore, know, *Bella*, that I not only permit him to love you, but I also expect you should endeavour to return his Affection; and look upon him as the Man whom I design for your Husband: There's his Letter, pursued he, putting it into her Hand. I blush for the Rudeness you have been guilty of; but endeavour to repair it, by a more obliging Behaviour for the future: I am going to send after him immediately to prevail upon him to return: Therefore, write him an Apology, I charge you; and have it done by the Time my Messenger is ready to set out.

Saying this, he went out of the Room; *Arabella* eagerly opened the Letter; and, finding it in a Style so different from what she expected, her Dislike of him returned with more Violence than ever.

Ah! the Traitor! said she aloud, Is it thus that he endeavours to move my Compassion? How greatly did I over-rate his Affection, when I imagined his Despair was capable of killing him? Disloyal Man! pursued she, walking about, Is it by Complaints to my Father that thou expectest to succeed? And dost thou imagine the Heart of *Arabella* is to be won by Violence and Injustice?

In this manner she wasted the Time allotted for her to write; and, when the Marquis sent for her Letter, having no Intention to comply, she went to his Chamber, conjuring him not to oblige her to a Condescension so unworthy of her.

The Marquis, being now excessively angry with her, rose up in a Fury, and, leading her to his Writing-Desk, ordered her, instantly, to write to her Cousin.

If I must write, my Lord, said she, sobbing, pray be so good as to dictate what I must say.

Apologize for your rude Behaviour, said the Marquis; and desire him, in the most obliging manner you can, to return.

Arabella, seeing there was a necessity for obeying, took up the Pen, and wrote the following Billet:

> The *unfortunate* Arabella, *to the most ungenerous* Glanville.
>
> It is not by the Power I have over you, that I command you to return, for I disclaim any Empire over so unworthy a Subject; but, since it is my Father's Pleasure I should invite you back, I must let you know, that I repeal your Banishment, and expect you will immediately return with the Messenger who brings this; however, to spare your Acknowledgments, know, that it is in Obedience to my Father's absolute Commands, that you receive this Mandate from
>
>   *Arabella.*

Having finished this Billet, she gave it to the Marquis to read; who, finding a great deal of his own Haughtiness of Temper in it, could not resolve to check her for a Disposition so like his own: Yet he told her, her Stile was very uncommon: And pray, added he smiling, who taught you to superscribe your Letters thus, 'The unfortunate *Arabella*, to the most ungenerous *Glanville*?' Why, *Bella*, this Superscription is wholly calculated for the Bearer's Information: But come, alter it immediately; for I don't choose my Messenger should know, that you are unfortunate, or that my Nephew is ungenerous.

Pray, my Lord, replied *Arabella*, content yourself with what I have already done in Obedience to your Commands, and suffer my Letter to remain as it is: Methinks it is but reasonable I should express some little Resentment at the Complaint my Cousin has been pleased to make to you against me; nor can I possibly make my Letter more obliging, without being guilty of an unpardonable Meanness.

You are a strange Girl, replied the Marquis, taking the Letter, and inclosing it in one from himself; in which he earnestly intreated his Nephew to return, threatning him with his Displeasure, if he disobeyed; and assuring him, that his Daughter would receive him as well as he could possibly desire.

The Messenger being dispatched, with Orders to ride Post, and overtake the young Gentleman, he obeyed his Orders so well, that he came up with him at ——, where he intended to lodge that Night.

Mr. *Glanville*, who expected his Uncle would make use of some Methods to recall him, opened his Letter without any great Emotion; but seeing another inclosed, his Heart leaped to his Mouth, not doubting but it was a Letter from *Arabella*; but the Contents surprised him so much, that he hardly knew whether he ought to look upon them as an Invitation to return, or a new Affront, her Words were so distant and haughty. The Superscription being much the same with a Billet he had received from her in the Garden, which had made him conclude her in Jest, he knew not what to think of it: One would swear this dear Girl's Head is turned, said he to himself, if she had not more *Wit* than her whole Sex besides.

After reading *Arabella*'s Letter several times, he at last opened his Uncle's; and, seeing the pressing Instances he made him to return, he resolved to obey; and the next Morning set out for the Castle.

Arabella, during the time her Cousin was expected, appeared so melancholy and reserved, that the Marquis was extremely uneasy: You have never, said he to her, disobeyed me in any one Action of your Life; and I may with reason expect you will conform to my Will in the Choice I have made of a Husband for you, since it is impossible to make any Objection either to his Person or Mind; and, being the Son of my Sister, he is certainly not unworthy of you, tho' he has not a Title.[27]

My first Wish, my Lord, replied *Arabella*, is to live single,[28] not being desirous of entering into any Engagement which may hinder my Solicitude and Cares, and lessen my Attendance, upon the best of Fathers, who, till now, has always most tenderly complied with my Inclinations in every thing: But if it is your absolute Command, that I should marry, give me not to one who, tho' he has the Honour to be allied to you, has neither merited your Esteem, or my Favour, by any Action worthy of his Birth, or the Passion he pretends to have for me; for, in fine, my Lord, by what Services has he deserved the Distinction with which you honour him? Has he ever delivered you from any considerable Danger? Has he saved your Life, and hazarded his own, for you, upon any Occasion whatever? Has he merited my Esteem, by his Sufferings, Fidelity, and Respect; or, by any great and generous Action, given me a Testimony of his Love, which should oblige me to reward him with my Affection? Ah! my Lord, I beseech you, think not so unworthily of your Daughter, as to bestow her upon one who has done so little to deserve her: If my Happiness be dear to you, do not precipitate me into a State from whence you cannot recal me, with a Person whom I can never affect.[29]

She would have gone on, but the Marquis interrupted her sternly: I'll hear no more, said he, of your foolish and ridiculous Objections: What Stuff is this you talk of? What Service am I to expect from my Nephew? And by what Sufferings is he to merit your Esteem? Assure yourself, *Arabella*, continued he, that I will never pardon you, if you presume to treat my Nephew in the Manner you have done: I perceive you have no real Objection to make to him; therefore I expect you will endeavour to obey me without Reluctance; for, since you seem to be so little acquainted with what will most conduce to your own Happiness, you must not think it strange, if I insist upon directing your Choice in the most important Business of your Life.

Arabella was going to reply; but the Marquis ordered her to be silent; and she went to her own Apartment in so much

Affliction, that she thought her Misfortunes were not exceeded
by any she had ever read.

CHAPTER XI

*In which a logical Argument is unseasonably
interrupted.*

The Marquis was also extremely uneasy at her Obstinacy: He
desired nothing more ardently than to marry her to his Nephew;
but he could not resolve to force her Consent; and, however
determined he appeared to her, yet, in Reality, he intended only
to use Persuasions to effect what he desired; and, from the
natural Sweetness of her Temper, he was sometimes not without
Hopes, that she might, at last, be prevailed upon to comply.

His Nephew's Return restored him to Part of his usual Tranquillity: After he had gently chid him for suffering himself to
be so far transported with his Resentment at the little Humours
of a Lady, as to leave his House, without acquainting him,
he bid him go to *Arabella*, and endeavour to make his Peace
with her.

Mr. *Glanville* accordingly went to her Apartment, resolving
to oblige her to come to some Explanation with him concerning
the Offence she complained of; but that fair incensed Lady,
who had taken Shelter in her Closet, ordered *Lucy* to tell him
she was indisposed, and could not see him.

Glanville, however, comforted himself for this Disappointment by the Hopes of seeing her at Supper; and accordingly she
came, when the Supper-Bell rung, and, making a very cool
Compliment to her Cousin, placed herself at Table: The soft
Languor that appeared in her Eyes, gave such an additional
Charm to one of the loveliest Faces in the World, that *Glanville*,
who sat opposite to her, could not help gazing on her with a
very particular Attention; he often spoke to her, and asked her
trifling Questions, for the sake of hearing the Sound of her
Voice, which Sorrow had made inchantingly sweet.

When Supper was over, she would have retired; but the Marquis desired her to stay and entertain her Cousin, while he went to look over some Dispatches he had received from *London*.

Arabella blushed with Anger at this Command; but not daring to disobey, she kept her Eyes fixed on the Ground, as if she dreaded to hear something that would displease her.

Well, Cousin, said *Glanville*, tho' you desire to have no Empire over so unworthy a Subject as myself, yet I hope you are not displeased at my returning, in Obedience to your Commands.

Since I am not allowed any Will of my own, said she, sighing, it matters not whether I am pleased, or displeased; nor is it of any Consequence to you to know.

Indeed but it is, Lady *Bella*, interrupted he; for if I knew how to please you, I would never, if I could help it, offend. Therefore, I beg you, tell me how I have disobliged you; for, certainly, you have treated me as harshly as if I had been guilty of some very terrible Offence.

You had the Boldness, said she, to talk to me of Love; and you well know that Persons of my Sex and Quality are not permitted to listen to such Discourses; and if, for that Offence, I banished you my Presence, I did no more than Decency required of me; and which I would yet do, were I Mistress of my own Actions.

But is it possible, Cousin, said *Glanville*, that you can be angry with any one for loving you? Is that a Crime of so high a Nature as to merit an eternal Banishment from your Presence?

Without telling you, said *Arabella*, blushing, whether I am angry at being loved, 'tis sufficient you know, that I will not pardon the Man who shall have the Presumption to tell me he loves me.

But, Madam, interrupted *Glanville*, if the Person who tells you he loves you, be of a Rank not beneath you, I conceive you are not at all injured by the favourable Sentiments he feels for you; and, tho' you are not disposed to make any Returns to his Passion, yet you are certainly obliged to him for his good Opinion.

Since Love is not voluntary, replied *Arabella*, I am not obliged to any Person for loving me; for, questionless, if he could help it, he would.

If it is not a voluntary Favour, interrupted *Glanville*, it is not a voluntary offence; and, if you do not think yourself obliged by the one, neither are you at Liberty to be offended with the other.

The Question, said *Arabella*, is not whether I ought to be offended at being loved, but whether it is not an Offence to be told I am so.

If there is nothing criminal in the Passion itself, Madam, resumed *Glanville*, certainly there can be no Crime in declaring it.

However specious your Arguments may appear, interrupted *Arabella*, I am persuaded it is an unpardonable Crime to tell a Lady you love her; and, tho' I had nothing else to plead, yet the Authority of Custom is sufficient to prove it.

Custom, Lady *Bella*, said *Glanville*, smiling, is wholly on my Side; for the Ladies are so far from being displeased at the Addresses of their Lovers, that their chiefest Care is to gain them, and their greatest Triumph to hear them talk of their Passion: So, Madam, I hope you'll allow that Argument has no Force.

I don't know, answered *Arabella*, what Sort of Ladies they are who allow such unbecoming Liberties, but I am certain, that *Statira*, *Parisatis*, *Clelia*, *Mandana*,[30] and all the illustrious Heroines of Antiquity, whom it is a Glory to resemble, would never admit of such Discourses.

Ah for Heaven's sake, Cousin, interrupted *Glanville*, endeavouring to stifle a Laugh, do not suffer yourself to be governed by such antiquated Maxims! The World is quite different to what it was in those Days; and the Ladies in this Age would as soon follow the Fashions of the *Greek* and *Roman* Ladies, as mimick their Manners; and I believe they would become one as ill as the other.

I am sure, replied *Arabella*, the World is not more virtuous now than it was in their Days, and there is good Reason to believe it is not much wiser; and I don't see why the Manners of this Age are to be preferred to those of former ones, unless they are wiser and better: However, I cannot be persuaded, that Things are as you say, but that when I am a little better acquainted with the World, I shall find as many Persons who resemble *Oroondates, Artaxerxes*, and the illustrious Lover of *Clelia*,[31] as those who are like *Tiribases, Artaxes*,[32] and the presuming and insolent *Glanville*.

By the Epithets you give me, Madam, said *Glanville*, I find you have placed me in very bad Company: But pray, Madam, if the illustrious Lover of *Clelia* had never discovered his Passion, how would the World have come to the Knowledge of it?

He did not discover his Passion, Sir, resumed *Arabella*, till, by the Services he did the noble *Clelius*, and his incomparable Daughter, he could plead some Title to their Esteem: He several times preserved the Life of that renowned *Roman*; delivered the beautiful *Clelia* when she was a Captive; and, in fine, conferred so many Obligations upon them, and all their Friends, as he might well expect to be pardoned by the divine *Clelia* for daring to love her. Nevertheless, she used him very harshly, when he first declared his Passion, and banished him also from her Presence; and it was a long time before she could prevail upon herself to compassionate his Sufferings.

The Marquis coming in interrupted *Arabella*; upon which she took Occasion to retire; leaving *Glanville* more captivated with her than ever.

He found her Usage of him was grounded upon Examples she thought it her Duty to follow; and, strange as her Notions of Life appeared, yet they were supported with so much Wit and Delicacy, that he could not help admiring her, while he foresaw, the Oddity of her Humour would throw innumerable Difficulties in his Way, before he should be able to obtain her.

However, as he was really passionately in Love with her, he resolved to accommodate himself, as much as possible, to her Taste, and endeavour to gain her Heart by a Behaviour most agreeable to her: He therefore assumed an Air of great Distance and Respect; never mentioned his Affection, nor the Intentions of her Father in his Favour; and the Marquis, observing his Daughter conversed with him with less Reluctance than usual,

leaving to Time, and the Merit of his Nephew, to dispose
her to comply with his Desires, resolved not to interpose his
Authority in an Affair upon which her own Happiness so much
depended.

CHAPTER XII

In which the Reader will find a Specimen of the true Pathetic, in a Speech of Oroondates. — *The Adventures of the Books.*

Arabella saw the Change in her Cousin's Behaviour with a great
deal of Satisfaction; for she did not doubt but his Passion was
as strong as ever; but that he forebore, thro' Respect, from
entertaining her with any Expressions of it: Therefore she now
conversed with him with the greatest Sweetness and Complaisance: She would walk with him for several Hours in the Garden,
leaning upon his Arm; and charmed him to the last Degree of
Admiration by the agreeable Sallies of her Wit, and her fine
Reasoning upon every Subject he proposed.

It was with the greatest Difficulty he restrained himself from
telling her a Thousand times a Day that he loved her to Excess,
and conjuring her to give her Consent to her Father's Designs
in his Favour: But, tho' he could get over his Fears of offending
her, yet it was impossible to express any Sentiments of this
Nature to her, without having her Women Witnesses of his
Discourse; for when he walked with her in the Garden, *Lucy,*
and another Attendant, always followed her: If he sat with her
in her own Chamber, her Women were always at one End of
it: And, when they were both in the Marquis's Apartment,
where her Women did not follow her, poor *Glanville* found
himself embarrassed by his Presence; for, conceiving his
Nephew had Opportunities enough of talking to his Daughter
in private, he always partook of their Conversation.

He passed some Weeks in this Manner, extremely chagrined
at the little Progress he made; and was beginning to be heartily

weary of the Constraint he laid upon himself, when *Arabella*, one Day, furnished him, without designing it, with an Opportunity of talking to her on the Subject he wished for.

When I reflect, said she, laughing, upon the Difference there was between us some Days ago, and the Familiarity in which we live at present, I cannot imagine by what means you have arrived to a good Fortune you had so little Reason to expect; for, in fine, you have given me no Signs of Repentance for the Fault you committed, which moved me to banish you; and I am not certain whether, in conversing with you in the manner I do, I give you not as much Reason to find Fault with my too great Easiness, as you did me to be displeased with your Presumption.

Since, returned *Glanville*, I have not persisted in the Commission of those Faults which displeased you, what greater Signs of Repentance can you desire, than this Reformation in my Behaviour?

But Repentance ought to precede Reformation, replied *Arabella*; otherwise, there is great room to suspect it is only feigned: And a sincere Repentance shews itself in such visible Marks, that one can hardly be deceived in that which is genuine. I have read of many indiscreet Lovers, who not succeeding in their Addresses, have pretended to repent, and acted as you do; that is, without giving any Signs of Contrition for the Fault they had committed, have eat and slept well, never lost their Colour, or grew one bit thinner, by their Sorrow; but contented themselves with saying they repented; and, without changing their Disposition to renew their Fault, only concealed their Intention, for fear of losing any favourable Opportunity of committing it again: But true Repentance, as I was saying, not only produces Reformation, but the Person who is possessed of it voluntarily punishes himself for the Faults he has been guilty of. Thus *Mazares*, deeply repenting of the Crime his Passion for the divine *Mandana* had forced him to commit; as a Punishment, obliged himself to follow the Fortune of his glorious Rival; obey all his Commands; and, fighting under his Banners, assist him to gain the Possession of his adored Mistress.[33] Such a glorious Instance of Self-denial was, indeed, a sufficient Proof of his Repentance; and infinitely more convincing than the Silence he imposed upon himself with respect to his Passion.

Oroondates, to punish himself for his Presumption, in daring to tell the admirable *Statira*, that he loved her, resolved to die, to expiate his Crime; and, doubtless, would have done so, if his fair Mistress, at the Intreaty of her Brother, had not commanded him to live.[34]

But pray, Lady *Bella*, interrupted *Glanville*, were not these Gentlemen happy at last in the Possession of their Mistresses?

Doubtless they were, Sir, resumed she; but it was not till after numberless Misfortunes, infinite Services, and many dangerous Adventures, in which their Fidelity was put to the strongest Trials imaginable.

I am glad, however, said *Glanville*, that the Ladies were not insensible; for, since you do not disapprove of their Compassion for their Lovers, it is to be hoped you will not be always as inexorable as you are now.

When I shall be so fortunate, interrupted she, to meet with a Lover who shall have as pure and perfect a Passion for me, as *Oroondates* had for *Statira*; and give me as many glorious Proofs of his Constancy and Affection, doubtless I shall not be ungrateful: But, since I have not the Merits of *Statira*, I ought not to pretend to her good Fortune; and shall be very well contented if I escape the Persecutions which Persons of my Sex, who are not frightfully ugly, are always exposed to, without hoping to inspire such a Passion as that of *Oroondates*.

I should be glad to be better acquainted with the Actions of this happy Lover, Madam, said *Glanville*; that, forming myself upon his Example, I may hope to please a Lady as worthy of my Regard as *Statira* was of his.

For Heaven's sake, Cousin, resumed *Arabella*, laughing, how have you spent your Time; and to what Studies have you devoted all your Hours, that you could find none to spare for the Perusal of Books from which all useful Knowledge may be drawn; which give us the most shining Examples of Generosity, Courage, Virtue, and Love; which regulate our Actions, form our Manners, and inspire us with a noble Desire of emulating those great, heroic, and virtuous Actions, which made those

Persons so glorious in their Age, and so worthy Imitation in ours? However, as it is never too late to improve, suffer me to recommend to you the reading of these Books, which will soon make you discover the Improprieties you have been guilty of; and will, probably, induce you to avoid them for the future.

I shall certainly read them, if you desire it, said *Glanville*; and I have so great an Inclination to be agreeable to you, that I shall embrace every Opportunity of becoming so; and will therefore take my Instructions from these Books, if you think proper, or from yourself; which, indeed, will be the quickest method of teaching me.

Arabella having ordered one of her Women to bring *Cleopatra, Cassandra, Clelia,* and the Grand *Cyrus*, from her Library, *Glanville* no sooner saw the Girl return, sinking under the Weight of those voluminous Romances,[35] but he began to tremble at the Apprehension of his Cousin laying her Commands upon him to read them; and repented of his Complaisance, which exposed him to the cruel Necessity of performing what to him appeared an *Herculean* Labour, or else incurring her Anger by his Refusal.

Arabella, making her Women place the Books upon a Table before her, opened them, one after another, with Eyes sparkling with Delight; while *Glanville* sat wrapt in Admiration at the Sight of so many huge Folio's written, as he conceived, upon the most trifling Subjects imaginable.

I have chosen out these few, said *Arabella* (not observing his Consternation) from a great many others, which compose the most valuable Part of my Library; and, by that time you have gone thro' these, I imagine you will be considerably improved.

Certainly, Madam, replied *Glanville*, turning over the Leaves in great Confusion, one may, as you say, be greatly improved; for these Books contain a great deal: And, looking over a Page of *Cassandra*, without any Design, read these Words, which were Part of *Oroondates*'s Soliloquy when he received a cruel Sentence from *Statira*:

"Ah cruel! (says this miserable Lover,) and what have I done to merit it? Examine the Nature of my Offence, and you will see I am not so guilty, but that my Death may free me from

Part of that Severity: Shall your Hatred last longer than my Life? And can you detest a Soul that forsakes its Body only to obey you? No, no, you are not so hard-hearted; that Satisfaction will, doubtless, content you: And, when I shall cease to be, doubtless I shall cease to be odious to you."

Upon my Soul, said *Granville*, stifling a Laugh with great Difficulty, I cannot help blaming the Lady this sorrowful Lover complains of, for her great Cruelty; for here he gives one Reason to suspect, that she will not even be contented with his dying in Obedience to her Commands, but will hate him after Death; an Impiety quite inexcusable in a Christian!

You condemn this illustrious Princess with very little Reason, interrupted *Arabella*, smiling at his Mistake; for, besides that she was not a Christian, and ignorant of those Divine Maxims of Charity and Forgiveness, which Christians, by their Profession, are obliged to practise, she was very far from desiring the Death of *Oroondates*; for, if you will take the Pains to read the succeeding Passages, you will find, that she expresses herself in the most obliging Manner in the World; for when *Oroondates* tells her he would live, if she would consent he should, the Princess most sweetly replies, "I not only consent, but also intreat it; and, if I have any Power, command it." However, lest you should fall into the other Extreme, and blame this great Princess for her Easiness (as you before condemned her for her Cruelty), 'tis necessary you should know how she was induced to this favourable Behaviour to her Lover: Therefore pray read the whole Transaction. Stay! here it begins, continued she; turning over a good many Pages, and marking where he should begin to read.

Glanville, having no great Stomach to the Task, endeavoured to evade it, by intreating his Cousin to relate the Passages she desired he should be acquainted with: But she declining it, he was obliged to obey; and began to read where she directed him: And, to leave him at Liberty to read with the greater Attention, she left him, and went to a Window at another End of the Chamber.

Mr. *Glanville*, who was not willing to displease her, examined the Task she had set him, resolving, if it was not a very hard one, to comply; but, counting the Pages, he was quite terrified at the Number, and could not prevail upon himself to read them: Therefore glancing them over, he pretended to be deeply engaged in reading, when, in Reality, he was contemplating the surprising Effect these Books had produced in the Mind of his Cousin; who, had she been untainted with the ridiculous Whims they created in her Imagination, was, in his Opinion, one of the most accomplished Ladies in the World.

When he had sat long enough to make her believe he had read what she had desired, he rose up, and joining her at the Window, began to talk of the Pleasantness of the Evening, instead of the Rigour of *Statira*.

Arabella coloured with Vexation at his extreme Indifference in a Matter which was of such prodigious Consequence, in her Opinion; but disdaining to put him in mind of his Rudeness, in quitting a Subject they had not thoroughly discussed, and which she had taken so much Pains to make him comprehend, she continued silent; and would not condescend to afford him an Answer to any thing he said.

Glanville, by her Silence and Frowns, was made sensible of his Fault; and, to repair it, began to talk of the inexorable *Statira*, though, indeed, he did not well know what to say.

Arabella, clearing up a little, did not disdain to answer him upon her favourite Topic: I knew, said she, you would be ready to blame this Princess equally for her Rigour and her Kindness; but it must be remembered that, what she did in Favour of *Oroondates*, was wholly owing to the Generosity of *Artaxerxes*.

Here she stopped, expecting *Glanville* to give his Opinion; who, strangely puzzled, replied at random, To be sure, Madam, he was a very generous Rival.

Rival! cried *Arabella*; *Artaxerxes* the Rival of *Oroondates*! Why certainly you have lost your Wits: He was *Statira*'s Brother; and it was to his Mediation that *Oroondates*, or *Orontes*, owed his Happiness.

Certainly, Madam, replied *Glanville*, it was very generous in *Artaxerxes*, as he was Brother to *Statira*, to interpose in the Behalf of an unfortunate Lover; and both *Oroondates*, and *Orontes*, were extremely obliged to him.

Orontes, replied *Arabella*, was more obliged to him than *Oroondates*; since the Quality of *Orontes* was infinitely below that of *Oroondates*.

But, Madam, interrupted *Glanville* (extremely pleased at his having so well got over the Difficulty he had been in), which of these two Lovers did *Statira* make happy?

This unlucky Question immediately informed *Arabella*, that she had been all this time the Dupe of her Cousin; who, if he had read a single Page, would have known that *Orontes* and *Oroondates* was the same Person; the Name of *Orontes* being assumed by *Oroondates*, to conceal his real Name and Quality.

The Shame and Rage she conceived at so glaring a Proof of his Disrespect, and the Ridicule to which she had exposed herself, were so great, that she could not find Words severe enough to express her Resentment; but, protesting that no Consideration whatever should oblige her to converse with him again, she ordered him instantly to quit her Chamber; and assured him, if he ever attempted to approach her again, she would submit to the most terrible Effects of her Father's Resentment, rather than be obliged to see a Person who had, by his unworthy Behaviour, made himself her Scorn and Aversion.

Glanville, who saw himself going to be discarded a second time, attempted, with great Submission, to move her to recal her cruel Sentence; but *Arabella*, bursting into Tears, complained so pathetically of the Cruelty of her Destiny, in exposing her to the hated Importunities of a Man she despised, and whose Presence was so insupportable, that *Glanville*, thinking it best to let her Rage evaporate a little before he attempted to pacify her, quitted her Chamber; cursing *Statira* and *Orontes* a thousand times, and loading the Authors of those Books with all the Imprecations his Rage could suggest.

CHAPTER XIII

The Adventure of the Books continued.

In this Temper he went to the Gardens to pass over the Chagrin this unfortunate Accident had given him; when, meeting the Marquis, who insisted upon knowing the Cause of that ill Humour, so visible in his Countenance, *Glanville* related all that had passed, but, in Spite of his Anger, it was impossible for him to repeat the Circumstances of his Disgrace without laughing, as well as the Marquis; who thought the Story so extremely diverting, that he would needs hear it over again.

However, *Charles*, said he, though I shall do what I can to gain your Pardon from *Bella*, yet I shall not scruple to own you acted extremely wrong, in not reading what she desired you; for, besides losing an Opportunity of obliging her, you drew yourself into a terrible Dilemma; for how was it possible for you to evade a Discovery of the Cheat you put upon her, when she began to talk with you upon those Passages she had desired you to read?

I acknowledge my Error, my Lord, answered *Glanville*; but if you restore me to my Cousin's Favour again, I promise you to repair it by a different Behaviour for the future.

I'll see what I can do for you, said the Marquis; leaving him, to go to *Arabella*'s Apartment, who had retired to her Closet, extremely afflicted at this new Insult she had received from her Cousin: Her Grief was the more poignant, as she was beginning to imagine, by the Alteration in his Behaviour, that he would prove such a Lover as she wished; for Mr. *Glanville*'s Person and Qualifications had attracted her particular Notice: And, to speak in the Language of Romance, she did not hate him; but, on the contrary, was very much disposed to wish him well: Therefore, it was no Wonder she extremely resented the Affront she had received from him.

The Marquis not finding her in her Chamber, proceeded to her Closet, where her Women informed him she was retired; and, knocking gently at the Door, was admitted by *Arabella*, whom he immediately discerned to have been weeping very much; for her fine Eyes were red and swelled, and the Traces of her Tears might still be observed on her fair Face; which, at the Sight of the Marquis, was overspread with a Blush, as if she was conscious of her Weakness in lamenting the Crime her Cousin had been guilty of.

The Marquis drew a favourable Omen for his Nephew from her Tears and Confusion; but, not willing to increase it, by acknowledging he had observed it, he told her he was come, at Mr *Glanville*'s Request, to make up the Quarrel between them.

Ah! my Lord, interrupted *Arabella*, speak no more to me of that unworthy Man, who has so grosly abused my Favour, and the Privilege I allowed him: His Baseness and Ingratitude are but too manifest; and there is nothing I so much regret as my Weakness in restoring him to Part of my good Opinion, after he had once forfeited it, by an Insolence not to be paralleled.

Indeed, *Bella*, said the Marquis, smiling, you resent too deeply these slight Matters: I can't think my Nephew so guilty as you would have me believe he is; and you ought neither to be angry or surprised, that he preferred your Conversation before reading in a foolish old-fashioned Book that you put in his Hands.

If your Lordship had ever read these Books, replied *Arabella*, reddening with Vexation, 'tis probable you would have another Opinion of them; but however that may be, my Cousin is not to be excused for the Contempt he shewed to my Commands; and for daring, by the Cheat he put on me, to expose me to the Shame of feeing myself so ridiculously imposed upon.

However, you must forgive him, said the Marquis; and I insist upon it, before I quit your Apartment, that you receive him into Favour.

Pardon me, my Lord, replied *Arabella*; this is what I neither can, nor ought to do; and I hope you will not wrong me so much as to continue to desire it.

Nay, *Bella*, said he, this is carrying Things too far, and making trifling Disputes of too great Consequence: I am surprised at your Treatment of a Man whom, after all, if ever you intend to obey me, you must consent to marry.

There is no Question, my Lord, replied she, but it would be my Glory to obey you in whatever is possible; but this you command me now to do, not being so, I conceive you will rather impute my Refusal to Necessity, than Choice.

How! returned the Marquis, will you endeavour to persuade me, that it is not possible Mr. *Glanville* should be your Husband?

'Tis impossible he should be so with my Consent, resumed *Arabella*; and I cannot give it without wounding my own Quiet in a most sensible manner.

Come, come, *Bella*, said the Marquis (fretting at her extreme Obstinacy), this is too much: I am to blame to indulge your Foibles in this Manner: Your Cousin is worthy of your Affection, and you cannot refuse it to him without incurring my Displeasure.

Since my Affection is not in my own Power to bestow, said *Arabella*, weeping, I know not how to remove your Displeasure; but, questionless, I know how to die, to avoid the Effects of what would be to me the most terrible Misfortune in the World.

Foolish Girl! interrupted the Marquis, how strangely do you talk? Are the thoughts of Death become so familiar to you, that you speak of dying with so little Concern?

Since, my Lord, resumed she, in an exalted Tone, I do not yield, either in Virtue or Courage, to many others of my Sex, who, when persecuted like me, have fled to Death for Relief, I know not why I should be thought less capable of it than they; and if *Artimisa*, *Candace*, and the beautiful Daughter of *Cleopatra*,[36] could brave the Terrors of Death for the sake of the Men they loved, there is no Question but I also could imitate their Courage, to avoid the Man I have so much Reason to hate.

The Girl is certainly distracted, interrupted the Marquis, excessively enraged at the strange Speech she had uttered: These foolish Books my Nephew talks of have turned her Brain! Where are they? pursued he, going into her Chamber: I'll burn all I can lay my Hands upon.[37]

Arabella, trembling for the Fate of her Books, followed her Father into the Room; who seeing the Books which had caused this woful Adventure lying upon the Table, he ordered one of her Women to carry them into his Apartment, vowing he would commit them all to the Flames.

Arabella not daring, in the Fury he was in, to interpose, he went out of the Room, leaving her to bewail the Fate of so many illustrious Heroes and Heroines, who, by an Effect of a more cruel Tyranny than any they had ever experienced before, were going to be cast into the merciless Flames; which would, doubtless, pay very little Regard to the divine Beauties of the admirable *Clelia*, or the heroic Valour of the brave *Orontes*;[38] and the rest of those great Princes and Princesses, whose Actions *Arabella* proposed for the Model of hers.

Fortune, however, which never wholly forsook these illustrious Personages, rescued them from so unworthy a Fate, and brought Mr. *Glanville* into the Marquis's Chamber just as he was giving Orders to have them destroyed.

END of the FIRST BOOK.

BOOK II

CHAPTER I

In which the Adventure of the Books is happily concluded.

The Marquis, as soon as he saw Mr. *Glanville*, told him he was resolved to cure *Arabella* of her Whims, by burning the Books that had put them into her Head: I have seized upon some of them, pursued he, smiling; and you may, if you please, wreak your Spite upon these Authors of your Disgrace, by burning them yourself.

Though I have all the Reason in the World to be enraged with that Incendiary *Statira*, said *Glanville* laughing, for the Mischief she has done me; yet I cannot consent to put such an Affront upon my Cousin, as to burn her favourite Books: And now I think of it, my Lord, pursued he, I'll endeavour to make a Merit with Lady *Bella* by saving them: Therefore spare them, at my Request, and let me carry them to her. I shall be quite unhappy till we are Friends again.

You may do as you will, said the Marquis; but I think it encouraging her in her Follies to give them to her again.

Glanville, without replying, eagerly took up the Books, for fear the Marquis should change his Mind; and, highly delighted with the Opportunity he had got of making his Peace with Lady *Bella*, ran to her Apartment, loaded with these kind Intercessors; and, making his Way by *Lucy*, who would have opposed him, penetrated even into the Closet of the melancholy Fair-one, who was making bitter Reflections on the

Cruelty of her Destiny, and bewailing her Loss with a Deluge of Tears.

As ridiculous as the Occasion of these Tears was, yet *Glanville* could not behold them without being affected: Assuming, therefore, a Countenance as sad as he was able, he laid the Books before her; and told her, he hoped she would excuse his coming into her Presence without her Permission, since it was only to restore her those Books, whose Loss she seemed so greatly to lament; and added, that it was with much Difficulty he prevailed upon the Marquis not to burn them immediately; and his Fears, that he might really do as he threatened, made him snatch them up, and bring them, with so little Ceremony, into her Closet.

Arabella, whose Countenance brightened into a Smile of pleasing Surprize at the Sight of her recovered Treasure, turned her bright Eyes upon *Glanville* with a Look of Complacency that went to his Heart.

I well perceive, said she, that, in exaggerating the Merit of this little Service you have done me, you expect I should suffer it to cancel your past Offences: I am not ungrateful enough to be insensible of any Kindness that is shewn me; and, tho' I might be excused for suspecting it was rather Policy than Friendship, that induced you to seek my Satisfaction, by saving these innocent Victims of my Father's Displeasure, nevertheless I pardon you upon the Supposition, that you will, for the future, avoid all Occasion of offending me.

At these Words, she made a Sign to him to be gone, fearing the Extravagance of his Joy would make him throw himself at her Feet to thank her for the infinite Favour she had conferred upon him; but, finding he seemed disposed to stay longer, she called one of her Women into the Closet; and, by some very significant Frowns, gave *Glanville* to understand his Stay was displeasing; so that he left her, with a very low Bow, highly pleased at her having repealed his Banishment; and, assured the Marquis, that nothing could have happened more fortunate for him, than his intended Disposal of his Daughter's Books, since it had proved the Means of restoring him to her Favour.

CHAPTER II

Which contains a very natural Incident.

From this Time Mr. *Glanville*, tho' he was far from coming up to Lady *Bella*'s Idea of a Lover, yet, by the Pains he apparently seemed to be at in obliging her, made every Day some Progress in her Esteem. The Marquis was extremely pleased at the Harmony which subsisted between them; tho' he could have wished to have seen their Marriage advance a little faster; but *Glanville*, who was better acquainted with *Arabella*'s Foible than the Marquis, assured him, he would ruin all his Hopes, if he pressed her to marry; and intreated him to leave it intirely to him, to dispose her to consent to both their Wishes.

The Marquis was satisfied with his Reasons, and resolving not to importune his Daughter, upon that Subject, any more, they lived for some Months in a perfect Tranquillity; to which an Illness the Marquis was seized with, and which was, from the first, thought to be dangerous, gave a sad Interruption.

Arabella's extreme Tenderness upon this Occasion, her anxious Solicitude, her pious Cares, and never-ceasing Attendance at the Bedside of her sick Father, were so many new Charms, that engaged the Affection of *Glanville* more strongly. As the Marquis's Indisposition increased, so did her Care and Assiduity: She would not allow any one to give him any thing but herself; bore all the pettish Humours of a sick Man with a surprizing Sweetness and Patience; watched whole Nights, successively, by his Bedside; and when, at his Importunity, she consented to take any Rest, it was only upon a Couch in his Chamber, from whence no Intreaties could make her remove. Mr. *Glanville* partook with her in these Fatigues; and, by his Care of her Father, and Tenderness for her, confirmed her in the Esteem she had entertained of him.

The Marquis, who had struggled with the Violence of his Distemper for a Fortnight, died on the Fifteenth Day in the Arms of *Arabella*, who received his last Looks; his Eyes never removing themselves from her Face, till they were closed by

Death. Her Spirits, which the Desire she had of being useful to him, had alone supported, now failed her at once; and she fell upon the Bed, without Sense or Motion, as soon as she saw him expire.

Mr. *Glanville*, who was kneeling on the other Side, and had been holding one of his Uncle's Hands, started up in the most terrible Consternation, and, seeing the Condition she was in, flew to her Relief: Her Women, while he supported her, used all the Endeavours they could think of to recover her; but she continued so long in her Swoon, that they apprehended she was dead; and *Glanville* was resigning himself up to the most bitter Sorrow, when she opened her Eyes; but it was only to close them again. Her Faintings continued the whole Day; and the Physicians declaring she was in great Danger, from her extreme Weakness, she was carried to Bed in a Condition that seemed to promise very little Hopes of her Life.

The Care of the Marquis's Funeral devolving upon Mr *Glanville*, he sent a Messenger express for his Father, who was appointed Guardian to Lady *Bella*; the Marquis having first asked her if she was willing it should be so. This Gentleman arrived Time enough to be Witness of that sad Ceremony, which was performed with a Magnificence suitable to the Birth and Fortune of the Marquis.

Lady *Bella* kept her Bed several Days, and her Life was thought to be in Danger; but her Youth, and the Strength of her Constitution, overcame her Disease; and, when she was so well recovered as to be able to admit of a Visit from her Uncle, Mr. *Glanville* sent for Permission to introduce him: The afflicted *Arabella* granted his Request; but, being then more indisposed than usual, she intreated they would defer their Visit for an Hour or two, which they complied with; and, returning at the appointed Time, were conducted into her Dressing-Room by *Lucy*, who informed them her Lady was just fallen into a Slumber.

Mr. *Glanville*, who had not seen her for some Days, expected her waking with great Impatience; and pleased himself with describing her, with a Lover's Fondness, to his Father, when the Sound of her Voice in the next Room interrupted him.

CHAPTER III

Which treats of a consolatory Visit, and other grave Matters.

Arabella, being then awaked from her Slumber, was indulging her Grief by Complaints, which her Women were so used to hear, that they never offered to disturb her. Merciless Fate! said she, in the most moving Tone imaginable, Cruel Destiny! that, not contented with having deprived my Infancy of the soft Cares, and tender Indulgences, of a Mother's Fondness, has robbed me of the only Parent I had left, and exposed me, at these early Years, to the Grief of losing him, who was not only my Father, but my Friend, and Protector of my Youth!

Then, pausing a Moment, she renewed her Complaints with a deep Sigh: Dear Relics of the best of Fathers! pursued she, Why was it not permitted me to bathe you with my Tears? Why were those sacred Remains of him, from whom I drew my Life, snatched from my Eyes, ere they had poured their Tribute of Sorrow over them? Ah! pitiless Women! said she to her Attendants, you prevented me from performing the last pious Rites to my dear Father! You, by your cruel Care, hindered me from easing my sad Heart, by paying him the last Duties he could receive from me! Pardon, O dear and sacred Shade of my loved Father! pardon this unwilling Neglect of thy afflicted Child, who, to the last Moment of her wretched Life, will bewail thy Loss!

Here she ceased speaking; and Mr. *Glanville*, whom this Soliloquy had much less confounded than his Father, was preparing to go in, and comfort her; when the old Gentleman stopping him with a Look of great Concern: My Niece is certainly much worse than we apprehend, said he: She is in a Delirium: Our Presence may, perhaps, discompose her too much.

No, Sir, replied *Glanville*, extremely confused at this Suspicion; my Cousin is not so bad as you suppose: It is common enough for People in any great Affliction to ease themselves by Complaints.

But these, replied the Knight, are the strangest Complaints I ever heard, and favour so much of Phrensy, that I am persuaded her Head is not quite right.

Glanville was going to reply, when *Lucy*, entering, told them her Lady had ordered their Admission: Upon which they followed her into *Arabella*'s Chamber, who was lying negligently upon her Bed.

Her deep Mourning, and the black Gawse, which covered Part of her fair Face, was so advantageous to her Shape and Complexion, that Sir *Charles*, who had not seen her since she grew up, was struck with an extreme Surprize at her Beauty, while his Son was gazing on her so passionately, that he never thought of introducing his Father to her, who contemplated her with as much Admiration as his Son, though with less Passion.

Arabella, rising from her Bed, saluted her Uncle with a Grace that wholly charmed him; and turning to receive Mr. *Glanville*, she burst into Tears at the Remembrance of his having assisted her in her last Attendance upon her Father. Alas! Sir, said she, when we saw each other last, we were both engaged, in a very melancholy Office: Had it pleased Heaven to have spared my Father, he would, doubtless, have been extremely sensible of your generous Cares; nor shall you have any Reason to accuse me of Ingratitude, since I shall always acknowledge your Kindness as I ought.

If you think you owe me any Obligation, returned *Glanville*, pay me, dearest Cousin, by moderating your Sorrow: Indeed you suffer yourself to sink too much under an Affliction which is impossible to be remedied.

Alas! answered *Arabella*, my Grief is very slight, compared to that of many others upon the Death of their Relations: The Great *Sysigambis*, who, questionless, wanted neither Fortitude nor Courage, upon the News of her Grand-daughter's Death, wrapt herself up in her Veil; and, resolving never more to behold the Light, waited for Death in that Posture.[1]

Menecrates, upon the Loss of his Wife, built a magnificent Tomb for her; and, shutting himself up in it, resolved to pass away the Remainder of his Life with her Ashes.[2] These, indeed, were glorious Effects of Piety and Affection, and unfeigned

Signs of an excessive Sorrow: What are the few Tears I shed to such illustrious Instances of Grief and Affection, as these?

Glanville, finding his Cousin upon this Strain, blushed extremely, and would have changed the Subject; but the old Gentleman, who had never heard of these two Persons she mentioned, who expressed their Sorrow for their Losses in so strange a Manner, was surprised at it; and was resolved to know more about them.

Pray, Niece, said he, were you acquainted with these People, who could not submit to the Dispensation of Providence, but, as one may say, flew in the Face of Heaven by their Impatience?

I am very well acquainted with their History, resumed *Arabella*; and I can assure you, they were both very admirable Persons.

Oh! Oh! their History! interrupted the Knight! What, I warrant you, they are to be found in the *Fairy Tales*, and those sort of Books! Well, I never could like such Romances, not I; for they only spoil Youth, and put strange Notions into their Heads.

I am sorry, resumed *Arabella*, blushing with Anger, that we are like to differ in Opinion upon so important a Point.

Truly, Niece, said Sir *Charles*, if we never differ in any thing else, I shall be very easy about this slight Matter; tho' I think a young Lady of your fine Sense (for my Son praises you to the Skies for your *Wit*) should not be so fond of such ridiculous Nonsense as these Story-Books are filled with.

Upon my Word, Sir, resumed *Arabella*, all the Respect I owe you cannot hinder me from telling you, that I take it extremely ill you should, in my Presence, rail at the finest Productions in the World: I think we are infinitely obliged to these Authors, who have, in so sublime a Style, delivered down to Posterity the heroic Actions of the bravest Men, and most virtuous of Women: But for the inimitable Pen of the famous *Scudery*,[3] we had been ignorant of the Lives of many great and illustrious Persons: The war-like Actions of *Oroondates*, *Aronces*, *Juba*, and the renowned *Artaban*, had, haply, never been talked of in our Age; and those fair and chaste Ladies, who were the Objects of their pure and constant Passions, had still been buried in Obscurity; and neither their divine Beauties, or singular Virtue, been the Subject of our Admiration and Praise. But for the famous *Scudery*, we had not known the true Cause of that Action of *Clelia*'s, for which the Senate decreed her a Statue; namely, Her casting herself, with an unparalleled Courage, into the *Tyber*, a deep and rapid River, as you must certainly know, and swimming to the other Side. It was not, as the *Roman* Historians falsly report, a Stratagem to recover herself, and the other Hostages, from the Power of *Porsena*; it was to preserve her Honour from Violation by the impious *Sextus*, who was in the Camp.[4] But for *Scudery*, we had still thought the inimitable Poetess *Sappho* to be a loose Wanton, whose Verses breathed nothing but unchaste and irregular Fires: On the contrary, she was so remarkably chaste, that she would never even consent to marry; but, loving *Phaon*, only with a Platonic Passion, obliged him to restrain his Desires within the Compass of a Brother's Affection.[5] Numberless are the Mistakes he has cleared up of this Kind; and I question, if any other Historian, but himself, knew that *Cleopatra* was really married to *Julius Cæsar*;[6] or that *Cæsario*, her Son by this Marriage, was not murdered, as was supposed, by the Order of *Augustus*, but married the fair Queen of *Ethiopia*, in whose Dominions he took Refuge.[7] The prodigious Acts of Valour, which he has recounted of those accomplished Princes, have never been equalled by the Heroes, of either the *Greek* or *Roman* Historians: How poor and insignificant are the Actions of their Warriors to *Scudery*'s, where one of those admirable Heroes would put whole Armies into Terror, and with his single Arm oppose a Legion!

Indeed, Niece, said Sir *Charles*, no longer able to forbear interrupting her, these are all very improbable Tales. I remember, when I was a Boy, I was very fond of reading the History of *Jack the Giant killer*, and *Tom Thumb*;[8] and these Stories so filled my Head, that I really thought one of those little Fellows killed Men an hundred Feet high; and that the other, after a great many surprising Exploits, was swallowed up by a Cow.

You was very young, Sir, you say, interrupted *Arabella* tartly, when those Stories gained your Belief: However, your Judgment was certainly younger, if you ever believed them at all; for as credulous as you are pleased to think me, I should never, at any Age, have been persuaded such Things could have happened.

My Father, Madam, said *Glanville*, who was strangely confused all this Time, bore Arms in his Youth; and Soldiers, you know, never trouble themselves much with reading.

Has my Uncle been a Soldier, said *Arabella*, and does he hold in Contempt the Actions of the bravest Soldiers in the World?

The Soldiers you speak of, Niece, said Sir *Charles*, were indeed the bravest Soldiers in the World; for I don't believe, they ever had their Equals.

And yet, Sir, said *Arabella*, there are a great Number of such Soldiers to be found in *Scudery*.

Indeed, my dear Niece, interrupted Sir *Charles*, they are to be found no-where else, except in your Imagination, which, I am sorry to see, is filled with such *Whimsies*.

If you mean this to affront me, Sir, resumed *Arabella*, hardly able to forbear Tears, I know how far, as my Uncle, I ought to bear with you: But, methinks, it is highly unkind to aggravate my Sorrows by such cruel Jests; and, since I am not in an Humour to suffer them, don't take it ill, if I intreat you to leave me to myself.

Mr. *Glanville*, who knew nothing pleased his Cousin so much as paying an exact Obedience to her Commands, rose up immediately; and, bowing respectfully to her, asked his Father, If he should attend him into the Gardens?

The Baronet, who thought *Arabella*'s Behaviour bordered a good deal upon Rudeness, took his Leave with some Signs of Displeasure upon his Countenance; and, notwithstanding all his Son could say in Excuse for her, he was extremely offended.

What, said he, to Mr. *Glanville*, does she so little understand the Respect that is due to me as her Uncle, that she, so peremptorily, desired me to leave her Room? My Brother was to blame to take so little Care of her Education; she is quite a Rustic!

Ah! don't wrong your Judgment so much, Sir, said *Glanville*; my Cousin has as little of the Rustic as if she had passed all her Life in a Court: Her fine Sense, and the native Elegance of her Manners give an inimitable Grace to her Behaviour; and as much exceed the studied Politeness of other Ladies I have conversed with, as the Beauties of her Person do all I have ever seen.

She is very handsome, I confess, returned Sir *Charles*; but I cannot think so well of her *Wit* as you do; for methinks she talks very oddly, and has the strangest Conceits! Who, but herself, would think it probable that one Man could put a whole Army to Flight; or commend a foolish Fellow for living in a Tomb, because his Wife was buried in it? Fie, fie! these are silly and extravagant Notions, and will make her appear very ridiculous.

Mr. *Glanville* was so sensible of the Justness of this Remark, that he could not help sighing; which his Father observing, told him, That, since she was to be his Wife, it was his Business to produce a Reformation in her; for, added he, notwithstanding the immense Fortune she will bring you, I should be sorry to have a Daughter-in-law, for whom I should blush as often as she opens her Mouth.

I assure you, Sir, said Mr. *Glanville*, I have but very little Hopes, that I shall be so happy as to have my Cousin for a Wife; for tho' it was my Uncle's Command I should make my Addresses to her, she received me so ill, as a Lover, that I have never dared to talk to her upon that Subject since.

And pray, resumed Sir *Charles*, upon what Terms are you at present?

While I seem to pretend nothing to her, as a Lover, replied Mr. *Glanville*, she is very obliging, and we live in great Harmony together; but I am persuaded, if I exceed the Bounds of Friendship in my Professions, she will treat me extremely ill.

But, interrupted Sir *Charles*, when she shall know, that her Father has bequeathed you one Third of his Estate, provided she don't marry you, 'tis probable her Mind may change; and you may depend upon it, since your Heart is so much set upon her, that, as I am her Guardian, I shall press her to perform the Marquis's Will.

Ah! Sir, resumed Mr. *Glanville*, never attempt to lay any Constraint upon my Cousin in an Affair of this Nature: Permit me to tell you, it would be an Abuse of the Marquis's generous Confidence, and what I would never submit to.

Nay, nay, said the old Gentleman, you have no Reason to fear any Compulsion from me: Tho' her Father has left me her Guardian, till she is of Age, yet it is with such Restriction, that my Niece is quite her own Mistress in that Respect; for tho' she is directed to consult me in her Choice of an Husband, yet my Consent is not absolutely necessary. The Marquis has certainly had a great Opinion of his Daughter's Prudence; and I hope, she will prove herself worthy of it by her Conduct.

Mr. *Glanville* was so taken up with his Reflections upon the State of his Affairs, that he made but little Reply; and, as soon as he had disengaged himself, retired to his Chamber, to be at more Liberty to indulge his Meditations. As he could not flatter himself, with having made any Impression upon the Heart of *Arabella*, he foresaw a thousand Inconveniences from the Death of the Marquis; for, besides that he lost a powerful Mediator with his Cousin, he feared that, when she appeared in the World, her Beauty and Fortune would attract a Croud of Admirers, among whom, it was probable, she would find some one more agreeable to her Taste than himself. As he loved her with great Tenderness, this Thought made him extremely uneasy; and he would sometimes wish the Marquis had laid a stronger Injunction upon her in his Will to marry him; and regretted the little Power his Father had over her: But he was too generous, to dwell long upon these Thoughts, and contented himself with resolving to do all that was honourable to obtain her, without seeking for any Assistance from unjustifiable Methods.

CHAPTER IV

Which contains some common Occurrences, but placed in a new Light.

Arabella, in a few Days, leaving her Chamber, had so many Opportunities of charming her Uncle by her Conversation, which, when it did not turn upon any Incident in her Romances, was perfectly fine, easy, and entertaining, that he declared, he should quit the Castle with great Regret; and endeavoured to persuade her to accompany him to Town: But *Arabella*, who was determined to pass the Year of her Mourning, in the Retirement she had always lived in, absolutely refused, strong as her Curiosity was, to see *London*.

Mr. *Glanville* secretly rejoiced at this Resolution, tho' he seemed desirous of making her change it; but she was unalterable; and, therefore, the Baronet did not think proper to press her any more.

Her Father's Will being read to her, she seemed extremely pleased with the Article in favour of Mr. *Glanville*, wishing him Joy of the Estate that was bequeathed to him, with a most inchanting Sweetness.

Mr. *Glanville* sighed, and cast his Eyes on the Ground, as he returned her Compliment, with a very low Bow; and Sir *Charles*, observing his Confusion, told *Arabella*, that he thought it was a very bad Omen for his Son, to wish him Joy of an Estate, which he could not come to the Possession of, but by a very great Misfortune.

Arabella, understanding his Meaning, blushed; and, willing to change the Discourse, proceeded to consult her Uncle upon the Regulation of her House. Besides the Legacies her Father had bequeathed to his Servants, those, who were more immediately about his Person, she desired, might have their Salaries continued to them: She made no other Alteration, than discharging these Attendants, retaining all the others; and submitting to her Uncle the Management of her Estates, receiving the Allowance he thought proper to assign her, till she was of Age, of which she wanted three Years.

Every Thing being settled, Sir *Charles* prepared to return to Town. Mr. *Glanville*, who desired nothing so much as to stay some time longer with his Cousin in her Solitude, got his Father to intreat that Favour for him of *Arabella*: But she represented to her Uncle the Impropriety of a young Gentleman's staying with her, in her House, now her Father was dead, in a manner so genteel and convincing, that Sir *Charles* could press it no further; and all that Mr. *Glanville* could obtain, was a Permission to visit her some time after, provided he could prevail upon his Sister, Miss *Charlotte Glanville*, to accompany him.

The Day of their Departure being come, *Sir Charles* took his Leave of his charming Niece, with many Expressions of Esteem and Affection; and Mr. *Glanville* appeared so concerned, that *Arabella* could not help observing it; and bade him adieu with great Sweetness.

When they were gone, she found her Time hung heavy upon her Hands; her Father was continually in her Thoughts, and made her extremely melancholy: She recollected the many agreeable Conversations she had had with *Glanville*; and wished it had been consistent with Decency to have detained him. Her Books being the only Amusement she had left, she applied herself to reading with more Eagerness than ever; but, notwithstanding the Delight she took in this Employment, she had so many Hours of Solitude and Melancholy to indulge the Remembrance of her Father in, that she was very far from being happy.

As she wished for nothing more passionately than an agreeable Companion of her own Sex and Rank, an Accident threw a Person in her Way, who, for some Days, afforded her a little Amusement. Stepping one Day out of her Coach, to go into Church, she saw a young Lady enter, accompanied with a middle-aged Woman, who seemed to be an Attendant. As *Arabella* had never seen any one, above the Rank of a Gentleman Farmer's Daughter, in this Church, her Attention was immediately engaged by the Appearance of this Stranger, who was very magnificently dressed: Tho' she did not seem to be more than eighteen Years of Age, her Stature was above the ordinary Size of Women; and, being rather too plump to be delicate, her Mien was so majestic, and such an Air of Grandeur was diffused over her whole Person, joined to the Charms of a very lovely Face, that *Arabella* could hardly help thinking she saw the beautiful *Candace*[9] before her, who, by *Scudery*'s Description, very much resembled this Fair one.

Arabella, having needfully observed her Looks, thought she saw a great Appearance of Melancholy in her Eyes, which filled her with a generous Concern for the Misfortunes of so admirable a Person; but, the Service beginning, she was not at

Liberty to indulge her Reflections upon this Occasion, as she never suffered any Thoughts, but those of Religion, to intrude upon her Mind, during these pious Rites.

As she was going out of Church she observed the young Lady, attended only with the Woman who came with her, preparing to walk home, and therefore stept forward, and, saluting her with a Grace peculiar to herself, intreated her to come into her Coach, and give her the Pleasure of setting her down at her own House: So obliging an Offer from a Person of *Arabella*'s Rank could not fail of being received with great Respect by the young Lady, who was not ignorant of all the Forms of Good-breeding; and, accepting her Invitation, she stepped into the Coach; *Arabella* obliging her Woman to come in also, for whom, as she had that Day only *Lucy* along with her, there was Room enough.

As they were going home, *Arabella*, who longed to be better acquainted, intreated the fair Stranger, as she called her, to go to the Castle, and spend the Day with her; and she consenting, they passed by the House where she lodged, and alighted at the Castle, where *Arabella* welcomed her, with the most obliging Expressions of Civility and Respect. The young Lady, tho' perfectly versed in the Modes of Town-Breeding, and *nothing-meaning* Ceremony, was at a Loss how to make proper Returns to the Civilities of *Arabella*: The native Elegance and Simplicity of her Manners were accompanied with so much real Benevolence of Heart, such insinuating Tenderness, and Graces so irresistible, that she was quite oppressed with them; and, having spent most of her Time between her Toilet and Quadrille,[10] was so little qualified for partaking a Conversation so refined as *Arabella*'s, that her Discourse appeared quite tedious to her, since it was neither upon Fashions, Assemblies,[11] Cards, or Scandal.

Her Silence, and that Absence of Mind, which she betrayed, made *Arabella* conclude, she was under some very great Affliction; and, to amuse her after Dinner, led her into the Gardens, supposing a Person, whose Uneasiness, as she did not doubt, proceeded from Love, would be pleased with the Sight of Groves and Streams, and be tempted to disclose her Misfortunes, while they wandered in that agreeable Privacy. In this, however, she was deceived; for, tho' the young Lady sighed several times, yet, when she did speak, it was only of indifferent things, and not at all in the manner of an afflicted Heroine.

After observing upon a thousand Trifles, she told *Arabella* at last, to whom she was desirous of making known her Alliance to Quality, that these Gardens were extremely like those of her Father's in-Law, the Duke of —— at ——

At this Intimation, she expected *Arabella* would be extremely surprised; but that Lady, whose Thoughts were always familiarized to Objects of Grandeur, and would not have been astonished, if she had understood her Guest was the Daughter of a King, appeared so little moved, that the Lady was piqued by her Indifference; and, after a few Moment's Silence, began to mention going away.

Arabella, who was desirous of retaining her a few Days, intreated her so obligingly to favour her with her Company, for some time, in her Solitude, that the other could not refuse; and, dispatching her Woman to the House where she lodged, to inform them of her Stay at the Castle, would have dispensed with her coming again to attend her, had not *Arabella* insisted upon the contrary.

The Reserve, which the Daughter-in-Law of the Duke of —— still continued to maintain, notwithstanding the repeated Expressions of Friendship *Arabella* used to her, increased her Curiosity to know her Adventures, which she was extremely surprised, she had never offered to relate; but, attributing her Silence, upon this Head, to her Modesty, she was resolved, as was the Custom in those Cases, to oblige her Woman, who, she presumed, was her Confidante, to relate her Lady's History to her; and sending for this Person one Day, when she was alone, to attend her in her Closet, she gave Orders to her Women, if the fair Stranger came to inquire for her, to say she was then busy, but would wait on her as soon as possible.

After this Caution, she ordered Mrs. *Morris* to be admitted; and, obliging her to sit down, told her, she sent for her in order to hear from her the History of her Lady's Life, which she was extremely desirous of knowing.

Mrs. *Morris*, who was a Person of Sense, and had seen the World, was extremely surprised at this Request of *Arabella*, which was quite contrary to the Laws of Good-breeding; and, as she thought, betrayed a great deal of impertinent Curiosity: She could not tell how to account for the free Manner in which she desired her to give up her Lady's Secrets, which, indeed, were not of a Nature to be told; and appeared so much confused, that *Arabella* took Notice of it; and, supposing it was her Bashfulness which caused her Embarrassment, she endeavoured to re-assure her by the most affable Behaviour imaginable.

Mrs. *Morris*, who was not capable of much Fidelity for her Lady, being but lately taken into her Service, and not extremely fond of her, thought she had now a fine Opportunity of recommending herself to *Arabella*, by telling her all she knew of Miss *Groves*, for that was her Name; and, therefore, told her, since she was pleased to command it, she would give her what Account she was able to her Lady; but intreated her to be secret, because it was of great Consequence to her, that her Affairs should not be known.

I always imagined, said *Arabella*, that your beautiful Mistress had some particular Reason for not making herself known, and for coming in this private Manner into this Part of the Country: You may assure yourself therefore, that I will protect her as far as I am able, and offer her all the Assistance in my Power to give her: Therefore you may acquaint me with her Adventures, without being apprehensive of a Discovery that would be prejudicial to her.

Mrs. *Morris*, who had been much better pleased with the Assurances of a Reward for the Intelligence she was going to give her, looked a little foolish at these fine Promises, in which she had no Share; and *Arabella*, supposing she was endeavouring to recollect all the Passages of her Lady's Life, told her, She need not give herself the Trouble to acquaint her with any thing that passed during the Infancy of her Lady, but proceed to acquaint her with Matters of greater Importance: And since, said she, you have, no doubt, been most favoured with her Confidence, you will do me a Pleasure to describe to me, exactly, all the Thoughts of her Soul, as she has communicated them to you, that I may the better comprehend her History.

CHAPTER V

The History of Miss Groves, interspersed with some very curious Observations.

Though, Madam, said Mrs. *Morris*, I have not been long in Miss *Groves*'s Service, yet I know a great many Things by the means of her former Woman, who told them to me, tho' my Lady thinks I am ignorant of them; and I know that this is her second Trip into the Country.

Pray, interrupted *Arabella*, do me the Favour to relate Things methodically: Of what Use is it to me to know that this is your Lady's second Trip, as you call it, into the Country, if I know not the Occasion of it? Therefore begin with informing me, who were the Parents of this admirable young Person.

Her Father, Madam, said Mrs. *Morris*, was a Merchant; and, at his Death, left her a large Fortune, and so considerable a Jointure to his Wife, that the Duke of ——, being then a Widower, was tempted to make his Addresses to her. Mrs. *Groves* was one of the proudest Women in the World; and, this Offer flattering her Ambition more than ever she had Reason to expect, she married the Duke after a very short Courtship; and carried Miss *Groves* down with her to ——, where the Duke had a fine Seat, and where she was received by his Grace's Daughters, who were much about her own Age, with great Civility. Miss *Groves*, Madam, was then about twelve Years old, and was educated with the Duke's Daughters, who, in a little time, became quite disgusted with their new Sister; for Miss *Groves*, who inherited her Mother's Pride, tho' not her Understanding, in all things affected an Equality with those young Ladies, who, Conscious of the Superiority of their Birth, could but ill bear with her Insolence and Presumption. As they grew older, the Difference of their Inclinations caused perpetual

Quarrels amongst them; for his Grace's Daughters were serious, reserved, and pious. Miss *Groves* affected noisy Mirth, was a great Romp, and delighted in masculine Exercises.

The Duchess was often reflected on for suffering her Daughter, without any other Company than two or three Servants, to spend great Part of the Day in riding about the Country, leaping over Hedges and Ditches, exposing her fair Face to the Injuries of the Sun and Wind; and, by those coarse Exercises, contracting a masculine and robust Air not becoming her Sex, and tender Years:[12] Yet she could not be prevailed upon to restrain her from this Diversion, till it was reported, she had listened to the Addresses of a young Sportsman, who used to mix in her Train, when she went upon those Rambles, and procured frequent Opportunities of conversing with her.

There is a great Difference, interrupted *Arabella*, in suffering Addresses, and being betrayed into an involuntary Hearing of them, and this last, I conceive to have been the Case of your Lady; for it is not very probable she would so far forget what she owed to her own Glory, as to be induced to listen quietly to Discourses like those you mention.

However, Madam, resumed Mrs. *Morris*, the Duchess thought it necessary to keep her more at home; but, even here she was not without meeting Adventures, and found a Lover in the Person who taught her to write.

That, indeed, was a very notable Adventure, said *Arabella*; but it is not strange, that Love should produce such Metamorphoses: 'Tis not very long ago, that I heard of a Man of Quality, who disguised himself in a poor Habit, and worked in the Gardens of a certain Nobleman, whose Daughter he was enamoured with: These things happen every day.

The Person I speak of, Madam, said Mrs. *Morris*, was never discovered to be any thing better than a Writing-master; and yet, for all that, Miss was *smitten* with his fine Person, and was taking Measures to run away with him, when the Intrigue was discovered, the Lover dismissed, and the young Lady, whose faulty Conduct had drawn upon her her Mother's Dislike, was sent up to *London*, and allowed to be her own Mistress at Sixteen; to which unpardonable Neglect of her

Mother she owes the Misfortunes that have since befallen her.

Whatever may be the common Opinion of this Matter, interrupted *Arabella* again, I am persuaded the Writing-master, as you call him, was some Person of Quality, who made use of that Device to get Access to his beautiful Mistress. Love is ingenious in Artifices: Who would have thought, that, under the Name of *Alcippus*, a simple Attendant of the fair *Artemisa* Princess of *Armenia*, the gallant *Alexander* Son of the great and unfortunate *Antony*, by Queen *Cleopatra*, was concealed, who took upon himself that mean Condition for the sake of seeing his adored Princess? Yet the Contrivance of *Orontes*, Prince of the *Massagetes*, was far more ingenious, and even dangerous; for this valiant and young Prince, happening to see the Picture of the beautiful *Thalestris*, Daughter of the Queen of the *Amazons*, he fell passionately in Love with her; and, knowing that the Entrance into that Country was forbid to Men, he dressed himself in Womens Apparel; and, finding means to be introduced to the Queen, and her fair Daughter, whose Amity he gained by some very singular Services in the Wars, he lived several Years undiscovered in their Court:[13] I see, therefore, no Reason to the contrary, but that this Writing-master might have been some illustrious Person, whom Love had disguised; and, I am persuaded, added she, smiling, that I shall hear more of him anon, in a very different Character.

Indeed, Madam, said Mrs. *Morris*, whom this Speech of *Arabella* had extremely surprised, I never heard any thing more about him, than what I have related; and, for what I know, he continues still to teach Writing; for I don't suppose the Duchess's Displeasure could affect him.

How is it possible, said *Arabella*, that you can suppose such an Offence to Probability? In my Opinion, 'tis much more likely, that this unfortunate Lover is dead thro' Despair; or, perhaps, wandering over the World in Search of that Fair one, who was snatched from his Hopes.

If it was his Design to seek for her, Madam, resumed Mrs. *Morris*, he need not have gone far, since she was only sent to *London*, whither he might easily have followed her.

There is no accounting for these Things, said *Arabella*:

Perhaps he has been imposed upon, and made to believe, that it was she herself that banished him from her Presence: 'Tis probable too, that he was jealous, and thought she preferred someone of his Rivals to him. Jealousy is inseparable from true Love; and the slightest Matters imaginable will occasion it: And, what is still more wonderful, this Passion creates the greatest Disorders in the most sensible and delicate Hearts. Never was there a more refined and faithful Passion, than that of the renowned *Artamenes* for *Mandana*; and yet this Prince was driven almost to Distraction by a Smile, which, he fansied, he saw in the Face of his Divine Mistress, at a time when she had some Reason to believe he was dead; and he was so transported with Grief and Rage, that, tho' he was a Prisoner in his Enemy's Camp, where the Knowledge of his Quality would have procured him certain Death, yet he determined to hazard all Things for the sake of presenting himself before *Mandana*, and upbraiding her with her Infidelity; when, in Reality, nothing was farther from the Thoughts of that fair and virtuous Princess, than the Lightness he accused her of:[14] So that, as I said before, it is not at all to be wondered at, if this disguised Lover of your Lady was driven to Despair by Suspicions as groundless, perhaps, as those of *Artamenes*, yet not the less cruel and tormenting.

Mrs. *Morris*, finding *Arabella* held her Peace at these Words, went on with her History in this manner: — Miss *Groves*, Madam, being directed by her Woman in all things, took up her Lodgings in her Father's House, who was a broken Tradesman, and obliged to keep himself concealed for fear of his Creditors: Here she formed her Equipage, which consisted of a Chair, one Footman, a Cook, and her Woman: As she was indulged with the Command of what Money she pleased, her Extravagance was boundless: She lavished away large Sums at Gaming, which was her favourite Diversion;[15] kept such a Number of different Animals for Favourites, that their Maintenance amounted to a considerable Sum every Year: Her Woman's whole Family were supported at her Expence; and, as she frequented all public Places, and surpassed Ladies of the first Quality in Finery, her Dress alone consumed great Part of her Income. I need not tell you, Madam, that my Lady was a celebrated Beauty: You have yourself being pleased to say, that she is very handsome. When she first appeared at Court, her Beauty, and the uncommon Dignity of her Person, at such early Years, made her the Object of general Admiration. The King was particularly struck with her; and declared to those about him, that Miss *Groves* was the finest Woman at Court. The Ladies, however, found means to explain away all that was flattering in this Distinction: They said, Miss *Groves* was clumsy; and it was her Resemblance to the *unwieldy German* Ladies that made her so much admired by his Majesty.[16] Her Pride, and the Quality Airs she affected, were the Subject of great Ridicule to those that envied her Charms: Some Censures were maliciously cast on her Birth; for, as she was always styled the Duchess of ——'s Daughter, a Custom she introduced herself, she seemed to disclaim all Title to a legal Father. Miss *Groves*, as universally admired as she was, yet made but very few particular Conquests. Her Fortune was known to be very considerable, and her Mother's Jointure was to descend to her after her Death: Yet there was no Gentleman, who would venture upon a Wife of Miss *Groves*'s Taste for Expence, as very few Estates, *to which she could pretend*, would support her Extravagance. — The Honourable Mr. *L*——, Brother to the Earl of ——, was the only one, amidst a Croud of Admirers, who made any particular Address to her. This Gentleman was tolerably handsome, and had the Art of making himself agreeable to the Ladies, by a certain Air of Softness and Tenderness, which never failed to make some Impression upon those he desired to deceive.

Miss *Groves* was ravished with her Conquest, and boasted of it so openly, that People, who were acquainted with this Gentleman's Character, foreseeing her Fate, could not help pitying her.

A very few Months Courtship completed the Ruin of poor Miss *Groves*: She fell a Sacrifice to Oaths which had been often prostituted for the same inhuman Purposes; and became so fond of her Betrayer, that it was with great Difficulty he could persuade her not to give him, even in public, the most ridiculous

Proofs of her *Tenderness*. Her Woman pretends, that she was ignorant of this Intrigue, till Miss *Groves* growing big with Child, it could no longer be concealed; it was at length agreed, she should lie-in at her own Lodgings, to prevent any Suspicions from her retreating into the Country; but that Scheme was over ruled by her Woman's Mother, who advised her to conceal herself in some Village, not far from Town, till the Affair was over.

Miss *Groves* approved of this second Proposal, but took Advantage of her Shape, which, being far from delicate, would not easily discover any growing Bigness, to stay in Town as long as she possibly could. When her Removal was necessary, she went to the Lodgings provided for her, a few Miles distant from *London*: And, notwithstanding the Excuses which were framed for this sudden Absence, the true Cause was more than suspected by some busy People, who industriously inquired into her Affairs.

Mr. *L——* saw her but seldom during her Illness: The Fear of being discovered was his Pretence: But her Friends easily saw through this Disguise, and were persuaded Miss *Groves* was waning in his Affections.

As she had a very strong Constitution, she returned to Town at the End of three Weeks: The Child was dead, and she looked handsomer than ever. Mr. *L——* continued his Visits; and the Town to make Remarks of them. All this time the Duchess never troubled herself about the Conduct of this unfortunate young Creature: And the People she was with had not the Goodness to give her any Hint of her Misconduct, and the Waste of her Fortune: On the contrary, they almost turned her Head with their Flatteries, preyed upon her Fortune, and winked at her Irregularities.

She was now a second time with Child: Her Character was pretty severely handled by her Enemies: Mr. *L——* began openly to slight her: And she was several thousand Pounds in Debt.[17] The Mother and Sisters of her Woman, in whose House she still was, were base enough to whisper the Fault she had been guilty of to all their Acquaintances. Her Story became generally known: She was shunned and neglected by every body; and even Mr. *L*——, who had been the Cause of her Ruin, intirely abandoned her,[18] and boasted openly of the Favours he had received from her.

Miss *Groves* protested to her Friends, That he had promised her Marriage; but Mr. *L*—— constantly denied it; and never scrupled to say, when he was questioned about it, That he found Miss *Groves* too easy a Conquest to make any Perjury necessary. Her Tenderness, however, for this base Man, was so great, that she never could bear to hear him railed at in her Presence; but would quarrel with the only Friends she had left, if they said any thing to his Disadvantage. As she was now pretty far advanced with Child, she would have retired into the Country; but the bad Condition of her Affairs made her Removal impossible: In this Extremity she had Recourse to her Uncle, a rich Merchant in the City, who, having taken all the necessary Precautions for his own Security, paid Miss *Groves*'s Debts, carrying on, in her Name, a Law-suit with the Duchess, for some Lands, which were to be put into her Hands, when she was of Age, and which that great Lady detained. Miss *Groves*, being reduced to live upon something less than an Hundred a Year,[19] quitted *London*, and came into this Part of the Country, where she was received by Mrs. *Barnet*, one of her Woman's Sisters, who is married to a Country Gentleman of some Fortune: In her House she lay-in of a Girl, which Mr. *L*—— sent to demand, and will not be persuaded to inform her how, or in what manner, he has disposed of the Child.

Her former Woman leaving her, I was received in her Place, from whom I learnt all these Particulars: And Miss *Groves* having gained the Affections of Mr. *Barnet*'s Brother, her Beauty, and the large Fortune which she has in Reversion, has induced him, notwithstanding the Knowledge of her past unhappy Conduct, to marry her. But their Marriage is yet a Secret, Miss *Groves* being apprehensive of her Uncle's Displeasure for not consulting him in her Choice.

Her Husband is gone to *London*, with an Intention to acquaint him with it; and, when he returns, their Marriage will be publicly owned.

CHAPTER VI

Containing what a judicious Reader will hardly approve.

Mrs. *Morris* ending her Narration, *Arabella*, who had not been able to restrain her Tears at some Parts of it, thanked her for the Trouble she had been at; and assured her of her Secrecy: Your Lady's Case, said she, is much to be lamented; and greatly resembles the unfortunate *Cleopatra*'s, whom *Julius Cæsar* privately marrying, with a Promise to own her for his Wife, when he should be peaceable Master of the *Roman* Empire, left that great Queen big with Child, and, never intending to perform his Promise, suffered her to be exposed to the Censures the World has so freely cast upon her; and which she so little deserved.

Mrs. *Morris*, seeing the favourable Light in which *Arabella* viewed the Actions of her *Lady*, did not think proper to say any thing to undeceive her; but went out of the Closet, not a little mortified at her Disappointment: For she saw she was likely to receive nothing for betraying her Lady's Secrets, from *Arabella*: Who seemed so little sensible of the Pleasure of Scandal, as to be wholly ignorant of its Nature; and not to know it when it was told her.

Miss *Groves*, who was just come to Lady *Bella*'s Chamber-door, to inquire for her, was surprised to see her Woman come out of it; and who, upon meeting her, expressed great Confusion. As she was going to ask her some Questions concerning her Business there, *Arabella* came out of the Closet; and, seeing Miss *Groves* in her Chamber, asked her Pardon for staying so long from her.

I have been listening to your History, said she, with great Frankness, which your Woman has been relating: And I assure you I am extremely sensible of your Misfortunes.

Miss *Groves*, at these Words, blushed with extreme Confusion; and Mrs. *Morris* turned pale with Astonishment and Fear. *Arabella*, not sensible that she had been guilty of any Indiscretion, proceeded to make Reflections upon some Part of her Story; which, though they were not at all disadvantageous to that young Lady, she received as so many Insults: And asked Lady *Bella*, If she was not ashamed to tamper with a Servant to betray the Secrets of her Mistress?

Arabella, a little surprised at so rude a Question, answered, however, with great Sweetness; and protested to her, that she would make no ill Use of what she had learned of her Affairs: For, in fine, Madam, said she, do you think I am less fit to be trusted with your Secrets, than the Princess of the *Leontines* was with those of *Clelia*;[20] between whom there was no greater Amity and Acquaintance, than with us? And you must certainly know, that the Secrets which that admirable Person entrusted with *Lysimena*, were of a Nature to be more dangerous, if revealed, than yours. The Happiness of *Clelia* depended upon *Lysimena*'s Fidelity: And the Liberty, nay, haply, the Life, of *Aronces*, would have been in Danger, if she had betrayed them. Though I do not intend to arrogate to myself the Possession of those admirable Qualities which adorned the Princess of the *Leontines*, yet I will not yield to her, or any one else, in Generosity and Fidelity: And if you will be pleased to repose as much Confidence in me, as those illustrious Lovers did in her, you shall be convinced I will labour as earnestly for your Interest, as that fair Princess did for those of *Aronces* and *Clelia*.

Miss *Groves* was so busied in reflecting upon the Baseness of her Woman in exposing her, that she heard not a Word of this fine Harangue (at which Mrs. *Morris*, notwithstanding the Cause she had for Uneasiness, could hardly help laughing); but, assuming some of that Haughtiness in her Looks, for which she used to be remarkable, she told Lady *Bella*, that she imputed her impertinent Curiosity to her Country Ignorance, and ill Breeding: And she did not doubt but she would be served in her own *kind*, and meet with as bad Fortune as she had done; and, perhaps, deserve it *worse* than she did: For there are more false Men in the World besides Mr. *L*——; and she was no handsomer than other People.

Saying this, she flung out of the Room, her Woman following, leaving *Arabella* in such Confusion at a Behaviour of which she had never before had an Idea, that for some Moments she remained immoveable.

Recollecting herself, at last, and conceiving, that Civility required she should endeavour to appease this incensed Lady, she went down Stairs after her; and, stopping her just as she was going out of the House, intreated her to be calm, and suffer her to vindicate herself from the Imputation of being impertinently curious to know her Affairs.

Miss *Groves*, quite transported with Shame and Anger, refused absolutely to stay.

At least, Madam, said *Arabella*, stay till my Coach can be got ready; and don't think of walking home, so slightly attended.

This Offer was as sullenly answered as the other: And *Arabella*, finding she was determined to venture home, with no other Guard than her Woman, who silently followed her, ordered two of her Footmen to attend her at a small Distance; and to defend her, if there should be Occasion.

For who knows, said she to *Lucy*, what Accident may happen? Some one or other of her insolent Lovers may take this Opportunity to carry her away; and I should never forgive myself for being the Cause of such a Misfortune to her.

Mrs. *Morris* having found it easy to reconcile herself to her Lady, by assuring her, that Lady *Bella* was acquainted with great Part of her Story before; and that what she told her, tended only to justify her Conduct, as she might have been convinced by what Lady *Bella* said; they both went home with a Resolution to say nothing of what had passed, with relation to the Cause of the Disgust Miss *Groves* had received: But only said, in general, that Lady *Bella* was the most ridiculous Creature in the World; and was so totally ignorant of good Breeding, that it was impossible to converse with her.

CHAPTER VII

Which treats of the Olympic Games.

While *Arabella* was ruminating on the unaccountable Behaviour of her new Acquaintance, she received a Letter from her

Uncle, informing her (for she had expresly forbid Mr. *Glanville* to write to her), that his Son and Daughter intended to set out for her Seat in a few Days.

This News was received with great Satisfaction by *Arabella*, who hoped to find an agreeable Companion in her Cousin; and was not so insensible of Mr. *Glanville*'s Merit, as not to feel some kind of Pleasure at the Thought of seeing him again.

This Letter was soon followed, by the Arrival of Mr. *Glanville*, and his Sister; who, upon the Sight of *Arabella*, discovered some Appearance of Astonishment and Chagrin; for, notwithstanding all her Brother had told her of her Accomplishments, she could not conceive it possible for a young Lady, bred up in the Country, to be so perfectly elegant and genteel as she found her Cousin.

As Miss *Charlotte* had a large Share of Coquetry in her Composition, and was fond of Beauty in none of her own Sex but herself, she was sorry to see Lady *Bella* possessed of so great a Share; and, being in Hopes her Brother had drawn a flattering Figure of her Cousin, she was extremely disappointed at finding the Original so handsome.

Arabella, on the contrary, was highly pleased with Miss *Glanville*; and, finding her Person very agreeable, did not fail to commend her Beauty: A sort of Complaisance mightily in Use among the Heroines, who knew not what Envy or Emulation meant.

Miss *Glanville* received her Praises with great Politeness, but could not find in her Heart to return them: And, as soon as these Compliments were over, Mr. *Glanville* told Lady *Bella*, how tedious he had found the short Absence she had forced him to, and how great was his Satisfaction at seeing her again.

I shall not dispute the Truth of your last Assertion, replied *Arabella*, smiling, since I verily believe, you are mighty well satisfied at present; but I know not how you will make it appear, that an Absence, which you allow to be short, has seemed so tedious to you; for this is a manifest Contradiction: However, pursued she, preventing his Reply, you look so well, and so much at Ease, that I am apt to believe, Absence has agreed very well with you.

And yet I assure you, Madam, said Mr. *Glanville*, interrupting her, that I have suffered more Uneasiness during this Absence, than I fear you will permit me to tell you.

Since, replied *Arabella*, that Uneasiness has neither made you thinner, nor paler, I don't think you ought to be pitied: For, to say the Truth, in these Sort of Matters, a Person's bare Testimony has but little Weight.

Mr. *Glanville* was going to make her some Answer; when Miss *Glanville*, who, while they had been speaking, was adjusting her Dress at the Glass, came up to them, and made the Conversation more general.

After Dinner, they adjourned to the Gardens, where the gay Miss *Glanville*, running eagerly from one Walk to another, gave her Brother as many Opportunities of talking to Lady *Bella* as he could wish: However, he stood in such Awe of her, and dreaded so much another Banishment, that he did not dare, otherwise than by distant Hints, to mention his Passion; and *Arabella*, well enough pleased with a Respect that in some measure came up to her Expectation, discovered no Resentment at Insinuations she was at Liberty to dissemble the Knowledge of: And if he could not, by her Behaviour, flatter himself with any great Hopes, yet he found as little Reason, in *Arabella*'s Language, to despair.

Miss *Glanville*, at the End of a few Weeks, was so tired of the magnificent Solitude she lived in, that she heartily repented her Journey; and insinuated to her Brother, her Inclination to return to Town.

Mr. *Glanville*, knowing his Stay was regulated by his Sister's, intreated her not to expose him to the Mortification of leaving *Arabella* so soon; and promised her he would contrive some Amusements for her, which should make her relish the Country better than she had yet done.

Accordingly, he proposed to *Arabella* to go to the Races, which were to be held at —— a few Miles from the Castle: She would have excused herself, upon account of her Mourning; but Miss *Glanville* discovered so great an Inclination to be present at this Diversion, that *Arabella* could no longer refuse to accompany her.

Since, said she to Miss *Glanville*, you are fond of public Diversions, it happens very luckily, that these Races are to be held at the Time you are here: I never heard of them before, and I presume 'tis a good many Years since they were last celebrated. Pray, Sir, pursued she, turning to *Glanville*, do not these Races, in some Degree, resemble the *Olympic* Games? Do the Candidates ride in Chariots?[21]

No, Madam, replied *Glanville*; the Jockeys are mounted upon the fleetest Coursers they can procure; and he who first reaches the Goal obtains the Prize.

And who is the fair Lady that is to bestow it? resumed *Arabella*: I dare engage one of her Lovers will enter the Lists; she will, doubtless, be in no less Anxiety than he; and the Shame of being overcome, will hardly affect him with more Concern, than herself; that is, provided he be so happy as to have gained her Affections. I cannot help thinking the fair *Elismonda* was extremely happy in this Particular: For she had the Satisfaction to see her secret Admirer Victor in all the Exercises at the *Olympic* Games, and carry away the Prize from many Princes, and Persons of rare Quality, who were Candidates with him; and he had also the Glory to receive three Crowns in one Day, from the Hands of his adored Princess; who, questionless, bestowed them upon him with an infinite deal of Joy.

What Sort of Races were those, Madam? said Miss *Glanville*; whose Reading had been very confined.

The *Olympic* Games, Miss, said *Arabella*, so called from *Olympia*, a City near which they were performed, in the Plains of *Elis*, consisted of Foot and Chariot Races; Combats with the Cestus;[22] Wrestling, and other Sports. They were instituted in Honour of the Gods and Heroes; and were therefore termed sacred, and were considered as a Part of Religion.

They were a kind of School, or military Apprenticeship; in which the Courage of the Youth found constant Employment: And the Reason why Victory in those Games was attended with such extraordinary Applause, was, that their Minds might be quickened with great and noble Prospects, when, in this Image of War, they arrived to a Pitch of Glory, approaching, in some Respects, to that of the most famous Conquerors. They thought this Sort of Triumph one of the greatest Parts of Happiness of which Human Nature was capable: So that when *Diagoras* had seen his Sons crowned in the *Olympic* Games, one of his Friends made him this Compliment, Now, *Diagoras*, you may die satisfied; since you can't be a God. It would tire you, perhaps, was I to describe all the Exercises performed there: But you may form a general Notion of them, from what you have doubtless read of Justs and Tournaments.[23]

Really, said Miss *Glanville*, I never read about any such Things.

No! replied *Arabella*, surprized: Well, then, I must tell you, that they hold a middle Place, between a Diversion and a Combat; but the *Olympic* Games were attended with a much greater Pomp and Variety: And not only all *Greece*, but other neighbouring Nations, were in a manner drained, to furnish out the Appearance.

Well, for my Part, said Miss *Glanville*, I never before heard of these Sort of Races; those I have been at were quite different. I know the Prizes and Bets are sometimes very considerable.

And, doubtless, interrupted *Arabella*, there are a great many Heroes who signalize themselves at these Races; not for the sake of the Prize, which would be unworthy of great Souls, but to satisfy that burning Desire of Glory, which spurs them on to every Occasion of gaining it.

As for the Heroes, or Jockeys, said Miss *Glanville*, call them what you please, I believe they have very little Share, either of the Profit or Glory: For their Masters have the one, and the Horses the other.

Their Masters! interrupted *Arabella*: What, I suppose a great many foreign Princes send their Favourites to Combat, in their Name? I remember to have read, that *Alcibiades* triumphed three times successively at the *Olympic* Games, by means of one of his Domestics, who, in his Master's Name, entered the Lists.[24]

Mr. *Glanville*, fearing his Sister would make some absurd Answer, and thereby disoblige his Cousin, took up the Discourse: And, turning it upon the *Grecian* History, engrossed her Conversation for two Hours, wholly to himself; while

Miss *Glanville* (to whom all they said was quite unintelligible) diverted herself with humming a Tune, and tinkling her Cousin's Harpsichord; which proved no Interruption to the more rational Entertainment of her Brother and *Arabella*.

CHAPTER VIII

Which concludes with an excellent moral Sentence.

The Day being come on which they designed to be present at the Races (or, as *Arabella* called them, the *Games*), Miss *Glanville*, having spent four long Hours in dressing herself to the greatest Advantage, in order, if possible, to eclipse her lovely Cousin, whose Mourning, being much deeper, was less capable of Ornaments, came into her Chamber; and, finding her still in her Morning Dress, For Heaven's sake, Lady *Bella*, said she,[25] when do you purpose to be ready? Why it is almost time to be gone, my Brother says, and here you are not a bit dressed!

Don't be uneasy, said *Arabella*, smiling; and, going to her Toilet, I shan't make you wait long.

Miss *Glanville*, seating herself near the Table, resolved to be present while her Cousin was dressing, that she might have an Opportunity to make some Remarks to her Disadvantage: But she was extremely mortified, to observe the Haste and Negligence she made her Women use in this important Employment; and that, notwithstanding her Indifference, nothing could appear more lovely and genteel.[26]

Miss *Glanville*, however, pleased herself with the Certainty of seeing her Cousin's Dress extremely ridiculed, for the peculiar Fashion of her Gown: And the Veil, which, as becoming as it was, would, by its Novelty, occasion great Diversion among the Ladies, helped to comfort her for the Superiority of her Charms; which, partial as she was to her own, she could not help secretly confessing.

Arabella being dressed in much less Time than her Cousin, Mr. *Glanville* was admitted, who led her down Stairs to her

Coach. His Sister, (secretly repining at the Advantage *Arabella*
had over her, in having so respectful an Adorer) followed: And,
being placed in the Coach, they set out with great Appearance
of Good-humour on all Sides.

They got to —— but just time enough to see the Beginning
of the first Course: *Arabella*, who fansied the Jockeys were
Persons of great Distinction, soon became interested in the Fate
of one of them, whose Appearance pleased her more than
the others. Accordingly, she made Vows for his Success, and
appeared so extremely rejoiced at the Advantage he had gained,
that Miss *Glanville* maliciously told her, People would make
Remarks at the Joy she expressed, and fansy she had a more
than ordinary Interest in that Jockey, who had first reached the
Goal.

Mr. *Glanville*, whom this impertinent Insinuation of his
sister had filled with Confusion and Spite, sat biting his Lips,
trembling for the Effect it would produce in *Arabella*: But she,
giving quite another Turn to her Cousin's Words, I assure you,
said she, with a Smile, I am not any farther interested in the
Fate of this Person, who has hitherto been successful, than what
the Handsomeness of his Garb, and the Superiority of his Skill,
may demand, from an unprejudiced Spectator: And, though I
perceive you imagine he is some concealed Lover of mine, yet I
don't remember to have ever seen him: And I am confident it is
not for my sake that he entered the Lists; nor is it my Presence
which animates him.

Lord bless me, Madam! replied Miss *Glanville*, Who would
ever think of such strange Things as these you talk of? No-body
will pretend to deny that you are very handsome, to be sure;
but yet, thank Heaven, the Sight of you is not so dangerous,
but that such sort of People, as these are, may escape your
Chains.

Arabella was so wholly taken up with the Event of the Races,
that she gave but very little Heed to this sarcastic Answer of
Miss *Glanville*; whose Brother, taking Advantage of an Opportunity which *Arabella* gave him by putting her Head quite out
of the Coach, chid her very severely for the Liberty she took
with her Cousin. *Arabella*, by looking earnestly out of the

Window, had given so full a View of her fine Person to a young Baronet,[27] who was not many Paces from the Coach, that, being struck with Admiration at the Sight of so lovely a Creature, he was going up to some of her Attendants to ask who she was, when he perceived Mr. *Glanville*, with whom he was intimately acquainted, in the Coach with her: Immediately he made himself known to his Friend, being excessively rejoiced at having got an Opportunity of beginning an Acquaintance with a Lady whose Sight had so charmed him.

Mr. *Glanville*, who had observed the profound Bow he made to *Arabella*, accompanied with a Glance that shewed an extreme Admiration of her, was very little pleased at this Meeting; yet he dissembled his Thoughts well enough in his Reception of him. But Miss *Glanville* was quite overjoyed, hoping she would now have her Turn of Gallantry and Compliment: Therefore, accosting him in her free Manner, Dear Sir *George*, said she, you come in a lucky Time to brighten up the Conversation: Relations are such dull Company for one another, 'tis half a Minute since we have exchanged a Word.

My Cousin, said *Arabella* smiling, has so strange a Disposition for Mirth, that she thinks all her Moments are lost, in which she finds nothing to laugh at: For my part, I do so earnestly long to know, to which of these Pretenders Fortune will give the Victory, that I can suffer my Cares for them to receive no Interruption from my Cousin's agreeable Gaiety.

Mr. *Glanville*, observing the Baronet gazed upon *Arabella* earnestly while she was speaking those few words, resolved to hinder him from making any Reply, by asking him several Questions concerning the Racers, their Owners, and the Bets which were laid; to which *Arabella* added, And pray, Sir, said she, do me the Favour to tell me, if you know who that gallant Man is, who has already won the first Course.

I don't know really, Madam, said Sir *George*, what his Name is, extremely surprized at her Manner of asking.

The Jockey had now gained the Goal a Second time; and *Arabella* could not conceal her Satisfaction. Questionless, said she, he is a very extraordinary Person; but I am afraid we shall not have the Pleasure of knowing who he is; for if he has any Reason for keeping himself concealed, he will evade any Inquiries after him, by slipping out of the Lists while this Hurry and Tumult lasts, as *Hortensius* did at the *Olympic* Games; yet, notwithstanding all his Care, he was discovered by being obliged to fight a single Combat with one of the Persons whom he had worsted at those Games.[28]

Mr. *Glanville*, who saw his Sister, by her little Coquetries with Sir *George*, had prevented him from hearing great Part of this odd Speech, proposed returning to the Castle; to which *Arabella* agreed: But, conceiving Civility obliged her to offer the Convenience of a Lodging to a Stranger of Sir *George*'s Appearance, and who was an Acquaintance of her Cousins, You must permit me, said she to Mr. *Glanville*, to intreat your noble Friend will accompany us to the Castle, where he will meet with better Accommodations than at any Inn he can find; for I conceive, that, coming only to be a Spectator of these Games, he is wholly unprovided with a Lodging.

The Baronet, surprized at so uncommon a Civility,[29] was at a Loss what Answer to make her at first; but recollecting himself, he told her that he would, if she pleased, do himself the Honour to attend her home; but as his House was at no great Distance from ——, he would be put to no Inconveniency for a Lodging.

Miss *Glanville*, who was not willing to part so soon with the Baronet, insisted, with her Cousin's Leave, upon his coming into the Coach; which he accordingly did, giving his Horse to the Care of his Servant; and they proceeded together to the Castle; *Arabella* still continuing to talk of the Games, as she called them, while poor *Glanville*, who was excessively confused, endeavoured to change the Discourse, not without an Apprehension, that every Subject he could think of, would afford *Arabella* an Occasion of shewing her Foible; which, notwithstanding the Pain it gave him, could not lessen his Love.

Sir *George*, whose Admiration of Lady *Bella* increased the longer he saw her, was extremely pleased with the Opportunity she had given him of cultivating an Acquaintance with her: He therefore lengthened out his Visit, in hopes of being able to say some fine Things to her before he went away; but Miss *Glan-ville*, who strove by all the little Arts she was Mistress of, to engage his Conversation wholly to herself, put it absolutely out of his Power; so that he was obliged to take his Leave without having the Satisfaction of even pressing the fair Hand of *Arabella*; so closely was he observed by her Cousin. Happy was it for him, that he was prevented by her Vigilance from attempting a Piece of Gallantry, which would, undoubtedly, have procured him a Banishment from her Presence; but, ignorant, how kind Fortune was to him in balking his Designs, he was ungrateful enough to go away in a mighty ill Humour with this fickle Goddess: So little capable are poor Mortals of knowing what is best for them!

CHAPTER IX

Containing some curious Anecdotes.

Lady *Bella*, from the Familiarity with which Miss *Glanville* treated this gay Gentleman, concluding him her Lover, and one who was apparently well received by her, had a strong Curiosity to know her Adventures; and as they were walking the next Morning in the Garden, she told her, that she thought it was very strange they had hitherto observed such a Reserve to each other, as to banish mutual Trust and Confidence from their Conversation: Whence comes it, Cousin, added she, being so young and lovely as you are, that you, questionless, have been engaged in many Adventures, you have never reposed Trust enough in me to favour me with a Recital of them?

Engaged in many Adventures,[30] Madam! returned Miss *Glanville*, not liking the Phrase: I believe I have been engaged in as few as your Ladyship.

You are too obliging, returned *Arabella*, who mistook what she said for a Compliment; for since you have more Beauty than I, and have also had more Opportunities of making yourself beloved, questionless you have a greater Number of Admirers.

As for Admirers, said Miss *Charlotte* bridling, I fansy I have had my Share! Thank God, I never found myself neglected; but, I assure you, Madam, I have had no Adventures, as you call them, with any of them.

No, really, interrupted *Arabella*, innocently.

No, really, Madam, reported Miss *Glanville*; and I am surprised you should think so.

Indeed, my dear, said *Arabella*, you are very happy in this respect, and also very singular; for I believe there are few young Ladies in the World, who have any Pretensions to Beauty, that have not given Rise to a great many Adventures; and some of them haply very fatal.

If you knew more of the World, Lady *Bella*, said Miss *Glanville* pertly, you would not be so apt to think, that young Ladies engage themselves in troublesome Adventures: Truly the Ladies that are brought up in Town are not to ready to run away with every Man they see.

No, certainly, interrupted *Arabella*; they do not give their Consent to such Proceedings; but for all that, they are, doubtless, run away with many times; for truly there are some Men, whose Passions are so unbridled, that they will have recourse to the most violent Methods to possess themselves of the Objects they love. Pray do you remember how often *Mandana* was run away with?[31]

Not I indeed, Madam, replied Miss *Glanville*; I know nothing about her; but I suppose she is a *Jew*, by her outlandish Name.

She was no *Jew*, said *Arabella*, tho' she favoured that People very much; for she obtained the Liberty of great Numbers of them from *Cyrus*, who had taken them Captives, and could deny her nothing she asked.[32]

Well, said Miss *Glanville*; and I suppose she denied *him* nothing he asked; and so they were even.

Indeed but she did tho', resumed *Arabella*; for she refused to give him a glorious Scarf which she wore, tho' he begged it on his Knees.[33]

And she was very much in the right, said Miss *Glanville*; for I see no Reason why a Lover should expect a Gift of any Value from his Mistress.

Doubtless, said *Arabella*, such a Gift was worth a Million of Services; and, had he obtained it, it would have been a glorious Distinction for him: However, *Mandana* refused it; and, severely virtuous as you are, I am persuaded you can't help thinking, she was a little too rigorous in denying a Favour to a Lover like him —

Severely virtuous, Lady *Bella*! said Miss *Glanville*, reddening with Anger: Pray what do you mean by that? Have you any Reason to imagine, I would grant any Favour to a Lover?

Why, if I did, Cousin, said *Arabella*, would it derogate so much from your Glory, think you, to bestow a Favour upon a Lover worthy your Esteem, and from whom you had received a thousand Marks of a most pure and faithful Passion, and also a great Number of very singular Services?

I hope, Madam, said Miss *Glanville*, it will never be my Fate to be so much obliged to any Lover, as to be under a Necessity of granting him Favours in Requital.

I vow, Cousin, interrupted *Arabella*, you put me in mind of the fair and virtuous *Antonia*, who was so rigid and austere, that she thought all Expressions of Love were criminal; and was so far from granting any Person Permission to love her, that she thought it a mortal Offence to be adored even in private.[34]

Miss *Glanville*, who could not imagine *Arabella* spoke this seriously, but that it was designed to sneer at her great Eagerness to make Conquests, and the Liberties she allowed herself in, which had probably come to her Knowledge, was so extremely vexed at the malicious Jest, as she thought it, that, not being able to revenge herself, she burst into Tears.

Arabella's Good-nature made her be greatly affected at this Sight; and, asking her Pardon for having undesignedly occasioned her so much Uneasiness, begged her to be composed, and tell her in what she had offended her, that she might be able to justify herself in her Apprehensions.

You have made no Scruple to own, Madam, said she, that you think me capable of granting Favours to Lovers, when, Heaven knows, I never granted a Kiss without a great deal of Confusion.

And you had certainly much Reason for Confusion, said *Arabella*, excessively surprised at such a Confession: I assure you I never injured you so much in my Thoughts, as to suppose you ever granted a Favour of so criminal a Nature.

Look you there now! said Miss *Glanville*, weeping more violently than before: I knew what all your round-about Speeches would come to: All you have said in Vindication of granting Favours, was only to draw me into a Confession of what I have done: How ungenerous was that!

The Favours I spoke of, Madam, said *Arabella*, were quite of another Nature, than those it seems you have so liberally granted: Such as giving a Scarf, a Bracelet, or some such Thing, to a Lover, who had haply sighed whole Years in Silence, and did not presume to declare his Passion, till he had lost best Part of his Blood in Defence of the Fair-one he loved: It was when you maintained, that *Mandana* was in the right to refuse her magnificent Scarf to the illustrious *Cyrus*, that I took upon me to oppose your Rigidness; and so much mistaken was I in your Temper, that I foolishly compared you to the fair and wise *Antonia*, whose Severity was so remarkable; but really, by what I understand from your own Confession, your Disposition resembles that of the inconsiderate[35] *Julia*, who would receive a Declaration of Love without Anger from any one; and was not over-shy, any more than yourself, of granting Favours almost as considerable as that you have mentioned.

While *Arabella* was speaking, Miss *Glanville*, having dried up her Tears, sat silently swelling with Rage, not knowing whether she should openly avow her Resentment for the injurious Language her Cousin had used to her, by going away immediately, or, by making up the Matter, appear still to be her Friend, that she might have the more Opportunities of revengeing herself. The Impetuosity of her Temper made her most inclined to the former; but the Knowledge that Sir *George* was to stay yet some Months in the Country, made her unwilling to leave a Place, where she might often see a Man whose fine Person had made some Impression upon her Heart; and, not enduring to leave such a charming Conquest to *Arabella*, she resolved to suppress her Resentment for the present; and listened, without any Appearance of Discomposure, to a fine Harangue of her Cousin upon the Necessity of Reserve, and distant Behaviour, to Men who presumed to declare themselves Lovers, enforcing her Precepts with Examples drawn from all the Romances she had ever read; at the End of which she embraced her, and assured her, if she had said any thing harsh, it proceeded from her great Regard to her Glory, of which she ardently wished to see her as fond as herself.

Miss *Glanville* constrained herself to make a Reply that might not appear disagreeable: And they were upon these Terms, when Mr. *Glanville* came up to them, and told Lady *Bella*, Sir *George* had sent to intreat their Company at his House that Day: But, added he, as I presume you will not think proper to go, on account of your Mourning, neither my Sister nor I will accept the Invitation.

I dare say, interrupted Miss *Glanville* hastily, Lady *Bella* will not expect such a needless Piece of Ceremony from us; and, if she don't think proper to go, she won't confine *us*.

By no means, Cousin, said *Arabella*, smiling; and, being persuaded Sir *George* makes the Entertainment purely for your Sake, it would not be kind in me to deprive him of your Company.

Mr. *Glanville*, being pleased to find his Cousin discovered no Inclination to go, would have persuaded his Sister not to leave Lady *Bella*: But Miss *Glanville* looked so much displeased at his Request, that he was obliged to insist upon it no more; and, both retiring to dress, Lady *Bella* went up to her Apartment, and betook herself to her Books, which supplied the Place of all Company to her.

Miss *Glanville*, having taken more than ordinary Pains in dressing herself, in order to appear charming in the Eyes of Sir *George*, came in to pay her Compliments to Lady *Bella* before she went, not doubting but she would be chagrined to see her look so well: But Lady *Bella*, on the contrary, praised the Clearness of her Complexion, and the Sparkling of her Eyes.

I question not, said she, but you will give Fetters to more Persons than one To-day; but remember, I charge you, added she smiling, while you are taking away the Liberty of others, to have a special Care of your own.

Miss *Glanville*, who could not think it possible, one Woman could praise another with any Sincerity, cast a Glance at the Glass, fearing it was rather because she looked but indifferently, that her Cousin was so lavish in her Praises; and, while she was settling her Features in a Mirror which every Day represented a Face infinitely more lovely than her own, Mr. *Glanville* came in, who, after having very respectfully taken Leave of Lady *Bella*, led his Sister to the Coach.

Sir *George*, who was extremely mortified to find Lady *Bella* not in it, handed Miss *Glanville* out with an Air so reserved, that she raillied him upon it; and gave her Brother a very unpleasing Emotion, by telling Sir *George*, she hoped Lady *Bella*'s not coming along with them, would not make him bad Company.

As he was too gallant to suffer an handsome young Lady, who spread all her Attractions for him, to believe he regretted the Absence of another when she was present; he coquetted with her so much, that Mr. *Glanville* was in hopes his Sister would wholly engage him from Lady *Bella*.

CHAPTER X

*In which our Heroine is engaged in a very
perilous Adventure.*

In the mean time, that solitary Fair-one was alarmed by a Fear of a very unaccountable Nature; for being in the Evening in her Closet, the Windows of which had a Prospect of the Gardens, she saw her illustrious concealed Lover, who went by the Name of *Edward*, while he was in her Father's Service, talking with great Emotion to her House-Steward, who seemed earnestly to listen to some Propositions he was making to him. Her Surprise at this Sight was so great, that she had not Power to observe them any longer; but, seating herself in her Chair, she had just Spirits enough to call *Lucy* to her Assistance; who, extremely frighted at the pale Looks of her Lady, gave her a Smelling-bottle, and was preparing to cut her Lace,[36] when *Arabella*, preventing her, told her, in a low Voice, that she feared she should be betrayed into the Hands of an insolent Lover, who was come to steal her away. Yes, added she with great Emotion, I have seen this presumptuous Man holding a Conversation with one of my Servants; and tho' I could not possibly, at this Distance, hear their Discourse, yet the Gestures they used in speaking, explained it too well to me; and I have Reason to expect, I shall suffer the same Violence that many illustrious Ladies have done before me; and be carried away by Force from my own House, as they were.

Alas! Madam! said *Lucy*, terrified at this Discourse, who is it that intends to carry your Ladyship away? Sure no Robbers will attempt any Mischief at such a time as this!

Yes, *Lucy*, replied *Arabella*, with great Gravity, the worst kind of Robbers; Robbers who do not prey upon Gold and Jewels; but, what is infinitely more precious, Liberty and Honour. Do you know that Person who called himself *Edward*, and worked in these Gardens like a common Gardener, is now in the House, corrupting my Servants; and, questionless, preparing to force open my Chamber, and carry me away? And Heaven knows when I shall be delivered from his Chains.

God forbid, said *Lucy*, sobbing, that ever such a Lady should have such hard Hap! What Crime, I wonder, can you be guilty of, to deserve to be in Chains?

My Crime, resumed *Arabella*, is to have Attractions which expose me to these inevitable Misfortunes, which even the greatest Princesses have not escaped. — But, dear *Lucy*, can you not think of some Methods by which I may avoid the Evil which waits me? Who knows but that he may, within these few Moments, force a Passage into my Apartment? These slight Locks can make but a poor Resistance to the Violence he will be capable of using.

Oh, dear Madam! cried *Lucy*, trembling, and pressing near her, what shall we do?

I asked your Advice, said she; but I perceive you are less able than myself to think of any thing to save me. — Ah! *Glanville*, pursued she, sighing, would to Heaven thou wert here now!

Yes, Madam, said *Lucy*, Mr. *Glanville*, I am sure, would not suffer any one to hurt your Ladyship.

As thou valuest my Friendship, said *Arabella*, with great Earnestness, never acquaint him with what has just now escaped my Lips: True, I did call upon him in this Perplexity; I did pronounce his Name; and that, haply, with a Sigh, which involuntarily forced its Way: And, questionless, if he knew his good Fortune, even amidst the Danger of losing me for ever, he would resent some Emotions of Joy: But I should die with Shame at having so indiscreetly contributed to his Satisfaction; And, therefore, again I charge you, conceal, with the utmost Care, what I have said.

Indeed, Madam, said *Lucy*, I shall tell him nothing but what your Ladyship bids me; and I am so frighted, that I can think of nothing but that terrible Man, that wants to carry you away. Mercy on us! added she, starting, I think I hear somebody on the Stairs!

Do not be alarmed, said *Arabella*, in a majestic Tone: It is I who have most Reason to fear: Nevertheless, I hope the Grandeur of my Courage will not sink under this Accident. Hark, somebody knocks at the Door of my Antechamber: — My own Virtue shall support me: — Go, *Lucy*, and ask who it is.

Indeed I can't, Madam, said she, clinging to her: Pray pardon me: Indeed I am so afraid, I cannot stir.

Weak-souled Wench! said *Arabella*, How unfit art thou for Accidents like these! Ah! had *Cylenia* and *Martesia* been like thee, the fair *Berenice*, and the Divine Princess of *Media*, had not so eagerly intreated their Ravishers to afford them their Company in their Captivity:[37] But go, I order you, and ask who it is that is at the Door of my Apartment: They knock again: Offer at no Excuses; but do your Duty.

Lucy, seeing her Lady was really angry, went trembling out of the Closet; but would go no farther than her Bedchamber, from whence she called out to know who was at the Door.

I have some Business with your Lady, said the House-Steward (for it was he that knocked:) Can I speak with her at present?

Lucy, a little re-assured by his Voice, made no Answer; but, creeping softly to the Door of the Antechamber, double-locked it; and then cried out in a Transport, No, I will take Care you shall not come to my Lady.

And why, pray, Mrs. *Lucy*? said the Steward: What have I done, that you are so much my Enemy?

You are a Rogue, said *Lucy*, growing very courageous, because the Door was locked between them.

A Rogue! said he, What Reason have you for calling me a Rogue? I assure you I will acquaint my Lady with your Insolence. I came to speak to her Ladyship about *Edward*; who prayed me to intercede for him, that he may be taken again into her Service: For he says, my Lady never believed any thing against him; and that was my Business: But, when I see her, I'll know whether you are allowed to abuse me in this manner.

Arabella, by this time, was advanced as far as the Bedchamber, longing to know what sort of Conference *Lucy* was holding with her intended Ravisher: When that faithful Confidant, seeing her, came running to her, and whispered her, that the House-Steward was at the Door, and said he wanted to intercede for *Edward*.

Ah! the Traitor! said *Arabella*, retiring again: Has he, then, really bargained with that disloyal Man, to deliver up his Mistress? I am undone, *Lucy*, said she, unless I can find a Way to escape out of the House. They will, questionless, soon force the Doors of my Apartment.

Suppose, said *Lucy*, your Ladyship went down the Stairs that lead from your Dressing-room into the Garden; and you may hide yourself in the Gardener's House till Mr. *Glanville* come.

I approve, said *Arabella*, of one Part of your Proposal: But I shall not trust myself in the Gardener's House; who, questionless, is in the Plot with the rest of my perfidious Servants, since none of them have endeavoured to advertise me of my Danger. If we can gain the Gardens undiscovered, we may get out by that Door at the Foot of the Terrace, which leads into the Fields; for you know I always keep the Key of that private Door: So, *Lucy*, let us commend ourselves to the Direction of Providence, and be gone immediately.

But what shall we do, Madam, said *Lucy*, when we are got out?

Why, said *Arabella*, you shall conduct me to your Brother's; and, probably, we may meet with some generous Cavalier by the Way, who will protect us till we get thither: However, as I have as great a Danger to fear within Doors, as without, I will venture to make my Escape, though I should not be so fortunate as to meet with any Knight who will undertake to protect me from the Danger which I may apprehend in the Fields.

Saying this, she gave the Key of the Door to *Lucy*, whose Heart beat violently with Fear; and, covering herself with some black Cypress,[38] which she wore in the Nature of a Veil, went softly down the little Staircase to the Terrace, followed by *Lucy* (who looked eagerly about her every Step that she went;) and, having gained the Garden-door, hastily unlocked it, and fled, as fast as possible, cross the Fields, in order to procure a Sanctuary at *William*'s House: *Arabella*, begging Heaven to throw some generous Cavalier in her Way, whose Protection she might implore, and, taking every Tree at a Distance for a Horse and Knight, hastened her Steps to meet her approaching Succour; which as soon as she came near, miserably balked her Expectations.

Though *William*'s Farm was not more than two Miles from the Castle; yet *Arabella*, unused to such a rude Way of Travelling, began to be greatly fatigued: The Fear she was in of being pursued by her apprehended Ravisher, had so violent an Effect upon her Spirits, that she was hardly able to prosecute her Flight; and, to complete her Misfortunes, happening to stumble over a Stump of a Tree that lay in her Way, she strained her Ancle; and the violent Anguish she felt, threw her into a Swoon.

Lucy, upon whose Arm she leaned, perceiving her fainting, screamed out aloud, not knowing what to do with her in that Condition: she placed her upon the Ground; and, supporting her Head against that fatal Stump, began to rub her Temples, weeping excessively all the Time. Her Swoon still continuing, the poor Girl was in inconceivable Terror: Her Brother's House was now but a little Way off; but it being impossible for her to carry her Lady thither without some Help, she knew not what to resolve upon.

At length, thinking it better to leave her for a few Moments, to run for Assistance, than to sit by her and see her perish for want of it, she left her, though not without extreme Agony; and flew, with the utmost Eagerness, to her Brother's. She was lucky enough to meet him just coming out of his Door; and, telling him the Condition in which she left her Lady, he, without asking any Questions about the Occasion of so strange an Accident, notwithstanding his Amazement, ran with all Speed to the Place where *Lucy* had left her: But, to their Astonishment and Sorrow, she was not to be found: They walked a long time in Search of her; and *Lucy*, being almost distracted with Fear lest she had been carried away, made Complaints that so puzzled her Brother he knew not what to say to her. But, finding their Search fruitless, they agreed to go home to the Castle, supposing, with some Appearance of Reason, that they might hear of her there.

Here they found nothing but Grief and Confusion. Mr. *Glanville* and his Sister were just returned, and had been at Lady *Bella*'s Apartment; but, not finding her there, they asked her Women where she was, who, not knowing any thing of her Flight, concluded she was in the Garden with *Lucy*. Mr. *Glanville*, surprised at her being at that Hour in the Garden, ran eagerly to engage her to come in, being apprehensive she would take Cold, by staying so late in the Air: But, not finding her in any of her usual Walks, he ordered several of the Servants to assist him in searching the whole Garden, sending them to different Places: But they all returned without Success; which filled him with the utmost Consternation.

He was returning, excessively uneasy, to the House, when he saw *Lucy*; who had been just told, in answer to her Inquiries about her Lady, that they were gone to look for her in the Garden; and running up to Mr. *Glanville*, who hoped to hear News of Lady *Bella* from her, Oh! Sir, said she, is my Lady found?

What! *Lucy*, said Mr. *Glanville* (more alarmed than before), do not you know where she is? I thought you had been with her.

Oh! dear, cried *Lucy*, wringing her Hands; for certain my poor Lady was stolen away while she was in that fainting Fit.

Sir, said she to *Glanville*, I know who the Person is that my
Lady said (and almost broke my Heart) would keep her in
Chains: He was in the House not many Hours ago.

Mr. *Glanville*, suspecting this was some new Whim of
Arabella's, would not suffer *Lucy* to say any more before the
Servants, who stood gaping with Astonishment at the strange
Things she uttered; but bid her follow him to his Apartment,
and he would hear what she could inform him concerning this
Accident. He would, if possible, have prevented his Sister from
being present at the Story; but, not being able to form any
Excuse for not suffering her to hear every thing that related to
her Cousin, they all three went into his Chamber; where he
desired *Lucy* to tell him what she knew about her Lady.

You must know, Sir, said *Lucy*, sobbing, that there came a
Man here to take away my Lady: A great Man he is, though he
worked in the Gardens; for he was in Love with her: And so he
would not own who he was.

And pray, interrupted Miss *Glanville*, Who told you he was
a great Man, as you say?

My Lady told me, said *Lucy*: But, *howsomever*, he was turned
away; for the Gardener says he catched him stealing Carp.

A very great Man, indeed, said Miss *Glanville*, that would
steal Carp!

You must know, Madam, said she, that was only a Pretence:
For he went there, my Lady says, to drown himself.

Bless me! cried Miss *Glanville*, laughing; the Girl's distracted, sure. Lord! Brother, don't listen to her nonsensical
Tales; we shall never find my Cousin by her.

Leave her to me, said Mr. *Glanville*, whispering: Perhaps I
may discover something by her Discourse, that will give us
some Light into this Affair.

Nay, I'll stay, I am resolved, answered she; for I long to
know where my Cousin is: Tho', do you think what this Girl
says is true, about a great Man disguised in the Gardens? Sure
my Cousin could never tell her such Stuff: But, now I think of
it, added she, Lady *Bella*, when we were speaking about the
Jockey, talked something about a Lover: I vow I believe it is as
the Girl says. Pray let's hear her out.

Mr. *Glanville* was ready to die with Vexation, at the Charmer of his Soul's being thus exposed; but there was no Help for it.

Pray, said he to *Lucy*, tell us no more about this Man: But, if you can guess where your Lady is, let me know.

Indeed I can't, Sir, said she; for my Lady and I both stole out of the House, for fear *Edward* should break open the Doors of her Apartment; and we were running as fast as possible to my Brother's House (where she said she would hide herself till you came); but my poor dear Lady fell down and hurt herself so much, that she fainted away: I tried what I could to fetch her again; but she did not open her Eyes: So I ran like Lightning to my Brother, to come and help me to carry her to the Farm; but, when we came back, she was gone.

What do you say? cried Mr. *Glanville*, with a distracted Look: Did you leave her in that Condition in the Fields? And was she not to be found when you came back?

No, indeed, Sir, said *Lucy*, weeping, we could not find her, though we wandered about a long time.

Oh! Heavens! said he, walking about the Room in a violent Emotion, Where can she be? What is become of her? Dear Sister, pursued he, order somebody to saddle my Horse: I'll traverse the Country all Night in quest of her.

You had best inquire, Sir, said *Lucy*, if *Edward* is in the House: He knows, may be, where my Lady is.

Who is he? cried *Glanville*.

Why the great Man, Sir, said *Lucy*, whom we thought to be a Gardener, who came to carry my Lady away; which made her get out of the House as fast as she could.

This is the strangest Story, said Miss *Glanville*, that ever I heard: Sure nobody would be so mad to attempt such an Action; my Cousin has the oddest Whims!

Mr. *Glanville*, not able to listen any longer, charged *Lucy* to say nothing of this Matter to any one; and then ran eagerly out of the Room, ordering two or three of the Servants to go in Search of their Lady: He then mounted his Horse in great Anguish of Mind, not knowing whither to direct his Course.

CHAPTER XI

In which the Lady is wonderfully delivered.

But to return to *Arabella*, whom we left in a very melancholy
Situation: *Lucy* had not been gone long from her before she
opened her Eyes; and, beginning to come perfectly to herself,
was surprised to find her Woman not near her: The Moon
shining very bright, she looked round her, and called *Lucy* as
loud as she was able, but not seeing her, or hearing any Answer,
her Fears became so powerful, that she had like to have relapsed
into her Swoon.

Alas! unfortunate Maid that I am! cried she, weeping excessively, questionless I am betrayed by her on whose Fidelity I
relied, and who was acquainted with my most secret Thoughts:
She is now with my Ravisher, directing his Pursuit, and I have
no Means of escaping from his Hands! Cruel and ungrateful
Wench, thy unparalled Treachery grieves me no less than all
my other Misfortunes: But why do I say, Her Treachery is
unparalleled? Did not the wicked *Arianta* betray her Mistress
into the Power of her insolent Lover?[39] Ah! *Arabella*, thou art
not single in thy Misery, since the divine *Mandana* was, like
thyself, the Dupe of a mercenary Servant.

Having given a Moment or two to these sad Reflections, she
rose from the Ground with an Intention to walk on; but her
Ancle was so painful, that she could hardly move: Her Tears
began now to flow with greater Violence: She expected every
Moment to see *Edward* approach her; and was resigning herself
up to Despair, when a Chaise, driven by a young Gentleman,
passed by her. *Arabella*, thanking Heaven for sending this
Relief, called out as loud as she could, conjuring him to stay.

The Gentleman, hearing a Woman's Voice, stopped immediately, and asked what she wanted.

Generous Stranger, said *Arabella*, advancing as well as she
was able, do not refuse your Assistance to save me from a most
terrible Danger: I am pursued by a Person whom, for very
urgent Reasons, I desire to avoid. I conjure you, therefore,

in the Name of her you love best, to protect me; and may you be crowned with the Enjoyment of all your Wishes, for so charitable an Action!

If the Gentleman was surprised at this Address, he was much more astonished at the Beauty of her who made it: Her Stature; her Shape, her inimitable Complexion; the Lustre of her fine Eyes, and the thousand Charms that adorned her whole Person, kept him a Minute silently gazing upon her, without having the Power to make her an Answer.

Arabella, finding he did not speak, was extremely disappointed. Ah! Sir, said she, What do you deliberate upon? Is it possible you can deny so reasonable a Request, to a Lady in my Circumstances?

For God's sake, Madam, said the Gentleman, alighting, and approaching her, let me know who you are, and how I can be of any Service to you.

As for my Quality, said *Arabella*, be assured it is not mean; and let this Knowledge suffice at present: The Service I desire of you is, to convey me to some Place where I may be in Safety for this Night: To-morrow I will intreat you to let some Persons, whom I shall name to you, know where I am; to the end they may take proper Measures to secure me from the Attempts of an insolent Man, who has driven me from my own House, by the Designs he was going to execute.

The Gentleman saw there was some Mystery in her Case, which she did not choose to explain; and, being extremely glad at having so beautiful a Creature in his Power, told her she might command him in all she pleased; and, helping her into the Chaise, drove off as fast as he could; *Arabella* suffering no Apprehensions from being alone with a Stranger, since nothing was more common to Heroines than such Adventures;[40] all her Fears being of *Edward*, whom she fansied every Moment she saw pursuing them: And, being extremely anxious to be in some Place of Safety, she urged her Protector to drive as fast as possible; who, willing to have her at his own House, complied with her Request; but was so unlucky in his Haste, as to overturn the Chaise. Though neither *Arabella* nor himself were hurt by the Fall, yet the Necessity there was to stay some time to put

the Chaise in a Condition to carry them any farther, filled her
with a thousand Apprehensions, lest they should be overtaken.

In the mean time, the Servants of *Arabella*, among whom
Edward, not knowing how much he was concerned in her
Flight, was resolved to distinguish himself by his Zeal in search-
ing for her, had dispersed themselves about in different Places:
Chance conducted *Edward* to the very Spot where she was:
When *Arabella*, perceiving him while he was two or three Paces
off, Oh! Sir, cried she, behold my Persecutor! Can you resolve
to defend me against the Violence he comes to offer me?

The Gentleman, looking up, and seeing a Man in Livery
approaching them, asked her, If that was the Person she complained of; and if he was her Servant?

If he is my Servant, Sir, replied she, blushing, he never had
my Permission to be so. And, indeed, no one else can boast of
my having granted them such a Liberty.

Do you know whose Servant he is, then, Madam? replied
the Gentleman, a little surprised at her Answer; which he could
not well understand.

You throw me into a great Embarrassment, Sir, resumed
Arabella, blushing more than before: Questionless, he appears
to be mine; but, since, as I told you before, he never discovered
himself to me, and I never permitted him to assume that Title,
his Services, if ever I received any from him, were not at all
considered by me, as Things for which I was obliged to him.

The Gentleman, still more amazed at Answers so little to the
Purpose, was going to desire her to explain herself upon this
strange Affair; when *Edward*, coming up close to *Arabella*,
cried out in a Transport, Oh! Madam! thank God you are
found.

Hold, impious Man! said *Arabella*, and do not give Thanks
for that which, haply, may prove thy Punishment. If I am found,
thou wilt be no better for it: And, if thou continuest to persecute
me, thou wilt probably meet with thy Death, where thou thinkest thou hast found thy Happiness.

The poor Fellow, who understood not a Word of this Discourse, stared upon her like one that had lost his Wits; when
the Protector of *Arabella*, approaching him, asked him, with a

stern Look, What he had to say to that Lady, and why he presumed to follow her?

As the Man was going to answer him, Mr. *Glanville* came galloping up; and *Edward*, seeing him, ran up to him, and informed him, that he had met with Lady *Bella*, and a Gentleman, who seemed to have been overturned in a Chaise, which he was endeavouring to refit; and that her Ladyship was offended with him for coming up to her; and also, that the Gentleman had used some threatening Language to him upon that Account.

Mr. *Glanville*, excessively surprised at what he heard, stopped; and, ordering a Servant who came along with him, to run back to the Castle, and bring a Chaise thither to carry Lady *Bella* home, he asked *Edward* several more Questions relating to what she and the Gentleman had said to him: And, notwithstanding his Knowledge of her ridiculous Humour, he could not help being alarmed by her Behaviour, nor concluding that there was something very mysterious in the Affair.

While he was thus conversing with *Edward*, *Arabella*, who had spied him almost as soon, was filled with Apprehension to see him hold so quiet a Parly with her Ravisher: The more she reflected upon this Accident, the more her Suspicions increased; and, persuading herself at last, that Mr. *Glanville* was privy to his Designs, this Belief, however improbable, wrought so powerfully upon her Imagination, that she could not restrain her Tears.

Doubtless, said she, I am betrayed, and the perjured *Glanville* is no longer either my Friend or Lover: He is this Moment concerting Measures with my Ravisher, how to deliver me into his Power; and, like *Philidaspes*, is glad of an Opportunity, by this Treachery, to be rid of a Woman whom his Parents and hers had destined for his Wife.[41]

Mr. *Glanville*, having learned all he could from *Edward*, alighted; and, giving him his Horse to hold, came up to *Arabella*: And, after expressing his Joy at meeting with her, begged her to let him know what Accident had brought her, unattended, from the Castle, at that time of Night.

If by this Question, said the incensed *Arabella*, you would persuade me you are ignorant of the Cause of my Flight, know, your Dissimulation will not succeed; and that, having Reason to believe you are equally guilty with him from whose intended Violence I fled, I shall have recourse to the Valour of this Knight you see with me, to defend me, as well against you, as that Ravisher, with whom I see you leagued. — Ah! unworthy Cousin, pursued she, What dost thou propose to thyself by so black a Treachery? What is to be the Price of my Liberty, which thou so freely disposest of? Has thy Friend there, said she (pointing to *Edward*), a Sister, or any Relation, for whom thou barterest, by delivering me up to him? But, assure thyself, this Stratagem shall be of no Use to thee: For, if thou art base enough to oppress my valiant Deliverer with Numbers, and thinkest, by Violence, to get me into thy Power, my Cries shall arm Heaven and Earth in my Defence. Providence may, haply, send some generous Cavaliers to my Rescue; and, if Providence fails me, my own Hand shall give me Freedom; for that Moment thou offerest to seize me, that Moment shall be the last of my Life.

While *Arabella* was speaking, the young Gentleman and *Edward*, who listened to her, eagerly, thought her Brain was disturbed: But Mr. *Glanville* was in a terrible Confusion, and silently cursed his ill Fate, to make him in Love with a Woman so ridiculous.

For Heaven's sake, Cousin, said he, striving to repress some Part of his Disorder, Do not give way to these extravagant Notions: There is nobody intends to do you any Wrong.

What! interrupted she, would you persuade me, that that Impostor there, pointing to *Edward*, has not a Design to carry me away; which you, by supporting him, are not equally guilty of?

Who? I! Madam! cried out *Edward*: Sure your Ladyship does not suspect me of such a strange Design! God knows I never thought of such a Thing!

Ah! Dissembler! interrupted *Arabella*, do not make use of that sacred Name to mask thy impious Falshoods: Confess with what Intent you came into my Father's Service disguised.

I never came disguised, Madam, returned *Edward*.

No! said *Arabella*: What means that Dress in which I see you, then?

'Tis the Marquis's Livery, Madam, said *Edward*, which he did not order to be taken from me when I left his Service.

And with what Purpose didst thou wear it? said she, Do not your Thoughts accuse you of your Crime?

I always hoped, Madam —— said he.

You hoped! interrupted *Arabella*: frowning, Did I ever give you Reason to hope? I will not deny but I had Compassion on you; but even That you was ignorant of.

I know, Madam, you had Compassion on me, said *Edward*; for your Ladyship, I always thought, did not believe me guilty.

I was weak enough, said she, to have Compassion on you, though I *did* believe you guilty.

Indeed, Madam, returned *Edward*, I always hoped, as I said before (but your Ladyship would not hear me out), that you did not believe any malicious Reports; and therefore you had Compassion on me.

I had no Reports of you, said she, but what my own Observation gave me; and that was sufficient to convince me of your Fault.

Why, Madam, said *Edward*, did your Ladyship see me steal the Carp then, which was the Fault unjustly laid to my Charge?

Mr. *Glanville*, as much Cause as he had for Uneasiness, could with great Difficulty restrain Laughter at this ludicrous Circumstance; for he guessed what Crime *Arabella* was accusing him of: As for the young Gentleman, he could not conceive what she meant, and longed to hear what would be the End of such a strange Conference. But poor *Arabella* was prodigiously confounded at his mentioning so low an Affair; not being able to endure that *Glanville* and her Protector should know a Lover of her's could be suspected of so base a Theft.

The Shame she conceived at it, kept her silent for a Moment: But, recovering herself at last, No, said she, I knew you better than to give any Credit to such an idle Report: Persons of your Condition do not commit such paltry Crimes.

Upon my Soul, Madam, said the young Gentleman, Persons of his Condition often do worse.

I don't deny it, Sir, said *Arabella*; and the Design he meditated of carrying me away was infinitely worse.

Really, Madam, returned the Gentleman, if you are such a
Person as I apprehend, I don't see how he durst make such an
Attempt.

It is very possible, Sir, said she, that I might be carried away,
though I was of greater Quality than I am: Were not *Mandana*,
Candace, *Clelia*, and many other Ladies who underwent the
same Fate,[42] of a Quality more illustrious than mine?

Really, Madam, said he, I know none of these Ladies.

No, Sir! said *Arabella*; extremely mortified.

Let me intreat you, Cousin, interrupted *Glanville* (who
feared this Conversation would be very tedious), to expose
yourself no longer to the Air at this time of Night: Suffer me to
conduct you home.

It concerns my Honour, said she, that this generous Stranger
should not think I am the only one that was ever exposed to
these Insolent Attempts. You say, Sir, pursued she, that you
don't know any of these Ladies I mentioned before: Let me ask
you, then, If you are acquainted with *Parthenissa*, or *Cleopatra*?[43] who were both, for some Months, in the Hands of
their Ravishers.

As for *Parthenissa*, Madam, said he, neither have I heard of
her; nor do I remember to have heard of any more than one
Cleopatra: But she was never ravished, I am certain; for she
was too willing.

How! Sir, said *Arabella*: Was *Cleopatra* ever willing to run
away with her Ravisher?

Cleopatra was a Whore, was she not, Madam? said he.

Hold thy Peace, unworthy Man, said *Arabella*; and profane
not the Memory of that fair and glorious Queen, by such
injurious Language: That Queen, I say, whose Courage was
equal to her Beauty; and her Virtue surpassed by neither. Good
Heavens! What a black Defamer have I chosen for my Protector!

Mr. *Glanville*, rejoicing to see *Arabella* in a Disposition to
be offended with her new Acquaintance, resolved to soothe her
a little, in hopes of prevailing upon her to return home. Sir,
said he to the Gentleman, who could not conceive why the

Lady should so warmly defend *Cleopatra*, you were in the Wrong to cast such Reflections upon that great Queen (repeating what he had heard his Cousin say before): For all the World, pursued he, knows she was married to *Julius Cæsar*.

Though I commend you, said *Arabella*, for taking the Part of a Lady so basely vilified; yet let not your Zeal for her Honour induce you to say more than is true for its Justification; for thereby you weaken, instead of strengthening, what may be said in her Defence. One Falshood always supposes another, and renders all you can say suspected: Whereas pure, unmixed Truth, carries Conviction along with it, and never fails to produce its desired Effect.

Suffer me, Cousin, interrupted *Glanville*, again to represent to you, the Inconveniency you will certainly feel, by staying so late in the Air: Leave the Justification of *Cleopatra* to some other Opportunity; and take care of your own Preservation.

What is it you require of me? said *Arabella*.

Only, resumed *Glanville*, that you would be pleased to return to the Castle, where my Sister, and all your Servants, are inconsolable for your Absence.

But who can assure me, answered she, that I shall not, by returning home, enter voluntarily into my Prison? The same Treachery which made the Palace of *Candace* the Place of her Confinement, may turn the Castle of *Arabella* into her Jayl.[44] For, to say the Truth, I still more than suspect you abet the Designs of this Man; since I behold you in his Party, and ready, no doubt, to draw your Sword in his Defence: How will you be able to clear yourself of this Crime? Yet I will venture to return to my House, provided you will swear to me, you will offer me no Violence, with regard to your Friend there: And also I insist, that he, from this Moment, disclaim all Intentions of persecuting me, and banish himself from my Presence for ever. Upon this Condition I pardon him, and will likewise pray to Heaven to pardon him also. Speak, presumptuous Unknown, said she to *Edward*, Wilt thou accept of my Pardon upon the Terms I offer it thee? And wilt thou take thyself to some Place where I may never behold thee again?

Since your Ladyship, said *Edward*, is resolved not to receive

me into your Service, I shan't trouble you any more: But I think
it hard to be punished for a Crime I was not guilty of.

'Tis better, said *Arabella*, turning from him, that thou
shouldst complain of my Rigour, than the World tax me with
Lightness and Indiscretion. And now, Sir, said she to *Glanville*,
I must trust myself to your Honour, which I confess I do a little
suspect: But, however, 'tis possible you have repented, like the
poor Prince *Thrasybulus*, when he submitted to the Suggestions
of a wicked Friend, to carry away the fair *Alcionida*, whom he
afterwards restored.[45] Speak, *Glanville*, pursued she, are you
desirous of imitating that virtuous Prince, or do you still retain
your former Sentiments?

Upon my Word, Madam, said *Glanville*, you will make me
quite mad, if you go on in this manner: Pray let me see you safe
home; and then, if you please, you may forbid my Entrance into
the Castle, if you suspect me of any bad Intentions towards you.

'Tis enough, said she; I will trust you. As for you, Sir, speaking to the young Gentleman, you are so unworthy, in my Apprehensions, by the Calumnies you have uttered against a Person
of that Sex which merits all your Admiration and Reverence,
that I hold you very unfit to be a Protector of any of it: Therefore
I dispense with your Services upon this Occasion; and think it
better to trust myself to the Conduct of a Person, who, like
Thrasybulus, by his Repentance, has restored himself to my
Confidence, than to one, who, though, indeed, he has never
betrayed me, yet seems very capable of doing so, if he had the
Power.

Saying this, she gave her Hand to *Glanville*, who helped her
into the Chaise that was come from the Castle; and the Servant,
who brought it, mounting his Horse, Mr. *Glanville* drove her
Home, leaving the Gentleman, who, by this time, had refitted
his Chaise, in the greatest Astonishment imaginable at her
unaccountable Behaviour.

END *of the* SECOND BOOK.

BOOK III

CHAPTER I

Two Conversations, out of which the Reader may pick up a great deal.

Arabella, continuing to ruminate upon her Adventure during their little Journey, appeared so low-spirited and reserved, that Mr. *Glanville*, tho' he ardently wished to know all the Particulars of her Flight, and Meeting with that Gentleman, whose Company he found her in, was obliged to suppress his Curiosity for the present, out of a Fear of displeasing her. As soon as they alighted at the Castle, her Servants ran to receive her at the Gates, expressing their Joy to see her again, by a thousand confused Exclamations.

Miss *Glanville*, being at her Toilet when she heard of her Arrival, ran down to welcome her, in her Hurry forgetting, that as her Woman had been curling her Hair, she had no Cap on.

Arabella received her Compliments with a little Coolness; for, observing that her Grief for her Absence had not made her neglect any of her usual Solicitude about her Person, she could not conceive it had been very great: Therefore, when she had made some slight Answer to the hundred Questions she asked in a Breath, she went up to her Apartment; and, calling *Lucy*, who was crying with Joy for her Return, she questioned her strictly concerning her leaving her in the Fields, acknowledging to her, that she suspected her Fidelity, tho' she wished, at the same time, she might be able to clear herself.

Lucy, in her Justification, related, after her punctual Way, all that had happened: By which, *Arabella* was convinced she had not betrayed her; and was also in some Doubt, whether Mr. *Glanville* was guilty of any Design against her.

Since, said she to *Lucy*, thou art restored to my good Opinion, I will, as I have always done, unmask my Thoughts to thee. I confess then, with Shame and Confusion, that I cannot think of Mr. *Glanville*'s assisting the Unknown to carry me away, without *resenting* a most poignant Grief: Questionless, my Weakness will surprise thee; and could I conceal it from myself, I would from thee; but, alas! it is certain, that I do not hate him; and I believe I never shall, guilty as he may be in my Apprehensions.

Hate him! Madam, said *Lucy*: God forbid you should ever hate Mr. *Glanville*, who, I am sure, loves your Ladyship as well as he does his own Sister!

You are very confident, *Lucy*, said *Arabella* blushing, to mention the Word Love to me: If I thought my Cousin had bribed thee to it, I should be greatly incensed: However, tho' I forbid you to talk of his Passion, yet I permit you to tell me the Violence of his Transports when I was missing; the Threats he uttered against my Ravishers; the Complaints he made against Fortune; the Vows he offered for my Preservation; and, in fine, whatever Extravagances the Excess of his Sorrow forced him to commit.

I assure you, Madam, said *Lucy*, I did not hear him say any of all this.

What! interrupted *Arabella*: And didst thou not observe the Tears trickle from his Eyes, which, haply, he strove to conceal? Did he not strike his Bosom with the Vehemence of his Grief; and cast his accusing and despairing Eyes to Heaven, which had permitted such a Misfortune to befal me?

Indeed, Madam, I did not, resumed *Lucy*; but he seemed to be very sorry; and said, He would go and look for your Ladyship.

Ah! the Traitor! interrupted *Arabella* in a Rage: Fain would I have found out some Excuse for him, and justified him in my Apprehensions; but he is unworthy of these favourable Thoughts: Speak of him no more, I command you; he is guilty of assisting my Ravisher to carry me away; and therefore merits my eternal Displeasure: But tho' I could find Reasons to clear him even of that Crime, yet he is guilty of Indifference and Insensibility for my Loss, since he neither died with Grief at the News of it; nor needed the Interposition of his Sister, or the Desire of delivering me, to make him live.

Arabella, when she had said this, was silent; but could not prevent some Tears stealing down her fair Face: Therefore, to conceal her Uneasiness, or to be at more Liberty to indulge it, she ordered *Lucy* to make haste and undress her; and, going to-bed, passed the small Remainder of the Night, not in Rest, which she very much needed, but, in Reflections on all the Passages of the preceding Day: And, finding, or imagining she found, new Reasons for condemning Mr. *Glanville,* her Mind was very far from being at Ease.

In the Morning, lying later than usual, she received a Message from Mr. *Glanville,* inquiring after her Health; to which she answered, That he was too little concerned in the Preservation of it, to make it necessary to acquaint him.

Miss *Glanville* soon after sent to desire Permission to drink her Chocolate[1] by her Bedside; which as she could not in Civility refuse, she was very much perplexed how to hide her Melancholy from the Eyes of that discerning Lady, who, she questioned not, would interpret it in favour of her Brother.

Upon Miss *Glanville*'s Appearance, she forced herself to assume a chearful Look, asking her Pardon, for receiving her in Bed; and complaining of bad Rest, which had occasioned her lying late.

Miss *Glanville,* after answering her Compliments with almost equal Politeness, proceeded to ask her an hundred Questions concerning the Cause of her Absence from the Castle: Your Woman, pursued she, laughing, told us a strange Medley of Stuff about a great Man, who was a Gardener; and wanted to carry you away: Sure there was nothing in it! Was there?

You must excuse me, Cousin, said *Arabella,* if I do not answer your Questions precisely now: 'Tis sufficient that I tell you, Certain Reasons obliged me to act in the Manner I did, for my own Preservation; and that, another time, you shall know my History; which will explain many Things you seem to be surprised at, at present.

Your History, said Miss *Glanville*! Why, will you write your own History then?

I shall not write it, said *Arabella*; tho', questionless, it will be written after my Death.

And must I wait till then for it, resumed Miss *Glanville*, gaily?

No, no, interrupted *Arabella*: I mean to gratify your Curiosity sooner; but it will not be yet a good time; and, haply, not till you have acquainted me with yours.

Mine! said Miss *Glanville*: It would not be worth your hearing; for really I have nothing to tell, that would make an History.

You have, questionless, returned *Arabella*, gained many Victories over Hearts; have occasioned many Quarrels between your Servants, by favouring some one, more than the others: Probably, you have caused some Bloodshed; and have not escaped being carried away once or twice: You have also, I suppose, undergone some Persecution, from those who have the Disposal of you, in Favour of a Lover whom you have an Aversion to; and lastly, there is haply some one among your Admirers, who is happy enough not to be hated by you.

I assure you, interrupted Miss *Glanville*, I hate none of my Admirers; and I can't help thinking you very unkind to use my Brother as you do: I am sure, there is not one Man in an hundred, that would take so much from your Hands as he does.

Then there is not one Man in an hundred, resumed *Arabella*, whom I should think worthy to serve me: But, pray, Madam, What ill Usage is it your Brother complains of? I have treated him with much less Severity than he had Reason to expect; and, notwithstanding he had the Presumption to talk to me of Love, I have endured him in my Sight; an Indulgence, for which I may haply be blamed in After-ages.

Why, sure, Lady *Bella*, said Miss *Glanville*, it would be no such Crime for my Brother to love you!

But it was a mortal Crime to tell me so, interrupted *Arabella*. And why was it such a mortal Crime to tell you so, said Miss

Glanville? Are you the first Woman by Millions, that has been told so?

Doubtless, returned *Arabella*, I am the first Woman of my Quality, that ever was told so by any Man, till after an infinite Number of Services, and secret Sufferings: And truly, I am of the illustrious *Mandana*'s Mind; for she said, That she should think it an unpardonable Presumption, for the greatest King on Earth to tell her he loved her, tho' after Ten Years of the most faithful Services, and concealed Torments.[2]

Ten Years! cried out Miss *Glanville*, in Amazement; Did she consider what Alterations Ten Years would make in her Face, and how much older she would be at the End of Ten Years, than she was before?

Truly, said *Arabella*, it is not usual to consider such little Matters so nicely; one never has the Idea of an Heroine older than Eighteen, tho' her History begins at that Age; and the Events, which compose it, contain the Space of Twenty more.

But, dear Cousin, resumed Miss *Glanville*, do you resolve to be Ten Years a courting? Or rather, will you be loved in Silence Ten Years, and be courted the other Ten; and so marry when you are an old Woman?

Pardon me, Cousin, resumed *Arabella*; I must really find Fault with the Coarseness of your Language. Courting, and Old Woman! What strange Terms! Let us, I beseech you, end this Dispute: If you have any thing to say in Justification of your Brother, which, I suppose, was the chief Intention of your Visit, I shall not be rude enough to restrain you; tho' I could wish you would not lay me under the Necessity of hearing what I cannot persuade myself to believe.

Since, returned Miss *Glanville*, I know of no Crime my Brother has been guilty of, I have nothing to say in his Justification: I only know, that he is very much mortified at the Message you sent him this Morning; for I was with him when he received it: But pray, What has he done to offend you?

If Mr. *Glanville*, interrupted *Arabella*, hopes for my Pardon, he must purchase it by his Repentance, and a sincere Confession of his Fault; which you may much better understand from himself, than from me: And, for this Purpose, I will condescend

.to grant him a private Audience, at which I desire you would be present; and also, I should take it well, if you will let him know, that he owes this Favour wholly to your Interposition.

Miss *Glanville*, who knew her Brother was extremely desirous of seeing *Arabella*, was glad to accept of these strange Terms; and left her Chamber, in order to acquaint him with that Lady's Intentions.

CHAPTER II

A solemn Interview.

In the mean time, that Fair-one, being risen, and negligently dressed, as was her Custom, went into her Closet, sending to give Miss *Glanville* Notice, That she was ready to see her. This Message immediately brought both the Brother and the Sister to her Apartment: And Miss *Glanville*, at her Brother's Request, staying in the Chamber, where she busied herself in looking at her Cousin's Jewels, which lay upon the Toilet, he came alone into the Closet, in so much Confusion at the Thoughts of the ridiculous Figure he made in complying with *Arabella*'s fantastical Humours, that his Looks persuading her there was some great Agitation in his Mind, she expected to see him fall at her Feet, and endeavour to deprecate her Wrath by a Deluge of Tears.

Mr. *Glanville* however disappointed her in that respect; for, taking a Seat near her, he began to intreat her, with a smiling Countenance, to tell him in what he had offended her; protesting, that he was not conscious of doing or saying any thing to displease her.

Arabella was greatly confused at this Question, which she thought she had no Reason to expect; it not being possible for her to tell him she was offended, that he was not in absolute Despair for her Absence, without, at the same time, confessing she looked upon him in the Light of a Lover, whose Expressions of a violent Passion would not have displeased her: Therefore,

to disengage herself from the Perplexity his Question threw her
into, she was obliged to offer some Violence to her Ingenu-
ousness; and, contrary to her real Belief tax him again with a
Design of betraying her into the Power of the Unknown.

Mr. *Glanville*, tho' excessively vexed at her persisting in so
ridiculous an Error, could hardly help smiling at the stern
Manner in which she spoke, but, knowing of what fatal Consequence it would be to him, if he indulged any Gaiety in so
solemn a Conference, he composed his Looks to a Gravity
suitable to the Occasion; and asked her in a very submissive
Tone, What Motive she was pleased to assign for so extraordinary a Piece of Villainy, as that she supposed him guilty of?

Truly, answered she blushing, I do not pretend to account
for the Actions of wicked and ungenerous Persons.

But, Madam, resumed *Glanville*, if I must needs be suspected
of a Design to seize upon your Person, methinks it would
have been more reasonable to suppose, I would rather use that
Violence in Favour of my own Pretensions, than those of any
other whatever; for, tho' you have expresly forbid me to tell
you I love you, yet I hope, you still continue to think I do.

I assure you, returned *Arabella*, assuming a severe Look, I
never gave myself the Trouble to examine your Behaviour with
Care enough to be sensible, if you still were guilty of the Weakness, which displeased me; but, upon a Supposition, that you
repented of your Fault, I was willing to live with you upon
Terms of Civility and Friendship, as became Persons in that
Degree of Relationship in which we are: Therefore, if you are
wise, you will not renew the Remembrance of those Follies I
have long since pardoned; nor seek Occasions of offending me
by new ones of the same kind, lest it produce a more severe
Sentence than that I formerly laid upon you.

However, Madam, returned Mr. *Glanville*, you must suffer
me to assure you, That my own Interest, which was greatly
concerned in your Safety, and my Principles of Honour, would
never allow me to engage in so villainous an Enterprize, as that
of abetting any Person in stealing you away: Nor can I conceive,
how you possibly could imagine a Fellow who was your menial
Servant, could form so presumptuous and dangerous a Design.

By your Manner of speaking, resumed *Arabella*, one would imagine you were really ignorant, both of the Quality of that presumptuous Man, as well as his designed Offence: But yet, 'tis certain, I saw you in his Company; and saw you ready to draw your Sword in his Defence, against my Deliverer. Had I not the Evidence of my own Senses, for your Guilt, I must confess, I could not be persuaded of it by any other Means: Therefore, since Appearances are certainly against you, it is not strange, if I cannot consent to acquit you in my Apprehensions, till I have more certain Confirmation of your Innocence, than your bare Testimony only, which, at present, has not all the Weight with me it had some time ago.

I protest, Madam, said Mr. *Glanville*, who was strangely perplexed, I have Reason to think my Case extremely hard, since I have brought myself to be suspected by you, only through my Eagerness to find you, and Solicitude for your Welfare.

Doubtless, interrupted *Arabella*, if you are innocent, your Case is extremely hard; yet it is not singular; and therefore you have less Reason to complain: The valiant *Coriolanus*, who was the most passionate and faithful Lover imaginable, having, by his admirable Valour, assisted the Ravishers of his adored *Cleopatra*, against those who came to rescue her; and, by his Arm alone, opposed to great Numbers of their Enemies, facilitated the Execution of their Design, had the Mortification afterwards to know, that he had, all that time been fighting against that Divine Princess, who, loaded him with the most cruel Reproaches for the Injury he had done her: Yet Fortune was so kind, as to give him the Means of repairing his Fault, and restoring him to some Part of her good Opinion; for, covered with Wounds as he was, and fatigued with fighting, before, yet he undertook, in that Condition, to prevent her Ravishers from carrying her off; and, for several Hours, continued fighting alone with near Two hundred Men, who were not able to overcome him, notwithstanding his extreme Weariness, and the Multitude of Blows which they aimed at him:[3] Therefore, *Glanville*, considering you, as *Cleopatra* did that unfortunate Prince, who was before suspected by her, as neither guilty nor innocent, I can only, like her, wish you may find some Occasion of justifying yourself, from the Crime laid to your Charge: Till then, I must be under a Necessity of banishing you from my Presence, with the same consolatory Speech she used to that unfortunate Prince: — "Go, therefore, *Glanville*, go, and endeavour your own Justification; I desire you should effect it, no less than you do yourself; and, if my Prayers can obtain from Heaven this Favour for you, I shall not scruple to offer some *in your Behalf*"[4]

CHAPTER III

In which the Interview is ended, not much to the Lover's Satisfaction, but exactly conformable to the Rules of Romance.

Arabella, when she had pronounced these Words, blushed excessively, thinking she had said too much: But, not seeing any Signs of extreme Joy in the Face of *Glanville*, who was silently cursing *Cleopatra*, and the Authors of those Romances, that had ruined so noble a Mind; and exposed him to perpetual Vexations, by the unaccountable Whims they had raised — Why are you not gone, said she, while I am in an Humour not to repent of the Favour I have shewn you?

You must excuse me, Cousin, said Mr. *Glanville*, peevishly, if I do not think so highly as you do of the Favour. Pray how am I obliged to you for depriving me of the Pleasure of seeing you, and sending me on a Wild-goose Chace, after Occasions to justify myself of a Crime I am wholly innocent of, and would scorn to commit?

Though, resumed *Arabella*, with great Calmness, I have Reason to be dissatisfied with the cool and unthankful manner in which you receive my Indulgence, yet I shall not change the favourable Disposition I am in towards you, unless you provoke me to it by new Acts of Disobedience: Therefore, in the Language of *Cleopatra*, I shall tell you. —

Upon my Soul, Madam, interrupted *Glanville*, I have no Patience with that rigorous Gipsy, whose Example you follow so exactly, to my Sorrow: Speak in your own Language, I beseech you; for I am sure neither hers, nor any one's upon Earth, can excel it.

Yet, said *Arabella*, striving to repress some Inclination to smile at this Sally, notwithstanding your unjust Prohibitions, I shall make use of the Language of that incomparable Lady, to tell you my Thoughts; which are, That 'tis possible you might be sufficiently justified in my Apprehensions, by the Anxiety it now appears you had for my Safety, by the Probability which I find in your Discourse, and the good Opinion I have of you, were it not requisite to make your Innocence apparent to the World, that so it might be lawful for *Arabella* to readmit you, with Honour, into her former Esteem and Friendship.

Mr. *Glanville*, seeing it would be in vain to attempt to make her alter her fantastical Determination at this time, went out of the Closet without deigning to make any Reply to his Sentence, though delivered in the Language of the admirable *Cleopatra*: But his ill Humour was so visible in his Face, that *Arabella*, who mistook it for an Excess of Despair, could not help feeling some kind of Pity for the Rigour which the Laws of Honour and Romance obliged her to use him with. And while she sat meditating upon the Scene which had just passed, Mr. *Glanville* returned to his own Room, glad that his Sister, not being in *Arabella*'s Chamber, where he had left her, had no Opportunity of observing his Discontent, which she would not fail to inquire the Cause of.

Here he sat, ruminating upon the Follies of *Arabella*, which he found grew more glaring every Day: Every thing furnished Matter for some new Extravagance; her Character was so ridiculous, that he could propose nothing to himself but eternal Shame and Disquiet, in the Possession of a Woman, for whom he must always blush, and be in Pain. But her Beauty had made a deep Impression on his Heart: He admired the Strength of her Understanding; her lively Wit; the Sweetness of her Temper; and a Thousand amiable Qualities which distinguished her from the rest of her Sex: Her Follies, when opposed to all those

Charms of Mind and Person, seemed inconsiderable and weak; and, though they were capable of giving him great Uneasiness, yet they could not lessen a Passion which every Sight of her so much the more confirmed.

As he feared it was impossible to help loving her, his Happiness depended upon curing her of her romantic Notions; and, though he knew not how to effect such a Change in her as was necessary to complete it, yet he would not despair, but comforted himself with Hopes of what he had not Courage to attempt. Sometimes he fansied Company, and an Acquaintance with the World, would produce the Alteration he wished: Yet he dreaded to see her exposed to Ridicule by her fantastical Behaviour, and become the Jest of Persons who were not possessed of half her Understanding.

While he traversed his Chamber, wholly engrossed by these Reflections, Miss *Glanville* was entertaining Sir *George*, of whose coming she was informed while she was in *Arabella*'s Chamber.

CHAPTER IV

In which our Heroine is greatly disappointed.

Miss *Glanville*, supposing her Brother would be glad not to be interrupted in his Conference with Lady *Bella*, did not allow any one to acquaint them with Sir *George*'s Visit; and, telling the Baronet her Cousin was indisposed, had, by these means, all his Conversation to herself.

Sir *George*, who ardently wished to see Lady *Bella*, protracted his Visit, in hopes that he should have that Satisfaction before he went away. And that fair Lady, whose Thoughts were a little discomposed by the Despair she apprehended Mr. *Glanville* was in, and fearful of the Consequences, when she had sat some time after he left her, ruminating upon what had happened, quitted her Closet, to go and inquire of Miss *Glanville*, in what Condition his Mind seemed to be when he went away; for she never doubted but that he was gone, like *Coriolanus*, to seek out for some Occasion to manifest his Innocence.

Hearing, therefore, the Voice of that Lady, who was talking and laughing very loud in one of the Summer-parlours, and being terrified with the Apprehension, that it was her Brother with whom she was thus diverting herself, she opened the Door of the Room precipitately; and by her Entrance, filled Sir *George* with extreme Pleasure; while her unexpected Sight produced a quite contrary Effect on Miss *Glanville*.

Arabella, eased of her Fear, that it was Mr. *Glanville*, who, instead of dying with Despair, was giving Occasion for that noisy Laugh of his Sister, saluted the Baronet with great Civility; and, turning to Miss *Glanville*, I must needs chide you, said she, for the Insensibility with which it appears you have parted with your Brother.

Bless me, Madam, interrupted Miss *Glanville*, what do you mean? Whither is my Brother gone?

That, indeed, I am quite ignorant of, resumed *Arabella*; and I suppose he himself hardly knows what Course he shall take: But he has been with you, doubtless, to take his Leave.

Take his Leave! repeated Miss *Glanville*: Has he left the Castle so suddenly then, and gone away without me?

The Enterprize upon which he is gone, said *Arabella*, would not admit of a Lady's Company: And, since he has left so considerable an Hostage with me as yourself, I expect he will not be long before he return; and, I hope, to the Satisfaction of us both.

Miss *Glanville*, who could not penetrate into the Meaning of her Cousin's Words, began to be strangely alarmed: But, presently, supposing she had a mind to divert herself with her Fears, she recovered herself, and told her she would go up to her Brother's Chamber, and look for him.

Arabella did not offer to prevent her, being very desirous of knowing, whether he had not left a Letter for her upon his Table, as was the Custom in those Cases: And, while she was gone, Sir *George* seized the Opportunity of saying an hundred gallant Things to her, which she received with great Indifference; the most extravagant Compliments being what she expected from all Men: And, provided they did not directly presume to tell her they loved her, no Sort of Flattery or Adulation could displease her.

In the mean time, Miss *Glanville*, having found her Brother in his Chamber, repeated to him what Lady *Bella* had said, as she supposed, to fright her.

Mr. *Glanville*, hearing this, and that Sir *George* was with her, hastened to them as fast as possible, that he might interrupt the foolish Stories he did not doubt she was telling.

Upon Miss *Glanville*'s Appearance with her Brother, *Arabella* was astonished.

I apprehended, Sir, said she, that you were some Miles from the Castle by this time: But your Delay and Indifference convince me, you neither expect nor wish to find the Means of being justified in my Opinion.

Pray, Cousin, interrupted *Glanville* (speaking softly to her) let us leave this Dispute to some other Time.

No, Sir, resumed she, aloud, my Honour is concerned in your Justification: Nor is it fit I should submit to have the Appearance of Amity for a Person who has not yet sufficiently cleared himself of a Crime, with too much Reason laid to his Charge. Did *Coriolanus*, think you, act in this Manner? Ah! if he had, doubtless, *Cleopatra* would never have pardoned him: Nor will I any longer suffer you to give me repeated Causes of Discontent.

Sir *George*, seeing Confusion in Mr. *Glanville*'s Countenance, and Rage in *Arabella*'s, began to think, that what he had at first took for a Jest, was a serious Quarrel between them, at which it was not proper he should be present; and was preparing to go: When *Arabella*, stopping him with a graceful Action —

If, noble Stranger, said she, you are so partial to the Failings of a Friend, that you will undertake to defend any unjustifiable Action he may be guilty of, you are at Liberty to depart: But, if you will promise to be an unprejudiced Hearer of the Dispute between Mr. *Glanville* and myself, you shall know the Adventure which has given Rise to it; and will be Judge of the Reasonableness of the Commands I have laid on him.

Though, Madam, said Sir *George*, (bowing very low to her), Mr. *Glanville* is my Friend, yet there is no Likelihood I shall espouse his Interest against yours: And a very strong

Prepossession I feel in Favour of you, already persuades me, that I shall give Sentence on your Side, since you have honoured me so far, as to constitute me Judge of this Difference.

The solemn manner in which Sir *George* (who began to suspect Lady *Bella's* peculiar Turn) spoke this, pleased her infinitely; while Mr. *Glanville*, vexed as he was, could hardly forbear laughing: When *Arabella*, after a Look of Approbation to Sir *George*, replied;

I find I have unwillingly engaged myself to more than I first intended: For, to enable you to judge clearly of the Matter in Dispute, 'tis necessary you should know my whole History.

Mr. *Glanville*, at this Word, not being able to constrain himself, uttered a Groan, of the same Nature with those which are often heard in the Pit⁵ at the Representation of a new Play. Sir *George* understood him perfectly well; yet seemed surprised: And *Arabella*, starting up,

Since, said she, I have given you no new Cause of Complaint, pray, from whence proceeds this Increase of Affliction?

I assure you, Cousin, answered he, my Affliction, if you please to term it so, increases every Day; and I believe it will make me mad at last: For this unaccountable Humour of yours is not to be borne.

You do not seem, replied *Arabella*, to be far from Madness already: And if your Friend here, upon hearing the Passages between us, should pronounce you guilty, I shall be at a Loss, whether I ought to treat you as a Madman, or a Criminal. Sir, added she, turning to Sir *George*, you will excuse me, if, for certain Reasons, I can neither give you my History myself, nor be present at the Relation of it: One of my Women, who is most in my Confidence, shall acquaint you with all the Particulars of my Life: After which I expect Mr. *Glanville* will abide by your Decision, as, I assure myself, I shall be contented to do.

Saying this, she went out of the Parlour, in order to prepare *Lucy* for the Recital she was to make.

Mr. *Glanville*, resolving not to be present at this new Absurdity, ran out after her; and went into the Garden, with a strong Inclination to hate the lovely Visionary who gave him such perpetual Uneasiness; leaving his Sister alone with the Baronet, who diverted herself extremely with the Thoughts of hearing her Cousin's History; assuring the Baronet, that he might expect something very curious in it, and find Matter sufficient to laugh at; for she was the most whimsical Woman in the World.

Sir *George*, who resolved to profit by the Knowlege of her Foible, made very little Reply to Miss *Glanville*'s Sneers; but waited patiently for the promised History, which was much longer coming than he imagined.

CHAPTER V

Some curious Instructions for relating an History.

Arabella, as soon as she left them, went up to her Apartment; and, calling *Lucy* into her Closet, told her that she had made Choice of her, since she was best acquainted with her Thoughts, to relate her History to her Cousins, and a Person of Quality who was with them.

Sure your Ladyship jests with me, said *Lucy*: How can I make a History about your Ladyship?

There is no Occasion, replied *Arabella*, for you to make a History: There are Accidents enough in my Life to afford Matter for a long one: All you have to do is to relate them as exactly as possible. You have lived with me from my Childhood, and are instructed in all my Adventures; so that you must be certainly very capable of executing the Task I have honoured you with.

Indeed, said *Lucy*, I must beg your Ladyship will excuse me: I never could tell how to repeat a Story when I have read it; And I know it is not such simple Girls as I can tell Histories: It is only fit for Clerks, and such Sort of People, that are very learned.

You are learned enough for that purpose, said *Arabella*; and, if you make so much Difficulty in performing this Part of your Duty, pray how came you to imagine you were fit for my Service, and the Distinction I have favoured you with? Did you

ever hear of any Woman that refused to relate her Lady's Story,
when desired? Therefore, if you hope to possess my Favour
and Confidence any longer, acquit yourself handsomely of this
Task, to which I have preferred you.

Lucy, terrified at the Displeasure she saw in her Lady's Countenance, begged her to tell her what she must say.

Well! exclaimed *Arabella*: I am certainly the most unfortunate Woman in the World! Every thing happens to me in a
contrary Manner from any other Person! Here, instead of my
desiring you to soften those Parts of my History where you
have greatest Room to flatter; and to conceal, if possible, some
of those Disorders my Beauty has occasioned; you ask me
to tell you what you must say; as if it was not necessary you
should know as well as myself, and be able, not only to recount
all my Words and Actions, even the smallest and most inconsiderable, but also all my Thoughts, however instantaneous; relate
exactly every Change of my Countenance; number all my
Smiles, Half-smiles, Blushes, Turnings pale, Glances, Pauses,
Full-stops, Interruptions; the Rise and Falling of my Voice;
every Motion of my Eyes; and every Gesture which I have used
for these Ten Years past; nor omit the smallest Circumstance
that relates to me.

Lord bless me! Madam, said *Lucy*, excessively astonished, I
never, till this Moment, it seems, knew the hundredth thou-
sandth Part of what was expected from me: I am sure, if I had,
I would never have gone to Service; for I might well know I
was not fit for such Slavery.

There is no such great Slavery in doing all I have mentioned
to you, interrupted *Arabella*: It requires, indeed, a good
Memory, in which I never thought you deficient; for you are
punctual to the greatest Degree of Exactness in recounting every
thing one desires to hear from you.

Lucy, whom this Praise soothed into good Humour, and
flattered with a Belief, that she was able, with a little Instruction,
to perform what her Lady required, told her, if she pleased only
to put her in a Way how to tell her History, she would engage,
after doing it once, to tell it again whenever she was desired.

Arabella, being obliged to comply with this odd Request, for

which there was no Precedent in all the Romances her Library
was stuffed with, began to inform her in this manner:

First, said she, you must relate my Birth, which you know is
very illustrious; and, because I am willing to spare you the
Trouble of repeating Things, that are not absolutely necessary,
you must apologize to your Hearers for slipping over what
passed in my Infancy, and the first Eight or Ten Years of my
Life; not failing, however, to remark, that, from some sprightly
Sallies of Imagination, at those early Years, those about me
conceived marvellous Hopes of my future Understanding: From
thence you must proceed to an accurate Description of my
Person.

What! Madam, interrupted *Lucy*, must I tell what Sort of
Person you have, to People who have seen you but a Moment
ago?

Questionless you must, replied *Arabella*; and herein you
follow the Examples of all the 'Squires and Maids who relate
their Masters and Ladies Histories: For, though it be to a
Brother, or near Relation, who has seen them a thousand times,
yet they never omit an exact Account of their Persons.

Very well, Madam, said *Lucy*: I shall be sure not to forget
that Part of my Story. I wish I was as perfect in all the rest.

Then, *Lucy*, you must repeat all the Conversations I have
ever held with you upon the Subjects of Love and Gallantry,
that your Audience may be so well acquainted with my
Humour, as to know exactly, before they are told, how I shall
behave, in whatever Adventures befal me. — After that, you
may proceed to tell them, how a noble Unknown saw me at
Church; how prodigiously he was struck with my Appearance;
the tumultuous Thoughts that this first View of me occasioned
in his Mind. —

Indeed, Madam, interrupted *Lucy* again, I can't pretend to
tell his Thoughts: For how should I know what they were?
None but himself can tell that.

However that may be, said *Arabella*, I expect you should
decypher all his Thoughts, as plainly as he himself could do;
otherwise my History will be very imperfect: Well, I suppose
you are at no loss about that whole Adventure, in which you

yourself bore so great a Share; so need not give you any further Instructions concerning it: Only you must be sure, as I said before, not to omit the least Circumstance in my Behaviour, but relate every thing I did, said, and thought, upon that Occasion. The disguised Gardener must appear next in your Story: Here you will of necessity be a little deficient, since you are not able to acquaint your Hearers with his true Name and Quality; which, questionless, is very illustrious. However, above all, I must charge you not to mention that egregious Mistake about the Carp; for, you know how —

Here Miss *Glanville*'s Entrance put a Stop to the Instructions *Lucy* was receiving: For she told *Arabella*, that Sir *George* was gone.

How! returned she, is he gone? Truly I am not much obliged to him for the Indifference he has shewed to hear my Story.

Why, really, Madam, said Miss *Glanville*, neither of us expected you would be as good as your Word, you were so long in sending your Woman down: And my Brother persuaded Sir *George* you were only in Jest; and Sir *George* has carried him home to Dinner.

And is it at Sir *George*'s, replied *Arabella*, that your Brother hopes to meet with an Occasion of clearing himself? He is either very insensible of my Anger, or very conscious of his own Innocence.

Miss *Glanville*, having nothing to say in Answer to an Accusation she did not understand, changed the Discourse: And the two Ladies passed the rest of the Day together, with tolerable Good-humour on Miss *Glanville*'s Side; who was in great Hopes of making a Conquest of the Baronet, before whom *Arabella* had made herself ridiculous enough: But that Lady was far from being at ease; she had laid herself under a Necessity of banishing Mr. *Glanville*, if he did not give her some convincing Proof of his Innocence; which, as Matters stood, she thought would be very hard for him to procure; and, as she could not absolutely believe him guilty, she was concerned she had gone so far.

CHAPTER VI

A very Heroic Chapter.

Mr. *Glanville*, coming home in the Evening, a little elevated with the Wine, of which he had drank too freely at Sir *George*'s, being told the Ladies were together, entered the Room where they were sitting; and, beholding *Arabella*, whose Pensiveness had given an inchanting Softness to her Face, with a Look of extreme Admiration —

Upon my Soul, Cousin, said he, if you continue to treat me so cruelly, you'll drive me mad. How I could adore you this Moment, added he, gazing passionately at her, if I might but hope you did not hate me!

Arabella, who did not perceive the Condition he was in, was better pleased with this Address than any he had ever used; and, therefore, instead of chiding him, as she was wont, for the Freedom of his Expressions, she cast her bright Eyes upon the Ground, with so charming a Confusion, that *Glanville*, quite transported, threw himself on his Knees before her; and, taking her Hand, attempted to press it to his Lips: But she, hastily withdrawing it —

From whence is this new Boldness? said she. And what is it you would implore by that prostrate Posture? I have told you already upon what Conditions I will grant you my Pardon. Clear yourself of being an Accomplice with my designed Ravisher, and I am ready to restore you to my Esteem.

Let me perish, Madam, returned *Glanville*, if I would not die to please you, this Moment!

It is not your Death that I require, said she: And though you should never be able to justify yourself in my Opinion, yet you might, haply, expiate your Crime, by a less Punishment than Death.

What shall I do, then, my Angelic Cousin? resumed he.

Truly, said she, the Sense of your Offence ought so mortally to afflict you, that you should invent some strange kind of Penance for yourself, severe enough to prove your Penitence sincere. — You know, I suppose, what the unfortunate *Orontes* did, when he found he had wronged his adored *Thalestris* by an injurious Suspicion.⁶

I wish he had hanged himself, said Mr. *Glanville*, rising up in a Passion, at seeing her again in her Altitudes.

And why, pray, Sir, said *Arabella*, are you so severe upon that poor Prince; who was, haply, infinitely more innocent than yourself.

Severe, Madam! said *Glanville*, fearing he had offended her: Why, to be sure, he was a sad Scoundrel, to use his adored *Thalestris* as he did: And I think one cannot be too severe upon him.

But, returned *Arabella*, Appearances were against her; and he had some Shadow of Reason for his Jealousy and Rage: Then, you know, amidst all his Transports, he could not be prevailed upon to draw his Sword against her.

What did that signify? said *Glanville*: I suppose he scorned to draw his Sword upon a Woman: That would have been a Shame indeed.

That Woman, Sir, resumed *Arabella*, was not such a contemptible Antagonist as you think her: And Men, as valiant, possibly, as *Orontes* (though, questionless, he was one of the most valiant Men in the World), have been cut in Pieces by the Sword of that brave *Amazon*.

Lord bless me! said Miss *Glanville*, I should be afraid to look at such a terrible Woman: I am sure she must be a very masculine Sort of Creature.

You are much mistaken, Miss, said *Arabella*: For *Thalestris*, though the most stout and courageous of her Sex, was, nevertheless, a perfect Beauty; and had as much Harmony and Softness in her Looks and Person, as she had Courage in her Heart, and Strength in her Blows.

Indeed, Madam, resumed Miss *Glanville*, you can never persuade me, that a Woman who can fight, and cut People to Pieces with their Blows, can have any Softness in her Person: She must needs have very masculine Hands, that could give such terrible Blows: And I can have no Notion of the Harmony of a Person's Looks, who, by what you say, must have the

Heart of a Tyger. But, indeed, I don't think there ever could be such a Woman.

What! Miss, interrupted *Arabella*: Do you pretend to doubt, that there ever was such a Person as *Thalestris*, Queen of the *Amazons*? Does not all the World know the Adventures of that illustrious Princess; her Affection for the unjust *Orontes*, who accused her of having a scandalous Intrigue with *Alexander*, whom she went to meet, with a very different Design, upon the Borders of her Kingdom; The injurious Letter he wrote her, upon this Suspicion, made her resolve to seek for him all over the World, to give him that Death he had merited, by her own Hand: And it was in those Rencounters that he had with her, while she was thus incensed, that he forbore to defend himself against her, though her Sword was often pointed to his Breast.

But, Madam, interrupted Mr. *Glanville*, pray what became of this Queen of the *Amazons*? Was she not killed at the Siege of *Troy*?[7] She never was at the Siege of *Troy*, returned *Arabella*: But she assisted the Princes who besieged *Babylon*, to recover the Liberty of *Statyra* and *Parisatis*: And it was in the opposite Party that she met with her faithless Lover.

If he was faithless, Madam, said Mr. *Glanville*, he deserved to die: And I wish, with all my Soul, she had cut him in Pieces with that famous Sword of hers that had done such Wonders.

Yet this faithless Man, resumed *Arabella*, whom you seem to have such an Aversion to, gave so glorious a Proof of his Repentance and Sorrow, that the fair Queen restored him to her Favour, and held him in much dearer Affection than ever: For, after he was convinced of her Innocence, he was resolved to punish himself with a Rigour equal to the Fault he had been guilty of; and, retiring to the Woods, abandoned for ever the Society of Men; dwelling in a Cave, and living upon bitter Herbs, passing the Days and Nights in continual Tears and Sorrow for his Crime: And here he proposed to end his Life, had not the fair *Thalestris* found him out in this Solitude; and, struck with the Sincerity of his Repentance, pardoned him; and, as I have said before, restored him to her Favour.

And, to shew you, said *Glanville*, that I am capable of doing as much for you; I will, if you insist upon it, seek out for some Cave, and do Penance in it, like that *Orontes*, provided you will come and fetch me out of it, as that same fair Queen did him.

I do not require so much of you, said *Arabella*; for I told you before, that, haply, you are justified already in my Opinion; but yet it is necessary, you should find out some Method of convincing the World of your Innocence; otherwise it is not fit I should live with you upon Terms of Friendship and Civility.

Well, well, Madam, said *Glanville*, I'll convince you of my Innocence, by bringing that Rascal's Head to you, whom you suspect I was inclined to assist in stealing you away.

If you do that, resumed *Arabella*, doubtless you will be justified in my Opinion, and the World's also; and I shall have no Scruple to treat you with as much Friendship as I did before.

My Brother is much obliged to you, Madam, interrupted Miss *Glanville*, for putting him upon an Action, that would cost him his Life!

I have so good an Opinion of your Brother's Valour, said *Arabella*, that I am persuaded he will find no Difficulty in performing his Promise; and I make no question but I shall see him covered with the Spoils of that Impostor, who would have betrayed me; and I flatter myself, he will be in a Condition to bring me his Head, as he bravely promises, without endangering his own Life.

Does your Ladyship consider, said Miss *Glanville*, that my Brother can take away no Person's Life whatever, without endangering his own?

I consider, Madam, said *Arabella*, your Brother as a Man possessed of Virtue and Courage enough to undertake to kill all my Enemies and Persecutors, though I had ever so many; and I presume, he would be able to perform as many glorious Actions for my Service, as either *Juba*, *Cæsario*, *Artamenes*, or *Artaban*,[8] who, though not a Prince, was greater than any of them.

If those Persons you have named, said Miss *Glanville*, were Murderers, and made a Practice of killing People, I hope my Brother will be too wise to follow their Examples: A strange kind of Virtue and Courage indeed, to take away the Lives of one's Fellow-Creatures! How did such Wretches escape the Gallows, I wonder?

I perceive, interrupted *Arabella*, what kind of Apprehensions you have: I suppose you think, if your Brother was to kill my Enemy, the Law would punish him for it: But pray undeceive yourself, Miss: The Law has no Power over Heroes; they may kill as many Men as they please, without being called to any Account for it; and the more Lives they take away, the greater is their Reputation for Virtue and Glory. The illustrious *Artaban*, from the Condition of a private Man, raised himself to the sublimest Pitch of Glory by his Valour; for he not only would win half a dozen Battles in a Day; but, to shew that Victory followed him where-ever he went, he would change Parties, and immediately the Vanquished became Conquerors; then, returning to the Side he had quitted, changed the Laurels of his former Friends into Chains. He made nothing of tumbling Kings from their Thrones, and giving away half a dozen Crowns in a Morning; for his Generosity was equal to his Courage; and to this Height of Power did he raise himself by his Sword. Beginning at first with petty Conquests, and not disdaining to oppose his glorious Arm to sometimes less than a Score of his Enemies; so, by degrees, enuring himself to conquer inconsiderable Numbers, he came at last to be the Terror of whole Armies, who would fly at the Sight of his single Sword.

This is all very astonishing indeed, said Miss *Glanville*: However, I must intreat you, not to insist upon my Brother's quarrelling and fighting with People, since it will be neither for your Honour, nor his Safety; for I am afraid, if he was to commit Murder to please you, the Laws would make him suffer for it; and the World would be very free with its Censures on your Ladyship's Reputation, for putting him upon such shocking Crimes.

By your Discourse, Miss, replied *Arabella*, one would imagine, you knew as little in what the good Reputation of a Lady consists, as the Safety of a Man; for certainly the one depends intirely upon his Sword, and the other upon the Noise and Bustle she makes in the World.[9] The Blood that is shed for a Lady, enhances the Value of her Charms; and the more Men a Hero kills, the greater his Glory, and, by Consequence, the more secure he is. If to be the Cause of a great many Deaths, can make a Lady infamous; certainly none were ever more so, than *Mandana*, *Cleopatra*, and *Statira*, the most illustrious Names in Antiquity; for each of whom, haply, an hundred thousand Men were killed: Yet none were ever so unjust, as to profane the Virtue of those Divine Beauties, by casting any Censures upon them for these glorious Effects of their Charms, and the heroic Valour of their Admirers.

I must confess, interrupted Miss *Glanville*, I should not be sorry to have a Duel or Two fought for me in *Hyde-Park*;[10] but then I would not have any Blood shed for the World.

Glanville here interrupting his Sister with a Laugh, *Arabella*, also could not forbear smiling at the harmless Kind of Combats her Cousin was fond of.

But to put an End to the Conversation, and the Dispute which gave Rise to it, she obliged Mr. *Glanville* to promise to fight with the Impostor *Edward*, whenever he found him; and either take away his Life, or force him to confess, he had no Part in the Design he had meditated against her.

This being agreed upon, *Arabella*, conducting Miss *Glanville* to her Chamber, retired to her own; and passed the Night with much greater Tranquillity, than she had done the preceding; being satisfied with the Care she had taken of her own Glory, and persuaded that *Glanville* was not unfaithful; a Circumstance, that was of more Consequence to her Happiness, than she was yet aware of.

CHAPTER VII

In which our Heroine is suspected of Insensibility.

While these things passed at the Castle, Sir *George* was meditating on the Means he should use to acquire the Esteem of Lady *Bella*, of whose Person he was a little enamoured, but of her Fortune a great deal more.

By the Observations he had made on her Behaviour, he discovered her peculiar Turn: He was well read in Romances himself, and had actually employed himself some Weeks in giving a new Version of the *Grand Cyrus*; but the prodigious Length of the Task he had undertaken, terrified him so much, that he gave it over: Nevertheless, he was perfectly well acquainted with the chief Characters in most of the *French* Romances; could tell every thing that was borrowed from them, in all the new Novels that came out; and, being a very accurate Critic, and a mortal Hater of *Dryden*, ridiculed him for want of Invention, as it appeared by his having recourse to these Books for the most shining Characters and Incidents in his Plays. *Almanzor*, he would say, was the Copy of the famous *Artaban* in *Cleopatra*, whose Exploits *Arabella* had expatiated upon to Miss *Glanville*, and her Brother: His admired Character of *Melantha* in Marriage *à-la-mode*, was drawn from *Berissa* in the *Grand Cyrus*; and the Story of *Osmyn* and *Bensayda*, in his Conquest of *Granada*, taken from *Sesostris* and *Timerilla* in that Romance.[11]

Fraught therefore with the Knowlege of all the Extravagances and Peculiarities in those Books, he resolved to make his Addresses to *Arabella* in the Form they prescribed; and, not having Delicacy enough to be disgusted with the Ridicule[12] in her Character, served himself with her Foible, to effect his Designs.

It being necessary, in order to his better Acquaintance with *Arabella*, to be upon very friendly Terms with Miss *Glanville* and her Brother, he said a thousand gallant Things to the one, and seemed so little offended with the Gloom he observed upon the Countenance of the other, who positively assured him, that *Arabella* meant only to laugh at him, when she promised him her History, that he intreated him, with the most obliging Earnestness, to favour him with his Company at his House, where he omitted no sort of Civility, to confirm their Friendship and Intimacy; and persuaded him, by several little and seemingly unguarded Expressions, that he was not so great an Admirer of Lady *Bella*, as her agreeable Cousin Miss *Glanville*.

Having thus secured a Footing in the Castle, he furnished

his Memory with all the necessary Rules of making Love in *Arabella*'s Taste, and deferred his next Visit no longer than till the following Day; but Mr. *Glanville* being indisposed, and not able to see Company, he knew it would be in vain to expect to see *Arabella*, since it was not to be imagined, Miss *Glanville* could admit of a Visit, her Brother being ill; and Lady *Bella* must be also necessarily engaged with her.

Contenting himself, therefore, with having inquired after the Health of the Two Ladies, he returned home, not a little vexed at his Disappointment.

Mr. *Glanville*'s Indisposition, increasing every Day, grew at last dangerous enough to fill his Sister with extreme Apprehensions. *Arabella*, keeping up to her Forms, sent regularly every Day, to inquire after his Health; but did not offer to go into his Chamber, though Miss *Glanville* was almost always there.

As she conceived his Sickness to be occasioned by the Violence of his Passion for her, she expected some Overture should be made her by his Sister, to engage her to make him a Visit; such a Favour being never granted by any Lady to a sick Lover, till she was previously informed, her Presence was necessary to hinder the Increase of his Distemper.

Miss *Glanville* would not have failed to represent to her Cousin the Incivility and Carelesness of her Behaviour, in not deigning to come and see her Brother in his Indisposition, had not Mr. *Glanville*, imputing this Neglect to the Nicety of her Notions, which he had upon other Occasions experienced, absolutely forbid her to say any thing to her Cousin upon this Subject.

Miss *Glanville* being thus forced to Silence, by the Fear of giving her Brother Uneasiness, *Arabella* was extremely disappointed to find, that, in Five Days Illness, no Application had been made to her, either by the sick Lover, or his Sister, who she thought interested herself too little in his Recovery; so that her Glory obliging her to lay some Constraint upon herself, she behaved with a Coolness and Insensibility, that increased Miss *Glanville*'s Aversion to her, while, in reality, she was extremely concerned for her Cousin's Illness; but not supposing it dangerous, since they had not recourse to the usual Remedy, of beseeching a Visit from the Person whose Presence was alone able to work a Cure, she resolved to wait patiently the Event.

However, she never failed in her Respect to Miss *Glanville*, whom she visited every Morning, before she went to her Brother; and also constantly dined with her in her own Apartment, inquiring always, with great Sweetness, concerning her Brother's Health; when perceiving her in Tears one Day, as she came in, as usual, to dine with her, she was extremely alarmed; and asked with great Precipitation, If Mr. *Glanville* was worse?

He is so bad, Madam, returned Miss *Glanville*, that I believe it will be necessary to send for my Papa, for fear he should die, and he not see him.

Die, Miss! interrupted *Arabella* eagerly: No, he must not die; and shall not, if the Pity of *Arabella* is powerful enough to make him live. Let us go then, Cousin, said she, her Eyes streaming with Tears; let us go and visit this dear Brother, whom you lament: Haply my Sight may repair the Evils my Rigour has caused him; and since, as I imagine, he has forborn, through the profound Respect he has for me, to request the Favour of a Visit, I will voluntarily bestow it on him, as well for the Affection I bear you, as because I do not wish his Death.

You do not wish his Death, Madam! said Miss *Glanville*, excessively angry at a Speech, in her Opinion, extremely insolent: Is it such a mighty Favour, pray, not to wish the Death of my Brother, who never injured you? I am sure, your Behaviour has been so extremely inhuman, that I have repented a thousand times, we ever came to the Castle.

Let us not waste the Time in idle Reproaches, said *Arabella*: If my Rigour has brought your Brother into this Condition, my Compassion can draw him out of it: It is no more than what all do suffer, who are possessed of a violent Passion; and few Lovers ever arrive to the Possession of their Mistresses, without being several times brought almost to their Graves, either by their Severity, or some other Cause: But nothing is more easy, than to work a Cure, in these Cases; for the very Sight of the Person beloved sometimes does it, as it happened to *Artamenes*, when the Divine *Mandana* condescended to visit him: A few kind Words, spoken by the fair Princess of *Persia* to *Oroondates*, recalled him from the Gates of Death;[13] and one Line from *Parisatis*'s Hand, which brought a Command to *Lysimachus* to live, made him not only resolve, but even able, to obey her. —

Miss *Glanville*, quite out of Patience at this tedious Harangue, without any Regard to Ceremony, flounced out of the Room; and ran to her Brother's Chamber, followed by *Arabella*, who imputed her rude Haste to a Suspicion, that her Brother was worse.

CHAPTER VIII

By which we hope the Reader will be differently affected.

At their Entrance into the Room, Miss *Glanville* inquired of the Physician, just going out, How he found her Brother? Who replied, that his Fever was increased since last Night; and that it would not (seeing *Arabella* preparing to go to his Bedside) be proper to disturb him.

Saying this, he bow'd, and went out; and Miss *Glanville*, repeating what the Physician had said, begged her to defer speaking to him till another time.

I know, said she, that he apprehends, the Sight of me will cause so many tumultuous Motions in the Soul of his Patient, as may prove prejudicial to him: Nevertheless, since his Disorder is, questionless, more in his Mind than Body, I may prove, haply, a better Physician than he; since I am more likely, than he, to cure an Illness I have caused —

Saying this, she walked up to Mr. *Glanville*'s Bed-side, who, seeing her, thanked her, with a weak Voice, for coming to see him; assuring her, he was very sensible of the Favour she did him —

You must not, said she, blushing, thank me too much, lest I think the Favour I have done you, is really of more Consequence than I imagined, since it merits so many Acknowledgements:

Your Physician tells us, pursued she, that your Life is in Danger; but I persuade myself, you will value it so much from this Moment, that you will not protract your Cure any longer.

Are you mad, Madam, whispered Miss *Glanville*, who stood behind her, to tell my Brother, that the Physician says he is in Danger? I suppose you really wish he may die, or you would not talk so.

If, answered she, whispering again to Miss *Glanville*, you are not satisfied with what I have already done for your Brother, I will go as far as Modesty will permit me: And gently pulling open the Curtains;

Glanville, said she, with a Voice too much raised for a sick Person's Ear, I grant to your Sister's Solicitations, what the fair *Statira* did to an Interest yet more powerful, since, as you know, it was her own Brother, who pleaded in Favour of the dying *Orontes*:[14] Therefore, considering you in a Condition haply no less dangerous, than that of that passionate Prince, I condescend, like her, to tell you, that I do not wish your Death; that I intreat you to live; and, lastly, by all the Power I have over you, I command you to recover.

Ending these Words, she closed the Curtain, that her transported Lover might not see her Blushes and Confusion, which were so great, that, to conceal them, even from Miss *Glanville*, she hurried out of the Room, and retired to her own Apartment, expecting, in a little time, to receive a Billet, under the sick Man's Hand, importing, that, in Obedience to her Commands, he was recovered, and ready to throw himself at her Feet, to thank her for that Life she had bestowed upon him, and to dedicate the Remains of it to her Service.

Miss *Glanville*, who stayed behind her, in a strange Surprize at her ridiculous Behaviour; though she longed to know what her Brother thought of it, finding he continued silent, would not disturb him. The Shame he conceived at hearing so absurd a Speech from a Woman he passionately loved; and the Desire he had, not to hear his Sister's Sentiments upon it; made him counterfeit Sleep, to avoid any Discourse with her upon so disagreeable a Subject.

That Day his Fever increased; and the next, the Physician

pronouncing him in great Danger, a Messenger was dispatched to Town, to hasten the Coming of Sir *Charles*; and poor Miss *Glanville* was quite inconsoleable, under the Apprehensions of losing him.

Arabella, not to derogate from her Character, affected great Firmness of Mind upon this Occasion; she used the most persuasive Eloquence to moderate her Cousin's Affliction, and caused all imaginable Care to be taken of Mr. *Glanville*: While any one was present, her Looks discovered only a calm and decent[15] Sorrow; yet when she was alone, or had only her dear *Lucy* with her, she gave free Vent to her Tears; and discovered a Grief for Mr. *Glanville*'s Illness, little different from that she had felt for her Father's.

As she now visited him constantly every Day, she took an Opportunity, when she was alone by his Bed-side, to chide him for his Disobedience, in not recovering, as she had commanded him.

Dear Cousin, answered he faintly, Can you imagine, Health is not my Choice? And do you think, I would suffer these Pains, if I could possibly ease myself of them?

Those Pains, replied *Arabella*, mistaking his Complaint, ought to have ceased, when the Cause of them did; and when I was no longer rigorous, you ought no longer to have suffered: But tell me, since you are, questionless, one of the strangest Men in the World, and the hardest to be comforted; nay, and I may add, the most disobedient of all, that ever wore the Fetters of Love; Tell me, I say, what must I do to content you?

If I live, Cousin, said *Glanville*—

Nay, interrupted *Arabella*, since my Empire over you is not so absolute as I thought; and since you think fit to reserve to yourself the Liberty of dying, contrary to my Desire; I think I had better resolve, not to make any Treaty with you: However, as I have gone thus far, I will do something more; and tell you, since I have commanded you to live, I will also permit you to love me, in order to make the Life I have bestowed on you, worthy your Acceptance. Make me no Reply, said she, putting her Hand on his Mouth; but begin from this Moment to obey me.

Saying this, she went out of the Room—

A few Hours after, his Fever being come to a Height, he grew delirious, and talked very wildly; but a favourable Crisis ensuing, he fell into a sound and quiet Sleep, and continued in it for several Hours: Upon his waking, the Physician declared, his Fever was greatly abated; and the next Morning, pronounced him out of Danger —

Miss *Glanville*, transported with Joy, ran to Lady *Bella*, and informed her of this good News; but as she did not make her the Acknowlegements she expected, for being the Cause of his Recovery, she behaved with more Reserve than Miss *Glanville* thought was necessary: Which renewed her former Disgusts; yet, dreading to displease her Brother, she concealed it from the Observation of her Cousin —

Arabella, being desirous of completing her Lover's Cure by some more favourable Expressions, went to his Chamber, accompanied by Miss *Glanville*.

I see, said she, approaching to his Bed-side, with an inchanting Smile, that you know how to be obedient, when you please; and I begin to know, by the Price you set upon your Obedience, that small Favours will not content you.

Indeed, my dearest Cousin, said *Glanville*, who had found her more interested in his Recovery than he expected, you have been very obliging, and I will always most gratefully own it.

I am glad, interrupted *Arabella*, that Gratitude is not banished from all your Family; and that that Person in it, for whom I have the most Sensibility, is not intirely divested of it —

I hope, said Mr. *Glanville*, my Sister has given you no Cause to complain of her.

Indeed but she has, replied *Arabella*; for, notwithstanding she is obliged to me for the Life of a Brother, whom questionless she loves very well; nevertheless, she did not deign to make me the least Acknowledgement for what I have done in your Favour: However, *Glanville*, provided you continue to observe that Respect and Fidelity towards me, which I have Reason to hope for from you, your Condition shall be never the worse for Miss *Glanville*'s unacknowleging Temper; and I now confirm the Grant I Yesterday made you, and repeat it again; That I permit you to love me, and promise you not to be displeased at

any Testimonies you will give me of your Passion, provided
you serve me with an inviolable Fidelity.

But, Madam, returned Mr. *Glanville*, to make my Happiness
complete, you must also promise to love me; or else what
signifies the Permission you give me to love you?

You are almost as unacknowleging as your Sister, resumed
Arabella, blushing; and if your Health was perfectly re-
established, questionless, I should chide you for your Presumption; but since something must be allowed to sick Persons,
whose Reason, one may suppose, is weakened by their Indisposition, I will pardon your Indiscretion at this time, and counsel
you to wait patiently for what Heaven will determine in your
Favour: Therefore endeavour to merit my Affection by your
Respect, Fidelity, and Services; and hope from my Justice, whatever it ought to bestow —

Ending this Speech, with a Solemnity of Accent, that gave
Mr. *Glanville* to understand, any Reply would offend her, he
silently kissed her fair Hand, which she held out to him; a
Favour, his Sickness, and the Terms upon which they now were,
gave him a Right to expect — And, finishing her Visit for that
time, left him to his Repose; being extremely pleased at the
Prospect of his Recovery, and very well satisfied at having so
gracefully got over so great a Difficulty, as that of giving him
Permission to love her: For by the Laws of Romance, when a
Lady has once given her Lover that Permission, she may law-
fully allow him to talk to her upon the Subject of his Passion,
accept all his Gallantries, and claim an absolute Empire over
all his Actions; reserving to herself the Right of fixing the Time
when she may own her Affection: And when that important.
Step is taken, and his Constancy put to a few Years more
Trial; when he has killed all his Rivals, and rescued her from a
thousand Dangers; she at last condescends to reward him with
her Hand; and all her Adventures are at an End for the future.

END of the THIRD BOOK.

BOOK IV

CHAPTER I

In which our Heroine discovers her Knowlege in Astronomy.

Sir *George*, who had never missed a Day, during Mr. *Glanville*'s Illness, in sending to the Castle, now he was able to see Company, visited him very frequently; and sometimes had the Happiness to meet with *Arabella* in his Chamber: But, knowing the Conditions of her Father's Will, and Mr. *Glanville*'s Pretensions, he was obliged to lay so much Constraint upon himself, in the Presence of Miss *Glanville*, and her Brother, that he hardly durst trust his Eyes, to express his Admiration of her, for Fear of alarming them with any Suspicion of his Designs: However, he did not fail to recommend himself to her Esteem, by a Behaviour to her full of the most perfect Respect; and very often, ere he was aware, uttered some of the extravagant Compliments, that the Gallants in the *French* Romances use to their Mistresses.

If he walked with her in the Gardens, he would observe, that the Flowers, which were before languishing and pale, bloomed with fresh Beauty at her Approach; that the Sun shined out with double Brightness, to exceed if possible, the Lustre of her Eyes; and that the Wind, fond of kissing her celestial Countenance, played with her fair Hair; and, by gentle Murmurs, declared its Happiness —

If Miss *Glanville* happened to be present, when he talked to her in this Strain, she would suppose he was ridiculing her

Cousin's fantastical Turn; and when she had an Opportunity
of speaking to him alone, would chide him, with a great deal
of good Humour, for giving her so much Diversion at her
Cousin's Expence.

Sir *George*, improving this Hint, persuaded Miss *Glanville*
by his Answers, that he really laughed at *Arabella*; and, being
now less fearful of giving any Suspicion to the gay Coquet,
since she assisted him to deceive her, he applied himself, with
more Assiduity than ever, to insinuate himself into *Arabella*'s
Favour.

However, the Necessity he was under of being always of
Arabella's Opinion, sometimes drew him into little Difficulties
with Miss *Glanville*. Knowing that young Lady was extremely
fond of Scandal, he told her, as a most agreeable Piece of
News, one Afternoon when he was there, that he had seen Miss
Groves, who, he supposed, had come into the Country upon
the same Account as she had done a Twelvemonth before: Her
Marriage being yet a Secret, the complaisant Baronet threw out
an Hint or two, concerning the Familiarity and Correspondence
there was between her and the Gentleman to whom she was
really secretly married.

Miss *Glanville*, making the most of this Intelligence, said a
thousand severe Things against the unfortunate Miss *Groves*;
which *Arabella*, always benevolent and kind, could not bear.

I persuade myself, said she to her Cousin, that you have
been misinformed concerning this Beauty, whose Misfortunes
you aggravate by your cruel Censures; and whoever has given
you the History of her Life, has, haply, done it with great
Injustice —

Why, Madam, interrupted Miss *Glanville*, do you think you
are better acquainted with her History, as you call it, who have
never been in Town, where her Follies made her so remarkable,
than Persons who were Eye-witnesses of all her ridiculous
Actions?

I apprehend, said *Arabella*, that I, who have had a Relation
made to me of all the Passages of her Life, and have been told
all her most secret Thoughts, may know as much, if not more,
than Persons who have lived in the same Place with her, and

have not had that Advantage; and I think, I know enough to vindicate her from many cruel Aspersions.

Pray, Madam, returned Miss *Glanville*, will your Ladyship pretend to defend her scandalous Commerce with Mr. *L*——?

I know not, Miss, said *Arabella*, why you call her Intercourse with that perjured Man by so unjust an Epithet. If Miss *Groves* be unchaste, so was the renowned *Cleopatra*, whose Marriage with *Julius Cæsar* is controverted to this Day.

And what Reasons, Madam, said Miss *Glanville*, have you for supposing, Miss *Groves* was married to Mr. *L*——, since all the World knows to the contrary?

Very sufficient ones, said *Arabella*; since it is hardly possible to suppose, a young Lady of Miss *Groves*'s Quality would stain the Lustre of her Descent by so shameful an Intrigue; and also, since there are Examples enough to be found of Persons, who suffered under the same unhappy Circumstances as herself; yet were perfectly innocent, as was that great Queen I have mentioned; who questionless, you, Sir, are sufficiently convinced, was married to that illustrious Conqueror; who, by betraying so great and so fair a Queen, in great measure tarnished the Glory of his Laurels —

Married, Madam! replied Sir *George*: Who presumes to say, that fair Queen was not married to that illustrious Conqueror?

Nay, you know, Sir, interrupted *Arabella*, many People did say, even while she was living, that she was not married; and have branded her Memory with infamous Calumnies, upon Account of the Son she had by *Cæsar*, the brave *Cæsario*, who, under the Name of *Cleomedon*, performed such Miracles of Valour in *Ethiopia*.[1]

I assure you, Madam, said Sir *George*, I was always a great Admirer of the famous *Cleomedon*, who was certainly the greatest Hero in the World.

Pardon me, Sir, said *Arabella*; *Cleomedon* was, questionless, a very valiant Man; but he, and all the Heroes that ever were, must give place to the unequalled Prince of *Mauritania*;[2] that illustrious, and for a long time unfortunate, Lover of the Divine *Cleopatra*, who was Daughter, as you questionless know, of the great Queen we have been speaking of —

Dear Heart! said Miss *Glanville*, What is all this to the Purpose? I would fain know, whether Sir *George* believes, Miss *Groves* was ever married to Mr. *L——*.

Doubtless, I do, said he; for, as Lady *Bella* says, she is in the same unhappy Circumstance with the great *Cleopatra*; and if *Julius Cæsar* could be guilty of denying his Marriage with that Queen, I see no Reason to suppose, why Mr. *L——* might not be guilty of the same kind of Injustice.

So then, interrupted Miss *Glanville*, reddening with Spite, you will really offer to maintain, that Miss *Groves* was married? Ridiculous! How such a Report would be laughed at in *London*!

I assure you, replied *Arabella*, if ever I go to *London*, I shall not scruple to maintain that Opinion to every one, who will mention that Fair-one to me; and use all my Endeavours to confirm them in it.

Your Ladyship would do well, said Miss *Glanville*, to persuade People, that Miss *Groves*, at fifteen, did not want to run away with her Writing-master.

As I am persuaded myself, said *Arabella*, that Writing-master was some noble Stranger in Disguise, who was passionately in Love with her, I shall not suffer any body, in my Hearing, to propagate such an unlikely Story; but since he was a Person worthy of her Affection, if she had run away with him, her Fault was not without Example, and even Excuse: You know what the fair *Artemisa* did for *Alexander*, Sir, pursued she, turning to Sir *George*: I would fain know your Sentiments upon the Action of that Princess, which some have not scrupled to condemn[3] —

Whoever they are, Madam, said Sir *George*, who condemn the fair *Artemisa* for what she did for *Alexander*, are Miscreants and Slanderers; and though that beautiful Princess has been dead more than two thousand Years, I would draw my Sword in Defence of her Character, against all who should presume, in my Presence, to cast any Censures upon it.

Since you are so courageous, said Miss *Glanville*, laughing excessively at this Sally, which, she thought, was to ridicule her Cousin; it is to be hoped, you will defend a living Lady's Character, who may thank you for it; and make the World believe, that her Correspondence with Mr. *L——* was intirely innocent; and that she never had any Design to run away with her Writing-master.

Are you resolved, Cousin, said Lady *Bella*, to persist in that ridiculous Mistake, and take a Nobleman for a Writing-master only because his Love put him upon such a Stratagem to obtain his Mistress?

Indeed, Lady *Bella*, said Miss *Glanville*, smileing, you may as well persuade me, the Moon is made of a Cream Cheese, as that any Nobleman turned himself into a Writing-master, to obtain Miss *Groves* —

Is it possible, Miss, said *Arabella*, that you can offer such an Affront to my Understanding, as to suppose, I would argue upon such a ridiculous System; and compare the second glorious Luminary of the Heavens to so unworthy a Resemblance? I have taken some Pains to contemplate the heavenly Bodies; and, by Reading and Observation, am able to comprehend some Part of their Excellence: Therefore it is not probable, I should descend to such trivial Comparisons; and liken a planet, which, haply, is not much less than our Earth, to a thing so inconsiderable, as that you name —

Pardon me, dear Cousin, interrupted Miss *Glanville*, laughing louder than before, if I divert myself a little with the Extravagance of your Notions. Really, I think, you have no Reason to be angry, if I supposed you might make a Comparison between the Moon and a Cream Cheese; since you say, that same Moon, which don't appear broader than your Gardener's Face, is not much less than the whole World: Why, certainly, I have more Reason to trust my own Eyes, than such whimsical Notions as these.

Arabella, unwilling to expose her Cousin's Ignorance, by a longer Dispute upon this Subject, begged her to let it drop for the present; and, turning to Sir *George*, I am very glad, said she, that having always had some Inclination to excuse, and even defend, the Flight of *Artemisa* with *Alexander*, my Opinion is warranted by that of a Person so generous as yourself: Indeed, when we consider, that this Princess forsook her Brother's Dominions, and fled away with a Lover whom she did not hate; questionless, her Enemies accuse her, with some Appearance of Reason, of too great Imbecility.

But, Madam, replied Sir *George*, her Enemies will not take the Pains to examine her Reasons for this Conduct —

True, Sir, resumed *Arabella*; for she was in Danger of seeing a Prince, who loved her, put to a cruel and infamous Death upon a public Scaffold; and she did not resolve to fly with him, till all her Tears and Prayers were found ineffectual to move the King her Brother to Mercy.

Tho', replied Sir *George*, I am extremely angry with the indiscreet *Cepio*, who discovered *Alexander* to the *Armenian* King; yet what does your Ladyship think of that gallant Action of his, when he saw him upon the Scaffold, and the Executioner ready to cut off his Head? How brave it was of him, to pass undauntedly thro' the prodigious Number of Guards that environed the Scaffold; and, with his drawn Sword, run the Executioner through the Body, in the Sight of them all! Then giving the Prince another Sword, engage more than Two thousand Men in his Defence!

Questionless, replied *Arabella*, it was a glorious Action; and when I think, how the King of *Armenia* was enraged to see such a Multitude of Soldiers fly from the Swords of two Men, I cannot chuse but divert myself with the Consternation he was in: Yet that was nothing to the horrible Despair, which tormented him afterwards, when he found, that *Alexander*, after being again taken and imprisoned, had broken his Chains, and carried away with him the Princess *Artemisa* his Sister.

CHAPTER II

In which a very pleasing Conversation is left unfinished.

As *Arabella* was in this Part of her Discourse, a Servant came to inform her, that Sir *Charles Glanville* was just alighted. Upon which, Miss *Glanville* flew to receive her Father; and *Arabella*, walking a little slower after her, gave Sir *George* an Opportunity of holding a little longer Conversation with her.

I dare believe, Madam, said he, when you read the Story of

the unfortunate *Alexander*, your fair Eyes did not refuse to shed some Tears at the barbarous and shameful Death he was going to suffer: Yet I assure you, melancholy as his Situation was, it was also very glorious for him, since he had the sublime Satisfaction of dying for the Person he adored; and had the ravishing Pleasure to know, that his Fate would draw Tears from that lovely Princess, for whom he sacrificed his Life: Such a Condition, Madam, ought to be envied rather than pitied; for, next to the Happiness of possessing the Person one adores, certainly the Glory of dying for her is most to be coveted.

Arabella, pleasingly surprized to hear Language so conformable to her own Ideas, looked for a Moment upon the Baronet, with a most inchanting Complacency in her Eyes —

It must be confessed, Sir, says she, that you speak very rationally upon these Matters; and by the Tenderness and Generosity of your Sentiments, you give me cause to believe, that your Heart is prepossessed with some Object worthy of inspiring them.

Sir *George* seeming as if he struggled to suppress a Sigh; You are in the right, Madam, said he, to suppose, that if my Heart be prepossessed with any Object, it is with one, who is capable of inspiring a very sublime Passion; and I assure you, if ever it submits to any Fetters, they shall be imposed on me by the fairest Person in the World —

Since Love is not voluntary, replied *Arabella*, smiling, it may happen, that your Heart may be surprised by a meaner Beauty, than such a one as you describe: However, as a Lover has always an extraordinary Partiality for the beloved Object, 'tis probable, what you say may come to pass; and you may be in Love with the fairest Person in the World, in your own Opinion.

They were now so near the House, that Sir *George* could reply no other ways, than by a very passionate Glance, which *Arabella* did not observe, being in haste to pay her Respects to her Uncle, whom she met just going to Mr. *Glanville*. Her Looks were directed to him. Sir *Charles* saluting her with great Affection, they all went into Mr. *Glanville*'s Chamber, who received his Father with the utmost Respect and Tenderness; extremely regretting the Trouble he had been at in taking a

Journey to the Castle upon his Account; and gently blaming his Sister for her Precipitancy in alarming him so soon.

Sir *Charles*, extremely overjoyed to find him so well recovered, would not allow him to blame Miss *Glanville* for what she had done; but, addressing himself to his Niece, he thanked her for the Care she had taken of Mr. *Glanville*, in very obliging Terms.

Arabella could not help blushing at her Uncle's Compliment, supposing he thanked her for having restored her Cousin to his Health.

I assure you, Sir, said she, Mr. *Glanville* is less obliged to my Commands, than to the Goodness of his Constitution, for his Recovery; and herein he was not so obedient, as many Persons I could name to him.

Mr. *Glanville*, willing to prevent the Company's Observation upon this Speech, began to acquaint his Father with the Rise and Progress of his Distemper: But though the old Gentleman listened with great Attention to his Son, while he was speaking; yet not having lost a Word of what *Arabella* had said, as soon as he was done, he turned to his Niece, and asked her, how she could be so unjust, to accuse his Son of Disobedience, because he did not recover, when she commanded him? Why, Madam, added he, you want to carry your Power farther than ever any Beauty did before you; since you pretend to make People sick and well, whenever you please.

Really, Sir, replied *Arabella*, I pretend to no more Power, than what I presume all others of my Sex have upon the like Occasions; and since nothing is more common, than for a Gentleman, though ever so sick, to recover in Obedience to the Commands of that Person, who has an absolute Power over his Life, I conceive, I have a Right to think myself injured, if Mr. *Glanville*, contrary to mine, had thought proper to die —

Since, said the old Gentleman, smiling, my Son has so well obeyed your Commands in recovering his Health, I shall tremble, lest, in Obedience to a contrary Command of yours, he should die, and deprive me of an Heir; a Misfortune, which, if it should happen, I should place to your Account.

I assure you, Sir, said *Arabella*, very gravely, I have too great an Esteem for Mr. *Glanville*, to condemn him to so severe a Punishment as Death for light Offences: And since it is not very probable, that he will ever commit such Crimes against me, as can be only expiated by his Death; such as Infidelity, Disobedience, and the like; you have no Reason to fear such a Misfortune by my Means —

Alas! replied Sir *George*, you Beauties make very nice Distinctions in these Cases; and think, if you do not directly command your Lovers to die, you are no-ways accountable for their Death: And when a Lover, as it often happens, dies through Despair of ever being able to make himself beloved; or, being doomed to Banishment or Silence, falls into a Fever, from which nothing but Kindness can recover him; and, that being denied, he patiently expires; I say, when these things happen, as they certainly do every Day; how can you hold yourselves guiltless of their Deaths, which are apparently occasioned, either by your Scorn or Insensibility?

Sir *Charles* and Miss *Glanville* were extremely diverted at this Speech of Sir *George*'s; and Mr. *Glanville*, though he would have wished he had been rallying any other Person's Follies than his Cousin's, yet could not help smiling at the solemn Accent, in which he delivered himself —

Arabella, mightily pleased with his Manner of talking, was resolved to furnish him with more Occasions of diverting the Company at her Expence.

I see, answered she, you are one of those Persons, who call a just Decorum, which all Ladies, who love Glory as they ought to do, are obliged to preserve, by the Name of Severity: But pray, what would you have a Lady do, whom an importunate Lover presumes to declare his Passion to? You know it is not permitted us to listen to such Discourses; and you know also, whoever is guilty of such an Offence, merits a most rigorous Punishment: Moreover, you find, that when a Sentence of Banishment or Silence is pronounced upon them, these unhappy Criminals are so conscious of the Justice of their Doom, that they never murmur against their Judge who condemns them; and therefore, whatever are their Fates, in Consequence of that Anger they have incurred, the Ladies, thus offended, ought not to be charged with it, as any cruel Exertion of their Power.

Such Eloquence as yours, Madam, replied Sir *George*, might defend Things yet more unjustifiable: However, you must give me leave, as being interested in the Safety of my Sex, still to be of Opinion, that no Man ought to be hated, because he adores a beautiful Object, and consecrates all his Moments to her Service.

Questionless, resumed *Arabella*, he will not be hated, while, out of the Respect and Reverence he bears her, he carefully conceals his Passion from her Knowlege; but as soon as ever he breaks through the Bounds, which that Respect prescribes him, and lets her understand his true Sentiments, he has Reason to expect a most rigorous Sentence, since he certainly, by that Presumption, has greatly deserved it.

If the Ladies, replied Sir *George*, were more equitable, and would make some Distinction between those who really love them in a passionate and respectful Silence, and others who do not feel the Power of their Charms, they might spare themselves the Trouble of hearing what so mortally offends them: But when a Lady sees a Man every Day, who by his Looks, Sighs, and Sollicitude to please her, by his numberless Services, and constant Attendance of her, makes it evident, that his Soul is possessed with a violent Passion for her; I say, when a Lady sees, and yet will not see, all this, and persists in using a passionate Adorer with all the Indifference due to a Man wholly insensible of the Power of her Charms; what must he do in such a mortifying Situation, but make known his Torments to her that occasions them, in order to prevail upon her to have some Sense of what he does and feels hourly for her sake?

But since he gains nothing by the Discovery of his Passion, resumed *Arabella*; but, on the contrary, loses the Advantages he was before possessed of, which were very great, since he might see and discourse with his Mistress every Day; and, haply, have the Honour to do her a great many petty Services, and receive some of her Commands; all these Advantages he loses, when he declares he loves: And, truly, I think, a Man who is so unwise as to hazard a certain Happiness for a very improbable Hope, deserves to be punished, as well for his Folly as Presumption; and, upon both these Accounts, Banishment is not too rigorous a Sentence.

CHAPTER III

Definition of Love and Beauty — The necessary Qualities of a Hero and Heroine.

Though, replied Mr. *Glanville*, you are very severe in the Treatment you think it necessary our Sex should receive from yours; yet I wish some of our Town Beauties were, if not altogether of your Opinion, yet sufficiently so, as to make it not a Slavery for a Man to be in their Company; for unless one talks of Love to these fair Coquets the whole time one is with them, they are quite displeased, and look upon a Man who can think any thing, but themselves, worthy his Thoughts or Observation, with the utmost Contempt. How often have you and I, Sir *George*, pursued he, pitied the Condition of the few Men of Sense, who are sometimes among the Crowd of Beaux, who attend the Two celebrated Beauties[4] to all Places of polite Diversion in Town? For those Ladies think it a mortal Injury done to their Charms, if the Men about them have Eyes or Ears for any Object but their Faces, or any Sound but that of their Voices: So that the Connoisseurs in Music, who attend them to *Ranelagh*,[5] must stop their Ears, like *Ulysses*, when the *Siren Frasi* sings;[6] and the Wits, who gallant them to the Side-box,[7] must lay a much greater Constraint upon themselves, in order to resist the Soul-moving *Garrick*;[8] and appear insensible, while he is upon the Stage.

Upon my Soul, added Sir *George* (forgetting the Character he assumed) when I have seen some Persons of my Acquaintance talking to the eldest of these Ladies, while one of *Congreve*'s Comedies[9] has been acting; his Face quite turned from the Stage, and hers overspread with an eternal Smile; her fine Eyes sometimes lifted up in a beautiful Surprize, and a little enchanting Giggle half-hid with her Fan; in spite of their Inattention, I have been ready to imagine, he was entertaining her with Remarks upon the Play, which she was judicious enough to understand; and yet I have afterwards been informed by himself, that nothing was less in their Thoughts; and all that Variety in her Face, and that extreme seeming Earnestness in his Discourse, was occasioned by the most trifling Subjects imaginable: He perhaps had been telling her, how the Sight of her Squirrel, which peeped out of her Pocket, surprised some Ladies she was visiting; and what they said upon her Fondness for it, when she was gone; blaming them at the same time for their Want of Delicacy, in not knowing how to set a right Value upon such pleasing Animals: Hence proceeded her Smiles, the lifting up of her Eyes, the half-stifled Laugh, and all the pretty Gestures that appeared so wonderfully charming to all those who did not hear their Discourse: And it is upon such Trifles as these, or else on the inexhaustible Subject of their Charms, that all who are ambitious of being near these Miracles, are under a Necessity of talking.

And pray, interrupted *Arabella*, What Subjects afford Matter for a more pleasing Variety of Conversation, than those of Beauty and Love? Can we speak of any Object so capable of delighting as Beauty, or of any Passion of the Mind more sublime and pleasing than Love?

With Submission, Madam, said *Glanville*, I conceive, all that can be said, either of Beauty, or of Love, may be comprised in a very few Words: All who have Eyes, and behold true Beauty, will be ready to confess it is a very pleasing Object; and all that can be said of it, may be said in a very few Words; for when we have run over the Catalogue of Charms, and mentioned fine Eyes, fine Hair, delicate Complexion, regular Features, and an elegant Shape, we can only add a few Epithets more, such as Lovely, Dangerous, Inchanting, Irresistible, and the like; and every thing that can be said of Beauty is exhausted. And so likewise it is with Love; we know that Admiration precedes it, that Beauty kindles it, Hope keeps it alive, and Despair puts an End to it; and that Subject may be as soon discussed as the other, by the judicious Use of proper Words; such as Wounds, Darts, Fires, Languishings, Dyings, Torture, Rack, Jealousy, and a few more of no Signification, but upon this Subject.

Certainly, Sir, said *Arabella*, you have not well considered what you say, since you maintain, that Love and Beauty are Subjects easily and quickly discussed: Take the Pains, I beseech you, to reflect a little upon those numerous and long Conversations,[10] which these Subjects have given Rise to in *Clelia*, and the *Grand Cyrus*, where the most illustrious and greatest Personages in the World manage the Disputes; and the agreeable Diversity of their Sentiments on those Heads affords a most pleasing and rational Entertainment: You will there find, that the greatest Conquerors, and Heroes of invincible Valour, reason with the most exact and scrupulous Nicety upon Love and Beauty; the Superiority of fair and brown Hair controverted by Warriors, with as much Eagerness as they dispute for Victory in the Field; and the different Effects of that Passion upon different Hearts defined with the utmost Accuracy and Eloquence.

I must own, interrupted Sir *Charles*, I should have but a mean Opinion of those Warriors, as you call them, who could busy themselves in talking of such Trifles; and be apt to imagine such insignificant Fellows, who could wrangle about the Colour of their Mistresses Hair, would be the first to turn their Backs upon the Enemy in Battle.

Is it possible, Sir, resumed *Arabella*, glowing with Indignation, that you can entertain such unworthy Thoughts of Heroes, who merit the Admiration and Praise of all Ages for their inestimable Valour, whom the Spears of a whole Army opposed to each of their single Swords would not oblige to fly? What think you, Sir, pursued she, looking at Sir *George*, of the injurious Words my Uncle has uttered against those heroic Princes, whose Courage, I believe, you are as well acquainted with as myself? The great *Oroondates*, the invincible *Artaban*, the valiant and fortunate *Artamenes*, the irresistible *Juba*, the incomparable *Cleomedon*, and an hundred other Heroes I could name, are all injured by this unjust Assertion of my Uncle; since certainly they were not more famous for their noble and wonderful Actions in War, than for the Sublimity and Constancy of their Affections in Love.

Some of these Heroes you have named, replied Sir *George*,

had the Misfortune, even in their Lives, to be very cruelly vilified: The great *Oroondates* was a long time accused of Treachery to his Divine Princess;[11] the valiant and unfortunate *Artamenes* was suspected of Inconstancy;[12] and the irresistible *Juba* reproached with Infidelity and Baseness, by both his Mistress and Friend.[13]

I never knew you was so well acquainted with these Persons, interrupted Mr. *Glanville*; and I fansy it is but very lately that you have given yourself the Trouble to read Romances.

I am not of your Opinion, said *Arabella*. Sir *George*, questionless, has appropriated great Part of his Time to the Perusal of those Books, so capable of improving him in all useful Knowlege; the Sublimity of Love, and the Quintessence of Valour; which two Qualities, if possessed in a superlative Degree, form a true and perfect Hero, as the Perfection of Beauty, Wit, and Virtue, make a Heroine worthy to be served by such an illustrious Personage; and I dare say, Sir *George* has profited so much by the great Examples of Fidelity and Courage he has placed before his Eyes, that no Consideration whatever could make him for one Moment fail in his Constancy to the Divine Beauty he adores; and, inspired by her Charms, he would scorn to turn his Back, as my Uncle phrases it, upon an Army of an hundred thousand Men.

I am extremely obliged to you, Madam, said Sir *George*, bowing his Head to the Ground, to hide a Smile he could not possibly restrain, for the good Opinion you have of my Courage and Fidelity.

As for Sir *George*'s Courage, Cousin, said Mr. *Glanville* laughing, I never disputed it: And though it be indeed a very extraordinary Exertion of it, to fight singly against an Army of an hundred thousand Men; yet since you are pleased to think it probable, I am as willing to believe Sir *George* may do it as any other Man; but, as for his Fidelity in Matters of Love, I greatly suspect it, since he has been charged with some very flagrant Crimes of that Nature.

How, Sir! resumed *Arabella*, Have you ever been faithless then? and, after having sworn, haply, to devote your whole Life to the Service of some Beauty, have you ever violated your Oaths, and been base enough to forsake her?

I have too much Complaisance, Madam, said Sir *George*, to contradict Mr. *Glanville*, who has been pleased positively to assert, that I have been faithless, as you most unkindly phrase it.

Nay, Sir, replied *Arabella*, this Accusation is not of a Nature to be neglected; and though a King should say it, I conceive, if you are innocent, you have a Right to contradict him, and clear yourself: Do you consider how deeply this Assertion wounds your Honour and Happiness for the future? What Lady, think you, will receive your Services, loaded as you are with the terrible Imputation of Inconstancy?

Oh! as for that, Madam, said Miss *Glanville*, I believe no Lady will think the worse of Sir *George* for being faithless: For my Part, I declare nothing pleases me so much, as gaining a Lover from another Lady; which is a greater Compliment to one's Beauty, than the Addresses of a Man that never was in Love before —

You may remember, Cousin, replied *Arabella*, that I said once before, your Spirit and Humour resembled a certain great Princess very much; and I repeat it again, never was there a greater Conformity in Tempers and Inclinations.[14]

My Daughter, said Sir *Charles*, is mightily obliged to you, Lady *Bella*, for comparing her to a great Princess: Undoubtedly you mean it as a Compliment.

If you think, said *Arabella*, that barely comparing her to a Princess be a Compliment, I must take the Liberty to differ from you: My Cousin is not so many Degrees below a Princess, as that such a Comparison should be thought extraordinary; for if her Ancestors did not wear a Crown, they might, haply, have deserved it; and her Beauty may one Day procure her a Servant, whose Sword, like that of the great *Artaban*, may win her a Sceptre; who, with a noble Confidence, told his Princess, when the Want of a Crown was objected to him, I wear a Sword, Madam, that can perform things more difficult than what you require; and if a Crown be all that I want to make me worthy of you, tell me what Kingdom in the World you choose to reign in, and I will lay it at your Feet.[15]

That was a Promise, replied Sir *George*, fit only for the great

Artaban to make: But, Madam, if you will permit me to make any Comparison between that renowned Warrior and myself, I would venture to tell you, that even the great *Artaban* was not exempted from the Character of Inconstancy any more than myself, since, as you certainly know, he was in Love with Three great Princesses successively.[16]

I grant you, replied *Arabella*, that *Artaban* did wear the Chains of Three Princesses successively: But it must also be remembered in his Justification, that the Two First of these Beauties refused his Adorations, and treated him with Contempt, because he was not a Prince: Therefore, recovering his Liberty, by those Disdains they cast on him, he preserved that illustrious Heart from Despair, to tender it with more passionate Fidelity to the Divine Princess of the *Parthians*; who, though greatly their Superior in Quality and Beauty, did permit him to love her. However, I must confess, I find something like Levity in the Facility he found in breaking his Fetters so often; and when I consider, that among all those great Heroes, whose Histories I have read, none but himself ever bore without dying, the Cruelties he experienced from those Princesses, I am sometimes tempted to accuse him myself of Inconstancy: But indeed every thing we read of that Prodigy of Valour is wholly miraculous; and since the Performance of Impossibilities was reserved for him, I conclude this Miracle also, among many others, was possible to him, whom nothing was ever able to resist upon Earth. However, pursued she, rising, I shall not absolutely condemn you, till I have heard your Adventures from your own Mouth, at a convenient Time, when I shall be able to judge how far you merit the odious Appellation of Inconstancy.

Saying this, she saluted her Uncle, who had for some time been conversing in a low Voice with his Son, with a Grace wholly charming, and retired to her Apartment. Miss *Glanville* following her a few Moments after (the Compliment, extravagant as it was, which she had paid her, having procured her some Good-will from the vain and interested Miss *Glanville*,) they conversed together with a great deal of good Humour till Dinner-time, which, because Mr. *Glanville* was not absolutely recovered, was served in his Chamber.

CHAPTER IV

In which our Heroine is engaged in a new Adventure.

As Mr. *Glanville* took a great deal of Pains to turn the Discourse upon Subjects, on which the charming *Arabella* could expatiate, without any Mixture of that Absurdity, which mingled itself in a great many others; the rest of that Day and several others, were passed very agreeably: At the End of which, Mr. *Glanville* being perfectly recovered, and able to go abroad; the Baronet proposed to take the Diversion of Hunting; which *Arabella*, who was used to it, consented to partake of; but being informed, that Miss *Glanville* could not ride, and chose to stay at Home, she would have kept her Company, had not Sir *Charles* insisted upon the contrary.

As Sir *George*, and some other Gentlemen, had invited themselves to be of the Party; *Arabella*, on her coming down to mount her Horse, found a great many young Gallants, ready to offer her their Assistance upon this Occasion: Accepting therefore, with great Politeness, this Help from a Stranger, who was nearest her, she mounted her Horse, giving Occasion to every one that was present, to admire the Grace with which she sat and managed him. Her Shape being as perfect as any Shape could possibly be, her Riding-Habit discovered all its Beauties: Her Hat, and the white Feather waving over Part of her fine black Hair, gave a peculiar Charm to her lovely Face: And she appeared with so many Advantages in this Dress and Posture, that Mr. *Glanville*, forgetting all her Absurdities, was wholly lost in the Contemplation of so many Charms, as her whole Person was adorned with.[17]

Sir *George*, though he really admired *Arabella*, was not so passionately in Love as Mr. *Glanville*; and, being a keen Sportsman, eagerly pursued the Game, with the rest of the Hunters; but Mr. *Glanville* minded nothing but his Cousin, and kept close by her.

After having rode a long time, *Arabella*, conceiving it a Piece of Cruelty, not to give her Lover an Opportunity of talking to her, as, by his extreme Solicitude, he seemed ardently to desire, coming to a delightful Valley, she stopped; and told Mr. *Glanville*, that, being weary of the Chace, she should alight, and repose herself a little under the Shade of those Trees.

Mr. *Glanville*, extremely pleased at this Proposition, dismounted; and, having helped her to alight, seated himself by her on the Grass.

Arabella, expecting he would begin to talk to her of his Passion, could not help blushing at the Thoughts of having given him such an Opportunity; and Mr. *Glanville*, endeavouring to accommodate himself to her Ideas of a Lover, expressed himself in Terms extravagant enough to have made a reasonable Woman think he was making a Jest of her: All which, however, *Arabella* was extremely pleased with; and she observed such a just Decorum in her Answers, that, as the Writers of Romance phrase it, if she did not give him any absolute Hopes of being beloved, yet she said enough to make him conclude she did not hate him.

They had conversed in this manner near a Quarter of an Hour, when *Arabella*, perceiving a Man at a little Distance, walking very composedly, shrieked out aloud; and, rising with the utmost Precipitation, flew from Mr. *Glanville*, and went to untie her Horse; while his Astonishment being so great at her Behaviour, that he could not, for a Moment or two, ask her the Cause of her Fear —

Do you not see, said she, out of Breath with the Violence of her Apprehensions, the Person who is coming towards us? It is the same, who, some Months ago, attempted to carry me away, when I was riding out with only Two Attendants: I escaped, for that time, the Danger that threatened me; but, questionless, he comes now to renew his Attempts: Therefore can you wonder at my Fear?

If it should be as you say, Madam, interrupted *Glanville*, What Reason have you to fear? Do you not think I am able to defend you?

Ah! without doubt, you are able to defend me, answered she; and though, if you offer to resist the Violence he comes to use against me, he will, haply, call Two or Three Dozen armed

Men to his Assistance, who are, I suppose, concealed here-
abouts, yet I am not apprehensive, that you will be worsted by
them: But as it happened to the brave *Juba*, and *Cleomedon*,
while they were fighting with some hundred Men, who wanted
to carry away their Princesses before their Faces; and were
giving Death at every Blow, in order to preserve them; the
Commander of these Ravishers, seeing the Two Princesses sitting, as I was, under a Tree, ordered them to be seized by Two
of his Men, and carried away, while the Two Princes were
losing best Part of their Blood in their Defence;[18] therefore, to
prevent such an Accident happening, while you are fighting for
my Rescue, I think it will be the safest Way for me to get on
Horseback, that I may be in a Condition to escape; and that
you may not employ your Valour to no Purpose.

Saying this, having, with Mr. *Glanville*'s Assistance, loosed
her Horse from the Tree, he helped her to mount, and then
remounted his own.

Your Antagonist, said *Arabella*, is on Foot; and therefore,
though I prize your Life extremely, yet I cannot dispense with
myself from telling you, that 'tis against the Laws of Knight-
hood to take any Advantage of that kind over your Enemy; nor
will I permit your Concern for my Safety to make you forget
what you owe to your own Reputation.

Mr. *Glanville*, fretting excessively at her Folly, begged her
not to make herself uneasy about things that were never likely
to happen.

The Gentleman yonder, added he, seems to have no Designs
to make any Attempt against you: If he should, I shall know
how to deal with him: But, since he neither offers to assault
me, nor affront you, I think we ought not to give him any
Reason to imagine we suspect him, by gazing on him thus; and
letting him understand by your Manner, that he is the Subject
of our Conversation. If you please, Madam, we will endeavour
to join our Company.

Arabella, while he was speaking, kept her Eyes fixed upon his
Face, with Looks which expressed her Thoughts were labouring
upon some very important Point: And, after a Pause of some
Moments, Is it possible, said she, with a Tone of extreme

Surprize, that I should be so mistaken in you? Do you really want Courage enough to defend me against that Ravisher?

Oh Heavens! Madam, interrupted *Glanville*, try not my Temper thus: Courage enough to defend you! 'Sdeath! you will make me mad! Who, in the Name of Wonder, is going to molest you?

He whom you see there, replied *Arabella*, pointing to him with her Finger: For know, cold and insensible as thou art to the Danger which threatens me, yonder Knight is thy Rival, and a Rival, haply, who deserves my Esteem better than thou dost; since, if he has Courage enough to get me by Violence into his Power, that same Courage would make him defend me against any Injuries I might be offered from another: And since nothing is so contemptible in the Eyes of a Woman, as a Lover who wants Spirit to die in her Defence; know, I can sooner pardon him, whom thou would cowardly fly from, for the Violence which he meditates against me, than thyself for the Pusillanimity thou hast betrayed in my Sight.

With these Words, she galloped away from her astonished Lover; who, not daring to follow her, for fear of increasing her Suspicions of his Cowardice, flung himself off his Horse in a violent Rage; and, forgetting that the Stranger was observing, and now within Hearing, he fell a cursing and exclaiming against the Books, that had turned his Cousin's Brain; and railing at his own ill Fate, that condemned him to the Punishment of loving her. Mr. *Hervey* (for it really was he, whom an Affair of Consequence had brought again into the Country) hearing some of Mr. *Glanville*'s last Words, and observing the Gestures he used, concluded he had been treated like himself by *Arabella*, Whom he knew again at a Distance. Therefore coming up to Mr. *Glanville*, laughing —

Though I have not the Honour of knowing you, Sir, said he, I must beg the Favour you will inform me, if you are not disturbed at the ridiculous Folly of the Lady I saw with you just now? She is the most fantastical Creature that ever lived, and, in my Opinion, fit for a Mad-house: Pray, are you acquainted with her?

Mr. *Glanville*, being in a very ill Humour, could not brook the Freedom of this Language against his Cousin, whose Follies he could not bear any one should rail at but himself; and, being provoked at his Sneers, and the Interruption he had given to their Conversation, he looked upon him with a disdainful Frown, and told him in an haughty Tone, That he was very impertinent to speak of a Lady of her Quality and Merit so rudely.

Oh! Sir, I beg your Pardon, replied Mr. *Hervey*, laughing more than before; What, I suppose you are the Champion of this fair Lady! But, I assure myself, if you intend to quarrel with every one that will laugh at her, you will have more Business upon your Hands than you can well manage.

Mr. *Glanville*, transported with Rage at this Insolence, hit him such a Blow with the But-End of his Whip, that it stunned him for a Moment; but recovering himself, he drew his Sword, and, mad with the Affront he had received, made a Push at *Glanville*; who, avoiding it with great Dexterity, had recourse to his Hanger for his Defence.

Arabella, in the mean time, who had not rid far, concealing herself behind some Trees, saw all the Actions of her Lover, and intended Ravisher; and, being possessed with an Opinion of her Cousin's Cowardice, was extremely rejoiced to see him fall upon his Enemy first, and that with so much Fury, that she had no longer any Reason to doubt his Courage: Her Suspicions, therefore, being removed, her Tenderness for him returned; and when she saw them engaged with their Swords (for, at that Distance, she did not plainly perceive the Difference of their Weapons), her Apprehensions for her Cousin were so strong, that, though she did not doubt his Valour, she could not bear to see him expose his Life for her: And, without making any Reflections upon the Singularity of her Design, she was going to ride up to them, and endeavour to part them; when she saw several Men come towards them, whom she took to be the Assistants of her Ravisher, though they were, in reality, Haymakers; who, at a Distance, having seen the Beginning of their Quarrel, had hastened to part them.

Terrified, therefore, at this Reinforcement, which she thought would expose her Cousin to great Danger, she galloped, with all Speed, after the Hunters, being directed by the Sound of the Horn. Her Anxiety for her Cousin made her regardless of her own Danger, so that she rode with a surprising Swiftness; and, overtaking the Company, she would have spoken, to tell them of her Cousin's Situation; when her Spirits failing her, she could only make a Sign with her Hand, and sunk down in a Swoon, in the Arms of Sir *George*, who eagerly galloped up to her; and, supporting her as well as he was able till some others came to her Relief, they took her off her Horse, and placed her upon the Ground; when, by the Help of some Water they brought from a Spring near them, in a little time she came to herself.

Sir *Charles*, who, seeing her come up to them without his Son, and by her fainting, concluded some Misfortune had happened to him, the Moment she opened her Eyes, asked her eagerly, Where he was?

Your Son, said *Arabella*, sighing, with a Valour equal to that of the brave *Cleomedon*, is this Moment fighting in my Defence against a Croud of Enemies; and is, haply, shedding the last Drop of his Blood in my Quarrel.

Shedding the last Drop of his Blood, *haply!* repeated Sir *Charles*, excessively grieved; and, not a little enraged at *Arabella*, supposing she had introduced him into some Quarrel, It may be *happy* for you, Madam; but I am sure it will make me very miserable, if my Son comes to any Harm.

If it be the Will of Heaven he should fall in this Combat, resumed *Arabella*, he can never have a more glorious Destiny: And as that Consideration will, doubtless, sweeten his last Moments, so it ought to be your Consolation: However, I beg you'll lose no time, but haste to his Assistance; for since he has a considerable Number of Enemies to deal with, 'tis not improbable but he may be overpowered at last.

Where did you leave my Son, Madam? cried Sir *Charles*, eagerly.

He is not far off, replied *Arabella*: And you will, doubtless, be directed to the Place, by the Sight of the Blood of his Enemies, which he has spilt. Go that way, pursued she, pointing with her Finger towards the Place where she had left her Cousin: There

you will meet with him, amidst a Croud of Foes, which he is
sacrificing to my Safety, and his just Resentment.

Sir *Charles*, not knowing what to think, galloped away,
followed by most Part of the Company; Sir *George* telling Lady
Bella, that he would stay to defend her against any Attempts that
might be made on her Liberty, by any of her Ravisher's Servants,
who were, probably, straggling about. *Arabella*, however, being
perfectly recovered, insisted upon following her Uncle.

There is no Question, said she, but Mr. *Glanville* is victorious: I am only apprehensive for the dangerous Wounds he may
have received in the Combat, which will require all our Care
and Assistance.

Sir *George*, who wanted to engross her Company a little to
himself, in vain represented to her, that, amidst the Horrors of
a Fight so bloody as that must certainly be, in which Mr.
Glanville and his Friends would be now engaged, it would be
dangerous for her to venture her Person: Yet she would not be
persuaded; but, having mounted her Horse, with his Assistance,
she rode as fast as she was able after the rest of the Company.

CHAPTER V

Being a Chapter of Mistakes.

Sir *Charles*, who, by this Time, had got to the Place she directed
him to, but saw no Appearance of fighting, and only a few
Haymakers in Discourse together, inquired, If there had been
any Quarrel between two Gentlemen in that Place?

One of them, at this Question, advancing, told Sir *Charles*,
that two Gentlemen had quarrelled there, and were fighting
with Swords; but that they had parted them; and that one of
them, having an Horse tied to a Tree, mounted him, and rode
away: That the other, they believed, was not far off; and that
there had been no Bloodshed, they having come time enough
to prevent it.

Sir *Charles* was extremely satisfied with this Account; and, giving the Haymakers some Money for the good Office they did in parting the two Combatants, rode up to meet Lady *Bella*; and informed her, that his Son was safe.

I cannot imagine he is safe, replied she, when I see some of his Enemies (pointing to the Haymakers) still alive: It is not customary, in those Cases, to suffer any to escape: And, questionless, my Cousin is either dead, or a Prisoner, since all his Adversaries are not vanquished.

Why, you dream, Madam, replied Sir *Charles*: Those Fellows yonder are Haymakers: What should make them Enemies to my Son? They were lucky enough to come in time to prevent him and another Gentleman from doing each other a Mischief. I cannot imagine for what Reason my Son quarrelled with that Person they speak of: Perhaps you can inform me.

Certainly, Sir, said *Arabella*, I can inform you, since I was the Cause of their Quarrel. The Story is too long to tell you now; and, besides, it is so connected with the other Accidents of my Life, that 'tis necessary you should be accquainted with my whole History, in order to comprehend it: But, if those Persons are what you say, and did really part my Cousin and his Antagonist, truly I believe they have done him a very ill Office: For, I am persuaded, my Cousin will never be at Rest, till, by his Rival's Death, he has freed himself from one, capable of the most daring Enterprizes to get me into his Power: And, since I cannot be in Security while he lives, and persists in the Resolution he has taken to persecute me, it had been better if he had suffered all the Effects of my Cousin's Resentment at that time, than to give him the Trouble to hunt him through the World, in order to sacrifice him to the Interest of his Love and Vengeance.

Sir *Charles*, no less astonished than alarmed at this Discovery of his Niece's sanguinary Sentiments, told her, he was sorry to see a Lady so far forget the Gentleness of her Sex, as to encourage and incite Men to such Extremities, upon her Account. And, for the future, added he, I must intreat you, Niece, to spare me the Affliction of seeing my Son exposed to these dangerous Quarrels: For, though his Life is so little regarded by you, yet it is of the utmost Consequence to me.

Arabella, who found Matter sufficient in the Beginning of this Speech, to be offended with her Uncle, yet, mistaking the latter Part of it for a pathetic Complaint of her Cruelty, replied very gravely, That her Cousin's Safety was not so indifferent to her as he imagined: And that she did not hate him so much, but that his Death would affect her very sensibly.

Arabella, in speaking these Words, blushed with Shame, as thinking they were rather too tender: And Sir *Charles*, who coloured likewise, from a very different Motive, was opening his Mouth, to tell her, that he did not think his Son was much obliged to her for not hating him; when *Arabella*, supposing he designed to press her to a further Explanation of the favourable Sentiments she felt for Mr. *Glanville*, stopped him with Precipitation: Press me no more, said she, upon this Subject: And, as I have already spoken too much, haply, before so many Witnesses, seek not to enhance my Confusion, by prolonging a Discourse that at present must needs be disagreeable to me.

I shall readily agree with you, Madam, replied Sir *Charles*, that you have spoken too much: And, if I had thought you capable of speaking in the manner you have done, I would have been more cautious in giving you an Occasion for it.

I should imagine, Sir, said *Arabella*, blushing with Anger, as she before did with Shame, that you would be the last Person in the World who could think I had spoken too much upon this Occasion: And, since you are pleased to tell me so, I think it fit to let you know, that I have not, in my Opinion, transgressed the Laws of Decency and Decorum, in what I have said in my Cousin's Favour: And I can produce many Examples of greater Freedom of Speech, in Princesses, and Ladies of the highest Quality: However, I shall learn such a Lesson of Moderation in this respect, from your Reproof, that I promise you, neither yourself, or Mr. *Glanville*, shall have any Cause, for the future, to complain of my want of Discretion.

Sir *Charles*, who was very polite and good-natured, was half angry with himself, for having obliged his Niece to such a Submission, as he thought it; and, apologizing for the Rudeness of his Reprehension, assured her, that he was perfectly convinced of her Discretion in all things; and did not doubt but her Conduct would be always agreeable to him.

Arabella, who, from what her Uncle had said, began to entertain Suspicions, that would never have entered any Imagination but hers, looked earnestly upon him for half a Moment, as if she wished to penetrate into the most secret Recesses of his Heart: But, fansying she saw something in his Looks that confirmed her Apprehensions, she removed her Eyes from his Face, and, fastening them on the Ground, remained for some Moments in Confusion. — Sir *Charles*, whom her apparent Disturbance made very uneasy, proposed returning to the Castle; telling Lady *Bella* he expected to find his Son already there.

'Tis more than probable, said she, turning to Sir *George*, that my Cousin is gone in Pursuit of my Ravisher; and the Interruption that has been given to his designed Vengeance, making him more furious than before, 'tis not likely he will return till he has punished his Insolence by that Death he so justly merits.

Mr. *Glanville* is already so happy in your Opinion, said Sir *George*, with a very profound Sigh, that there is no need of his rendering you this small Service, to increase your Esteem: But, if my Prayers are heard, the Punishment of your Ravisher will be reserved for a Person less fortunate, indeed, than Mr. *Glanville*, tho' not less devoted to your Interest, and concerned in your Preservation.

Sir *George* counterfeiting a Look of extreme Confusion and Fear, as he ended these Words;

Arabella, who perfectly comprehended the Meaning they were designed to convey, thought herself obliged to take no Notice of them: And, therefore, without making any Reply to the young Baronet, who ventured slowly to lift his Eyes to her Face, in order to discover if there were any Signs of Anger in it, she told Sir *Charles* she inclined to go home: And Sir *George*, with the rest of the Company, attended them to the Castle; where, as soon as they arrived, they took their Leave.

Sir *George*, notwithstanding *Arabella*'s Care to deprive him of an Opportunity of speaking to her, told her, in a Whisper, having eagerly alighted to help her off her Horse,

I am going, Madam, to find out that insolent Man, who has dared to offer Violence to the fairest Person in the World: And, if I am so happy as to meet with him, he shall either take my Life, or I will put him into a Condition never to commit any more Offences of that Nature.

Saying this, he made a low Bow; and, being desirous to prevent her Answer, remounted his Horse, and went away with the Rest of the Company.

Arabella, who, upon this Occasion, was to be all Confusion, mixed with some little Resentment, discovered so much Emotion in her Looks, while Sir *George* was whispering to her, that her Uncle, as he was handing her into the House, asked her, If she was offended at any thing Sir *George* had said to her?

Arabella, construing this Question as she had done some other things her Uncle had said to her, replied, in a reserved manner, Since my Looks, contrary to my Intention, have betrayed my Thoughts to you, I will not scruple to confess, that I have some Cause to be offended with Sir *George*; and that, in two Instances To-day, he has seemed to forget the Respect he owes me.

Sir *Charles* was fired at this Account: Is it possible, said he, that Sir *George* has had the Assurance to say any thing to offend you, and that before my Face too? This Affront is not to be borne.

I am sorry, replied *Arabella*, eying him heedfully, to see you so much concerned at it.

Don't be uneasy, interrupted Sir *Charles*: There will be no bad Consequences happen from it: But he shall hear of it, added he, raising his Voice with Passion: I'll force him this Night to explain himself.

You must pardon me, Sir, said *Arabella*, more and more confirmed in her Notions, if I tell you, that I am extremely offended at your uncommon Zeal upon this Occasion: And also I must assure you, that a little more Calmness would be less liable to Suspicion.

Miss *Glanville* coming to meet them, Sir *Charles*, who did not take much Notice of what *Arabella* said, eagerly inquired for his Son; and, hearing he was not come home, was apprehensive of his meeting again with the Person he had quarrelled with: But his Fears did not last long; for Mr. *Glanville* came in, having purposely avoided the Company, to hide the Uneasiness Lady *Bella*'s tormenting Folly had given him.

CHAPTER VI

In which the Mistakes are continued.

As soon as Mr. *Glanville* appeared, the two Ladies retired; Miss *Glanville* asking *Arabella* a hundred Questions concerning their Diversion, the Drift of which was, to know how Sir *George* behaved to her: But that fair Lady, whose Thoughts were wholly employed on the strange Accidents which had happened to her that Day, longed to be at Liberty to indulge her Reflections; and, complaining of extreme Weariness, under Pretence of reposing herself till Dinner, got quit of Miss *Glanville*'s Company, which, at that time, she thought very tedious.

As soon as she was left to herself, her Imagination running over all that had happened, she could not help confessing, that few Women ever met with such a Variety of Adventures in one Day: In Danger of being carried off by Violence, by one Lover; delivered by another; Insinuations of Love from a Third, who, she thought, was enamoured of her Cousin; and, what was still more surprising a Discovery, that her Uncle was not insensible of her Charms, but was become the Rival of his own Son.

As extravagant as this Notion was, *Arabella* found Precedents in her Romances of Passions full as strange and unjustifiable; and confirmed herself in that Opinion, by recollecting several Examples of unlawful Love. Why should I not believe, said she, that my Charms can work as powerful Effects as those of *Olympia*, Princess of *Thrace*, whose Brother was passionately enamoured of her?[19]

Did not the Divine *Clelia* inspire *Maherbal* with a violent Passion for her, who, though discovered to be her Brother, did not, nevertheless, cease to adore her?[20] And, to bring an Instance still nearer to my own Case, was not the Uncle of the fair *Alcyone* in Love with her? And did he not endeavour to win her Heart by all the Methods in his Power?[21]

Ah! then, pursued she, let us doubt no more of our Misfortune: And, since our fatal Beauty has raised this impious Flame, let us stifle it with our Rigour, and not allow an ill-timed Pity, or Respect, to encourage a Passion which may, one Day, cast a Blemish upon our Glory.

Arabella, having settled this Point, proceeded to reflect on the Conquest she had made of Sir *George*: She examined his Words over and over, and found them so exactly conformable to the Language of an *Oroondates* or *Orontes*, that she could not choose but be pleased: But, recollecting that it behoved her, like all other Heroines, to be extremely troubled and perplexed at an Insinuation of Love, she began to lament the cruel Necessity of parting with an agreeable Friend; who, if he persisted in making her acquainted with his Thoughts, would expose himself to the Treatment Persons so indiscreet always meet with; nor was she less concerned, lest, if Mr. *Glanville* had not already dispatched her Ravisher, Sir *George*, by wandering in Search of him, and, haply, sacrificing him to his eager Desire of serving her, should, by that means, lay her under an Obligation to him, which, considering him as a Lover, would be a great Mortification.

Sir *George*, however, was gone home to his own House, with no Thoughts of pursuing *Arabella*'s Ravisher: And Mr. *Glanville*, being questioned by his Father concerning his Quarrel, invented some trifling Excuse for it; which not agreeing with the Account the Baronet had received from *Arabella*, he told his Son, that he had concealed the Truth from him; and that there was more in that Affair than he had owned. You quarrelled, added he, upon *Arabella*'s Account; and she did not scruple to affirm it before all the Company.

Mr. *Glanville*, who had vainly flattered himself with an Hope, that his Cousin had not acquainted the Company with her whimsical Apprehensions, was extremely vexed when he found she had exposed herself to their Ridicule, and that it was probable even he had not escaped: But, willing to know from

her own Mouth how far she had carried her Folly, he went up
to her Chamber; and, being immediately admitted, she began
to congratulate him upon the Conquest he had gained, as she
supposed, over his Enemy; and thanked him very solemnly for
the Security he had procured for her.

Mr. *Glanville*, after assuring her, that she was in no Danger
of ever being carried away by that Person whom she feared,
proceeded to inquire into all that had passed between her and
the Company whom she had joined, when she left him; and
Arabella, relating every Particular, gave him the Mortification
to know, that her Folly had been sufficiently exposed: But she
touched upon her Fears for him with so much Delicacy, and
mentioned her Fainting in such a manner, as insinuated a much
greater Tenderness than he before had Reason to hope for; and
this Knowlege destroying all his Intentions to quarrel with her
for what she had said, he appeared so easy and satisfied, that
Arabella, reflecting upon the Misfortune his Father's new-born
Passion would probably be the Occasion of to him, could not
help sighing at the Apprehension; looking on him, at the same
time, with a kind of pitying Complacency; which did not escape
Mr. *Glanville*'s Notice.

I must know the Reason of that Sigh, Cousin, said he, smiling, and taking her Hand.

If you are wise, replied *Arabella*, gravely, you will be contented to remain in the pleasing Ignorance you are at present;
and not seek to know a thing which will, haply, afford you but
little Satisfaction.

You have increased my Curiosity so much by this Advice,
resumed he, accommodating his Looks to *Arabella*'s, that I
shall not be at Rest till I know what it is you conceal from me:
And, since I am so much concerned in it, even by your own
Confession, I have a Right to press you to explain yourself.

Since you are so importunate, replied *Arabella*, I must tell
you, that I will not do you so great a Diskindness, as to explain
myself; nor will I be the first who shall acquaint you with
your Misfortune, since you will, haply, too soon arrive at the
Knowledge of it, by other means.

Glanville, who imagined this was some new Whim that had

got into her Head, was but little perplexed at an Insinuation, which, had he been ignorant of her Foible, would have given him great Uneasiness: But, being sensible that she expected he would press her to disclose herself, and appear extremely concerned at her refusing him that Satisfaction, he counterfeited so well, that she was at a loss how to evade the Arguments he used to make her unfold the terrible Mystery; when the Dinner-bell ringing, and relieving her for the present, Mr. *Glanville* led her down to the Parlour; where Sir *Charles* and his Daughter attended their coming.

CHAPTER VII

In which the Mistakes are not yet cleared up.

The Baronet, who had been put into a bad Humour by *Arabella*'s Insinuations, that Sir *George* had affronted her, appeared reserved and uneasy; and, being resolved to question her about it, was willing first to know exactly what it was his Niece had been offended at: But as he feared, if it came to his Son's Knowlege, it would produce a Quarrel between the young Gentlemen, that might have dangerous Consequences, he was desirous of speaking to her alone; and, as soon as Dinner was over, asked her to take a Walk with him upon the Terrace, telling her he had something to say to her in private. *Arabella*, whose Fears had been considerably increased by the Pensiveness which appeared in her Uncle's Looks during Dinner, and supposing he wanted a private Conversation, only to explain himself more clearly to her, than he had yet done, was excessively alarmed at this Request; and, casting her Eyes down to the Ground, blushed in such a manner as betrayed her Confusion; and made Miss *Glanville* and her Brother believe, that she suspected her Uncle had a Design to press her soon to give her Hand to Mr. *Glanville*, which occasioned her apparent Disorder.

Sir *Charles*, however, who had not so heedfully observed her Behaviour, repeated his Request; adding, with a Smile, upon her giving him no Answer, Sure Lady *Bella*, you are not afraid to be alone with your Uncle.

No, Sir, replied *Arabella*, giving him a piercing Look; I am not afraid of being alone with my Uncle; and, as long as he pretends to be no more than my Uncle, I shall not scruple to hear what he has to say to me.

Sir *Charles*, a little vexed at an Answer which insinuated, as he thought, a Complaint of his having pretended to more Authority over her than he ought, told her, he hoped she had no Cause to believe he would displease her, by any improper Exertion of that Power over her, with which her Father had intrusted him: For I assure you, added he, I would rather you should follow my Advice as an Uncle, than obey me as a Guardian; and, since my Affection for you is, perhaps, greater than what many People have for a Niece, my Solicitude ought to be imputed to that Motive.

I have all the Sense I ought to have of that Affection you honour me with, replied *Arabella*; and since I hope it will be always what it should be, without wishing for its Increase, I am contented with those Testimonies I have already received of it; and do not desire any other.

Sir *Charles*, a little puzzled to understand the Meaning of these Words, which the grave Looks of *Arabella* made yet more mysterious, rose from his Seat with an Air of Discontent: I should have been glad to have spoken a Word in private to you, Niece, said he; but, since you think proper to make so much Ceremony in such a Trifle, I'll defer it till you are in a better Humour.

Miss *Glanville*, seeing her Father going out of the Room, stepped before him: Nay, Papa, said she, if you want to speak with my Cousin, my Brother and I will go out, and leave you to yourselves.

You will do me a very great Displeasure, said *Arabella*; for, I am sure, my Uncle has not any thing of Consequence to say to me: However, added she, seeing Miss *Glanville* go away, I am resolved, I will not be left alone; and therefore, Mr. *Glanville*, since I can pretend to some Power over you, I command you to stay.

You may remember, Madam, said Mr. *Glanville*, with a Smile, you refused to gratify my Curiosity, with regard to something you hinted to me some time ago; and, to punish you, added he, going out of the Room, I am resolved you shall listen to what my Father has to say to you; for, by your Unwillingness to hear it, I imagine you suspect already what it is.

Arabella, finding she had no way to avoid hearing what she dreaded so much, and observing her Uncle had resumed his Chair, prepared to give him Audience; but, in order to deprive him of all Hope, that she would receive his Discourse favourably, she assumed the severest Look she was capable of; and, casting her Eyes on the Ground, with a Mixture of Anger and Shame, waited with a kind of Fear and Impatience for what he had to say.

I see, Madam, said the Baronet, observing her Confusion, that you apprehend what I am going to say to you; but, I beseech you, do not fear I have any Intentions, but such as you'll approve.

You are certainly in the right, Sir, said *Arabella*, in the Interpretation you have put on my Looks: I am really in Pain about the Purport of your Discourse: And you would particularly oblige me, if you would dispense with me from hearing it.

I see, replied Sir *Charles*, that, out of a mistaken Fear, you are unwilling to hear me, in order to avoid coming to the Explanation I desire: But I tell you, once again, you have nothing to apprehend.

I have every thing to apprehend, Sir, resumed *Arabella*, tartly, while you persist in your Design of disobliging me; and you cannot give me a greater Proof of the Badness of your Intentions, than by thus forcing me to listen to Discourses I ought to avoid.

Since my Word has no Weight with you, replied Sir *Charles*, I'll condescend to assure you, by the most sacred Oath, That I do not mean to come to any Extremities with Sir *George*, concerning what you already told me: All I desire to know is, If you think you had any Reason to be offended with him for any thing he said? And, in that Case, I cannot dispense with myself from expostulating with him about it.

You would do me a Favour, Sir, resumed *Arabella*, if you would interest yourself a little less in what Sir *George* said to me: The Offence was committed against me only; and none but myself has any Right to resent it.

'Tis enough, Niece, said Sir *Charles*, rising: You acknowledge sufficient to make me resolve to oblige him to ask Pardon for the Affront you have received: However, I beg you may make yourself easy; no ill Consequences will happen from this Affair, provided my Son does not know it: And I know you have too much Discretion to acquaint him with it.

Saying this, he went out of the Room, leaving *Arabella* in great Confusion at what he had said; which, in her Opinion, had amounted almost to a plain Declaration of his Passion; and his Design of putting an End to Sir *George*'s Pretensions, whom, it was probable, he looked upon as a more dangerous Rival than his Son, confirmed her in the Opinion of his Resolution to persecute her.

Full of the Reflections this Accident had occasioned, she went to walk in the Garden, where Mr. *Glanville*, his Sister having just left him, joined her.

As he imagined, his Father's Design, in speaking to her alone, was to prevail upon her to consent to marry him before she left the Country, which was what he most earnestly wished, he drew a bad Omen from the Discontent which appeared in her Eyes.

Is it with me, Cousin, said he, or with what my Father has been saying to you, that you are angry?

With both, replied *Arabella*, hastily; for if you had staid in the Room, as I commanded you, I should not have been exposed to the Pain of hearing Things so disagreeable.

Since I knew what would be the Purport of my Father's Discourse, said Mr. *Glanville*, you ought not to be surprised I could not resolve to give any Interruption to it, by my Presence: And, being so much interested in the Success of his Solicitations, I could not choose but give him an Opportunity of speaking to you alone, as he desired.

It seems then, resumed *Arabella*, you know what was the Subject of his Conversation.

I believe I can guess, interrupted Mr. *Glanville*, smiling.

Is it possible, cried *Arabella*, starting back in great Surprize, that, knowing, as you say you do, your Father's Intentions, you would resolve to furnish him with an Opportunity of disclosing them?

Can you blame me, said Mr. *Glanville*, for suffering him to undertake what I durst not myself? I know your Delicacy, or rather your Severity, so well, that I am sensible, if I had taken the Liberty to say what my Father has said, you would have been extremely offended; and punished me, as you have often done, with a Banishment from your Presence: Nay, pursued he, seeing Astonishment and Anger in her Countenance, I perceive you are, at this Moment, going to pronounce some terrible Sentence against me.

You are deceived, said *Arabella*, with a forced Calmness; I am so far from being offended with you, that I am ready to acknowledge, you merit very extraordinary Praises for the perfect Resignation you shew to the Will, and, for your Credit, I will suppose, the Commands, of your Father: But I would advise you to be contented with the Reputation of being a dutiful Son; and, for the future, never aspire to that of being a faithful Lover.

Speaking these Words, which were wholly unintelligible to her amazed Admirer, she left him, and went to her own Apartment, strangely surprised at the Indifference of Mr. *Glanville*; who, as she understood what he had said, was not only willing to resign her to his Father, but also took upon him to mediate in his behalf.

As she was unwilling to acknowledge, even to herself, that the Grief she felt at this Discovery, proceeded from any Affection for her Cousin, she imputed it to the Shame of seeing herself so basely forsaken and neglected; and, not being able to find a Precedent for such an Indignity offered to the Charms of any Lady in her Romances, the Singularity of her Fate, in this respect, seemed to demand all her Uneasiness.

CHAPTER VIII

Which contains some necessary Consequences of the foregoing Mistakes — A Soliloquy on a Love-Letter.

While *Arabella* passed her Time in her Closet, in the most disagreeable Reflections, *Glanville* was racking his Brain to find out the Meaning of those mysterious Words she had uttered at leaving him: He examined them twenty times over, but could not possibly penetrate into their Sense: But, supposing at last, that they really meant nothing at all, or were occasioned by some new Flight of her Imagination, he went to find out his Father, in order to know what had passed between him and *Arabella*.

Sir *Charles*, however, was not to be found; he had ordered his Horse to be made ready, under Pretence of taking a little Ride after Dinner; and, passing by Sir *George*'s House, alighted to pay him a Visit.

The young Baronet, being at home, received him with great Politeness: And Sir *Charles*, whose peculiar Disposition was, to be nicely tenacious of every thing which, he imagined, had any Relation to the Honour of his Family, took the first Opportunity to question him, concerning the Confusion his Whisper had occasioned in Lady *Bella*; adding, That she had confessed, he had given her Reason to take ill what he had said to her.

Sir *George*, who was by no means willing to quarrel with the Uncle of *Arabella*, received the old Gentleman's Remonstrances with a great deal of Calmness; and, finding *Arabella* had not discovered the Purport of that Whisper which had offended her, he told Sir *Charles*, That the Confusion he saw in her Countenance was occasioned by his raillying her upon the Fright she had been in upon Mr. *Glanville*'s Account: He added some other Particulars that intirely taking away all Inclination in Sir *Charles* to pursue the Matter any farther, they parted upon very good Terms; Sir *George* promising, very soon, to return his Visit at the Castle.

Mr. *Glanville*, upon his Father's Return, being impatient to know what he had said to *Arabella*, inquired with so much Precipitation, concerning the Conversation they had had together, that Sir *Charles*, unwilling to tell him the Truth, and not having time to consider of an Answer, evaded his Question in such a manner, that Mr. *Glanville* could not help making some Observation upon it; and, comparing this Circumstance with what *Arabella* had said, tho' he could not comprehend the Meaning that seemed to be concealed under their Behaviour, he immediately concluded, there was some Mystery, which it concerned him to find out.

Possessed with this Opinion, he longed for an Opportunity to talk with *Arabella* alone; but he was not so happy to obtain one; for, tho' that Fair-one presided at the Tea-table, as usual, and also appeared at Supper, yet she so industriously avoided all Occasions of being alone with him, tho' but for a Moment, and appeared so reserved and uneasy, that it was impossible for him to speak to her upon that Subject.

As soon as it was time to retire, having resolved to request the Favour of a few Moments Conversation with her, in her own Apartment; and when he had, as was his Custom, handed her up Stairs; instead of wishing her a good Night, at her Chamber-door, he was going to desire Permission to enter it with her; when *Lucy*, coming to meet her Lady, whispered her in the Ear; upon which, *Arabella*, turning towards him, gave him an hasty Salute, and hurried into her Apartment.

Glanville, no less vexed at this Disappointment, than perplexed at that Whisper, which had caused such a visible Emotion in *Arabella*, retired to his own Room, tormented with a thousand uneasy Suspicions, for which he could not exactly assign a Cause; and wishing impatiently for the next Day, in which he hoped to procure some Explanation of what at present greatly perplexed him.

In the mean time, *Arabella*, who had been informed by *Lucy*, in that Whisper, who was eager to let her know it, that a Messenger had brought a Letter from Sir *George*, and, late as it was at Night, waited for an Answer, was debating with herself, whether she should open this Billet or not: She had a strong Inclination to see what it contained; but, fearful of transgressing the Laws of Romance, by indulging a Curiosity not justifiable by Example, she resolved to return this Letter unopened.

Here, said she to *Lucy*, give this Letter to the Messenger that brought it, and tell him, I was excessively offended with you, for receiving it from his Hands.

Lucy, taking the Letter, was going to obey her Orders; when, recollecting herself, she bid her stay.

Since Sir *George*, said she to herself, is no declared Lover of mine, I may, without any Offence to Decorum, see what this Letter contains: To refuse receiving it, will be to acknowlege, that his Sentiments are not unknown to me; and, by consequence, to lay myself under a Necessity of banishing him: Nor is it fit, that I should allow him to believe I am so ready to apprehend the Meaning of every gallant Speech, which is used to me; and to construe such Insinuations, as he took the Liberty to make me, into Declarations of Love.

Allowing, therefore, the Justice of these Reasons, she took the Letter out of *Lucy*'s Hand; and, being upon the Point of opening it, a sudden Thought controuled her Designs: She threw it suddenly upon her Toilet; and, looking very earnestly upon it,

Presumptuous Paper! said she, speaking with great Emotion to the Letter: Bold Repository of thy Master's daring Thoughts! Shall I not be blamed by all, who hereafter will hear, or read, my History, if, contrary to the Apprehensions I have, that thou containest a Confession that will displease me, I open thy Seal, and become accessary to thy Writer's Guilt, by deigning to make myself acquainted with it? And thou, too indiscreet and unwary Friend, whose Folds contain the Acknowlegement of his Crime! What will it advantage thee or him, if, torn by my resenting Hand, I make thee suffer, for the Part thou bearest in thy Master's Fault; and teach him, by thy Fate, how little Kindness he has to expect from me! Yet, to spare myself the Trouble of reading what will, questionless, greatly displease me, I will return thee, uninjured, into thy Master's Hands; and, by that Moderation, make him repent the Presumption he has been guilty of!

CHAPTER IX

Containing a Love-Letter in the Heroic Stile; with some occasional Reasonings by Lucy, full of Wit and Simplicity.

Our fair Heroine, having ended the foregoing Soliloquy, took up the Letter, and gave it to *Lucy*, who had, all the time she was speaking, observed a profound Silence, mixed with a most eager Attention.

Here, pursued she, carry it to the Person who brought it; and bid him tell his Master, that, lest I should find any thing in it, which may offend me, I have chosen not to read it: And, if he is wise, he will profit by my Concern for him, and take care how he hazards displeasing me a Second time by an Importunity of this kind, which I shall not so easily pardon him.

Lucy, who had taken particular Notice of this Speech, in order to remember every Word of it, when she repeated it again, went conning her Lesson to the Place where she had desired the Servant to wait her coming: But he was gone; such being indeed his Master's Orders; for he was apprehensive, that, following the Custom of the Ladies in Romances, *Arabella* would return his Letter; and therefore, to deprive her of an Opportunity of sending it back that Night, he ordered his Man to say, he waited for an Answer; but, as soon as he conveniently could, to come away without one.

Lucy, in a great Surprize at the Servant's going away, returned to her Lady with the Letter in her Hand, telling her she must needs read it now, since the Person, who brought it, was gone.

It must be confessed, said *Arabella*, taking the Letter from her, with a Smile, he has fallen upon an ingenious Device, to make me keep it for this Night; and, since, haply, I may be mistaken in the Contents, I have a mind to open it.

Lucy did not fail to confirm her Lady in this Design: And *Arabella*, making as if she yielded to the Importunities of her Confidante, opened the Letter; which she found as follows:

The unfortunate and despairing Bellmour, *to the Divine* Arabella.

Madam,
Since it is, doubtless, not only with your Permission, but even by
your Commands, that your Uncle, Sir *Charles Glanville*, comes
to pronounce the Sentence of my Death, in the Denunciation of
your Anger, I submit, Madam, without repining at the Rigour of
that Doom you have inflicted on me. Yes, Madam, this Criminal,
who has dared to adore you, with the most sublime and perfect
Passion that ever was, acknowleges the Justice of his Punishment;
and, since it is impossible to cease loving you, or to live without
telling you he does so, he is going, voluntarily, to run upon that
Death your Severity makes him wish for, and the Greatness of
his Crime demands. Let my Death then, O Divine *Arabella*,
expiate the Offence I have been guilty of! And let me hope those
fair Eyes, that have beheld me with Scorn when alive, will not
refuse to shed some Tears upon my Tomb! And that, when you
remember my Crime of loving you, you will also be pleased to
remember, that I died for that Crime; and wish for no other
Comfort in Death, but the Hope of your not hating, when he is
no more,

                                        The unhappy Bellmour.

Arabella, who had read this Letter aloud, sighed gently at
the Conclusion of it; but poor *Lucy*, who was greatly affected
at so dolorous an Epistle, could not restrain her Tears; but
sobbed so often, and with so much Violence, as, at length,
recalled her Lady from the Reverie, into which she was plunged.

What ails you? said she to her Confidante, greatly surprised:
What is the Cause of this unseemly Sorrow?

Oh! Madam! cried *Lucy*, her Sobs making a frequent and
unpleasing Interruption in her Words; I shall break my Heart
to be sure: Never was such a sad mournful Letter in the World:
I could cry my Eyes out for the poor Gentleman. Pray excuse
me, Madam; but, indeed, I can't help saying, You are the most
hard-heartedest Lady I ever knew in my born Days: Why, to be
sure, you don't care, if an hundred fine Gentlemen should die
for you, tho' their Spirits were to haunt you every Night! Well!

I would not have what your Ladyship has to answer for, for all the World!

You are a foolish Wench! replied *Arabella*, smiling at her Simplicity: Do you think I have any Cause to accuse myself, tho' Five thousand Men were to die for me! 'Tis very certain, my Beauty has produced very deplorable Effects: The unhappy *Hervey* has expiated, by his Death, the Violence his too desperate Passion forced him to meditate against me: The no less guilty, the noble Unknown, *Edward*, is wandering about the World, in a tormenting Despair; and stands exposed to the Vengeance of my Cousin, who has vowed his Death. My Charms have made another Person, whose Character ought to be sacred to me, forget all the Ties of Consanguinity; and become the Rival of his Son, whose Interest he once endeavoured to support: And, lastly, the unfortunate *Bellmour* consumes away in an hopeless Passion; and, conscious of his Crime, dooms himself, haply, with more Severity than I desire, to a voluntary Death; in hopes, thereby, of procuring my Pardon and Compassion, when he is no more. All these, *Lucy*, as I said before, are very deplorable Effects of my Beauty; but you must observe, that my Will has no Part in the Miseries, that unfortunate Beauty occasions; and that, tho' I could even wish myself less fair, in order to avoid giving so much Unhappiness to others, yet these Wishes would not avail; and since, by a fatal Necessity, all these Things will happen, whether I would or no, I must comfort myself under the Uneasiness, which the Sensibility of my Temper makes me feel, by the Reflection, that, with my own Consent, I contribute nothing to the Misfortune of those who love me.

Will your Ladyship then let poor Sir *George* die? said *Lucy*, who had listened very attentively to this fine Harangue, without understanding what it meant.

Questionless, he must die, replied *Arabella*, if he persists in his Design of loving me.

But, pray, Madam, resumed *Lucy*, cannot your Ladyship command him to live, as you did Mr. *Hervey*, and Mr. *Glanville*, who both did as you bid them?

I may command him to live, said *Arabella*; and there is no

Question but he would obey me, if I likewise permit him to love me; but, this last not being fit for me to do, I see no way to prevent the sad Resolution he has taken.

To be sure, Madam, returned *Lucy*, your Ladyship knows what you ought to do better than I can advise your Ladyship, being that you are more learned than me: But, for all that, I think it's better to save Life than to kill, as the Bible-Book says; and, since I am sure your Ladyship is a good Christian, if the Gentleman dies for the Want of a few kind Words, or so, I am sure you will be troubled in Mind about it.

It must be confessed, said *Arabella*, smiling, that, tho' your Solicitations are not very eloquent, they are very earnest and affecting; and I promise you, I will think about it; and, if I can persuade myself, I am doing no wrong Thing, by concerning myself about his Preservation, I will dispatch you To-morrow Morning, with my Orders to him, to live, or, at least, to proceed no further in his Design of dying, till he has further Cause.

Lucy, being extremely glad she had gained her Point, called in her Lady's other Women, who, having assisted her to undress, left her in her Closet, to which she always retired for an Hour, before she went to Bed.

END of the FIRST VOLUME.

THE

Female QUIXOTE;

OR, THE
ADVENTURES
OF

ARABELLA.

VOL. II.

The SECOND EDITION:
Revised and Corrected.

LONDON:

Printed for A. MILLAR, over-againſt
Catharine-ſtreet in the *Strand.*

M.DCC.LII.

THE

Female QUIXOTE

OR, THE

ADVENTURES

OF

ARABELLA.

VOL. II.

THE SECOND EDITION.

Revised and Corrected.

LONDON:

Printed for A. MILLAR, over-against

Catharine-Street in the Strand.

MDCCLIII.

BOOK V

CHAPTER I

*A Dispute very learnedly handled by two Ladies, in
which the Reader may take what Part he pleases.*

Mr. *Glanville*, who was too much in Love to pass the Night
with any great Degree of Tranquillity, under the Apprehensions
he felt; it being the Nature of that Passion, to magnify the most
inconsiderable Trifles into Things of the greatest Importance,
when they concern the beloved Object; did not fail to torment
himself with a thousand different Fears, which the mysterious
Behaviour of his Father, and the more mysterious Words of his
Mistress, gave rise to. Among many various Conjectures, all
equally unreasonable, he fixed upon one, no way advantageous
to Sir *Charles*; for, supposing that the Folly of *Arabella* had
really disgusted him, and made him desirous of breaking off
the designed Match between them; he was, as he thought, taking
Measures to bring this about, knowing, that if Lady *Bella*
refused to fulfil her Father's Desire in this Particular, a very
considerable Estate would descend to him.

Upon any other Occasion, Mr. *Glanville* would not have
suspected his Father of so ungenerous an Action; but Lovers
think every thing possible, which they fear; and being prepossessed with this Opinion, he resolved the next Morning to
sound his Father's Inclinations, by intreating him to endeavour
to prevail upon Lady *Bella* to marry him before her Year of
Mourning for the Marquis was expired.

Attending him, therefore, at Breakfast, in his own Chamber,

he made his designed Request, not without heedfully observing his Countenance at the same time; and trembling, lest he should make him an Answer, that might confirm his uneasy Suspicion.

Sir *Charles*, however, agreeably surprised him, by promising to comply with his Desire that Day; for, added he, tho' my Niece has some odd Ways, yet upon the whole, she is a very accomplished Woman; and when you are her Husband, you may probably find the Means of curing her of those little Follies, which at present are conspicuous enough; but being occasioned by a Country Education, and a perfect Ignorance of the World, the Instruction, which then you will not scruple to give her, and which, from a Husband, without any Offence to her Delicacy, she may receive, may reform her Conduct; and make her Behaviour as complete, as, it must be confessed, both her Person and Mind now are.

Mr. *Glanville* having acquiesced in the Justice of this Remark, as soon as Breakfast was over, went to visit the two Ladies, who generally drank their Chocolate together.

Miss *Glanville* being then in Lady *Bella*'s Apartment, he was immediately admitted, where he found them engaged in a high Dispute; and, much against his Will, was obliged to be Arbitrator in the Affair, they having, upon his Entrance, both appealed to him.

But, in order to place this momentous Affair in a true Light, 'tis necessary to go back a little, and acquaint the Reader with what had passed in the Apartment; and also, following the Custom of the Romance and Novel-Writers, in the Heart of our Heroine.

No sooner were her fair Eyes open in the Morning, than the unfortunate Sir *George* presenting himself to her Imagination, her Thoughts, to use *Scudery*'s Phrase, were at a cruel War with each other: She wished to prevent the Death of this obsequious Lover; but she could not resolve to preserve his Life, by giving him that Hope he required; and without which, she feared, it would be impossible for him to live.

After pondering a few Hours upon the Necessity of his Case, and what a just Regard to her own Honour required of her, Decorum prevailed so much over Compassion, that she resolved to abandon the miserable Sir *George* to all the Rigour of his Destiny; when, happily for the disconsolate Lover, the History of the fair *Amalazontha*[1] coming into her Mind, she remembered, that this haughty Princess, having refused to marry the Person, her Father recommended to her, because he had not a Crown upon his Head; nevertheless, when he was dying for Love of her, condescended to visit him, and even to give him a little Hope, in order to preserve his Life: She conceived it could be no Blemish to her Character, if she followed the Example of this most glorious Princess; and suffered herself to relax a little in her Severity, to prevent the Effects of her Lover's Despair.

Fear not, *Arabella*, said she to herself; fear not to obey the Dictates of thy Compassion, since the glorious *Amalazontha* justifies, by her Example, the Means thou wilt use to preserve a noble Life, which depends upon a few Words thou shalt utter.

When she had taken this Resolution, she rung her Bell for her Women; and as soon as she was dressed, she dismissed them all but *Lucy*, whom she ordered to bring her Paper and Pens, telling her, she would write an Answer to Sir *George*'s Letter.

Lucy obeyed with great Joy; but by that Time she had brought her Lady all the Materials for Writing, her Mind was changed; she having reflected, that *Amalazontha*, whose Example, in order to avoid the Censure of future Ages, she was resolved exactly to follow, did not write to *Ambiomer*, but paid him a Visit, she resolved to do the like; and therefore bid *Lucy* take them away again, telling her: She had thought better of it, and would not write to him.

Lucy, extremely concerned at this Resolution, obeyed her very slowly, and with great seeming Regret.

I perceive, said *Arabella*, you are afraid, I shall abandon the unfortunate Man you solicit for, to the Violence of his Despair; but tho' I do not intend to write to him, yet I'll make use of a Method, perhaps as effectual; for, to speak truly, I mean to make him a Visit; his Fever I suppose being violent enough by this Time to make him keep his Bed.

And will you be so good, Madam, said *Lucy*, to go and see the poor Gentleman? I warrant you, he will be ready to die for Joy, when he sees you.

'Tis probable what you say may happen, replied *Arabella*, but there must be proper Precautions used to prevent those Consequences, which the sudden and unexpected Sight of me may produce. Those about him, I suppose, will have Discretion enough for that: Therefore give Orders for the Coach to be made ready, and tell my Women, they must attend me; and be sure you give them Directions, when I enter Sir *George's* Chamber, to stay at a convenient Distance, in order to leave me an Opportunity of speaking to him, without being heard: As for you, you may approach the Bed-side with me; since, being my Confident, you may hear all we have to say.

Arabella, having thus settled the Ceremonial of her Visit, according to the Rules prescribed by Romances, sat down to her Tea-table, having sent to know, if Miss *Glanville* was up, and received for Answer, that she would attend her at Breakfast.

Arabella, who had at first determined to say nothing of this Affair to her Cousin, could not resist the Desire she had of talking upon a Subject so interesting; and, telling her with a Smile, that she was about to make a very charitable Visit that Morning, asked her, if she was disposed to bear her Company in it.

I know you Country Ladies, said Miss *Glanville*, are very fond of visiting your sick Neighbours: For my Part, I do not love such a grave kind of Amusement; yet, for the sake of the Airing,[2] I shall be very willing to attend you.

I think, said *Arabella*, with a more serious Air than before, it behoves every generous Person to compassionate the Misfortunes of their Acquaintance and Friends, and to relieve them as far as lies in their Power; but those Miseries we ourselves occasion to others, demand, in a more particular Manner, our Pity; and, if consistent with Honour, our Relief.

And pray, returned Miss *Glanville*, who is it you have done any Mischief to, which you are to repair by this charitable Visit, as you call it?

The Mischief I have done, replied *Arabella*, blushing, and casting down her Eyes, was not voluntary, I assure you: Yet I will not scruple to repair it, if I can; tho', since my Power is confined by certain unavoidable Laws, my Endeavours may not haply have all the Success I could wish.

Well, but, dear Cousin, interrupted Miss *Glanville*, tell me in plain *English*, what this Mischief is, which you have done; and to what Purpose you are going out this Morning?

I am going to pay a Visit to Sir *George Bellmour*, replied *Arabella*; and I intreat you, fair Cousin, to pardon me for robbing you of so accomplished a Lover. I really always thought he was in Love with you, till I was undeceived by some Words he spoke Yesterday; and a Letter I received from him last Night, in which he has been bold enough to declare his Passion to me, and, through the Apprehension of my Anger, is this Moment dying with Grief; and 'tis to reconcile him to Life, that I have prevailed upon myself to make him a Visit; in which charitable Design, as I said before, I should be glad of your Company.

Miss *Glanville*, who believed not a Word Lady *Bella* had said, burst out a laughing, at a Speech, that appeared to her so extremely false and ridiculous.

I see, said *Arabella*, you are of a Humour to divert yourself with the Miseries of a despairing Lover; and in this Particular, you greatly resemble the fair and witty *Doralisa*,[3] who always jested at such Maladies as are occasioned by Love: However, this Insensibility does not become you so well as her, since all her Conduct was conformable to it, no Man in the World being bold enough to talk to her of Love; but you, Cousin, are ready, even by your own Confession, to listen to such Discourses from any body; and therefore this Behaviour, in you, may be with more Justice termed Levity, than Indifference.

I perceive, Cousin, said Miss *Glanville*, I have always the worst of those Comparisons you are pleased to make between me and other People; but, I assure you, as free and indiscreet as you think me, I should very much scruple to visit a Man, upon any Occasion whatever.

I am quite astonished, Miss *Glanville*, resumed *Arabella*, to hear you assume a Character of so much Severity; you, who have granted Favours of a Kind in a very great Degree criminal.

Favours! interrupted Miss *Glanville*, criminal Favours! Pray explain yourself, Madam.

Yes, Cousin, said *Arabella*, I repeat it again; criminal Favours, such as allowing Persons to talk to you of Love; not forbidding them to write to you; giving them Opportunities of being alone with you for several Moments together; and several other Civilities of the like Nature, which no Man can possibly merit, under many Years Services, Fidelity, and Pains: All these are criminal Favours, and highly blameable in a Lady, who has any Regard for her Reputation.

All these, replied Miss *Glanville*, are nothing in Comparison of making them Visits; and no Woman, who has any Reputation at all, will be guilty of taking such Liberties.[4]

What! Miss, replied *Arabella*, will you dare, by this Insinuation, to cast any Censures upon the Virtue of the divine *Mandana*, the haughty *Amalazontha*, the fair *Statira*, the cold and rigid *Parisatis*, and many other illustrious Ladies, who did not scruple to visit their Lovers, when confined to their Beds, either by the Wounds they received in Battle, or the more cruel and dangerous ones they suffered from their Eyes? These chaste Ladies, who never granted a Kiss of their Hand to a Lover, till he was upon the Point of being their Husband,[5] would nevertheless most charitably condescend to approach their Bedside, and speak some compassionate Words to them, in order to promote their Cure, and make them submit to live; nay, these divine Beauties would not refuse to grant the same Favour to Persons whom they did not love, to prevent the fatal Consequences of their Despair.

Lord, Madam! interrupted Miss *Glanville*, I wonder you can talk so blasphemously, to call a Parcel of confident Creatures divine, and such terrible Words.

Do you know, Miss, said *Arabella*, with a stern Look, that 'tis of the greatest Princesses that ever were, whom you speak in this irreverent Manner! Is it possible, that you can be ignorant of the sublime Quality of *Mandana*, who was the Heiress of two powerful Kingdoms?[6] Are you not sensible, that *Amalazontha* was Queen of *Turringia*? And will you pretend to deny the glorious Extraction of *Statira* and *Parisatis*, Princesses of *Persia*?

I shall not trouble myself to deny any thing about them,

Madam, said Miss *Glanville*; for I never heard of them before; and really I do not choose to be always talking of Queens and Princesses, as if I thought none but such great People were worthy my Notice: It looks so affected, I should imagine every one laughed at me, that heard me.

Since you are so very scrupulous, returned *Arabella*, that you dare not imitate the sublimest among Mortals, I can furnish you with many Examples, from the Conduct of Persons, whose Quality was not much superior to yours, which may reconcile you to an Action, you at present, with so little Reason, condemn: And, to name but One among some Thousands, the fair *Cleonice*, the most rigid and austere Beauty in all *Sardis*, paid several Visits to the passionate *Ligdamis*, when his Melancholy, at the ill Success of his Passion, threw him into a Fever, that confined him to his Bed.[7]

And pray, Madam, who was that *Cleonice*? said Miss *Glanville*; and where did she live?

In *Sardis*, I tell you, said *Arabella*, in the Kingdom of *Lydia*.

Oh! then it is not in our Kingdom, said Miss *Glanville*: What signifies what Foreigners do? I shall never form my Conduct, upon the Example of Outlandish People; what is common enough in their Countries, would be very particular here; and you can never persuade me, that it is seemly for Ladies to pay Visits to Men in their Beds.

A Lady, said *Arabella*, extremely angry at her Cousin's Obstinacy, who will suffer Men to press her Hand, write to her, and talk to her of Love, ought to be ashamed of such an affected Niceness, as that you pretend to.

I insist upon it, Madam, said Miss *Glanville*, that all those innocent Liberties you rail at, may be taken by any Woman, without giving the World room to censure her: But, without being very bold and impudent, she cannot go to see Men in their Beds; a Freedom that only becomes a Sister, or near Relation.

So then, replied *Arabella*, reddening with Vexation, you will persist in affirming the divine *Mandana* was impudent?

If she made such indiscreet Visits as those, she was, said Miss *Glanville*.

Oh Heavens! cried *Arabella*, have I lived to hear the most

illustrious Princess that ever was in the World, so shamefully reflected on?

Bless me, Madam! said Miss *Glanville*, what Reason have you to defend the Character of this Princess so much? She will hardly thank you for your Pains, I fancy.

Were you acquainted with the Character of that most generous Princess, said *Arabella*, you would be convinced, that she was sensible of the smallest Benefits; but it is not with a View of acquiring her Favour, that I defend her against your inhuman Aspersions, since it is more than Two thousand Years since she died; yet common Justice obliges me to vindicate a Person so illustrious for her Birth and Virtue; and were you not my Cousin, I should express my Resentment in another Manner, for the Injury you do her.

Truly, said Miss *Glanville*, I am not much obliged to you, Madam, for not downright quarrelling with me for one that has been in her Grave Two thousand Years: However, nothing shall make me change my Opinion, and I am sure most People will be of my Side of the Argument.

That Moment Mr. *Glanville* sending for Permission to wait upon *Arabella*, she ordered him to be admitted, telling Miss *Glanville*, she would acquaint her Brother with the Dispute: To which she consented.

CHAPTER II

Which inculcates, by a very good Example, that a Person ought not to be too hasty in deciding a question he does not perfectly understand.

You are come very opportunely, Sir, said *Arabella*, when he entered the Room, to be Judge of a great Controversy between Miss *Glanville* and myself. I beseech you therefore, let us have your Opinion upon the Matter.

Miss *Glanville* maintains, that it is less criminal in a Lady to hear Persons talk to her of Love, allow them to kiss her Hand,

and permit them to write to her, than to make a charitable Visit to a Man who is confined to his Bed through the Violence of his Passion and Despair; the Intent of this Visit being only to prevent the Death of an unfortunate Lover, and, if necessary, to lay her Commands upon him to live.

And this latter is your Opinion, is it not Madam? said Mr. *Glanville*.

Certainly, Sir, replied *Arabella*, and in this I am justified by all the Heroines of Antiquity.

Then you must be in the Right, Madam, returned Mr. *Glanville*, both because your own Judgment tells you so, and also the Example of these Heroines you mention.

Well, Madam, interrupted Miss *Glanville* hastily, since my Brother has given Sentence on your Side, I hope you will not delay your Visit to Sir *George* any longer.

How! said Mr. *Glanville*, surprised, is Lady *Bella* going to visit Sir *George*? Pray, Madam, may I presume to enquire the Reason for your doing him this extraordinary Favour?

You are not very wise, said *Arabella*, looking gravely upon Miss *Glanville*, to discover a Thing, which may haply create a Quarrel between your Brother, and the unfortunate Person you speak of: Yet since this Indiscretion cannot be recalled, we must endeavour to prevent the Consequences of it.

I assure you, Madam, interrupted Mr. *Glanville*, extremely impatient to know the Meaning of these Hints, you have nothing to fear from me: Therefore you need not think yourself under any Necessity of concealing this Affair from me.

You are not, haply, so moderate as you pretend, said *Arabella*, (who would not have been displeased to have seen him in all the jealous Transports of an enraged *Orontes*[8]); but whatever ensues, I can no longer keep from your Knowledge, a Truth your Sister has begun to discover; but in telling you what you desire to know, I expect you will suppress all Inclinations to Revenge, and trust the Care of your Interest to my Generosity.

You are to know then, that in the Person of your Friend Sir *George*, you have a Rival, haply the more to be feared, as his Passion is no less respectful than violent: I possibly tell you more than I ought, pursued she, blushing, and casting down her

Eyes, when I confess, that for certain Considerations, wherein perhaps you are concerned, I have received the first Insinuation of this Passion with Disdain enough; and I assure myself, that you are too generous to desire any Revenge upon a miserable Rival, of whom Death is going to free you.

Then, taking Sir *George*'s Letter out of her Cabinet, she presented it to Mr. *Glanville*.

Read this, added she; but read it without suffering yourself to be transported with any violent Motions of Anger: And as in Fight, I am persuaded you would not oppress a fallen and vanquished Foe; so in Love, I may hope, an unfortunate Rival will merit your Compassion.

Never doubt it, Madam, replied Mr. *Glanville*, receiving the Letter, which Miss *Glanville*, with a beating Heart, earnestly desired to hear read. Her Brother, after asking Permission of *Arabella*, prepared to gratify her Curiosity; but he no sooner read the first Sentence, than, notwithstanding all his Endeavours, a Smile appeared in his Face; and Miss *Glanville*, less able, and indeed less concerned to restrain her Mirth at the uncommon Stile, burst out a laughing, with so much Violence, as obliged her Brother to stop, and counterfeit a terrible Fit of Coughing, in order to avoid giving *Arabella* the like Offence.

The Astonishment of this Lady, at the surprising and unexpected Effect her Lover's Letter produced on Miss *Glanville*, kept her in a profound Silence, her Eyes wandering from the Sister to the Brother; who, continuing his Cough, was not able, for some Moments, to go on with his Reading.

Arabella, during this Interval, having recovered herself a little, asked Miss *Glanville*, if she found any thing in a Lover's Despair, capable of diverting her so much, as she seemed to be with that of the unfortunate Sir *George*?

My Sister, Madam, said Mr. *Glanville*, preventing her Reply, knows so many of Sir *George*'s Infidelities, that she cannot persuade herself he is really in such a dangerous Way as he insinuates: Therefore you ought not to be surprised, if she is rather disposed to laugh at this Epistle, than to be moved with any Concern for the Writer, who, though he is my Rival, I must say, appears to be in a deplorable Condition.

Pray, Sir, resumed *Arabella*, a little composed by those Words, finish the Letter: Your Sister may possibly find more Cause for Pity than Contempt, in the latter Part of it.

Mr. *Glanville*, giving a Look to his Sister, sufficient to make her comprehend, that he would have her restrain her Mirth for the future, proceeded in his reading; but every Line increasing his strong Inclination to laugh, when he came to the pathetic Wish, that her fair Eyes might shed some Tears upon his Tomb, no longer able to keep his assumed Gravity, he threw down the Letter in a counterfeited Rage.

Curse the stupid Fellow! cried he, is he mad, to call the finest black Eyes in the Universe, fair. Ah! Cousin, said he to *Arabella*, he must be little acquainted with the Influence of your Eyes, since he can so egregiously mistake their Colour.

And it is very plain, replied *Arabella*, that you are little acquainted with the sublime Language in which he writes, since you find Fault with an Epithet, which marks the Beauty, not the Colour, of those Eyes he praises; for, in fine, Fair is indifferently applied, as well to black and brown Eyes, as to light and blue ones, when they are either really lovely in themselves, or by the Lover's Imagination created so: And therefore, since Sir *George*'s Prepossession has made him see Charms in my Eyes, which questionless are not there; by calling them fair, he has very happily expressed himself, since therein he has the Sanction of those great Historians, who wrote the Histories of Lovers he seems to imitate, as well in his Actions as Stile.

I find my Rival is very happy in your Opinion, Madam, said Mr. *Glanville*; and I am apt to believe, I shall have more Reason to envy than pity his Situation.

If you keep within the Bounds I prescribe you, replied *Arabella*, you shall have no Reason to envy his Situation, but, considering the Condition to which his Despair has by this Time certainly reduced him, Humanity requires that we should take some Care of him; and, to shew you how great my Opinion of your Generosity is, I will even entreat you to accompany me in the Visit I am going to make him.

Mr. *Glanville*, being determined, if possible, to prevent her exposing herself, affected to be extremely moved at this Request;

and, rising from his Chair in great seeming Agitation, traversed the Room for some Moments, without speaking a Word: Then suddenly stopping;

And can you, Madam, said he, looking upon *Arabella*, suppose, that I will consent to your visiting my Rival; and that I will be mean enough to attend you myself to his House? Do you think, that *Orontes* you have often reproached me with, would act in such a Manner?

I don't know how *Orontes* would have acted in this Case, said *Arabella*, because it never happened that such a Proof of his Submission was ever desired of him; but, considering that he was of a very fiery and jealous Disposition, it is probable he might act as you do.

I always understood, Madam, said Mr. *Glanville*, that *Orontes* was a Favourite of yours, but it seems I was mistaken.

You will be very unjust, said *Arabella*, to draw any unfavourable Conclusion from what I have said, to the Prejudice of that valiant Prince, for whom I confess I have a great Esteem; and truly whoever reflects upon the great Actions he did in the Wars between the *Amazons* and the fierce *Naobarzanes* King of the *Cilicians*,[9] must needs conceive a very high Idea of his Virtue; but if I cannot bring the Example of *Orontes* to influence you in the present Case, I can mention those of other Persons, no less illustrious for their Birth and Courage, than him. Did not the brave *Memnon*, when his Rival *Oxyatres* was sick, intreat the beautiful *Barsina* to favour him with a Visit?[10] And the complaisant Husband of the divine *Parisatis* was not contented with barely desiring her to visit *Lysimachus*, who was dying with Despair at their Marriage, but would many times bring her himself to the Bed-side of this unfortunate Lover, and, leaving her there, give him an Opportunity of telling her what he suffered for her Sake.[11]

I am afraid, Madam, said Mr. *Glanville*, I shall never be capable of imitating either the brave *Memnon*, nor the complaisant *Lysimachus*, in this Case, and the Humour of *Orontes* seems to me the most commendable.

Nevertheless, said *Arabella*, the Humour of *Orontes* cost him an infinite Number of Pains; and it may happen, you will as near resemble him in his Fortune as you do in his Disposition: But pray let us end this Dispute at present. If you are not generous enough to visit an unfortunate Rival, you shall not put a Stop to the Charity of my Intentions; and since Miss *Glanville* is all of a sudden become so severe, that she will not accompany me in this Visit, I shall be contented with the Attendance of my Women.

Saying this, she rose from her Seat, calling *Lucy*, and ordered her to bid her Companions attend.

Mr. *Glanville*, seeing her thus determined, was almost mad with Vexation.

Upon my Soul, Madam, said he, seizing her Hand, you must not go.

How, Sir! said *Arabella*, sternly.

Not without seeing me die first, resumed he, in a languishing Tone.

You must not die, replied *Arabella*, gravely, nor must you pretend to hinder me from going.

Nay, Madam, said *Glanville*, one of these two Things will certainly happen: Either you must resolve not to visit Sir *George*, or else be contented to see me die at your Feet.

Was ever any Lady in so cruel a Dilemma? said *Arabella*, throwing herself into the Chair in a languishing Posture: What can I do to prevent the Fate of two Persons, one of whom I infinitely pity, and the other, obstinate as he is, I cannot hate? Shall I resolve to let the miserable *Bellmour* die, rather than grant him a Favour the most rigid Virtue would not refuse him? or shall I, by opposing the impetuous Humour of a Lover, to whom I am somewhat obliged, make myself the Author of his Death? Fatal Necessity! which obliges me either to be cruel or unjust; and, with a Disposition to neither, makes me, in some Degree, guilty of both.

CHAPTER III

In which our Heroine is in some little Confusion.

While *Arabella* was uttering this pathetic Complaint, Mr. *Glan-ville*, with great Difficulty, kept himself from smiling; and, by some supplicating Looks to his Sister, prevented her laughing out; yet she giggled in secret behind her Fan: But *Arabella* was so lost in her melancholy Reflections, that she kept her Eyes immoveably fixed on the Ground for some Moments: At last, casting an upbraiding Glance at *Glanville*;

Is it possible, cruel Person that you are! said she to him, that you can, without Pity, see me suffer so much Uneasiness; and, knowing the Sensibility of my Temper, can expose me to the Grief of being accessary to the Death of an unfortunate Man, guilty indeed of a too violent Passion, which merits a gentler Punishment, than that you doom him to?

Don't be uneasy, dear Cousin, interrupted Miss *Glanville*; I dare assure you Sir *George* won't die.

It is impossible to think that, said *Arabella*, since he has not so much as received a Command from me to live; but tell me truly, pursued she, do you believe it probable, that he will obey me, and live?

Indeed, Madam, said Miss *Glanville*, I could swear for him that he will.

Well, replied *Arabella*, I will content myself with sending him my Commands in Writing; but it is to be feared they will not have so much Efficacy upon his Spirit.

Mr. *Glanville*, extremely pleased that she had laid aside her Design of visiting Sir *George*, did not oppose her writing to him, though he was plotting how to prevent the Letter reaching his Hands; and while she went into her Closet to write, he conferred with his Sister upon the Means he should use, express-ing, at the same Time, great Resentment against Sir *George*, for endeavouring to supplant him in his Cousin's Affection.

What then, said Miss *Glanville*, do you really imagine Sir *George* is in Love with Lady *Bella*?

He is either in Love with her Person or Estate, replied Mr. *Glanville*, or perhaps with both; for she is handsome enough to gain a Lover of his Merit, though she had no Fortune; and she has Fortune enough to do it, though she had no Beauty.

My Cousin is well enough, to be sure, said Miss *Glanville*; but I never could think her a Beauty.

If, replied Mr. *Glanville*, a most lovely Complection, regular Features, a fine Stature, an elegant Shape, and an inexpressible Grace in all her Motions, can form a Beauty, Lady *Bella* may pretend to that Character, without any Dispute.

Though she was all that you say, returned Miss *Glanville*, I am certain Sir *George* is not in Love with her.

I wish I was certain of that, replied Mr. *Glanville*; for 'tis very probable you are mistaken.

You may see by his Letter, interrupted Miss *Glanville*, what a Jest he makes of her; and if you had heard how he talked to her the other Day in the Garden, you would have died with Laughing; yet my poor Cousin thought he was very serious, and was so foolishly pleased!

I assure you, *Charlotte*, said Mr. *Glanville*, gravely, I shall take it very ill, if you make so free with your Cousin's little Foibles; and if Sir *George* presumes to make a Jest of her, as you say, I shall teach him better Manners.

You are the strangest Creature in the World! said Miss *Glanville*: A Minute or two ago, you was wishing to be sure he was not in Love with her; and now you are angry, when I assure you he is only in Jest.

Arabella, that Moment coming out of her Closet, broke off their Discourse. I have written to Sir *George*, said she, addressing herself to Mr. *Glanville*; and you are at Liberty, if you please, to read my Letter, which I propose to send away immediately.

Mr. *Glanville*, taking the Letter out of her Hand, with a low Bow, began to read it to himself; but *Arabella*, willing his Sister should also be acquainted with the Contents, obliged him, much against his Will, to read it aloud. It was as follows:

Arabella, *To* Bellmour.

WHATEVER Offence your presumptuous Declaration may
have given me, yet my Resentment will be appeased with a less
Punishment than Death: And that Grief and Submission you have
testified in your Letter, may haply have already procured you
Pardon for your Fault, provided you do not forfeit it by Disobedience.

I therefore command you to live, and command you by all
that Power you have given me over you.

Remember I require no more of you, than *Parisatis* did of
Lysimachus, in a more cruel and insupportable Misfortune:[12]
Imitate then the Obedience and Submission of that illustrious
Prince; and, tho' you should be as unfortunate as he, let your
Courage also be equal to his; and, like him, be contented with the
Esteem that is offered you, since it is all that can be bestowed, by

Arabella.

Mr. *Glanville*, finding by this Epistle, that *Arabella* did not
design to encourage the Addresses of Sir *George*, would not
have been against his receiving it, had he not feared the Consequence of his having such a convincing Proof of the Peculiarity
of her Temper in his Possession; and while he kept the Letter
in his Hand, as if he wanted to consider it a little better, he
meditated on the Means to prevent its ever being delivered; and
had possibly fixed upon some successful Contrivance, when a
Servant coming in, to inform the Ladies, that Sir *George* was
come to wait on them, put an End to his Schemes; and he
immediately ran down to receive him, not being willing to
increase, by his Stay, the Astonishment and Confusion which
appeared in the Countenance of *Arabella*, at hearing a Man,
whom she had believed and represented to be dying, was come
to pay her a Visit.

CHAPTER IV

Where the Lady extricates herself out of her former
Confusion, to the great Astonishment, we will suppose,
of the Reader.

Miss *Glanville*, not having so much Delicacy as her Brother, could not help exulting a little upon this Occasion.

After the terrible Fright you have been in, Madam, said she, upon Sir *George*'s Account, I wonder you do not rather think it is his Ghost than himself that is come to see us.

There is no Question, but it is himself that is come, said *Arabella*, (who had already reconciled this Visit to her first Thoughts of him;) and it is, haply, to execute his fatal Design in my Presence, that has brought him here; and, like the unfortunate *Agilmond*, he means to convince me of his Fidelity and Love, by falling upon his Sword before my Eyes.[13]

Bless me, Madam, said Miss *Glanville*, what horrid Things come into your Head! I vow you terrify me out of my Wits, to hear you.

There is no Occasion for your Fears, interrupted *Arabella*: Since we already suspect his Designs, it will be very easy to prevent them: Had the Princess of the *Sarmatians* known the fatal Intentions of her despairing Lover, doubtless, she would have used some Precautions to hinder him from executing them; for want of which, she saw the miserable *Agilmond* weltering in his Blood at her Feet; and with Reason accused herself of being the Cause of so deplorable a Spectacle.

The Astonishment Miss *Glanville* was in, to hear her Cousin talk in this Manner, kept her from giving her any Interruption, while she related several other terrible Instances of Despair.

In the mean time, Sir *George*, who was impatient to go up to Lady *Bella*'s Apartment, having flattered himself into a Belief, that his Letter was favourably received; and that he should be permitted to *hope* at least; made a short Visit to Sir *Charles* in his own Room; and, accompanied by Mr. *Glanville*, who was resolved to see in what Manner *Arabella* received him, went to her Apartment.

As he had taken Care, at his Entrance, to accommodate his Looks to the Character he had assumed of an humble despairing Lover, *Arabella* no sooner saw him, but her Countenance changed; and, making a Sign to Mr. *Glanville*, who could not comprehend what she meant, to seize upon the Guard of his Sword, she hastily stept forward to meet him.

I am too well convinced, said she to Sir *George*, that the Intent of your coming hither To-day, is to commit some Violence against yourself before my Eyes: But listen not, I beseech you, to the Dictates of your Despair: Live; I command you, live; and since you say, I have the absolute Disposal of your Life, do not deprive yourself of it, without the Consent of her, on whom you profess to have bestowed it.

Sir *George*, who did not imagine *Arabella* would communicate his Letter to her Cousins, and only expected some distant Hints from her concerning it, was so confounded at this Reception before them, that he was not able to reply: he blushed, and turned pale alternately; and, not daring to look, either upon Miss *Glanville*, or her Brother, or to meet the Eyes of the fair Visionary, who with great Impatience, expected his Answer, he hung down his Head in a very silly Posture; and, by his Silence, confirmed *Arabella* in her Opinion.

As he did not want for Wit and Assurance, during that Interval of Silence, and Expectation from all Parties; his Imagination suggested to him the Means of extricating himself out of the ridiculous Perplexity he was in; and as it concerned him greatly to avoid any Quarrel with the Brother and Sister, he determined to turn the whole Matter into a Jest: but, if possible, to manage it so, that *Arabella* should not enter into his Meaning.

Raising therefore his Eyes, and looking upon *Arabella* with a melancholy Air;

You are not deceived, Madam, said he: This Criminal, with whom you are so justly offended, comes with an Intention to die at your Feet, and breath out his miserable Life, to expiate those Crimes of which you accuse him: But since your severe Compassion will oblige me to live, I obey, oh! most divine, but cruel *Arabella*! I obey your harsh Commands; and, by endeavouring to live, give you a more convincing Proof of that Respect and Submission I shall always have for your Will.

I expected no less from your Courage and Generosity, said *Arabella*, with a Look of great Complacency; and since you so well know how to imitate the great *Lysimachus* in your Obedience, I shall be no less acknowleging than the fair *Parisatis*;[14] but will have for you an Esteem equal to that Virtue I have observed in you.

Sir *George*, having received this gracious Promise, with a most profound Bow, turned to Mr. *Glanville*, with a kind of chastened Smile upon his Countenance.

And, you, fortunate and deserving Knight, said he, happy in the Affections of the fairest Person in the World! grudge me not this small Alleviation of my Misfortunes; and envy me not that Esteem, which alone is able to make me suffer Life, while you possess, in the Heart of the divine *Arabella*, a Felicity that might be envied by the greatest Monarchs in the World.

As diverting as this Scene was, Mr. *Glanville* was extremely uneasy: For though Sir *George*'s Stratagem took, and he believed he was only indulging the Gaiety of his Humour, by carrying on this Farce; yet he could not endure, he should divert himself at *Arabella*'s Expence. The solemn Speech he had made him, did indeed force him to smile; but he soon assumed a graver Look, and told Sir *George*, in a low Voice, that when he had finished his Visit he should be glad to take a Turn with him in the Garden.

Sir *George* promised to follow him, and Mr. *Glanville* left the Room, and went into the Gardens; where the Baronet, having taken a respectful Leave of *Arabella*, and, by a sly Glance, convinced Miss *Glanville*, he had sacrificed her Cousin to her Mirth, went to join her Brother.

Mr. *Glanville*, as soon as he saw him, walked to meet him with a very reserved Air: Which Sir *George* observing, and being resolved to keep up his Humour;

What, inhuman, but too happy Lover, said he, what, am I to understand by that Cloud upon your Brow? Is it possible, that thou canst envy me the small Comfort I have received; and, not satisfied with the glorious Advantages thou possessest, wilt thou still deny me that Esteem, which the divine *Arabella* has been pleased to bestow upon me?

Pray, Sir *George*, said Mr. *Glanville*, lay aside this pompous Style: I am not disposed to be merry at present, and have not all the Relish for this kind of Wit, that you seem to expect. I desired to see you here, that I might tell you without Witnesses, I take it extremely ill, you should presume to make my Cousin the Object of your Mirth. Lady *Bella*, Sir, is not a Person, with whom such Liberties ought to be taken; nor will I, in the double Character of her Lover and Relation, suffer it from any one whatever.

Cruel Fortune! said Sir *George*, stepping back a little, and lifting up his Eyes, shall I always be exposed to thy Persecutions? And must I, without any apparent Cause, behold an Enemy in the Person of my Friend; who, though, without murmuring, I resign to him the adorable *Arabella*, is yet resolved to dispute with me, a Satisfaction, which does not deprive him of any Part of that glorious Fortune to which he is destined? Since it is so, unjust and cruel Friend, pursued he, strike this Breast which carries the Image of the divine *Arabella*; but think not, that I will offer to defend myself, or lift my Sword, against a Man beloved by her.

This is all very fine, returned Mr. *Glanville*, hardly able to forbear laughing; but 'tis impossible, with all your Gaiety, to hinder me from being serious upon this Business.

Then be as serious as thou wilt, dear *Charles*, interrupted Sir *George*, provided you will allow me to be gay; and not pretend to infect me with thy unbecoming Gravity.

I have but a few Words to say to you, then, Sir, replied Mr. *Glanville*: Either behave with more Respect to my Cousin; or prepare to give me Satisfaction, for the Insults you offer her.

Oh! I understand you, Sir, said Sir *George*; and because you have taken it into your Head to be offended at a Trifle of no Consequence in the World, I must give you a fair Chance to run me through the Body! There is something very foolish, faith, in such an extravagant Expectation: But since Custom has made it necessary, that a Man must venture his Soul and Body upon these important Occasions; because I will not be out of the Fashion, you shall command me whenever you think fit; though I shall fight with my Schoolfellow with a very ill Will, I assure you.

There is no Necessity for fighting, said Mr. *Glanville*, blushing at the ludicrous Light, in which the gay Baronet had placed his Challenge:[15] The Concession I have required, is very small, and not worth the contesting for, on your Side. Lady *Bella*'s Peculiarity, to which you contribute so much, can afford you, at best, but an ill-natured Diversion, while it gives me a real Pain; and sure, you must acknowledge, you are doing me a very great Injury, when you endeavour to confirm a Lady, who is to be my Wife, in a Behaviour that excites your Mirth, and makes her a fit Object for your Ridicule, and Contempt.

You do Lady *Bella* a much greater Injury than I do, replied Sir *George*, by supposing, she can ever be an Object of Ridicule and Contempt: I think very highly of her Understanding; and though the Bent of her Studies has given her Mind a romantic Turn, yet the Singularity of her Manners is far less disagreeable, than the lighter Follies of most of her Sex.

But to be absolutely perfect, interrupted Mr. *Glanville*, I must cure her of that Singularity; and therefore I beg you will not persist in assuming a Behaviour conformable to her romantic Ideas; but rather help me to banish them from her Imagination.

Well, replied Sir *George*, since you no longer threaten, I'll do what I can to content you; but I must quit my Heroics by Degrees, and sink with Decency into my own Character; otherwise she will never endure me in her Presence.

Arabella and Miss *Glanville*, appearing in the Walk, broke off the Conversation. The Baronet and Mr. *Glanville* walked forward to meet them; but *Arabella*, who did not desire Company, struck into another Walk, whither Mr. *Glanville* following, proposed to join her; when he saw his Father, who had been taking a Turn there alone, make up to *Arabella*; and, supposing he would take that Opportunity to talk to her concerning him, he went back to his Sister and Sir *George*, whose Conversation he interrupted, to the great Regret of Miss *Glanville*.

CHAPTER V

*In which will be found one of the former Mistakes
pursued, and another cleared up, to the great
Satisfaction of Two Persons; among whom, the
Reader, we expect, will make a Third.*

Arabella no sooner saw Sir *Charles* advancing towards her,
when, sensible of the Consequence of being alone with a Person
whom she did not doubt, would make use of that Advantage,
to talk to her of Love, she endeavoured to avoid him, but in
vain; for Sir *Charles*, guessing her Intentions, walked hastily up
to her; and, taking hold of her Hand,

You must not go away, Lady *Bella*, said he: I have something
to say to you.

Arabella, extremely discomposed at this Behaviour, struggled to free her Hand from her Uncle; and giving him a Look,
on which Disdain and Fear were visibly painted,

Unhand me, Sir, said she, and force me not to forget the
Respect I owe you, as my Uncle, by treating you with a Severity
such uncommon Insolence demands.

Sir *Charles*, letting go her Hand in a great Surprize, at the
Word Insolent, which she had used, asked her if she knew to
whom she was speaking?

Questionless, I am speaking to my Uncle, replied she; and
'tis with great Regret I see myself obliged to make use of Expressions no way conformable to the Respect I bear that sacred
Character.

And, pray, Madam, said Sir *Charles*, somewhat softened by
this Speech, who is it that obliges you to lay aside that Respect
you seem to acknowledge is due to your Uncle?

You do, Sir, replied she; and 'tis with infinite Sorrow, that I
beheld you assuming a Character unbecoming the Brother of
my Father.

This is pretty plain, indeed, interrupted Sir *Charles*: But pray,
Madam, inform me, what it is you complain of.

You, questionless, know much better than I can tell you,

replied *Arabella*, blushing, the Offence I accuse you of; nor is it proper for me to mention, what it would not become me to suffer.

Zounds! cried Sir *Charles*, no longer able to suppress his growing Anger, this is enough to make a Man mad.

Ah! I beseech you, Sir, resumed *Arabella*, suffer not an unfortunate and ill-judged Passion to be the Bane of all your Happiness and Virtue: Recall your wandering Thoughts; reflect upon the Dishonour you will bring upon yourself, by persisting in such unjustifiable Sentiments.

I do not know how it is possible to avoid it, said Sir *Charles*; and, notwithstanding all this fine Reasoning, there are few People but would fly into greater Extremities; but my Affection for you makes me —

Hold, hold, I conjure you, Sir, interrupted *Arabella*; force me not to listen to such injurious Language; carry that odious Affection somewhere else; and do not persecute an unfortunate Maid, who has contributed nothing to thy Fault, and is only guilty of too much Compassion for thy Weakness.

Good God, cried Sir *Charles*, starting back, and looking upon *Arabella* with Astonishment; how I pity my Son! What would I not give, if he did not love this Girl?

Think not, replied *Arabella*, that the Passion your Son has for me, makes your Condition a bit the worse; for I would be such as I am, with respect to you, were there no Mr. *Glanville* in the World.

I never thought, Niece, said Sir *Charles*, after a little Pause, that any Part of my Behaviour could give you the Offence you complain of, or authorize that Hatred and Contempt you take the Liberty to express for me: But since it is so, I promise you, I will quit your House, and leave you to yourself; I have always been solicitous for your Welfare; and, ungrateful as you are —

Call me not ungrateful, interrupted *Arabella* again: Heaven is my Witness, that had you not forgot I was your Niece, I would have always remembered you was my Uncle; and not only have regarded you as such, but have looked upon you as another Father, under whose Direction Providence had placed me, since it had deprived me of my real Father; and whose

Tenderness and Care, might have in some measure supplied the
Loss I had of him: But Heaven has decreed it otherwise; and
since it is its Will, that I should be deprived of the Comfort and
Assistance my Orphan State requires, I must submit, without
murmuring, to my Destiny. Go then, unfortunate and lamented
Uncle, pursued she, wiping some Tears from her fine Eyes; go,
and endeavour by Reason and Absence to recover thy Repose;
and be assured, whenever you can convince me you have triumphed over these Sentiments which now cause both our
Unhappiness, you shall have no Cause to complain of my Conduct towards you.

Finishing these Words, she left him with so much Speed, that
it would have been impossible for him to have stopped her,
though he had intended it: But indeed, he was so lost in Wonder
and Confusion at a Behaviour for which he was not able to
assign any other Cause than Madness, that he remained fixed
in the same Posture of Surprize, in which she had left him; and
from which he was first interrupted by the Voice of his Son,
who, seeing *Arabella* flying towards the House in great seeming
Emotion, came to know the Result of their Conversation.

Sir, said Mr. *Glanville*, who had spoken to his Father before,
but had no Answer, will you not inform me, what Success you
have had with my Cousin? How did she receive your Proposal?

Speak of her no more, said Sir *Charles*, she is a proud
ungrateful Girl, and unworthy the Affection you have for her.

Mr. *Glanville*, who trembled to hear so unfavourable an
Answer to his Inquiries, was struck dumb with his Surprize and
Grief; when Sir *Charles* taking Notice of the Alteration in his
Countenance;

I am sorry, said he, to find you have set your Heart upon
this fantastic Girl: If ever she be your Wife, which I very much
doubt, she will make you very unhappy: But, *Charles*, pursued
he, I would advise you to think no more of her; content yourself
with the Estate you gain by her Refusal of you: With that
Addition to your own Fortune, you may pretend[16] to any Lady
whatever; and you will find many that are full as agreeable as
your Cousin, who will be proud of your Addresses.

Indeed, Sir, said Mr. *Glanville*, with a Sigh, there is no

Woman upon Earth whom I would choose to marry, but Lady *Bella*: I flattered myself, I had been happy enough to have made some Progress in her Affection; but it seems, I was mistaken; however, I should be glad to know, if she gave you any Reasons for refusing me.

Reasons! said Sir *Charles*: There is no making her hear Reason, or expecting Reason from her; I never knew so strange a Woman in my Life: She would not allow me to speak what I intended concerning you; but interrupted me, every Moment, with some high-flown Stuff or other.

Then I have not lost all Hopes of her, cried Mr. *Glanville* eagerly; for since she did not hear what you had to say, she could not possibly deny you.

But she behaved in a very impertinent Manner to me, interrupted Sir *Charles*; complained of my harsh Treatment of her; and said several other Things, which, because of her uncommon Style, I could not perfectly understand; yet they seemed shocking; and, upon the Whole, treated me so rudely, that I am determined to leave her to herself, and trouble my Head no more about her.

For God's sake, dear Sir, said Mr. *Glanville*, alarmed at this Resolution, suspend your Anger, till I have seen my Cousin: There is some Mistake, I am persuaded, in all this. I know she has some very odd Humours, which you are not so well acquainted with, as I am. I'll go to her, and prevail upon her to explain herself.

You may do so, if you please, replied Sir *Charles*; but I fear it will be to very little Purpose; for I really suspect her Head is a little turned: I do not know what to do with her: It is not fit she should have the Management of herself; and yet 'tis impossible to live upon easy Terms with her.

Mr. *Glanville*, who did not doubt but *Arabella* had been guilty of some very ridiculous Folly, offered nothing more in her Justification; but, having attended his Father to his own Chamber went to *Arabella*'s Apartment.

He found the pensive Fair-one, in a melancholy Posture, her Head reclined upon one of her fair Hands; and though her Eyes were fixed upon a Book she held in the other, yet she did not seem to read, but rather to be wholly buried in Contemplation.

Mr. *Glanville* having so happily found her alone (for her Women were not then in her Chamber) seated himself near her; having first asked Pardon for the Interruption he had given to her Studies; and *Arabella*, throwing aside her Book, prepared to listen to his Discourse; which by the Agitation, which appeared in his Looks, she imagined, would be upon some extraordinary Subject.

I left my Father just now, said he, in a great deal of Uneasiness, on account of something you said to him, Lady *Bella*: He apprehends you are disobliged, and he would willingly know how.

Has your Father then acquainted you with the Subject of our Conversation? interrupted *Arabella*.

I know what would have been the Subject of your Conversation, replied Mr. *Glanville*, if you had been pleased to listen to what Sir *Charles* intended to say to you on my Behalf.

On your Behalf? interrupted *Arabella*: Ah poor deceived *Glanville*! how I pity thy blind Sincerity! But it is not for me to undeceive thee: only thus much I may say to you, Beware of committing your Interests to a Person, who will be a much better Advocate for another than for you.

Mr. *Glanville*, rejoiced to find by these Words, that her Resentment against his Father was occasioned by a Suspicion so favourable for him, assured her, that Sir *Charles* wished for nothing more earnestly, than that he might be able to merit her Esteem; and that it was to dispose her to listen to his Addresses, that he wanted to discourse with her that Morning.

Mr. *Glanville*, being obliged, through his Knowledge of his Cousin's Temper, to speak to her in this distant Manner, went on with his Assurances of his Father's Candour in this Respect; and *Arabella*, who would not declare her Reasons for doubting it, only replied, that she wished Sir *Charles* meant all that he had said to him; but that she could not persuade herself to believe him sincere, till his future Actions had convinced her he was so.

Mr. *Glanville*, impatient to let his Father know, how greatly he had been mistaken in the Cause of *Arabella*'s Behaviour, made his Visit shorter than he would otherwise have done, in order to undeceive him.

Is it possible, said Sir *Charles*, when his Son had repeated the Conversation he had just had with *Arabella*, that she could be so foolish, as to imagine, I had a Design to propose any one else to her but you? What Reason have I ever given her, to think I would not be glad to have her for my Daughter-in-law? Indeed, she has some odd Ways that are very disagreeable; but she is one of the best Matches in *England* for all that: Poor Girl! pursued he, she had Reason to be angry, if that was the Case; and now I remember, she cried, when I told her I would leave the House; yet her Spirit was so great, that she told me, I might go. Well, I'll go and make it up with her; but who could have imagined, she would have been so foolish? Sir *Charles*, at the Repetition of these Words, hurried away to *Arabella*'s Apartment.

Niece, said he at his Entrance, I am come to ask your Pardon, for having led you into a Belief, that I meant —

'Tis enough, Sir, interrupted *Arabella*; I grant you my Pardon for what is past; and as it does not become me to receive Submissions from my Uncle, while he remembers he is so, I will dispense with your Acknowledgments at present: Only to convince me, that this sudden Alteration is sincere, avoid, I beseech you, for the future, all Occasions of displeasing me.

I protest, cried Sir *Charles*, that I never intended —

I will not hear you say a Word more of your past Intentions, interrupted *Arabella* again; I have forgot them all; and, while you continue to regard me as your Niece, I will never remember them to your Disadvantage.

Then I may hope, said Sir *Charles* —

Oh! Heavens! cried *Arabella*, not suffering him to proceed; do you come to insult me thus, with a mock Repentance? And has my Easiness in being so ready to forget the Injury you would have done me, made you presumptuous enough to cherish an insolent Hope that I will ever change my Resolution?

How vexatious is this! replied Sir *Charles*, fretting to see her continually mistaking him. I swear to you, by all that is sacred, that 'tis my Son, for whom I would sollicit your Consent.

How! said *Arabella*, astonished, Will you then be just at last? And can you resolve to plead for that Son, whose Interest, but a Moment ago, you would have destroyed?

I see, said Sir *Charles*, it is impossible to convince you.

No, no, interrupted *Arabella*, hastily; it is not impossible but my own ardent Wishes that it may be so, will help to convince me of the Truth of what you say: For, in fine, do you think, I shall not be as glad as yourself, to find you capable of acting honourably by your Son; and to see myself no longer the Cause of the most unjustifiable Conduct imaginable?

Sir *Charles* was opening his Mouth, to press her in Favour of Mr. *Glanville*; whom, notwithstanding her strange Behaviour, he was glad to find, she loved; when *Arabella* preventing him,

Seek not, I beseech you, said she, to destroy that Belief I am willing to give your Words, by any more Attempts at this Time to persuade me; for truly, I shall interpret your Sollicitude no way in your Favour; therefore, if you desire I should be convinced you are sincere, let the Silence I require of you, be one Proof of it.

Sir *Charles*, who looked excessively out of Countenance at such a peremptory Command from his Niece, was going out of her Chamber in a very ill Humour, when the Dinner-bell ringing, she gave him her Hand, with a very gracious Air; and permitted him to lead her into the Dining-room, where they found Mr. *Glanville*, his Sister, and Sir *George*, who had been detained to Dinner by Miss *Glanville*, expecting their coming.

CHAPTER VI

Containing some Account of Thalestris, *Queen of the* Amazons, *with other curious Anecdotes.*

Lady *Bella* having recovered her usual Chearfulness, thro' the Satisfaction she felt at her Uncle's returning to Reason, and the Abatement she perceived in Sir *George*'s extreme Melancholy, mixed in the Conversation with that Wit and Vivacity which was natural to her, and which so absolutely charmed the whole Company, that not one of them remembered any of her former Extravagancies.

Mr. *Glanville* gazed on her with a passionate Tenderness, Sir *George* with Admiration, and the old Baronet with Wonder and Delight.

But Miss *Glanville*, who was inwardly vexed at the Superiority her Cousin's Wit gave her over herself, wished for nothing more than an Opportunity of interrupting a Conversation in which she could have no Share; and, willing to put them in mind of some of *Arabella*'s strange Notions, when she observed them disputing concerning some of the Actions of the antient *Romans*, she very innocently asked Sir *George*, whether in former Times Women went to the Wars, and fought like Men? For my Cousin, added she, talks of one *Thaltris*, a Woman, that was as couragious as any Soldier whatever.

Mr. *Glanville*, horridly vexed at a Question that was likely to engage *Arabella* in a Discourse very different from that she had been so capable of pleasing in, frowned very intelligibly at his Sister; and, to prevent any Answer being given to her absurd Demand, directed some other Conversation to *Arabella*: But she, who saw a favourite Subject started, took no Notice of what Mr. *Glanville* was saying to her; but, directing her Looks to Sir *George*,

Though Miss *Glanville*, said she, be a little mistaken in the Name of that fair Queen she has mentioned; yet I am persuaded you know whom she means; and that it is the renowned *Thalestris*, whose Valour staggers her Belief, and of whom she wants to be informed.

Ay, ay, *Thalestris*, said Miss *Glanville*: It is such a strange Name I could not remember it; but, pray, was there ever such a Person?

Certainly, Madam, there was, replied Sir *George*: She was Queen of the *Amazons*, a war-like Nation of Women, who possessed great Part of *Cappadocia*, and extended their Conquests so far, that they became formidable to all their Neighbours.

You find, Miss, said *Arabella*, I did not attempt to impose upon you, when I told you of the admirable Valour of that beautiful Queen; which indeed was so great, that the united Princes, in whose Cause she fought, looked upon her Assistance to be equal to that of a whole Army; and they honoured her accordingly, with the most distinguishing Marks of their Esteem and Acknowlegement, and offered her the chief Command of their Forces.[17]

O shameful! cried Sir *Charles*, offer a Woman the Command of an Army! Brave Fellows indeed, that would be commanded by a Woman! Sure you mistake, Niece; there never was such a thing heard of in the World.

What, Sir, said *Arabella*, will you contradict a Fact attested by the greatest Historians that ever were? You may as well pretend to say, there were never such Persons as *Oroondates* or *Juba*, as dispute the Existence of the famous *Thalestris*.

Why, pray, Madam, said Sir *Charles*, who were those?

One of them, replied *Arabella*, was the great King of *Scythia*; and the other, Prince of the Two *Mauritanias*.

Ods-heart! interrupted Sir *Charles*, I believe their Kingdoms are in the Moon: I never heard of *Scythia*, or the Two *Mauritanias*, before.

And yet, Sir, replied *Arabella*, those Kingdoms are doubtless as well known, as *France* or *England*; and there is no Question, but the Descendants of the great *Oroondates*, and the valiant *Juba*, sway the Sceptres of them to this Day.

I must confess, said Sir *George*, I have a very great Admiration for those Two renowned Princes, and have read their beautiful Exploits with infinite Pleasure; notwithstanding which, I am more inclined to esteem the great *Artaban*, than either of them.

Though *Artaban*, replied *Arabella*, is without Question, a Warrior equal to either of them, and haply no Person in the World possessed so sublime a Courage as his was; yet, it may be, your Partiality proceeds from another Cause; and you having the Honour to resemble him in some little Infidelities he was accused of, with less Justice than yourself perhaps, induces you to favour him more than any other.

Arabella blushed when she ended these Words: And Sir *George* replied, with a Sigh;

I have, indeed, the Honour, Madam, to resemble the great *Artaban*, in having dared to raise my Thoughts towards a Divine Person, who, with Reason, condemns my Adorations.

Hey-day! cried Sir *Charles*, are you going to speak of Divine Things, after all the Fables you have been talking of? Troth, I love to hear young Men enter upon such Subjects: But pray, Niece, who told you Sir *George* was an Infidel?

Mr. *Glanville*, replied *Arabella*: And I am inclined to think he spoke Truth; for Sir *George* has never pretended to deny it.

How! interrupted Sir *Charles*; I am sorry to hear that. I hope you have never, added he, looking at the young Baronet, endeavoured to corrupt my Son with any of your Free-thinking Principles: I am for every body having Liberty of Conscience; but I cannot endure to hear People of your Stamp endeavouring to propagate your mischievous Notions; and because you have no Regard for your own future Happiness, disturbing other People in the laudible Pursuit of theirs.

We will not absolutely condemn Sir *George*, said *Arabella*, till we have heard his History from his own Mouth, which he promised, some Time ago, to relate when I desired it.

I do not imagine his History is fit to be heard by Ladies, said Sir *Charles*; for your Infidels live a strange kind of Life.

However that may be, replied *Arabella*, we must not dispense with Sir *George* from performing his Promise: I dare say there are no Ladies here, who will think the worse of him for freely confessing his Faults.

You may answer for yourself, if you please, Madam, said Sir *Charles*; but I hope my Girl there, will not say as much.

I dare say my Cousin is not so rigid, said *Arabella*: She has too much the Spirit of *Julia* in her, to find Fault with a little Infidelity.[18]

I am always obliged to you for your Comparisons, Cousin, said Miss *Glanville*: I suppose this is greatly to my Advantage too.

I assure you, Madam, said Sir *George*, Lady *Bella* has done you no Injury by the Comparison she has just now made; for *Julia* was one of the finest Princesses in the World.

Yet she was not free from the Suspicion of Infidelity, replied *Arabella*; but though I do not pretend to tax my Cousin with that Fault, yet it is with a great deal of Reason that I say she resembles her in her volatile Humour.

I was never thought to be ill-humoured in my Life, Madam, said Miss *Glanville*, colouring; and I cannot imagine what Reason I have given you for saying I am.

Nay, Cousin, said *Arabella*, I am not condemning your Humour; for to say the Truth, there are a great many Charms in a volatile Disposition; and, notwithstanding the admirable Beauty of *Julia*, it is possible she made as many Slaves by her light and airy Carriage, as she did by her Eyes, though they were the fairest in the World, except the divine *Cleopatra*'s.

Cleopatra! cried Sir *Charles*: Why she was a Gypsey,[19] was she not?

I never heard her called so, said *Arabella*, gravely; and I am apt to believe you are not at all acquainted with her: But pray, pursued she, let us wave this Discourse at present, and prepare to listen to Sir *George*'s Relation of his Life: which, I dare say, is full of very extraordinary Events: However, Sir, added she, directing her Speech to the young Baronet, I am afraid your Modesty will induce you to speak with less Candour than you ought, of those great Actions, which questionless you have performed: Therefore we shall hear your History, with greater Satisfaction, from the Mouth of your faithful Squire, who will not have the same Reasons that you have, for suppressing what is most admirable in the Adventures of your Life.

Since it is your Pleasure, Madam, replied Sir *George*, to hear my Adventures, I will recount them as well as I am able myself, to the End that I may have an Opportunity of obliging you by doing some Violence to my natural Modesty, which will not suffer me to relate Things the World have been pleased to speak of to my Advantage, without some little Confusion.

Then, casting down his Eyes, he seemed to be recollecting the most material Passages in his Life. Mr. *Glanville*, though he could have wished he had not indulged *Arabella* in her ridiculous Request, was not able to deny himself the Diversion of hearing what kind of History he would invent; and therefore resolved to stay and listen to him.

Miss *Glanville* was also highly delighted with the Proposal; but Sir *Charles*, who could not conceive there could be any thing worth listening to, in a young Rake's[20] Account of himself, got up with an Intention to walk in the Garden; when, perceiving it rained, he changed his Resolution, and resuming his Seat, prepared to listen, as every one else did, to the expected Story.

When Sir *George*, after having paused a Quarter of an Hour longer, during which all the Company observed a profound Silence, began his Relation in this Manner, addressing himself to *Arabella*.

END of the fifth BOOK.

BOOK VI

Containing the Beginning of Sir George's *History; in which the ingenious Relator has exactly copied the Stile of Romance.*

Though at present, Madam, you behold me in the Quality of a private Gentleman, in the Possession only of a tolerable Estate; yet my Birth is illustrious enough: My Ancestors having formerly worn a Crown; which, as they won by their Valour, so they lost by their Misfortune only.

How, interrupted Sir *Charles*, are you descended from Kings? Why, I never heard you say so before: Pray, Sir, how far are you removed from Royal Blood? and which of your Forefathers was it that wore a Crown?

Sir, replied Sir *George*, it is not much more than eight Hundred Years since my Ancestors, who were *Saxons*, swayed the Sceptre of *Kent*; and from the first Monarch of that mighty Kingdom, am I lineally descended.

Pray where may that Kingdom of *Kent* lie? said Sir *Charles*.

Sir, replied Sir *George*, it is bounded by *Sussex* on the South-West; *Surry* on the West; the *English* Channel on the South; *Dover* Streights on the South East; and the *Downs* on the East; and it is divided from *Middlesex* and *Essex* on the North by the *Thames*.

A mighty Kingdom, indeed! said Sir *Charles*: Why, it makes but a very small Part of the Kingdom of *Britain* now: Well, if your Ancestors were Kings of that County, as it is now called, it must be confessed their Dominions were very small.

However that may be, said *Arabella*, it raises Sir *George* greatly in my Esteem, to hear he is descended from Kings; for, truly, a Royal Extraction does infinitely set off noble and valiant Actions, and inspires only lofty and generous Sentiments: Therefore, illustrious Prince (for in that Light I shall always consider you), be assured, though Fortune has despoiled you of your Dominions, yet since she cannot deprive you of your Courage and Virtue, Providence will one Day assist your noble Endeavours to recover your Rights, and place you upon the Throne of your Ancestors, from whence you have been so inhumanly driven: Or, haply, to repair that Loss, your Valour may procure you other Kingdoms, no less considerable than that to which you was born.

For Heaven's sake, Niece, said Sir *Charles*, How come such improbable Things into your Head? Is it such an easy Matter, think you, to conquer Kingdoms, that you can flatter a young Man, who has neither Fleets nor Armies, with such strange Hopes?

The great *Artaban*, Sir, resumed *Arabella*, had neither Fleets nor Armies, and was Master only of a single Sword; yet he soon saw himself greater than any King, disposing the Destinies of Monarchs by his Will, and deciding the Fates of Empires by a single Word: But pray let this Dispute rest where it is, and permit Sir *George* to continue his Relation.

It is not necessary, Madam, resumed Sir *George*, to acquaint you with the Misfortunes of my Family, or relate the several Progressions it made towards the private Condition in which it now is: For, betides that reciting the Events of so many Hundred Years may haply, in some Measure, try your Patience, I should be glad if you would dispense with me from entering into a Detail of Accidents that would sensibly afflict me: It shall suffice, therefore, to inform you, that my Father, being a peaceable Man, fond of Retirement and Tranquillity, made no Attempts to recover the Sovereignty from which his Ancestors had been unjustly expelled; but quietly beheld the Kingdom of *Kent* in the Possession of other Masters, while he contented himself with the Improvement of that small Pittance of Ground, which was all that the unhappy Prince *Veridomer*, my Grandfather, was able to bequeath to him.[1]

Hey-day! cried Sir *Charles*, will you new-christen your Grandfather, when he has been in his Grave these Forty Years? I knew honest Sir *Edward Bellmour* very well, though I was but a Youth when he died; but I believe no Person in *Kent* ever gave him the Title of Prince *Veridomer*: Fie! fie! these are idle Brags.

Sir *George*, without taking Notice of the old Baronet's Heat, went on with his Narration in this Manner:

Things were in this State, Madam, when I was born. I will not trouble you with the Relation of what I did in my Infancy.

No, pray skip over all that, interrupted Sir *Charles*; I suppose your Infancy was like other People's; what can there be worth hearing in that?

You are deceived, Sir, said *Arabella*: The Infancy of illustrious Personages has always something very extraordinary in it; and from their childish Words and Actions there have been often Presages drawn of their future Greatness and Glory.

Not to disoblige Sir *Charles*, however, said the young Prince of *Kent*, I will not repeat many things, which I said and did in the first Years of my Life, that those about me thought very surprising; and from them prognosticated, that very strange Accidents would befal me.

I have been a Witness of some very unfavourable Prognostics of you, said Sir *Charles*, smiling; for you was the most unlucky bold Spark, that ever I knew in my Life.

'Tis very certain, pursued Sir *George*, that the Forwardness of my Spirit gave great Uneasiness to my Father; who, being, as I said before, inclinable to a peaceable and sedentary Life, endeavoured as much as possible to repress that Vivacity in my Disposition, which he feared might involve me in dangerous Enterprizes. The Pains he took in my Education, I recompensed by a more than ordinary Docility; and, before I was Thirteen, performed all my Exercises with a marvellous Grace; and, if I may dare say so, was, at those early Years, the Admiration and Wonder of all that saw me.

Lady *Bella* had some Reason to fear your Modesty, I find,

said Sir *Charles*, smiling; for, methinks you really speak too slightly of your Excellencies.

However that may be, resumed Sir *George*; my Father saw these early Instances of a towering Genius in me, with a Pleasure, chastened by his Fears, that the Grandeur of my Courage would lead me to attempt something for the Recovery of that Kingdom, which was my Due; and which might haply occasion his losing me.

Possessed with these Thoughts, he carefully avoided saying any thing to me concerning the glorious Pretences, to which my Birth gave me a Right; and often wished it had been possible for him to conceal from me, that I was the true and lawful Heir of the Kingdom of *Kent*; a Circumstance he never chose to mention to any Person, and would have been glad, if it had always remained a Secret.

And so it was a Secret, interrupted Sir *Charles*; for, till this Day, I never heard of it; and it might still have been a Secret, if you had pleased; for nobody, I dare say, would suspect such a Thing; and very few, I believe, will be inclined to think there is any thing in such an improbable Tale.

Notwithstanding all my Father's Endeavours to the contrary, Madam, pursued Sir *George*, I cherished those towering Sentiments, the Knowledge of my Birth inspired me with; and it was not without the utmost Impatience, that I brooked the private Condition, to which I found myself reduced.

Cruel Fate! would I sometimes cry; was it not enough to deprive me of that Kingdom, which is my Due, and subject me to a mean, and inglorious State; but, to make that Condition infinitely more grievous, must thou give me a Soul towering above my abject Fortune? A Soul, that cannot but disdain the base Submission, I must pay to those, who triumph in the Spoils of my ruined House? A Soul, which sees nothing above its Hopes and Expectations? And, in fine, a Soul, that excites me daily to attempt Things worthy of my Birth, and those noble Sentiments I inherit from my great Forefathers? Ah! pursued I, unhappy *Bellmour*; what hinders thee from making thyself known and acknowledged for what thou art? What hinders thee from boldly asserting thy just and natural Rights; and from defying the Usurper, who detains them from thee? What hinders thee, I say?

What? Interrupted Sir *Charles*, why the Fear of a Halter,[2] I suppose: There is nothing more easy than to answer that Question.

Such, Madam, said Sir *George*, were the Thoughts, which continually disturbed my Imagination; and, doubtless, they had not failed to push me on to some hazardous Enterprize, had not a fatal Passion interposed, and by its sweet, but dangerous Allurements, stifled for a while that Flame, which Ambition, and the Love of Glory, kindled in my Soul.

Sir *George* here pausing, and fixing his Eyes with a melancholy Air on the Ground, as if prest with a tender Remembrance;

Mr. *Glanville* asked him, smiling, If the Thoughts of poor *Dolly* disturbed him? Pray, added he, give us the History of your first Love, without any Mixture of Fable; or shall I take the Trouble off you? For you know, I am very well acquainted with your Affair with the pretty Milk-maid,[3] and can tell it very succinctly.

'Tis true, Sir, said Sir *George*, sighing, I cannot recall the Idea of *Dorothea*, into my Remembrance, without some Pain: That fair, but unfaithful Sheperdess, who first taught me to sigh, and repaid my Tenderness with the blackest Infidelity: Yet I will endeavour to compose myself, and go on with my Narration.

Be pleased to know then, Madam, pursued Sir *George*, that having my Thoughts, in this manner, wholly employed with the Disasters of my Family, I had arrived to my seventeenth Year, without being sensible of the Power of Love; but the Moment now arrived, which was to prove fatal to my Liberty. Following the Chace one Day with my Father, and some other Gentlemen, I happened to lag a little behind them; and, being taken up with my ordinary Reflections, I lost my Way, and wandered a long time, without knowing or considering whither I was going. Chance at last conducted me to a pleasant Valley, surrounded with Trees: and, being tired with riding, I lighted, and tying my Horse to a Tree, walked forward, with an Inten-

tion to repose myself a few Moments under the Shade of one
of those Trees, that had attracted my Observation: But while
I was looking for the most convenient Place, I spied, at the
Distance of some few Yards from me, a Woman lying asleep
upon the Grass: Curiosity tempted me to go nearer this Person;
and, advancing softly, that I might not disturb her, I got near
enough to have a View of her Person: But, ah! Heavens! what
Wonders did my Eyes encounter in this View! — The Age of
this fair Sleeper seemed not to exceed Sixteen; her Shape was
formed with the exactest Symmetry; one of her Hands supported her Head; the other, as it lay carelesly stretched at her
Side, gave me an Opportunity of admiring its admirable Colour
and Proportion: The thin Covering upon her Neck discovered
Part of its inimitable Beauty to my Eyes; but her Face, her lovely
Face, fixed all my Attention.

Certain it is, Madam, that, out of this Company, it would
be hard to find any thing so perfect, as what I now viewed. Her
Complexion was the purest White imaginable, heightened by
the inchanting Glow, which dyed her fair Cheeks with a Colour
like that of a new-blown Rose: Her Lips, formed with the
greatest Perfection, and of a deeper Red, seemed to receive new
Beauties from the Fragrance of that Breath that parted from
them. Her auburn Hair fell in loose Ringlets over her Neck;
and some straggling Curls, that played upon her fair Forehead,
set off by a charming Contrast the Whiteness of that Skin it
partly hid: Her Eyes indeed were closed; and though I knew
not whether their Colour and Beauty were equal to those other
Miracles in her Face, yet their Proportion seemed to be large;
and the snowy Lids, which covered them, were admirably set
off by those long and sable Lashes that adorned them.

For some Moments I gazed upon this lovely Sleeper, wholly
lost in Wonder and Admiration.

Where, whispered I, where has this Miracle been concealed,
that my Eyes were never blessed with the Sight of her before?
These Words, though I uttered them softly, and with the utmost
Caution; yet by the murmuring Noise they made, caused an
Emotion in the beauteous Sleeper, that she started, and pres-
ently after opened her Eyes: But what Words shall I find to

express the Wonder, the Astonishment, and Rapture, which the sight of those bright Stars inspired me with? The Flames which darted from those glorious Orbs, cast such a dazling Splendor upon a Sight too weak to bear a Radiance so unusual, that, stepping back a few Paces, I contemplated at a Distance, that Brightness, which began already to kindle a consuming Fire in my Soul.

Bless me! interrupted Sir *Charles*, confounded at so pompous a Description; who could this be?

The pretty Milk-maid, *Dolly Acorn*, replied Mr. *Glanville* gravely: Did you never see her, Sir, when you was at your Seat, at ——? She used often to bring Cream to my Lady.

Aye, aye, replied Sir *Charles*, I remember her: She was a very pretty Girl: And so it was from her Eyes, that all those Splendors and Flames came, that had like to have burnt you up, Sir *George*: Well, well, I guess how the Story will end: Pray let us hear it out.

I have already told you, Madam, resumed Sir *George*, the marvelous Effects the Sight of those bright Eyes produced upon my Spirit: I remained fixed in a Posture of Astonishment and Delight; and all the Faculties of my Soul were so absorbed in the Contemplation of the Miracles before me, that I believe, had she still continued before my Eyes, I should never have moved from the Place where I then stood: But the fair Virgin, who had spied me at the small Distance to which I was retired, turned hastily about, and flew away with extraordinary Swiftness.

When Love, now lending me Wings, whom Admiration had before made motionless, I persued her so eagerly, that at last I overtook her; and, throwing myself upon my Knees before her,

Stay, I conjure you, cried I; and if you be a Divinity, as your celestial Beauty makes me believe, do not refuse the Adoration I offer you: But if, as I most ardently wish, you are a Mortal, though sure the fairest that ever graced the Earth; stop a Moment, to look upon a Man, whose Respects for you as a Mortal fall little short of those Adorations he offers you as a Goddess.

I can't but think, cried Sir *Charles*, laughing, how poor *Dolly* must be surprised at such a rhodomontade Speech![4]

Oh, Sir! replied Mr. *Glanville*, you will find she will make as good a one.

Will she, by my Troth, said Sir *Charles*: I don't know how to believe it.

This Action, pursued Sir *George*, and the Words I uttered, a little surprised that fair Maid, and brought a Blush into her lovely Cheeks; but recovering herself, she replied with an admirable Grace,

I am no Divinity, said she; and therefore your Adorations are misplaced: But if, as you say, my Countenance moves you to any Respect for me, give me a Proof of it, by not endeavouring to hold any further Discourse with me, which is not permitted me from one of your Sex and Appearance.

A very wise Answer, indeed! interrupted Sir *Charles* again: Very few Town Ladies would have disclaimed the Title of Goddess, if their Lovers had thought proper to bestow it upon them. I am mightily pleased with the Girl for her Ingenuity.

The Discretion of so young a Damsel, resumed Sir *George*, charmed me no less than her Beauty; and I besought her, with the utmost Earnestness, to permit me a longer Conversation with her.

Fear not, lovely Virgin, said I, to listen to the Vows of a Man, who, till he saw you, never learnt to sigh: My Heart, which defended its Liberty against the Charms of many admirable Ladies, yields, without Reluctance, to the pleasing Violence your Beauties lay upon me. Yes, too charming and dangerous Stranger, I am no longer my own Master: It is in your Power to dispose of my Destiny: Consider therefore, I beseech you, whether you can consent to see me die? For I swear to you, by the most sacred Oaths, unless you promise to have some Compassion on me, I will no longer behold the Light of Day.

You may easily conceive, Madam, that, considering this lovely Maid in the Character of a Shepherdess, in which she appeared, I made her a Declaration of my Passion, without thinking myself obliged to observe those Respects, which, to a Person of equal Rank with myself, Decorum would not have permitted me to forget.[5]

However, she repelled my Boldness with so charming a

Modesty, that I began to believe, she might be a Person of illustrious Birth, disguised under the mean Habit she wore: But, having requested her to inform me who she was, she told me her Name was *Dorothea*; and that she was Daughter to a Farmer, that lived in the neighbouring Valley. This Knowledge increasing my Confidence, I talked to her of my Passion, without being the least afraid of offending her.

And therein you was greatly to blame, said *Arabella*: For, truly, though the fair *Dorothea* told you, she was Daughter to a Farmer; yet, in all Probability, she was of a much higher Extraction, if the Picture you have drawn of her be true.

The fair *Arsinoe*, Princess of *Armenia*, was constrained for a while to conceal her true Name and Quality, and pass for a simple Country-woman, under the Name of *Delia*: Yet the generous *Philadelph*, Prince of *Cilicia*, who saw and loved her under that Disguise, treated her with all the Respect he would have done, had he known she was the Daughter of a King.[6] In like manner, Prince *Philoxipes*, who fell in Love with the beautiful *Policrete*, before he knew she was the Daughter of the great *Solon*; and while he looked upon her as a poor Stranger, born of mean Parents; nevertheless, his Love supplying the Want of those Advantages of Birth and Fortune, he wooed her with a Passion as full of Awe and Delicacy, as if her Extraction had been equal to his own.[7] And therefore those admirable Qualities the fair *Dorothea* possessed, might also have convinced you, she was not what she seemed, but haply, some great Princess in Disguise.

To tell you the Truth, Madam, replied Sir *George*, notwithstanding the fair *Dorothea* informed me, she was of a mean Descent, I could not easily forego the Opinion, that she was of an illustrious Birth: And the Histories of those fair Princesses you have mentioned, coming into my Mind, I also thought it very possible, that this divine Person might either be the Daughter of a great King, or Lawgiver, like them; but, being wholly engrossed by the Violence of my new-born Affection, I listened to nothing, but what most flattered my Hopes; and, addressing my lovely Shepherdess with all the Freedom of a Person who thinks his Birth much superior to hers; she listened to my

Protestations, without any seeming Reluctance, and condescended to assure me before we parted, that she did not hate me. So fair a Beginning, seemed to promise me the most favourable Fortune I could with Reason expect. I parted from my fair Shepherdess with a thousand Vows of Fidelity; exacting a Promise from her, that she would meet me as often as she conveniently could, and have the Goodness to listen to those Assurances of inviolable Tenderness my Passion prompted me to offer her. When she left me, it seemed as if my Soul had forsaken my Body to go after her: My Eyes pursued her Steps as long as she was in Sight; I envied the Ground she prest as she went along, and the Breezes that kissed that celestial Countenance in their Flight.

For some Hours I stood in the same Posture in which she had left me; contemplating the sudden Change I had experienced in my Heart, and the Beauty of that divine Image, which was now engraven in it. Night drawing on, I began to think of going home; and, untying my Horse, I returned the Way I had come; and at last struck into a Road, which brought me to the Place where I parted from the Company; from whence I easily found my Way home, so changed both in my Looks and Carriage, that my Father, and all my Friends, observed the Alteration with some Surprize.

CHAPTER II

In which Sir George, *continuing his surprising History, relates a most stupendous Instance of a Valour only to be parallelled by that of the great* Oroondates, Cæsareo, *&c. &c. &c.*

For some Months, continued Sir *George*, I prosecuted my Addresses to the admirable *Dorothea*; and I flattered myself with a Hope, that I had made some Progress in her Heart: But, alas! this deceitful Fair-one, who only laughed at the Torments she made me endure, at the Time she vowed eternal Constancy to me, gave her Hand to a Lover of her Father's providing, and abandoned me, without Remorse, to the most cruel Despair.

I will not trouble you, Madam, with the Repetition of those Complaints, which this perfidious Action drew from me for a long Time. At length, my Courage enabling me to overcome the Violence of my Grief, I resolved to think of the ungrateful *Dorothea* no more; and the Sight of another Beauty compleating my Cure, I no longer remembred the unfaithful Shepherdess, but with Indifference.

Thus, Madam, have I faithfully related one of those Infidelities, wherewith my Enemies slander me; who can support their Assertion, with no better Proof, than that I did not die, when *Dorothea* abandoned me: But I submit it to your Candour, whether an unfaithful Mistress deserved such an Instance of Affection, from a Lover she had betrayed?

Why, really, replied *Arabella*, after a little Pause, you had some Excuse to plead for your Failure in this Point: And though you cannot be called, the most perfect amongst Lovers, seeing you neither died, nor was in Danger of dying; yet neither ought you to be ranked among those who are most culpable: But pray proceed in your Story; I shall be better able to form a right Judgment of your Merit as a Lover, when I have heard all your Adventures.

My Passion for *Dorothea*, resumed Sir *George*, being cured by her Treachery towards me, the Love of Glory began again to revive in my Soul. I panted after some Occasion to signalize my Valour, which yet I had met with no Opportunity of doing; but, hearing, that a mighty Army was preparing to march upon a secret Expedition, I privately quitted my Father's Seat; and attended only by my faithful 'Squire, I took the same Route the Army had taken, and arrived the Day before the terrible Battle of —— was fought, where, without making myself known, I performed such Prodigies of Valour, as astonished all who beheld me. Without doubt, I should have been highly caressed by the Commander, who certainly would have given me the Honour of a Victory my Sword alone had procured for him; but, having unwittingly engaged myself too far in Pursuit of the flying Enemy, I found myself alone, encompassed with a Party of about Five hundred Men; who seeing they were pursued only by a single Man, faced about, and prepared to kill or take me Prisoner.

Pray, Sir, interrupted Sir *Charles*, when did all this happen? and how came it to pass, that your Friends have been ignorant to this Moment of those Prodigies of Valour you performed at that Battle? I never heard you was ever in a Battle: Fame has done you great Injustice, by concealing the Part you had in that famous Victory.

The great Care I took to conceal myself, replied Sir *George*, was one Reason why my Friends did not attribute to me the Exploits, which the Knight in black Armour, who was no other than myself, performed; and the Accident I am going to relate, prevented my being discovered, while the Memory of those great Exploits were yet fresh in the Minds of those I had so greatly obliged.

Be pleased to know, therefore, Madam, that seeing myself about to be encompassed by this Party of the Enemy, I disdained to fly; and, though I was alone, resolved to sustain their Attack, and sell my Life as dear as possible.

Why, if you did so, you was a Madman, cried Sir *Charles* in a Heat: The bravest Man that ever lived, would not have presumed to fight with so great a Number of Enemies. What could you expect, but to be cut in Pieces? Pooh! pooh! don't think any body will credit such a ridiculous Tale: I never knew you was so addicted to —

Lying, perhaps, the good Knight would have said; but Sir *George*, who was concerned he was present at his Legend, and could not blame him for doubting his Veracity, prevented his Utterance of a Word he would be obliged to take ill, by abruptly going on with his Story.

Placing my Back therefore against a Tree, pursued he, to prevent my being assaulted behind, I presented my Shield to the boldest of these Assailants; who, having struck an impotent Blow upon it, as he was lifting up his Arm to renew his Attack, I cut it off with one Stroke of my Sword; and the same Instant plunged it to the Hilt in the Breast of another, and clove the Scull of a third, who was making at me, in two Parts.

Sir *Charles*, at this Relation, burst into a loud Fit of Laughter;

and, being more inclined to divert himself, than be offended at the Folly and Vanity of the young Baronet, he permitted him to go on with his surprising Story, without giving him any other Interruption.

These three Executions, Madam, pursued Sir *George*, were the Effects only of so many Blows; which raised such Indignation in my Enemies, that they prest forward in great Numbers to destroy me; but, having, as I before said, posted myself so advantageously, that I could only be assaulted before, not more than Three or Four could attack me at one time. The Desire of lengthening out my Life, till happily some Succour might come to my Relief, so invigorated my Arm, and added to my ordinary Strength an almost irresistible Force, that I dealt Death at every Blow; and in less than a quarter of an Hour, saw more than Fifty of my Enemies at my Feet, whose Bodies served for a Bulwark against their Fellows Swords.

The Commander of this little Body, not having Generosity enough to be moved with those prodigious Effects of Valour in my Favour, was transported with Rage at my Resistance; and the Sight of so many of his Men slain before his Face, served only to encrease his Fury; and that Moment, seeing, that, with Two more Blows, I had sent two of his most valiant Soldiers to the Shades, and that the rest fearing to come within the Length of my Sword, had given me a few Moments Respite,

Ah! Cowards! cried he, are you afraid of a single Man? And will you suffer *him* to escape from your Vengeance, who has slain so many of your brave Comrades before your Eyes?

These Words inspiring them with a Fierceness, such as he desired, they advanced towards me with more Fury than before: By this Time, I had received several large Wounds, and my Blood ran down from many Parts of my Body: yet was I not sensible of any Decay of Strength, nor did the settled Designs of my Enemies to destroy me daunt me in the least: I still relied upon the Assistance I expected Providence would send to my Relief, and determined, if possible, to preserve my Life, till it arrived.

I fought, therefore, with a Resolution, which astonished my Enemies, but did not move them to any Regard for my Safety:

And, observing their brutal Commander, a few Paces from me, encouraging his Men, both with his Cries and Gestures, Indignation against this inhuman Wretch so transported me out of my Discretion, that I quitted my Post, in order to sacrifice him to my Revenge.

Seeing me advance furiously towards him, he turned pale with Fear, and endeavoured to shelter himself in the midst of his Men; who, more valiant than himself, opposed themselves to my Rage, to favour his Retreat: But quickly clearing myself a Way with my Sword, I pressed towards the barbarous Coward; and, ere he could avoid the Blow I aimed at him, it struck him senseless at my Feet.

My particular Revenge thus satisfied, I was sensible of the Fault I had committed in quitting my Post, by which I exposed myself to be surrounded by the Enemy. I endeavoured to regain it, but in vain: I was beset on all Sides, and now despaired of any Safety; and therefore only sought to die couragiously, and make as many of my Enemies as I could, attend my Fall.

Exasperated by the Misfortune of their Commander, they pressed upon me with redoubled Fury. Faint as I was, with the Loss of Blood, and so fatigued with the past Action, and the obstinate Fight I had maintained so long with such a considerable Number, I could hardly any longer lift up my Arm; and, to complete, my Misfortune, having thrust my Sword into the Body of one of the forwardest of my Enemies, in my endeavouring to regain it, it broke in Pieces, and the Hilt only remained in my Hand.

This Accident completed my Defeat: Deprived of my Sword, I was no longer capable of making any Defence: several of them pressed upon me at once; and, throwing me down, tied my Hands together behind me. Shame and Rage at this Indignity worked so forcibly upon my Spirits, weakened as I then was, that I fell into a Swoon. What happened till my Recovery, I am not able to tell; but, at the Return of my Senses, I found myself laid on a Bed in a tolerable Chamber, and some Persons with me, who kept a profound Silence.

CHAPTER III

A Love-Adventure, after the Romantic Taste.

Recollecting in a few Moments all that happened to me, I could not choose but be surprised at finding myself treated with so little Severity, considering I was Prisoner to Persons who had been Witnesses of the great Quantity of Blood I had shed in my own Defence. My Wounds had been dressed while I continued in my Swoon; and the Faces of those Persons who were about me, expressed nothing of Unkindness.

After reflecting some Time longer on my Situation, I called to a young Man, who sat near my Bed-side, and intreated him to inform me, where I was, and to whom I was a Prisoner? But could get no other Answer to those Questions, than a most civil Intreaty to compose myself, and not protract the Cure of my Wounds by talking, which the Surgeons had declared, would be of a bad Consequence; and had therefore ordered me to be as little disturbed as possible.

Notwithstanding this Remonstrance, I repeated my Request, promising to be entirely governed by them for the future in what regarded my Health, provided they would satisfy me in those Particulars: But my Attendant did not so much as reply to those Importunities; but to prevent the Continuance of them, rose from his Seat, and retired to the other End of the Chamber.

I passed that Day, and several others, without being able to learn the Truth of my Condition: All this Time, I was diligently waited on by the two Persons I had first seen, neither of whom I could prevail upon to inform me of what I desired to know; and, judging, by this obstinate Reserve, and the Manner of my Treatment, that there was some Mystery in the Case, I forbore to ask them any more Questions, conceiving they had particular Orders not to answer them.

The Care that was taken to forward my Cure, in three Weeks entirely restored me to Health: I longed impatiently to know, what was to be my Destiny; and busied myself in conjecturing it, in vain; when one Morning, an elderly Lady entered my Chamber, at whose Appearance my two Attendants retired.

After she had saluted me very civilly, and inquired after my Health, she seated herself in a Chair near my Bedside, and spoke to me in this Manner:

I make no Question, Sir, but you are surprised at the Manner in which you have been treated, and the Care there has been taken to prevent discovering to you the Place where you now are; but you will doubtless be more surprized, to hear you are in the Fortress of ———, and in the House of Prince *Marcomire*, whose Party you fought against alone; and whom you so dangerously wounded, before you was taken Prisoner by his Men.

Is it possible, Madam, said I, who, from the first Moment of her Appearance, had been in a strange Perplexity, is it possible, I am in the House of a Man, whose Life I endeavoured so eagerly to destroy? And is it to him, who oppressed me so basely with Numbers, that I am obliged for the Succour I have received?

It is not to him, replied the Lady, that you are obliged for the favourable Treatment you have had; but listen to me patiently, and I will disclose the Truth of your Adventure.

Prince *Marcomire*, who was the Person that headed that Party against which you so valiantly defended yourself, after the Loss of the Battle, was hastening to throw himself into this Place, where his Sister, and many Ladies of Quality, had come for Security: Your indiscreet Pursuit engaged you in the most unequal Combat that ever was fought; and ———

Nay, Sir, interrupted *Arabella*, though I do not refuse to give you all the Praises your gallant Defence of yourself against Five Hundred Men deserves; yet I cannot agree with that Lady, in saying, it was the most unequal Combat that ever was fought: For, do but reflect, I beseech you, upon that which the brave Prince of *Mauritania* sustained against twice that Number of Men, with no other Arms than his Sword; and, you having been in Battle that Day, was, as I conceive, completely armed. The young Prince of *Egypt*, accompanied only by the valiant, but indiscreet, *Cepio* his Friend, engaged all the King of *Armenia*'s

Guards, and put them all to Flight. The courageous *Ariobasanes* scorned to turn his Back upon a whole Army; not to mention the invincible *Artaban*, whom a Thousand Armies together could not have made to turn.[8]

Be pleased to observe, Madam, said Sir *George*, that to the End I may faithfully recount my History, I am under a Necessity of repeating Things, which, haply, may seem too advantageous for a Man to say of himself: Therefore I indeed greatly approve of the Custom, which, no doubt, this Inconveniency introduced, of a 'Squire, who is thoroughly instructed with the Secrets of his Master's Heart, relating his Adventures, and giving a proper Eulogium of his rare Valour, without being in Danger of offending the Modesty of the renowned Knight; who, as you know, Madam, upon those Occasions, commodiously slips away.

It being, however, this Lady's Opinion, that no Man ever undertook a more hazardous Combat, or with greater Odds, against him, she did not fail to express her Admiration of it, in very high Terms.

The Noise of this Accident, pursued she, was soon spread over the whole Town; and the beautiful *Sydimiris*, *Marcomire*'s Sister, hearing that her Brother was wounded, as it was thought to Death, and that the Person who killed him, was taken Prisoner; she flew out to meet her wounded Brother, distracted with Grief, and vowing to have the severest Tortures executed on him, who had thus barbarously murdered her Brother. Those who bore that unhappy Prince, having brought him into the House, his Wounds were searched; and the Surgeons declared, they were very dangerous.

Sydimiris, hearing this, redoubled her Complaints and Vows of Vengeance against you: Her Brother having then the chief Authority in the Place, she commanded, in his Name, to have you brought hither, and to be most strictly guarded; determined, if her Brother died, to sacrifice you to his Ghost.

Full of these sanguinary Resolutions, she left his Chamber, having seen him laid in Bed; and his Wounds dressed; but passing along a Gallery to her own Apartment, she met the Persons who were bringing you to the Room that was to be your Prison: You was not, pursued the Lady, yet recovered from your Swoon, so that they carried you like one that was dead: They had taken off your Helmet to give you Air; by which means your Face being quite uncovered, pale, languishing, and your Eyes closed, as if in Death, presented the most moving, and, at the same Time, most pleasing Object in the World.

Sydimiris, who stopt, and for a Moment eagerly gazed upon you, lost all of a sudden the Fierceness which before had animated her against you: And lifting up her Eyes to view those Men that carried you;

Are you sure, said she to them, that this is the Person who wounded my Brother?

Yes, Madam, replied one of them; this must be he, since there was no other in his Company; and he alone sustained the Attack of Five hundred Men; and would probably not have left one of them alive, had not his Sword, by breaking, put it into our Power to take him Prisoner.

Carry him away, said *Sydimiris*; but let his Wounds be dressed, and let him be carefully looked to, that, if my Brother dies, he may be punished as he deserves.

Pronouncing these Words in a low and faltering Voice, she turned her Eyes a second time upon you; then, hastily averting her Looks, she hurried to her own Chamber, and threw herself into a Chair, with all the Marks of a very great Disturbance.

The Affection I have for her, being the Person who had brought her up, and most favoured with her Confidence, made me behold her in this Condition with great Concern; and supposing it was her Brother that disquieted her, I besought her not to give way to the Violence of her Grief, but to hope that Heaven would restore him to her Prayers.

Alas! my dear *Urinoe*, said she, I am more culpable than you can imagine; and I grieve less for the Condition to which I see *Marcomire* reduced, than for that Moderation wherewith I am constrained, spite of myself, to behold his Enemy.

Yes, dear *Urinoe*, pursued she, blushing, and casting down her Eyes, the Actions of this Unknown appear to me in quite another Light, since I have seen him; and, instead of looking upon him as the Murderer of my Brother, I cannot help admiring that rare Valour, with which he defended himself against so great a Number of Enemies; and am even ready to condemn the furious *Marcomire*, for oppressing so brave a Man.

As I had never approved of those violent Transports of Grief and Rage, which she had expressed upon the first News of her Brother's Misfortune; and as I looked upon your glorious Defence with the utmost Admiration; so, far from condemning the Change of her Thoughts, I confirmed her in the favourable Opinion she began to entertain of you; and, continuing to make Remarks upon all the Particulars of the Combat, which had come to our Knowledge, we found nothing in your Behaviour, but what increased our Admiration.

Sydimiris therefore, following the Dictates of her own Generosity, as well as my Advice, placed Two Persons about you, whose Fidelity we could rely on; and gave them Orders to treat you with all imaginable Care and Respect, but not to inform you of the Place in which you was, or to whom you was Prisoner.

In the mean Time, *Marcomire*, whose Wounds had been again examined, was declared out of Danger by the Surgeons; and he having understood the Excess of his Sister's Grief, and the Revenge she had vowed against you, gave her Thanks for those Expressions of her Tenderness; and also uttered some Threats, which intimated a violent Hatred against you; and a Design of prosecuting his Revenge upon you, as soon as he was in a Condition to leave his Chamber.

Sydimiris, who heard him, could with Difficulty dissemble her Concern.

Ah! *Urinoe*, said she to me, when we were alone; 'tis now, that I more than ever repent of that Excess of Rage, which transported me against the brave Unknown. I have thereby put him intirely into my Brother's Power, and shall be haply accessary to that Death he is meditating for him, or else a perpetual Imprisonment.

This Reflection gave her so much Pain, that I could not choose but pity her; and considering, that the only Way to preserve you, was for her to dissemble a Rage equal to *Marcomire*'s against you, in order to prevent being suspected of any Design in your Favour, I persuaded her to join with him in every Thing he said; while, in the mean time, we would endeavour to get you cured of your Wounds, that you might at least be in a Condition once more to defend yourself with that miraculous Valour Heaven has bestowed on you.

Sydimiris perceiving her Brother would soon be in a Condition to execute his Threats, resolved to hazard every thing, rather than to expose you to his Rage: She therefore communicated to me her Design of giving you Liberty, and, by presenting a sufficient Reward to your Guard, inducing them to favour your Escape.

I undertook to manage this Business in her Name, and have done it so effectually, that you will this Night be at Liberty, and may depart the Town immediately, in which it will be dangerous to stay any Time, for Fear of being discovered.

Sydimiris forbad me to let you know the Person to whom you would be obliged for your Freedom; but I could not endure, that you should unjustly involve the Sister of *Marcomire*, in that Resentment you will questionless always preserve against *him*; and to keep you from being innocently guilty of Ingratitude, I resolved to acquaint you with the Nature of those Obligations you owe to her.

CHAPTER IV

The Adventure continued.

Ah! Madam, said I, perceiving she had finished her Discourse, doubt not but I shall most gratefully preserve the Remembrance of what the generous *Sydimiris* has done for me; and shall always be ready to lose that Life in her Defence, which she has had the superlative Goodness to take so much Care of. But, Madam, pursued I, with an earnest Look, do not, I beseech you, refuse me one Favour, without which I shall depart with inconceivable Sorrow.

Depend upon it, valiant Sir, replied she, that if what you will require of me, be in my Power, and fit for me to grant, I shall very willingly oblige you.

It is then, resumed I, trembling at the Boldness of my Request, that you would condescend to intreat the most generous *Sydimiris* to favour me with an Interview, and give me an Opportunity of throwing myself at her Feet, to thank her for all those Favours I have received from her Compassion.

I cannot promise you, replied the Lady, rising, to prevail upon *Sydimiris* to grant you an Audience; but I assure you, that I will endeavour to dispose her to do you this Favour; and it shall not be my Fault, if you are not satisfied.

Saying this, she went out of my Chamber, I having followed her to the Door, with Protestations that I would never forget her Kindness upon this Occasion.

I past the rest of that Day in an anxious Impatience for Night, divided between Fear and Hope, and more taken up with the Thoughts of seeing *Sydimiris*, than with my expected Liberty.

Night came at last, and the Door of my Apartment opening, I saw the Lady who had been with me in the Morning, enter.

I have prevailed upon *Sydimiris* to see you, said she; and she is willing, at my Intreaty, to grant that Favour to a Person, who, she with Reason thinks, has been inhumanly treated by her Brother.

Then, giving me her Hand, she conducted me along a large Gallery, to a stately Apartment; and after traversing several Rooms, she led me into one, where *Sydimiris* herself was: Who, as soon as she perceived me, rose from her Seat, and received me with great Civility.

In the Transport I then was, I know not how I returned the graceful Salute the incomparable *Sydimiris* gave me; for most certain it is, that I was so lost in Wonder, at the Sight of the many Charms I beheld in her Person, that I could not unlock my Tongue, or remove my Eyes from her inchanting Face; but remained fixed in a Posture, which at once expressed my Admiration and Delight.

To give you a Description of that Beauty which I then contemplated, I must inform you, Madam, that *Sydimiris* is tall, of a handsome Stature, and admirably proportioned; her Hair was of the finest Black in the World; her Complexion marvelously fair; all the Lineaments of her Visage were perfectly beautiful; and her Eyes, which were large and black, sparkled with so quick and piercing a Fire, that no Heart was able to resist their powerful Glances: Moreover, *Sydimiris* is admirably shaped; her Port is high and noble; and her Air so free, yet so commanding, that there are few Persons in the World, with whom she may not dispute the Priority of Beauty:[9] In fine, Madam, *Sydimiris* appeared with so many Advantages to a Spirit prepossessed already with the most grateful Sense of her Favours, that I could not resist the sweet Violence wherewith her Charms took Possession of my Heart: I yielded therefore, without Reluctance, to my Destiny, and resigned myself, in an Instant, to those Fetters, which the Sight of the Divine *Sydimiris* prepared for me: Recovering therefore a little from that Admiration, which had so totally engrossed all my Faculties, I threw myself at her Feet, with an Action wholly composed of Transport.

Divine *Sydimiris*, said I, beholding her with Eyes, in which the Letters of my new-born Passion might very plainly be read, see at your Feet a Man devoted to your Service, by all the Ties of Gratitude and Respect. I come, Madam, to declare to you, that from the first Moment you gave me Liberty, I had devoted that and my Life to you; and at your Feet I confirm the Gift; protesting by all that is most dear and sacred to me, that since I hold my Life from the Divine *Sydimiris*, she alone shall have the absolute Disposal of it for the future; and should she please again to demand it, either to appease her Brother's Fury, or to sacrifice it to her own Security, I will most faithfully perform her Will, and shed the last Drop of that Blood at her Command, which I would with Transport lose in her Defence.

A fine high flown Speech indeed! said Sir *Charles*, laughing: but I hope you did not intend to keep your Word.

Sure, Sir, replied *Arabella*, you do not imagine, that Sir *George* would have failed in executing all he had promised to the beautiful and generous *Sydimiris*: What could he possibly have said less? And indeed what less could she have expected from a Man, whom at the Hazard of her own Life and Happiness, she had given Freedom to?

I accompanied these Words, Madam, pursued Sir *George*,

with so passionate a Look and Accent, that the fair *Sydimiris* blushed, and, for a Moment, cast down her Eyes with a visible Confusion. At last,

Sir, replied she, I am too well satisfied with what I have done, with respect to your Safety, to require any Proofs of your Gratitude, that might be dangerous to it; and shall remain extremely well satisfied, if the Obligations you think you owe me, may induce you to moderate your Resentment against my Brother, for the cruel Treatment you received from him.

Doubt not, Madam, interrupted I, eagerly, but I shall, in the Person of *Marcomire*, regard the Brother of the divine *Sydimiris*; and that Consideration will be sufficient, not only to make me forget all the Violences he committed against me, but even to defend his Life, if need be, with the Hazard of my own.

Excessively generous indeed! said Sir *Charles*: I never heard any thing like it.

Oh! dear Sir, replied *Arabella*, there are numberless Instances of equal, and even superior Generosity, to be met with in the Lives of the Heroes of Antiquity: You will there see a Lover, whose Mistress has been taken from him, either by Treachery or Force, venture his Life in Defence of the injurious Husband who possesses her; and though all his Felicity depends upon his Death, yet he will rescue him from it, at the Expence of the greater Part of his Blood.[10]

Another, who after a long and bloody War, has, by taking his Enemy Prisoner, an Opportunity of terminating it honourably; yet, thro' an heroic Principle of Generosity, he gives his Captive Liberty, without making any Conditions, and has all his Work to do over again.[11]

A Third having contracted a violent Friendship with the Enemies of his Country, through the same generous Sentiments, draws his Sword in their Defence, and makes no Scruple to fight against an Army, where the King his Father is in Person.[12]

I must confess, said Sir *Charles*, that Generosity seems to me very peculiar, that will make a Man fight for his Enemies against his own Father.

It is in that Peculiarity, Sir, said *Arabella*, that his Generosity consists; for certainly there is nothing extraordinary in fighting for one's Father, and one's Country; but when a Man has arrived to such a Pitch of Greatness of Soul, as to neglect those mean and selfish Considerations, and, loving Virtue in the Persons of his Enemies, can prefer their Glory before his own particular Interest, he is then a perfect Hero indeed: Such an one was *Oroondates*, *Artaxerxes*, and many others I could name, who all gave eminent Proofs of their Disinterestedness and Greatness of Soul, upon the like Occasions: Therefore, not to detract from Sir *George's* Merit, I must still insist, that in the Resolutions he had taken to defend his Enemy's Life at the Expence of his own, he did no more than what any Man of ordinary Generosity ought to do, and what he was particularly obliged to, by what the amiable *Sydimiris* had done for him.

I was so happy, however, Madam, continued Sir *George*, to find that those Expressions of my Gratitude wrought somewhat upon the Heart of the lovely *Sydimiris* in my Favour: Her Words discovered as much, and her Eyes spoke yet more intelligibly: but our Conversation was interrupted by the discreet *Urinoe*, who, fearing the Consequence of so long a Stay in her Chamber, represented to me, that it was Time to take my Leave.

I turned pale at this cruel Sound; and, beholding. *Sydimiris* with a languishing Look,

Would to Heaven, Madam, said I, that instead of giving me Liberty, you would keep me eternally your Prisoner; for though a Dungeon was to be the Place of my Confinement, yet if it was near you, it would seem a Palace to me; for indeed I am no longer in a Condition to relish that Freedom you bestow upon me, since it must remove me farther from you: But I beseech you, Madam, to believe, that in delivering me from your Brother's Fetters, you have cast me into your own, and that I am more a Prisoner than ever, but a Prisoner to so lovely a Conqueror, that I do not wish to break my Chains, and prefer the sweet and glorious Captivity I am in, to all the Crowns in the World.

You are very bold, said *Sydimiris*, blushing, to entertain me with such Discourse; yet I pardon this Offence, in Consideration of what you have suffered from my Brother, and on Condition that you will depart immediately, without speaking another Word.

Sydimiris spoke this so earnestly, that I durst not disobey her; and, kissing the Hem of her Robe, with a passionate Air, I left her Chamber, conducted by *Urinoe*; who having brought me to a private Door, which carried us into the Street, I there found a Man waiting for me, whom I knew to be the same that had attended me during my Stay in that House.

Urinoe having recommended to him to see me safe out of the Town, I took Leave of her, with the most grateful Acknowledgements for her Kindness; and followed my Conductor, so oppressed with Grief at the Thoughts of leaving the Place where *Sydimiris* was, that I had hardly Strength to walk.

CHAPTER V

*An extraordinary Instance of Generosity in a Lover,
somewhat resembling that of the great* Artaxerxes
in Cassandra.[13]

The farther I went, continued Sir *George*, the more my Regret increased; and, finding it would be impossible to live, and quit the divine *Sydimiris*, I all at once took a Resolution to remain in the Town concealed; and, communicating my Design to my Guide, I engaged him to assist me in it, by a Present of a considerable Sum, which he could not resist: Accordingly he left me in a remote Part of the Town, and went to find out a convenient Lodging for me; which he soon procured, and also a Suit of Cloaths to disguise me, my own being very rich and magnificent.

Having recommended me as a Relation of his, who was newly arrived, I was received very civilly by the People with whom he placed me; and, finding this young Man to be very witty and discreet, and also very capable of serving me, I communicated to him my Intentions by staying, which were only to be near the divine *Sydimiris*, and to have the Happiness of sometimes seeing her, when she went abroad.

This Man entering into my Meaning, assured me, he would faithfully keep my Secret; and that he would not fail to bring me Intelligence of all that passed in the Palace of *Marcomire*.

I could with Difficulty keep myself from falling at his Feet, to express my Sense of his kind and generous Offers; but I contented myself with presenting him another Sum of Money, larger than the first, and assured him of my future Gratitude.

He then took Leave, and left me to my Reflections, which were wholly upon the Image of the Divine *Sydimiris*, and the Happiness of being so near the Object I adored.

My Confidant came to me the next Day; but brought me no other News, than that my Escape was not yet known to *Marcomire*. I inquired if he had seen *Sydimiris*; but he replied he had not, and that *Urinoe* had only asked him, if he had conducted me safe out of Town: To which he had answered as we had agreed, that I had got out safe and undiscovered.

A Day or two after, he brought me News more pleasing; for he told me, that *Sydimiris* had sent for him into her Chamber, and asked him several Questions concerning me: That she appeared very melancholy, and even blushed, whenever she mentioned my Name.

This Account gave sufficient Matter for my Thoughts to work upon for several Days. I interpreted *Sydimiris*'s Blush a Thousand different Ways; I reflected upon all the different Causes to which it might be owing, and busied myself with all those innumerable Conjectures, which, as you know, Madam, such an Incident always gives rise to in a Lover's Imagination. At length I explained it to my own Advantage, and felt thereby a considerable Increase of my Affection.

A whole Week having elapsed, without another Sight of my Confidant, I began to be greatly alarmed; when, on the Eighth Day of this cruel Suspense, I saw him appear; but with so many Marks of Disturbance in his Face, that I trembled to hear what he had to acquaint me with.

Oh! Sir, said he, as soon as his Concern suffered him to speak, *Marcomire* has discovered your Escape, and the Means by which it was procured: One of those in whom *Urinoe* confided, has betrayed it to him; and the beauteous *Sydimiris* is likely to feel the most terrible Effects of his Displeasure: He has confined her to her Chamber, and vows to sacrifice her Life to the Honour of his Family; which, he says, she has stained; and he loads that admirable Lady with so many Reproaches, that it is thought, her Grief for such undeserved Calumnies will occasion her Death.

Scarce had he finished these cruel Words, when I, who all the time he had been speaking, beheld him with a dying Eye, sunk down at his Feet in a Swoon; which continued so long, that he began to think me quite dead: However I at last opened my Eyes; but it was only to pour forth a River of Tears, and to utter Complaints, which might have moved the most obdurate Heart.

After having a long Time tormented myself in weeping and complaining, I at last took a Resolution, which offered me some Alleviation of my Grief; and the faithful *Toxares*, seeing me a little composed, left me to myself, with a Promise to return soon, and acquaint me with what passed further in the Palace of *Marcomire*.

As soon as he was gone, I rose from my Bed; and, dressing myself in those Cloaths I wore when I was taken Prisoner, I went to the Palace of *Marcomire*; and, demanding to see him, I was told he was in the Apartment of *Sydimiris*; and, at my earnest Desire, they conducted me thither.

When I entered the Room, I beheld that incomparable Beauty stretched upon a Couch, dissolved in Tears; and *Urinoe* upon her Knees, before her, accompanying with her own, those precious Drops which fell from the bright Eyes of her Mistress.

Marcomire, who was walking furiously about the Room, exclaiming with the utmost Violence against that fair Sufferer, did not observe my Entrance; so that I had an Opportunity of going towards *Sydimiris*, who lifting up her Eyes to look upon me, gave a loud Shriek; and, by a Look of extreme Anguish, let me understand, how great her Apprehensions were upon my Account.

I am come, Madam, said I, to perform Part of the Promise I made you, and by dying, to prove your Innocence; and, freeing you from the Reproaches you suffer on my Account, I shall have the Happiness to convince you, that my Life is infinitely less dear to me, than your Tranquillity. *Sydimiris*, who hearkened to me with great Emotion, was going to make some Answer, when *Marcomire*, alarmed by his Sister's Shriek, came towards us, and, viewing me at first with Astonishment, and then with a Smile of Cruelty and Revenge,

Is it possible, said he, that I behold my designed Murderer again in my Power?

I am in thy Power, said I, because I am willing to be so; and came voluntarily to put myself into your Hands, to free that excellent Lady from the Imputation you have laid on her: Know, *Marcomire*, that it is to myself alone I owed my Liberty, which I would still preserve against all the Forces thou couldst bring to deprive me of it; and this Sword, which left thee Life enough to threaten mine, would haply once more put yours in Danger, were I not restrained by a powerful Consideration, which leaves me not the Liberty of even wishing you ill.

Ah! Dissembler, said *Marcomire*, in a Rage, think not to impose upon me by thy counterfeited Mildness: Thou art my Prisoner once more, and I shall take Care to prevent your escaping a second Time.

I am not your Prisoner, replied I, while I possess this Sword, which has already defended me against greater Numbers than you have here to oppose me; but, continued I, throwing down my Sword at *Sydimiris*'s Feet, I resign my Liberty to restore that Lady to your good Opinion, and to free her from those base Aspersions thou hast unjustly loaded her with, upon my Account.

It matters not, said the brutal Brother, taking up my Sword, whether thou hast resigned, or I have deprived thee of Liberty; but since thou art in my Power, thou shalt feel all the Effects of my Resentment: Take him away, pursued he, to some of his People; put him into the worst Dungeon you can find; and let him be guarded carefully, upon Pain of Death, if he again escapes.

With these Words, several Men offered to lead me out of the Room; but I repulsed them with Disdain; and making a low Reverence to *Sydimiris*, whose Countenance expressed the

Extremes of Fear and Anguish, I followed my Conductors to
the Prison allotted for me; which, hideous as it was, I contemplated with a secret Pleasure, since I had by that Action, which
had brought me into it, given a Testimony of my Love for the
adorable *Sydimiris*.

CHAPTER VI

In which it will be seen, that the Lady is as generous as her Lover.

I passed some Days in this Confinement, melancholy enough:
My Ignorance of the Destiny of *Sydimiris* gave me more Pain
than the Sense of my own Misfortunes; and one Evening, when
I was more than usually disquieted, one of my Guard entered
my Prison, and, giving me a Letter, retired, without speaking a
Word: I opened this Letter, with Precipitation, and by the Light
of a Lamp which was allowed me, I read the following Words.

Sydimiris, *To the most generous* Bellmour.

It is not enough to tell you, that the Method you took to free me
from my Brother's Severity, has filled me with the utmost Esteem
and Admiration. So generous an Action merits a greater
Acknowledgement, and I will make no Scruple to confess, that
my Heart is most sensibly touched by it: Yes, *Bellmour*, I have
received this glorious Testimony of your Affection with such a
Gratitude, as you yourself could have wished to inspire me with;
and it shall not be long, before you will have a convincing Proof
of the Effect it has had upon the Spirit of

Sydimiris.

This Letter, Madam, pursued Sir *George*, being wholly calcu-
lated to make me hope that I was not hated by the divine
Sydimiris; and that she meditated something in my Favour,
I resigned myself up to the most delightful Expectations.

What! cried I, transported with the Excess of my Joy: Does

the most admirable *Sydimiris* condescend to assure me, that I have touched her Heart? And does she promise me, that I shall receive some convincing Proof of her Acknowledgement?

Ah! too happy, and too fortunate *Bellmour*, to what a glorious Destiny hast thou been reserved! And how oughtest thou to adore these Fetters, that have procured thee the Esteem of the Divine *Sydimiris*! —

Such, Madam, were the Apprehensions which the Billet I had received, inspired me with. I continually flattered myself with the most pleasing Hopes; and during three Weeks longer, in which I heard no more from *Sydimiris*, my Imagination was wholly filled with those sweet Thoughts which her Letter had made me entertain.

At length, on the Evening of a Day which I had wholly spent in reading over *Sydimiris*'s Letter; and interpreting the Sense of it a thousand different Ways, but all agreeable to my ardent Wishes; I saw the sage *Urinoe* enter my Prison, accompanied by *Toxares*, whom I had not seen during my last Confinement. Wholly transported at the Sight of these Two Friends, and not doubting but they had brought me the most agreeable News, I ran towards them; and throwing myself at *Urinoe*'s Feet, I begged her, in an Extacy of Joy, to accquaint me with *Sydimiris*'s Commands.

Urinoe, in some Confusion at this Action, intreated me to rise. 'Tis fit, cried I, in a Transport I could not master, that in this Posture I should receive the Knowledge of that Felicity *Sydimiris* has had the Goodness to promise me. *Urinoe* sighed at these Words; and beholding me with a Look of Compassion and Tenderness,

Would to God, said she, that all I have to say, were as agreeable, as the first News I have to tell you; which is, that you are free, and at Liberty to leave the Town this Moment! *Sydimiris*, continued she, has bought your Freedom, at the Expence of her own; and, to deliver you from her Brother's Chains, she has put on others, haply more cruel than those you have worn: In fine, she has married a Man, whom she detested, to procure your Liberty; her Brother having granted it to her upon that Condition alone.

Scarce had *Urinoe* finished these Words, when I fell, without Sense or Motion, at her Feet. *Toxares* and she, who had foreseen what might happen, having provided themselves with Cordials necessary to restore me, brought me to myself with infinite Trouble.

Cruel! said I to them, with a Tone and Look, which witnessed the Excess of my Despair, Why have you hindered me from dying, at once to prevent the thousand Deaths I shall suffer from my Grief? Is this the Confirmation of those glorious Hopes *Sydimiris* had permitted me to entertain? Is this that Proof of the Acknowlegements I was to expect? And is it by throwing herself into the Arms of my Rival, that she repays those Obligations she thinks she owes me?

Ah! inhuman *Sydimiris*! was it to make my Despair more poignant, that thou flatterest me with such a Prospect of Happiness? And was it necessary to the Grandeur of thy Nuptials, that my Life should be the Sacrifice?

But, how unjust am I, cried I, repenting in an Instant of those injurious Suspicions; How unjust am I, to accuse the divine *Sydimiris* of Inhumanity? Was it not to give me Freedom, that she bestowed herself upon a Man she hates? And has she not made herself miserable for ever, to procure me a fansied Happiness?

Ah! if it be so, what a Wretch am I? I, who have been the only Cause of that Misery, to which she has doomed herself? Ah! Liberty! pursued I, how I detest thee, since purchased by the Misfortune of *Sydimiris*! And how far more sweet and glorious were those Chains, which I wore for her Sake!

My Sighs and Tears leaving me no longer the Power of Speech, I sunk down on my Bed, oppressed with a mortal Grief.

Urinoe and *Toxares* drew near to comfort me, and said all that sensible and discreet Persons could think of to alleviate my Despair.

Though I have heard that *Sydimiris* is married, replied I, without dying immediately; yet do not imagine, that I will suffer this odious Life to continue long. If Sorrow do not quickly dispatch me, I will seek Death by other Means; for since *Sydimiris* is lost, I have no more Business in the World.

The charitable *Urinoe* and *Toxares* endeavoured in vain to divert me from this sad Resolution, when *Urinoe*, finding all their Reasonings ineffectual, drew a Letter out of her Pocket, and, presenting it to me, I had Orders, said she, not to let this Letter be delivered to you, till you had left the Town; but the Despair, to which I see you reduced, does, I conceive, dispense with my rigorous Observation of those Directions.

While *Urinoe* was speaking, I opened this Letter trembling, and found it as follows.

CHAPTER VII

Containing an Incident full as probable as any in Scudery's *Romances.*

Sydimiris, *To* Bellmour.

If that Proof of my Gratitude, which I promised to give you, fall short of your Expectations; blame not the Defect of my Will, but the Rigour of my Destiny: It was by this only Way I could give you Liberty; nor is it too dearly bought by the Loss of all my Happiness, if you receive it as you ought: Had I been allowed to follow my own Inclinations, there is no Man in the World I would have preferred to yourself. I owe this Confession to the Remembrance of your Affection, of which you gave me so generous an Instance; and the Use I expect you will make of it, is to console you under a Misfortune, which is common to us both; though I haply have most Reason to complain, since I could not be just to you, without being cruel at the same Time, or confer a Benefit, without loading you with a Misfortune. If the Sacrifice I have made of myself for your sake, gives me any Claim to the Continuance of your Love, I command you, by the Power it gives me over you, to live, and not add to the Miseries of my Condition, the Grief of being the Cause of your Death. Remember, I will

look upon your Disobedience, as an Act of the most cruel Ingratitude; and your Compliance with this Request shall ever be
esteemed, as the dearest Mark you can give of that Passion you
have borne to the unfortunate

Sydimiris.

Ah! *Sydimiris*, cried I, having read this Letter, more cruel
in your Kindness than Severity! After having deprived me of
yourself, do you forbid me to die; and expose me by so rigorous
a Command to Ills infinitely more hard and painful than Death?

Yes, pursued I, after a little Pause; yes *Sydimiris*, thou shalt
be obeyed; we will not dye, since thou hast commanded us to
live; and, notwithstanding the Tortures to which thou con-
demnest us, we will obey this Command; and give thee a glorious Proof of our present Submission, by enduring that Life,
which the Loss of thee has rendered truly wretched.

Urinoe and *Toxares*, somewhat reassured, by the Resolution
I had taken, exhorted me by all the Persuasions, Friendship
could put in their Mouths, to persevere in it; and, *Urinoe*
bidding me farewel, I endeavoured to prevail upon her to procure me a Sight of *Sydimiris* once more, or at least to bear a
Letter from me to her; but she refused both these Requests so
obstinately, telling me, *Sydimiris* would neither consent to the
one nor the other, that I was obliged to be contented with the
Promise she made me, to represent my Affliction in a true Light
to her Mistress; and to assure her, that nothing but her absolute
Commands could have hindered me from dying. Then, taking
leave of me with much Tenderness, she went out of the Prison,
leaving *Toxares* with me, who assisted me to dress, and conducted me out of that miserable Place, where I had passed so many
sad, and also joyful Hours. At a Gate to which he brought me,
I found a Horse waiting; and, having embraced this faithful
Confidant, with many Expressions of Gratitude, I bestowed a
Ring of some Value upon him to remember me by; and, mounting my Horse, with a breaking Heart, I took the first Road
which presented itself to my Eyes, and galloped away, without
knowing whither I went. I rode the whole Night, so totally
engrossed by my Despair, that I did not perceive my Horse was

so tired, it could hardly carry me a Step farther: At last the poor Beast fell down under me, so that I was obliged to dismount; and, looking about me, perceived I was in a Forest, without seeing the least Appearance of any Habitation.

The Wildness and Solitude of the Place, flattered[14] my Despair, and while my Horse was feeding upon what Grass he could find, I wandered about: The Morning just breaking, gave me Light enough to direct my Steps. Chance at last conducted me to a Cave, which seemed to have been the Residence of some Hermit, or unfortunate Lover like myself. It was dug at the Side of a Rock, the Entrance to it thick set with Bushes, which hid it from View. I descended by a few Steps cut rudely enough, and was convinced, it had formerly served for a Habitation for some religious or melancholy Person; for there were Seats of Turf raised on each Side of it, a Kind of Bed composed of dried Leaves and Rushes, and a Hole made artificially at the Top, to admit the Light.[15]

While I considered this Place attentively, I all at once took up a Resolution, inspired by my Despair; which was, to continue there, and indulge my Melancholy in a Retirement so fitted for my Purpose.

Giving my Horse therefore Liberty to go where he pleased, and hanging up my Arms upon a Tree near my Cave, I took Possession of this solitary Mansion, with a gloomy Kind of Satisfaction, and devoted all my Hours to the Contemplation of my Misfortunes.

I lived in this Manner, Madam, for ten Months, without feeling the least Desire to change my Habitation; and, during all that time, no Mortal approached my Solitude, so that I lived perfectly secure and undiscovered.

Sir *George* pausing here to take Breath, the old Baronet said what will be found in the following Chapter.

CHAPTER VIII

A single Combat fought with prodigious Valour, and described with amazing Accuracy.

Give me Leave, Sir, said Sir *Charles*, to ask, if you eat in all this Time?

Alas! Sir, replied Sir *George*, Sighs and Tears were all my Sustenance.

Sir *Charles*, Mr. *Glanville*, and Miss, laughing at this Answer, *Arabella* seemed greatly confused:

It is not to be imagined, said she, that Sir *George*; or, to say better, Prince *Viridomer*, lived ten Months without eating anything to support Nature; but such trifling Circumstances are always left out, in the Relations of Histories; and truly an Audience must be very dull and unapprehensive, that cannot conceive, without being told, that a Man must necessarily eat in the Space of ten Months.

But the Food Sir *George* lived on, replied the Baronet, was very unsubstantial, and would not afford him much Nourishment.

I suppose, resumed *Arabella*, he lived upon such Provisions as the Forest afforded him; such as wild Fruits, Herbs, bitter Sallads, and the like; which, considering the Melancholy that possessed him, would appear a voluptuous Repast; and which the unfortunate *Orontes*, when he was in the same Situation, thought infinitely too good for him.

Sir *Charles*, finding *Arabella*, took no Notice of the Historian's Hyperbole of living upon his Sighs and Tears, passed it over, for Fear of offending her; and Sir *George*, who had been in some Anxiety how to bring himself off, when he perceived *Arabella* was reasonable enough to suppose he must have eat during his Abode in the Forest, went on with his Relation in this Manner.

I lived, as I before observed to you, Madam, in this Cave for ten Months; and truly I was so reconciled to that solitary way of Life, and found so much Sweetness in it, that I believe, I should have remained there till this Day, but for the Adventure which I am going to recount.

It being my Custom to walk out every Evening in the Forest; returning to my Cave, something later than usual, I heard the Cries of a Woman at some Distance, who seemed to be in Distress: I stopped to listen from what Side those Cries proceeded; and, perceiving they seemed to approach nearer to me, I took down my Armour from the Tree where I had hung it; and hastily arming myself, shaped my Course towards the Place from whence those Complaints seemed to come, resolving to assist that unknown Person with all the Strength that was left me.

Having gone some Paces, I spied through the Branches of the Trees a Man on Horseback with a Lady, who struggled to get loose, and at Times calling aloud for Succour.

This Sight inflaming me with Rage against that impious Ravisher; I flew towards him: And when I came within hearing;

Hold, Wretch! cried I, and cease to offer Violence to that Lady, whom thou bearest away by Force; or prepare to defend thyself against one, who will die, before he will suffer thee to prosecute thy unjust Designs.

The Man, without answering me, clapped Spurs to his Horse; and it would have been impossible to have overtaken him, had not my own Horse, which had never quitted the Forest, appeared in my View: I quickly mounted him, and followed the Track the Ravisher had taken, with such Speed, that I came up with him in a Moment.

Caitiff! said I, release the Lady, and defend thyself. These Words, which I accompanied with a thundering Blow upon his Head-piece, obliged him to set down the Lady, who implored Heaven, with the utmost Ardour, to grant me the Victory: And, recoiling back a few Paces, to take a View of me,

I know not, said he, for what Reason thou settest thyself to oppose my Designs; but I well know, that thou shalt dearly repent of thy Temerity.

Saying this, he advanced furiously towards me, and aimed so heavy a Blow at my Head, that, had I not received it on my Shield, I might haply have no longer been in a Condition to defend the distressed Lady: But, having with the greatest Dexterity imaginable, avoided this Blow, I made at him with so much Fierceness, and directed my Aims so well, that in a few Moments I wounded him in several Places; and his Arms were all dyed with his Blood.

This good Success redoubled my Vigour; and having, by a lucky Stroke with my Sword, cut the Strings of his Head-piece, it fell off: And his Head being bare, I was going to let fall a dreadful Blow upon it, which doubtless would have shivered it in a thousand Pieces, when he cried out for Quarter, and, letting fall his Sword, by that Action assured me my Victory was intire.

Live Wretch, cried I, since thou art base enough to value Life after being vanquished: but swear upon my Sword, that thou wilt never more attempt the Liberty of that Lady.

While I was speaking, I perceived he was no longer able to sit his Horse: But, staggering a Moment, he fell off, and lay extended without Motion upon the Ground. Touched with Compassion at this Sight, I alighted, and, supposing him to be in a Swoon, was preparing to give him some Assistance; but, upon my nearer Approach, I found he was quite dead.

Leaving therefore this mournful Object, I turned about, with an Intention to go and offer the distressed Lady my further Help; but I perceived her already at my Feet.

Valiant Knight, said she, with a Tone of Voice so bewitching, that all my Faculties were suspended, as by Inchantment, suffer me, on my Knees, to thank you, for the Deliverance you have procured me from that base Man; since to your admirable Valour I owe not only the Preservation of my Life; but, what is infinitely dearer to me, my Honour.

The Astonishment, wherewith I beheld the miraculous Beauty that appeared before me, kept me a Moment in such an attentive Gaze, that I forgot she was at my Feet: Recollecting myself, however, with some Confusion at my Neglect,

Oh! rise, Madam, cried I, helping her up with infinite Respect, and debase not such Perfection to a Posture, in which all the Monarchs on the Earth might glory to appear before it.

That you may the better conceive the Alteration which the Sight of this fair Unknown produced in my Soul, I will endeavour, to give you a Description of her Beauty, which was altogether miraculous.

CHAPTER IX

In which the Reader will find a Description of a Beauty,
in a Style truly sublime.

The new fallen Snow, pursued Sir *George*, was tanned, in Comparison of the refined Purity of that White which made up the Ground of her Complexion; and, though Fear had a little gathered the Carnations of her Cheeks, yet her Joy at being delivered seemed to plant them there with such fresh Advantages, that any Eye might shrink at the Brightness of that mingled Lustre: Her Mouth, as well for Shape as Colour, might shame the Imitation of the best Pencils, and the liveliest Tints; and though through some petty Intervals of Joy, it wanted the Smiles, which Grief and Terror sequestred, yet she never opened it, but like the East, at the Birth of a beautiful Day, and then discovered Treasures, whose excelling Whiteness made the Price inestimable: All the Features of her Face had so near a Kindred to Proportion and Symmetry, as the several Masters of *Apelles*'s Art[16] might have called it his Glory to have copied Beauties from her, as the best of Models: The Circumference of her Visage shewed the Extremes of an imperfect Circle, and almost formed it to a perfect Oval: And this Abridgment of Marvels was tapered by a Pair of the brightest Stars, that ever were lighted up by the Hand of Nature: As their Colour was the same with the Heavens, there was a spherical Harmony in their Motion; and that mingled with a Vivacity so penetrating, as neither the firmest Eye, nor the strongest Soul, could arm themselves with a Resistance of Proof against those pointed Glories: Her Head was crowned with a prodigious Quantity of fair long Hair, which Colour as fitly suited the Beauty of her Eyes, as Imagination could make it: To these Marvels of Face were joined the rest of her Neck, Hands, and Shape; and there seemed a Contest between the Form and Whiteness of the two former, which had the largest Commission from Nature to work Wonders.

In fine, her Beauty was miraculous, and could not fail of producing a sudden Effect upon a Heart like mine.

Having passed in an Instant from the extremest Admiration, to something yet more tender, I reiterated my Offers of Service to the fair Unknown; who told me, she feared her Father had Occasion for some Assistance, her Ravisher having left his Men to engage him, and keep off his Pursuit, while he rode off with his Prize: Hereupon I begg'd her to direct me to the Place where she left her Father, assuring her I would gladly venture my Life a Second time, to preserve his; and she desiring to go with me, I placed her before me on my Horse, and had the exquisite Pleasure of supporting with my Arms the fairest and most admirable Creature in the World.

In less than half an Hour, which had appeared to me but a Moment, we got to the Place where she had been torn from her Father; whom we beheld with three of his Servants, maintaining a Fight against twice as many of their Enemies.

Having gently set down the beauteous Unknown upon the Grass, I flew to the Relief of her Father; and, throwing myself furiously among his Assailants, dispatched two of them with so many Blows: The others, seeing so unexpected an Assistance, gave back a little; and I took Advantage of their Consternation, to redouble my Blows, and brought Two more of them at my Feet.

There remained now but Four to overcome; and my Arrival having given new Vigour to those whose Part I had taken, they seconded me so well, that we soon had nothing more left to do; for the rest, seeing their Comrades slain, sought their Safety in Flight: We were too generous to pursue them, the Blood of such Wretches being unworthy to be shed by our Swords.

The fair Unknown, seeing us Conquerors, flew to embrace her Father; who, holding her pressed between his Arms, turned his Eyes upon me; then quitting her, came towards me, and in the most obliging Terms imaginable, returned me Thanks for the Assistance I had brought him; and being informed by his

Daughter, of what I had done for her Preservation, this old Gentleman renewed his Acknowlegements, calling me the Preserver of his Life, the valiant Defender of his Daughter's Honour, his tutelary Angel, and the Guardian of his House.

In fine, he loaded me with so many Thanks and Praises, that I could not choose but be in some Confusion; and, to put an End to them, I begged he would inform me, by what Means he came into that Misfortune.

He told me, that, residing in a Castle at the Extremity of this Forest, the Charms of his Daughter had captivated a neighbouring Lord, whose Character and Person being disagreeable both to her and himself, he had absolutely refused to give her to him: Thereupon he had set upon them as they were going to visit a Relation at some Distance, and dragging *Philonice* out of the Coach, put her before him on his Horse, and carried her away, leaving Eight of his Men to engage him, and his Servants; who, being but Four in Number, must inevitably have perished, had I not come to his Relief, and, by my miraculous Valour, vanquished all his Enemies.

Saying this, he desired me to go home with him to the Castle; and having led his Daughter to the Coach, insisted upon my placing myself next her; and, getting in himself, ordered them to return home.

This Accident having altered his Design of making the Visit which had been the Occasion of this Journey.

The Baron, for that I found was his Title, entertained me, all the Way, with repeated Expressions of Acknowledgements and Tenderness; and the incomparable *Philonice* condescended also to assure me of her Gratitude for the Service I had done her.

At our Arrival at the Castle, I perceived it was very large and magnificent: The Baron conducted me to one of the best Apartments, and would stay in the Room till my Armour was taken off, that he might be assured I had received no Hurts: Having rendered him the like Civility in his own Chamber, and satisfied myself he was not wounded, we returned to the beautiful *Philonice*; and this second Sight having finished my Defeat, I remained so absolutely her Slave, that neither *Dorothea* nor *Sydimiris* were more passionately beloved.

At the earnest Intreaty of the Baron, I staid some Weeks in the Castle; during which, the daily Sight of *Philonice* so augmented my Flames, that I was no longer in a Condition to conceal them; but, fearing to displease that Divine Beauty by a Confession of my Passion, I languished in secret; and the Constraint I laid upon myself, gave me such Torments, that I fell into a profound Melancholy, and looked so pale and dejected, that the Baron was sensible of the Alteration, and conjured me in the most pressing Terms, to acquaint him with the Cause of my Uneasiness: But though I continued obstinately silent with my Tongue, yet my Eyes spoke intelligibly enough; and the Blushes which appeared in the fair Cheeks of *Philonice*, whenever she spoke to me on the Subject of my Grief, convinced me she was not ignorant of my Passion.

At length the Agitation of my Mind throwing me into a Fever, the Baron, who was firmly persuaded, that my Illness proceeded from some concealed Vexation, pressed me continually to declare myself; and, finding all his Intreaties ineffectual, he commanded his Daughter to endeavour to find out the Cause of that Grief which had put me into such a Condition.

For that Purpose therefore, having brought the fair *Philonice* into my Chamber, he staid a few Minutes, and leaving the Room, under Pretence of Business, *Philonice* remained alone by my Bedside, her Women, out of Respect, staying at the other End of the Chamber.

This Divine Person, seeing herself alone with me, and remembering her Father's Command, blushed, and cast down her Eyes in such apparent Confusion, that I could not help observing it: And interpreting it to the Displeasure she took in being so near me,

Whatever Joy I take in the Honour your Visit does me, Madam, said I, in a weak Voice; yet since nothing is so dear to me, as your Satisfaction, I would rather dispense with this Mark of your Goodness to an unfortunate Wretch, than see you in the least Constraint.

And why, replied she, with a Tone full of Sweetness, do you suppose that I am here by Constraint, when it would be more just to believe, that in visiting the valiant Defender of my

Honour, and the Life of my Father, I only follow my own Inclinations?

Ah! Madam, said I, transported with Joy at so favourable a Speech, the little Service I had the Happiness to do you, does not merit so infinite a Favour; and tho' I had lost the best Part of my Blood in your Defence, I should have been well rewarded with your Safety.

Since you do not repent of what you have done, replied she, I am willing to be obliged to you for another Favour; and ask it with the greater Hope of obtaining it, as I must acquaint you, it is by my Father's Command I take that Liberty, who is much interested in my Success.

There is no Occasion, Madam, returned I, to make use of any Interest but your own, to engage me to obey you, since that is, and ever will be, all-powerful with me: Speak then, Madam, and let me know what it is you desire of me, that I may, once in my Life, have the Glory of obeying you.

It is, said she, blushing still more than before, that you will acquaint us with the Cause of that Melancholy, which has, as we imagine, occasioned your present Illness.

At these Words I trembled, turned pale; and, not daring to discover the true Cause of my Affliction, I remained in a profound Silence.

I see, said the beautiful *Philonice*, that you have no Inclination to obey me; and since my Request has, as I perceive, given you some Disturbance, I will prevail upon my Father to press you no farther upon this Subject.

No Madam, said I, eagerly; the Baron shall be satisfied, and you shall be obeyed; though, after the Knowledge of my Crime, you doom me to that Death I so justly merit.

Yes Madam, this unfortunate Man, who has had the Glory to acquire your Esteem by the little Service he did you, has cancelled the Merit of that Service by daring to adore you.

I love you, divine *Philonice*; and, not being able either to repent, or cease to be guilty of loving you, I am resolved to die, and spare you the Trouble of pronouncing my Sentence. I beseech you therefore to believe, that I would have died in Silence, but for your Command to declare myself, and you should never have known the Excess of my Love and Despair, had not my Obedience to your Will obliged me to confess it.

I finished these Words with so much Fear and Confusion, that I durst not lift my Eyes up to the fair Face of *Philonice*, to observe how she received this Discourse: I waited therefore, trembling, for her Answer; but finding that in several Minutes she spoke not a Word, I ventured at last, to cast a languishing Glance upon the Visage I adored, and saw so many Marks of Disorder upon it, that I was almost dead with the Apprehensions of having offended her beyond even the Hope of procuring her Pardon by my Death.

CHAPTER X

Wherein Sir George concludes his History; which produces an unexpected Effect.

The Silence of *Philonice*, continued Sir *George*, pierced me to the Heart; and when I saw her rise from her Seat, and prepare to go away without speaking, Grief took such Possession of my Spirits, that, uttering a Cry, I fell into a Swoon, which, as I afterwards was informed, greatly alarmed the beautiful *Philonice*; who, resuming her Seat, had the Goodness to assist her Women in bringing me to myself; and, when I opened my Eyes, I had the Satisfaction to behold her still by me, and all the Signs of Compassion in her Face.

This Sight a little re-assuring me; I ask your Pardon, Madam, said I, for the Condition in which I have appeared before you, and also for that I am not yet dead, as is doubtless your Wish: But I will make Haste, pursued I, sighing, to fulfil your Desires; and you shall soon be freed from the Sight of a miserable Wretch, who, to his last Moment, will not cease to adore you.

It is not your Death that I desire, said the fair *Philonice*; and, after having preserved both my Father and me from Death, it is not reasonable, that we should suffer you to die, if we can help it.

Live therefore, *Bellmour*, pursued she, blushing; and live, if possible, without continuing in that Weakness I cannot choose but condemn: Yet whatever are your Thoughts for the future, remember that your Death will be a Fault I cannot resolve to pardon.

Speaking these Words without giving me Time to answer, she left my Chamber; and I found something so sweet and favourable in them, that I resolved to obey her, and forward my Cure as much as I was able: However, the Agitation of Spirits increased my Fever so much, that my Life was despaired of.

The Baron hardly ever left my Bed-side. *Philonice* came every Day to see me, and seemed extremely moved at the Danger I was in. One Day, when I was worse than usual, she came close to the Bedside; and, opening the Courtain,

What *Bellmour*, said she, do you pay so little Obedience to my Commands, that you resolve to die?

Heaven is my Witness, Madam, said I, faintly, that nothing is so dear and sacred to me as your Commands; and since, out of your superlative Goodness, you are pleased to have some Care for my Life, I would preserve it to obey you, were it in my Power; but, alas! Madam, I strive in vain to repel the Violence of my Distemper.

In a few Days more, I was reduced to the last Extremity: it was then that the fair *Philonice* discovered, that she did not hate me; for she made no Scruple to weep before me; and those Tears she so liberally shed, had so powerful an Effect upon my Mind, that the Contentment I felt, communicated itself to my Body, and gave such a Turn to my Distemper, that my Recovery was not only hoped, but expected.

The Baron expressed his Satisfaction at this Alteration, by the most affectionate Expressions; and though the fair *Philonice* said very little, yet I perceived by the Joy that appeared in her fair Eyes, that she was not less interested in my Recovery, than her Father.

The Physicians having declared me out of Danger, the Baron, who had taken his Resolutions long before, came one Day into my Chamber; and ordering those who attended me, to leave us alone,

Prince, said he, for in recounting my History to him, I had disclosed my true Quality, I am not ignorant of that Affection you bear my Daughter; and am sensible it has occasioned the Extremity to which we have seen you reduced: Had you been pleased to acquaint me with your Sentiments, you would have avoided those Displeasures you have suffered; for though your Birth were not so illustrious as it is, yet, preferring Virtue to all other Advantages, I should have esteemed my Daughter honoured by your Love, and have freely bestowed her on you: But since to those rare Qualities wherewith Heaven has so liberally endowed you, you add also that of a Birth so noble, doubt not but I shall think myself highly favoured by your Alliance: If therefore your Thoughts of my Daughter be not changed, and you esteem her worthy to be your Bride, I here solemnly promise you to bestow her upon you, as soon as you are perfectly recovered.

I leave you to guess, Madam, the Joy which I felt at this Discourse: It was so great, that it would not permit me to thank him, as I should have done, for the inestimable Blessing he bestowed on me.

I saw *Philonice* a few Minutes after; and, being commanded by her Father to give me her Hand, she did so without any Marks of Reluctance, and, having respectfully kissed it, I vowed to be her Slave for ever.

Who would have imagined, continued Sir *George*, with a profound Sigh, that Fortune, while she thus seemed to flatter me, was preparing to make me suffer the severest Torments? I began now to leave my Bed, and was able to walk about my Chamber. The Baron was making great Preparations for our Nuptials; when one Night I was alarmed with the Cries of *Philonice*'s Women; and, a few Moments after, the Baron came into my Chamber, with a distracted Air.

O! Son, cried he, for so he always called me, now *Philonice* is lost both to you and me. She is carried off by Force, and I am preparing to follow and rescue her, if possible: but I fear my Endeavours will be fruitless, since I know not which Way her Ravishers have taken.

Oh! Sir, cried I, transported both with Grief and Rage, you shall not go alone: Her Rescue belongs to me; and I will effect it, or perish in the Attempt.

The Baron, having earnestly conjured me not to expose myself to the Danger of a Relapse, by so imprudent a Resolution, was obliged to quit me, Word being brought him, that his Horse was ready: And as soon as he was gone out of the Room, in spite of all that could be said to prevent me, by my Attendants, I made them put on my Armour; and, mounting a Horse I had caused to be made ready, sallied furiously out of the Castle, breathing out Vows of Vengeance against the Wretch who had robbed me of *Philonice.*

I rode the whole Night without stopping. Day appeared, when I found myself near a small Village. I entered it, and made strict Enquiry after the Ravisher of *Philonice,* describing that fair Creature, and offering vast Rewards to any who could bring me the least Intelligence of her: But all was in vain; I could make no Discovery.

After travelling several Days, to no Purpose, I returned to the Castle, in order to know if the Baron had been more successful in his Pursuit than myself; but I found him oppressed with Grief: He had heard no Tidings of his Daughter, and had suffered no small Apprehensions upon my Account. Having assured him I found myself very able to travel, I took an affectionate Leave of him, promising him never to give over my Search, till I had found the Divine *Philonice*: But Heaven has not permitted me that Happiness; and though I have spent several Years in searching for her, I have never been able to discover where she is: Time has not cured me of my Grief for her Loss; and, though by an Effect of my Destiny, another Object possesses my Soul, yet I do not cease to deplore her Misfortune, and to offer up Vows for her Happiness.

And is this all you have to say? said *Arabella,* whom the latter Part of his History had extremely surprised; or are we to expect a Continuance of your Adventures?

I have faithfully related all my Adventures, that are worthy your hearing, Madam, returned Sir *George*; and I flatter myself, you will do me the Justice to own, that I have been rather unfortunate than faithless; and that Mr. *Glanville* had little Reason to tax me with Inconstancy.

In my Opinion, resumed *Arabella*, Mr. *Glanville* spoke too favourably of you, when he called you only inconstant; and if he had added the Epithet of Ungrateful and Unjust, he would have marked your Character better.

For, in fine, Sir, pursued she, you will never persuade any reasonable Person, that your being able to lose the Remembrance of the fair and generous *Sydimiris*, in your new Passion for *Philonice*, was not an Excess of Levity: But your suffering so tamely the Loss of this last Beauty, and allowing her to remain in the Hands of her Ravisher, while you permit another Affection to take Possession of your Soul, is such an Outrage to all Truth and Constancy, that you deserve to be ranked among the falsest of Mankind.

Alas! Madam, replied Sir *George*, who had not foreseen the Inference *Arabella* would draw from this last Adventure, What would you have an unfortunate Man, whose Hopes have been so often, and so cruelly, disappointed, do? I have bewailed the Loss of *Philonice*, with a Deluge of Tears; I have taken infinite Pains to find her, but to no Purpose; and when Heaven compassionating my Sufferings, presented to my Eyes, an Object, to whom the whole World ought to pay Adoration, how could I resist that powerful Impulse, which forced me to love what appeared so worthy of my Affection?

Call not, interrupted *Arabella*, that an irresistible Impulse, which was only the Effect of thy own changing Humour: The same Excuse might be pleaded for all the Faults we see committed in the World; and Men would no longer be answerable for their own Crimes. Had you imitated the illustrious Heroes of Antiquity, as well in the Constancy of their Affections, as, it must be confessed, you have done in their admirable Valour; you would now be either sighing in your Cave for the Loss of the generous *Sydimiris*, or wandering through the World in Search of the beautiful *Philonice*. Had you persevered in your Affection, and continued your Pursuit of that Fair-one; you would, perhaps, ere this, have found her sleeping under the

Shade of a Tree in some lone Forest, as *Philodaspes* did his admirable *Delia*, or disguised in a Slave's Habit, as *Ariobarsanes* saw his Divine *Olympia*; or bound haply in a Chariot, and have had the Glory of freeing her, as *Ambriomer* did the beauteous *Agione*;[17] or in a Ship in the Hands of Pirates, like the incomparable *Eliza*;[18] or —

Enough, dear Niece, interrupted Sir *Charles*; you have quoted Examples sufficient, if this inconstant Man would have the Grace to follow them.

True, Sir, replied *Arabella*; and I would recommend to his Consideration the Conduct of those illustrious Persons I have named, to the end that, pursuing their Steps, he may arrive at their Glory and Happiness, that is the Reputation of being perfectly constant, and the Possession of his Mistress: And be assured, Sir, pursued *Arabella*, looking at Sir *George*, that Heaven will never restore you the Crown of your Ancestors, and place you upon the Throne to which you pretend, while you make yourself unworthy of its Protection, by so shameful an Inconstancy.

I perhaps speak with too much Freedom to a great Prince; whom though Fortune has despoiled of his Dominions, is intitled to a certain Degree of Respect: But I conceive, it belongs to me, in a particular manner, to resent the Baseness of that Crime, to which you are pleased to make me the Excuse; and, looking upon myself as dishonoured by those often prostituted Vows you have offered me, I am to tell you, that I am highly disobliged; and forbid you to appear in my Presence again, till you have resumed those Thoughts, which are worthy your noble Extraction; and are capable of treating me with that Respect, that is my Due.

Saying this, she rose from her Seat, and walked very majestically out of the Room, leaving Sir *George* overwhelm'd with Shame and Vexation at having conducted the latter Part of his Narration so ill; and drawn upon himself a Sentence, which deprived him of all his Hopes.

CHAPTER XI

Containing only a few Inferences, drawn from the foregoing Chapters.

Mr. *Glanville*, excessively delighted with this Event, could not help laughing at the unfortunate Baronet; who seemed, by his Silence, and down-cast Looks, to expect it.

Who would have imagined, said he, that so renowned a Hero would have tarnished the Glory of his Lawrels, as my Cousin says, by so base an Ingratitude? Indeed Prince, pursued he, laughing, you must resolve to recover your Reputation, either by retiring again to your Cave, and living upon bitter Herbs, for the generous *Sydimiris*; or else wander through the World, in search of the Divine *Philonice*.

Don't triumph, dear *Charles*, replied Sir *George*, laughing in his Turn; have a little Compassion upon me, and confess, that nothing could be more unfortunate, than that damn'd Slip I made at the latter End of my History: But for that, my Reputation for Courage and Constancy had been as high as the Great *Oroondates*, or *Juba*.

Since you have so fertile an Invention, said Sir *Charles*, you may easily repair this Mistake. Ods heart! It is pity you are not poor enough to be an Author; you would occupy a Garret in *Grub-street*,[19] with great Fame to yourself, and Diversion to the Public.

Oh! Sir, cried Sir *George*, I have Stock enough by me, to set up for an Author To-morrow, if I please: I have no less than Five Tragedies, some quite, others almost finished; Three or four Essays on *Virtue*, *Happiness*, &c. Three thousand Lines of an Epic Poem; half a Dozen Epitaphs; a few Acrostics; and a long String of Puns, that would serve to embellish a Daily Paper, if I was disposed to write one.

Nay, then, interrupted Mr. *Glanville*, you are qualified for a Critic at the *Bedford* Coffee-house;[20] where with the rest of your Brothers, Demy-wits, you may sit in Judgment upon the Productions of a *Young*, a *Richardson*, or a *Johnson*. Rail with premeditated Malice at the *Rambler*; and, for the want of Faults, turn even its inimitable Beauties into Ridicule: The Language, because it reaches to Perfection, may be called stiff, laboured, and pedantic; the Criticisms, when they let in more Light than your weak Judgment can bear, superficial and ostentatious Glitter; and because those Papers contain the finest System of Ethics yet extant, damn the queer Fellow, for over-propping Virtue; an excellent new Phrase! which those who can find no Meaning in, may accommodate with one of their own; then give shrewd Hints, that some Persons, though they do not publish their Performances, may have more Merit, than those that do.[21]

Upon my Soul, *Charles*, said Sir *George*, thou art such an ill-natured Fellow, that I am afraid, thou wilt be sneering at me when I am gone; and wilt endeavour, to persuade Lady *Bella*, that not a Syllable of my Story is true. Speak, pursued he, wilt thou have the Cruelty to deprive me of my lawful Claim to the great Kingdom of *Kent*; and rob me of the Glory of fighting singly against Five hundred Men?

I do not know, said Sir *Charles*, whether my Niece be really imposed upon, by the Gravity with which you told your surprising History; but I protest, I thought you were in earnest at first; and that you meant to make us believe it all to be Fact.

You are so fitly punished, said Mr. *Glanville*, for that ill-judged Adventure you related last, by the bad Opinion Lady *Bella* entertains of you, that I need not add to your Misfortune: And therefore, you shall be Prince *Veridomer*, if you please; since, under that Character, you are obliged not to pretend to any Lady, but the incomparable *Philonice*.

Sir *George*, who understood his Meaning, went home, to think of some Means, by which he might draw himself out of the Embarrassment he was in; and Mr. *Glanville*, as he had promised, did not endeavour to undeceive Lady *Bella*, with regard to the History he had feigned; being very well satisfied with his having put it out of his Power to make his Addresses to her, since she now looked upon him as the Lover of *Philonice*.

As for Sir *Charles*, he did not penetrate into the Meaning of Sir *George*'s Story; and only imagined, that by relating such a

Heap of Adventures, he had a Design to entertain the Company, and give a Proof of the Facility of his Invention; and Miss *Glanville*, who supposed, he had been ridiculing her Cousin's strange Notions, was better pleased with him than ever.

Arabella, however, was less satisfied than any of them: She could not endure to see so brave a Knight, who drew his Birth from a Race of Kings, tarnish the Glory of his gallant Actions by so base a Perfidy.

Alas! said she to herself, How much Reason has the beautiful *Philonice* to accuse me for all the Anguish she suffers? Since I am the Cause, that the ungrateful Prince, on whom she bestows her Affections, suffers her to remain quietly, in the Hands of her Ravisher, without endeavouring to rescue her: But, Oh! too lovely, and unfortunate Fair-one, said she, as if she had been present, and listening to her, distinguish, I beseech you, between those Faults, which the Will, and those which Necessity makes us commit. I am the Cause, 'tis true, of thy Lover's Infidelity; but I am the innocent Cause; and would repair the Evils, my fatal Beauty gives rise to, by any Sacrifice in my Power to make.

While *Arabella*, by her romantic Generosity, bewailed the imaginary Afflictions of the full as imaginary *Philonice*; Mr. *Glanville*, who thought the Solitude she lived in, confirmed her in her absurd and ridiculous Notions, desired his Father to press her to go to *London*.

Sir *Charles* complied with his Request, and earnestly intreated her to leave the Castle, and spend a few Months in Town. Her Year of Mourning being now expired, she consented to go; but Sir *Charles*, who did not think his Son's Health absolutely confirmed, proposed to spend a few Weeks at *Bath*;[22] which was readily complied with by *Arabella*.

The End of BOOK VI.

BOOK VII

CHAPTER I

For the Shortness of which the Length of the next shall make some Amends.

Sir *George*, to gratify *Arabella*'s Humour, had not presumed to come to the Castle for several Days; but, hearing that they were preparing to leave the Country, he wrote a short Billet to her; and in the Style of Romance, most humbly intreated her to grant him a Moment's Audience.

Arabella being informed by *Lucy*, to whom Sir *George*'s Gentleman had addressed himself, that he had brought a Letter from his Master, she ordered her to bring him to her Apartment, and as soon as he appeared,

How comes it, said she, that the Prince your Master, has had the Presumption to importune me again, after my absolute Commands to the contrary?

The Prince, my Master, Madam! said the Man, excessively surprised.

Ay! said *Arabella*, Are you not Sir *George*'s 'Squire? And does he not trust you with his most secret Thoughts?

I belong to Sir *George Bellmour*, Madam, replied the Man, who did not understand what she meant: I have not the Honour to be a 'Squire.

No! interrupted *Arabella*; 'tis strange then, that he should have honoured you with his Commission; Pray, what is it you come to request for him?

My Master, Madam, said he, ordered me to get this Letter delivered to your Ladyship, and to stay for your Commands.

You would persuade me, said she, sternly, being provoked that he did not deliver the Letter upon his Knees, as was the Custom in Romances, that you are not acquainted with the Purport of this audacious Billet, since you express so little Fear of my Displeasure; but know, presumptuous, that I am mortally offended with your Master, for his daring to suppose I would read this Proof at once of his Insolence and Infidelity; and was you worth my Resentment, I would haply make you suffer for your Want of Respect to me.

The poor Man, surprised and confounded at her Anger, and puzzled extremely to understand what she meant, was opening his Mouth to say something, 'tis probable in his own Defence, when *Arabella*, preventing him,

I know what thou wouldst say, said she: Thou wouldst abuse my Patience by a false Detail of thy Master's Sighs, Tears, Exclamations, and Despair.

Indeed, Madam, I don't intend to say any such Thing, replied the Man.

No! repeated *Arabella*, a little disappointed, Bear back this presumptuous Billet then, which I suppose contains the melancholy Account; and tell him, He that could so soon forget the generous *Sydimiris* for *Philonice*, and could afterwards be false to that incomparable Beauty, is not a Person worthy to adore *Arabella*.

The Man, who could not tell what to make of this Message, and feared he should forget these two hard Names, humbly intreated her to be pleased to acquaint his Master, by a Line, with her Intentions. *Arabella*, supposing he meant to importune her still more, made a Sign with her Hand, very majestically, for him to be gone; but he, not able to comprehend her Meaning, stood still, with an Air of Perplexity, not daring to beg her to explain herself; supposing, she, by that Sign, required something of him.

Why dost thou not obey my Commands? said *Arabella*, finding he did not go.

I will, to be sure, Madam, replied he; wishing at the same Time secretly, she would let him know what they were.

And yet, said she hastily, thou art disobeying me this Moment: Did I not bid you get out of my Presence, and to speak no more of your inconstant Master, whose Crimes have rendered him the Detestation of all generous Persons whatever?

Sir *George*'s Messenger, extremely surprised at so harsh a Character of his Master, and the Rage with which the Lady seemed to be actuated, made haste to get out of her Apartment; and, at his Return, informed his Master, very exactly, of the Reception he had met with, repeating all Lady *Bella*'s Words; which, notwithstanding the Blunders he made in the Names of *Sydimiris* and *Philonice*, Sir *George* understood well enough; and found new Occasion of wondering at the Excess of *Arabella*'s Extravagance, who he never imagined would have explained herself in that Manner to his Servant.

Without endeavouring therefore to see *Arabella*, he went to pay his Compliments to Sir *Charles*, Mr. *Glanville*, and Miss *Glanville*; to the last of whom he said some soft Things, that made her extremely regret his staying behind them in the Country.

CHAPTER II

Not so long as was first intended; but contains, however, a surprising Adventure on the Road.

The Day of their Departure being come, they set out in a Coach and Six,[1] attended by several Servants on Horseback. The first Day's Journey passed off, without any Accident worthy relating; but, towards the Close of the Second, they were alarmed by the Appearance of three Highwaymen, well mounted, at a small Distance.

One of the Servants, who had first spied them, immediately rode up to the Coach; and, for fear of alarming the Ladies, whispered Mr. *Glanville* in the Ear.

Sir *Charles*, who was sitting next his Son, and had heard it, cried out with too little Caution, How's this? Are we in any Danger of being attacked, say you?

Mr. *Glanville*, without replying, jumped out of the Coach; at which Miss *Glanville* screamed out; and, lest her Father should follow, sprung into her Brother's Seat, and held him fast by the Coat.

Arabella, being in a strange Consternation at all this, put her Head out of the Coach, to see what was the Matter; and, observing Three or Four Men of a genteel Appearance, on Horseback, who seemed to halt, and gaze on them, without offering to advance;

Sir, said she to her Uncle, are yonder Knights the Persons whom you suppose will attack us?

Ay, ay, said Sir *Charles*, they are Knights of the Road² indeed: I suppose we shall have a Bout with them; for it will be scandalous to deliver, since we have the Odds of our Side, and are more than a Match for them.

Arabella, interpreting these Words in her own Way, looked out again; and, seeing the Robbers, who had by this Time taken their Resolution, galloping towards them, her Cousin and the Servants ranging themselves of each Side of the Coach, as if to defend them,

Hold, hold, valiant Men, said she, as loud as she could speak, addressing herself to the Highwaymen; do not, by a mistaken Generosity, hazard your Lives in a Combat, to which the Laws of Honour do not oblige you: We are not violently carried away, as you falsely suppose; we go willingly along with these Persons, who are our Friends and Relations.

Hey-day! cried Sir *Charles*, staring at her with great Surprize; what's the Meaning of all this? Do you think these Fellows will mind your fine Speeches, Niece?

I hope they will, Sir, said she: Then, pulling her Cousin, Shew yourself, for Heaven's Sake, Miss, pursued she, and second my Assurances, that we are not forced away: These generous Men come to fight for our Deliverance.

The Highwaymen, who were near enough to hear *Arabella*'s Voice, though they could not distinguish her Words, gazed on her with great Surprize; and, finding they would be very well received, thought fit to abandon their Enterprize, and galloped away as fast as they were able. Some of the Servants made a Motion to pursue them; but Mr. *Glanville* forbad it; and, entering again into the Coach, congratulated the Ladies upon the Escape they had had.

Since these Men, said *Arabella*, did not come to deliver us, out of a mistaken Notion, that we were carried away by Force, it must necessarily follow, they had some bad Design; and I protest I know not who to suspect is the Author of it, unless the Person you vanquished, said she to Mr. *Glanville*, the other Day in a single Combat; for the disguised *Edward*, you assured me, was dead: But perhaps, continued she, it was some Lover of Miss *Glanville*'s who designed to make an Attempt to carry her away: Methinks he was too slenderly attended for such an hazardous Undertaking.

I'll assure you Madam, said Miss *Glanville*, I have no Lovers among Highwaymen.

Highwaymen! repeated *Arabella*.

Why, ay, to be sure, Madam, rejoined Sir *Charles*: What do you take them for?

For Persons of Quality, Sir, resumed *Arabella*; and though they came, questionless, either upon a good or bad Design, yet it cannot be doubted, but that their Birth is illustrious; otherwise they would never pretend either to fight in our Defence, or to carry us away.

I vow, Niece, said Sir *Charles*, I can't possibly understand you.

My Cousin, Sir, interrupted Mr. *Glanville*, has been mistaken in these Persons; and has not yet, possibly, believed them to be Highwaymen, who came to rob us.

There is no Question, Sir, said *Arabella*, smiling, that if they did not come to defend us, they came to rob you: But it is hard to guess, which of us it was of whom they designed to deprive you; for it may very possibly be for my Cousin's Sake, as well as mine, that this Enterprize was undertaken.

Pardon me, Madam, said Mr. *Glanville*, who was willing to prevent his Father from answering her Absurdities; these Men had no other Design than to rob us of our Money.

How! said *Arabella*: Were these Cavaliers, who appeared to be in so handsome a Garb, that I took them for Persons of prime Quality, were they Robbers? I have been strangely mistaken, it seems: However, I apprehend there is no Certainty, that your Suspicions are true; and it may still be as I say, that they either came to rescue or carry us away.

Mr. *Glanville*, to avoid a longer Dispute, changed the Discourse; having observed with Confusion, that Sir *Charles*, and his Sister, seemed to look upon his beloved Cousin as one that was out of her Senses.

CHAPTER III

Which concludes with an authentic Piece of History.

Arabella, during the rest of this Journey, was so wholly taken up in contemplating upon the last Adventure, that she mixed but little in the Conversation. Upon their drawing near *Bath*, the Situation of that City afforded her the Means of making a Comparison between the Valley in which it was placed (with the amphitheatrical View of the Hills around it) and the Valley of *Tempe*.

'T was in such a Place as this, said she, pursuing her Comparison, that the fair *Andronice* delivered the valiant *Hortensius*:[3] And really I could wish, our Entrance into that City might be preceded by an Act of equal Humanity with that of that fair Princess.

For the Gratification of that Wish, Madam, said Mr. *Glanville*, it is necessary some Person should meet with a Misfortune, out of which you might be able to relieve him; but I suppose the Benevolence of your Disposition may be equally satisfied with not finding any Occasion, as of exercising it, when it is found.

Though it be not my Fortune to meet with those Occasions, replied *Arabella*, there is no Reason to doubt but others do, who possibly have less Inclination to afford their Assistance than myself: And it is possible, if any other than the Princess of *Messina* had happened to pass by, when *Hortensius* was in the Hands of the *Thessalians*, he would not have been rescued from the ignominious Death he was destined to, merely for killing a Stork.

How! interrupted Sir *Charles*, put a Man to Death for killing a Stork! Ridiculous! Pray, in what Part of the World did that happen? Among the *Indians* of *America*,[4] I suppose.

No, Sir, said *Arabella*, in *Thessaly*; the fairest Part in all *Macedonia*, famous for the beautiful Valley of *Tempe*, which excited the Curiosity of all Travellers whatever.

No, not all, Madam, returned Sir *Charles*; for I am acquainted with several Travellers, who never saw it, nor even mentioned it; and if it is so famous as you say, I am surprised I never heard of it before.

I don't know, said *Arabella*, what those Travellers thought worthy of their Notice; but I am certain, that if any Chance should conduct me into *Macedonia*, I would not leave it till I saw the Valley of *Tempe*, so celebrated by all the Poets and Historians.

Dear Cousin, cried *Glanville*, who could hardly forbear smiling, what Chance, in the Name of Wonder, should take you into *Turky*, at so great a Distance from your own Country?

And so, said Sir *Charles*, this famous Valley of *Tempe* is in *Turky*.[5] Why you must be very fond of travelling, indeed, Lady *Bella*, if you would go into the *Great Mogul*'s Country,[6] where the People are all Pagans, they say, and worship the Devil.

The Country my Cousin speaks of, said Mr. *Glanville*, is in the Grand Signor's Dominions: The Great Mogul, you know, Sir ——

Well, interrupted Sir *Charles*, the Great Mogul, or the Grand Signor, I know not what you call him: But I hope my Niece does not propose to go thither.

Not unless I am forcibly carried thither, said *Arabella*; but I do determine, if that Misfortune should ever happen to me, that I would, if possible, visit the Valley of *Tempe*, which is in that Part of *Greece* they call *Macedonia*.

Then I am persuaded, replied Sir *Charles*, you'll never see

that famous Vale you talk of; for it is not very likely you should
be forcibly carried away into *Turky*.

And why do you think it unlikely, that I should be carried
thither? interrupted *Arabella*. Do not the same Things happen
now, that did formerly? And is any thing more common, than
Ladies being carried, by their Ravishers, into Countries far
distant from their own? May not the same Accidents happen
to me, that have happened to so many illustrious Ladies before
me? And may I not be carried into *Macedonia* by a Similitude
of Destiny with that of a great many beautiful Princesses, who,
though born in the most distant Quarters of the World, chanced
to meet at one time in the City of *Alexandria*, and related their
miraculous Adventures to each other?[7]

And it was for that very Purpose they met, Madam, said Mr.
Glanville, smiling.

Why, truly, said *Arabella*, it happened very luckily for each
of them, that they were brought into a Place where they found
so many illustrious Companions in Misfortune, to whom they
might freely communicate their Adventures, which otherwise
might, haply, have been concealed, or, at least, have been imper-
fectly delivered down to us: However, added she, smiling, if I
am carried into *Macedonia*, and by that means have an Opportunity of visiting the famous Vale of *Tempe*, I shall take care
not to draw the Resentment of the *Thessalians* upon me, by an
Indiscretion like that of *Hortensius*.

For be pleased to know, Sir, said she, addressing herself to
her Uncle, that his killing a Stork, however inconsiderable a
Matter it may appear to us, was yet looked upon as a Crime of
a very atrocious Nature among the *Thessalians*; for they have
a Law, which forbids, upon Pain of Death, the killing of Storks;
the Reason for which is, that *Thessaly* being subject to be
infested with a prodigious Multitude of Serpents, which are a
delightful Food to these sort of Fowls, they look upon them as
sacred Birds, sent by the Gods to deliver them from these
Serpents and Vipers: and though *Hortensius*, being a Stranger,
was pardoned through the Intercession of the Princess *Andronice*, they made him promise to send another Stork into *Thessaly*,
to the End that he might be reputed innocent.

CHAPTER IV

*In which one of our Heroine's Whims is justified, by
some others full as whimsical.*

This Piece of History, with Sir *Charles*'s Remarks upon it,
brought them into *Bath*. Their Lodgings being provided before-
hand, the Ladies retired to their different Chambers, to repose
themselves after the Fatigue of their Journey, and did not meet
again till Supper was on Table; when Miss *Glanville*, who had
eagerly enquired what Company was then in the Place, and
heard there were a great many Persons of Fashion just arrived,
prest *Arabella* to go to the Pump-Room[8] the next Morning,
assuring her she would find a very agreeable Amusement.

Arabella accordingly consented to accompany her; and,
being told the Ladies went in an Undress[9] of a Morning, she
accommodated herself to the Custom, and went in a negligent
Dress; but instead of a Capuchin, she wore something like a
Veil, of black Gauze,[10] which covered almost all her Face, and
Part of her Waist, and gave her a very singular Appearance.

Miss *Glanville* was too envious of her Cousin's Superiority
in point of Beauty, to inform her of any Oddity in her Dress,
which she thought might expose her to the Ridicule of those
that saw her; and Mr. *Glanville* was too little a Critic in Ladies
Apparel, to be sensible that *Arabella* was not in the Fashion;
and since every Thing she wore became her extremely, he could
not choose but think she drest admirably well: He handed her
therefore, with a great deal of Satisfaction, into the Pump-
Room, which happened to be greatly crouded that Morning.

The Attention of most Part of the Company was immediately
engaged by the Appearance Lady *Bella* made. Strangers are
here most strictly criticized, and every new Object affords a
delicious Feast of Raillery and Scandal.

The Ladies, alarmed at the Singularity of her Dress, crouded
together in Parties; and the Words, Who can she be? Strange
Creature! Ridiculous! and other Exclamations of the same
Kind, were whispered very intelligibly.

The Men were struck with her Figure, veiled as she was: Her fine Stature, the beautiful Turn of her Person, the Grace and Elegance of her Motion, attracted all their Notice: The Phænomena of the Veil, however, gave them great Disturbance. So lovely a Person seemed to promise the Owner had a Face not unworthy of it; but that was totally hid from their View: For, *Arabella*, at her Entrance into the Room, had pulled the Gauze quite over her Face, following therein the Custom of the Ladies in *Clelia*, and the *Grand Cyrus*, who, in mixed Companies, always hid their Faces with great Care.

The Wits and Pretty-Fellows,[11] railed at the envious Covering, and compared her to the Sun obscured by a Cloud; while the Beaux *dem'd* the horrid Innovation, and expressed a Fear, lest it should grow into a Fashion.

Some of the wiser Sort took her for a Foreigner; others, of still more Sagacity, supposed her a *Scots* Lady, covered with her Plaid; and a third Sort, infinitely wiser than either, concluded she was a *Spanish* Nun, that had escaped from a Convent, and had not yet quitted her Veil.

Arabella, ignorant of the Diversity of Opinions, to which her Appearance gave Rise, was taken up in discoursing with Mr. *Glanville* upon the medicinal Virtue of the Springs, the Oeconomy of the Baths, the Nature of the Diversions, and such other Topicks, as the Objects around them furnished her with.

In the mean Time, Miss *Glanville* was got amidst a Croud of her Acquaintance, who had hardly paid the Civilities of a first Meeting, before they eagerly enquired, who that Lady she brought with her was.

Miss *Glanville* informed them, that she was her Cousin, and Daughter to the deceased Marquis of —— adding with a Sneer, That she had been brought up in the Country; knew nothing of the World; and had some very peculiar Notions, as you may see, said she, by that odd kind of Covering she wears.

Her Name and Quality were presently whispered all over the Room: The Men, hearing she was a great Heiress, found greater Beauties to admire in her Person: The Ladies, aw'd by the Sanction of Quality, dropt their Ridicule on her Dress, and begun to quote Examples of Whims full as inexcusable.

One remembered, that Lady *J——* *F——* always wore her Ruffles reversed; that the Countess of —— went to Court in a Farthingale;[12] that the Dutchess of —— sat astride upon a Horse;[13] and a certain Lady of great Fortune, and nearly allied to Quality, because she was not dignified with a Title, invented a new one for herself; and directed her Servants to say in speaking to her, *Your Honouress*, which afterwards became a Custom among all her Acquaintance; who mortally offended her if they omitted that Instance of Respect.

CHAPTER V

Containing some historical Anecdotes, the Truth of which may possibly be doubted, as they are not to be found in any of the Historians.

After a short Stay in the Room, *Arabella* expressing a Desire to return home, Mr. *Glanville* conducted her out. Two Gentlemen of his Acquaintance attending Miss *Glanville*, Sir *Charles* detained them to Breakfast; by which Means they had an Opportunity of satisfying their Curiosity; and beheld *Arabella*, divested of that Veil, which had, as they said, and 'tis probable they said no more than they thought, concealed one of the finest Faces in the World.

Miss *Glanville* had the Mortification to see both the Gentlemen so charmed with the Sight of her Cousin's Face, that for a long time she sat wholly neglected; but the Seriousness of her Behaviour, giving some little Disgust to the youngest of them, who was what the Ladies call a pretty Fellow, a dear Creature, and the most diverting Man in the World; he applied himself wholly to Miss *Glanville*, and soon engaged her in a particular Conversation.

Mr. *Selvin*, so was the other Gentleman called, was of a much graver Cast: He affected to be thought deep-read in History, and never failed to take all Opportunities of displaying his Knowledge of Antiquity, which was indeed but very superficial; but

having some few Anecdotes by Heart, which he would take
Occasion to introduce as often as he could, he passed among
many Persons for one, who, by Application and Study, had
acquired an universal Knowledge of antient History.

Speaking of any particular Circumstance, he would fix
the Time, by computing the Year with the Number of the
Olympiads.[14]

It happened, he would say; in the 141st Olympiad.

Such an amazing Exactness, had a suitable Effect on his
Audience, and always procured him a great Degree of Attention.

This Gentleman hitherto had no Opportunity of displaying
his Knowledge of History, the Discourse having wholly turned
upon News, and other Trifles; when *Arabella*, after some more
Enquiries concerning the Place, remarked, that there was a very
great Difference between the medicinal Waters at *Bath*, and the
fine Springs at the Foot of the Mountain *Thermopylæ* in *Greece*,
as well in their Qualities, as manner of using them; and I am of
Opinion, added she, that *Bath*, famous as it is for restoring
Health, is less frequented by infirm Persons, than the famous
Springs of *Thermopylæ* were by the Beauties of *Greece*, to
whom those Waters have the Reputation of giving new Lustre.[15]

Mr. *Selvin*, who, with all his Reading, had never met with
any Account of these celebrated *Grecian* Springs, was extremely
disconcerted at not being able to continue a Conversation,
which the Silence of the rest of the Company made him imagine,
was directed wholly to him.

The Shame he conceived at seeing himself posed[16] by a Girl,
in a Matter which so immediately belonged to him, made him
resolve to draw himself out of this Dilemna at any Rate; and,
though he was far from being convinced, that there were no
such Springs at *Thermopylæ*[17] as *Arabella* mentioned; yet he
resolutely maintained that she must be mistaken in their Situation; for, to his certain Knowledge, there were no medicinal
Waters at the Foot of that Mountain.

Arabella, who could not endure to be contradicted in what
she took to be so incontestable a Fact, reddened with Vexation
at his unexpected Denial.

It should seem, said she, by your Discourse, that you are

unacquainted with many material Passages, that passed among very illustrious Persons there; and if you knew any thing of *Pisistratus* the *Athenian*, you would know, that an Adventure he had at those Baths, laid the Foundation of all those great Designs, which he afterwards effected, to the total Subversion of the *Athenian* Government.

Mr. *Selvin*, surprised that this Piece of History had likewise escaped his Observation, resolved, however, not to give up his Point.

I think, Madam, replied he, with great Self-sufficiency, that I am pretty well acquainted with every thing which relates to the Affairs of the *Athenian* Commonwealth; and know by what Steps *Pisistratus* advanced himself to the Sovereignty. It was indeed a great Stroke of Policy in him, said he, turning to Mr. *Glanville*, to wound himself, in order to get a Guard assigned him.

You are mistaken, Sir, said *Arabella*, if you believe, there was any Truth in the Report of his having wounded himself: It was done, either by his Rival *Lycurgus* or *Theocrites*; who believing him still to be in Love with the fair *Cerinthe*, whom he courted, took that Way to get rid of him: Neither is it true, that Ambition alone inspired *Pisistratus* with a Design of enslaving his Country: Those Authors who say so, must know little of the Springs and Motives of his Conduct. It was neither Ambition nor Revenge, that made him act as he did; it was the violent Affection he conceived for the beautiful *Cleorante*, whom he first saw at the famous Baths of *Thermopylæ*, which put him upon those Designs; for, seeing that *Lycurgus*, who was not his Rival in Ambition, but Love, would certainly become the Possessor of *Cleorante*, unless he made himself Tyrant of *Athens*, he had Recourse to that violent Method, in order to preserve her for himself.

I protest, Madam, said Mr. *Selvin*, casting down his Eyes in great Confusion at her superior Knowledge in History, these Particulars have all escaped my Notice; and this is the first time I ever understood, that *Pisistratus* was violently in Love; and that it was not Ambition, which made him aspire to Sovereignty.

I do not remember any Mention of this in *Plutarch*,

continued he, rubbing his Forehead, or any of the Authors who have treated on the Affairs of *Greece*.

Very likely, Sir, replied *Arabella*; but you will see the whole Story of *Pisistratus*'s Love for *Cleorante*, with the Effects it produced, related at large in *Scudery*.

Scudery, Madam! said the sage Mr. *Selvin*, I never read that Historian.

No, Sir! replied *Arabella*, then your Reading has been very confined.

I know, Madam, said he, that *Herodotus, Thucydides*, and *Plutarch*, have indeed quoted him frequently.[18]

I am surprised, Sir, said Mr. *Glanville*, who was excessively diverted at this Discovery of his great Ignorance and Affectation, that you have not read that famous Historian; especially, as the Writers you have mentioned quote him so often.

Why, to tell you the Truth, Sir, said he; though he was a *Roman*; yet it is objected to him, that he wrote but indifferent *Latin*; with no Purity or Elegance; and —

You are quite mistaken, Sir, interrupted *Arabella*; the great *Scudery* was a *Frenchman*; and both his *Clelia* and *Artamenes* were written in *French*.

A *Frenchman* was he? said Mr. *Selvin*, with a lofty Air: Oh! then, 'tis not surprising, that I have not read him: I read no Authors, but the Antients, Madam, added he, with a Look of Self-applause; I cannot relish the Moderns at all: I have no Taste for their Way of Writing.

But *Scudery* must needs be more ancient than *Thucydides*, and the rest of those *Greek* Historians you mentioned, said Mr. *Glanville*: How else could they quote him?

Mr. *Selvin* was here so utterly at a Loss, that he could not conceal his Confusion: He held down his Head, and continued silent; while the Beau, who had listened to the latter Part of their Discourse; exerted his supposed Talent of Raillery against the unhappy Admirer of the antient Authors; and increased his Confusion by a thousand Sarcasms, which gave more Diversion to himself, than any Body else.

CHAPTER VI

Which contains some excellent Rules for Raillery.[19]

Mr. *Glanville*, who had too much Politeness and Good-nature to insist too long upon the Ridicule in the Character of his Acquaintance, changed the Discourse: And *Arabella*, who had observed, with some Concern, the ill-judged Raillery of the young Beau,[20] took Occasion to decry that Species of Wit; and gave it as her Opinion, that it was very dangerous and unpleasing.

For, truly, said she, it is almost impossible to use it without being hated or feared; and whoever gets a Habit of it, is in Danger of wronging all the Laws of Friendship and Humanity.

Certainly, pursued she, looking at the Beau, it is extremely unjust to railly one's Friends, and particular Acquaintance: First, choose them well, and be as nice as you please in the Choice; but when you have chosen them, by no means play upon them: 'Tis cruel and malicious, to divert one's self at the Expence of one's Friend.

However, Madam, said Mr. *Glanville*, who was charmed to hear her talk so rationally, you may give People Leave to railly their Enemies.

Truly, resumed *Arabella*, I cannot allow that, any more than upon Friends; for Raillery is the poorest kind of Revenge that can be taken: Methinks, it is mean to railly Persons who have a small Share of Merit; since, haply, their Defects were born with them, and not of their own acquiring; and it is great Injustice to descant upon one slight Fault in Men of Parts, to the Prejudice of a thousand good Qualities.

For aught I see, Madam, said the Beau, you will not allow one to railly any Body.

I am of Opinion, Sir, said *Arabella*, that there are very few proper Objects for Raillery; and still fewer, who can railly well: The Talent of Raillery ought to be born with a Person; no Art can infuse it; and those who endeavour to railly in spite of Nature, will be so far from diverting others, that they will become the Objects of Ridicule themselves.

Many other pleasing Qualities of Wit may be acquired by
Pains and Study, but Raillery must be the Gift of Nature: It is
not enough to have many lively and agreeable Thoughts; but
there must be such an Expression, as must convey their full
Force and Meaning; the Air, the Aspect, the Tone of the Voice,
and every Part in general, must contribute to its Perfection.

There ought also to be a great Distance between Raillery and
Satire, so that one may never be mistaken for the other: Raillery
ought indeed to surprise, and sensibly touch, those to whom it
is directed; but I would not have the Wounds it makes, either
deep or lasting: Let those who feel it, be hurt like Persons, who,
gathering Roses, are pricked by the Thorns, and find a sweet
Smell to make amends.

I would have Raillery raise the Fancy, and quicken the
Imagination, the Fire of its Wit should only enable us to trace
its Original, and shine as the Stars do, but not burn. Yet, after
all, I cannot greatly approve of Raillery, or cease to think it
dangerous; and, to pursue my Comparison, said she, with an
inchanting Smile, Persons who possess the true Talent of Raillery, are like Comets; they are seldom seen, and are at once
admir'd and fear'd.

I protest, Lady *Bella*, said Sir *Charles*, who had listen'd to
her with many Signs of Admiration, you speak like an Orator.

One would not imagine, interrupted Mr. *Glanville*, who saw
Arabella in some Confusion at the coarse Praise her Uncle gave
her, that my Cousin could speak so accurately of a Quality she
never practises: And 'tis easy to judge by what she has said,
that no body can railly finer than herself, if she pleases.

Mr. *Selvin*, tho' he bore her a Grudge for knowing more
History than he did, yet assur'd her, that she had given the best
Rules imaginable for raillying well. But the Beau, whom she had
silenc'd by her Reproof, was extremely angry; and, supposing it
would mortify her to see him pay Court to her Cousin, he
redoubled his Assiduities to Miss *Glanville*, who was highly
delighted at seeing *Arabella* less taken Notice of by this gay
Gentleman, than herself.

CHAPTER VII

In which the Author condescends to be very minute in the Description of our Heroine's Dress.

The Indifference of Mr. *Tinsel*, convincing Miss *Glanville*, that *Arabella* was less to be dreaded than she imagin'd, she had no Reluctance at seeing her prepare for her publick Appearance the next Ball Night.

Having consulted her Fancy in a rich Silver Stuff, she had bought for that Purpose, a Person was sent for to make it; and *Arabella*, who follow'd no Fashion but her own Taste, which was form'd on the manners of the Heroines, order'd the Woman to make her a Robe after the same Model as the Princess *Julia*'s.[21]

The Mantua-maker,[22] who thought it might do her great Prejudice with her new Customer, to acknowledge she knew nothing of the Princess *Julia*, or the Fashion of her Gown, replied at Random, and with great Pertness,

That, that Taste was quite out; and, she would advise her Ladyship to have her Cloaths made in the present Mode, which was far more becoming.

You can never persuade me, said *Arabella*, that any Fashion can be more becoming than that of the Princess *Julia*'s, who was the most gallant Princess upon Earth, and knew better than any other, how to set off her Charms. It may indeed be a little obsolete now, pursued she, for the Fashion could not but alter a little in the Compass of near two thousand Years.

Two thousand Years! Madam, said the Woman, in a great Surprize; Lord help us Trades-people, if they did not alter a thousand Times in as many Days! I thought your Ladyship was speaking of the last Month's Taste; which, as I said before, is quite out now.

Well, replied *Arabella*, let the present Mode be what it will, I insist upon having my Cloaths made after the Pattern of the beautiful Daughter of *Augustus*; being convinced, that none other can be half so becoming.

What Fashion was that, pray, Madam, said the Woman? I never saw it.

How, replied *Arabella*, have you already forgot the Fashion of the Princess *Julia*'s Robe, which you said was wore but last Month? Or, are you ignorant that the Princess *Julia*, and the Daughter of *Augustus*, is the same Person?

I protest, Madam, said the Woman, extremely confus'd, I had forgot that, till you called it to my Mind.

Well, said *Arabella*, make me a Robe in the same Taste.

The Mantua-maker was now wholly at a Loss in what Manner to behave; for, being conscious that she knew nothing of the Princess *Julia*'s Fashion, she could not undertake to make it without Directions; and she was afraid of discovering her Ignorance by asking for any; so that her Silence and Embarrassment persuading *Arabella* she knew nothing of the Matter, she dismist her with a small Present, for the Trouble she had given her, and had Recourse to her usual Expedient, which was, to make one of her Women, who understood a little of the Mantua-making Business, make a Robe for her, after her own Directions.

Miss *Glanville*, who imagin'd she had sent for Work-women, in order to have Cloaths made in the modern Taste, was surpriz'd at her Entrance into her Chamber, to see her dressing for the Ball, in a Habit singular to the last Degree.

She wore no Hoop, and the Blue and Silver Stuff of her Robe, was only kept by its own Richness, from hanging close about her. It was quite open round her Breast, which was shaded with a rich Border of Lace; and clasping close to her Waist, by small Knots of Diamonds, descended in a sweeping Train on the Ground.

The Sleeves were short, wide, and slash'd, fastned in different Places with Diamonds, and her Arms were partly hid by half a Dozen Falls of Ruffles. Her Hair, which fell in very easy Ringlets on her Neck, was plac'd with great Care and Exactness round her lovely Face; and the Jewels and Ribbons, which were all her Head-dress, dispos'd to the greatest Advantage.[23]

Upon the whole, nothing could be more singularly becoming than her Dress; or set off with greater Advantage the striking Beauties of her Person.

Miss *Glanville*, tho' she was not displeas'd to see her persist in her Singularity of Dress; yet could not behold her look so lovely in it, without feeling a secret Uneasiness; but consoling herself with the Hopes of the Ridicule she would occasion, she assum'd a chearful Air, approv'd her Taste in the Choice of her Colours, and went with her at the usual Hour, to the Rooms, attended by Mr. *Glanville*, Mr. *Selvin*, and the young Beau we have formerly mention'd.

The Surprize *Arabella*'s unusual Appearance gave to the whole Company, was very visible to every one but herself.

The Moment she enter'd the Room, everyone whisper'd the Person next to them; and for some Moments, nothing was heard but the Words, the Princess *Julia*; which was eccho'd at every Corner, and at last attracted her Observation.

Mr. *Glanville*, and the rest of the Company with her, were in some Confusion at the universal Exclamation, which they imagin'd was occasion'd by the Singularity of her Habit; tho' they could not conceive, why they gave her that Title. Had they known the Adventure of the Mantua-maker, it would doubtless have easily occur'd to them; for the Woman had no sooner left *Arabella*, than she related the Conference she had with a Lady newly arriv'd, who had requir'd her to make a Robe in the Manner of the Princess *Julia's*; and dismiss'd her, because she did not understand the Fashions that prevail'd two thousand Years ago.

This Story was quickly dispers'd, and for its Novelty, afforded a great deal of Diversion; every one long'd to see a Fashion of such Antiquity; and expected the Appearance of the Princess *Julia* with great Impatience.

It is not to be doubted but much Mirth was treasur'd up for her Appearance; and the occasional Humourist had already prepared his accustom'd Jest, when the Sight of the devoted fair One repell'd his Vivacity, and the design'd Ridicule of the whole Assembly.

Scarce had the tumultuous Whisper escap'd the Lips of each Individual, when they found themselves aw'd to Respect by that irresistable Charm in the Person of *Arabella*, which commanded Reverence and Love from all who beheld her.

Her noble Air, the native Dignity in her Looks, the inexpressible Grace which accompany'd all her Motions, and the consummate Loveliness of her Form, drew the Admiration of the whole Assembly.

A respectful Silence succeeded, and the Astonishment her Beauty occasion'd, left them no Room to descant on the Absurdity of her Dress.

Miss *Glanville*, who felt a malicious Joy at the Sneers she expected would be cast on her Cousin, was greatly disappointed at the Deference which seem'd to be paid her; and to vent some Part of her Spleen, took occasion to mention her Surprize, at the Behaviour of the Company on their Entrance; wondering what they could mean by whispering the Princess *Julia* to one another.

I assure you, said *Arabella*, smiling, I am not less surpriz'd than you at it; and since they directed their Looks to me at the same Time, I fancy they either took me for some Princess of the Name of *Julia*, who is expected here to-Night, or else flatter me with some Resemblance to the beautiful Daughter of *Augustus*.

The Comparison, Madam, said Mr. *Selvin*, who took all Occasions to shew his Reading, is too injurious to you, for I am of Opinion you as much excel that licentious Lady in the Beauties of your Person, as you do in the Qualities of your Mind.

I never heard Licentiousness imputed to the Daughter of *Augustus Cæsar*, said *Arabella*; and the most her Enemies can say of her, is, that she loved Admiration, and would permit herself to be beloved, and to be told so, without shewing any Signs of Displeasure.

Bless me, Madam, interrupted Mr. *Selvin*, how strangely do you mistake the Character of *Julia*: Tho' the Daughter of an Emperor, she was, pardon the Expression, the most abandon'd Prostitute in *Rome*; many of her Intrigues are recorded in History; but to mention only one, Was not her infamous Commerce with *Ovid*, the Cause of his Banishment?[24]

CHAPTER VIII

Some Reflexions very fit, and others very unfit for an Assembly-Room.

You speak in strange Terms, replied *Arabella*, blushing, of a Princess, who if she was not the most reserv'd and severe Person in the World, was yet nevertheless, absolutely chaste.

I know there were People who represented her Partiality for *Ovid* in a very unfavourable Light; but that ingenious Poet, when he related his History to the great *Agrippa*, told him in Confidence all that had pass'd between him and the Princess *Julia*, than which nothing could be more innocent, tho' a little indiscreet. For, 'tis certain that she permitted him to love her, and did not condemn him to any rigorous Punishment for daring to tell her so; yet, for all this, as I said before, tho' she was not altogether so austere as she ought to have been, yet she was nevertheless a most virtuous Princess.

Mr. *Selvin*, not daring to contradict a Lady whose extensive Reading had furnish'd her with Anecdotes unknown almost to any Body else, by his Silence confess'd her Superiority. But Mr. *Glanville*, who knew all these Anecdotes were drawn from Romances, which he found contradicted the known Facts in History, and assign'd the most ridiculous Causes for Things of the greatest Importance; could not help smiling at the Facility with which Mr. *Selvin* gave into those idle Absurdities. For notwithstanding his Affectation of great Reading, his superficial Knowledge of History made it extremely easy to deceive him; and as it was his Custom to mark in his Pocket-Book all the Scraps of History he heard introduced into Conversation, and retail them again in other Company; he did not doubt but he would make a Figure with the curious Circumstances *Arabella* had furnish'd him with.

Arabella observing Mr. *Tinsel* by his familiar Bows, significant Smiles, and easy Salutations, was acquainted with the greatest Part of the Assembly, told him, that she did not doubt but he knew the Adventures of many Persons whom they were viewing; and that he would do her a Pleasure, if he would relate some of them.

Mr. *Tinsel* was charm'd with a Request which afforded him an Opportunity of gratifying a favourite Inclination, and seating himself near her immediately, was beginning to obey her Injunctions, when she gracefully intreated him to stay a Moment; and calling to Mr. *Glanville*, and his Sister, who were talking to Mr. *Selvin*, ask'd them if they chose to partake of a more rational Amusement than Dancing, and listen to the Adventures of some illustrious Persons, which Mr. *Tinsel* had promis'd to relate.

I assure you, Madam, said Mr. *Glanville*, smiling, you will find that a less innocent Amusement than Dancing.

Why so, Sir, replied *Arabella*, since it is not an indiscreet Curiosity which prompts me to a Desire of hearing the Histories Mr. *Tinsel* has promis'd to entertain me with; but rather a Hope of hearing something which may at once improve and delight me; something which may excite my Admiration, engage my Esteem, or influence my Practice.

'T was doubtless, with such Motives as these, that we find Princesses and Ladies of the most illustrious Rank, in *Clelia* and the Grand *Cyrus*, listning to the Adventures of Persons, in whom they were probably as little interested, as we are in these around us. Kings, Princes and Commanders of Armies, thought it was no Waste of their Time, in the midst of the Hurry and Clamour of a Camp, to listen many Hours to the Relation of one single History, and not fill'd with any extraordinary Events; but haply a simple Recital of common Occurrences: The great *Cyrus* while he was busy in reducing all *Asia* to his Yoke, heard nevertheless, the Histories of all the considerable Persons in the Camp, besides those of Strangers, and even his Enemies. If there was therefore any thing either criminal or mean, in hearing the Adventures of others, do you imagine so many great and illustrious Persons would have given in to such an Amusement?

After this *Arabella* turn'd gravely about to Mr. *Tinsel*, and told him, he was at Liberty to begin his Recital.

The Beau, a little disconcerted by the Solemnity with which she requested his Information, knew not how to begin with the

Formality that he saw was required of him; and therefore sat silent for a few Moments; which *Arabella* suppos'd was to recall to his Memory all the Passages he propos'd to relate.

His Perplexity would probably have increas'd instead of lessening by the profound Silence which she observed, had not Miss *Glanville* seated herself with a sprightly Air on the other Side of him, and directing his Eyes to a tall handsome Woman that had just enter'd, ask'd him pleasantly, to tell her History if he knew it.

Mr. *Tinsel*, brought into his usual Track by this Question, answer'd smiling, That the History of that Lady was yet a Secret, or known but to a very few; but my Intelligence, added he, is generally the earliest, and may always be depended on.

Perhaps, said *Arabella*, the Lady is one of your Acquaintances, and favour'd you with the Recital of her Adventures from her own Mouth.

No, really, Madam, answer'd Mr. *Tinsel*, surpriz'd at the great Simplicity of *Arabella*, for so he understood it; the Lady, I believe, is not so communicative: And to say the Truth, I should not chuse to hear her Adventures from herself, since she certainly would suppress the most material Circumstances.

In a Word, said he, lowering his Voice, That Lady was for many Years the Mistress of a young military Nobleman, whom she was so complaisant to follow in all his Campaigns, Marches, Sieges, and every Inconveniency of War: He married her in *Gibraltar*,[25] from whence he is lately arriv'd, and introduc'd his new Lady to his noble Brother, by whom she was not unfavourably receiv'd. 'Tis worth remarking, that this same haughty Peer thought fit to resent with implacable Obstinacy, the Marriage of another of his Brothers, with the Widow of a brave Officer, of considerable Rank in the Army. 'Tis true, she was several Years older than the young Lord, and had no Fortune; but the Duke assign'd other Reasons for his Displeasure: He complain'd loudly, that his Brother had dishonour'd the Nobility of his Birth, by this Alliance, and continued his Resentment till the Death of the young Hero, who gave many remarkable Proofs of his Courage and Fortitude upon several Occasions, and died gloriously before the Walls of

Carthagena;[26] leaving his disconsolate Lady a Widow a second Time, with the Acquisition of a Title indeed, but a very small Addition to her Fortune.

Observe that gay, splendid Lady, I beseech you, Madam, pursued he, turning to *Arabella*; how affectedly she looks and talks, and throws her Eyes around the Room, with a haughty Self-sufficiency in her Aspect, and insolent Contempt for every Thing but herself. Her Habit, her Speech, her Motions, are all *French;*[27] nothing in *England* is able to please her; the People so dull, so aukwardly polite, the Manners so gross; no Delicacy, no Elegance, no Magnificence in their Persons, Houses, or Diversions; every thing is so distasteful, there is no living in such a Place. One may crawl about, indeed, she says, and make a shift to breathe in the odious Country, but one cannot be said to live; and with all the Requisites to render Life delightful, here, one can only suffer, not enjoy it.

Would one not imagine, pursued he, this fine Lady was a Person of very exalted Rank, who has the Sanction of Birth, Riches, and Grandeur for her extraordinary Pride; and yet she is no other than the Daughter of an Inn-Keeper at *Spa*, and had the exalted Post assign'd her of attending new Lodgers to their Apartments, acquainting them with all the Conveniences of the Place, answering an humble Question or two concerning what Company was in the Town, what Scandal was stirring, and the like.

One of our great Sea Commanders[28] going thither for his Health, happen'd to lodge at this Inn; and was so struck with her Charms, that he marry'd her in a few Weeks, and soon after brought her to *England*.

Such was the Origin of this fantastick Lady; whose insupportable Pride and ridiculous Affectation, draws Contempt and Aversion wherever she appears.

Did I not tell you, Madam, interrupted Mr. *Glanville*, that the Amusement you had chose was not so innocent as Dancing? What a deal of Scandal has Mr. *Tinsel* utter'd in the Compass of a few Minutes?

I assure you, replied *Arabella*, I know not what to make of the Histories he has been relating. I think they do not deserve that Name, and are rather detatched Pieces of Satire on particular Persons,[29] than a serious Relation of Facts. I confess my Expectations from this Gentleman have not been answer'd.

I think, however, Madam, said Mr. *Glanville*, we may allow that there is a negative Merit in the Relations Mr. *Tinsel* has made; for, if he has not shewn us any Thing to approve, he has at least shewn us what to condemn.

The Ugliness of Vice, reply'd *Arabella*, ought only to be represented to the Vicious; to whom Satire, like a magnifying Glass, may aggravate every Defect, in order to make its Deformity appear more hideous; but since its End is only to reprove and amend, it should never be address'd to any but those who come within its Correction, and may be the better for it: A virtuous Mind need not be shewn the Deformity of Vice, to make it be hated and avoided; the more pure and uncorrupted our Ideas are, the less shall we be influenc'd by Example. A natural Propensity to Virtue or Vice often determines the Choice: 'Tis sufficient therefore to shew a good Mind what it ought to pursue, though a bad one must be told what to avoid. In a Word, one ought to be always incited, the other always restrain'd.[30]

I vow, Lady *Bella*, said Miss *Glanville*, you'd make one think one came here to hear a Sermon; you are so very grave, and talk upon such high-flown Subjects. What Harm was there in what Mr. *Tinsel* was telling us? It would be hard indeed, if one might not divert one's self with other Peoples Faults.

I am afraid, Miss, said *Arabella*, those who can divert themselves with the Faults of others, are not behind hand in affording Diversion. And that very Inclination, added she, smilingly, to hear other Peoples Faults, may by those very People, be condemned as one, and afford them the same Kind of ill-natur'd Pleasure you are so desirous of.

Nay, Madam, return'd Miss *Glanville*, your Ladyship was the first who introduc'd the Discourse you condemn so much. Did not you desire Mr. *Tinsel* to tell you Histories about the Company; and ask my Brother and me, to come and hear them?

'Tis true, reply'd *Arabella*, that I did desire you to partake with me of a pleasing and rational Amusement, for such I imagin'd

Mr. *Tinsel's* Histories might afford; far from a Detail of Vices, Follies, and Irregularities, I expected to have heard the Adventures of some illustrious Personages related; between whose Actions, and those of the Heroes and Heroines of Antiquity, I might have found some Resemblance.

For Instance, I hop'd to have heard imitated the sublime Courage of a *Clelia*, who, to save her Honour from the Attempts of the impious *Tarquin*, leapt into the River *Tyber*, and swam to the other Side;[31] or the noble Resolution of the incomparable *Candace*, who, to escape out of the Hands of her Ravisher, the Pirate *Zenadorus*, set Fire to his Vessel with her own Hands, and committed herself to the Mercy of the Waves:[32] Or, the Constancy and Affection of a *Mandana*, who, for the Sake of a *Cyrus*, refused the richest Crowns in the World, and braved the Terrors of Death to preserve herself for him.[33]

As for the Men, I hoped to have heard of some who might have almost equall'd the great *Oroondates*, the invincible *Artaban*, the valiant *Juba*, the renowned *Alcamenes*,[34] and many thousand Heroes of Antiquity; whose glorious Exploits in War, and unshaken Constancy in Love, have given them immortal Fame.

While *Arabella* was uttering this long Speech, with great Emotion, Miss *Glanville*, with a sly Look at the Beau, gave him to understand, that was her Cousin's Foible.

Mr. *Tinsel*, however, not able to comprehend the Meaning of what she said, listen'd to her with many Signs of Perplexity and Wonder.

Mr. *Selvin* in secret repin'd at her prodigious Knowledge of History; and Mr. *Glanville*, with his Eyes fix'd on the Ground, bit his Lips almost through with Madness.

In the mean Time, several among the Company, desirous of hearing what the strange Lady was saying so loud, and with so much Eagerness and Emotion, gather'd round them; which Mr. *Glanville* observing, and fearing *Arabella* would expose herself still farther, whisper'd his Sister to get her away, if possible.

Miss *Glanville*, tho' very unwilling, obey'd his Injunctions; and complaining of a sudden Head-ach, *Arabella* immediately propos'd retiring, which was joyfully complied with by Mr. *Glanville*, who with the other Gentlemen attended them home.

CHAPTER IX

Being a Chapter of the Satyrical Kind.

At their Return, Sir *Charles* told his Niece, That she had now had a Specimen of the World, and some of the fashionable Amusements; and ask'd her, how she had been entertain'd.

Why, truly, Sir, replied she, smiling, I have brought away no great Relish for a Renewal of the Amusement I have partaken of To-night. If the World, in which you seem to think I am but new initiated, affords only these Kinds of Pleasures, I shall very soon regret the Solitude and Books I have quitted.

Why pray, said Miss *Glanville?* What Kind of Amusements did your Ladyship expect to find in the World? And what was there disagreeable in your Entertainment to Night? I am sure there is no Place in *England*, except *London*, where there is so much good Company to be met with, as here. The Assembly was very numerous and brililant, and one can be at no Loss for Amusements: The Pump-Room in the Morning, the Parade, and the Rooms,[35] in the Evening, with little occasional Parties of Pleasure, will find one sufficient Employment, and leave none of one's Time to lye useless upon one's Hand.

I am of Opinion, replied *Arabella*, that one's Time is far from being well employ'd in the Manner you portion it out: And People who spend theirs in such trifling Amusements, must certainly live to very little Purpose.

What room, I pray you, does a Lady give for high and noble Adventures, who consumes her Days in Dressing, Dancing, listening to Songs, and ranging the Walks with People as thoughtless as herself? How mean and contemptible a Figure must a Life spent in such idle Amusements make in History? Or rather, are not such Persons always buried in Oblivion, and can any Pen be found who would condescend to record such inconsiderable Actions?

Nor can I persuade myself, added she, that any of those Men whom I saw at the Assembly, with Figures so feminine, Voices so soft, such tripping Steps, and unmeaning Gestures, have ever signalized either their Courage or Constancy; but might be overcome by their Enemy in Battle, or be false to their Mistress in Love.

Law! Cousin, reply'd Miss *Glanville*, you are always talking of Battles and Fighting. Do you expect that Persons of Quality, and fine Gentlemen, will go to the Wars? What Business have they to fight? That belongs to the Officers.

Then every fine Gentleman is an Officer, said *Arabella*; and some other Title ought to be found out for Men who do nothing but Dance and Dress.

I could never have imagined, interrupted Mr. *Tinsel*, surveying *Arabella*, that a Lady so elegant and gay in her own Appearance, should have an Aversion to Pleasure and Magnificence.

I assure you, Sir, replied *Arabella*, I have an Aversion to neither: On the contrary, I am a great Admirer of both. But my Ideas of Amusements and Grandeur are probably different from yours.

I will allow the Ladies to be sollicitous about their Habits, and dress with all the Care and Elegance they are capable of; but such Trifles are below the Consideration of a Man, who ought not to owe the Dignity of his Appearance to the Embroidery on his Coat, but to his high and noble Air, the Grandeur of his Courage, the Elevation of his Sentiments, and the many heroick Actions he has perform'd.

Such a Man will dress his Person with a graceful Simplicity, and lavish all his Gold and Embroidery upon his Armour, to render him conspicuous in the Day of Battle. The Plumes in his Helmet will look more graceful in the Field, than the Feather in his Hat at a Ball; and Jewels blaze with more Propriety on his Shield and Cuirass in Battle, than glittering on his Finger in a Dance.

Do not imagine, however, pursued she, that I absolutely condemn Dancing, and think it a Diversion wholly unworthy of a Hero.

History has recorded some very famous Balls, at which the most illustrious Persons in the World have appear'd.

Cyrus the Great, we are inform'd, open'd a Ball with the divine *Mandana* at *Sardis*.[36] The renown'd King of *Scythia* danc'd with the Princess *Cleopatra* at *Alexandria*.[37] The brave *Cleomedon* with the fair *Candace* at *Ethiopia*;[38] but these Diversions were taken but seldom, and consider'd indeed as an Amusement, not as a Part of the Business of Life.

How would so many glorious Battles have been fought, Cities taken, Ladies rescu'd, and other great and noble Adventures been atchiev'd, if the Men, sunk in Sloth and Effeminacy, had continually followed the Sound of a Fiddle, saunter'd in publick Walks, or tattled over a Tea-table.

I vow, Cousin, said Miss *Glanville*, you are infinitely more severe in your Censures than Mr. *Tinsel* was at the Assembly. You had little Reason methinks to be angry with him.

All I have said, reply'd *Arabella*, was the natural Inference from your own Account of the Manner in which People live here. When Actions are a Censure upon themselves, the Reciter will always be consider'd as a Satirist.

CHAPTER X

In which our Heroine justifies her own Notions by some very illustrious Examples.

Mr. *Selvin* and Mr. *Tinsel*, who had listen'd attentively to this Discourse of *Arabella*, took Leave as soon as it was ended, and went away with very different Opinions of her.

Mr. *Tinsel* declaring she was a Fool, and had no Knowledge of the World, and Mr. *Selvin* convinc'd she was a Wit, and very learn'd in Antiquity.

Certainly, said Mr. *Selvin*, in Support of his Opinion, the Lady has great Judgment; has been capable of prodigious Application, as is apparent by her extensive Reading: Then her Memory is quite miraculous. I protest, I am quite charm'd with her: I never met with such a Woman in my Life.

Her Cousin, in my Opinion, reply'd Mr. *Tinsel*, is infinitely beyond her in every Merit, but Beauty. How sprightly and free her Conversation? What a thorough Knowledge of the World?

So true a Taste for polite Amusements, and a Fund of Spirits that sets Vapours and Spleen at Defiance.

This Speech bringing on a Comparison between the Ladies, the Champions for each grew so warm in the Dispute, that they had like to have quarrell'd. However, by the Interposition of some other Gentlemen who were with them, they parted tolerable Friends that Night, and renew'd their Visits to Sir *Charles* in the Morning.

They found only Miss *Glanville* with her Father and Brother. *Arabella* generally spent the Mornings in her own Chamber, where Reading and the Labours of the Toilet employ'd her Time till Dinner: Tho' it must be confess'd to her Honour, that the latter engross'd but a very small Part of it.

Miss *Glanville*, with whom the Beau had a long Conversation at one of the Windows; in which he recounted his Dispute with Mr. *Selvin*, and the Danger he ran of being pink'd in a Duel,[39] that was his Phrase, for her Sake, at last propos'd a Walk; to which she consented, and engaged to prevail upon *Arabella* to accompany them.

That Lady at first positively refused, alleging in Excuse, That she was so extremely interested in the Fate of the Princess *Melisintha*,[40] whose Story she was reading, that she could not stir till she had finish'd it.

That poor Princess, continu'd she, is at present in a most terrible Situation. She has just set Fire to the Palace, in order to avoid the Embraces of a King who forced her to marry him. I am in Pain to know how she escapes the Flames.

Pshaw, interrupted Miss *Glanville*, let her perish there, if she will: Don't let her hinder our Walk.

Who is it you doom with so much Cruelty to perish, said *Arabella*, closing the Book, and looking stedfastly on her Cousin? Is it the beautiful *Melisintha*, that Princess, whose Fortitude and Patience have justly render'd her the Admiration of the whole World? That Princess, descended from a Race of Heroes, whose heroick Virtues all glowed in her own beauteous Breast; that Princess, who, when taken Captive with the King her Father, bore her Imprisonment and Chains with a marvellous Constancy; and who, when she had enslaved her Con-

queror, and given Fetters to the Prince who held her Father and
herself in Bonds, nobly refus'd the Diadem he profer'd her, and
devoted herself to Destruction, in order to punish the Enemy
of her House. I am not able to relate the rest of her History,
seeing I have read no further myself; but if you will be pleased
to sit down and listen to me while I read what remains, I am
persuaded you will find new Cause to love and admire this
amiable Princess.

Pardon me, Madam, said Miss *Glanville*, I have heard
enough; and I could have been very well satisfied not to have
heard so much. I think we waste a great deal of Time talking
about People we know nothing of. The Morning will be quite
lost, if we don't make Haste. Come, added she, you must go:
You have a new Lover below, who waits to go with us; he'll
die if I don't bring you.

A new Lover! return'd *Arabella*, surpriz'd.

Aye, aye, said Miss *Glanville*, the learned Mr. *Selvin*; I assure
you, he had almost quarrell'd with Mr. *Tinsel* last Night about
your Ladyship.

Arabella, at this Intelligence, casting down her Eyes, discover'd many Signs of Anger and Confusion: And after a Silence
of some Moments, during which, Miss *Glanville* had been
employ'd in adjusting her Dress at the Glass, addressing herself
to her Cousin with an Accent somewhat less sweet than before,

Had any other than yourself, Miss, said she, acquainted me
with the Presumption of that unfortunate Person, I should haply
have discover'd my Resentment in other Terms: But, as it is,
must inform you, that I take it extremely ill, you should be
accessary to giving me this Offence.

Hey day! said Miss *Glanville*, turning about hastily, How
have I offended your Ladyship, pray?

I am willing to hope, Cousin, reply'd *Arabella*, that it was
only to divert yourself with the Trouble and Confusion in which
you see me, that you have indiscreetly told Things which ought
to have been buried in Silence.

And what is all this mighty Trouble and Confusion about
then, Madam, said Miss *Glanville*, smiling? Is it because I told
you, Mr. *Selvin* was a Lover of your Ladyship?

Certainly, said *Arabella*, such an Information is sufficient to give one a great deal of Perplexity. Is it such a little Matter, think you, to be told that a Man has the Presumption to love one?

A meer Trifle, replied Miss *Glanville*, laughing; a hundred Lovers are not worth a Moment's Thought, when one's sure of them, for then the Trouble is all over. And as for this unfortunate Person, as your Ladyship called him, let him die at his Leisure, while we go to the Parade.

Your Levity, Cousin, said *Arabella*, forces me to smile, notwithstanding the Cause I have to be incens'd; however, I have Charity enough to make me not desire the Death of Mr. *Selvin*, who may repair the Crime he has been guilty of by Repentance and Discontinuation.

Well then, said Miss *Glanville*, you are resolved to go to the Parade: Shall I reach you your odd Kind of Capuchin?

How, said *Arabella*, can I with any Propriety see a Man who has discover'd himself to have a Passion for me? Will he not construe such a Favour into a Permission for him to hope?

Oh! no, interrupted Miss *Glanville*, he does not imagine I have told your Ladyship he loves you; for indeed he don't know that I am acquainted with his Passion.

Then he is less culpable than I thought him, reply'd *Arabella*; and if you think I am in no Danger of hearing a Confession of his Fault from his own Mouth, I'll comply with your Request, and go with you to the Parade. But added she, I must first engage you to promise not to leave me alone a Moment, lest he should take Advantage of such an Opportunity, to give some Hint of his Passion, that would force me to treat him very rigorously.

Miss *Glanville* answer'd laughing, That she would be sure to mind her Directions. However, said she, your Ladyship need not be apprehensive he will say any fine Things to you; for I knew a young Lady he was formerly in Love with, and the odious Creature visited her a Twelve-month before he found Courage enough to tell her she was handsome.

Doubtless, reply'd *Arabella*, he was much to be commended for his Respect. A Lover should never have the Presumption to declare his Passion to his Mistress, unless in certain Circumstances, which may at the same Time in part disarm her Anger. For Instance, he must struggle with the Violence of his Passion, till it has cast him into a Fever. His Physicians must give him over, pronouncing his Distemper incurable, since the Cause of it being in his Mind, all their Art is incapable of removing it. Thus he must suffer, rejoicing at the Approach of Death, which will free him from all his Torments, without violating the Respect he owes to the Divine Object of his Flame. At length, when he has but a few Hours to live, his Mistress, with many Signs of Compassion, conjures him to tell her the Cause of his Despair. The Lover, conscious of his Crime, evades all her Inquiries; but the Lady laying at last a peremptory Command upon him to disclose the Secret, he dares not disobey her, and acknowledges his Passion with the utmost Contrition for having offended her; bidding her take the small Remainder of his Life to expiate his Crime; and finishes his Discourse by falling into a Swoon.

The Lady is touch'd at his Condition, commands him to live; and if necessary, permits him to hope.

This is the most common Way in which such Declarations are, and ought to be brought about. However, there are others, which are as well calculated for sparing a Lady's Confusion, and deprecating her Wrath.

The Lover, for Example, like the Prince of the *Massagetes*, after having buried his Passion in Silence for many Years, may chance to be walking with his Confidant in a retir'd Place; to whom, with a Deluge of Tears, he relates the Excess of his Passion and Despair. And while he is thus unbosoming his Griefs, not in the least suspecting he is overheard, his Princess, who had been listning to him in much Trouble and Confusion, by some little Rustling she makes, unawares discovers herself.

The surpriz'd Lover throws himself at her Feet, begs Pardon for his Rashness, observes that he had never presum'd to discover his Passion to her; and implores her Leave to die before her, as a Punishment for his undesign'd Offence.[41]

The Method which the great *Artamenes* took to let the Princess of *Media* know he adored her, was not less respectful. This valiant Prince, who had long loved her, being to fight a great

Battle, in which he had some secret Presages he should fall, which however deceiv'd him, wrote a long Letter to the divine *Mandana*, wherein he discover'd his Passion, and the Resolution his Respect had inspir'd him with, to consume in Silence, and never presume to disclose his Love while he lived; acquainting her, that he had order'd that Letter not to be deliver'd to her, till it was certainly known that he was dead.

Accordingly he receiv'd several Wounds in the Fight, which brought him to the Ground, and his Body not being found, they concluded it was in the Enemy's Possession.

His faithful 'Squire, who had receiv'd his Instructions before the Battle, hastens to the Princess, who, with all the Court, is mightily affected at his Death.

He presents her the Letter, which she makes no Scruple to receive, since the Writer is no more. She reads it, and her whole Soul is melted with Compassion; she bewails his Fate with the most tender and affectionate Marks of Grief.

Her Confidant asks why she is so much affected, since in all Probability, she would not have pardon'd him for loving her, had he been alive?

She acknowledges the Truth of her Observation, takes Notice that his Death having cancell'd his Crime, his respectful Passion alone employs her Thoughts; she is resolv'd to bewail as innocent and worthy of Compassion when dead, him whom living she would treat as a Criminal, and insinuates, that her Heart had entertain'd an Affection for him.

Her Confidant treasures up this Hint, and endeavours to console her, but in vain, till News is brought, that *Artamenes*, who had been carry'd for dead out of the Field, and by a very surprizing Adventure conceal'd all this Time, is return'd.

The Princess is cover'd with Confusion, and tho' glad he is alive, resolves to banish him for his Crime.

Her Confidant pleads his Cause so well, that she consents to see him; and, since he can no longer conceal his Passion, he confirms the Confession in his Letter, humbly begging Pardon for being still alive.

The Princess, who cannot plead Ignorance of his Passion, nor deny the Sorrow she testify'd for his Death, condescends to

pardon him, and he is also permitted to hope.[42] In like Manner
the great Prince of *Persia*[43] —

Does your Ladyship consider how late it is? interrupted Miss
Glanville, who had hitherto very impatiently listen'd to her.
Don't let us keep the Gentlemen waiting any longer for us.

I must inform you how the Prince of *Persia* declar'd his Love
for the incomparable *Berenice*, said *Arabella*.

Another Time, dear Cousin, said Miss *Glanville*; methinks
we have talk'd long enough upon this Subject.

I am sorry the Time has seem'd so tedious to you, said
Arabella, smiling; and therefore I'll trespass no longer upon
your Patience. Then ordering *Lucy* to bring her Hat and Gloves,
she went down Stairs, follow'd by Miss *Glanville*, who was
greatly disappointed at her not putting on her Veil.

CHAPTER XI

*In which our Heroine being mistaken herself, gives
Occasion for a great many other Mistakes.*

As soon as the Ladies enter'd the Room, Mr. *Selvin*, with more
Gaiety than usual, advanc'd towards *Arabella*, who put on so
cold and severe a Countenance at his Approach, that the poor
Man extremely confus'd, drew back, and remain'd in great
Perplexity, fearing he had offended her.

Mr. *Tinsel*, seeing Mr. *Selvin*'s Reception, and aw'd by the
becoming Majesty in her Person, notwithstanding all his Assurance, accosted her with less Confidence than was his Custom;
but *Arabella* softning her Looks with the most engaging Smiles,
made an Apology for detaining them so long from the Parade,
gave her Hand to the Beau, as being not a suspected Person,
and permitted him to lead her out, Mr. *Glanville*, to whom she
always allow'd the Preference on those Occasions, being a little
indispos'd, and not able to attend her.

Mr. *Tinsel*, whose Vanity was greatly flatter'd by the Preference *Arabella* gave him to his Companion, proceeded, according

to his usual Custom, to examine her Looks and Behaviour with more Care; conceiving such a Preference must proceed, from a latent Motive which was not unfavourable for him. His Discernment on these Occasions being very surprising, he soon discover'd in the bright Eyes of *Arabella* a secret Approbation of his Person, which he endeavour'd to increase by displaying it with all the Address he was Master of, and did not fail to talk her into an Opinion of his Wit, by ridiculing every Body that pass'd them, and directing several study'd Compliments to herself.

Miss *Glanville*, who was not so agreeably entertain'd by the grave Mr. *Selvin*, saw these Advances to a Gallantry with her Cousin with great Disturbance: She was resolved to interrupt it, if possible, and being convinc'd Mr. *Selvin* preferr'd *Arabella*'s Conversation to hers, she plotted how to pair them together, and have the Beau to herself.

As they walk'd a few Paces behind her Cousin and Mr. *Tinsel*, she was in no Danger of being over-heard; and taking Occasion to put Mr. *Selvin* in mind of *Arabella*'s Behaviour to him, when he accosted her; she ask'd him, if he was conscious of having done any thing to offend her?

I protest, Madam, reply'd Mr. *Selvin*, I know not of any thing I have done to displease her. I never fail'd, to my Knowledge, in my Respects towards her Ladyship, for whom indeed I have a most profound Veneration.

I know so much of her Temper, resum'd Miss *Glanville*, as to be certain, if she has taken it into her Head to be angry with you, she will be ten times more so at your Indifference: And if you hope for her Favour, you must ask her Pardon with the most earnest Submission imaginable.

If I knew I had offended her, reply'd Mr. *Selvin*, I would very willingly ask her Pardon; but really, since I have not been guilty of any Fault towards her Ladyship, I don't know how to acknowledge it.

Well, said Miss *Glanville* coldly, I only took the Liberty to give you some friendly Advice, which you may follow, or not, as you please. I know my Cousin is angry at something, and I wish you were Friends again, that's all.

I am mightily oblig'd to you, Madam, said Mr. *Selvin*; and since you assure me her Ladyship is angry, I'll ask her Pardon tho', really, as I said before, I don't know for what.

Well, interrupted Miss *Glanville*, we'll join them at the End of the Parade; and to give you an Opportunity of speaking to my Cousin, I'll engage Mr. *Tinsel* myself.

Mr. *Selvin*, who thought himself greatly oblig'd to Miss *Glanville* for her good Intentions, tho' in reality she had a View of exposing her Cousin, as well as an Inclination to engage Mr. *Tinsel*, took Courage as they turn'd, to get on the other Side of *Arabella*, whom he had not dar'd before to approach, while Miss *Glanville*, addressing a Whisper of no great Importance to her Cousin, parted her from the Beau, and slackning her Pace a little, fell into a particular Discourse with him, which *Arabella* being too polite to interrupt, remain'd in a very perplexing Situation, dreading every Moment that Mr. *Selvin* would explain himself. Alarm'd at his Silence, yet resolv'd to interrupt him if he began to speak, and afraid of beginning a Conversation first, lest he should construe it to his Advantage.

Mr. *Selvin* being naturally timid in the Company of Ladies, the Circumstance of Disgrace which he was in with *Arabella*, her Silence and Reserve so added to his accustom'd Diffidence, that tho' he endeavour'd several times to speak, he was not able to bring out any thing but a preluding Hem; which he observ'd, to his extreme Confusion, seem'd always to encrease *Arabella*'s Constraint.

Indeed, that Lady, upon any Suspicion that he was going to break his mysterious Silence, always contracted her Brow into a Frown, cast down her Eyes with an Air of Perplexity, endeavour'd to hide her Blushes with her Fan; and to shew her Inattention, directed her Looks to the contrary Side.

The Lady and Gentleman being in equal Confusion, no Advances were made on either Side towards a Conversation, and they had reach'd almost the End of the Parade in an uninterrupted Silence; when Mr. *Selvin*, fearing he should never again have so good an Opportunity of making his Peace, collected all his Resolution, and with an Accent trembling under the Importance of the Speech he was going to make, began,

Madam, Since I have had the Honour of walking with your Ladyship, I have observed so many Signs of Constraint in your Manner, that I hardly dare intreat you to grant me a Moment's Hearing while I —

Sir, interrupted *Arabella*, before you go any further, I must inform you, that what you are going to say will mortally offend me. Take heed then how you commit an Indiscretion which will force me to treat you very rigorously.

If your Ladyship will not allow me to speak in my own Justification, said Mr. *Selvin*, yet I hope you will not refuse to tell me my Offence, since I —

You are very confident, indeed, interrupted *Arabella* again, to suppose I will repeat what would be infinitely grievous for me to hear. Against my Will, pursued she, I must give you the Satisfaction to know, that I am not ignorant of your Crime, but I also assure you that I am highly incens'd; and that not only with the Thoughts you have dar'd to entertain of me, but likewise with your Presumption in going about to disclose them.

Mr. *Selvin*, whom the seeming Contradictions in this Speech astonish'd, yet imagin'd in general it hinted at the Dispute between him and Mr. *Tinsel*; and supposing the Story had been told to his Disadvantage, which was the Cause of her Anger, reply'd in great Emotion at the Injustice done him,

Since somebody has been so officious to acquaint your Ladyship with an Affair which ought to have been kept from your Knowledge; 'tis a Pity they did not inform you, that Mr. *Tinsel* was the Person that had the least Respect for your Ladyship, and is more worthy of your Resentment.

If Mr. *Tinsel*, replied *Arabella*, is guilty of an Offence like yours, yet since he has conceal'd it better, he is less culpable than you; and you have done that for him; which haply he would never have had Courage enough to do for himself as long as he lived.

Poor *Selvin*, quite confounded at these intricate Words, would have begg'd her to explain herself, had she not silenc'd him with a dreadful Frown: And making a Stop till Miss *Glanville* and Mr. *Tinsel* came up to them, she told her Cousin with a peevish Accent, that she had perform'd her Promise very ill;

and whisper'd her, that she was to blame for all the Mortifications she had suffer'd.

Mr. *Tinsel*, supposing the Alteration in *Arabella*'s Humour
proceeded from being so long depriv'd of his Company; endeavour'd to make her Amends by a Profusion of Compliments;
which she receiv'd with such an Air of Displeasure, that the
Beau, vex'd at the ill Success of his Gallantry, told her, he was
afraid Mr. *Selvin*'s Gravity had infected her Ladyship.

Say rather, reply'd *Arabella*, that his Indiscretion has
offended me.

Mr. *Tinsel*, charm'd with this beginning Confidence, which
confirm'd his Hopes of having made some Impression on her
Heart; conjur'd her very earnestly to tell him how Mr. *Selvin*
had offended her.

'Tis sufficient, resum'd she, that I tell you he has offended
me, without declaring the Nature of his Crime, since doubtless
it has not escaped your Observation, which, if I may believe
him, is not wholly disinterested. To confess yet more, 'tis true
that he hath told me something concerning you, which —

Let me perish, Madam, interrupted the beau, if one Syllable
he has said be true.

How, said *Arabella*, a little disconcerted, Will you always
persist in a Denial then?

Deny it, Madam, return'd Mr. *Tinsel*, I'll deny what he has
said with my last Breath, 'tis all a scandalous Forgery: No Man
living is less likely to think of your Ladyship in that Manner. If
you knew my Thoughts, Madam, you would be convinc'd
nothing is more impossible, and —

Sir, interrupted *Arabella*, extremely mortify'd, methinks you
are very eager in your Justification. I promise you, I do not
think you guilty of the Offence he charg'd you with; if I did,
you would haply experience my Resentment in such a Manner,
as would make you repent of your Presumption.

Arabella, in finishing these Words, interrupted Miss *Glanville*'s Discourse with Mr. *Selvin*, to tell her, she desir'd to
return Home; to which that young Lady, who had not been at
all pleas'd with the Morning's Walk, consented.

CHAPTER XII

In which our Heroine reconciles herself to a mortifying Incident, by recollecting an Adventure in a Romance, Similar to her own.

As soon as the Ladies were come to their Lodgings, *Arabella* went up her own Apartment to meditate upon what had pass'd, and Miss *Glanville* retir'd to dress for Dinner; while the two Gentlemen, who thought they had great Reason to be dissatisfy'd with each other on Account of Lady *Bella*'s Behaviour, went to a Coffee-house, in order to come to some Explanation about it.

Well, Sir, said the Beau, with a sarcastick Air, I am greatly oblig'd to you for the Endeavours you have us'd to ruin me in Lady *Bella*'s Opinion. Rat me, if it is not the greatest Misfortune in the World, to give occasion for Envy.

Envy, Sir, interrupted Mr. *Selvin*; I protest I do really admire your great Skill in Stratagems, but I do not envy you the Possession of it. You have, indeed, very wittily contriv'd to put your own Sentiments of that Lady, which you deliver'd so freely the other Night, into my Mouth. 'Twas a Master-piece of Cunning, indeed; and, as I said before, I admire your Skill prodigiously.

I don't know what you mean, reply'd *Tinsel*, you talk in Riddles. Did you not yourself acquaint Lady *Bella* with the Preference I gave Miss *Glanville* to her? What would you propose by such a Piece of Treachery? You have ruin'd all my Hopes by it: The Lady resents it excessively, and 'tis no Wonder, 'faith, it must certainly mortify her. Upon my Soul, I can never forgive thee for so *mal a propos*[44] a Discovery.

Forgive me, Sir, replied *Selvin*, in a Rage, I don't want your Forgiveness. I have done nothing unbecoming a Man of Honour. The Lady was so prejudiced by your Insinuations, that she would not give me Leave to speak; otherwise, I would have fully inform'd her of her Mistake, that she might have known how much she was oblig'd to you.

So she would not hear thee, interrupted *Tinsel* laughing, dear Soul, how very kind was that? 'Faith, I don't know how it is, but I am very lucky, without deserving to be so. Thou art a Witness for me, *Frank*, I took no great Pains to gain this fine Creature's Heart; but it was damn'd malicious tho', to attempt to make Discoveries. I see she is a little piqu'd, but I'll set all to rights again with a *Billet-doux*.[45] I've an excellent Hand, tho' I say it, at a *Billet-doux*. I never knew one of mine fail in my Life.

Harkee, Sir, said *Selvin* whispering, any more Attempts to shift your Sentiments upon me, and you shall hear of it. In the mean Time, be assur'd, I'll clear myself, and put the Saddle upon the right Horse.

Demme, if thou art not a queer Fellow, said *Tinsel*, endeavouring to hide his Discomposure at this Threat under a forc'd Laugh.

Selvin, without making any Reply, retir'd to write to *Arabella*; which *Tinsel* suspecting, resolv'd to be before-hand with him; and without leaving the Coffee-house, call'd for Paper, and wrote a Billet to her, which he dispatch'd away immediately.

The Messenger had just got Admittance to *Lucy*, when another arriv'd from *Selvin*.

They both presented their Letters, but *Lucy* refus'd them, saying, her Lady would turn her away, if she receiv'd such Sort of Letters.

Such Sort of Letters, return'd *Tinsel*'s Man! Why do you know what they contain, then?

To be sure, I do, reply'd *Lucy*; they are Love-Letters; and my Lady has charg'd me never to receive any more.

Well, reply'd *Selvin*'s Servant, you may take my Letter; for my Master desir'd me to tell you, it was about Business of Consequence, which your Lady must be acquainted with.

Since you assure me it is not a Love-Letter, I'll take it, said *Lucy*.

And, pray take mine too, said *Tinsel*'s *Mercury*;[46] for I assure you, it is not a Love Letter neither; 'tis only a *Billet doux*.

Are you sure of that, reply'd *Lucy*; because I may venture to take it, I fancy, if 'tis what you say.

I'll swear it, said the Man, delivering it to her. Well, said she, receiving it, I'll take them both up. But what did you call this, pursu'd she? I must not forget it, or else my Lady will think it a Love-Letter.

A *Billet-doux*, said the Man.

Lucy, for fear she should forget it, repeated the Words *Billet-doux* several Times as she went up Stairs; but entering her Lady's Apartment, she perceiving the Letters in her Hand, ask'd her so sternly, how she durst presume to bring them into her Presence, that the poor Girl, in her Fright, forgot the Lesson she had been conning; and endeavouring to recal it into her Memory, took no Notice of her Lady's Question, which she repeated several times, but to no Purpose.

Arabella, surpriz'd at her Inattention, reiterated her Commands, in a Tone somewhat louder than usual; asking her at the same Time, why she did not obey her immediately?

Indeed, Madam, reply'd *Lucy*, your Ladyship would not order me to take back the Letters, if you knew what they were: They are not Love-Letters; I was resolv'd to be sure of that before I took them. This, Madam, is a Letter about Business of Consequence; and the other — Oh dear! I can't think what the Man call'd it! But it is not a Love-Letter, indeed, Madam.

You are a simple Wench, said *Arabella* smiling: You may depend upon it, all Letters directed to me, must contain Matters of Love and Gallantry; and those I am not permitted to receive. Take them away then immediately. But stay, pursued she, seeing she was about to obey her, one of them, you say, was deliver'd to you as a Letter of Consequence; perhaps it is so: Indeed it may contain an Advertisement of some Design to carry me away. How do I know, but Mr. *Selvin*, incited by his Love and Despair, may intend to make such an Attempt? Give me that Letter, *Lucy*, I am resolved to open it. As for the other — yet who knows but the other may also bring me Warning of the same Danger from another Quarter. The Pains Mr. *Tinsel* took to conceal his Passion, nay, almost as I think, to deny it, amounts to a Proof that he is meditating some Way to make sure of me. 'Tis certainly so: Give me that Letter, *Lucy*; I should be accessary to their intended Violence, if I neglected this timely Discovery.

Well, cried she, taking one of the Letters, this is exactly like what happen'd to the beautiful Princess of *Cappadocia*;[47] who, like me, in one and the same Day, receiv'd Advice that two of her Lovers intended to carry her off.

As she pronounc'd these Words Miss *Glanville* entered the Room, to whom *Arabella* immediately recounted the Adventure of the Letters; telling her, she did not doubt, but they contain'd a Discovery of some Conspiracy to carry her away.

And whom does your Ladyship suspect of such a strange Design, pray, said Miss *Glanville* smiling?

At present, reply'd *Arabella*, the two Cavaliers who walk'd with us To-day, are the Persons who seem the most likely to attempt that Violence.

I dare answer for Mr. *Tinsel*, replied Miss *Glanville*, he thinks of no such Thing.

Well, said *Arabella*, to convince you of your Mistake, I must inform you, that Mr. *Selvin*, having the Presumption to begin a Declaration of Love to me on the Parade this Morning, I reprov'd him severely for his Want of Respect, and threatned him with my Displeasure; in the Rage of his Jealousy, at seeing me treat Mr. *Tinsel* well, he discover'd to me, that he also was as criminal as himself, in order to oblige me to a severer Usage of him.

So he told you Mr. *Tinsel* was in Love with you, interrupted Miss *Glanville*?

He told it me in other Words, reply'd *Arabella*; for he said, Mr. *Tinsel* was guilty of that Offence, which I resented so severely to him.

Miss *Glanville* beginning to comprehend the Mystery, with great Difficulty forbore laughing at her Cousin's Mistake; for she well knew the Offence Mr. *Selvin* hinted at, and desirous of knowing what those Letters contain'd, she begg'd her to delay opening them no longer.

Arabella, pleas'd at her Solicitude, open'd one of the Letters; but glancing her Eye to the Bottom, and seeing the Name of *Selvin*, she threw it hastily upon the Table, and averting her Eyes, What a Mortification have I avoided, said she, that Letter is from *Selvin*; and questionless, contains an Avowal of his Crime.

Nay, you must read it, cried Miss *Glanville*, taking it up; since you have open'd it, 'tis the same Thing: You can never persuade him but you have seen it. However, to spare your Nicety, I'll read it to you. Which accordingly she did, and found it as follows.

MADAM,

I know not what Insinuations have been made use of to persuade you I was guilty of the Offence, which, with Justice, occasion'd your Resentment this Morning; but I assure you, nothing was ever more false. My Thoughts of your Ladyship are very different, and full of the profoundest Respect and Veneration. I have Reason to suspect Mr. *Tinsel* is the Person who has thus endeavoured to prejudice me with your Ladyship; therefore I am excusable if I tell you, that those very Sentiments, too disrespectful to be named, which he would persuade you are mine, he discover'd himself. He then, Madam, is the Person guilty of that Offence he so falsly lays to the Charge of him, who, is, with the utmost Respect and Esteem,

Madam,

Your Ladyship's

most obedient, and

most humble Servant,

F. SELVIN.

How's this, cry'd Miss *Glanville?* Why, Madam, you are certainly mistaken. You see Mr. *Selvin* utterly denies the Crime of loving you. He has suffer'd very innocently in your Opinion. Indeed, your Ladyship was too hasty in condemning him.

If what he says be true, replied *Arabella*, who had been in extreme Confusion, while a Letter so different from what she expected was reading; I have indeed unjustly condemn'd him. Nevertheless, I am still inclin'd to believe this is all Artifice; and that he is really guilty of entertaining a Passion for me.

But why should he take so much Pains to deny it, Madam, said Miss *Glanville?* Methinks that looks very odd.

Not at all, interrupted *Arabella*, whose Spirits were rais'd by recollecting an Adventure in her Romance, similar to this, Mr. *Selvin* has fallen upon the very same Stratagem with *Seramenes*;[48] who being in Love with the beautiful *Cleobuline*, Princess of *Corinth*, took all imaginable Pains to conceal his Passion, in order to be near that fair Princess; who would have banish'd him from her Presence, had she known he was in Love with her. Nay, he went so far in his Dissimulation, as to pretend Love to one of the Ladies of her Court; that his Passion for the Princess might be the less taken notice of. In these Cases therefore, the more resolutely a Man denies his Passion, the more pure and violent it is.

Then Mr. *Selvin*'s Passion is certainly very violent, reply'd Miss *Glanville*, for he denies it very resolutely; and I believe none but your Ladyship would have discover'd his Artifice. But shall we not open the other Letter? I have a strong Notion it comes from *Tinsel*.

For that very Reason I would not be acquainted with the Contents, reply'd *Arabella*. You see, Mr. *Selvin* accuses him of being guilty of that Offence which he denies: I shall doubtless, meet with a Confirmation of his Love in that Letter. Do not, I beseech you, added she, seeing her Cousin preparing to open the Letter, expose me to the Pain of hearing a presumptuous Declaration of Love. Nay, pursued she, rising in great Emotion, if you are resolved to persecute me by reading it, I'll endeavour to get out of the hearing of it.

You shan't, I declare, said Miss *Glanville*, laughing and holding her, I'll oblige you to hear it.

I vow, Cousin, said *Arabella* smiling, you use me just as the Princess *Cleopatra* did the fair and wise *Antonia*.[49] However, if by this you mean to do any Kindness to the unfortunate Person who wrote that Billet, you are greatly mistaken; since, if you oblige me to listen to a Declaration of his Crime, you will lay me under a Necessity to banish him. A Sentence he would have avoided, while I remained ignorant of it.

To this Miss *Glanville* made no other Reply than by opening the Billet, the Contents of which may be found in the following Chapter.

CHAPTER XIII

*In which our Heroine's Extravagance will be thought,
perhaps, to be carried to an extravagant Length.*

MADAM,

I had the Honour to assure you this Morning on the Parade,
that the Insinuations Mr. *Selvin* made use of to rob me of the
superlative Happiness of your Esteem were entirely false and
groundless. May the Beams of your bright Eyes never shine on
me more, if there is any Truth in what he said to prejudice me
with your Ladyship. If I am permitted to attend you to the Rooms
this Evening, I hope to convince you, that it was absolutely
impossible I could have been capable of such a Crime, who am,
with the most profound Respect,

Your Ladyship's
most devoted, & *c.*
D. TINSEL.

Well, Madam, said Miss *Glanville*, when she had read this
Epistle, I fancy you need not pronounce a Sentence of Banishment upon poor Mr. *Tinsel*; he seems to be quite innocent of
the Offence your Ladyship suspects him of.

Why, really, return'd *Arabella*, blushing with extreme Confusion at this second Disappointment, I am greatly perplexed
to know how I ought to act on this Occasion. I am much in the
same Situation with the Princess *Serena*.[50] For you must know,
this Princess — Here *Lucy* entering, inform'd the Ladies Dinner
was serv'd — I shall defer till another Opportunity, said
Arabella, upon this Interruption, the Relation of the Princess
Serena's Adventures; which you will find, added she, in a low
Voice, bears a very great Resemblance to mine.

Miss *Glanville* reply'd, she would hear it whenever she
pleas'd, and then follow'd *Arabella* to the Dining Room.

The Cloth was scarce remov'd, when Mr. *Selvin* came in.
Arabella blush'd at his Appearance, and discover'd so much
Perplexity in her Behaviour, that Mr. *Selvin* was apprehensive

he had not yet sufficiently justify'd himself; and therefore took the first Opportunity to approach her.

I shall think myself very unhappy, Madam, said he bowing, if the Letter I did myself the Honour to write to you this Morning —

Sir, interrupted *Arabella*, I perceive you are going to forget the Contents of that Letter, and preparing again to offend me by a presumptuous Declaration of Love.

Who I, Madam, reply'd he, in great Astonishment and Confusion, I-I-I protest — tho' I-I have a very great Respect for your Ladyship, yet–yet I never presum'd to–to–to —

You have presum'd too much, replied *Arabella*, and I should forget what I ow'd to my own Glory, if I furnish'd you with any more Occasions of offending me. — Know then, I absolutely forbid you to appear before me again, at least, till I am convinc'd you have chang'd your Sentiments.

Saying this, she rose from her Seat, and making a Sign to him not to follow her, which indeed he had no Intention to do, she quitted the Room, highly satisfy'd with her own Conduct upon this Occasion, which was exactly conformable to the Laws of Romance.

Mr. *Tinsel*, who had just alighted from his Chair, having a Glimpse of her, as she pass'd to her own Apartment, resolv'd, if possible, to procure a private Interview; for he did not doubt but his Billet had done Wonders in his Favour.

For that Purpose he ventur'd up to her Anti-Chamber, where he found *Lucy* in waiting, whom he desir'd to acquaint her Lady, that he intreated a Moment's Speech with her.

Lucy, after hesitating a Moment, and looking earnestly at him, replied, Sir, if you'll promise me faithfully, you are not in Love with my Lady, I'll go and deliver your Message.

Duce take me, said *Tinsel*, if that is not a very whimsical Condition truly — Pray, my Dear, how came it into thy little Brain, to suspect I was in Love with thy Lady? But, suppose I should be in Love with her, what then?

Why, then 'tis likely you would die, that's all, said *Lucy*, without my Lady would be se kind to command you to live.

I vow thou hast mighty pretty Notions, Child, said *Tinsel*

smiling; hast thou been reading any Play-Book lately? But pray, dost think thy Lady would have Compassion on me, if I was in Love with her? Come, I know thou art in her Confidence? Hast thou ever heard her talk of me? Does she not tell thee all her Secrets?

Here *Arabella*'s Bell ringing, the Beau slipp'd half a Guinea into her Hand, which *Lucy* not willing to refuse, went immediately to her Lady; to whom with a trembling Accent, she repeated Mr. *Tinsel*'s Request.

Imprudent Girl, cried *Arabella*, for I am loth to suspect thee of Disloyalty to thy Mistress, Dost thou know the Nature and Extent of the Request thou hast deliver'd? Art thou ignorant that the presumptuous Man whom thou sollicitest this Favour for, has mortally offended me?

Indeed, Madam, said *Lucy* frighted out of her Wits, I don't sollicit for him. I scorn to do any such Thing. I would not offend your Ladyship for the World: For, before I would deliver his Message to your Ladyship, I made him assure me, that he was not in Love with your Ladyship.

That was very wisely done, indeed, replied *Arabella*, smiling: And do you believe he spoke the Truth?

Yes, indeed, I am sure of it, said *Lucy* eagerly, if your Ladyship will but be pleas'd to see him, he is only in the next Room; I dare promise —

How, interrupted *Arabella*! What have you done? Have you brought him into my Apartment then? I protest this Adventure is exactly like what befel the beautiful *Statira*, when, by a Stratagem of the same Kind *Oroondates* was introduc'd into her Presence. *Lucy*, thou art another *Barsina*, I think; but I hope thy Intentions are not less innocent than hers was.[51]

Indeed, Madam, reply'd *Lucy*, almost weeping, I am very innocent. I am no *Barsina*, as your Ladyship calls me.

I dare answer for thee, said *Arabella* smiling at the Turn she gave to her Words, thou art no *Barsina*; and I should wrong thee very much to compare thee with that wise Princess; for thou art certainly one of the most simple Wenches in the World. But since thou hast gone so far, let me know what the unfortunate Person desires of me; for, since I am neither more rigid, nor pretend to more Virtue than *Statira*, I may do at least as much for him, as that great Queen did for *Oroondates*.

He desires, Madam, said *Lucy*, that your Ladyship would be pleas'd to let him speak with you.

Or, in his Words, I suppose, replied *Arabella*, He humbly implor'd a Moment's Audience.

I told your Ladyship his very Words, indeed, Madam, said *Lucy*.

I tell thee, Girl, thou art mistaken, said *Arabella*; 'tis impossible he should sue for such a Favour in Terms like those: Therefore, go back, and let him know that I consent to grant him a short Audience upon these Conditions.

First, Provided he does not abuse my Indulgence by offending me with any Protestations of his Passion.

Secondly, That he engages to fulfil the Injunctions I shall lay upon him, however cruel and terrible they may appear.

Lastly, That his Despair must not prompt him to any Act of Desperation against himself.

Lucy having received this Message, quitted the Room hastily, for fear she should forget it.

Well, my pretty Ambassadress, said *Tinsel*, when he saw her enter the Anti-chamber, Will your Lady see me?

No, Sir, replied *Lucy*.

No, interrupted *Tinsel*, that's kind 'faith, after waiting so long.

Pray, Sir, said *Lucy*, don't put me out so; I shall forget what my Lady ordered me to tell you.

Oh! I ask your Pardon, Child, said *Tinsel*. Come, let me hear your Message.

Sir, said *Lucy*, adopting the Solemnity of her Lady's Accent — My Lady bad me say, that she will grant — No, that she consents to grant you a short Dience.

Audience you would say, Child, said *Tinsel*: But how came you to tell me before she would not see me? —

I vow and protest, Sir, said *Lucy*, you have put all my Lady's Words clean out of my Head — I don't know what comes next —

Oh, no matter, said *Tinsel*, you have told me enough: I'll wait upon her directly.

Lucy, who saw him making towards the Door, prest between it and him; and having all her Lady's Whims in her Head, suppos'd he was going to carry her away — Possess'd with this Thought, she scream'd out, Help! Help! for Heaven's Sake! My Lady will be carry'd away!

Arabella hearing this Exclamation of her Woman's, eccho'd her Screams, tho' with a Voice infinitely more delicate; and seeing *Tinsel*, who, confounded to the last Degree at the Cries of both the Lady and her Woman, had got into her Chamber he knew not how, she gave herself over for lost, and fell back in her Chair in a Swoon, or something she took for a Swoon, for she was persuaded it could happen no otherwise; since all Ladies in the same Circumstances are terrified into a fainting Fit,[52] and seldom recover till they are conveniently carried away; and when they awake, find themselves many Miles off in the Power of their Ravisher.

Arabella's other Women, alarm'd by her Cries, came running into the Room; and seeing Mr. *Tinsel* there, and their Lady in a Swoon, concluded some very extraordinary Accident had happen'd.

What is your Business here, cry'd they all at a Time? Is it you that has frighted her Ladyship?

Devil take me, said *Tinsel* amaz'd, if I can tell what all this means.

By this Time Sir *Charles*, Mr. *Glanville*, and his Sister, came running astonished up Stairs. *Arabella* still continued motionless in her Chair, her Eyes closed, and her Head reclined upon *Lucy*, who with her other Women, was endeavouring to recover her.

Mr. *Glanville* eagerly ran to her Assistance, while Sir *Charles* and his Daughter as eagerly interrogated Mr. *Tinsel*, who stood motionless with Surprize, concerning the Cause of her Disorder.

Arabella then first discovering some Signs of Life, half opened her Eyes.

Inhuman Wretch, cry'd she, with a faint Voice, supposing herself in the Hands of her Ravisher, think not thy cruel Violence shall procure thee what thy Submissions could not obtain; and if when thou hadst only my Indifference to surmount, thou didst find it so difficult to overcome my Resolution, now that by this unjust Attempt, thou hast added Aversion to that Indifference, never hope for any Thing but the most bitter Reproaches from me. —

Why, Niece, said Sir *Charles*, approaching her, what's the Matter? Look up, I beseech you, no-body is attempting to do you any Hurt; here's none but Friends about you.

Arabella, raising her Head at the Sound of her Uncle's Voice, and casting a confused Look on the Persons about her,

May I believe my Senses? Am I rescued, and in my own Chamber? To whose Valour is my Deliverance owing? Without doubt, 'tis to my Cousin's; but where is he? Let me assure him of my Gratitude.

Mr. *Glanville*, who had retired to a Window in great Confusion, as soon as he heard her call for him, came towards her, and in a Whisper begg'd her to be compos'd; that she was in no Danger.

And pray, Niece, said Sir *Charles*, now you are a little recovered, be so good to inform us of the Cause of your Fright. What has happen'd to occasion all this Confusion?

How, Sir, said *Arabella*, don't you know then what has happen'd? — Pray how was I brought again into my Chamber, and by what Means was I rescu'd?

I protest, said Sir *Charles*, I don't know that you have been out of it.

Alas, replied *Arabella*, I perceive you are quite ignorant of what has befallen me; nor am I able to give you any Information: All I can tell you is, that alarm'd by my Women's Cries, and the Sight of my Ravisher, who came into my Chamber, I fainted away, and so facilitated his Enterprize; since doubtless it was very easy for him to carry me away while I remained in that senseless Condition. How I was rescued, or by whom, one of my Women can haply inform you; since its probable one of them was also forced away with me — Oh Heav'ns! cry'd she, seeing *Tinsel*, who all this while stood gazing like one distracted; what makes that impious Man in my Presence! What am I to think of this? Am I really deliver'd or no?

What can this mean, cried Sir *Charles*, turning to *Tinsel*? Have you, Sir, had any Hand in frighting my Niece?

I, Sir, said *Tinsel*! Let me perish if ever I was so confounded in my Life: The Lady's Brain is disordered, I believe.

Mr. *Glanville*, who was convinced all this Confusion was caus'd by some of *Arabella*'s usual Whims, dreaded lest an Explanation would the more expose her; and therefore told his Father, that it would be best to retire, and leave his Cousin to the Care of his Sister and her Women; adding, that she was not yet quite recover'd, and their Presence did but discompose her.

Then addressing himself to *Tinsel*, told him he would wait upon him down Stairs.

Arabella seeing them going away together, and supposing they intended to dispute the Possession of her with their Swords, call'd out to them to stay.

Mr. *Glanville*, however, without minding her, press'd Mr. *Tinsel* to walk down.

Nay, pray, Sir, said the Beau, let us go in again; she may grow outrageous if we disoblige her.

Outrageous, Sir, said *Glanville*, do you suppose my Cousin is mad?

Upon my Soul, Sir, replied *Tinsel*, if she is not mad, she is certainly a little out of her Senses, or so —

Arabella having reiterated her Commands for her Lovers to return, and finding they did not obey her, ran to her Chamber-door, where they were holding a surly Sort of Conference, especially on *Glanville*'s Side, who was horridly out of Humour.

I perceive by your Looks, said *Arabella* to her Cousin, the Design you are meditating; but know that I absolutely forbid you, by all the Power I have over you, not to engage in Combat with my Ravisher here.

Madam, interrupted *Glanville*, I beseech you do not —

I know, said she, you will object to me the Examples of *Artamenes*, *Aronces*,[53] and many others, who were so generous as to promise their Rivals not to refuse them that Satisfaction whenever they demanded it — but consider, you have not the same Obligations to Mr. *Tinsel* that *Artamenes* had to the King of *Assyria*, or that *Aronces* had to —

For God's Sake, Cousin, said *Glanville*, what's all this to the Purpose? Curse on *Aronces* and the King of *Assyria*, I say —

The Astonishment of *Arabella* at this intemperate Speech of her Cousin, kept her for a Moment immoveable, when Sir *Charles*, who during this Discourse, had been collecting all the Information he could from *Lucy*, concerning this perplexed Affair, came towards *Tinsel*, and giving him an angry Look, told him, he should take it well if he forbore visiting any of his Family for the future.

Oh! Your most obedient Servant, Sir, said *Tinsel*: You expect, I suppose, I should be excessively chagrin'd at this Prohibition? But upon my Soul, I am greatly oblig'd to you. Agad! I have no great Mind to a Halter: And since this Lady is so apt to think People have a Design to ravish her, the wisest Thing a Man can do, is to keep out of her Way.

Sir, replied *Glanville*, who had followed him to the Door, I believe there has been some little Mistake in what has happened To-day — However, I expect you'll take no unbecoming Liberties with the Character of Lady *Bella* —

Oh! Sir said *Tinsel*, I give you my Honour I shall always speak of the Lady with the most profound Veneration. She is a most accomplish'd, incomprehensible Lady: And the Devil take me, if I think there is her Fellow in the World — And so, Sir, I am your most obedient —

A Word with you before you go, said *Glanville* stopping him — No more of these Sneers, as you value that smooth Face of yours, or I'll despoil it of a Nose.

Oh! Your humble Servant, said the Beau, retiring in great Confusion, with something betwixt a Smile and a Grin upon his Countenance, which he took Care however Mr. *Glanville* should not see; who as soon as he quitted him went again to *Arabella*'s Apartment, in order to prevail upon his Father and Sister to leave her a little to herself, for he dreaded lest some more Instances of her Extravagance would put it into his Father's Head, that she was really out of her Senses.

Well, Sir, said *Arabella* upon his Entrance, you have I suppose, given your Rival his Liberty. I assure you this Generosity is highly agreeable to me — And herein you imitate the noble *Artamenes*, who upon a like Occasion, acted as you have done.[54] For when Fortune had put the Ravisher of *Mandana* in his Power, and he became the Vanquisher of his Rival, who endeavour'd by Violence to possess that divine Princess; this truly generous Hero relinquished the Right he had of disposing of his Prisoner, and instead of sacrificing his Life to his just and reasonable Vengeance, he gave a Proof of his admirable Virtue and Clemency by dismissing him in Safety, as you have done. However, added she, I hope you have made him swear upon your Sword, that he will never make a second Attempt upon my Liberty. I perceive, pursued she, seeing Mr. *Glanville* continued silent, with his Eyes bent on the Ground, for indeed he was ashamed to look up; that you would willingly avoid the Praise due to the heroic Action you have just performed — Nay, I suppose you are resolved to keep it secret, if possible; yet I must tell you, that you will not escape the Glory due to it. Glory is as necessarily the Result of a virtuous Action, as Light is an Effect of the Sun which causeth it, and has no Dependance on any other Cause; since a virtuous Action continues still the same, tho' it be done without Testimony; and Glory, which is, as one may say, born with it, constantly attends it, tho' the Action be not known.

I protest, Niece, said Sir *Charles*, that's very prettily said.

In my Opinion, Sir, pursued *Arabella*, if any thing can weaken the Glory of a good Action, 'tis the Care a Person takes to make it known: As if one did not do Good for the Sake of Good, but for the Praise that generally follows it. Those then that are govern'd by so interested a Motive, ought to be considered as sordid rather than generous Persons; who making a Kind of Traffick between Virtue and Glory, barter just so much of the one for the other, and expect, like other Merchants, to make Advantage by the Exchange.

Mr. *Glanville*, who was charm'd into an Extacy at this sensible Speech of *Arabella*'s, forgot in an Instant all her Absurdities. He did not fail to express his Admiration of her Understanding in Terms that brought a Blush into her fair Face, and obliged her to lay her Commands upon him to cease his excessive Commendations. Then making a Sign to them to leave her alone, Mr. *Glanville*, who understood her, took his Father and Sister down Stairs, leaving *Arabella* with her faithful *Lucy*, whom she immediately commanded to give her a Relation of what had happened to her from the Time of her swooning till she recovered.

CHAPTER XIV

A Dialogue between Arabella and Lucy, in which the latter seems to have the Advantage.

Why, Madam, said *Lucy*, all I can tell your Ladyship is, that we were all excessively frighted, to be sure, when you fainted, especially myself; and that we did what we could to recover you — And so accordingly your Ladyship did recover.

What's this to the Purpose? said *Arabella*, perceiving she stop'd here. I know that I fainted, and 'tis also very plain that I recover'd again — I ask you what happened to me in the intermediate Time between my Fainting and Recovery. Give me a faithful Relation of all the Accidents, to which by my Fainting I am quite a Stranger; and which no doubt, are very considerable —

Indeed, Madam, replied *Lucy*, I have given your Ladyship a faithful Relation of all I can remember.

When, resum'd *Arabella* surpriz'd?

This Moment, Madam, said *Lucy*.

Why, sure thou dream'st, Wench, replied she, Hast thou told me how I was seiz'd and carry'd off! How I was rescued again? And —

No, indeed, Madam, interrupted *Lucy*, I don't dream; I never told your Ladyship that you was carry'd off.

Well, said *Arabella*, and why dost thou not satisfy my Curiosity? Is it not fit I should be acquainted with such a momentous Part of my History?

I can't, indeed, and please your Ladyship, said *Lucy*.

What, can'st thou not? said *Arabella*, enrag'd at her Stupidity.

Why, Madam, said *Lucy*, sobbing, I can't make a History of nothing.

Of nothing, Wench, resumed *Arabella*, in a greater Rage than before: Dost thou call an Adventure to which thou was a Witness, and borest haply so great a Share in, nothing? — An Adventure which hereafter will make a considerable Figure in the Relation of my Life, dost thou look upon as trifling and of no Consequence?

No, indeed I don't, Madam, said *Lucy*.

Why then, pursued *Arabella*, dost thou wilfully neglect to relate it? Suppose, as there is nothing more likely, thou wert commanded by some Persons of considerable Quality, or haply some great Princes and Princesses, to recount the Adventures of my Life, would'st thou omit a Circumstance of so much Moment?

No indeed, Madam, said *Lucy*.

I am glad to hear thou art so discreet, said *Arabella*; and pray do me the Favour to relate this Adventure to me, as thou would'st do to those Princes and Princesses, if thou wert commanded.

Here, *Arabella* making a full Stop, fixed her Eyes upon her Woman, expecting every Moment she would begin the desired Narrative — But finding she continued silent longer than she thought was necessary for recalling the several Circumstances of the Story into her Mind,

I find, said she, it will be necessary to caution you against making your Audience wait too long for your Relation; it looks as if you was to make a studied Speech, not a simple Relation of Facts, which ought to be free from all Affectation of Labour and Art; and be told with that graceful Negligence which is so becoming to Truth.

This I thought proper to tell you, added she, that you may not fall into that Mistake when you are called upon to relate my Adventures — Well, now if you please to begin —

What, pray, Madam, said *Lucy*?

What, repeated *Arabella*? Why, the Adventures which happened to me so lately. Relate to me every Circumstance of my being carried away, and how my Deliverance was effected by my Cousin.

Indeed, Madam, said *Lucy*, I know nothing about your Ladyship's being carried away.

Begone, cried *Arabella*, losing all Patience at her Obstinacy, get out of my Presence this Moment. Wretch, unworthy of my Confidence and Favour, thy Treason is too manifest, thou art brib'd by that presumptuous Man to conceal all the Circumstances of his Attempt from my Knowledge, to the End that I may not have a full Conviction of his Guilt.

Lucy, who never saw her Lady so much offended before, and knew not the Occasion of it, burst into Tears; which so affected the tender Heart of *Arabella*, that losing insensibly all her Anger, she told her with a Voice soften'd to a Tone of the utmost Sweetness and Condescension, that provided she would confess how far she had been prevail'd upon by his rich Presents, to forget her Duty, she would pardon and receive her again into Favour —

Speak, added she, and be not afraid, after this Promise, to let me know what Mr. *Tinsel* requir'd of thee, and what were the Gifts with which he purchas'd thy Services; doubtless, he presented thee with Jewels of a considerable Value —

Since your Ladyship, said *Lucy* sobbing, has promis'd not to be angry, I don't care if I do tell your Ladyship what he gave me. He gave me this Half Guinea, Madam, indeed he did; but for all that, when he would come into your Chamber, I struggled with him, and cry'd out, for fear he should carry your Ladyship away —

Arabella, lost in Astonishment and Shame at hearing of so inconsiderable a Present made to her Woman, the like of which not one of her Romances could furnish her, order'd her immediately to withdraw, not being willing she should observe the Confusion this strange Bribe had given her.

After she had been gone some Time, she endeavour'd to compose her Looks, and went down to the Dining-Room, where Sir *Charles* and his Son and Daughter had been engag'd in a Conversation concerning her, the Particulars of which may be found in the first Chapter of the next Book.

The End *of the* Seventh BOOK.

BOOK VIII

Contains the Conversation refer'd to in the last Chapter of the preceding Book.

Miss *Glanville*, who with a malicious Pleasure had secretly triumph'd in the Extravagances her beautiful Cousin had been guilty of, was now sensibly disappointed to find they had had so little Effect on her Father and Brother; for instead of reflecting upon the Absurdities to which they had been a Witness, Mr. *Glanville* artfully pursu'd the Subject *Arabella*. had just before been expatiating upon, taking notice frequently of some Observations of hers, and by a well contriv'd Repetition of her Words, oblig'd his Father a second Time to declare that his Niece had spoken extremely well.

Mr. *Glanville* taking the Word, launch'd out into such Praises of her Wit, that Miss *Glanville*, no longer able to listen patiently, reply'd,

'Twas true Lady *Bella* sometimes said very sensible Things; that 'twas a great Pity she was not always in a reasonable Way of thinking, or that her Intervals were not longer —

Her Intervals, Miss, said *Glanville*, pray what do you mean by that Expression? —

Why, pray, said Miss *Glanville*, don't you think my Cousin is sometimes a little wrong in the Head?

Mr. *Glanville* at these Words starting from his Chair, took a Turn a-cross the Room in great Discomposure, then stopping all of a sudden, and giving his Sister a furious Look — *Charlotte*, said he, don't give me Cause to think you are envious of your Cousin's superior Excellencies —

Envious! repeated Miss *Glanville*, I envious of my Cousin — I vow I should never have thought of that — Indeed, Brother, you are much mistaken; my Cousin's superior Excellencies never gave me a Moment's Disturbance — Tho' I must confess her unaccountable Whims have often excited my Pity —

No more of this, *Charlotte*, interrupted Mr. *Glanville*, as you value my Friendship — No more of it —

Why, really Son, said Sir *Charles*, my Niece has very strange Whimsies sometimes. How it came into her Head to think Mr. *Tinsel* would attempt to carry her away, I can't imagine? For after all, he only prest rather too rudely into her Chamber, for which, as you see, I have forbidden his Visits.

That was of a Piece, said Miss *Glanville* sneeringly to her Brother, with her asking you if you had made Mr. *Tinsel* swear upon your Sword, that he would never again attempt to carry her away; and applauding you for having given him his Liberty, as the generous *Atermens* did on the same Occasion.

I would advise you, *Charlotte*, said Mr. *Glanville*, not to aim at repeating your Cousin's Words, till you know how to pronounce them properly.

Oh! that's one of her superior Excellencies, said Miss *Glanville*.

Indeed, Miss, said *Glanville* very provokingly, she is superior to you in many Things; and as much so in the Goodness of her Heart, as in the Beauty of her Person —

Come, come, *Charles*, said the Baronet, who observ'd his Daughter sat swelling and biting her Lip at this Reproach, personal Reflections are better avoided. Your Sister is very well, and not to be disparag'd; tho, to be sure, Lady *Bella* is the finest Woman I ever saw in my Life.

Miss *Glanville*, was if possible, more disgusted at her Father's Palliation than her Brother's Reproaches; and, in order to give a Loose to her Passion, accus'd Mr *Glanville* of a Decrease in his Affection for her, since he had been in Love with her Cousin; and having found this Excuse for her Tears, very freely gave vent to them —

Mr. *Glanville* being softned by this Sight, sacrificed a few Compliments to her Vanity, which soon restor'd her to her usual Tranquillity; then turning the Discourse on his beloved *Arabella*, pronounc'd a Panegyrick on her Virtues and Accomplishments of an Hour long; which, if it did not absolutely persuade his Sister to change her Opinion, it certainly convinc'd his Father, that his Niece was not only perfectly well in her Understanding, but even better than most others of her Sex.

Mr. *Glanville* had just finish'd her Eulogium, when *Arabella* appear'd; Joy danc'd in his Eyes at her Approach; he gaz'd upon her with a Kind of conscious Triumph in his Looks; her consummate Loveliness justifying his Passion, and being in his Opinion, more than an Excuse for all her Extravagancies.

CHAPTER II

In which our Heroine, as we presume, shews herself in two very different Lights.

Arabella, who at her Entrance had perceiv'd some Traces of Uneasiness upon Miss *Glanville*'s Countenance, tenderly ask'd her the Cause; to which that young Lady answering in a cold and reserv'd Manner, Mr. *Glanville*, to divert her Reflexions on it, very freely accus'd himself of having given his Sister some Offence. To be sure, Brother, said Miss *Glanville*, you are very vehement in your Temper, and are as violently carry'd away about Things of little Importance as of the greatest; and then, whatever you have a Fancy for, you love so obstinately.

I am oblig'd to you, Miss, interrupted Mr. *Glanville*, for endeavouring to give Lady *Bella* so unfavourable an Opinion of me —

I assure you, said *Arabella*, Miss *Glanville* has said nothing to your Disadvantage: For, in my Opinion, the Temperament of great Minds ought to be such as she represents yours to be. For there is nothing at so great a Distance from true and heroick Virtue, as that Indifference which obliges some People to be pleas'd with all Things or nothing: Whence it comes to pass, that they neither entertain great Desires of Glory, nor Fear of Infamy; that they neither love nor hate; that they are wholly influenc'd by Custom, and are sensible only of the Afflictions of the Body, their Minds being in a Manner insensible —

To say the Truth, I am inclin'd to conceive a greater Hope of a Man, who in the Beginning of his Life is hurry'd away by some evil Habit, than one that fastens on nothing: The Mind that cannot be brought to detest Vice, will never be persuaded to love Virtue; but one who is capable of loving or hating irreconcileably, by having, when young, his Passions directed to proper Objects, will remain fix'd in his Choice of what is good. But with him who is incapable of any violent Attraction, and whose Heart is chilled by a general Indifference, Precept or Example will have no Force — And Philosophy itself, which boasts it hath Remedies for all Indispositions of the Soul, never had any that can cure an indifferent Mind — Nay, added she, I am persuaded that Indifference is generally the inseparable Companion of a weak and imperfect Judgment. For it is so natural to a Person to be carry'd towards that which he believes to be good, that if indifferent People were able to judge of things, they would fasten on something. But certain it is, that this Lukewarmness of Soul, which sends forth but feeble Desires, sends also but feeble Lights; so that those who are guilty of it, not knowing any thing clearly, cannot fasten on any thing with Perseverance.

Mr. *Glanville*, when *Arabella* had finish'd this Speech, cast a triumphing Glance at his Sister, who had affected great Inattention all the while she had been speaking. Sir *Charles*, in his Way, express'd much Admiration of her Wit, telling her, if she had been a Man, she would have made a great Figure in Parliament, and that her Speeches might have come perhaps to be printed in time.

This Compliment, odd as it was, gave great Joy to *Glanville*, when the Conversation was interrupted by the Arrival of Mr. *Selvin*, who had slipt away unobserv'd at the Time that *Arabella*'s Indisposition had alarm'd them, and now came to enquire after her Health; and also if an Opportunity offer'd to

set her right with Regard to the Suspicions she had entertain'd
of his designing to pay his Addresses to her.

Arabella, as soon as he had sent in his Name, appear'd to be
in great Disturbance; and upon his Entrance, offer'd immediately to withdraw, telling Mr. *Glanville*, who would have
detain'd her, that she found no Place was likely to secure her
from the Persecutions of that Gentleman.

Glanville star'd, and look'd strangely perplex'd at this
Speech; Miss *Glanville* smil'd, and poor *Selvin*, with a very silly
Look — hem'd two or three times, and then with a faultring
Accent said, Madam, I am very much concern'd to find your
Ladyship resolv'd to persist in —

Sir, interrupted *Arabella*, my Resolutions are unalterable. I
told you so before, and am surpriz'd, after the Knowledge of
my Intentions, you presume to appear in my Presence again,
from whence I had so positively banish'd you.

Pray, Niece, said Sir *Charles*, what has Mr. *Selvin* done to
disoblige you?

Sir, reply'd *Arabella*, Mr. *Selvin*'s Offence can admit of no
other Reparation than that which I requir'd of him, which was
a voluntary Banishment from my Presence: And in this, pursu'd
she, I am guilty of no more Severity to you, than the Princess
Udosia was to the unfortunate *Thrasimedes*. For the Passion of
this Prince having come to her Knowledge, notwithstanding the
Pains he took to conceal it, this fair and wise Princess thought
it not enough to forbid his speaking to her, but also banish'd
him from her Presence; laying a peremptory Command upon
him, never to appear before her again till he was perfectly cur'd
of that unhappy Love he had entertain'd for her[1] — Imitate
therefore the meritorious Obedience of this poor Prince, and if
that Passion you profess for me —

How, Sir, interrupted Sir *Charles*, Do you make Love to my
Niece then? —

Sir, replied Mr. *Selvin*, who was strangely confounded at
Arabella's Speech, tho' I really admire the Perfections this Lady
is possess'd of, yet I assure you, upon my Honour, I never had
a Thought of making any Addresses to her; and I can't imagine
why her Ladyship persists in accusing me of such Presumption.

So formal a Denial, after what *Arabella* had said, extremely perplex'd Sir *Charles*, and fill'd Mr. *Glanville* with inconceivable Shame —

Miss *Glanville* enjoy'd their Disturbance, and full of an ill-natur'd Triumph, endeavour'd to look *Arabella* into Confusion: But that Lady not being at all discompos'd by this Declaration of Mr. *Selvin*'s, having accounted for it already, replied with great Calmness,

Sir, 'Tis easy to see thro' the Artifice of your disclaiming any Passion for me — Upon any other Occasion questionless, you would rather sacrifice your Life, than consent to disavow these Sentiments, which unhappily for your Peace you have entertain'd. At present the Desire of continuing near me, obliges you to lay this Constraint upon yourself; however you know *Thrasimedes* fell upon the same Stratagem to no Purpose. The rigid *Udosia* saw thro' the Disguise, and would not dispense with herself from banishing him from *Rome*, as I do you from *England* —

How, Madam! interrupted *Selvin* amaz'd —

Yes, Sir, replied *Arabella* hastily, nothing less can satisfy what I owe to the Consideration of my own Glory.

Upon my Word, Madam, said *Selvin*, half angry, and yet strongly inclin'd to laugh, I don't see the Necessity of my quitting my native Country, to satisfy what you owe to the Consideration of your own Glory. Pray, how does my staying in *England* affect your Ladyship's Glory?

To answer your Question with another, said *Arabella*, Pray how did the Stay of *Thrasimedes* in *Rome*, affect the Glory of the Empress *Udosia*?

Mr. *Selvin* was struck dumb with this Speech, for he was not willing to be thought so deficient in the Knowledge of History, as not to be acquainted with the Reasons why *Thrasimedes* should not stay in *Rome*.

His Silence therefore seeming to *Arabella* to be a tacit Confession of the Justice of her Commands, a Sentiment of Compassion for this unfortunate Lover, intruded itself into her Mind; and turning her bright Eyes, full of a soft Complacency upon *Selvin*, who star'd at her as if he had lost his Wits —

I will not, said she, wrong the Sublimity of your Passion for me so much, as to doubt your being ready to sacrifice the Repose of your own Life to the Satisfaction of mine: Nor will I do so much Injustice to your Generosity, as to suppose the Glory of obeying my Commands, will not in some Measure soften the Rigour of your Destiny — I know not whether it may be lawful for me to tell you, that your Misfortune does really cause me some Affliction; but I am willing to give you this Consolation, and also to assure you, that to whatever Part of the World your Despair will carry you, the good Wishes and Compassion of *Arabella* shall follow you —

Having said this, with one of her fair Hands she cover'd her Face, to hide the Blushes which so compassionate a Speech had caus'd — Holding the other extended with a careless Air, supposing he would kneel to kiss it, and bathe it with his Tears, as was the Custom on such melancholy Occasions, her Head at the same Time turned another Way, as if reluctantly and with Confusion she granted this Favour. — But after standing a Moment in this Posture, and finding her Hand untouch'd, she concluded Grief had depriv'd him of his Senses, and that he would shortly fall into a Swoon as *Thrasimedes* did: And to prevent being a Witness of so doleful a Sight, she hurry'd out of the Room without once turning about, and having reach'd her own Apartment, sunk into a Chair, not a little affected with the deplorable Condition in which she had left her suppos'd miserable Lover.

CHAPTER III
The Contrast continued.

The Company she had left behind her being all, except Mr. *Glanville*, to the last Degree surpriz'd at her strange Words and Actions, continued mute for several Minutes after she was gone, staring upon one another, as if each wish'd to know the other's Opinion of such an unaccountable Behaviour. At last Miss

Glanville, who observed her Brother's Back was towards her, told Mr. *Selvin* in a low Voice, that she hop'd he would call and take his Leave of them before he set out for the Place where his Despair would carry him. —

Mr. *Selvin*, in spite of his natural Gravity, could not forbear laughing at this Speech of Miss *Glanville*'s, which shock'd her Brother, and not being able to stay where *Arabella* was ridicul'd, nor intitled to resent it, which would have been a manifest Injustice on that Occasion, he retir'd to his own Apartment to give vent to that Spleen which in those Moments made him out of Humour with all the World.

Sir *Charles*, when he was gone, indulg'd himself in a little Mirth on his Niece's Extravagance, protesting he did not know what to do with her. Upon which Miss *Glanville* observ'd, that it was a Pity there were not such Things as Protestant Nunneries;[2] giving it as her Opinion, that her Cousin ought to be confin'd in one of those Places, and never suffer'd to see any Company, by which Means she would avoid exposing herself in the Manner she did now.

Mr. *Selvin*, who possibly thought this a reasonable Scheme of Miss *Glanville*'s, seem'd by his Silence to assent to her Opinion; but Sir *Charles* was greatly displeas'd with his Daughter for expressing herself so freely; alledging that *Arabella*, when she was out of those Whims, was a very sensible young Lady, and sometimes talk'd as learnedly as a Divine. To which Mr. *Selvin* also added, that she had a great Knowledge of History, and had a most surprizing Memory; and after some more Discourse to the same Purpose, he took his Leave, earnestly entreating Sir *Charles* to believe that he never entertain'd any Design of making his Addresses to Lady *Bella*.

In the mean Time, that Lady after having given near half an Hour to those Reflexions which occur to Heroines in the same Situation with herself, call'd for *Lucy*, and order'd her to go to the Dining-Room, and see in what Condition Mr. *Selvin* was, telling her she had certainly left him in a Swoon, as also the Occasion of it; and bid her give him all the Consolation in her Power.

Lucy, with Tears in her Eyes at this Recital, went down as she was order'd, and entering the Room without any Ceremony, her Thoughts being wholly fix'd on the melancholy Circumstance her Lady had been telling her; she look'd eagerly round the Room without speaking a Word, till Sir *Charles* and Miss *Glanville*, who thought she had been sent with some Message from *Arabella*, ask'd her both at the same Instant, What she wanted? —

I came, Sir, said *Lucy*, repeating her Lady's Words, to see in what Condition Mr. *Selvin* is in, and to give him all the Solation in my Power.

Sir *Charles*, laughing heartily at this Speech, ask'd her what she could do for Mr. *Selvin?* To which she reply'd, she did not know; but her Lady had told her to give him all the Solation in her Power.

Consolation thou would'st say, I suppose, said Sir *Charles*.

Yes, Sir, said *Lucy* curtseying. Well, Child, added he, go up and tell your Lady, Mr. *Selvin* does not need any Consolation.

Lucy accordingly return'd with this Message, and was met at the Chamber-Door by *Arabella*, who hastily asked her if Mr. *Selvin* was recover'd from his Swoon: To which *Lucy* reply'd that she did not know; but that Sir *Charles* bid her tell her Ladyship, Mr. *Selvin* did not need any Consolation.

Oh Heavens! cry'd *Arabella*, throwing herself into a Chair as pale as Death — He is dead, he has fallen upon his Sword, and put an End to his Life and Miseries at once — Oh! how unhappy am I, cry'd she, bursting into Tears, to be the Cause of so cruel an Accident — Was ever any Fate so terrible as mine — Was ever Beauty so fatal — Was ever Rigour so unfortunate — How will the Quiet of my future Days be disturbed by the sad Remembrance of a Man whose Death was caused by my Disdain — But why, resum'd she after a little Pause — Why do I thus afflict myself for what has happened by an unavoidable Necessity? Nor am I singular in the Misfortune which has befallen me — Did not the sad *Perinthus* die for the beautiful *Panthea*[3] — Did not the Rigour of *Barsina* bring the miserable *Oxyatres* to the Grave[4] — And the Severity of *Statira* make *Oroondates* fall upon his Sword in her Presence, tho' happily he escap'd being kill'd by it[5] — Let us then not afflict ourselves unreasonably at this sad Accident — Let us lament as we ought the fatal Effects of our Charms — But let us comfort ourselves with the Thought that we have only acted conformable to our Duty.

Arabella having pronounc'd these last Words with a solemn and lofty Accent, order'd *Lucy*, who listen'd to her with Eyes drown'd in Tears, to go down and ask if the Body was remov'd — for added she, all my Constancy will not be sufficient to support me against that pitiful Sight.

Lucy accordingly deliver'd her Message to Sir *Charles* and Miss *Glanville*, who were still together, discoursing on the fantastical Turn of *Arabella*, when the Knight, who could not possibly comprehend what she meant by asking if the Body was removed, bid her tell her Lady he desired to speak with her.

Arabella, upon receiving this Summons, set herself to consider what could be the Intent of it. If Mr. *Selvin* be dead, said she, what Good can my Presence do among them? Surely it cannot be to upbraid me with my Severity, that my Uncle desires to see me — No, it would be unjust to suppose it. Questionless my unhappy Lover is still struggling with the Pangs of Death, and for a Consolation in his last Moments, implores the Favour of resigning up his Life in my Sight. Pausing a little at these Words, she rose from her Seat with a Resolution to give the unhappy *Selvin* her Pardon before he dy'd. Meeting Mr. *Glanville* as he was returning from his Chamber to the Dining-Room, she told him, she hop'd the Charity she was going to discover towards his Rival, would not give him any Uneasiness; and preventing his Reply by going hastily into the Room, he follow'd her dreading some new Extravagance, yet not able to prevent it, endeavour'd to conceal his Confusion from her Observation — *Arabella*, after breathing a gentle Sigh, told Sir *Charles*, that she was come to grant Mr. *Selvin* her Pardon for the Offence he had been guilty of, that he might depart in Peace.

Well, well, said Sir *Charles*, he is departed in Peace without it.

How, Sir, interrupted *Arabella*, is he dead then already? Alas! Why had he not the Satisfaction of seeing me before he expir'd, that his Soul might have departed in Peace? He would have been assur'd not only of my Pardon, but Pity also; and that

Assurance would have made him happy in his last Moments.

Why, Niece, interrupted Sir *Charles* staring, you surprize me prodigiously: Are you in earnest?

Questionless I am, Sir, said she, nor ought you to be surpriz'd at the Concern I express for the Fate of this unhappy Man, nor at the Pardon I propos'd to have granted him; since herein I am justified by the Example of many great and virtuous Princesses, who have done as much, nay, haply more than I intended to have done, for Persons whose Offences were greater than Mr. *Selvin*'s.

I am very sorry, Madam, said Sir *Charles*, to hear you talk in this Manner: 'Tis really enough to make one suspect you are —

You do me great Injustice, Sir, interrupted *Arabella*, if you suspect me to be guilty of any unbecoming Weakness for this Man: if barely expressing my Compassion for his Misfortunes be esteem'd so great a Favour, what would you have thought if I had supported his Head on my Knees while he was dying, shed Tears over him, and discover'd all the Tokens of a sincere Affection for him?

Good God! said Sir *Charles*, lifting up his Eyes, Did any body ever hear of any thing like this?

What, Sir, said *Arabella*, with as great an Appearance of Surprize in her Countenance as his had discover'd, Do you say you never heard of any thing like this? Then you never heard of the Princess of *Media*, I suppose —

No, not I, Madam, said Sir *Charles* peevishly.

Then, Sir, resum'd *Arabella*, permit me to tell you, that this fair and virtuous Princess condescended to do all I have mention'd for the fierce *Labynet*, Prince of *Assyria*; who tho' he had mortally offended her by stealing her away out of the Court of the King her Father, nevertheless, when he was wounded to Death in her Presence, and humbly implor'd her Pardon before he died, she condescended as I have said, to support him on her Knees, and shed Tears for his Disaster[6] — I could produce many more Instances of the like Compassion in Ladies almost as highly born as herself, tho' perhaps their Quality was not quite so illustrious, she being the Heiress of two powerful Kingdoms. Yet to mention only these —

Good Heavens! cry'd Mr. *Glanville* here, being quite out of Patience, I shall go distracted —

Arabella surpriz'd at this Exclamation, look'd earnestly at him for a Moment — and then ask'd him, Whether any thing she had said had given him Uneasiness?

Yes, upon my Soul, Madam, said *Glanville*, so vex'd and confus'd that he hardly knew what he said —

I am sorry for it, reply'd *Arabella* gravely, and also am greatly concern'd to find that in Geneosity you are so much exceeded by the illustrious *Cyrus*; who was so far from taking Umbrage at *Mandana*'s Behaviour to the dying Prince, that he commended her for the Compassion she had shewn him. So also did the brave and generous *Oroondates*, when the fair *Statira* —

By Heavens! cry'd *Glanville* rising in a Passion, there's no hearing this. Pardon me, Madam, but upon my Soul, you'll make me hang myself.

Hang yourself, repeated *Arabella*, sure you know not what you say? You meant, I suppose, that you'll fall upon your Sword. What Hero ever threatned to give himself so vulgar a Death? But pray let me know the Cause of your Despair, so sudden and so violent.

Mr. *Glanville* continuing in a Sort of sullen Silence, *Arabella* raising her Voice went on:

Tho' I do not conceive myself oblig'd to give you an Account of my Conduct, seeing that I have only permitted you yet to hope for my Favour; yet I owe to myself and my own Honour the Justification I am going to make. Know then, that however suspicious my Compassion for Mr. *Selvin* may appear to your mistaken Judgment, yet it has its Foundation only in the Generosity of my Disposition, which inclines me to pardon the Fault when the unhappy Criminal repents; and to afford him my Pity when his Circumstances require it. Let not therefore the Charity I have discover'd towards your Rival, be the Cause of your Dispair, since my Sentiments for him, were he living, would be what they were before; that is, full of Indifference, nay, haply Disdain. And suffer not yourself to be so carried away by a violent and unjust Jealousy, as to threaten your own Death, which if you really had any Ground for your Suspicions, and truly lov'd me, would come unsought for, tho' not undesir'd — For indeed, was your Despair reasonable, Death would necessarily follow it; for what Lover can live under so desperate a Misfortune. In that Case you may meet Death undauntedly when it comes, nay, embrace it with Joy; but truly the killing one's self is but a false Picture of true Courage, proceeding rather from Fear of a further Evil, than Contempt of that you fly to: For if it were a Contempt of Pain, the same Principle would make you resolve to bear patiently and fearlesly all Kinds of Pains; and Hope being of all other the most contrary Thing to Fear, this being an utter Banishment of Hope, seems to have its Ground in Fear.

CHAPTER IV

In which Mr. Glanville makes an unsuccessful Attempt upon Arabella.

Arabella, when she had finish'd these Words, which banish'd in part Mr. *Glanville*'s Confusion, went to her own Apartment, follow'd by Miss *Glanville*, to whom she had made a Sign for that Purpose; and throwing herself into a Chair, burst into Tears, which greatly surprizing Miss *Glanville*, she prest her to tell her the Cause.

Alas! reply'd *Arabella*, have I not Cause to think myself extremely unhappy? The deplorable Death of Mr. *Selvin*, the Despair to which I see your Brother reduc'd, with the fatal Consequences which may attend it, fills me with a mortal Uneasiness.

Well, said Miss *Glanville*, your Ladyship may make yourself quite easy as to both these Matters; for Mr. *Selvin* is not dead, nor is my Brother in Despair that I know of.

What do you say, Miss, interrupted *Arabella*, is not Mr. *Selvin* dead? Was the Wound he gave himself not mortal then?

I know of no Wound that he gave himself, not I, said Miss *Glanville*; what makes your Ladyship suppose he gave himself a Wound? Lord bless me, what strange Thoughts come into your Head.

Truly I am rejoic'd to hear it, reply'd *Arabella*; and in order to prevent the Effects of his Despair, I'll instantly dispatch my Commands to him to live.

I dare answer for his Obedience, Madam, said Miss *Glanville* smiling.

Arabella then gave Orders for Paper and Pens to be brought her, and seeing Mr. *Glanville* enter the Room, very formally acquainted him with her Intention, telling him, that he ought to be satisfy'd with the Banishment to which she had doom'd his unhappy Rival, and not require his Death, since he had nothing to fear from his Pretensions.

I assure you, Madam, said Mr. *Glanville*, I am perfectly easy upon that Account: And in order to spare you the Trouble of sending to Mr. *Selvin*, I may venture to assure you that he is in no Danger of dying.

'Tis impossible, Sir, reply'd *Arabella*, according to the Nature of Things, 'tis impossible but he must already be very near Death — You know the Rigour of my Sentence, you know —

I know, Madam, said Mr. *Glanville*, that Mr. *Selvin* does not think himself under a Necessity of obeying your Sentence; and has the Impudence to question your Authority for banishing him from his native Country.

My Authority, Sir, said *Arabella* strangely surpriz'd, is founded upon the absolute Power he has given me over him.

He denies that, Madam, said *Glanville*, and says that he neither can give, nor you exercise an absolute Power over him; since you are both accountable to the King, whose Subjects you are, and both restrain'd by the Laws under whose Sanction you live.

Arabella's apparent Confusion at these Words giving Mr. *Glanville* Hopes that he had fallen upon a proper Method to cure her of some of her strange Notions, he was going to pursue his Arguments, when *Arabella* looking a little sternly upon him,

The Empire of Love, said she, like the Empire of Honour, is govern'd by Laws of its own, which have no Dependence upon, or Relation to any other.

Pardon me, Madam, said *Glanville*, if I presume to differ from you. Our Laws have fix'd the Boundaries of Honour as well as those of Love.

How is that possible, reply'd *Arabella*, when they differ so widely, that a Man may be justify'd by the one, and yet condemn'd by the other? For Instance, pursued she, you are not permitted by the Laws of the Land to take away the Life of any Person whatever; yet the Laws of Honour oblige you to hunt your Enemy thro' the World, in order to sacrifice him to your Vengeance. Since it is impossible then for the same Actions to be at once just and unjust, it must necessarily follow, that the Law which condemns it, and that which justifies it is not the same, but directly opposite — And now, added she, after a little Pause, I hope I have entirely clear'd up that Point to you.

You have indeed, Madam, reply'd Mr. *Glanville*, proved to a Demonstration, that what is called Honour is something distinct from Justice, since they command Things absolutely opposite to each other.

Arabella without reflecting on this Inference, went on to prove the independent Sovereignty of Love, which, said she, may be collected from all the Words and Actions of those Heroes who were inspir'd by this Passion. We see it in them, pursued she, triumphing not only over all natural and avow'd Allegiance, but superior even to Friendship, Duty, and Honour itself. This the Actions of *Oroondates*, *Artaxerxes*, *Spitridates*, and many other illustrious Princes sufficiently testify.[7]

Love requires a more unlimited Obedience from its Slaves, than any other Monarch can expect from his Subjects; an Obedience which is circumscrib'd by no Laws whatever, and dependent upon nothing but itself.

I shall live, Madam, says the renowned Prince of *Scythia* to the divine *Statira*, I shall live, since it is your Command I should do so; and Death can have no Power over a Life which you are pleas'd to take Care of[8] —

Say only that you wish I should conquer, said the great *Juba* to the incomparable *Cleopatra*, and my Enemies will be already vanquish'd — Victory will come over to the Side you favour — and an Army of a hundred thousand Men will not be able to overcome the Man who has your Commands to conquer —⁹

How mean and insignificant, pursued she, are the Titles bestow'd on other Monarchs compar'd with those which dignify the Sovereigns of Hearts, such as divine Arbitress of my Fate, Visible Divinity, Earthly Goddess, and many others equally sublime —

Mr. *Glanville* losing all Patience at her obstinate Folly, interrupted her here with a Question quite foreign to the Subject she was discussing, and soon after quitting her Chamber, retir'd to his own, more than ever despairing of her Recovery.

CHAPTER V

In which is introduc'd a very singular Character.

Miss *Glanville*, whose Envy and Dislike of her lovely Cousin was heighten'd by her Suspicions that she disputed with her the Possession of Sir *George*'s Heart, she having been long in reality a great Admirer of that gay Gentleman, was extremely delighted with the Ridicule her absurd Behaviour had drawn upon her at *Bath*, which she found by Enquiry was thro' Mr. *Tinsel*'s Representation grown almost general.

In order therefore to be at Liberty to go to the Publick Places un-eclips'd by the superior Beauty of *Arabella*, she acquainted her Father and Brother with Part of what she had heard, which determin'd them to prevent that young Lady's Appearance in Publick while they staid at *Bath*; this being no difficult Matter to bring about, since *Arabella* only went to the Rooms or Parade in Compliance with the Invitation of her Cousins.

Miss *Glanville* being by these Means rid of a Rival too powerful even to contend with, went with more than usual Gaiety to the Assembly, where the Extravagancies of *Arabella* afforded a perpetual Fund for Diversion. Her more than passive Behaviour upon this Occasion, bannishing all Restraint among those she convers'd with, the Jest circulated very freely at

Arabella's Expence. Nor did Miss *Glanville* fail to give new Poignancy to their Sarcasms, by artfully deploring the bent of her Cousin's Studies, and enumerating the many Absurdities they had made her guilty of.

Arabella's uncommon Beauty had gain'd her so many Enemies among the Ladies that compos'd this Assembly, that they seem'd to contend with each other who should ridicule her most. The celebrated Countess of ——[10] being then at *Bath*, approach'd a Circle of these fair Defamers, and listning a few Moments to the contemptuous Jests they threw out against the absent Beauty, declar'd herself in her Favour; which in a Moment, such was the Force of her universally acknowledg'd Merit, and the Deference always pay'd to her Opinion, silenc'd every pretty Impertinent around her.

This Lady, who among her own Sex had no Superior in Wit, Elegance, and Ease, was inferior to very few of the other in Sense, Learning, and Judgment. Her Skill in Poetry, Painting, and Musick, tho' incontestably great, was number'd among the least of her Accomplishments. Her Candour, her Sweetness, her Modesty and Benevolence, while they secur'd her from the Darts of Envy, render'd her superior to Praise, and made the one as unnecessary as the other ineffectual.

She had been a Witness of the Surprize *Arabella*'s extraordinary Appearance had occasion'd, and struck with that as well as the uncommon Charms of her Person, had prest near her with several others of the Company, when she was discoursing in the Manner we have related.

A Person of the Countess's nice Discernment could not fail of observing the Wit and Spirit, which tho' obscur'd, was not absolutely hid under the Absurdity of her Notions. And this Discovery adding Esteem to the Compassion she felt for the fair Visionary, she resolv'd to rescue her from the ill-natur'd Raillery of her Sex; praising therefore her Understanding, and the Beauty of her Person with a Sweetness and Generosity peculiar to herself, she accounted in the most delicate Manner imaginable for the Singularity of her Notions, from her Studies, her Retirement, her Ignorance of the World, and her lively Imagination. And to abate the Keenness of their Sarcasms, acknowledg'd, that she herself had, when very young, been deep read in Romances; and but for an early Acquaintance with the World, and being directed to other Studies, was likely to have been as much a Heroine as Lady *Bella*.

Miss *Glanville*, tho' she was secretly vex'd at this Defence of her Cousin, was however under a Necessity of seeming oblig'd to the Countess for it: And that Lady expressing a Desire to be acquainted with Lady *Bella*, Miss *Glanville* respectfully offer'd to attend her Cousin to her Lodgings, which the Countess as respectfully declin'd, saying, As Lady *Bella* was a Stranger, she would make her the first Visit.

Miss *Glanville* at her Return gave her Brother an Account of what had happen'd at the Assembly, and fill'd him with an inconceivable Joy at the Countess's Intention. He had always been a zealous Admirer of that Lady's Character, and flatter'd himself that the Conversation of so admirable a Woman would be of the utmost Use to *Arabella*.

That very Night he mention'd her to his beloved Cousin; and after enumerating all her fine Qualities, declar'd that she had already conceiv'd a Friendship for her, and was solicitous of her Acquaintance.

I think myself extremely fortunate, replied *Arabella*, in that I have (tho' questionless undeservedly) acquir'd the Amity of this lovely Person; and I beg you, pursued she to Miss *Glanville*, to tell her, that I long with Impatience to embrace her, and to give her that Share in my Heart which her transcendent Merit deserves.

Miss *Glanville* only bow'd her Head in Answer to this Request, giving her Brother at the same Time a significant Leer; who tho' used to *Arabella*'s Particularities, could not help being a little confounded at the heroic Speech she had made.

CHAPTER VI

*Containing something which at first Sight may possibly
puzzle the Reader.*

The Countess was as good as her Word, and two Days after
sent a Card to *Arabella*, importing her Design to wait on her
that Afternoon.

Our Heroine expected her with great Impatience, and the
Moment she enter'd the Room flew towards her with a graceful
Eagerness, and straining her in her Arms, embrac'd her with all
the Fervour of a long absent Friend.

Sir *Charles* and Mr. *Glanville* were equally embarrass'd at
the Familiarity of this Address; but observing that the Countess
seem'd not to be surpriz'd at it, but rather to receive it with
Pleasure, they were soon compos'd.

You cannot imagine, lovely Stranger, said *Arabella* to the
Countess, as soon as they were seated, with what Impatience I
have long'd to behold you, since the Knowledge I have receiv'd
of your rare Qualities, and the Friendship you have been pleas'd
to honour me with — And I may truly protest to you, that such
is my Admiration of your Virtues, that I would have gone to
the farthest Part of the World to render you that which you with
so much Generosity have condescended to bestow upon me.

Sir *Charles* star'd at this extraordinary Speech, and not being
able to comprehend a Word of it, was concern'd to think how
the Lady to whom it was address'd would understand it.

Mr. *Glanville* look'd down, and bit his Nails in extreme
Confusion; but the Countess who had not forgot the Language
of Romance, return'd the Compliment in a Strain as heroic
as hers.

The Favour I have receiv'd from Fortune, said she, in bringing me to the Happiness of your Acquaintance, charming
Arabella, is so great, that I may rationally expect some terrible
Misfortune will befall me: Seeing that in this Life our Pleasures
are so constantly succeeded by Pains, that we hardly ever enjoy
the one without suffering the other soon after.

Arabella was quite transported to hear the Countess express herself in Language so conformable to her own; but Mr. *Glanville* was greatly confounded, and began to suspect she was diverting herself with his Cousin's Singularities: And Sir *Charles* was within a little of thinking her as much out of the Way as his Niece.

Misfortunes, Madam, said *Arabella*, are too often the Lot of excellent Persons like yourself. The sublimest among Mortals both for Beauty and Virtue have experienc'd the Frowns of Fate. The Sufferings of the divine *Statira* or *Cassandra*, for she bore both Names, the Persecutions of the incomparable *Cleopatra*, the Distresses of the beautiful *Candace*, and the Afflictions of the fair and generous *Mandana*, are Proofs that the most illustrious Persons in the World have felt the Rage of Calamity.

It must be confess'd, said the Countess, that all those fair Princesses you have nam'd, were for a while extremely unfortunate: Yet in the Catalogue of these lovely and afflicted Persons you have forgot one who might with Justice dispute the Priority of Sufferings with them all — I mean the beautiful *Elisa*, Princess of *Parthia*.

Pardon me, Madam, reply'd *Arabella*, I cannot be of your Opinion. The Princess of *Parthia* may indeed justly be rank'd among the Number of unfortunate Persons, but she can by no means dispute the melancholy Precedence with the divine *Cleopatra* — For in fine, Madam, what Evils did the Princess of *Parthia* suffer which the fair *Cleopatra* did not likewise endure, and some of them haply in a greater Degree? If *Elisa* by the tyrannical Authority of the King her Father, saw herself upon the Point of becoming the Wife of a Prince she detested,[11] was not the beautiful Daughter of *Antony*, by the more unjustifiable Tyranny of *Augustus*, likely to be forced into the Arms of *Tyberius*, a proud and cruel Prince, who was odious to the whole World as well as to her?[12] If *Elisa* was for some time in the Power of Pyrates,[13] was not *Cleopatra* Captive to an inhuman King, who presented his Sword to the fair Breast[14] of that divine Princess worthy the Adoration of the whole Earth? And in fine, if *Elisa* had the Grief to see her dear *Artaban*

imprison'd by the Order of *Augustus, Cleopatra* beheld with
mortal Agonies, her beloved *Coriolanus* inclos'd amidst the
Guards of that enrag'd Prince, and doom'd to a cruel Death.[15]

'Tis certain, Madam, reply'd the Countess, that the Misfortunes of both these Princesses were very great, tho' as you have
shew'd me with some Inequality: And when one reflects upon
the dangerous Adventures to which Persons of their Quality
were expos'd in those Times, one cannot help rejoicing that we
live in an Age in which the Customs, Manners, Habits, and
Inclinations differ so widely from them, that 'tis impossible
such Adventures should even happen.

Such is the strange Alteration of Things, that some People I
dare say at present, cannot be persuaded to believe there ever
were Princesses wandering thro' the World by Land and Sea in
mean Disguises, carry'd away violently out of their Father's
Dominions by insolent Lovers — Some discover'd sleeping in
Forests, other shipwreck'd on desolate Islands, confin'd in
Castles, bound in Chariots, and even struggling amidst the
tempestuous Waves of the Sea, into which they had cast themselves to avoid the brutal Force of their Ravishers. Not one of
these Things having happen'd within the Compass of several
thousand Years, People unlearn'd in Antiquity would be apt to
deem them idle Tales, so improbable do they appear at present.

Arabella, tho' greatly surpriz'd at this Discourse, did not
think proper to express her Thoughts of it. She was unwilling
to appear absolutely ignorant of the present Customs of the
World, before a Lady whose good Opinion she was ardently
desirous of improving. Her Prepossessions in favour of the
Countess made her receive the new Lights she held out to her
with Respect, tho' not without Doubt and Irresolution. Her
Blushes, her Silence, and down-cast Eyes gave the Countess to
understand Part of her Thoughts; who for fear of alarming her
too much for that Time, dropt the Subject, and turning the
Conversation on others more general, gave *Arabella* an Opportunity of mingling in it with that Wit and Vivacity which was
natural to her when Romances were out of the Question.

CHAPTER VII

*In which, if the Reader has not anticipated it, he will
find an Explanation of some seeming Inconsistencies in
the foregoing Chapter.*

The Countess, charm'd with the Wit and good Sense of
Arabella, could not conceal her Admiration, but exprest it in
Terms the most obligingly imaginable: And *Arabella*, who was
excessively delighted with her, return'd the Compliments she
made her with the most respectful Tenderness.

In the midst of these mutual Civilities, *Arabella* in the Style
of Romance, intreated the Countess to favour her with the
Recital of her Adventures.

At the Mention of this Request, that Lady convey'd so much
Confusion into her Countenance, that *Arabella* extremely
embarrass'd by it, tho' she knew not why, thought it necessary
to apologize for the Disturbance she seem'd to have occasion'd
in her.

Pardon me, Madam, reply'd the Countess recovering herself,
if the Uncommoness of your Request made a Moment's
Reflexion necessary to convince me that a young Lady of your
Sense and Delicacy could mean no Offence to Decorum by
making it. The Word Adventures carries in it so free and licentious a Sound in the Apprehensions of People at this Period of
Time, that it can hardly with Propriety be apply'd to those few
and natural Incidents which compose the History of a Woman
of Honour. And when I tell you, pursued she with a Smile, that
I was born and christen'd, had a useful and proper Education,
receiv'd the Addresses of my Lord —— through the Recommendation of my Parents, and marry'd him with their Consents
and my own Inclination, and that since we have liv'd in great
Harmony together, I have told you all the material Passages of
my Life, which upon Enquiry you will find differ very little
from those of other Women of the same Rank, who have a
moderate Share of Sense, Prudence and Virtue.

Since you have already, Madam, replied *Arabella* blushing,

excus'd me for the Liberty I took with you, it will be unnecessary to tell you it was grounded upon the Customs of antient Times, when Ladies of the highest Rank and sublimest Virtue, were often expos'd to a Variety of cruel Adventures which they imparted in Confidence to each other, when Chance brought them together.

Custom, said the Countess smiling, changes the very Nature of Things, and what was honourable a thousand Years ago, may probably be look'd upon as infamous now — A Lady in the heroic Age you speak of, would not be thought to possess any great Share of Merit, if she had not been many times carried away by one or other of her insolent Lovers: Whereas a Beauty in this could not pass thro' the Hands of several different Ravishers, without bringing an Imputation on her Chastity.

The same Actions which made a Man a Hero in those Times, would constitute him a Murderer in These — And the same Steps which led him to a Throne Then, would infallibly conduct him to a Scaffold Now.

But Custom, Madam, said *Arabella*, cannot possibly change the Nature of Virtue or Vice: And since Virtue is the chief Characteristic of a Hero, a Hero in the last Age will be a Hero in this — Tho' the Natures of Virtue or Vice cannot be changed, replied the Countess, yet they may be mistaken; and different Principles, Customs, and Education, may probably change their Names, if not their Natures.

Sure, Madam, said *Arabella* a little moved, you do not intend by this Inference to prove *Oroondates*, *Artaxerxes*, *Juba*, *Artaban*, and the other Heroes of Antiquity, bad Men?

Judging them by the Rules of Christianity, and our present Notions of Honour, Justice, and Humanity, they certainly are, replied the Countess.

Did they not possess all the necessary Qualifications of Heroes, Madam, said *Arabella*, and each in a superlative Degree? — Was not their Valour invincible, their Generosity unbounded, and their Fidelity inviolable?

It cannot be denied, said the Countess, but that their Valour was invincible; and many thousand Men less courageous than themselves, felt the fatal Effects of that invincible Valour, which was perpetually seeking after Occasions to exert itself. *Oroondates* gave many extraordinary Proofs of that unbounded Generosity so natural to the Heroes of his Time. This Prince being sent by the King his Father, at the Head of an Army, to oppose the *Persian* Monarch, who had unjustly invaded his Dominions, and was destroying the Lives and Properties of his Subjects; having taken the Wives and Daughters of his Enemy Prisoners, had by these Means an Opportunity to put a Period to a War so destructive to his Country: Yet out of a Generosity truly heroic, he releas'd them immediately without any Conditions; and falling in Love with one of those Princesses, secretly quitted his Father's Court, resided several Years in that of the Enemy of his Father and Country, engag'd himself to his Daughter, and when the War broke out again between the two Kings, fought furiously against an Army in which the King his Father was in Person, and shed the Blood of his future Subjects without Remorse; tho' each of those Subjects, we are told, would have sacrific'd his Life to save that of their Prince, so much was he belov'd.[16] Such are the Actions which immortalize the Heroes of Romance, and are by the Authors of those Books styl'd glorious, godlike, and divine. Yet judging of them as Christians, we shall find them impious and base, and directly opposite to our present Notions of moral and relative Duties.

'Tis certain therefore, Madam, added the Countess with a Smile, that what was Virtue in those Days, is Vice in ours: And to form a Hero according to our Notions of 'em at present, 'tis necessary to give him Qualities very different from *Oroondates*.

The secret Charm in the Countenance, Voice, and Manner of the Countess, join'd to the Force of her Reasoning, could not fail of making some Impression on the Mind of *Arabella*; but it was such an Impression as came far short of Conviction. She was surpriz'd, embarrass'd, perplex'd, but not convinc'd. Heroism, romantic Heroism, was deeply rooted in her Heart; it was her Habit of thinking, a Principle imbib'd from Education. She could not separate her Ideas of Glory, Virtue, Courage, Generosity, and Honour, from the false Representations of them in the Actions of *Oroondates*, *Juba*, *Artaxerxes*, and the rest of the imaginary Heroes. The Countess's Discourse had rais'd a Kind of Tumult in her Thoughts, which gave an Air of Perplexity to her lovely Face, and made that Lady apprehensive she had gone too far, and lost that Ground in her Esteem, which she had endeavour'd to acquire by a Conformity to some of her Notions and Language. In this however, she was mistaken; *Arabella* felt a Tenderness for her that had already the Force of a long contracted Friendship, and an Esteem little less than Veneration.

When the Countess took Leave, the Professions of *Arabella*, tho' deliver'd in the Language of Romance, were very sincere and affecting, and were return'd with an equal Degree of Tenderness by the Countess, who had conceiv'd a more than ordinary Affection for her.

Mr. *Glanville*, who could have almost worship'd the Countess for the generous Design he saw she had entertain'd, took an Opportunity as he handed her to her Chair,[17] to intreat in a Manner as earnestly as polite, that she would continue the Happiness of her Acquaintance to his Cousin; which with a Smile of mingled Dignity and Sweetness she assur'd him of.

CHAPTER VIII
Which concludes Book the Eighth.

Mr. *Glanville* at his Return to the Dining-Room, finding *Arabella* retir'd, told his Father in an Rapture of Joy, that the charming Countess would certainly make a Convert of Lady *Bella*.

Methinks, said the Baronet, she has as strange Whims in her Head as my Niece. Ad's-heart what a deal of Stuff did she talk about! A Parcel of Heroes as she calls them, with confounded hard Names — In my Mind she is more likely to make Lady *Bella* worse than better.

Mr. *Glanville*, a little vex'd at his Father's Mis-apprehension, endeavour'd with as much Delicacy as he could, to set him right with Regard to the Countess; so that he brought him at last to confess she manag'd the Thing very well.

The Countess, who had resolv'd to take *Arabella* openly into her Protection, was thinking on Means to engage her to appear at the Assembly, whither she propos'd to accompany her in a modern Dress. But her good Intentions towards our lovely Heroine were suspended by the Account she receiv'd of her Mother's Indisposition, which commanded her immediate Attendance on her at her Seat in ——

Her sudden Departure gave *Arabella* an extreme Uneasiness, and proved a cruel Disappointment to Mr. *Glanville*, who had founded all his Hopes of her Recovery on the Conversation of that Lady.

Sir *Charles* having Affairs that requir'd his Presence in *London*, propos'd to his Niece the leaving *Bath* in a few Days, to which she consented; and accordingly they set out for *London* in *Arabella*'s Coach and Six, attended by several Servants on Horseback, her Women having been sent away before in the Stage.[18]

Nothing very remarkable happen'd during this Journey, so we shall not trouble our Readers with several small Mistakes of *Arabella*'s, such as her supposing a neat Country Girl who was riding behind a Man, to be some Lady or Princess in Disguise, forc'd away by a Lover she hated, and intreating Mr. *Glanville* to attempt her Rescue; which occasion'd some little Debate between her and Sir *Charles*, who could not be persuaded to believe it was as she said, and forbid his Son to meddle in other People's Affairs. Several of these Sort of Mistakes, as we said before, we omit, and will therefore, if our Reader pleases, bring our Heroine without further Delay to *London*.

The End *of the* Eighth BOOK.

BOOK IX

CHAPTER I

In which is related an admirable Adventure.

Miss *Glanville*, whose Spirits were greatly exhilerated at their Entrance into *London*, that Seat of Magnificence and Pleasure, congratulated her Cousin upon the Entertainment she would receive from the new and surprizing Objects which every Day for a considerable Time would furnish her with; and ran over the Catalogue of Diversions with such a Volubility of Tongue, as drew a gentle Reprimand from her Father, and made her keep a sullen Silence till they were set down in St. *James*'s Square,[1] the Place of their Residence in Town.

Sir *Charles* having order'd his late Lady's Apartment to be prepar'd for the Accommodation of his Niece; as soon as the first Civilities were over, she retired to her Chamber, where she employ'd herself in giving her Women Directions for placing her Books, of which she had brought a moderate Quantity to *London*, in her Closet.

Miss *Glanville* as soon as she had dispatch'd away some hundred Cards[2] to her Acquaintance, to give them Notice she was in Town, attended *Arabella* in her own Apartment; and as they sat at the Tea she begun to regulate the Diversions of the Week, naming the Drawing-Room, Park, Concert, *Ranelagh*,[3] Lady —— Assembly, the Dutchess of —— Rout,[4] *Vaux-Hall*,[5] and a long &c. of Visits; at which *Arabella*, with an Accent that express'd her Surprize, ask'd her, if she suppos'd she intended to stay in Town three or four Years ——

Law, Cousin, said Miss *Glanville*, all this is but the Amusement of a few Days.

Amusement, do you say, replied *Arabella*, methinks it seems to be the sole Employment of those Days: And what you call the Amusement, must of Necessity be the Business of Life.

You are always so grave, Cousin, said Miss *Glanville*, one does not know what to say to you. However, I shan't press you to go to Public Places against your Inclination, yet you'll condescend to receive a few Visits, I suppose?

Yes, replied *Arabella*, and if among the Ladies whom I shall see, I find any like the amiable Countess of ——, I shall not scruple to enter into the most tender Amity with them.

The Countess of —— is very well, to be sure, said Miss *Glanville*, yet I don't know how it is, she does not suit my Taste — She is very particular in a great many Things, and knows too much for a Lady, as I heard my Lord *Trifle* say one Day: Then she is quite unfashionable: She hates Cards, keeps no Assembly, is seen but seldom at Publick Places; and in my Opinion, as well as in a great many others, is the dullest Company in the World. I'm sure I met her at a Visit a little before I went down to your Seat, and she had not been a quarter of an Hour in the Room, before she set a whole Circle of Ladies a yawning.

Arabella, tho' she had a sincere Contempt for her Cousin's Manner of thinking, yet always politely conceal'd it; and vex'd as she was at her Sneers upon the Countess, she contented herself with gently defending her, telling her at the same Time, that till she met with a Lady who had more Merit than the Countess, she should always possess the first Place in her Esteem.

Arabella, who had from her Youth adopted the Resentments of her Father, refus'd to make her Appearance at Court, which Sir *Charles* gently intimated to her; yet being not wholly divested of the Curiosity natural to her Sex, she condescended to go *incog.*[6] to the Gallery on a Ball Night, accompanied by Mr. *Glanville* and his Sister, in order to behold the Splendor of the *British* Court.

As her Romances had long familiariz'd her Thoughts to Objects of Grandeur and Magnificence, she was not so much

struck as might have been expected, with those that now presented themselves to her View. Nor was she a little disappointed
to find that among the Men she saw none whose Appearance
came up to her Ideas of the Air and Port of an *Artaban*, *Oroondates*, or *Juba*; or any of the Ladies, who did not in her Opinion,
fall short of the Perfections of *Elisa*, *Mandana*, *Statira*, &c.
'Twas remarkable too, that she never enquir'd how often the
Princesses had been carried away by love-captivated Monarchs,
or how many Victories the King's Sons had gain'd; but seem'd
the whole Time she was there to have suspended all her Romantick Ideas of Glory, Beauty, Gallantry, and Love.

Mr. *Glanville* was highly pleas'd with her compos'd Behaviour, and a Day or two after intreated her to allow him the
Honour of shewing her what was remarkable and worthy of
her Observation in this great Metropolis. To this she also consented, and for the greater Privacy began their Travels in a hir'd
Coach.

Part of several Days were taken up in this Employment; but
Mr. *Glanville* had the Mortification to find she was full of
Allusions to her Romances upon every Occasion, such as her
asking the Person who shews the Armoury at the *Tower*, the
Names of the Knights to whom each Suit belong'd, and wondering there were no Devices on the Shields or Plumes of Feathers in
the Helmets: She observ'd that the Lion *Lysimachus* kill'd,[7] was,
according to the History of that Prince, much larger than any of
those she was shew'd in the *Tower*, and also much fiercer: Took
Notice that St. *Paul*'s was less magnificent in the Inside, than the
Temple in which *Cyrus*, when he went to *Mandana*, heard her
return Thanks for his suppos'd Death:[8] Enquir'd if it was not
customary for the King and his whole Court to sail in Barges
upon the *Thames*, as *Augustus* used to do upon the *Tyber*,[9]
whether they had not Musick and Collations in the Park, and
where they celebrated the Justs and Tournaments.

The Season for *Vaux-Hall* being not yet over,[10] she was
desirous of once seeing a Place, which by the Description she
had heard of it, greatly resembled the Gardens of *Lucullus* at
Rome, in which the Emperor, with all the Princes and Princesses
of his Court were so nobly entertain'd, and where so many

gallant Conversations had pass'd among those admirable Persons.[11]

The Singularity of her Dress, for she was cover'd with her Veil, drew a Number of Gazers after her, who prest round her with so little Respect, that she was greatly embarrass'd, and had Thoughts of quitting the Place, delightful as she own'd it, immediately, when her Attention was wholly engross'd by an Adventure in which she soon interested herself very deeply.

An Officer of Rank in the Sea Service had brought his Mistress disguis'd in a Suit of Man's or rather Boy's Cloaths, and a Hat and Feather, into the Gardens. The young Creature being a little intoxicated with the Wine she had taken too freely, was thrown so much off her Guard as to give Occasion to some of the Company to suspect her Sex; and a gay Fellow, in order to give them some Diversion at her Expence, pretending to be affronted at something she said, drew his Sword upon the disguis'd Fair One, which so alarm'd her, that she shriek'd out, She was a Woman, and ran for Protection to her Lover, who was so disorder'd with Liquor, that he was not able to defend her.

Miss *Glanville*, ever curious and inquisitive, demanded the Cause why the Company ran in Crouds to that particular Spot; and receiv'd for Answer, That a Gentleman had drawn his Sword upon a Lady disguis'd in a Man's Habit.

Oh Heav'ns! cry'd *Arabella*, this must certainly be a very notable Adventure. The Lady has doubtless some extraordinary Circumstances in her Story, and haply upon Enquiry, her Misfortunes will be found to resemble those which oblig'd the beautiful *Aspasia* to put on the same Disguise, who was by that Means murder'd by the cruel *Zenodorus* in a Fit of Jealousy at the Amity his Wife express'd for her.[12] But can I not see this unfortunate Fair One, added she, pressing in Spite of Mr. *Glanville*'s Intreaties thro' the Croud — I may haply be able to afford her some Consolation.

Mr. *Glanville* finding his Persuasions were not regarded, follow'd her with very little Difficulty: For her Veil falling back in her Hurry, she did not mind to replace it, and the Charms of her Face, join'd to the Majesty of her Person, and Singularity of her Dress, attracting every Person's Attention and Respect, they made Way for her to pass, not a little surpriz'd at the extreme Earnestness and Solemnity that appear'd in her Countenance upon an Event so diverting to every one else.

The disguis'd Lady whom she was endeavouring to approach, had thrown herself upon a Bench in one of the Boxes, trembling still with the Apprehension of the Sword, tho' her Antagonist was kneeling at her Feet, making Love to her in Mock-Heroicks[13] for the Diversion of the Company.

Her Hat and Peruke[14] had fallen off in her Fright, and her Hair which had been turn'd up under it, hung now loosely about her Neck, and gave such an Appearance of Woe to a Face, which notwithstanding the Paleness that Terror had overspread it with, was really extremely pretty, that *Arabella* was equally struck with Compassion and Admiration of her.

Lovely Unknown, said she to her with an Air of extreme Tenderness, tho' I am a Stranger both to your Name and History, yet your Aspect persuadeth me your Quality is not mean, and the Condition and Disguise in which I behold you, shewing that you are unfortunate, permit me to offer you all the Assistances in my Power, seeing that I am mov'd thereto by my Compassion for your Distress, and that Esteem which the Sight of you most necessarily inspire.

Mr. *Glanville* was struck dumb with Confusion at this strange Speech, and at the Whispers and Scoffs it occasion'd among the Spectators. He attempted to take hold of her Hand, in order to lead her away, but she disengag'd herself from him with a Frown of Displeasure; and taking no Notice of Miss *Glanville*, who whisper'd with great Emotion, Lord, Cousin, how you expose yourself! prest nearer to the beautiful Disguis'd, and again repeated her Offers of Service.

The Girl being perfectly recover'd from her Intoxication by the Fright she had been in, gaz'd upon *Arabella* with a Look of extreme Surprize: Yet being mov'd to respect by the Dignity of her Appearance, and strange as her Words seem'd to be by the obliging Purport of them, and the affecting Earnestness with which they were deliver'd, she rose from her Seat and thank'd her, with an Accent full of Regard and Submission.

Fair Maid, said *Arabella*, taking her Hand, let us quit this

Place, where your Discovery may probably subject you to more Dangers: If you will be pleas'd to put yourself into my Protection, and acquaint me with the History of your Misfortunes; I have Interest enough with a valiant Person who shall undertake to free you from your Persecutions, and re-establish the Repose of your Life.

The kneeling Hero, who as well as every one else that were present, had gaz'd with Astonishment at *Arabella* during all this Passage, perceiving she was about to rob him of the disguis'd Fair, seiz'd hold of the Hand she had at Liberty, and swore he would not part with her.

Mr. *Glanville* almost mad with Vexation, endeavour'd to get *Arabella* away.

Are you mad, Madam, said he in a Whisper, to make all this Rout about a Prostitute? Do you see how every Body stares at you? What will they think — For Heav'ns sake let us be gone.

What, Sir, replied *Arabella* in a Rage, Are you base enough to leave this admirable Creature in the Power of that Man, who is questionless her Ravisher; and will you not draw your Sword in her Defence?

Hey day! cry'd the Sea-Officer, wak'd out of his stupid Dose by the Clamour about him: What's the Matter here — What are you doing? Where's my *Lucy*? Zoons! Sir, said he to the young Fellow who held her, What Business have you with my *Lucy*? And uttering a dreadful Oath, drew out his Sword, and stagger'd towards his gay Rival, who observing the Weakness of his Antagonist, flourish'd with his Sword to shew his Courage and frighten the Ladies, who all ran away screaming. *Arabella* taking Miss *Glanville* under the Arm, cried out to Mr. *Glanville* as she left the Place, to take Care of the distress'd Lady, and while the two Combatants were disputing for her, to carry her away in Safety.

But Mr. *Glanville* without regarding this Injunction, hasten'd after her; and to pacify her, told her the Lady was rescu'd by her favourite Lover, and carry'd off in Triumph.

But are you sure, said *Arabella*, it was not some other of her Ravishers who carry'd her away, and not the Person whom she has haply favour'd with her Affection! May not the same Thing have happen'd to her, as did to the beautiful *Candace*, Queen of *Ethiopia*; who while two of her Ravishers were fighting for her, a third whom she took for her Deliverer, came and carry'd her away.[15]

But she went away willingly, I assure you, Madam, said Mr. *Glanville*: Pray don't be in any Concern about her —

If she went away willingly with him, reply'd *Arabella*, 'tis probable it may not be another Ravisher: And yet if this Person that rescu'd her happen'd to be in Armour, and the Vizor of his Helmet down, she might be mistaken as well as Queen *Candace*.

Well, well, he was not in Armour, Madam, said *Glanville* almost beside himself with Vexation at her Folly —

You seem to be disturb'd, Sir, said *Arabella* a little surpriz'd at his peevish Tone: Is there any Thing in this Adventure which concerns you? Nay, now I remember, you did not offer to defend the Beautiful Unknown. I am not willing to impute your In-action upon such an Occasion, to Want of Courage or Generosity; perhaps you are acquainted with her History, and from this Knowledge refus'd to engage in her Defence.

Mr. *Glanville* perceiving the Company gather from all Parts to the Walk they were in, told her he would acquaint her with all he knew concerning the disguis'd Lady when they were in the Coach on their Return Home; and *Arabella* impatient for the promis'd Story, propos'd to leave the Gardens immediately, which was gladly comply'd with by Mr. *Glanville*, who heartily repented his having carry'd her thither.

CHAPTER II

Which ends with a very unfavourable Prediction for our Heroine.

As soon as they were seated in the Coach she did not fail to call upon him to perform his Promise: But Mr. *Glanville*, excessively out of Humour at her exposing herself in the Gardens, reply'd, without considering whether he should not offend her, That he knew no more of the disguis'd Lady than any body else in the Place.

How, Sir, reply'd *Arabella*, Did you not promise to relate her Adventures to me? And would you have me believe you knew no more of them than the rest of the Cavaliers and Ladies in the Place?

Upon my Soul, I don't, Madam, said *Glanville*; yet what I know of her is sufficient to let me understand she was not worth the Consideration you seem'd to have for her.

She cannot sure be more indiscreet than the fair and unfortunate *Hermione*, reply'd *Arabella*; who like her put on Man's Apparel, through Despair at the ill Success of her Passion for *Alexander* — And certain it is, that tho' the beautiful *Hermione* was guilty of one great Error which lost her the Esteem of *Alexander*, yet she had a high and noble Soul; as was manifest by her Behaviour and Words when she was murder'd by the Sword of *Demetrius*. Oh! Death, cry'd she, as she was falling, how sweet do I find thee, and how much and how earnestly have I desir'd thee![16]

Oh Lord! oh Lord! cry'd Mr. *Glanville* hardly sensible of what he said, Was there ever any Thing so intolerable?

You pity the unhappy *Hermione*, Sir? said *Arabella* interpreting his Exclamation her own Way. Indeed she is well worthy of your Compassion. And if the bare Recital of the Words she utter'd at receiving her Death's Wound affects you so much, you may guess what would have been your Agonies, had you been *Demetrius* that gave it her.

Here Mr. *Glanville* groaning aloud thro' Impatience at her Absurdities —

This Subject affects you deeply, I perceive, said *Arabella*. There is no Question but you would have acted in the same Circumstance, as *Demetrius* did: Yet let me tell you, the Extravagancy of his Rage and Despair for what he had innocently committed, was imputed to him as a great Imbecillity, as was also the violent Passion he conceiv'd soon after for the Fair *Deidamia*. You know the Accident which brought that fair Princess into his Way.

Indeed, I do not, Madam, said *Glanville* peevishly.

Well, then I'll tell you, said *Arabella*, but pausing a little:

The Recital I have engag'd myself to make, added she, will necessarily take up some Hours Time, as upon Reflexion I have found: So if you will dispense with my beginning it at present, I will satisfy your Curiosity To-morrow, when I may be able to pursue it without Interruption.

To this Mr. *Glanville* made no other Answer than a Bow with his Head; and the Coach a few Moments after arriving at their own House, he led her to her Aparment, firmly resolv'd never to attend her to any more Publick Places while she continued in the same ridiculous Folly.

Sir *Charles*, who had several Times been in doubt whether *Arabella* was not really disorder'd in her Senses; upon Miss *Glanville*'s Account of her Behaviour at the Gardens, concluded she was absolutely mad, and held a short Debate with himself, Whether he ought not to bring a Commission of Lunacy[17] against her, rather than marry her to his Son, whom he was persuaded could never be happy with a Wife so unaccountably absurd. Tho' he only hinted at this to Mr. *Glanville*, in a Conversation he had with him while his Dissatisfaction was at its Height, concerning *Arabella*, yet the bare Supposition that his Father ever thought of such a Thing, threw the young Gentleman into such Agonies, that Sir *Charles* to compose him, protested he would do nothing in relation to his Niece that he would not approve of. Yet he expostulated with him on the Absurdity of her Behaviour, and the Ridicule to which she expos'd herself wherever she went; appealing to him, whether in a Wife he could think those Follies supportable, which in a Mistress occasion'd him so much Confusion.

Mr. *Glanville*, as much in Love as he was, felt all the Force of this Inference, and acknowledg'd to his Father, That he could not think of marrying *Arabella*, till the Whims her Romances had put into her Head, were eraz'd by a better Knowledge of Life and Manners. But he added with a Sigh, That he knew not how this Reformation would be effected; for she had such a strange Facility in reconciling every Incident to her own fantastick Ideas, that every new Object added Strength to the fatal Deception she laboured under.

CHAPTER III

In which Arabella meets with another admirable Adventure.

Our lovely Heroine had not been above a Fortnight in *London*, before the gross Air of that smoaky Town affected her Health so much,[18] that Sir *Charles* propos'd to her to go for a few Weeks to *Richmond*,[19] where he hir'd a House elegantly furnish'd for her Reception.

Miss *Glanville* had been too long out of that darling City, to pay her the Compliment of attending her constantly at *Richmond*; yet she promis'd to be as often as possible with her: And Sir *Charles*, having Affairs that could not dispense with his Absence from Town, plac'd his Steward in her House, being a Person whose Prudence and Fidelity he could rely upon; and he, with her Women, and some other menial Servants, made up her Equipage.

As it was not consistent with Decorum for Mr. *Glanville* to reside in her House, he contented himself with riding to *Richmond* generally every Day: And as long as *Arabella* was pleas'd with that Retirement, he resolv'd not to press her Return to Town till the Countess of —— arriv'd, in whose Conversation he grounded all his Hopes of her Cure.

At that Season of the Year *Richmond* not being quite deserted by Company, *Arabella* was visited by several Ladies of Fashion; who charm'd with her Affability, Politeness, and good Sense, were strangely perplex'd how to account for some Peculiarities in her Dress and Manner of thinking.

Some of the younger Sort from whom *Arabella*'s extraordinary Beauty took away all Pretensions to Equality on that Score, made themselves extremely merry with her Oddnesses, as they call'd them, and gave broad Intimations that her Head was not right.

As for *Arabella*, whose Taste was as delicate, Sentiments as refin'd, and Judgment as clear as any Person's could be who believ'd the Authenticity of *Scudery*'s Romances, she was strangely disappointed to find no Lady with whom she could converse with any tolerable Pleasure: And that instead of *Clelia*'s, *Statira*'s, *Mandana*'s, &c. she found only Miss *Glanville*'s among all she knew.

The Comparison she drew between such as these and the charming Countess of —— whom she had just begun to be acquainted with at *Bath*, increas'd her Regret for the Interruption that was given to so agreeable a Friendship: And it was with infinite Pleasure Mr. *Glanville* heard her repeatedly wish for the Arrival of that admirable Lady (as she always call'd her) in Town.

Not being able to relish the insipid Conversation of the young Ladies that visited her at *Richmond*, her chief Amusement was to walk in the Park there; which because of its Rural Privacy, was extremely agreeable to her Inclinations.

Here she indulg'd Contemplation, leaning on the Arm of her faithful *Lucy*, while her other Women walk'd at some Distance behind her, and two Men Servants kept her always in Sight.

One Evening when she was returning from her usual Walk, she heard the Sound of a Woman's Voice, which seem'd to proceed from a Tuft of Trees that hid her from her View. And stopping a Moment, distinguish'd some plaintive Accents, which increasing her Curiosity, she advanc'd towards the Place, telling *Lucy*, she was resolv'd if possible to discover who the distress'd Lady was, and what was the Subject of her Affliction.

As she drew nearer with softly treading Steps, she could distinguish through the Branches of the Trees, now despoil'd of great part of their Leaves, two Women seated on the Ground, their Backs towards her, and one of them with her Head gently reclin'd on the other's Shoulder, seem'd by her mournful Action to be weeping; for she often put her Handkerchief to her Eyes, breathing every Time a Sigh, which, as *Arabella* phras'd it, seem'd to proceed from the deepest Recesses of her Heart.

This Adventure, more worthy indeed to be styl'd an Adventure than all our Fair Heroine had ever yet met with, and so conformable to what she had read in Romances, fill'd her Heart with eager Expectation. She made a Sign to *Lucy* to make no Noise, and creeping still closer towards the Place where this afflicted Person sat, she heard her distinctly utter these Words, which however were often interrupted with her Sighs.

Ah! *Ariamenes*, whom I to my Misfortune have too much loved, and whom to my Misfortune I fear I shall never sufficiently hate, since that Heav'n and thy cruel Ingratitude hath ordain'd that thou shalt never be mine, and that so many sweet and dear Hopes are for ever taken from me, return me at least, ungrateful Man, return me those Testimonies of my innocent Affection, which were sometimes so dear and precious to thee. Return me those Favours, which all innocent as they were, are become Criminal by thy Crime. Return me, Cruel Man, return me those Reliques of my Heart which thou detainest in Despight of me, and which, notwithstanding thy Infidelity, I cannot recover.

Here her Tears interrupting her Speech, *Arabella* being impatient to know the History of this afflicted Person, came softly round to the other Side, and shewing herself, occasion'd some Disturbance to the sad Unknown; who rising from her Seat, with her Face averted, as if asham'd of having so far disclos'd her Sorrows in a Stranger's Hearing, endeavour'd to pass by her un-notic'd.

Arabella perceiving her Design, stop'd her with a very graceful Action, and with a Voice all compos'd of Sweetness, earnestly conjur'd her to relate her History.

Think not, Lovely Unknown, said she (for she was really very pretty) that my Endeavours to detain you proceed from an indiscreet Curiosity. 'Tis true, some Complaints which have fallen from your fair Mouth, have rais'd in me a Desire to be acquainted with your Adventures; but this Desire has its Foundation in that Compassion your Complaints have fill'd me with: And if I wish to know your Misfortunes, 'tis only with a View of affording you some Consolation.

Pardon me, Madam, said the Fair Afflicted, gazing on *Arabella* with many Signs of Admiration, if my Confusion at being over-heard in a Place I had chosen to bewail my Misfortunes, made me be guilty of some Appearance of Rudeness, not seeing the admirable Person I wanted to avoid. But, pursued she, hesitating a little, those Characters of Beauty I behold in

your Face, and the Gracefulness of your Deportment convincing
me you can be of no ordinary Rank, I will the less scruple to
acquaint you with my Adventures, and the Cause of those
Complaints you have heard proceed from my Mouth.

Arabella assuring her, that whatever her Misfortunes were,
she might depend upon all the Assistance in her Power, seated
herself near her at the Foot of the Tree where she had been
sitting, and giving *Lucy* Orders to join the rest of her Women,
and stay at a Distance till she made a Sign to them to advance,
she prepar'd to listen to the Adventures of the Fair Unknown,
who after some little Pause, began to relate them in this Manner.

CHAPTER IV

In which is related the History of the Princess of Gaul.

My Name, Madam, is *Cynecia*, my Birth illustrious enough,
seeing that I am the Daughter of a Sovereign Prince, who possesses a large and spacious Territory in what is now called
Antient *Gaul*.

What, Madam, interrupted *Arabella*, Are you a Princess
then?

Questionless I am, Madam, replied the Lady; and a Princess
happy and prosperous, till the Felicity of my Life was interrupted by the perfidious *Ariamenes*.

Pardon me, Madam, interrupted *Arabella* again, that my
Ignorance of your Quality made me be deficient in those
Respects which are due to your high Birth, and which not-
withstanding those Characters of Greatness I might read in the
Lineaments of your Visage, I yet neglected to pay —

Alas! Madam, said the Stranger, that little Beauty which
the Heavens bestow'd on me only to make me wretched, as by
the Event it has proved, has long since taken its Flight, and
together with my Happiness, I have lost that which made me
Unhappy. And certain it is, Grief has made such Ravages among
what might once have been thought tolerable in my Face, that

I should not be surpriz'd if my being no longer Fair, should make you with Difficulty believe I ever was so.

Arabella after a proper Compliment in Answer to this Speech, intreated the Princess to go on with her History, who hesitating a little, comply'd with her Request.

Be pleas'd to know then, Madam, said she, that being bred up with all imaginable Tenderness in my Father's Court, I had no sooner arriv'd to my Sixteenth Year than I saw myself surrounded with Lovers; who nevertheless, such was the Severity with which I behav'd myself, conceal'd their Passions under a respectful Silence, well knowing Banishment from my Presence was the least Punishment they had to expect, if they presum'd to declare their Sentiments to me.

I liv'd in this Fashion, Madam, for Two Years longer, rejoicing in the Insensibility of my own Heart, and triumphing in the Sufferings of others, when my Tranquillity was all at once interrupted by an Accident which I am going to relate to you.

The Princess stopt here to give Vent to some Sighs which a cruel Remembrance forc'd from her; and continuing in a deep Muse for five or fix Minutes, resum'd her Story in this Manner.

It being my Custom to walk in a Forest adjoining to one of my Father's Summer Residences, attended only by my Women, one Day when I was taking this Amusement, I perceiv'd at some Distance a Man lying on the Ground; and impell'd by a sudden Curiosity, I advanc'd towards this Person, whom upon a nearer View I perceiv'd to have been wounded very much, and fainted away through Loss of Blood. His Habit being very rich, I concluded by that he was of no mean Quality: But when I had look'd upon his Countenance, pale and languishing as it was, methought there appear'd so many Marks of Greatness, accompany'd with a Sweetness so happily blended, that my Attention was engag'd in an extraordinary Manner, and interested me so powerfully in his Safety, that I commanded some of my Women to run immediately for proper Assistance, and convey him to the Castle, while I directed others to throw some Water in his Face, and to apply some Linen to his Wounds, to stop the Bleeding.

These charitable Cares restor'd the wounded Stranger to his

Senses; he open'd his Eyes, and turning them slowly to the
Objects around him, fix'd at last their languishing Looks on
me: When mov'd, as it should seem, to some Respect by what
he saw in my Countenance, he rose with some Difficulty from
the Ground, and bowing almost down to it again, by that
Action seem'd to pay me his Acknowledgments for what he
suppos'd I had done for his Preservation.

His extreme Weakness having oblig'd him to creep towards
a Tree, against the Back of which he supported himself, I went
nearer to him, and having told him the Condition in which I
found him, and the Orders I had dispatch'd for Assistance,
requested him to acquaint me with his Name and Quality, and
the Adventure which had brought him into that Condition.

My Name, Madam, answer'd he, is *Ariamenes*, my Birth is
Noble enough; I have spent some Years in my Travels, and was
returning to my native Country, when passing thro' this Forest
I was seiz'd with an Inclination to sleep. I had ty'd my Horse
to a Tree, and retiring some few Paces off, stretch'd myself at the
Foot of a large Oak whose Branches promis'd me an agreeable
Shade. I had not yet clos'd my Eyes, when the Slumber I invited
was dissipated by the Sound of some Voices near me.

A Curiosity, not natural to me, made me listen to the Discourse of these Persons, whom by the Tone of their Voices, tho'
I could not see them, I knew to be Men.

In short, Madam, I was a Witness to a most horrible Scheme
which they concerted together; my Weakness will not permit
me to enter into an exact Detail of all I heard: The Result of
their Conference was, To seize the Princess of this Country and
carry her off.

Here, pursued *Cynecia*, I interrupted the Stranger with a
loud Cry, which giving him to understand who I was, he apolo-
giz'd in the most graceful Manner imaginable for the little
Respect he had hitherto paid me.

I then intreated him to tell me, If he had any Opportunity of
hearing the Name of my design'd Ravisher; to which he reply'd,
that he understood it to be *Taxander*.

This Man, Madam, was one of my Father's Favourites, and
had been long secretly in Love with me.

Ariamenes then inform'd me, that being enflam'd with Rage against these impious Villains, he rose from the Ground, remounted his Horse, and defy'd the two Traytors aloud, threatning them with Death, unless they abandon'd their impious Design.

Taxander made no Answer, but rush'd furiously upon him, and had the Baseness to suffer his wicked Associate to assist him: But the valiant *Ariamenes*, tho' he spoke modestly of his Victory, yet gave me to understand that he had made both the Villains abandon their wicked Enterprize, with their Lives; and that dismounting, in order to see if they were quite dead, he found himself so faint with the Wounds he had received from them both, that he had not Strength to re-mount his Horse; but crawling on, in Hopes of meeting with some Assistance, fainted away at last through Weariness and Loss of Blood.

While he was giving me this Account, the Chariot I had sent for arrived, and having made him such Acknowledgments as the Obligation I had received from him demanded, I caus'd him to get into the Chariot, and sending one with him to acquaint the Prince my Father with all that had happen'd, and the Merit of the valiant Stranger, I returned the same Way I came with my Women, my Thoughts being wholly engross'd by this Unknown.

The Service he had done me filled me with a Gratitude and Esteem for him, which prepar'd my Heart for those tender Sentiments I afterwards entertain'd, to the Ruin of my Repose.

I will not tire your Patience, Madam, with a minute Detail of all the succeeding Passages of my Story; it shall suffice to tell you, That *Ariamenes* was received with extraordinary Marks of Esteem by my Father; that his Cure was soon compleated; and that having vow'd himself to my Service, and declar'd an unalterable Passion for me, I permitted him to love me, and gave him that Share in my Heart, which I fear not all his Infidelities will ever deprive him of.

His Attachment to me was soon suspected by *Taxander*'s Relations, who having secretly vow'd his Ruin, endeavour'd to discover if I had admitted his Addresses, and having made themselves Masters of our Secrets, by means of the Treachery of one of my Women, procur'd Information to be given to my Father of our mutual Passion.

Alas! what Mischiefs did not this fatal Discovery produce: My Father, enrag'd to the last Degree at this Intelligence, confin'd me to my Apartments, and order'd *Ariamenes* to leave his Dominions within three Days.

Spare me, Madam, the Repetition of what pass'd at our last sad Interview, which by large Bribes to my Guards he obtain'd.

His Tears, his Agonies, his Vows of everlasting Fidelity, so sooth'd my Melancholy at parting with him, and persuaded me of his Constancy, that I waited for several Months with perfect Tranquillity for the Performance of the Promise he made me, to do my Father such considerable Services in the War he was engag'd in with one of his Neighbours, as should oblige him to give me to him for his Reward.

But, alas! two Years roll'd on without bringing back the unfaithful *Ariamenes*. My Father died, and my Brother who succeeded him, being about to force me to marry a Prince whom I detested, I secretly quitted the Court, and attended only by this faithful Confidant whom you behold with me, and some few of my trusty Domesticks, I came hither in Search of *Ariamenes*, he having told me this Country was the Place of his Birth.

Polenor, the most prudent and faithful of my Servants, undertook to find out the ungrateful *Ariamenes*, whom yet I was willing to find Excuses for; but all his Enquiries were to no Effect; the Name of *Ariamenes* was not known in this Part of the World.

Tir'd out with unsuccessful Enquiries, I resolv'd to seek out some obscure Place, where I might in secret lament my Misfortunes, and expect the End of them in Death. My Attendants found me out such a Retreat as I wanted, in a neighbouring Village, which they call *Twickenham*,[20] I think, from whence I often make Excursions to this Park, attended only as you see; and here indulge myself in Complaints upon the Cruelty of my Destiny.

The sorrowful *Cynecia* here ended her Story, to which in the Course of her Relation she had given a great many Interruptions through the Violence of her Grief: And *Arabella*, after having said every Thing she could think on to alleviate her Affliction, earnestly entreated her to accept of an Asylum at her House; where she should be treated with all the Respect due to her illustrious Birth.

The afflicted Lady, tho' she respectfully declin'd this Offer, yet express'd a great Desire of commencing a strict Amity with our fair Heroine, who on her Part, made her the most tender Protestations of Friendship.

The Evening being almost clos'd, they parted with great Reluctancy on both Sides; mutually promising to meet in the same Place the next Day.

Cynecia, having enjoin'd her new Friend absolute Secrecy, *Arabella* was under a Necessity of keeping this Adventure to herself. And tho' she long'd to tell Mr. *Glanville*, who came to visit her the next Day, that the Countess was extremely mistaken, when she maintain'd there were no more wandering Princesses in the World, yet the Engagement she had submitted to, kept her silent.

CHAPTER V

A very mysterious Chapter.

Arabella, who impatiently long'd for the Hour of meeting the fair Princess, with whom she was extremely delighted, consulted her Watch so often, and discovered so much Restlessness and Anxiety, that Mr. *Glanville* began to be surpriz'd; and the more, as she peremptorily commanded him not to attend her in her Evening Walk. This Prohibition, which, tho' he durst not dispute, he secretly resolv'd to disobey; and as soon as she set out for the Park with her usual Attendants, he slipp'd out by a Back-door, and keeping her in his Sight, himself unseen, he ventur'd to watch her Motions.

As he had expected to unravel some great Mystery, he was agreeably disappointed to find she continued her Walk in the Park with great Composure; and tho' she was soon join'd by the imaginary Princess, yet conceiving her to be some young Lady, with whom she had commenced an Acquaintance at *Richmond*, his Heart was at Rest; and for fear of displeasing her, he took a contrary Path from that she was in, that he might not meet her, yet resolv'd to stay till he thought she would be inclin'd to return, and then shew himself, and conduct her Home. A Solicitude for which he did not imagine she need be offended.

The two Ladies being met, after reciprocal Compliments, the Princess intreated *Arabella* to relate her Adventures; who not being willing to violate the Laws of Romance, which require an unbounded Confidence upon these Occasions, began very succinctly to recount the History of her Life; which, as she manag'd it, contain'd Events almost as Romantick and Incredible as any in her Romances; winding them up with a Confession that she did not hate Mr. *Glanville*, whom she acknowledg'd to be one of the most faithful and zealous of Lovers.

Cynecia with a Sigh, congratulated her upon the Fidelity of a Lover, who by her Description, was worthy the Place he possess'd in her Esteem: And expressing a Wish, that she could see, unobserv'd by him, this gallant and generous Person, *Arabella*, who that Moment espy'd him at a Distance, yet advancing towards them, told her, with a Blush that overspread all her Face, That her Curiosity might be satisfied in the Manner she wish'd, for yonder, added she, is the Person we have been talking of.

Cynecia, at these Words, looking towards the Place where her fair Friend had directed; no sooner cast her Eyes upon Mr. *Glanville*, than giving a loud Cry, she sunk into the Arms of *Arabella*, who, astonish'd and perplex'd as she was, eagerly held them out to support her.

Finding her in a Swoon, she dispatch'd *Lucy*, who was near her, to look for some Water to throw in her Face; but that Lady, breathing a deep Sigh, open'd her languishing Eyes, and fixing a melancholy Look upon *Arabella*,

Ah! Madam, said she, wonder not at my Affliction and Surprize, since in the Person of your Lover I behold the ungrateful *Ariamenes*.

Oh Heavens! my fair Princess, replied *Arabella*, What is it you say? Is it possible *Glanville* can be *Ariamenes*?

He, cried the afflicted Princess with a disorder'd Accent, He whom I now behold! and whom you call *Glanville*, was once *Ariamenes*, the perjur'd, the ungrateful *Ariamenes*. Adieu, Madam, I cannot bear his Sight; I will hide myself from the World for ever; nor need you fear a Rival or an Enemy in the unfortunate *Cynecia*, who if possible, will cease to love the unfaithful *Ariamenes*, and will never hate the beautiful *Arabella*.

Saying this, without giving her Time to answer, she took hold of her Confidant by the Arm, and went away with so much Swiftness, that she was out of Sight before *Arabella* was enough recover'd from her Astonishment to be able to intreat her Stay.

Our charming Heroine, ignorant till now of the true State of her Heart, was surpriz'd to find it assaulted at once by all the Passions which attend disappointed Love. Grief, Rage, Jealousy, and Despair made so cruel a War in her gentle Bosom, that, unable either to express or to conceal the strong Emotions with which she was agitated, she gave Way to a violent Burst of Tears, leaning her Head upon *Lucy*'s Shoulder, who wept as heartily as her Lady, tho' ignorant of the Cause of her Affliction.

Mr. *Glanville*, who was now near enough to take Notice of her Posture, came running with eager Haste to see what was the Matter; when *Arabella*, rous'd from her Extacy of Grief by the Sound of his Steps, lifted up her Head, and seeing him approach,

Lucy, cried she, trembling with the Violence of her Resentment, Tell that Traitor to keep out of my Sight. Tell him, I forbid him ever to appear before me again. And, tell him, added she, with a Sigh that shook her whole tender Frame, All the Blood in his Body is too little to wash away his Guilt, or to pacify my Indignation.

Then hastily turning away, she ran towards her other Attendants, who were at some Distance; and joining her Women, proceeded directly Home.

Mr. *Glanville*, amaz'd at this Action, was making after her as fast as he could, when *Lucy* crossing in his Way, cried out to him to stop.

My Lady, said she, bid me tell you, Traitor —

Hey day! interrupted *Glanville*, What the Devil does the Girl mean?

Pray, Sir, said she, let me deliver my Message: I shall forget if you speak to me till I have said it all — Stay, let me see, What comes next?

No more Traitor, I hope, said *Glanville*.

No, Sir, said *Lucy*; but there was something about washing in Blood, and you must keep out of her Sight, and not appear before the Nation — Oh dear! I have forgot it half: My Lady was in such a piteous Taking, I forgot it, I believe, as soon as she said it. What shall I do? —

No Matter, said *Glanville*, I'll overtake her, and ask —

No, no, Sir, said *Lucy*, Pray don't do that, Sir, my Lady will be very angry: I'll venture to ask her to tell me over again, and come back and let you know it.

But tell me, reply'd *Glanville*, Was any thing the Matter with your Lady? She was in a piteous Taking, you say.

Oh dear! yes, Sir, said *Lucy*; but I was not bid to say any thing about that. To be sure, my Lady did cry sadly, and sigh'd as if her Heart would break; but I don't know what was the Matter with her.

Well, said *Glanville*, excessively shock'd at this Intelligence, Go to your Lady; I am going Home — You may bring me her Message to my own Apartment.

Lucy did as she was desir'd; and Mr. *Glanville*, impatient as he was to unravel the Mystery, yet dreading lest his Presence should make *Arabella* be guilty of some Extravagance before the Servants who were with her, he follow'd slowly after her, resolving, if possible, to procure a private Interview with the lovely Visionary, for whose Sorrow, tho' he suspected it was owing to some ridiculous Cause, he could not help being affected.

CHAPTER VI

Not much plainer than the former.

Arabella, who had walk'd as fast as her Legs would carry her, got Home before *Lucy* could overtake her, and retiring to her Chamber, gave Way to a fresh Burst of Grief, and bewail'd the Infidelity of *Glanville* in Terms befitting a *Clelia* or *Mandana*.

As soon as she saw *Lucy* enter, she started from her Chair with great Emotion.

Thou comest, said she, I know, to intercede for that ungrateful Man, whose Infidelity I am weak enough to lament: But open not thy Mouth, I charge thee, in his Defence.

No, indeed, Madam, said *Lucy*.

Nor bring me any Account of his Tears, his Desperation, or his Despair, said *Arabella*, since questionless he will feign them all to deceive me.

Here *Glanville*, who had watch'd *Lucy*'s coming, and had follow'd her into *Arabella*'s Apartment, appear'd at the Door.

Oh Heavens! cried *Arabella*, lifting up her fine Eyes, Can it be that this disloyal Man, unaw'd by the Discovery of his Guilt, again presumes to approach me! —

Dearest Cousin, said *Glanville*, What is the Meaning of all this? — How have I disoblig'd you? — What is my Offence? I beseech you, tell me.

＊Ask the inconstant *Ariamenes*, replied *Arabella*, the Offence of the ungrateful *Glanville*. The Betrayer of *Cynecia* can best answer that Question to the Deceiver of *Arabella*. And the Guilt of the one can only be compar'd to the Crimes of the other.

Good God! interrupted Mr. *Glanville* fretting excessively, What am I to understand by all this? On my Soul, Madam, I don't know the Meaning of one Word you say.

Oh Dissembler! said *Arabella*, Is it thus that thou would'st

---

＊ This Enigmatical Way of speaking upon such Occasions, is of great Use in the voluminous *French* Romances; since the Doubt and Confusion it is Cause of, both to the Accus'd and Accuser, gives Rise to a great Number of succeeding Mistakes, and consequently Adventures.

impose upon my Incredulity? Does not the Name of *Ariamenes*
make thee tremble then? And can'st thou hear that of *Cynecia*
without Confusion?

Dear Lady *Bella*, said *Glanville* smiling, What are these
Names to me?

False Man, interrupted *Arabella*, Dost thou presume to sport
with thy Crimes then? Are not the Treacheries of *Ariamenes* the
Crimes of *Glanville*? Could *Ariamenes* be false to the Princess of
Gaul, and can *Glanville* be innocent towards *Arabella*?

Mr. *Glanville*, who had never heard her in his Opinion, talk
so ridiculously before, was so amaz'd at the incomprehensible
Stuff she utter'd with so much Emotion, that he began to fear
her Intellects were really touch'd. This Thought gave him a
Concern that spread itself in a Moment over his Countenance.
He gaz'd on her with a fix'd Attention, dreading, yet wishing
she would speak again; equally divided between his Hopes that
her next Speech would remove his Suspicion, and his Fears,
that it might more confirm them.

Arabella taking Notice of his pensive Posture, turn'd away
her Head, lest, by beholding him, she should relent, and treat
him with less Severity than she had intended; making at the
same Time a Sign to him to be gone.

Indeed, Lady *Bella*, said *Glanville* who understood her perfectly well, I cannot leave you in this Temper. I must know how
I have been so unfortunate as to offend you.

Arabella, no longer able to contain herself, burst into Tears
at this Question: With one Hand she made repeated Signs to
him to be gone, with the other she held her Handkerchief to
her Eyes, vex'd and asham'd of her Weakness.

But Mr. *Glanville*, excessively shock'd at this Sight, instead
of leaving her, threw himself on his Knees before her, and
taking her Hand, which he tenderly prest to his Lips,

Good God! my dearest Cousin, said he, How you distract
me by this Behaviour? Sure something extraordinary must be
the Matter. What can it be that thus afflicts you? — Am I the
Cause of these Tears? — Can I have offended you so much? —
Speak, dear Madam — Let me know my Crime. Yet may I
perish if I am conscious of any towards you —

Disloyal Man, said *Arabella* disengaging her Hand from his, Does then the Crime of *Ariamenes* seem so light in thy Apprehension, that thou can'st hope to be thought innocent by *Arabella*? No, no, ungrateful Man, the unfortunate *Cynecia* shall have no Cause to say, that I will triumph in her Spoils. I myself will be the Minister of her Revenge; and *Glanville* shall suffer for the Crime of *Ariamenes*.

Who the Devil is this *Ariamenes*, cry'd *Glanville* rising in a Passion? And why am I to suffer for his Crime, pray? For Heav'ns Sake, dear Cousin, don't let your Imagination wander thus. Upon my Soul, I don't believe there is any such Person as *Ariamenes* in the World.

Vile Equivocator, said *Arabella*; *Ariamenes*, tho' dead to *Cynecia*, is alive to the deluded *Arabella*. The Crimes of *Ariamenes* are the Guilt of *Glanville*: And if the one has made himself unworthy of the Princess of *Gaul*, by his Perfidy and Ingratitude, the other by his Baseness and Deceit, merits nothing but Contempt and Detestation from *Arabella*.

Frenzy, by my Soul, cry'd *Glanville* mutteringly between his Teeth: This is downright Frenzy. What shall I do? —

Hence, from my Presence, resum'd *Arabella*, false and ungrateful Man; persecute me no more with the hateful Offers of thy Love. From this Moment I banish thee from my Thoughts for ever; and neither as *Glanville* or as *Ariamenes*, will I ever behold thee more.

Stay, dear Cousin, said *Glanville* holding her (for she was endeavouring to rush by him, unwilling he should see the Tears that had overspread her Face as she pronounc'd those Words) hear me, I beg you, but one Word. Who is it you mean by *Ariamenes*? — Is it me? — Tell me, Madam, I beseech you — This is some horrid Mistake — You have been impos'd upon by some villainous Artifice — Speak, dear Lady *Bella* — Is it me you mean by *Ariamenes*? For so your last Words seem'd to hint —

Arabella, without regarding what he said, struggled violently to force her Hand from his: and finding him still earnest to detain her, told him with an enrag'd Voice, That she would call for Help, if he did not unhand her directly.

Poor *Glanville*, at this Menace, submissively dropt her Hand;

and the Moment she was free, she flew out of the Room, and locking herself up in her Closet, sent her Commands to him by one of her Women, whom she call'd to her, to leave her Apartment immediately.

CHAPTER VII

Containing indeed no great Matters, but being a Prelude to greater.

Mr. *Glanville*, who stood fix'd like a Statue in the Place where *Arabella* had left him, was rous'd by this Message, which tho' palliated a little by the Girl that deliver'd it, who was not quite so punctual as *Lucy*, nevertheless fill'd him with extreme Confusion. He obey'd however immediately, and retiring to his own Apartment, endeavoured to recall to his Memory all Lady *Bella* had said.

The Ambiguity of her Stile, which had led him into a Suspicion he had never entertain'd before, her last Words had partly explain'd, if as he understood she did, she meant him by *Ariamenes*. Taking this for granted, he easily conceiv'd some Plot grounded on her Romantick Notions had been laid, to prepossess her against him.

Sir *George*'s Behaviour to her rush'd that Moment into his Thoughts: He instantly recollected all his Fooleries, his History, his Letter, his Conversation, all apparently copied from those Books she was so fond of, and probably done with a View to some other Design upon her.

These Reflections, join'd to his new-awak'd Suspicions, that he was in Love with her, convinc'd him he was the Author of their present Misunderstanding; and that he had impos'd some new Fallacy upon *Arabella*, in order to promote a Quarrel between them.

Fir'd almost to Madness at this Thought, he stamp'd about his Room, vowing Revenge upon Sir *George*, execrating Romances, and cursing his own Stupidity, for not discovering Sir *George* was his Rival, and knowing his plotting Talent, not providing against his Artifices.

His first Resolutions were, to set out immediately for Sir *George*'s Seat, and force him to confess the Part he had acted against him: But a Moment's Consideration convinc'd him, that was not the most probable Place to find him in, since it was much more likely he was waiting the Success of his Schemes in *London*, or perhaps at *Richmond*.

Next to satiating his Vengeance, the Pleasure of detecting him in such a Manner, that he could not possibly deny or palliate his Guilt, was next his Heart.

He resolv'd therefore to give it out, that he was gone to *London*, to make Lady *Bella* believe it was in Obedience to her Commands that he had left her, with a Purpose not to return till he had clear'd his Innocence; but, in Reality, to conceal himself in his own Apartment, and see what Effects his reputed Absence would produce.

Having thus taken his Resolution, he sent for Mr. *Roberts* his Father's Steward, to whose Care he had entrusted Lady *Bella* in her Retirement, and acquainting him with Part of his Apprehensions with Regard to Sir *George*'s Attempts upon his Cousin; he imparted to him his Design of staying conceal'd there, in order to discover more effectually those Attempts, and to preserve Lady *Bella* from any Consequence of them.

Mr. *Roberts* approv'd of his Design; and assur'd him of his Vigilance and Care, both in concealing his Stay, and also in giving him Notice of every Thing that pass'd.

Mr. *Glanville* then wrote a short Billet to *Arabella*, expressing his Grief for her Displeasure, his Departure in Obedience to her Orders, and his Resolution not to appear in her Presence, till he could give her convincing Proofs of his Innocence.

This Letter he sent by *Roberts*, which *Arabella* condescended to read, but would return no Answer.

Mr. *Glanville* then mounting his Horse, which *Roberts* had order'd to be got ready, rode away, and leaving him at a House he sometimes put up at, return'd on Foot, and was let in by Mr. *Roberts* at the Garden-door, and conducted unseen to his Chamber.

While he pass'd that Night and great Part of the next Day, meditating on the Treachery of Sir *George*, and soothing his Uneasiness with the Hopes of Revenge, *Arabella*, no less disquieted, mused on the Infidelity of her Lover, the Despair of *Cynecia*, and the Impossibility of her ever being happy. Then ransacking her Memory for Instances in her Romances of Ladies equally unfortunate with herself, she would sometimes compare herself to one Lady, sometimes to another, adapting their Sentiments, and making Use of their Language in her Complaints.

Great Part of the Day being spent in this Manner, the uneasy Restlessness of her Mind made her wish to see *Cynecia* again. She long'd to ask her a hundred Questions about the unfaithful *Ariamenes*, which the Suddenness of her Departure, and her own Astonishment prevented her from doing, when she made that fatal Discovery, which had cost her so much Uneasiness.

Sometimes a faint Hope would arise in her Mind that *Cynecia* might be mistaken, thro' the great Resemblance that possibly was between *Ariamenes* and *Glanville*.

She remember'd that *Mandana* had been deceiv'd by the Likeness of *Cyrus* to *Spitridates*; and concluded that illustrious Prince inconstant, because *Spitridates*, whom she took for *Cyrus*, saw her carried away, without offering to rescue her.

Dwelling with Eagerness upon this Thought, because it afforded her a temporary Relief from others more tormenting, she resolved to go to the Park, tho' she had but little Hopes of finding *Cynecia* there; supposing it but too probable, that the Disturbance which the Sight, or fancied Sight of *Ariamenes* had given her, would confine her for some Days to her Chamber. Yet however small the Probability was of meeting with her, she could not resist the impatient Desire she felt of going to seek her.

Dispensing therefore with the Attendance of any other Servant but *Lucy*, she left her Apartment, with a Design of resuming her usual Walk, when she was met, at her stepping out of the Door, by Lady *L*——'s three Daughters, (who had visited her during her Residence at *Richmond*) and another young Lady.

These Ladies, who to vary the Scene of their Rural Diversions, were going to cross over to *Twickenham*, and walk there, prest Lady *Bella* to accompany them. Our melancholy Heroine refus'd them at first, but upon their repeated Importunity, recollecting that the Princess of *Gaul* had informed her she resided there, she consented to go, in Hopes some favourable Chance might bring her in their Way, or discover the Place of her Retreat, when she could easily find some Excuse for leaving her Companions, and going to her.

Mr. *Roberts*, who according to his Instructions, narrowly watch'd *Arabella*'s Motions, finding she did not command his Attendance as usual, resolv'd however to be privately of this Party. He had but just Time to run up and acquaint Mr. *Glanville*, and then follow'd the Ladies at a Distance, who taking Boat, pass'd over to *Twickenham*, which he also did as soon as he saw them landed.

CHAPTER VIII

Which acquaints the Reader with two very extraordinary Accidents.

Mr. *Glanville*, who did not doubt but *Roberts* would bring him some Intelligence, sat waiting with anxious Impatience for his Return. The Evening drew on apace, he number'd the Hours, and began to grow uneasy at *Arabella*'s long Stay. His Chamber-Window looking into the Garden, he thought he saw his Cousin, cover'd with her Veil as usual, hasten down one of the Walks; his Heart leap'd at this transient View, he threw up the Sash, and looking out, saw her very plainly strike into a cross Walk, and a Moment after saw Sir *George*, who came out of a little Summer-house, at her Feet. Transported with Rage at this Sight, he snatch'd up his Sword, flew down the Stairs into the Garden, and came running like a Madman up the Walk in which the Lovers were. The Lady observing him first, for Sir *George*'s Back was towards him, shriek'd aloud, and not knowing what she did, ran towards the House, crying for Help, and came back as fast, yet not Time enough to prevent Mischief:

For Mr. *Glanville*, actuated by an irresistible Fury, cried out to Sir *George* to defend himself, who had but just Time to draw his Sword, and make an ineffectual Pass at Mr. *Glanville*, when he receiv'd his into his Body, and fell to the Ground.[21]

Mr. *Glanville* losing his Resentment insensibly, at the Sight of his Rival's Blood, threw down his Sword, and endeavour'd to support him; while the Lady, who had lost her Veil in her running, and to the great Astonishment of Mr. *Glanville*, prov'd to be his Sister, came up to them, with Tears and Exclamations, blaming herself for all that had happen'd. Mr. *Glanville*, with a Heart throbbing with Remorse for what he had done, gaz'd on his Sister with an accusing Look, as she hung over the wounded Baronet with streaming Eyes, sometimes wringing her Hands, then clasping them together in an Agony of Grief.

Sir *George* having Strength enough left to observe her Disorder, and the generous Concern of *Glanville*, who holding him in his Arms, intreated his Sister to send for proper Assistance, Dear *Charles*, said he, you are too kind, I have us'd you very ill, I have deserved my Death from your Hand — You know not what I have been base enough to practise against you — If I can but live to clear your Innocence to Lady *Bella*, and free you from the Consequences of this Action, I shall die satisfy'd —

His Strength failing him at these Words, he fainted away in Mr. *Glanville*'s Arms; who tho' now convinc'd of his Treachery, was extremely shock'd at the Condition he saw him in.

Miss *Glanville* renewing her Tears and Exclamations at this Sight, he was oblig'd to lay Sir *George* gently upon the Ground, and ran to find out somebody to send for a Surgeon, and to help him to convey him into the House.

In his Way he was met by Mr. *Roberts*, who was coming to seek him; and with a Look of Terror and Confusion told him, Lady *Bella* was brought Home extremely ill — that her Life had been in Danger, and that she was but just recover'd from a terrible fainting Fit.

Mr. *Glanville*, tho' greatly alarm'd at this News, forgot not to take all possible Care of Sir *George*; directing *Roberts* to get some Person to carry him into the House, and giving him Orders to procure proper Assistance, flew to Lady *Bella*'s Apartment.

Her Women had just put her to Bed, raving as in a strong Delirium. Mr. *Glanville* approach'd her, and finding she was in a violent Fever, dispatch'd a Man and Horse immediately to Town, to get Physicians, and to acquaint his Father with what had happen'd.

Mr. *Roberts*, upon the Surgeon's Report that Sir *George* was not mortally wounded, came to inform him of this good News, but he found him incapable of listning to him, and in Agonies not to be exprest. 'Twas with Difficulty they forc'd him out of *Arabella*'s Chamber into his own; where throwing himself upon his Bed, he refus'd to see or speak to any Body, till he was told Sir *Charles* and the Physicians were arriv'd.

He then ran eagerly to hear their Opinions of his beloved Cousin, which he soon discover'd, by their significant Gestures and half-pronounc'd Words, to be very bad. They comforted him however, with Hopes that she might recover, and insisting upon her being kept very quiet, oblig'd him to quit the Room. While all the necessary Methods were taken to abate the Violence of the Disease, Sir *Charles*, who had been inform'd by his Steward of his Son's Duel with Sir *George*, was amaz'd to the last Degree at two such terrible Accidents.

Having seen his Son to his Chamber, and recommended him to be patient and compos'd, he went to visit the young Baronet, and was not a little surpriz'd to find his Daughter sitting at his Bed's Head, with all the Appearance of a violent Affliction.

Indeed Miss *Glanville*'s Cares were so wholly engross'd by Sir *George*, that she hardly ever thought of her Cousin *Arabella*, and had just stept into her Chamber while the Surgeons were dressing Sir *George*'s Wound, and renew'd her Attendance upon him as soon as that was over.

Miss *Glanville*, however, thought proper to make some trifling Excuses to her Father for her Solicitude about Sir *George*. And the young Baronet, on whom the Fear of Death produc'd its usual Effects, and made him extremely concern'd for the Errors of his past Life, and very desirous of attoning for them, if possible, assur'd Sir *Charles*, that if he liv'd he would offer himself to his Acceptance for a Son-in-law; declaring that he had basely trifled with the Esteem of his Daughter, but that she had wholly subdued him to herself by her forgiving Tenderness.

Sir *Charles* was very desirous of knowing the Occasion of his Quarrel with his Son, but Sir *George* was too weak to hold any farther Conversation; upon which Sir *Charles*, after a short Visit retir'd, taking Miss *Glanville* along with him.

That the Reader, whose Imagination is no doubt upon the Stretch to conceive the Meaning of these Two extraordinary Incidents, may be left no longer in Suspense, we think proper to explain them both in the following Chapter, that we may in the next pursue our History without Interruption.

CHAPTER IX

Which will be found to contain Information absolutely necessary for the right understanding of this History.

Our fair and afflicted Heroine, accompanied by the Ladies we have mention'd, having cross'd the River, pursu'd their Walk upon its winding Banks, entertaining themselves with the usual Topicks of Conversation among young Ladies, such as their Winnings and Losings at *Brag*,[22] the Prices of Silks, the newest Fashions, the best Hair-Cutter, the Scandal at the last Assembly, &c.

Arabella was so disgusted with this (as she thought) insipid Discourse, which gave no Relief to the Anxiety of her Mind, but added a Kind of Fretfulness and Impatience to her Grief, that she resolv'd to quit them, and with *Lucy*, go in quest of the Princess of *Gaul*'s Retreat.

The Ladies, however, insisted upon her not leaving them; and her Excuse that she was going in Search of an unfortunate Unknown, for whom she had vow'd a Friendship, made them all immediately resolve to accompany her, extremely diverted with the Oddity of the Design, and sacrificing her to their Mirth by sly Leers, Whispers, stifled Laughs, and a thousand little sprightly Sallies, which the disconsolate *Arabella* took no Notice of, so deeply were her Thoughts engag'd.

Tho' she knew not which Way to direct her Steps, yet concluding the melancholy *Cynecia* would certainly chuse some
very solitary Place for her Residence, she rambled about among
the least frequented Paths, follow'd by the young Ladies, who
ardently desir'd to see this unfortunate unknown; tho' at
Arabella's earnest Request, they promis'd not to shew themselves to the Lady, who, she inform'd them, for very urgent
Reasons, was oblig'd to keep herself conceal'd.

Fatiguing as this Ramble was to the delicate Spirits of
Arabella's Companions, they were enabled to support it by the
Diversion her Behaviour afforded them.

Every Peasant she met, she enquir'd if a Beautiful Lady
disguis'd did not dwell somewhere thereabout.

To some she gave a Description of her Person, to others an
Account of the Domesticks that were with her; not forgetting
her Dress, her Melancholy, and the great Care she took to keep
herself conceal'd.

These strange Enquiries, with the strange Language in which
they were made, not a little surpriz'd the good People to whom
she address'd herself, yet mov'd to Respect by the majestick
Loveliness of her Person, they answer'd her in the Negative,
without any Mixture of Scoff and Impertinence.

How unfavourable is Chance, said *Arabella* fretting at the
Disappointment, to Persons who have any Reliance upon it!
This Lady that I have been in Search of so long without Success,
may probably be found by others who do not seek her, whose
Presence she may wish to avoid, yet not be able.

The young Ladies finding it grew late, express'd their Apprehensions at being without any Attendants; and desir'd *Arabella*
to give over her Search for that Day. *Arabella* at this Hint
of Danger, enquir'd very earnestly, If they apprehended any
Attempts to carry them away? And without staying for an
Answer, urg'd them to walk Home as fast as possible, apologizing for the Danger into which she had so indiscreetly drawn
both them and herself; yet added her Hopes, that, if any Attempt
should be made upon their Liberty, some generous Cavalier
would pass by who would rescue them: A Thing so common,
that they had no Reason to despair of it.

Arabella construing the Silence with which her Companions heard these Assurances, into a Doubt of their being so favoured by Fortune, proceeded to inform them of several Instances wherein Ladies met with unexpected Relief and Deliverance from Ravishers.

She mentioned particularly the Rescue of *Statira* by her own Brother, whom she imagin'd for many Years dead; that of the Princess *Berenice* by an absolute Stranger,[23] and many others, whose Names, Characters and Adventures she occasionally run over; all which the young Ladies heard with inconceivable Astonishment. And the Detail had such an Effect upon *Arabella*'s Imagination, bewilder'd as it was in the Follies of Romances, that 'spying three or four Horsemen riding along the Road towards them, she immediately concluded they would be all seiz'd and carried off.

Posses'd with this Belief, she utter'd a loud Cry, and flew to the Water-side, which alarming the Ladies, who could not imagine what was the Matter, they ran after her as fast as possible.

Arabella stop'd when she came to the Water-side, and looking round about, and not perceiving any Boat to waft them over to *Richmond*, a Thought suddenly darted into her Mind, worthy those ingenious Books which gave it Birth.

Turning therefore to the Ladies, who all at once were enquiring the Cause of her Fright;

'Tis now, my fair Companions, said she, with a solemn Accent, that the Destinies have furnish'd you with an Opportunity of displaying in a Manner truly Heroick, the Sublimity of your Virtue, and the Grandeur of your Courage to the World.

The Action we have it in our Power to perform will immortalize our Fame, and raise us to a Pitch of Glory equal to that of the renown'd *Clelia* herself.

Like her, we may expect Statues erected to our Honour: Like her, be propos'd as Patterns to Heroines in ensuing Ages: And like her, perhaps, meet with Sceptres and Crowns for our Reward.

What that beauteous *Roman* Lady perform'd to preserve herself from Violation by the impious *Sextus*,[24] let us imitate to avoid the Violence our intended Ravishers yonder come to offer us.

Fortune, which has thrown us into this Exigence, presents us the Means of gloriously escaping: And the Admiration and Esteem of all Ages to come, will be the Recompence of our noble Daring.

Once more, my fair Companions, If your Honour be dear to you, if an immortal Glory be worth your seeking, follow the Example I shall set you, and equal with me the *Roman Clelia*.

Saying this, she plung'd into the *Thames*, intending to swim over it, as *Clelia* did the *Tyber*.[25]

The young Ladies, who had listened with silent Astonishment at the long Speech she had made them, the Purport of which not one of them understood, scream'd out aloud at this horrid Spectacle, and wringing their Hands, ran backwards and forwards like distracted Persons, crying for Help. *Lucy* tore her Hair, and was in the utmost Agony of Grief, when Mr. *Roberts*, who, as we have said before, kept them always in Sight, having observ'd *Arabella* running towards the Water-side, follow'd them as fast as he could, and came Time enough up to see her frantick Action. Jumping into the River immediately after her, he caught hold of her Gown, and drew her after him to the Shore. A Boat that Instant appearing, he put her into it, senseless, and to all Appearance dead. He and *Lucy* supporting her, they were wafted over in a few Moments to the other Side: Her House being near the River, Mr. *Roberts* carry'd her in his Arms to it; and as soon as he saw her shew Signs of returning Life, left her to the Care of the Women, who made haste to put her into a warm Bed, and ran to find out Mr. *Glanville*, as we have related.

There remains now only to account for Sir *George* and Miss *Glanville*'s sudden Appearance, which happen'd, gentle Reader, exactly as follows.

Miss *Glanville*, having set out pretty late in the Afternoon, with a Design of staying all Night at *Richmond*, as her Chaise drove up *Kew-Lane*,[26] saw one of her Cousin's Women, *Deborah* by Name, talking to a Gentleman, whom, notwithstanding the

Disguise of a Horseman's Coat, and a Hat slouch'd over his Face, she knew to be Sir *George Bellmour*.

This Sight alarming her Jealousy, and renewing all her former Suspicions, that her Cousin's Charms rival'd hers in his Heart, as soon as she alighted, finding *Arabella* was not at Home, she retir'd in great Anguish of Mind to her Chamber, revolving in her Mind every Particular of Sir *George*'s Behaviour to her Cousin in the Country, and finding new Cause for Suspicion in every Thing she recollected, and reflecting upon the Disguise in which she saw him, and his Conference with her Woman, she concluded herself had all along been the Dupe of his Artifice, and her Cousin the real Object of his Love.

This Thought throwing her into an Extremity of Rage, all her tenderest Emotions were lost in the Desire of Revenge. She imagin'd to herself so much Pleasure from exposing his Treachery, and putting it out of his Power to deny it, that she resolv'd, whatever it cost her, to have that Satisfaction.

Supposing therefore *Deborah* was now return'd she rung her Bell, and commanded her Attendance on her in her Chamber.

The stern Brow with which she receiv'd her, frighten'd the Girl, conscious of her Guilt, into a Disposition to confess all, even before she was tax'd with any thing.

Miss *Glanville* saw her Terror, and endeavour'd to heighten it, by entering at once into Complaints and Exclamations against her, threatning to acquaint her Father with her Plots to betray her Lady, and assuring her of a very severe Punishment for her Treachery.

The Girl, terrify'd extremely at these Menaces, begg'd Miss *Glanville*, with Tears, to forgive her, and not to acquaint Sir *Charles* or her Lady, with her Fault; adding, that she would confess all, and never while she liv'd, do such a Thing again.

Miss *Glanville* would make her no Promises, but urg'd her to confess: Upon which *Deborah* sobbing, own'd, That for the Sake of the Presents Sir *George* had made her, she consented to meet him privately from Time to Time, and give him an Account of every Thing that pass'd with Regard to her Lady; not think-ing there was any Harm in it. That according to his Desires, she had constantly acquainted him with all her Lady's Motions,

when, and where she went, how she and Mr. *Glanville* agreed,
and a hundred other Things which he enquir'd about. That that
Day in particular, he had intreated her to procure him the
Means of an Interview with her Lady, if possible; and understanding Mr. *Glanville* was not at *Richmond*, she had let him
privately into the Garden, where she hop'd to prevail upon her
Lady to go.

What, said Miss *Glanville* surpriz'd, Is Sir *George* waiting
for my Cousin in the Garden then?

Yes, indeed, Madam, said *Deborah*: But I'll go and tell him
to wait no longer; and never speak to him again, if your Ladyship will but be pleas'd to forgive me.

Miss *Glanville* having taken her Resolution, not only promis'd *Deborah* her Pardon, but also a Reward, provided she
would contrive it so, that she might meet Sir *George* instead of
her Cousin.

The Girl, having the true Chamber-Maid Spirit of Intrigue
in her, immediately propos'd her putting on one of her Lady's
Veils; which as it was now the Close of the Evening, would
disguise her sufficiently; to which Miss *Glanville*, transported
with the Thoughts of thus having an Opportunity of convincing
Sir *George* of his Perfidy, and reproaching him for it, consented,
and bid her bring it without being observ'd into her Chamber.

Deborah informing her, that Sir *George* was conceal'd in
the Summer-House, as soon as she had equip'd herself with
Arabella's Veil, she went into the Walk that led to it; and Sir
George, believing her to be that Lady, hasten'd to throw himself
at her Feet, and had scarce got through half a Speech he had
study'd for his present Purpose, when Mr. *Glanville* gave a fatal
Interruption to his Heroicks, in the Manner we have already
related.

CHAPTER X

A short Chapter indeed, but full of Matter.

Richmond was now a Scene of the utmost Confusion and
Distress. *Arabella*'s Fever was risen to such a Height, that she
was given over by the Physicians; and Sir *George*'s Wounds,
tho' not judg'd mortal at first, yet by the great Effusion of Blood
had left him in so weak a Condition, that he was thought to be
in great Danger.

Sir *Charles*, almost distracted with the Fears of the Consequences of Sir *George*'s Death, intreated his Son to quit the
Kingdom;[27] but Mr. *Glanville*, protesting he would rather die
than leave *Arabella* in that Illness, he was oblig'd to give Bail
for his Appearance, in case Sir *George* dy'd: This Affair, notwithstanding all Endeavours to prevent it, having made a great
Noise.

Poor Sir *Charles*, opprest as he was with the Weight of all
these Calamities, was yet oblig'd to labour incessantly to keep
up the Spirits of his Son and Daughter. The settled Despair of
the one, and the silent swelling Grief of the other, cut him to
the Heart. He omitted no Arguments his Paternal Affection
suggested to him, to moderate their Affliction. Mr. *Glanville*
often endeavour'd to assume a Composure he was very far
from feeling, in order to satisfy his Father. But Miss *Glanville*,
looking upon herself to be the Cause of Sir *George*'s Misfortune, declar'd, She should be miserable all her Life, if he died.

Arabella in her lucid Intervals, being sensible of her Danger,
prepar'd for Death, with great Piety and Constancy of Mind,
having solemnly assur'd Mr. *Glanville* of her Forgiveness, who
would not at that Time enter into an Explanation of the Affair
which had given her Offence for fear of perplexing her. She
permitted his Presence often in her Chamber, and desir'd with
great Earnestness the Assistance of some worthy Divine in her
Preparations for Death. The Pious and Learned Doctor —— at
Sir *Charles*'s[28] Intimation of his Niece's Desire, came constantly
twice a Day to attend her. Her Fever, by a favourable Crisis,

and the great Skill of her Physicians, left her in a Fortnight; but this violent Distemper had made such a Ravage in her delicate Constitution, and reduc'd her so low that there seem'd very little Probability of her Recovery. Doctor ——, in whom her unfeign'd Piety, her uncommon Firmness of Mind, had created a great Esteem and Tenderness for her, took all Opportunities of comforting, exhorting, and praying by her. The Occasion of her Illness being the Subject of every body's Conversation at *Richmond*, he gently hinted it to her, and urg'd her to explain her Reasons for so extravagant an Action.

In the Divine Frame *Arabella* was then in, this Action appear'd to her rash and vain-glorious, and she acknowledg'd it to be so to her pious Monitor: Yet she related the Motives which induc'd her to it, the Danger she was in of being carry'd away, the Parity of her Circumstances then with *Clelia*, and her emulous Desire of doing as much to preserve her Honour as that renown'd *Roman* Lady did for hers.

The good Doctor was extremely surpriz'd at this Discourse: He was beginning to think her again delirious; but *Arabella* added to this Account such sensible Reasoning on the Nature of that Fondness for Fame, which prompted her to so rash an Undertaking, that the Doctor left her in strange Embarrassment, not knowing how to account for a Mind at once so enlighten'd, and so ridiculous.

Mr. *Glanville*, meeting him as he came out of her Chamber, the Doctor took this Opportunity to acknowledge the Difficulties *Arabella*'s inconsistent Discourse had thrown him into. Mr. *Glanville* taking him into his own Apartment, explain'd the Nature of that seeming Inconsistency, and expatiated at large upon the Disorders Romances had occasion'd in her Imagination; several Instances of which he recounted, and fill'd the Doctor with the greatest Astonishment and Concern. He lamented pathetically the Ruin such a ridiculous Study had brought on so noble a Mind; and assur'd Mr. *Glanville*, he would spare no Endeavours to rescue it from so shocking a Delusion.

Mr. *Glanville* thank'd him for his good Design, with a Transport which his Fears of his Cousin's Danger almost mingled with Tears; and the Doctor and he agreed to expect for some few Days longer an Alteration for the better in the Health of her Body, before he attempted the Cure of her Mind. Mr. *Glanville*'s extreme Anxiety had made him in Appearance neglect the repentant Sir *George*, contenting himself with constantly sending twice a Day to enquire after his Health, but had not yet visited him.

No sooner had the Physicians declared that *Arabella* was no longer in Danger, than his Mind being freed from that tormenting Load of Suspence under which it had labour'd while her Recovery was yet doubtful, he went to Sir *George*'s Chamber, who by reason of his Weakness, tho' he was also upon the Recovery, still kept his Bed.

Sir *George*, tho' he ardently wish'd to see him, yet conscious of the Injuries he had both done and design'd him, could not receive his Visit without extreme Confusion: But entering into the Cause of their Quarrel, as soon as he was able to speak, he freely acknowledg'd his Fault, and all the Steps he had taken to supplant him in *Arabella*'s Affection.

Mr. *Glanville* understanding by this Means, that he had brib'd a young Actress to personate a Princess forsaken by him; and had taught her all that Heap of Absurdity with which she had impos'd upon *Arabella*, as has been related, desir'd only by Way of Reparation, That when his Cousin was in a Condition to be spoken to upon that Subject, he would condescend to own the Fraud to her; which Sir *George* faithfully promising, an Act of Oblivion pass'd on Mr. *Glanville*'s Side for all former Injuries, and a solemn Assurance from Sir *George* of inviolable Friendship for the future. An Assurance, however, which Mr. *Glanville* would willingly have dispens'd with: For tho' not of a vindictive Temper, it was one of his Maxims, That a Man who had once betray'd him, it would be an Error in Policy ever to trust again.

CHAPTER XI

Being in the Author's Opinion, the best Chapter in this History.[29]

The good Divine, who had the Cure of *Arabella*'s Mind greatly at Heart, no sooner perceiv'd that the Health of her Body was almost restor'd, and that he might talk to her without the Fear of any Inconvenience, than he introduce'd the Subject of her throwing herself into the River, which he had before lightly touch'd upon, and still declar'd himself dissatisfy'd with.

Arabella, now more dispos'd to defend this Point than when languishing under the Pressure of Pain and Dejection of Mind, endeavour'd by Arguments founded upon Romantick Heroism, to prove, That it was not only reasonable and just, but also great and glorious, and exactly conformable to the Rules of Heroick Virtue.

The Doctor listen'd to her with a mix'd Emotion, between Pity, Reverence, and Amazement: And tho' in the Performance of his Office he had been accustom'd to accommodate his Notions to every Understanding, and had therefore accumulated a great Variety of Topicks and Illustrations; yet he found himself now engag'd in a Controversy for which he was not so well prepar'd as he imagin'd, and was at a Loss for some leading Principle, by which he might introduce his Reasonings, and begin his Confutation.

Tho' he saw much to praise in her Discourse, he was afraid of confirming her Obstinacy by Commendation: And tho' he also found much to blame, he dreaded to give Pain to a Delicacy he rever'd.

Perceiving however, that *Arabella* was silent, as if expecting his Reply, he resolv'd not to bring upon himself the Guilt of abandoning her to her Mistake, and the Necessity of speaking forc'd him to find something to say.

Tho' it is not easy, Madam, said he, for any one that has the Honour of conversing with your Ladyship to preserve his Attention free to any other Idea, than such as your Discourse tends immediately to impress, yet I have not been able while you was speaking, to refrain from some very mortifying Reflections on the Imperfection of all human Happiness, and the uncertain Consequences of all those Advantages which we think ourselves not only at Liberty to desire, but oblig'd to cultivate.

Tho' I have known some Dangers and Distresses, reply'd *Arabella* gravely, yet I did not imagine myself such a Mirror of Calamity as could not be seen without Concern. If my Life has not been eminently fortunate, it has yet escap'd the great Evils of Persecution, Captivity, Shipwrecks and Dangers, to which many Ladies far more illustrious both by Birth and Merit than myself, have been expos'd. And indeed tho' I have sometimes rais'd Envy, or possibly incurr'd Hatred, yet I have no Reason to believe I was ever beheld with Pity before.

The Doctor saw he had not introduc'd his Discourse in the most acceptable Manner; but it was too late to repent.

Let me not, Madam, said he, be censur'd before I have fully explain'd my Sentiments.

That you have been envy'd, I can readily believe: For who that gives Way to natural Passions has not Reason to envy the Lady *Arabella*? But that you have been hated, I am indeed less willing to think, tho' I know how easily the greater Part of Mankind hate those by whom they are excell'd.

If the Misery of my Condition, reply'd *Arabella*, has been able to excite that Melancholy your first Words seem'd to imply, Flattery will contribute very little towards the Improvement of it. Nor do I expect from the Severity of the Sacerdotal Character, any of those Praises, which I hear perhaps with too much Pleasure, from the rest of the World.

Having been so lately on the Brink of that State, in which all Distinctions but that of Goodness are destroy'd, I have not recover'd so much Levity, but that I would yet rather hear Instructions than Compliments.

If therefore you have observ'd in me any dangerous Tenets, corrupt Passions, or criminal Desires, I conjure you discover me to myself. Let no false Civility restrain your Admonitions. Let me know this Evil which can strike a good Man with Horror, and which I dread the more, as I do not feel it.

I cannot suppose that a Man of your Order would be alarm'd at any other Misery than Guilt: Nor will I think so meanly of him whose Direction I have intreated, as to imagine he can think Virtue unhappy, however overwhelm'd by Disasters or Oppression.

Keep me therefore no longer in Suspence: I expect you will exert the Authority of your Function, and I promise you on my Part, Sincerity and Submission.

The good Man was now compleatly embarras'd; he saw his Meaning mistaken, but was afraid to explain it, lest he should seem to pay Court by a cowardly Retraction: He therefore paus'd a little, and *Arabella* supposed he was studying for such Expressions as might convey Censure without Offence.

Sir, said she, if you are not yet satisfy'd of my Willingness to hear your Reproofs, let me evince my Docility, by intreating you to consider yourself as dispens'd from all Ceremony upon this Occasion.

Your Imaginations, Madam, reply'd the Doctor, are too quick for Language; you conjecture too soon, what you do not wait to hear: and reason upon Suppositions which cannot be allow'd you.

When I mention'd my Reflections upon human Misery, I was far from concluding your Ladyship miserable, compar'd with the rest of Mankind; and though contemplating the abstracted Idea of possible Felicity, I thought that even You might be produc'd as an Instance that it is not attainable in this World, I did not impute the Imperfection of your State to Wickedness, but intended to observe, That though even Virtue be added to external Advantages, there will yet be something wanting to Happiness.

Whoever sees you, Madam, will immediately say, That nothing can hinder you from being the happiest of Mortals, but Want of Power to understand your own Advantages. And whoever is admitted to your Conversation, will be convinc'd that you enjoy all that Intellectual Excellence can confer; yet I see you harrass'd with innumerable Terrors and Perplexities, which never disturb the Peace of Poverty or Ignorance.

I cannot discover, said *Arabella*, how Poverty or Ignorance can be privileg'd from Casualty or Violence, from the Ravisher, the Robber, or the Enemy. I should hope rather that if Wealth and Knowledge can give nothing else, they at least confer Judgment to foresee Danger, and Power to oppose it.

They are not indeed, return'd the Doctor, secur'd against real Misfortunes, but they are happily defended from wild Imaginations: They do not suspect what cannot happen, nor figure Ravishers at a Distance, and leap into Rivers to escape them.

Do you suppose then, said *Arabella*, that I was frighted without Cause?

It is certain, Madam, reply'd he, that no Injury was intended you.

Disingenuity, Sir, said *Arabella*, does not become a Clergyman — I think too well of your Understanding to imagine your Fallacy deceives yourself: Why then should you hope that it will deceive me?

The Laws of Conference require that the Terms of the Question and Answer be the same.

I ask, if I had not Cause to be frighted? Why then am I answer'd that no Injury was intended?

Human Beings cannot penetrate Intentions, nor regulate their Conduct but by exterior Appearances. And surely there was sufficient Appearance of intended Injury, and that the greatest which my Sex can suffer.

Why, Madam, said the Doctor, should you still persist in so wild an Assertion?

A coarse Epithet, said *Arabella*, is no Confutation. It rests upon you to shew, That in giving Way to my Fears, even supposing them groundless, I departed from the Character of a reasonable Person.

I am afraid, replied the Doctor, of a Dispute with your Ladyship, not because I think myself in Danger of Defeat, but because being accustom'd to speak to Scholars with Scholastick Ruggedness, I may perhaps depart in the Heat of Argument, from that Respect to which you have so great a Right, and give Offence to a Person I am really afraid to displease.

But, if you will promise to excuse my Ardour, I will endeavour to prove that you have been frighted without Reason.

I should be content, replied *Arabella*, to obtain Truth upon harder Terms, and therefore intreat you to begin.

The Apprehension of any future Evil, Madam, said the Divine, which is called Terror, when the Danger is from natural Causes, and Suspicion, when it proceeds from a moral Agent, must always arise from Comparison.

We can judge of the Future only by the Past, and have therefore only Reason to fear or suspect, when we see the same Causes in Motion which have formerly produc'd Mischief, or the same Measures taken as have before been preparatory to a Crime.

Thus, when the Sailor in certain Latitudes sees the Clouds rise, Experience bids him expect a Storm. When any Monarch levies Armies, his Neighbours prepare to repel an Invasion.

This Power of Prognostication, may, by Reading and Conversation, be extended beyond our own Knowledge: And the great Use of Books, is that of participating without Labour or Hazard the Experience of others.

But upon this Principle how can you find any Reason for your late Fright.

Has it ever been known, that a Lady of your Rank was attack'd with such Intentions, in a Place so publick, without any Preparations made by the Violator for Defence or Escape?

Can it be imagin'd that any Man would so rashly expose himself to Infamy by Failure, and to the Gibbet by Success?

Does there in the Records of the World appear a single Instance of such hopeless Villany?

It is now Time, Sir, said *Arabella*, to answer your Questions, before they are too many to be remembered.

The Dignity of my Birth can very little defend me against an Insult to which the Heiresses of great and powerful Empires, the Daughters of valiant Princes, and the Wives of renowned Monarchs, have been a thousand Times exposed.

The Danger which you think so great, would hardly repel a determin'd Mind; for in Effect, Who would have attempted my Rescue, seeing that no Knight or valiant Cavalier was within View?

What then should have hinder'd him from placing me in a

Chariot? Driving it into the pathless Desert? And immuring me in a Castle, among Woods and Mountains? Or hiding me perhaps in the Caverns of a Rock? Or confining me in some Island of an immense Lake?

From all this, Madam, interrupted the Clergyman, he is hinder'd by Impossibility.

He cannot carry you to any of these dreadful Places, because there is no such Castle, Desart, Cavern, or Lake.

You will pardon me, Sir, said *Arabella,* if I recur to your own Principles:

You allow that Experience may be gain'd by Books: And certainly there is no Part of Knowledge in which we are oblig'd to trust them more than in Descriptive Geography.

The most restless Activity in the longest Life, can survey but a small Part of the habitable Globe: And the rest can only be known from the Report of others.

Universal Negatives are seldom safe, and are least to be allow'd when the Disputes are about Objects of Sense; where one Position cannot be inferr'd from another.

That there is a Castle, any Man who has seen it may safely affirm. But you cannot with equal Reason, maintain that there is no Castle, because you have not seen it.

Why should I imagine that the Face of the Earth is alter'd since the Time of those Heroines, who experienc'd so many Changes of uncouth Captivity?

Castles indeed, are the Works of Art; and are therefore subject to Decay. But Lakes, and Caverns, and Desarts, must always remain.

And why, since you call for Instances, should I not dread the Misfortunes which happen'd to the divine *Clelia,* who was carry'd to one of the Isles of the *Thrasymenian* Lake?[30]

Or those which befel the beautiful *Candace,* Queen of *Ethiopia,* whom the Pyrate *Zenedorus* wander'd with on the Seas?[31]

Or the Accidents which imbitter'd the Life of the incomparable *Cleopatra?*[32]

Or the Persecutions which made that of the fair *Elisa* miserable?[33]

Or, in fine, the various Distresses of many other fair and

virtuous Princesses: Such as those which happen'd to *Olympia*, *Bellamira*, *Parisatis*, *Berenice*, *Amalazantha*, *Agione*, *Albysinda*, *Placidia*, *Arsinoe*, *Deidamia*,[34] and a thousand others I could mention.

To the Names of many of these illustrious Sufferers I am an absolute Stranger, replied the Doctor.

The rest I faintly remember some Mention of in those contemptible Volumes, with which Children are sometimes injudiciously suffer'd to amuse their Imaginations; but which I little expected to hear quoted by your Ladyship in a serious Discourse.

And though I am very far from catching Occasions of Resentment, yet I think myself at Liberty to observe, That if I merited your Censure for one indelicate Epithet, we have engag'd on very unequal Terms, if I may not likewise complain of such contemptuous Ridicule as you are pleas'd to exercise upon my Opinions by opposing them with the Authority of Scriblers, not only of Fictions, but of senseless Fictions; which at once vitiate the Mind, and pervert the Understanding; and which if they are at any Time read with Safety, owe their Innocence only to their Absurdity.

From these Books, Sir, said *Arabella*, which you condemn with so much Ardour, though you acknowledge yourself little acquainted with them, I have learnt not to recede from the Conditions I have granted, and shall not therefore censure the Licence of your Language, which glances from the Books upon the Readers.

These Books, Sir, thus corrupt, thus absurd, thus dangerous alike to the Intellect and Morals, I have read; and that I hope without Injury to my Judgment, or my Virtue.

The Doctor, whose Vehemence had hinder'd him from discovering all the Consequences of his Position, now found himself entangled, and reply'd in a submissive Tone,

I confess, Madam, my Words imply an Accusation very remote from my Intention.

It has always been the Rule of my Life, not to justify any Words or Actions because they are mine.

I am asham'd of my Negligence, I am sorry for my Warmth,

and intreat your Ladyship to pardon a Fault which I hope never to repeat.

The Reparation, Sir, said *Arabella* smiling, over-balances the Offence, and by thus daring to own you have been in the Wrong, you have rais'd in me a much higher Esteem for you.

Yet I will not pardon you, added she, without enjoining you a Penance for the Fault you own you have committed; and this Penance shall be to prove,

First, That these Histories you condemn are Fictions.

Next, That they are absurd.

And Lastly, That they are Criminal.

The Doctor was pleas'd to find a Reconciliation offer'd upon so very easy Terms, with a Person whom he beheld at once with Reverence and Affection, and could not offend without extreme Regret.

He therefore answered with a very chearful Composure:

To prove those Narratives to be Fictions, Madam, is only difficult, because the Position is almost too evident for Proof.

Your Ladyship knows, I suppose to what Authors these Writings are ascrib'd?

To the *French* Wits of the last Century, said *Arabella*.

And at what Distance, Madam, are the Facts related in them from the Age of the Writer?

I was never exact in my Computation, replied *Arabella*; but I think most of the Events happen'd about two thousand Years ago.

How then, Madam, resum'd the Doctor, could these Events be so minutely known to Writers so far remote from the Time in which they happened?

By Records, Monuments, Memoirs, and Histories, answered the Lady.

But by what Accident, then, said the Doctor smiling, did it happen these Records and Monuments were kept universally secret to Mankind till the last Century?

What brought all the Memoirs of the remotest Nations and earliest Ages only to *France*?

Where were they hidden that none could consult them but a few obscure Authors?

And whither are they now vanished again that they can be found no more?

Arabella having sat silent a while, told him, That she found his Questions very difficult to be answer'd; and that though perhaps the Authors themselves could have told whence they borrowed their Materials, she should not at present require any other Evidence of the first Assertion:

But allow'd him to suppose them Fictions, and requir'd now that he should shew them to be absurd.

Your Ladyship, return'd he, has, I find, too much Understanding to struggle against Demonstration, and too much Veracity to deny your Convictions; therefore some of the Arguments by which I intended to shew the Falshood of these Narratives may be now used to prove their Absurdity.

You grant them, Madam, to be Fictions?

Sir, interrupted *Arabella* eagerly, You are again infringing the Laws of Disputation.

You are not to confound a Supposition of which I allow you only the present Use, with an unlimited and irrevocable Concession.

I am too well acquainted with my own Weakness to conclude an Opinion false, merely because I find myself unable to defend it.

But I am in haste to hear the Proof of the other Positions, not only because they may perhaps supply what is deficient in your Evidence of the first, but because I think it of more Importance to detect Corruption than Fiction.

Though indeed Falshood is a Species of Corruption, and what Falshood is more hateful than the Falshood of History.

Since you have drawn me back, Madam, to the first Question, returned the Doctor, Let me know what Arguments your Ladyship can produce for the Veracity of these Books.

That there are many Objections against it, you yourself have allowed, and the highest moral Evidence of Falshood appears when there are many Arguments against an Assertion, and none for it.

Sir, replied *Arabella*, I shall never think that any Narrative, which is not confuted by its own Absurdity, is without one Argument at least on its Side; there is a Love of Truth in the human Mind, if not naturally implanted, so easily obtained from Reason and Experience, that I should expect it universally to prevail where there is no strong Temptation to Deceit; we hate to be deceived, we therefore hate those that deceive us; we desire not to be hated, and therefore know that we are not to deceive. Shew me an equal Motive to Falshood, or confess that every Relation has some Right to Credit.

This may be allowed, Madam, said the Doctor, when we claim to be credited, but that seems not to be the Hope or Intention of these Writers.

Surely Sir, replied *Arabella*, you must mistake their Design; he that writes without Intention to be credited, must write to little Purpose; for what Pleasure or Advantage can arise from Facts that never happened? What Examples can be afforded by the Patience of those who never suffered, or the Chastity of those who were never solicited? The great End of History, is to shew how much human Nature can endure or perform. When we hear a Story in common Life that raises our Wonder or Compassion, the first Confutation stills our Emotions, and however we were touched before, we then chase it from the Memory with Contempt as a Trifle, or with Indignation as an Imposture. Prove, therefore, that the Books which I have hitherto read as Copies of Life, and Models of Conduct, are empty Fictions, and from this Hour I deliver them to Moths and Mould; and from this Time forward consider their Authors as Wretches who cheated me of those Hours I ought to have dedicated to Application and Improvement, and betrayed me to a Waste of those Years in which I might have laid up Knowledge for my future Life.

Shakespear, said the Doctor, calls just Resentment the Child of Integrity,[35] and therefore I do not wonder, that what Vehemence the Gentleness of your Ladyship's Temper allows, should be exerted upon this Occasion. Yet though I cannot forgive these Authors for having destroyed so much valuable Time, yet I cannot think them intentionally culpable, because I cannot believe they expected to be credited. Truth is not always injured by Fiction. An admirable* Writer of our own Time, has found

* *Richardson.*

the Way to convey the most solid Instructions, the noblest
Sentiments, and the most exalted Piety, in the pleasing Dress of
a* Novel, and, to use the Words of the greatest† Genius in the
present Age, "Has taught the Passions to move at the Command
of Virtue."[36] The Fables of *Æsop*, though never I suppose
believed, yet have been long considered as Lectures of moral
and domestic Wisdom, so well adapted to the Faculties of Man,
that they have been received by all civilized Nations; and the
Arabs themselves have honoured his Translator with the Appellation of *Locman* the Wise.[37]

The Fables of *Æsop*, said *Arabella*, are among those of which
the Absurdity discovers itself, and the Truth is comprised in the
Application; but what can be said of those Tales which are told
with the solemn Air of historical Truth, and if false convey no
Instruction?

That they cannot be defended, Madam, said the Doctor, it
is my Purpose to prove, and if to evince their Falshood be
sufficient to procure their Banishment from your Ladyship's
Closet, their Day of Grace is near an End. How is any oral, or
written Testimony, confuted or confirmed?

By comparing it, says the Lady, with the Testimony of others,
or with the natural Effects and standing Evidence of the Facts
related, and sometimes by comparing it with itself.

If then your Ladyship will abide by this last, returned he,
and compare these Books with antient Histories, you will not
only find innumerable Names, of which no Mention was ever
made before, but Persons who lived in different Ages, engaged
as the Friends or Rivals of each other. You will perceive that
your Authors have parcelled out the World at Discretion,
erected Palaces, and established Monarchies wherever the Conveniency of their Narrative required them, and set Kings and
Queens over imaginary Nations. Nor have they considered
themselves as invested with less Authority over the Works of
Nature, than the Institutions of Men; for they have distributed
Mountains and Desarts, Gulphs and Rocks, wherever they

* Clarissa.
† The Author of the Rambler.

wanted them, and whenever the Course of their Story required an Expedient, raised a gloomy Forest, or overflowed the Regions with a rapid Stream.

I suppose, said *Arabella*, you have no Intention to deceive me, and since, if what you have asserted be true, the Cause is undefensible, I shall trouble you no longer to argue on this Topic, but desire now to hear why, supposing them Fictions, and intended to be received as Fictions, you censure them as absurd?

The only Excellence of Falshood, answered he, is its Resemblance to Truth; as therefore any Narrative is more liable to be confuted by its Inconsistency with known Facts, it is at a greater Distance from the Perfection of Fiction; for there can be no Difficulty in framing a Tale, if we are left at Liberty to invert all History and Nature for our own Conveniency. When a Crime is to be concealed, it is easy to cover it with an imaginary Wood. When Virtue is to be rewarded, a Nation with a new Name may, without any Expence of Invention, raise her to the Throne. When *Ariosto*[38] was told of the Magnificence of his Palaces, he answered, that the Cost of poetical Architecture was very little; and still less is the Cost of Building without Art, than without Materials. But their historical Failures may be easily passed over, when we consider their physical or philosophical Absurdities; to bring Men together from different Countries does not shock with every inherent or demonstrable Absurdity, and therefore when we read only for Amusement, such Improprieties may be born: But who can forbear to throw away the Story that gives to one Man the Strength of Thousands; that puts Life or Death in a Smile or a Frown; that recounts Labours and Sufferings to which the Powers of Humanity are utterly unequal; that disfigures the whole Appearance of the World, and represents every Thing in a Form different from that which Experience has shewn. It is the Fault of the best Fictions, that they teach young Minds to expect strange Adventures and sudden Vicissitudes, and therefore encourage them often to trust to Chance. A long Life may be passed without a single Occurrence that can cause much Surprize, or produce any unexpected Consequence of great Importance; the Order of the

World is so established, that all human Affairs proceed in a regular Method, and very little Opportunity is left for Sallies or Hazards, for Assault or Rescue; but the Brave and the Coward, the Sprightly and the Dull, suffer themselves to be carried alike down the Stream of Custom.

Arabella, who had for some Time listened with a Wish to interrupt him, now took Advantage of a short Pause. I cannot imagine, Sir, said she, that you intend to deceive me, and therefore I am inclined to believe that you are yourself mistaken, and that your Application to Learning has hindered you from that Acquaintance with the World, in which these Authors excelled. I have not long conversed in Public, yet I have found that Life is subject to many Accidents. Do you count my late Escape for nothing? Is it to be numbered among daily and cursory Transactions, that a Woman flies from a Ravisher into a rapid Stream?

You must not, Madam, said the Doctor, urge as an Argument the Fact which is at present the Subject of Dispute.

Arabella blushing at the Absurdity she had been guilty of, and not attempting any Subterfuge or Excuse, the Doctor found himself at Liberty to proceed:

You must not imagine, Madam, continued he, that I intend to arrogate any Superiority, when I observe that your Ladyship must suffer me to decide, in some Measure authoritatively, whether Life is truly described in those Books; the Likeness of a Picture can only be determined by a Knowledge of the Original. You have yet had little Opportunity of knowing the Ways of Mankind, which cannot be learned but from Experience, and of which the highest Understanding, and the lowest, must enter the World in equal Ignorance. I have lived long in a public Character, and have thought it my Duty to study those whom I have undertaken to admonish or instruct. I have never been so rich as to affright Men into Disguise and Concealment, nor so poor as to be kept at a Distance too great for accurate Observation. I therefore presume to tell your Ladyship, with great Confidence, that your Writers have instituted a World of their own, and that nothing is more different from a human Being, than Heroes or Heroines.

I am afraid, Sir, said *Arabella*, that the Difference is not in Favour of the present World.

That, Madam, answered he, your own Penetration will enable you to judge when it shall have made you equally acquainted with both: I have no Desire to determine a Question, the Solution of which will give so little Pleasure to Purity and Benevolence.

The Silence of a Man who loves to praise is a Censure sufficiently severe, said the Lady. May it never happen that you should be unwilling to mention the Name of *Arabella*. I hope wherever Corruption prevails in the World, to live in it with Virtue, or, if I find myself too much endanger'd, to retire from it with Innocence. But if you can say so little in Commendation of Mankind, how will you prove these Histories to be vicious, which if they do not describe real Life, give us an Idea of a better Race of Beings than now inhabit the World.

It is of little Importance, Madam, replied the Doctor, to decide whether in the real or fictitious Life, most Wickedness is to be found. Books ought to supply an Antidote to Example, and if we retire to a Contemplation of Crimes, and continue in our Closets to inflame our Passions, at what time must we rectify our Words, or purify our Hearts? The immediate Tendency of these Books which your Ladyship must allow me to mention with some Severity, is to give new Fire to the Passions of Revenge and Love; two Passions which, even without such powerful Auxiliaries, it is one of the severest Labours of Reason and Piety to suppress, and which yet must be suppressed if we hope to be approved in the Sight of the only Being whose Approbation can make us happy. I am afraid your Ladyship will think me too serious. I have already learned too much from you, said *Arabella*, to presume to instruct you, yet suffer me to caution you never to dishonour your sacred Office by the Lowliness of Apologies. Then let me again observe, resumed he, that these Books soften the Heart to Love, and harden it to Murder. That they teach Women to exact Vengeance, and Men to execute it; teach Women to expect not only Worship, but the dreadful Worship of human Sacrifices. Every Page of these Volumes is filled with such extravagance of Praise, and expressions of Obedience as one human Being ought not to hear from another; or with Accounts of Battles, in which thousands are slaughtered for no other Purpose than to gain a Smile from the haughty Beauty, who sits a calm Spectatress of the Ruin and Desolation, Bloodshed and Misery, incited by herself.

It is impossible to read these Tales without lessening part of that Humility, which by preserving in us a Sense of our Alliance with all Human Nature, keeps us awake to Tenderness and Sympathy, or without impairing that Compassion which is implanted in us as an Incentive to Acts of Kindness. If there be any preserved by natural Softness, or early Education, from learning Pride and Cruelty, they are yet in danger of being betrayed to the Vanity of Beauty, and taught the Arts of Intrigue.

Love, Madam, is, you know, the Business, the sole Business of Ladies in Romances. *Arabella*'s Blushes now hinder'd him from proceeding as he had intended. I perceive, continued he, that my Arguments begin to be less agreeable to your Ladyship's Delicacy, I shall therefore insist no longer upon false Tenderness of Sentiment, but proceed to those Outrages of the violent Passions, which, though not more dangerous, are more generally hateful.

It is not necessary, Sir, interrupted *Arabella*, that you strengthen by any new Proof a Position which when calmly considered cannot be denied; my Heart yields to the Force of Truth, and I now wonder how the Blaze of Enthusiastic Bravery, could hinder me from remarking with Abhorrence the Crime of deliberate unnecessary Bloodshed.

I begin to perceive that I have hitherto at least trifled away my Time, and fear that I have already made some Approaches to the Crime of encouraging Violence and Revenge. I hope, Madam, said the good Man with Horror in his Looks, that no Life was ever lost by your Incitement. *Arabella* seeing him thus moved, burst into Tears, and could not immediately answer. Is it possible, cried the Doctor, that such Gentleness and Elegance should be stained with Blood? Be not too hasty in your Censure, said *Arabella*, recovering herself, I tremble indeed to think how nearly I have approached the Brink of Murder, when I thought myself only consulting my own Glory; but whatever I suffer, I will never more demand or instigate Vengeance, nor consider my Punctilios[39] as important enough to be ballanced against Life.

The Doctor confirmed her in her new Resolutions, and thinking Solitude was necessary to compose her Spirits after the Fatigue of so long a Conversation, he retired to acquaint Mr. *Glanville* with his Success, who in the Transport of his Joy was almost ready to throw himself at his Feet, to thank him for the Miracle, as he called it, that he had performed.

CHAPTER XII

In which the History is concluded.

Mr. *Glanville*, who fancied to himself the most ravishing Delight from conversing with his lovely Cousin, now recovered to the free Use of all her noble Powers of Reason, would have paid her a Visit that Afternoon, had not a Moment's Reflection convinced him that now was the Time, when her mind was labouring under the Force of Conviction, to introduce the repentant Sir *George* to her, who by confessing the ridiculous Farce he had invented to deceive her, might restore him to her good Opinion, and add to the Doctor's solid Arguments the poignant Sting of Ridicule which she would then perceive she had incurred.

Sir *George* being now able to leave his Chamber, and *Arabella* well enough recovered to admit a Visit in hers, Mr. *Glanville* intreated his Father to wait on her, and get Permission for Sir *George* to attend her upon a Business of some Consequence. Sir *Charles* no sooner mentioned this Request, than *Arabella* after a little Hesitation complied with it. As she had been kept a Stranger to all the Particulars of Mr. *Glanville*'s Quarrels with the young Baronet, her Thoughts were a little perplex'd concerning the Occasion of this Visit, and her Embarrassment was considerably increased by the Confusion which she perceived in the Countenance of Sir *George*. It was not without some Tokens of a painfully supprest Reluctance that Sir *George* consented to perform his Promise, when Mr. *Glanville* claim'd it, but the Disadvantages that would attend his Breach of it, dejected and humbled as he now was, presenting themselves in a forcible manner to his Imagination, confirmed his wavering Resolutions. And since he found himself obliged to be his own Accuser, he endeavoured to do it with the best Grace he could. Acknowledging therefore to Lady *Bella* all the Artifices her Deception by Romances had given him Encouragement to use upon her, and explaining very explicitly the last with relation to the pretended Princess of *Gaul*, he submissively asked her Pardon for the Offence it would now give her, as well as for the Trouble it had formerly.

Arabella struck with inconceivable Confusion, having only bowed her Head to his Apology, desired to be left alone, and continued for near two Hours afterwards wholly absorb'd in the most disagreeable Reflections on the Absurdity of her past Behaviour, and the Contempt and Ridicule to which she now saw plainly she had exposed herself. The Violence of these first Emotions having at length subsided, she sent for Sir *Charles*, and Mr. *Glanville*, and having with a noble Ingenuity expatiated upon the Follies her vitiated Judgment had led her into, she apologized to the first, for the frequent Causes she had given him of Uneasiness; and, turning to Mr. *Glanville*, whom she beheld with a Look of mingled Tenderness and Modesty, To give you myself, said she with all my remaining Imperfections, is making you but a poor Present in return for the Obligations your generous Affection has laid me under to you; yet since I am so happy as to be desired for a Partner for Life by a Man of your Sense and Honour, I will endeavour to make myself as worthy as I am able of such a favourable Distinction.

Mr. *Glanville* kissed the Hand she gave him with an emphatic Silence, while Sir *Charles*, in the most obliging Manner imaginable, thanked her for the Honour she conferred both on himself and Son by this Alliance.

Sir *George*, entangled in his own Artifices, saw himself under a Necessity of confirming the Promises he had made to Miss

Glanville during his Fit of Penitence, and was accordingly married to that young Lady, at the same Time that Mr. *Glanville* and *Arabella* were united.

We chuse, Reader, to express this Circumstance, though the same, in different Words, as well to avoid Repetition, as to intimate that the first mentioned Pair were indeed only married in the common Acceptation of the Word; that is, they were privileged to join Fortunes, Equipages,[40] Titles, and Expence; while Mr. *Glanville* and *Arabella* were united, as well in these, as in every Virtue and laudable Affection of the Mind.

FINIS.

Notes

The following titles are found throughout the Notes:

Artamenes   Madeleine de Scudéry, *Artamenes; or, the Grand
             Cyrus. That Excellent Romance* (1690–91)
Cassandra   Gauthier de Coste de la Calprenède, *Cassandra: the
             fam'd Romance* (1652)
Clarissa   Samuel Richardson, *Clarissa; Or the History of a
             Young Lady* (1747–9), 8 vols.
Clelia   Scudéry, *Clelia, an excellent new Romance* (1678)
Cleopatra   La Calprenède, *Hymen's Praeludia or Love's Master-
             peice. Being That so much admired Romance, intituled
             Cleopatra* (1674)
Pharamond   La Caprenède, *Pharamond: or, the History of France.
             A fam'd Romance* (1677)
OED   *Oxford English Dictionary*

[DEDICATION]

1.   *Earl of MIDDLESEX*: Charles Sackville, Earl of Middlesex
     (1711–69), later second Duke of Dorset. Variously described as
     'a lover of learning, and a patron of learned men' (*Gentleman's
     Magazine* 39 (1769), p. 54) and 'a dissolute and extravagant
     man of fashion' (*Dictionary of National Biography*), he had
     presented an ode written by Lennox to the Princess of Wales on
     her birthday in 1750. It is generally assumed, on internal evi-
     dence, that the dedication to the Earl of Middlesex was written
     by Samuel Johnson, as James Boswell first claimed (though he
     erroneously cited the year of publication as 1762; *The Life of
     Samuel Johnson* (1791; 1811), vol. 1, p. 340).

VOLUME I

BOOK I

1. *Cervantes*: Miguel de Cervantes (1547–1616), Spanish novelist, dramatist and poet, whose reputation rests almost exclusively on his novel *Don Quixote* (1605, 1615). It tells the story of Alonso Quijano, a gaunt, kindly country gentleman who lives in the region of La Mancha. His sense of reality severely impaired as a result of reading chivalric romances, he believes it is his duty to redress the wrongs of the whole world. Changing his name to Don Quixote de la Mancha, he is knighted by an innkeeper, whose miserable abode he mistakes for a castle. He later asks an ignorant rustic named Sancho Panza to be his squire, and together they set out on their quest – Don Quixote riding a bony old nag named Rocinante. Quixote's over-excited imagination persuades him that windmills are giants, flocks of sheep armies and galley-slaves oppressed gentlemen, but after many fruitless battles he returns home. Tired and disillusioned, shortly before his death he renounces all books of knight-errantry. Although the novel is generally regarded as a satire of exaggerated chivalric romances, it is seen by some as an ironic tale of an idealist frustrated and mocked in a materialist society. By the eighteenth century, quixotism had become a by-word for an innocent or uninformed idealism. In his review of *The Female Quixote*, Henry Fielding identifies five points in which Lennox's novel surpasses its model, four points in which Cervantes' text is superior and some points of equality; he thought that Arabella's gender was the novel's greatest strength, because it was more probable that a young girl rather than an elderly gentleman would be 'subverted by her reading Romances' ('The Covent-Garden Journal' (see Introduction note 20), p. 161).

2. *presided at the Council*: Founded in the fourteenth century, the Privy Council was a group of royal advisers who exercised great power during the sixteenth and seventeenth centuries (the forerunner of the Cabinet). It dealt with matters of state, and members sat upon the bench at sessions of the courts. As Lord President of the Privy Council, the Marquis would indeed have been one of the most powerful men in 'the whole Kingdom'.

3. *The most laborious Endeavours . . . Epitome of Arcadia*: Alluding to the English garden style of artful simplicity, which is implicitly contrasted to the formal ornateness of French gardens.

Similarly, Arabella's excesses are tied to her reading of French romances. Antagonism to things French was a significant aspect of British nationality throughout the eighteenth century, and was fostered by several prolonged military conflicts, including the War of the Austrian Succession (1740–48), King George's War (1744–8), the American part of the War of the Austrian Succession and the third of four French and Indian wars. Arcadia was a district of the Greek Peloponnesus, the home of pastoral simplicity and happiness, according to Virgil.

4. *Arabella*: The name is not unusual in eighteenth-century fiction: Clarissa's sister is an Arabella (Richardson, *Clarissa*), as is the Fool of Quality's wife (Henry Brooke, *The Fool of Quality* (1765–70)) and the Vicar of Wakefield's daughter-in-law (Oliver Goldsmith, *The Vicar of Wakefield* (1766)). But Wendy Motooka ('Coming to a Bad End', *Eighteenth-Century Fiction* 8.2 (1996), pp. 253–5) suggests that Lennox may have had in mind the Princess Arabella of England, whom she mentions as a potential bride for Henry the Great of France in a piece in the *Lady's Museum* (1760–61): she was related to the Lennox family, which suggests something of Lennox's investment in her romance heroine.

5. *perfect Mistress of the French and Italian Languages*: Arabella is an early example of the skills promoted by eighteenth-century conduct books for women. Hester Chapone, for example, claimed that 'Dancing and the knowledge of the French tongue are now so universal that they cannot be dispensed with in the education of a gentlewoman ... Italian would be easily learnt after French'; she found study of classical languages incompatible with femininity and unnecessary, 'since the English, French, or Italian tongues afford tolerable translations of all the most valuable productions of antiquity, besides the multitude of original authors which they furnish' (*Letters on the Improvement of the Mind, addressed to a Young Lady* (1773), in Vivien Jones, ed., *Women in the Eighteenth Century: Constructions of Femininity* (1990), pp. 104–5). For Chapone, see Introduction, note 4.

6. *great Store of Romances ... very bad Translations*: Though this was a common opinion, it was not necessarily accurate; many French romances were translated into English in the seventeenth century by Sir Charles Cotteral and John Davies, among others, and achieved great popularity.

7. *Singularity of her Dress*: The first of many references to Arabella's sartorial singularity; see the Introduction for discussion of the

heroine's 'cross-historical' dressing. Arabella would have been expected to wear a dress with a hoop and a tight bodice, and wide-brimmed hat to attend church.

8. *took their Places behind her*: According to the rules of social decorum, servants were expected to sit in the back of the church.

9. *Sarsenet Hood ... Veil*: 'Sarsenet is a very fine and soft silk material made both plain and twilled, in various colours' (*OED*). It was distinctly out of fashion to wear a veil and thus marks Arabella as being out of touch with the present day. Arabella copies the fashion from Mandana and other heroines of romance (cf. *Artamenes, Cleopatra*).

10. *called her favourite Woman ... confided her most secret Thoughts*: Arabella follows romance conventions in confiding in her personal servant, but female conduct literature of the period explicitly advised against making confidantes of one's servants for such relationships transgressed class boundaries, spoiled the servants and debased the mistress (see John Gregory, *A Father's Legacy to his Daughters* (1774), in *The Young Lady's Pocket Library, or Parental Monitor* (1790), ed. Vivien Jones (1995); p. 29).

11. *a couple of Guineas*: English gold coins issued from 1663 to 1813; the guinea was fixed in 1717 at 21 shillings (that is, one pound and one shilling).

12. *Master of no great Elegance in Letter-writing*: In this lack of skill, Hervey resembles Solmes, Clarissa's semi-literate suitor in Richardson's *Clarissa*, which was the most widely read novel of the period.

13. *Toilet*: A 'toilet-table' or 'dressing-table'; 'a table on which articles are placed that are required for or used in dressing' (*OED*).

14. *Closet*: 'A room for privacy or retirement; a private room; an inner chamber' (*OED*). Whereas decorum and custom would allow the Marquis and close family friends like Glanville to see Arabella in her 'Chamber' or 'Apartment', it was considered a breach of her privacy, and hence of decorum, if they were to 'penetrate' into her 'Closet' (see Book II, Chapter I).

15. *the only Diversion she was allowed*: Horseriding was an acceptable leisure pursuit for upper-class women, as evidenced by many portraits of women and horses; see note 17, Book IV for examples. As the century progressed, it was advocated as a healthy activity for middle-class women (see Gregory, *Father's Legacy*, p. 20).

16. *Hanger*: 'A kind of short sword, originally hung from the belt' (*OED*).

17. *Punctuality*: 'Minuteness; preciseness; circumstantialness' (*OED*).

18. *an Air very different from an Oroondates*: A model of physical and intellectual perfection, Oroondates, prince of Scythia, is the central character in *Cassandra*. Oroondates takes on the disguise of a gardener to be near Statira (who also goes by the name of Cassandra), the woman he loves, after she has been imprisoned by Alexander (*Cassandra*, I, iv). As an archetypal romantic hero, he is often mentioned by eighteenth-century authors, who seem to expect their readers to recognize the allusion.

19. *he was only going to make away with some of the Carp*: Ponds in the landscaped gardens surrounding stately homes in the country were often stocked with fish such as carp to provide a constant supply of fresh fish for the family. Edward is therefore stealing from the Marquis's larder, so to speak: hence the head gardener's stern response to Edward's 'evil Designs'. Poaching was a highly contentious issue at the time. Only persons who met specified property qualifications, essentially gentlemen and the aristocracy, could legally hunt game (such as deer, rabbits or pheasants), and any infringement of these rights was regarded as an attack on their property. For the poor, however, poaching was often a dire necessity. Because of the eighteenth-century enclosure movement many small farmers lost their land and became labourers, with no food supply of their own. They saw poaching as a compensation to which they were entitled – it was a 'social' crime, which most people did not regard as a crime at all.

20. *saluting*: Giving a formal kiss of greeting.

21. *Cavalier*: A gentleman attending upon or escorting a lady, a 'gallant'.

22. *The Heroines . . . short Absence*: In fact, romance heroines rarely condescend to embrace their admirers, and only do so at moments of great emotion and sadness (cf. *Cleopatra*, II, iii).

23. *Billet*: A short letter or note.

24. *Basilisk*: 'A fabulous reptile, also called a *cockatrice*, alleged to be hatched by a serpent from a cock's egg; ancient authors stated that its hissing drove away all other serpents, and that its breath, and even its look, was fatal' (*OED*).

25. *any Heroine that voluntarily left her Father's House, however persecuted she might be*: An ironic reference to Richardson's beleaguered heroine. Clarissa, as Lennox's first readers would remember, *did* leave her father's house, and was suspected of

eloping with what Arabella calls 'a favoured Lover'. Her flight has tragic consequences, culminating in her rape and death.

26. *resent*: 'To feel or experience (joy, sorrow, pain, etc.)' (*OED*), frequently used in romances in this sense, and as such, one of the peculiarities of Arabella's speech (highlighted by the use of italics).

27. *he is certainly not unworthy of you, tho' he has not a Title*: Glanville is by no means middle class, but his class status is beneath that of Arabella, the daughter of a marquis. Arabella, of course, is not concerned with his title but rather with his ignorance of romances and romance conventions.

28. *My first Wish ... is to live single*: Arabella repeats Clarissa's oft-repeated wish for a single life over an enforced marriage.

29. *affect*: 'Be drawn to, have affection or liking for; to take to, be fond of, show preference for; to fancy, like, or love' (*OED*).

30. *Statira, Parisatis, Clelia, Mandana*: Statira and Parisatis are the daughters of the king of Persia in *Cassandra*. Statira is also one of the heroines of the play *The Rival Queens; or, The Death of Alexander the Great* (1677) by Nathanial Lee, often revived in the eighteenth century. Clelia is the eponymous heroine of *Clelia*, and Mandana is the princess beloved by Artamenes in *Artamenes*. Statira and Clelia are invoked as models by the precocious eleven-year-old heroine at the beginning of Lennox's first novel, *The Life of Harriot Stuart* (1750).

31. *Artaxerxes ... Lover of Clelia*: Artaxerxes, prince of Persia, is a leading character in *Cassandra*. Clelia, the daughter of Clelius, had several virtuous lovers, but the lover referred to here is the one who finally won her heart, Aronces.

32. *Tiribases, Artaxes*: A typical romance villain, the treacherous Tiribasus appears in *Cleopatra*, notably in the story of Candace, queen of Ethiopia (III, i and ii). Artaxes is the corrupt and mendacious opponent of the eponymous hero in *Artamenes* (see I, i and III, ii).

33. *Thus Mazares ... his adored Mistress*: In *Artamenes*, Mazares is one of Mandana's abductors. When he repents his crime, Mandana forces him to join his rival, Cyrus, to test the sincerity of his repentance and to regain her esteem.

34. *Oroondates ... commanded him to live*: Oroondates, prince of Scythia, is in love with Princess Statira of Persia. Because the two states are at war, Oroondates visits his beloved at the Persian court disguised as Orontes, prince of the Massagetes. When his secret love for Statira causes his illness, he reveals the truth to the Princess. Because Orontes is a mere vassal prince, Statira is deeply

offended by this revelation and orders Orontes/Oroondates to
abstain from further impudence. Hereupon Oroondates' condition worsens and it is at this point that he delivers the soliloquy
from which Glanville quotes in the following scene (cf. *Cassandra*, I, ii). Eventually Oroondates reveals his true identity as
well as the cause of his illness to Statira's brother, Artaxerxes,
who informs his sister and encourages her to be merciful. She
then commands him to live. (This scene will later suggest to
Arabella that Glanville's and Sir George's illnesses can be cured
by a visit from her.)

35. *sinking under the Weight of those voluminous Romances*: Glanville's horror at the length of the romances is not unfounded:
Pope alludes slyly to their size in *The Rape of the Lock*, wherein
the 'alter' dedicated to 'Love' in Belinda's chamber is 'built, / Of
twelve vast French romances, neatly gilt' (Canto I, lines 37–8).
Hester Chapone claims that 'the prolixity and poverty of the
style is unsupportable. I have (and yet I am still alive) drudged
through Le Grand Cyrus, in twelve huge volumes, Cleopatra, in
eight or ten, Polexander, Ibrahim, Cleli, etc.' (quoted in Miriam
Rossiter Small, *Charlotte Ramsay Lennox* (1935), p. 91).

36. *Artimisa, Candace . . . Daughter of Cleopatra*: All three heroines
had lovers who were imprisoned and awaiting death, and all
three expressed their readiness to die with them – a sentiment
here echoed by Arabella.

37. *I'll burn all I can lay my Hands upon*: Probably a reference to
the burning of Don Quixote's books (ch. 6); that Arabella's
books are saved is one of Lennox's many comic revisions to
Cervantes' more tragic text.

38. *the heroic Valour of the brave Orontes*: A reference to the real
Orontes, prince of the Massagetes and lover of Thalestris, queen
of the Amazons, whose adventures are featured in *Cassandra*.

BOOK II

1. *The Great Sysigambis . . . in that Posture*: In *Cassandra* (II, ii),
Sysigambis responds in this way upon hearing of the death of
both (not one) of her granddaughters, Statira and Parisatis.

2. *Menecrates . . . with her Ashes*: There are two minor characters
called Menecrates in *Artamenes*, but given what she says about
him, Arabella is probably thinking of Menesteus, who built two
tombs after his wife's death, buried her in one and lived himself
for many years in the other (*Artamenes*, VIII, ii).

3. *But for the inimitable . . . Scudery*: Whether it is a mark of Lennox's carelessness or of her heroine's naivety, Arabella is here under the impression that the French romance writer Scudéry was a man, perhaps erroneously assuming that not Madeleine but her brother Georges de Scudéry was the author. She also mistakenly believes that it was Scudéry – not La Calprenède – who wrote *Cassandra* (in which Oroondates appears), *Cleopatra* (which features Juba, Artaban and Cleopatra herself, along with the historical figures here associated with her), and *Clelia* (in which Aronces is the hero).

4. *true Cause . . . in the Camp*: Clelia's swimming of the Tiber at the head of the hostages in order to escape the power of Porsena and her long-sought reunion with her lover Aronces is the climax of Scudéry's romance (*Clelia* V, ii, iii). Arabella's speculation that Clelia swam the Tiber to preserve her honour appears to be her own invention; but at the close of Scudéry's tale, Clelia *is* awarded a statue and other honours.

5. *inimitable Poetess Sappho . . . Brother's Affection*: Sappho (b. 612 BC) was a native of Lesbos and one of the most famous lyric poets of all time. The legend that she flung herself into the sea on being rejected by the beautiful youth Phaon has been the subject of many works. For 'The History of Sapho', see *Artamenes*, X, ii.

6. *that Cleopatra was really married to Julius Caesar*: Cf. *Cleopatra*, I, ii.

7. *that Caeserio . . . took Refuge*: Cf. *Cleopatra*, I, iii. Caesario's survival and his subsequent liaison with Candace, queen of Ethiopia, feature prominently in the romance.

8. *the History of Jack the Giant killer . . . Tom Thumb*: The 'Giant Killer' is mentioned in the first chapter of Henry Fielding's *Joseph Andrews* (1742), while Tom Thumb, the pygmy hero of a traditional nursery tale, is the eponymous hero of one of Fielding's best-known plays (1730), a brilliant satirical burlesque of heroic tragedy.

9. *Candace*: See note 32, Book I.

10. *Quadrille*: A card-game played by four persons.

11. *Assemblies*: 'The public assembly, which formed a regular feature of fashionable life in the 18th century, is described by Chambers (*Cyclopaedia*, 1751) as "a stated and general meeting of the polite persons of both sexes, for the sake of conversation, gallantry, news, and play"' (*OED*).

12. *to spend . . . in riding . . . tender Years*: Miss Groves approximates the social stereotype of the horsy Englishwoman, who was

already being mocked in the polite press. Addison in the *Spectator* makes fun of 'a rural *Andromache*, who ... makes nothing of leaping over a Six bar Gate' and 'If a Man tells her a waggish Story, she gives him a Push with her Hand in jest' (Joseph Addison, Richard Steele, et al., *The Spectator*, ed. Donald F. Bond, 5 vols. (1710–12; 1965), vol. 1, p. 241). Like Addison's Andromache, Miss Groves is a rural romp, who mistakenly assumes that physicality on horseback and with men is acceptable female behaviour. In addition, through all this outdoor exercise, she loses her pale complexion, which was not only a mark of fashion but of upper-class standing.

13. *Who would have thought ... in their Court*: Arabella draws on episodes of class and gender cross-dressing in *Cleopatra*, IV, I and *Cassandra*, II, iii and iv to validate the 'disguises' of the writing master and the gardener. See the Introduction for further discussion of the significance of such boundary crossings in the novel.

14. *and yet this Prince ... Lightness he accused her of*: When Spitridates, Artamenes' near-double, is killed, his head is shown to the distraught Mandana. Hiding in the enemy camp, Artamenes happens to see Mandana smile, and is overcome with anger and jealousy at her apparent infidelity (*Artamenes*, X, iii).

15. *Here she formed her Equipage ... favourite Diversion*: Miss Groves's staff of four enables her to function in fashionable society, where servants were an indicator of income. Her extravagant 'Gaming' was by no means unusual – throughout the century there is commentary on the nation's passion for gambling, and there is much anti-gambling literature. Elite women addicted to gambling were represented as betraying their social responsibilities and their public reputation, and coming dangerously close to prostitution (Steele argued that men could mortgage their estates to pay their debts, but women risked their bodies). Lennox's literary mentor Samuel Johnson devoted an early issue of his *Rambler* to the subject of gambling. Writing in the guise of the agony aunt 'Mr Rambler', Johnson observes:

> There is no grievance, publick or private, of which, since I took upon me the office of a periodical monitor, I have received so many, or so earnest complaints, as of the predominance of play; of a fatal passion for cards and dice, which seems to have overturned, not only the ambition of excellence, but the desire of pleasure; to have extinguished the flames of the lover, as well as of the patriot; and

threatens, in its further progress, to destroy all distinctions, both of
rank and sex, to crush all emulation but that of fraud, to corrupt
all those classes of our people, whose ancestors have, by their virtue,
their industry, or their parsimony, given them the power of living
in extravagance, idleness, and vice, and to leave them without
knowledge, but of the modish games, and without wishes, but for
lucky hands. (*Rambler* 15, 8 May 1750)

16. *unwieldy German Ladies ... his Majesty*: The court of King
George II (reigned 1727–60) and Queen Caroline (d. 1737) was
infamous for its improprieties. Lennox is characteristically critical of court society, of which she had first-hand unpleasant
experience in the period 1743–7, but she was not alone in her
criticism of the Georges. Like her readers, she would also have
remembered the scandalous court of George I. When he arrived
in Britain in September 1714, George was accompanied by a full
retinue of German friends, advisers and servants – all eager to
cash in on the venture. He had also arrived with two mistresses
but no wife (Sophia had been imprisoned for adultery). The
English took very unkindly to the two mistresses, labelling the
tall, thin Ehrengard Melusina von Schulenberg the 'maypole',
and the short, fat Charlotte Sophia Kielmansegge the 'elephant'.
The whole political episode, which includes Lennox's derogatory
reference to the king's mistresses, the king's attentions to Miss
Groves and the latter's affair with an earl's brother, provoked
her publisher Andrew Millar to ask for alterations; she writes to
Richardson that 'he assures me that the History of Miss Groves /
in the first Vol. will not be printed' (Duncan Isles, 'The Lennox
Collection' (1970), p. 339). As Isles speculates, 'the manuscript
version ... could have been more lethal' (p. 340).

17. *several thousand Pounds in Debt*: This was an enormous amount
of money – the wealthy gentry possessed a yearly income of
between £3,000 and £5,000, which gives some idea of the scale
of her debts. However, other elite women far surpassed Miss
Groves in this field: by 1792, Georgiana, Duchess of Devonshire,
owed £62,000.

18. *even Mr. L—— ... abandoned her*: The inset history of Miss
Groves mixes elements from the life stories of Sally Martin and
Polly Horton, Clarissa's antagonists at Mrs Sinclair's brothel,
including a negligent but indulgent mother, vanity and extrava-
gant gambling, as well as abandonment by her seducer. Miss
Groves avoids their fate and instead contracts a secret marriage

with a country gentleman related by marriage to her serving woman.

19. *being reduced to . . . less than an Hundred a Year*: With this level of income, Miss Groves must leave London for cheaper rural accommodation and seems to maintain only Mrs Morris to wait on her; it would be regarded as a meagre income, on the borders of gentility. John Trusler in the *Economist* (1774) estimated an annual income of £370 to maintain a household with two servants.

20. *do you think . . . those of Clelia*: In *Clelia*, it is Celeres, friend and confidante of Aronces, who tells Lysimena, princess of the Leontines, 'The History of Aronces and Clelia'. When his father wants to force Aronces into an unwelcome marriage, Lysimena allows him to feign love for her. Although Clelia is jealous, Lysimena is in fact loyal to both her and Aronces.

21. *do not these Races . . . ride in Chariots*: Arabella's 'Olympic Games' are based on the descriptions of Roman chariot races she had read in *Clelia*. In Scudéry's romance the races are part of 'The History of the Princess Elismonda', where they are turned into a tournament. Elismonda is thrilled to be able to award a crown (one, not three, as Arabella misremembers it) to her 'secret Admirer', Hortentius, who defeats, among others, two princes and a mysterious stranger, who were aspiring for her hand. If the country races they attend are not quite so grandiose as the Olympic Games, horse racing was, nevertheless, a very important eighteenth-century spectator sport. The races were sites for fashionable display and commerce (in the form of betting). Some racehorses attained celebrity status and many eighteenth-century paintings of racehorses, pre-eminently by George Stubbs, affirm the owner's status as well as a national appreciation for equine beauty (see, for example, 'Gimcrack on Newmarket Heath, with a Trainer, Jockey and a Stable-lad', *c.* 1765, painted for the horse's owner, the second Viscount Bolingbroke).

22. *Cestus*: 'A contrivance consisting of thongs of bull-hide, loaded with strips of iron and lead, and wound round the hands. Used by Roman boxers as a protection and to give greater weight to the blows' (*OED*).

23. *They were a kind of School . . . Justs and Tournaments*: Lennox's heroine is rephrasing a passage from Temple Stanyan's *Grecian History* (2nd edn, 1739), in which he gives an account of the Olympic Games. Stanyan himself makes the suggestion that the Games resembled medieval jousts and tournaments, belying

the tradition that women were not permitted to attend the Games. Diagoras of Rhodes, a boxer victorious in the 79th Olympiad, became a legend in his own time. He witnessed the victories of his two sons at the 83rd Olympiad.

24. *I remember to have read . . . entered the Lists*: Historical accounts of classical chariot races, available in Plutarch, Thucydides and others, confirm Arabella's observation that prominent men conventionally would have favoured domestics drive their chariots for them. Alcibiades (5th century BC) was an Athenian statesman and brilliant general. Accounts of his successful chariot racing appear in Thucydides and Plutarch, among others. It is not clear where Arabella read of his exploits, but in *Clelia* the heroes drive their own chariots.

25. *Morning Dress*: A woman's dress intended for informal day wear.

26. *Haste and Negligence . . . lovely and genteel*: Romance heroines often combined perfect beauty and taste in fashion with indifference to their appearance. Arabella transgresses conduct-book advice in so far as she is open to the charge of 'the affectation of singularity' in her dress, but conforms to it in that she spends as little time as possible in dressing (see Sarah Pennington, *An Unfortunate Mother's Advice to her Absent Daughters, in a Letter to Miss Pennington* (1761), in *The Young Lady's Pocket Library*, ed. Jones, pp. 82–3).

27. *a young Baronet*: A member of the lowest hereditary titled order, lower in rank than a baron, but above a knight.

28. *as Hortensius did . . . at those Games*: In fact, Hortensius did not keep 'himself concealed' at the Games. Arabella was probably thinking of the mysterious stranger (see also note 20), who was later discovered to be Attalus.

29. *surprized at so uncommon a Civility*: In romances it was conventional to bestow lavish hospitality upon complete strangers, but not in eighteenth-century polite English society.

30. *Engaged in many Adventures*: The clash between Arabella's discourse of romance and the discourse of eighteenth-century British social life frequently leads to hilarious misunderstandings between Arabella and other characters. In this case Miss Glanville is shocked at what she believes is Arabella's assumption that she must have had many amorous 'adventures'. Later in this chapter Miss Glanville, this time confused by Arabella's use of the word 'favour', confesses to 'only' having granted kisses to lovers, when her cousin was merely talking about giving small tokens of affection to lovers, like a scarf or a bracelet.

31. *Pray do you remember ... run away with*: Detractors of the genre often complained about the number of times the heroines were abducted. In *Artamenes*, the hero Cyrus/Artamenes has to rescue Mandana eight times. As the Countess later points out, unlike a romance heroine, 'a Beauty in this [age] could not pass thro' the Hands of several different Ravishers, without bringing an Imputation on her Chastity' (VIII, vii).

32. *She was no Jew ... nothing she asked*: In *Artamenes* (VIII, ii), the eponymous hero freed the Jewish captives held in Babylon, though not, as Arabella here suggests, at the behest of Mandana.

33. *for she refused ... on his Knees*: That Artamenes 'begged it on his Knees' is Arabella's embellishment of the scene (cf. *Artamenes*, I, ii).

34. *you put me in mind ... in private*: Antonia's extreme disinclination to any kind of expression of love is featured prominently in *Cleopatra*.

35. *inconsiderate*: Careless, thoughtless. The history of Augustus's daughter Julia is found in La Calprenède's *Cleopatra*.

36. *Smelling-bottle ... cut her Lace*: Lucy is probably planning to give Arabella smelling salts of carbonate of ammonia; the pungent smell restored people from fainting. Tightly laced corsets were already subject to criticism on health grounds, and cutting the laces which could constrict normal breathing is a common activity in eighteenth-century novels.

37. *Ah! had Cylenia and Martesia ... in their Captivity*: Arabella confuses two captivity scenes: Cyllenia is not with Berenice when the latter is held captive by Arsacomes, but they are together when Berenice is imprisoned by her father for refusing to marry the man of his choice (*Cassandra*, IV, iv and vi). Mandana's abductors are obliged to take her favourite waiting-woman, Martesia, with them not at Mandana's request but because Martesia clings onto her mistress's clothes.

38. *Cypress*: 'A light transparent material resembling cobweb lawn or crape; like the latter it was, when black, much used for habiliments of mourning' (*OED*).

39. *Did not the wicked Arianta ... insolent Lover*: It was because of the treachery of her waiting-woman Arianta that Mandana was carried off by the king of Assyria (*Artamenes*, II, i and ii).

40. *Arabella suffering ... such Adventures*: Newspapers of the period confirm that abductions and rapes occurred in real life, and novelists used such stories in their fiction, most famously, Richardson's *Clarissa*. In *The Female Spectator* (1744), Eliza

Haywood tells the tragic story of 'the Innocent *Erminia*', misled by a masquerade costume matching that of her brother's to go home with a stranger who rapes her, then blindfolds her and abandons her in a dirty London lane (see *Women in the Eighteenth Century*, ed. Jones, pp. 38–44).

41. *like Philidaspes . . . for his Wife*: In *Artamenes* (II, ii and VIII, i), Philidaspes is the name by which the king of Assyria is known at the court of Mandana's father, Ciaxares. Unhappy with his mother's choice of a wife for him, Philidaspes attempts to get rid of this proposed bride in various ways, including having her abducted by an associate.

42. *Mandana, Candace, Clelia . . . same Fate*: In *Artamenes*, Mandana is carried away by the king of Assyria, by Mazares, prince of Saces, by the king of Pontus and by Prince Ariantes. Candace, in *Cleopatra*, is carried away by the pirate Zenodorus. Clelia, finally, is carried away by Horatius, by Tarquin's men and by Sextus.

43. *Parthenissa, or Cleopatra*: The heroine of Roger Boyle's romance *Parthenissa* is locked up in a castle for some months by an unwanted suitor. Cleopatra is carried away by the king of Armenia, and kept prisoner on his ship (though in her case only for a couple of days, not months, as Arabella claims). The confusion between the gentleman and Arabella arises from the fact that the former is talking about Cleopatra, the queen of Egypt, and the latter about her daughter, the heroine of La Calprenède's romance.

44. *The same Treachery . . . her Jayl*: When Tiribasus gained control over the army, Candace, queen of Ethiopia, was put under house arrest (*Cleopatra*, III, ii).

45. *the poor Prince Thrasybulus . . . restored*: A reference to an episode in *Artamenes* (III, iii), in which Thrasibulus is tempted to abduct Alcionida, but he repents in time and restores her to her father, Euphranor.

BOOK III

1. *to drink her Chocolate*: A secret delight only known to the Spanish, chocolate was a novelty during the 1700s in England. Initially chocolate was served alongside coffee in coffee houses, but in the course of the eighteenth century the chocolate house gained rapid popularity as a place where the local intelligentsia could play cards, hear the latest news and enjoy 'the Spanish

treat'. A common way to prepare a chocolate drink was to stew the cocoa for several hours, thus removing the cocoa butter, and then to reboil it with milk, flavouring and cane sugar and thicken it with eggs just before serving. In the eighteenth century, choco-Late was commonly thought to work as a fertility drug for women.

2. *And truly ... concealed Torments*: Words to this effect are spoken by Mandana when she discovers that the king of Assyria is planning to carry her away (*Artamenes*, II, i).

3. *The valiant Coriolanus ... aimed at him*: cf. *Cleopatra*, IX, iv. Characteristically, Arabella embellishes the story of Coriolanus's adventures by adding a few colourful details of her own, such as his single combat against 'Two hundred Men'.

4. *Go, therefore, Glanville ... in your Behalf*. A partial quotation from Cleopatra's speech (*Cleopatra*, IX, iv).

5. *uttered a Groan ... in the Pit*: The pit is that part of the auditorium of a theatre which is on the floor of the house, next to the stage. In the early playhouses the stage and lower boxes were approximately at ground level and the whole space sunk between these was called the pit, from the Elizabethan cockpit used for cock-fighting. In the early nineteenth century, the old rows of pit seats were gradually replaced by the stalls. Pit seats were the cheapest seats in a theatre, and perhaps for that reason attracted some of the rowdiest theatre-goers, who were notorious for vociferously expressing their approval as well as their dissatisfaction with the performance, not infrequently punctuating their verbal comments by throwing missiles at the actors.

6. *You know ... injurious Suspicion*: Orontes, the lover of Thalestris, queen of the Amazons, unjustly suspected her of an amorous intrigue with Alexander; when he discovered his mistake, he withdrew from society and lived in a state of despondency in a cave, from which he only emerged from time to time to save Thalestris's life during the seige of Babylon.

7. *what became of this Queen ... Siege of Troy*: Glanville draws correctly on his classical education. The Amazons fought on the side of the Trojans, and Penthesilia, their queen, was killed by Achilles.

8. *Juba ... Artaban*: Juba is another name for Cleopatra's lover, Coriolanus, in La Calprenède's romance. Artaban, also a character in *Cleopatra*, turns out to be the son of Pompey the Great.

9. *good Reputation of a Lady ... Noise and Bustle she makes in the World*: Again, Arabella's views are completely contrary to eighteenth-century notions of female decorum, as epitomized by

John Gregory's pronouncement that 'One of the chief beauties in a female character, is that modest reserve, that retiring delicacy, which avoids the public eye' (*Father's Legacy*, p. 11).

10. *a Duel or Two fought for me in Hyde-Park*: Duelling was illegal in Britain (English Common Law treated the killing of someone in a duel as an act of murder), but it remained a common practice even at mid-century. Lennox, along with other writers such as Richardson, Fielding, Addison and Steele, criticized duelling, but the custom remained part of the upper classes' aristocratic code of honour until well into the second half of the nineteenth century. Hyde Park was a fashionable London park; a former royal hunting ground, the park was a well-known venue for duels.

11. *he was perfectly well acquainted . . . in that Romance*: Sir George is right: Dryden took many of his characters and plots from French romances. Thus the chief source for *Alamanzor and Almahide; or, The Conquest of Granada* (1670–71) was Scudéry's *Almahide* (1661–3). As Sir George says, the character of the hero, Almanzor, is also in part based on Artaban in La Caprenède's *Cleopatra* (which Dryden acknowledges in his essay 'Of Heroic Plays'). There appears to be little ground for Sir George's claim that the character of Melantha in Dryden's comedy *Marriage-à-la-Mode* (produced 1672; published 1673) is based on Berisa in Scudéry's *Artamenes*, nor that the characters of Ozmyn and Benzayda in *The Conquest of Granada* were derived from the story of Sesostris and Timareta (not 'Timerilla') in that romance. Yet the story of Sesostris and Timareta did provide Dryden with the material from which he moulded the serious plot of *Marriage-à-la-Mode*.

12. *the Ridicule*: 'A ridiculous or absurd thing, feature, characteristic, or habit; an absurdity' [now *rare*] (*OED*).

13. *as it happened to Artamenes . . . Gates of Death*: Although Mandana's visit and her 'few kind Words' had the extraordinary effect of healing his wounds, Artamenes was actually well out of danger by the time she visited him after he had been seriously wounded in battle (*Artamenes*, I, ii).

14. *fair Statira . . . dying Orontes*: In *Cassandra* (II, ii), Alexander wants to marry the Persian princess Parisatis to his friend Hephestion. Put in prison for attacking Hephestion, Lysimachus is determined to starve himself to death. Parisatis saves his life by writing him a letter in which she orders Lysimachus to live.

15. *decent*: 'Suitable, appropriate, or proper to the circumstances or special requirements of the case; seemly, fitting' (*OED*).

BOOK IV

1. *brave Caesario ... in Ethiopia*: Cf. *Cleopatra*, III, i and ii.
2. *unequalled Prince of Mauritania*: That is, Coriolanus, the hero of *Cleopatra*.
3. *what the fair Artemisa ... to condemn*: Cf. 'The History of Alexander and the Princess Artemisa' in *Cleopatra* (IV, i and ii). The 'Action of that Princess' that 'some have not scrupled to condemn' is a reference to Artemisa's decision – virtually unprecedented in French romance – to run away with her hero.
4. *Two celebrated Beauties*: The 'Two Sister Beauties' – as the first edition of the novel has it – were Maria (1733–60) and Elizabeth Gunning (1734–90). They came over from Ireland to London in 1750 where they caused a stir. Early in 1752 Elizabeth married the Duke of Hamilton and Maria the Earl of Coventry. See the Introduction for more information on the Gunning girls.
5. *Ranelagh*: A pleasure garden in Chelsea, where people might walk, admire the ornamental lake or Chinese pavilion, listen to concerts, attend masquerades or dances, play cards, watch fireworks or take tea in the rotunda.
6. *must stop their Ears ... Siren Frasi sings*: In Greek mythology, the sirens were sea-nymphs whose enticing song lured sailors to their death. Odysseus escaped from this ordeal by filling his companions' ears with wax and strapping himself to the mast of his ship. Signora Giulia Frasi (dates unknown) was a celebrated Italian soprano, who first appeared in London in 1743. She most likely sang the part of 'Pleasure' in Handel's one-act dramatic cantata 'The Choice of Hercules', which was first performed at Covent Garden on 1 March 1751 as 'an additional New Act' concluding a performance of the ode 'Alexander's Feast'.
7. *the Side-box*: The box seats at the theatre were more expensive than a place on the main floor, or pit, and thus were kept usually by upper-class patrons. Fashionable women in the boxes often came as much to display their finery and beauty as to watch the play – they were part of the theatre's spectacle.
8. *Soul-moving Garrick*: David Garrick (1717–79) was the most celebrated and respected actor of the period, perhaps of the century. He promoted a revolutionary 'natural' style of speech delivery and gesture, and his own respectability helped to raise the status of the profession. He was also a playwright, the author of light comedies, and he managed the Drury Lane Theatre during the height of his career, where he did much to revive Shake-

speare's popularity. Sarah Pennington, advising her daughters on
acceptable pursuits, advocated 'THE THEATRE, which, by the
indefatigable labour of the inimitable Mr. Garrick, has been
brought to a very great perfection, will afford you an equally
rational and improving entertainment' (*An Unfortunate Mother's
Advice*, ed. Jones, p. 90). Garrick was a friend of Lennox's
mentor Samuel Johnson, and Lennox knew and corresponded
with him over many years. Duncan Isles's 'The Lennox Collection' includes four letters from Garrick to Lennox between 1753
and 1774. Garrick resented Lennox's irreverent reading of his
idol in *Shakespear Illustrated*; he rejected *Philander* and *The
Sister* for production at Drury Lane, but praised her novel *Henrietta* and staged her adaptation *Old City Manners* at Drury Lane
in November 1775. Despite his failure to produce two of her
plays, they seem to have had a cordial relationship, and Lennox
acknowledges Garrick's 'friendly assistance' in the printed version of *Old City Manners*.

9.   *Congreve's Comedies*: The English dramatist William Congreve
(1670–1729) is often regarded as the greatest master of the
Restoration comedy of manners. Among his important stage
successes were the comedies *The Double Dealer* (1693), *Love
for Love* (1695) and *The Way of the World* (1700). Addison
and Steele, among others, objected to the sexual frankness of
Restoration comedy, and attempted to reform the English stage.
The plays, however, remained popular, and were performed
alongside the new 'sentimental' comedies.

10. *those numerous and long Conversations*: Scudéry's romances –
especially *Clelia* and *Artamenes* – are well known for their long
and digressive 'conversations' in which the 'greatest Conquerors
and Heroes' take part in 'Disputes' concerning topics such as the
ones mentioned here by Arabella.

11. *The great Oroondates ... Divine Princess*: In *Cassandra* (I, iv
and v), Princess Roxana is in love with Oroondates and in order
to drive a wedge between him and Princess Statira attempts to
convince the latter that Oroondates was unfaithful.

12. *the valiant and unfortunate Artamenes ... Inconstancy*: The
cause of this suspicion of 'Inconstancy' on the part of Mandana
was that when she was crying out for help as she was being
abducted by the king of Assyria, the person she thought was her
lover Artamenes was in fact Spitridates, to whom Artamenes
bore an uncanny likeness (*Artamenes*, VI, iii).

13. *the irresistible Juba ... Mistress and Friend*: In *Cleopatra* (II, iv

and V, ii), the reputation of Juba – or Coriolanus – is compro-
mised by his enemies' lies, which cause him to be distrusted by
both his mistress, Cleopatra, and his friend, Marcellus.

14. *I said once before ... Tempers and Inclinations*: Arabella made
this – uncomplimentary – comparison between Miss Glanville
and the Princess Julia before, in Book II, Chapter IX (see note
35, Book II).

15. *her Beauty ... lay it at your Feet*: Cf. *Cleopatra*, III, iii (although
there is no exact match for Artaban's speech in La Calprenède's
text).

16. *great Artaban ... successively*: The 'Three great Princesses' suc-
cessively loved by Artaban are Candace, queen of Ethiopia,
Arsinoe, princess of Armenia, and Elisa, princess of Parthia. As
Arabella suggests, in the world of the romance this would make
Artaban an inconstant hero.

17. *mounted her Horse ... adorned with*: Mid-eighteenth-century
riding habits were often showy, colourful costumes. A significant
tradition in English art shows English society ladies posing as
equestriennes, either on horseback or simply in riding costume
(equestrian paintings being the most expensive of the portrait
genre). Stubbs's painting of Sophia Musters (1777), and Reynolds's of Lady Charles Spencer with her horse (1775), and of
Lady Worsley, all show them in glorious ruby-red habits. *Lady
Worsley* (1780) wears a red military-inspired outfit with a theatrical beaver hat trimmed with ostrich feathers. The sexual allure
of such costumes is evident in the number of 'Gallants' who want
to help Arabella mount her horse, and Glanville's adulation of
her charms. Advice books for women riders were not available
until later in the century, but most emphasize the graceful visual
spectacle of a woman on horseback, a combination of elegance
and accomplishment. Throughout the century, there were anxi-
eties about women's participation in field sports – 'let not such
horrid joy / E'er stain the bosom of the British fair. / Far be the
spirit of the chase from them!', opined James Thomson in *The
Seasons* (1730, 1744; 'Autumn', line 573) – but many women
displayed their equestrian skills either in hare-coursing or fox-
hunting. That Miss Glanville is unable to ride is another sly
indication that she lacks some essential parts of a lady's education.

18. *But as it happened ... in their Defence*: This passage is a slightly
inaccurate rendering of an episode in *Cleopatra* (I, iv). Juba
(Coriolanus) and Cleomedon (Caesario) were facing fewer than

two dozen (not 'some hundred') men when their assailants' 'Commander', the pirate Zenodorus, carried away Candace and her woman Clitie (not Cleopatra and Candace, or Juba's and Cleomedon's 'Princesses').

19. *Olympia . . . enamoured of her*: Cf. 'The History of Olympia' in *Cleopatra* (VI, i).

20. *Maherbal . . . adore her*: In fact, it is Adherbal, prince of Numidia, who later turns out to be Clelia's long-lost brother Octavius, *not* Maherbal, who is briefly her lover at Carthage.

21. *the Uncle of . . . Alcyone . . . in his Power*: See 'The History of Alcione' in *Cassandra* (II, vi). It is actually not her uncle but the uncle of Alcione's husband, Theander, who is in love with her.

VOLUME II

BOOK V

1. *the fair Amalazontha*: In *Pharamond* (V, iii and iv), Amalazontha, the haughty princess of the Thuringians, resists the suit of Ambiomer, the man her father wanted her to marry. At her father's request, she does agree to visit the wounded and languishing hero.

2. *Airing*: 'A walk, ride, or drive to take the air' (*OED*).

3. *Doralisa*: Cf. *Artamenes*, V, i. In contrast to what Arabella claims, Doralisa does eventually listen to the lover's discourse of Prince Myrsiles, and subsequently agrees to marry him.

4. *you, who have granted Favours . . . such Liberties*: Again confusion arises because Arabella adheres to the courting rituals of French romances (which proscribe all sorts of socially acceptable eighteenth-century behaviour), while Miss Glanville is shocked that Arabella could consider visiting a man, unrelated by close blood ties, in his bedroom (which would be viewed as compromising the reputation of a modern woman).

5. *chaste Ladies . . . their Husband*: The heroines of romance are on the whole very chaste, especially in the work of Scudéry. There are some exceptions, for example, Statira and Oroondates kiss each other quite intimately, once their marriage has been arranged (*Cassandra*, I, iv).

6. *two powerful Kingdoms*: Cappadocia and Media.

7. *Cleonice . . . his Bed*: There is no such episode in 'The History of Ligdamus and Cleonice' in *Artamenes* (IV, iii).

8. *jealous Transports of an enraged Orontes*: See note 6, Book III.

9. *great Actions ... Cilicians*: In *Cassandra* (II, iv), Orontes, disguised as Orithia, valiantly leads the Amazon force against Naobarzanes and rescues his captive, Thalestris.

10. *Memnon ... a Visit*: When in *Cassandra* (V, iii) Prince Oxyatres falls seriously ill as a result of his unrequited love for Barsina, his rival, Memnon, resigns his amorous claims to her in order to relieve the plight of his prince (but he does not actually persuade Barsina to visit Oxyatres, as Arabella believes). In an equally chivalrous move, Oxyatres responds by conquering his love for Barsina.

11. *complaisant Husband ... for her Sake*: In *Cassandra* (II, ii), Hephestion insists his wife Parisatis visit her disappointed lover Lysimachus, who was languishing dangerously close to death following the marriage of Parisatis to his rival.

12. *Parisatis ... insupportable Misfortune*: See note 14, Book III.

13. *Agilmond ... before my Eyes*: In *Pharamond* (X, ii), Agilmond, king of Lombardy, and Gilismene, princess of the Sarmatians, are lovers. But when intriguers convince Gilismene that her lover is dishonest, Agilmond hurries to her and, to prove his 'Fidelity and Love', throws himself on his sword at her feet. Fortunately, he survives.

14. *since you so well know ... Parisatis*: Parisatis acts upon her grandmother's desire that she marry Hephestion, but that does not prevent her from informing Lysimachus that she esteems him at least as much as her husband.

15. *prepare to give me Satisfaction ... his Challenge*: Lennox, like other writers of the period, including Addison, Steele, Fielding and Richardson, found duelling a reprehensible practice. She often exposes its irresponsibility through making its participants look ridiculous (early in *Harriot Stuart*, Harriot's brother and Belmein attempt to fight a duel, but first their swords are whisked away by a doctor and then their pistols turn out to be uncharged – they end up torn between rage and a desire to laugh; see *The Life of Harriot Stuart*, ed. Susan Kubica Howard (1995), pp. 94–5).

16. *pretend*: 'To aspire to, aim at, make pretension to; to be a suitor or candidate for' (*OED*).

17. *offered her the chief Command of their Forces*: During the campaign to liberate Statira and Parisatis from their captivity by the Babylonians, Thalestris was called upon to take the command, but she declined, on account of her gender (*Cassandra*, III, iii).

18. *the Spirit of Julia ... Infidelity*: See note 14, Book IV.

19. *a Gypsey*: Sir Charles probably refers to Cleopatra's nationality as Egyptian (when they first appeared in England about the beginning of the sixteenth century, Gypsies were commonly believed to have come from Egypt and they continued to be classified as a separate race in England because of their dark skins).

20. *Rake*: A debauched man of fashion, whose career of seduction or reform is the subject of many eighteenth-century novels. Samuel Richardson constantly inveighed against the popular notion that a reformed rake made the best husband (for example, in *Familiar Letters on Important Occasions* (1741), a father reminds his daughter 'that the wild assertion, of a rake making a good husband, was the most dangerous opinion a young woman could imbibe', *Women in the Eighteenth Century*, ed. Jones, p. 38).

BOOK VI

1. *not much more than eight Hundred Years ... bequeath to him*: Acting on Richardson's advice, Lennox amended the manuscript to curtail somewhat Bellmour's genealogical pretensions to the kingdom of Kent. Rather than the manuscript's recent claim, the published novel makes Bellmour's family the rulers of Kent in the distant past, having lost the kingdom at some unspecified point. His grandfather is allowed to retain the title 'Prince Veridomer' but is reduced to being an improver of a 'small Pittance of Ground'. See Richardson's letter to Lennox of 8 or 15 November 1751 (Isles, 'The Lennox Collection' (1970), p. 338).

2. *Fear of a Halter*: That is, fear of hanging.

3. *your Affair with the pretty Milk-maid*: Both Glanville and Sir Charles are indulgent about Sir George's dalliance with the milk-maid, who turns out to be one *Dolly Acorn*; in the mid eighteenth century it was socially acceptable for upper-class men to have sexual liaisons with lower-class women, especially servants of the family, as Dolly appears to have been. The virtuous resistance of Richardson's Pamela to Mr B's seductions is unusual and ridiculed within the novel itself: as Sir Simon puts it, ' "Why, what is all this, my dear, but that our neighbour has a mind to his mother's waiting-maid! And if he takes care she wants for nothing, I don't see any great injury will be done her. He hurts no *family* by this" ' (*Pamela*, (1740), Vol. I, Letter XXXII).

4. *rhodomontade Speech*: Extravagant speech.

5. *I made her a declaration ... to forget*: Sir George's 'romance'

replicates eighteenth-century distinctions of rank and emphasizes the sexual vulnerability of rural women and domestic servants. Sir George's history constantly ignores romance codes of courtship and narrates a series of seductions; his inauthentic history of infidelity earns Arabella's dismissal.

6. *fair Arsinoe . . . Daughter of a King*: Cf. *Cleopatra* (IV, iii and iv), 'The History of Philadelph'.

7. *Philoxipes . . . equal to his own*: Cf. *Artamenes* (II, iii), 'The History of Philoxypes and Policrite'.

8. *do but reflect . . . made to turn*: Arabella's rendition of the exploits of the heroes of romance is not devoid of hyperbole. Thus, in *Cleopatra* (IX, iv), Coriolanus ('the brave Prince of Mauritania') defends Cleopatra and Artemisa armed only with his sword, but the number of his opponents is not revealed in La Calprenède's text. Alexander ('The young Prince of *Egypt*') and his friend Cepio indeed engage all of the king of Armenia's guards, but instead of putting them to flight, Cepio gets killed and Alexander is recaptured (IV, ii). Although Ariobasanes is certainly a brave man, we are told that during the defence of Byzantium his forces were seriously outnumbered by his opponents and were unable to resist them (VII, i). Arabella repeats her earlier exaggeration of Artaban's valour and prowess (see Book III, Chapter VI).

9. *To give you a Description . . . Priority of Beauty*: Sir George's Sydimiris is obviously modelled after Arabella.

10. *a Lover, whose Mistress . . . of his Blood*: Not identified.

11. *taking his Enemy Prisoner . . . over again*: In Roger Boyle's *Parthenissa* (IV, iv), Artabenes, king of Media, leads an army against Surena in order to secure the release of Parthenissa. Having captured Surena, Artabenes immediately sets him free again – releasing Parthenissa being his real mission. Surena subsequently refuses to let Parthenissa go, and Artabenes 'has all his Work to do over again'.

12. *violent Friendship . . . in Person*: His intense friendship for Artaxerxes, prince of Persia, and love of Statira, leads Oroondates, prince of Scythia, to fight with the Persians against his own people (*Cassandra*, I, ii). In the conflict between duty and love, the hero of romance chooses the latter.

13. *An extraordinary Instance . . . in Cassandra*: A reference to an episode in *Cassandra* (IV, v), in which Arsaces (Artaxerxes) surrenders himself to the king of Scythia in the hope that that might deter the King from marrying his daughter Berenice to the hateful

Arsacomes. The 'extraordinary Instance of Generosity' is mirrored a little later in this chapter in Bellmour giving himself up to Prince Marcomire in order 'to free that excellent Lady [Sydimiris, Marcomire's sister] from the Imputation you have laid on her'.

14. *flattered*: In this context, 'flattered' means that the place both mirrored and fostered his despair.

15. *Chance at last ... admit the Light*: Sir George's cave bears a general resemblance to the cave to which Orontes penitently retires after having misjudged Thalestris (*Cassandra*, V, ii).

16. *Apelles's Art*: Apelles (*c.* 352–308 BC) was born on Kos and was to become one of the most praised painters of the ancient world. Nothing of his work has survived, but we know about it through other writers' descriptions. He painted Alexander the Great many times, and one of these paintings hung in the temple of Artemis in Ephesus. Apelles also painted scenes from mythology, such as Venus Anadyomene and Calumny, personifying Ignorance, Suspicion and Envy. He is also credited with having painted the first self-portrait in the world.

17. *Agione*: Cf. *Pharamond*, IX, i.

18. *Delia ... Olympia ... Eliza*: Cf. *Cleopatra*, IV, iii; VI, iii; III, iv.

19. *Grub-street*: The former name of a street in London, famous in the eighteenth century for the needy literary hacks and struggling writers who lived there. Samuel Johnson defined 'Grub Street' in his *Dictionary* as 'much inhabited by writers of small histories, dictionaries, and temporary poems; whence any mean production is called grubstreet'.

20. *Bedford Coffee-house*: A famous coffee house near Covent Garden Theatre. Frequented by such prominent writers and actors as Pope, Fielding, Garrick, Sheridan and Horace Walpole, it was described by 'Mr Town', the 'Critic and Censor-General' of the *Connoisseur*, as 'every night crowded with men of parts. Almost every one you meet is a polite scholar and a wit. Jokes and *bon mots* are echo'd from box to box; every branch of literature is critically examined, and the merit of every production of the press, or performance at the theatres, weighed and determined' (31 January 1754, p. 4). But the patrons drank a lot more than just coffee, and thus the Bedford Coffee House became a byword for excessive drinking and rowdy behaviour.

21. *the rest of your Brothers ... more Merit, than those that do*: Mr Glanville defends the newly professionalized activity of authorship against dilettante writers and critics. Specifically, he valorizes

the work of Edward Young (1683–1765), writer of prose, satires, dramatic tragedies and poetry, most famously *Night Thoughts on Life, Death and Immortality* (1742–5); Samuel Richardson, successful printer and author of the phenomenally successful novels *Pamela* and *Clarissa*; and Samuel Johnson, English lexicographer, essayist, poet and moralist. The *Rambler* (1750–52) was a series of semi-weekly essays by Samuel Johnson, dealing with social mores and literature.

22. *Bath*: The town of Bath (about 100 miles west of London) became a fashionable health and pleasure resort during the reigns of George II (1727–60) and George III (1760–1820). Its natural hotspring waters were regarded as having medicinal qualities, but by the mid eighteenth century Bath serviced more than the sick. People could attend concerts and the theatre, engage in fashionable shopping and dance at the Assembly Rooms. Bath was the most famous of the English resorts in the eighteenth century, the favoured destination of royalty and aristocracy, but also attracting middle- and lower-class holiday-makers.

BOOK VII

1. *Coach and Six*: A large carriage drawn by six horses.

2. *Knights of the Road*: Highwaymen. Between 1650 and 1800 highwaymen were common in England, with many of them becoming legendary and romantic figures. In an age when travel was already hazardous due to the lack of decent roads, no one rode alone without fear of being robbed, and people often joined company or hired escorts. In fact, travellers would often write their wills before they set off. As this episode demonstrates once again, 'real life' turns out to be quite as adventurous as Arabella's romances.

3. *'T was in such a Place . . . Hortensius*: Scudéry describes the Vale of Tempe in *Clelia*, in 'The History of the Princess Elismonda' (IV, i), wherein appears Arabella's story about Andronice, the princess of Messina, who saves the life of Hortensius when he is condemned for killing a stork (storks were regarded as sacred in classical mythology and killing one was therefore considered a crime).

4. *Indians of America*: American Indians featured more prominently in Lennox's first novel, *Harriot Stuart*, in which the heroine at one point is taken into Indian captivity.

5. *in Turky*: When the novel appeared (1752), Macedonia was still

part of the Ottoman Empire. The Vale of Tempe was noted by many classical authors, and remains a celebrated tourist stop in Thessaly.

6. *Great Mogul's Country*: That is, India. The Great Mogul was the sovereign of the empire founded in India by the Moguls (Indian Muslims) in the sixteenth century. As Glanville points out, Sir Charles confuses the Great Mogul, the Emperor of Delhi, with the Grand Signior, or the Sultan of Turkey. Despite the benefits of a masculine education, Sir Charles's historical and geographical knowledge is limited, while Arabella, drawing her information from romances, appears well informed.

7. *a great many beautiful Princesses . . . each other*: The numbers are indicated by the conclusion of *Cleopatra*, when eleven princesses are married off in a single ceremony.

8. *Pump-Room*: A room at a spa where guests would drink the water of supposedly medicinal springs to improve or retain their health. However, many people would gather at the pump-rooms of resorts such as Bath or Bristol Hotwells to socialize, dance, gossip and to see and be seen as much as to 'take the waters'.

9. *went in an Undress*: Partial or incomplete dress, informal morning wear. To discard any item of full dress (a hoop, a periwig or a long gown) was to be 'undressed'.

10. *Capuchin . . . of Black Gauze*: A 'capuchin' was a soft hood, often worn by women in the eighteenth century. Arabella's decision to wear a veil clearly marks her out as being 'not in the fashion' (cf. note 9, Book I).

11. *Pretty-Fellows*: Fops

12. *Countess of —— went to Court in a Farthingale*: Perhaps an allusion to Maria Gunning, the Countess of Coventry; see the Introduction for an example of her play with fashion codes. A farthingale is a 'frame-work of hoops, usually of whalebone, worked into some kind of cloth, formerly used for extending the skirts of women's dresses' (*OED*). It was fashionable in the seventeenth century, but old-fashioned by the middle of the eighteenth century.

13. *Dutchess of —— sat astride upon a Horse*: No specific historical figure has been identified. The point of the allusion is the unconventionality of a lady riding astride, rather than side-saddle.

14. *Olympiad*: 'A period of four years reckoned from one celebration of the Olympic games to the next, by which the ancient Greeks computed time, the year 776 BC being taken as the first year of the first Olympiad' (*OED*).

15. *famous Springs . . . new Lustre*: The Springs of Thermopylae and the tale of Pisistratus, the Athenian, his rivals Lycurgus and Theocrites, 'the fair Cerinthe', and 'the beautiful Cleorante', to which Arabella subsequently refers, all occur in 'The History of Pisistrates' in *Artamenes* (IX, iii).

16. *posed*: Perplexed, nonplussed.

17. *Springs at Thermopylæ*: As the etymology of the name suggests, Arabella's romance-derived information may be correct. Institutions making use of the medicinal waters have long been established at Thermopylae.

18. *Herodotus, Thucydides, and Plutarch, have indeed quoted him frequently*: Herodotus (*c.* 480–*c.* 425 BC), a famous Greek historian, often called the Father of History; Thucydides (*c.* 460–*c.* 400 BC), an Athenian historian; and Plutarch (AD *c.* 46–*c.* 120), a Greek biographer. Arabella and Mr Selvin assume that Scudéry is a male writer, see note 3, Book II.

19. *Which contains some excellent Rules for Raillery*: Arabella's analysis of raillery in this chapter, as well as the remarks made by Mr Glanville, are based in part on a conversation on the same subject in 'The History of Pisistrates' in *Artamenes* (IX, iii).

20. *young Beau*: 'A man who gives particular, or excessive, attention to dress, mien, and social etiquette; an exquisite, a fop, a dandy' (*OED*). The pump-rooms at spa resorts like Bath and pleasure gardens like Ranelagh and Vauxhall were favourite haunts of beaux.

21. *Robe . . . Princess Julia's*: There is no such model of Princess Julia's robe in *Cleopatra*.

22. *Mantua-maker*: Dressmaker.

23. *She wore no Hoop . . . greatest Advantage*: Arabella's 'singular' dress lacks a fashionable hoop and the lace cap normally worn by women of her class; the profusion of diamonds advertises her wealth and status.

24. *Julia . . . Ovid . . . Banishment*: Ovid (43 BC–AD 17), Roman poet known for his *Ars amatoria* (*The Art of Love, c.* AD 1) and the *Metamorphoses* (AD 2 onwards), was banished from Rome by Augustus in AD 8 to Tomis on the Black Sea, possibly for having had an affair with a female relative of the emperor. Princess Julia, in whose affairs Ovid may have been involved, was the daughter of Emperor Augustus's daughter, also called Julia (39 BC–AD 14), whom her father had married off after her first husband's death to his chief military adviser, Agrippa (64–12 BC), a man older than her father. Ovid's account of his relation-

ship with Princess Julia is found in 'The History of Ovid, Cipassis, and Julia' (*Cleopatra*, VII, iii).

25. *Gibraltar*: The Rock of Gibraltar was seized by an Anglo-Dutch force led by Sir George Rooke in 1704. The territory was ceded to Great Britain by Spain in the 1713 Treaty of Utrecht as part of the settlement of the War of the Spanish Succession. However, the military and commercial rivalry between Britain and Spain, mainly involving conflicting territorial claims in America and the trade (including the slave trade) with the West Indies, continued to cause tensions between the two nations. From time to time hostilities would flare up, resulting in a string of military campaigns and several full-scale wars, in which the position of Gibraltar was invariably at stake. The War of the Quadruple Alliance (1718–20) had left the Rock firmly in possession of the British, and despite a Spanish siege of Gibraltar in 1727, the Anglo-Spanish War of 1727–9 did not change this. The Spanish besieged Gibraltar again in an attempt to wrest it from the British in 1739, as part of what is known as the War of Jenkins's Ear (1739–43).

26. *died gloriously before the Walls of Carthagena*: Cartagena is a city and port in the northwest of present-day Colombia, on the Bay of Cartagena in the Caribbean Sea. As part of the West Indian front of the War of Jenkins's Ear, a British fleet and troops landed at Playa Grande, near Cartagena, and began a two-month assault on the city's defences. The ultimate plan was to march across the Isthmus to capture Panama City in conjunction with Anson's Pacific fleet. However, the campaign ended in disaster, with most of the proposed actions called off due to the ravages of yellow fever and other diseases. Six hundred men of the British expeditionary force died before reaching the first action at Cartagena. The war sputtered out in 1742–3 for lack of troops to continue it.

27. *Her Habit . . . all French*: Part of a traditional anti-French critique, evident throughout the century. Disparaging views of imported French fashions had much to do with the economic competition that underpinned the persistent military conflict between the two nations. Critics, such as Addison, found the manners of Frenchwomen lacking proper feminine 'Discretion and Modesty' (*Spectator*, no. 45, 21 April 1711). The super-elegant Frenchwoman who despises English simplicity turns out to be the daughter of an innkeeper.

28. *One of our great Sea Commanders*: Possibly Admiral Charles Knowles, whose *Dictionary of National Biography* entry records his second marriage at Aix-la-Chapelle, near Spa, to Maria Mag-

dalena Teresa, daughter of the Comte de Bouget. Elsewhere she is described as of German origin. Tinsel's gossip perhaps plays on speculations about her background.

29. *detatched Pieces of Satire on particular Persons*: Tinsel's stories are reminiscent of the scandalous, racy narratives of Aphra Behn, Delarivier Manley and Eliza Haywood, Lennox's novelistic predecessors, which often involved recognizable figures from contemporary life, but they are also typical spa town fare.

30. *The Ugliness of Vice ... restrain'd*: Arabella's language recalls Samuel Johnson's similar sentiments about the undesirability of representing vice. Writing at a time when 'new' realistic novels such as Tobias Smollett's *Roderick Random* (1748) and Henry Fielding's *Tom Jones* (1749) had begun to eclipse the once popular romances that Arabella still adores, Johnson commented in *Rambler* 4 (31 March 1750):

> In narratives where historical veracity has no place, I cannot discover why there should not be exhibited the most perfect idea of virtue; of virtue not angelical, nor above probability, for what we cannot credit, we shall never imitate, but the highest and purest that humanity can reach, which, exercised in such trials as the various revolutions of things shall bring upon it, may, by conquering some calamities, and enduring others, teach us what we may hope, and what we can perform. Vice, for vice is necessary to be shewn, should always disgust; nor should the graces of gaiety, or the dignity of courage, be so united with it, as to reconcile it to the mind. Wherever it appears, it should raise hatred by the malignity of its practices, and contempt by the meanness of its stratagems: for while it is supported by either parts or spirit, it will be seldom heartily abhorred.

31. *sublime Courage ... other Side*: See note 4, Book II. (In fact, it is not Tarquin Clelia is trying to escape from, but his son, Sextus.)

32. *noble Resolution ... Mercy of the Waves*: Cf. *Cleopatra*, III, ii.

33. *Constancy ... for him*: As a mark of her constancy and fidelity to Cyrus, Mandana refused the kings of Assyria and Pontus, as well as several princes.

34. *Alcamenes*: See 'The History of Alcamenes and Melanippa' in *Cleopatra*, VIII, ii–iv.

35. *the Parade ... Rooms*: In the Spa town of Bath, the 'Parade' or Grand Parade was where the fashionable visitors walked, displaying their fine clothes; the 'Rooms' were the Assembly Rooms, where people met, danced and ate.

36. *Cyrus the Great ... at Sardis*: Arabella remembers this incorrectly, for Mandana had been carried away by the king of Pontus before Cyrus could dance with her (*Artamenes*, VIII, iii).

37. *King of Scythia ... at Alexandria*: Arabella misremembers the conversation of Alcamenes, king of Scythia, and Cleopatra at Alexandria as a dance.

38. *brave Cleomedon ... at Ethiopia*: Again, there is no parallel for this in 'The History of Caesario [Cleomedon], and the Queen Candace' (*Cleopatra*, I, iii and III, i).

39. *pink'd in a Duel*: Pierced with a bullet, or pricked ('pink'd') or stabbed with a pointed weapon.

40. *the Fate of the Princess Melisintha*: In *Pharamond* (VI, ii), Melisintha is saved from 'the Embraces of a King' by her father during a fire in the palace in which they were held.

41. *surpriz'd Lover ... undesign'd Offence*: In *Cassandra* (II, iii), Thalestris discovers that Orontes, prince of the Massagetes, is in love with her when she overhears his soliloquy, *not* a conversation with a confidante.

42. *The Method which the great Artamenes took ... permitted to hope*: The events are found in *Artamenes*, II, i.

43. *great Prince of Persia*: Artaxerxes, prince of Persia, at long last reveals his love (and true identity) to Berenice in *Cassandra*, IV, ii.

44. *mal a propos*: French, literally, 'ill to purpose' or 'inappropriate'.

45. *Billet-doux*: A love letter.

46. *Mercury*: The Roman equivalent of the Greek messenger god Hermes; a grandiose term for Tinsel's messenger.

47. *beautiful Princess of Cappadocia*: That is, Mandana.

48. *Seramenes*: There is no such character in 'The History of Cleobuline Queen of Corinth' (*Artamenes*, VII, ii).

49. *you use me ... wise Antonia*: In *Cleopatra*, the eponymous heroine asks Antonia to read a love letter to her (IX, ii).

50. *I am much in the same Situation with the Princess Serena*: In fact, Arabella's situation is quite dissimilar to that of Princess Serena. In *Pharamond* (VII, iii), Princess Serena has three real (not imagined) suitors, two of whom plot against the favoured lover.

51. *this Adventure ... than hers was*: Again Arabella's 'Adventure' is *not* 'exactly like what befel the beautiful *Statira*'. In Statira's case, she visited Barsina not knowing that Oroondates was staying with Barsina; Oroondates' 'Stratagem' was to hide in Barsina's closet and then throw himself at Statira's feet (*Cassandra*, I, vi).

52. *all Ladies ... fainting Fit*: The heroines of seventeenth-century

French romances faint a lot but so do the heroines of mid-eighteenth-century realist novels. Fainting, like blushing and weeping, became one of the dominant eighteenth-century cultural codes of femininity.

53. *Examples of Artamenes, Aronces*: In *Artamenes* (I. i), the hero promises his rival, the king of Assyria, that he will not marry Mandana before he has conquered him honourably in combat. In *Clelia* (V, iii), Aronces makes a similar promise to his rival Horatius with regard to the fate of the heroine.

54. *you imitate . . . as you have done*: In *Artamenes* (I, i), the hero spares the ravisher of Mandana, the king of Assyria, when he had both the opportunity and just cause to take his life.

BOOK VIII

1. *Princess Udosia . . . entertain'd for her*: When Thrasimond (not Thrasimedes), king of the Vandals, falls in love with Eudoxia at the court of Constantinople, she banishes him as soon as she finds out about it. Thrasimond later dies of lover's grief (*Pharamond*, VII, ii).

2. *Protestant Nunneries*: Mary Astell famously proposed a women's seminary, which would combine religion and rationality, in *A Serious Proposal to the Ladies, for the Advancement of their True and Greatest Interest* (1694); Sarah Scott's novel *Millenium Hall* (1762) offers an approximation of Astell's 'Monastery' in its portrait of a community of women. Millenium Hall functions as a retreat from the world and as a place of good works.

3. *Perinthus die for . . . Panthea*: The sorrowful tale of Perinthus is related in *Artamenes* (V, i).

4. *Barsina bring . . . to the Grave*: In *Cassandra* (V, iii), Oxyatres' violent fever is a consequence of his failure to woo her away from her other suitor.

5. *Statira . . . kill'd by it*: When Statira, after she has married Alexander, demands that Oroondates respect her virtue and her conjugal duty to her husband, he acquiesces; since he has now lost the sole reason to live, he decides to throw himself upon his sword – only to be saved in the nick of time by Barsina, who knocks the sword aside (*Cassandra*, I, vi).

6. *Princess of Media . . . his Disaster*: These adventures of Mandana are related in *Artamenes* (IX, i).

7. *Actions . . . testify*: The test these heroes of romance were facing was the choice between love and duty: between the women they

loved and their duty to their relatives and their country. For the choice faced by Oroondates, see note 12, Book VI. In *Cassandra*, Artaxerxes, prince of Persia, is in love with Berenice, princess of Scythia. In order to be with her, he lives in disguise at the Scythian court, and even fights alongside the Scythians while his own country is overrun by the Macedonians. In *Artamenes*, Spitridates, prince of Bithynia, is in love with Araminta, princess of Pontus, but because their countries are involved in a lengthy war he is forced to choose between his honour and his love.

8. *I shall live ... take Care of*: Arabella is apparently quoting from *Cassandra*, but the passage has not been identified.

9. *Say only ... to conquer*: Again, there is no exact match for this passage in *Cleopatra*.

10. *The celebrated Countess of——*: Not identified, though contemporary readers speculated about her identity. Lady Mary Wortley Montagu (1689–1762) begged her daughter, 'Tell me who is that accomplish'd Countess she celebrates. I left no such person in London' (Lady Mary Wortley Montagu, *Letters*, ed. Clare Brant (1992): letter from Adrianople, 1 April 1717). Montagu thought the novel was the work of Sarah Fielding.

11. *Elisa ... she detested*: The beautiful Elisa, princess of Parthia, is a character in *Cleopatra*. Her particular plight is that she is under pressure from her father to marry Tigranes, king of Media.

12. *Daughter of Antony ... to her*: In *Cleopatra*, Augustus tries to force Cleopatra 'into the Arms of *Tyberius*', a fate she narrowly escapes when Tiberius ultimately renounces his claim on her.

13. *Elisa ... Pyrates*: Cf. *Cleopatra*, III, iv.

14. *Cleopatra ... fair Breast*: Cleopatra was held captive by Artaxus, king of Armenia, on his ship; when her rescuers approached the ship, he held a sword to her breast to keep them at bay.

15. *And in fine ... cruel Death*: Arabella's point is clear: while Elisa's lover Artaban, though imprisoned, is not in mortal danger, both Cleopatra's brother, Caesario, and her lover, Coriolanus, are not only imprisoned by Augustus but also threatened with death (cf. *Cleopatra*, XII, iv).

16. *Oroondates ... was he belov'd*: See note 12, Book VI.

17. *Chair*: 'A light vehicle drawn by one horse; a chaise' (*OED*).

18. *her Women having been sent away before in the Stage*: Whereas the members of well-to-do families would travel by private coaches, servants usually travelled separately by public stage-coach (often sent on beforehand in order to investigate the route or to prepare the residence at which the family was going to stay).

BOOK IX

1. *St. James's Square*: Located just north of St James's Park, St James's Square, laid out by Henry Jermyn in the 1670s, was one of London's earliest squares. It was lined by exclusive houses for those people whose business made it essential to live near St James's Palace, and for fifty years was the most fashionable address in London, with seven dukes and seven earls in residence by the 1720s.

2. *Cards*: Part of the convention of paying social visits in the eighteenth century was to leave a card with a domestic servant, who would then announce your visit by presenting the card to the hosts, or to have one's card delivered in advance of one's visit.

3. *Ranelagh*: See note 5, Book IV.

4. *Rout*: 'Fashionable gathering or assembly, large evening party or reception' (*OED*).

5. *Vaux-Hall*: Vauxhall Gardens (known as 'New Spring Gardens' until 1785) were opened to the public in 1661. Jonathan Tyers bought the gardens in 1728 and developed them into the fashionable pleasure gardens they became by 1752. Vauxhall was located about two miles from the city of London, on the south side of the Thames – going across the water added to the gardens' rural appeal. Other attractions included outdoor concerts, a theatre, lighted gardens and refreshments. The Vauxhall crowds were mixed in terms of gender (it was a socially acceptable place for female leisure) and class (the price of admission being one shilling until 1792, when it was increased to two shillings). For some commentators, Vauxhall represented an ideal public space, while others reprobated its rowdiness and the illicit sexual encounters that took place in the dark walks.

6. *incog.*: Incognito.

7. *Lion Lysimachus kill'd*: See *Cassandra*, II, ii.

8. *Temple . . . suppos'd Death*: Because it had been foretold by the magi that Cyrus would one day be ruler over Media, there was much rejoicing among the Medes when the news of Cyrus's supposed death reached them. When Mandana is in the temple thanking the gods for his death, Cyrus (disguised as Artamenes) overhears her (*Artamenes*, I, i).

9. *sail in Barges . . . upon the Tyber*: Cf. *Cleopatra*, IX, ii.

10. *Season for Vaux-Hall being not yet over*: Vauxhall was open approximately three months of the year, usually from May to August. The last night of the season, in particular, was infamous

for the rowdy behaviour of the crowds. The drunken and aggressive naval officer and the intoxicated prostitute whom Arabella
encounters are plausible frequenters of Vauxhall.

11. *Gardens of Lucullus ... admirable Persons*: Arabella is thinking
of a scene in *Cleopatra* (IX, ii), in which Augustus entertains
Terentia, Maecenas's wife, with music and 'many gallant Conversations' in the famous Gardens of Lucullus in Rome.

12. *her Misfortunes ... express'd for her*: In *Cleopatra* (IX, iii),
Artesia (not Aspasia) escapes from the advances of Phraates, king
of Parthia, by disguising herself as a man.

13. *Mock-Heroicks*: In a manner ridiculing or burlesquing the heroic
style, character and discourse of the romance.

14. *Peruke*: A kind of wig worn from the seventeenth to the early
nineteenth century.

15. *Candace ... carry'd her away*: See note 18, Book IV.

16. *Hermione ... desir'd thee*: In *Cassandra* (III, iii, iv; V, i), Demetrius, prince of Phrygia, is attacked by an inexperienced warrior,
who, without inflicting any wounds on him, falls on the Prince's
sword, speaking the words here cited by Arabella ('Oh! Death
... desir'd thee!'). The warrior turns out to be a woman, Hermione, in a man's dress. She is mortally wounded, but lives long
enough for Demetrius to fall in love with her and for her to tell
at length of her passion for Alexander. At first torn by remorse,
rage and guilt, Demetrius later falls in love with Deidamia, who
herself was bemoaning the loss of Agis.

17. *Commission of Lunacy*: According to a thirteenth-century stat-
ute, De Praerogativa Regis (On the King's Prerogative) gave the
crown custody of the lands of natural fools and wardship of
the property of the insane during their insanity. The process of
establishing lunacy (before a jury) was sometimes known as a
'commission of lunacy'.

18. *gross Air ... Health so much*: Eighteenth-century London was
notorious for its intense air pollution. Because of the massive
burning of coal, the air over the city became filled with huge
amounts of smoke and soot containing sulphur dioxide and
nitrogen dioxide, which often made breathing difficult, if not
life-threatening. What made the situation worse was that the
smoke combined with London's equally notorious fog to create
what later came to be known as 'smog'.

19. *Richmond*: Then a small town in Surrey on the River Thames,
not far from London. Named after the fabulous Richmond Palace
that Henry VII had built there (around 1610), Richmond became

a fashionable resort after the opening of Richmond Wells in 1696. Apart from the palace and the many splendid homes, the town vaunted the luscious Richmond Park (once a favoured royal hunting ground) and Richmond Hill, which affords beautiful views over the Thames Valley.

20. *Twickenham*: A village in the present London borough of Richmond-upon-Thames. In the eighteenth century it became an exclusive retreat from court life, with the building of many elegant country houses. It was also popular with the foremost writers and artists. Henrietta Howard, mistress of George II and a friend of Horace Walpole, had Marble Hill House built for her and regularly entertained the greatest poets and wits of the day. Both Horace Walpole and Alexander Pope left their mark on Twickenham: Pope built his Grotto there, and, after he had bought Strawberry Hill in 1749, Walpole began to convert the modest home over the next fifty years into his own vision of a 'gothic fantasy' – thereby setting a new trend in gothic architecture.

21. *Mr. Glanville ... fell to the Ground*: This climactic duel is a farcical version of the duel in *Clarissa* between Colonel Morden and Lovelace; Bellmour, unlike Lovelace, does not have to die to expiate his sins, but he is condemned to marry the frivolous Charlotte Glanville.

22. *Brag*: 'A game at cards, essentially identical with the modern game of poker' (*OED*).

23. *Rescue of ... an absolute Stranger*: The rescues of Statira and Berenice are related in *Cassandra*, IV, v and IV, vi.

24. *that beauteous Roman Lady ... impious Sextus*: See note 42, Book II.

25. *she plung'd into the Thames ... Tyber*: At the end of Perdou de Subligny's *The Mock-Clelia: Being a Comical History of French Gallantries, and Novels, in Imitation of Dom Quixote* (which seems to have been one of the models for Lennox's novel), a deluded heroine rides her horse into a canal in imitation of Clelia's plunge into the Tiber. The mock-Clelia is partly cured by the cold water she imbibes (*The Mock-Clelia* (1678), p. 267).

26. *Kew-Lane*: A street in Richmond, at one time the home of the well-known poet James Thomson (1700–1748).

27. *quit the Kingdom*: Because English common law treated the killing of someone in a duel as an act of murder, those who had overcome their adversaries in a duel would often evade prosecution by fleeing to the continent or to one of the colonies.

28. *Pious and Learned Doctor* ——: This character is generally considered to be modelled on Lennox's mentor, Dr Samuel Johnson.

29. *Being in the Author's Opinion, the best Chapter in this History*:
Critics have speculated since the mid nineteenth century that
Samuel Johnson wrote this chapter but there is no conclusive
evidence. Recent critics, following Duncan Isles, have doubted
this theory (see Duncan Isles, Appendix to *The Female Quixote*,
ed. Dalziel (1989), pp. 419–28).

30. *Clelia ... Thrasymenian Lake*: A reference to an episode in
Clelia, in which the heroine is carried away by Horatius, who
keeps her on an island in Lake Trasimene.

31. *Candace ... on the Seas*: See *Cleopatra*, III, ii.

32. *Accidents ... Cleopatra*: Among the 'Accidents' that embittered
the life of Cleopatra was the fact that Augustus did not allow her
to marry the man she loved (Coriolanus), and that she was
abducted by Artaxus, king of Armenia, unwelcome or thwarted
love being the primary sufferings of a Romance heroine.

33. *Persecutions ... Elisa miserable*: The afflictions that beset the
'fair Elisa' were many. Thus, she was captured by pirates, married
against her will to Tigranes, king of Media, and was separated
from the man she loved, Artaban.

34. *Olympia ... Deidamia*: The sufferings that these heroines of
romance underwent are manifold but basically of two kinds:
facing various obstructions on the road to true love (notably
parental pressure, false rumours and abductions), and being
exposed to the unwelcome attentions of undesirable lovers.
Bellamira is the previously unmentioned heroine in *Pharamond*,
which also features the characters of Albysinda and Placidia.

35. *Child of Integrity*: A reference to Shakespeare's *Macbeth*. When
Malcolm, son of the murdered King Duncan of Scotland and
legitimate heir to the throne, confesses to the loyal Macduff that
he is too weak to oppose his father's murderer and usurper to
the throne, Macbeth, Macduff gives up all hope that Scotland
will ever be liberated from its tyrant ruler and breaks down in
deep and black despair. Malcolm is so touched by Macduff's
deeply felt patriotism, calling it 'this noble passion, / Child of
integrity' (IV.3.114–15), that he regains faith in his own abilities
to lead an army against Macbeth.

36. *Has taught the Passions to move at the Command of Virtue*:
This praise of Richardson by Johnson appears in the opening
lines of the *Rambler* 97 (19 February 1751); the rest of the
Rambler text is then turned over to a guest author, Samuel

Richardson himself. Lennox engages in complex and potentially ironic ways in the contemporary debate about novels versus romances. As David Marshall observes, 'At the moment that the author of the chapter evokes the example of Richardson – a model for the author who would write novels rather than romances – and cites the words and the authority of the author of the *Rambler*, she or he alludes to an instance in which "the author" has transferred the authority for his text to another author' ('Writing Masters', *Eighteenth-Century Fiction* 5.2 (1993), p. 128).

37. *Fables of Æsop ... Locman the Wise*: According to tradition, the author of *Aesop's Fables* was a Phrygian slave who probably lived from 620 to 560 BC. However, there is little information on Aesop's life, and some scholars even doubt whether he existed at all. The earliest extant collections of his work were made by Greek versifiers and Latin translators; tales from the Orient and from ancient sources were added to form what we now know as *Aesop's Fables*. Locman, or Lokman, who is said to have lived around 1050 BC, is one of the most celebrated sages of the East. A well-known collection of Arabic fables bears the name of Lokman. Since he was also black, and since Aesop appears to have adapted some of Lokman's fables for his own use, Lokman is often confused with Aesop. However, Aesop lived about 500 years later than Lokman.

38. *Ariosto*: Ludovico Ariosto (1474–1533), Italian poet and playwright, best known for his epic poem *Orlando Furioso* (1516, 1532).

39. *Punctilio*: 'A fine-drawn or fastidious objection, a scruple' (OED).

40. *Equipage*: All that is needed for a domestic establishment.

PENGUIN CLASSICS

CLARISSA, *OR* THE HISTORY OF A YOUNG LADY
SAMUEL RICHARDSON

'Oh thou savage-hearted monster! What work hast thou made in one guilty hour, for a whole age of repentance!'

Pressured by her unscrupulous family to marry a wealthy man she detests, Clarissa Harlowe flees with the witty and debonair Robert Lovelace and places herself under his protection. It soon transpires, however, that Lovelace is an untrustworthy rake whose vague promises of marriage are accompanied by unwelcome and increasingly brutal sexual advances. And yet, Clarissa finds his charm alluring, her scrupulous sense of virtue tinged with unconfessed desire. Told through a complex series of interweaving letters, *Clarissa* is a richly ambiguous study of a fatally attracted couple and a work of astonishing power and immediacy. A huge success when it first appeared in 1747, it remains one of the greatest of all European novels.

In his introduction, Angus Ross examines characterization, the epistolary style, the role of the family and the position of women in *Clarissa*. This edition also includes a chronology, suggestions for further reading, tables of letters, notes, a glossary and an appendix on the music for the 'Ode to Wisdom'.

'The first book in the world for the knowledge it displays of the human heart' Samuel Johnson

Edited with an introduction and notes by Angus Ross

PENGUIN CLASSICS

PAMELA   SAMUEL RICHARDSON

'I cannot be patient, I cannot be passive, when my virtue is in danger'

Fifteen-year-old Pamela Andrews, alone and unprotected, is relentlessly pursued by her dead mistress's son. Although she is attracted to young Mr B., she holds out against his demands and threats of abduction and rape, determined to defend her virginity and abide by her own moral standards. Psychologically acute in its investigations of sex, freedom and power, Richardson's first novel caused a sensation when it was first published, with its depiction of a servant heroine who dares to assert herself. Richly comic and full of lively scenes and descriptions, *Pamela* contains a diverse cast of characters, ranging from the vulgar and malevolent Mrs Jewkes to the aggressive but awkward country squire who serves this unusual love story as both its villain and its hero.

This edition incorporates all the revisions made by Richardson in his lifetime. Margaret A. Doody's introduction discusses the genre of epistolary novels, and examines characterization, the role of women and class differences in *Pamela*.

Edited by Peter Sabor with an introduction by Margaret A. Doody

PENGUIN CLASSICS

MOLL FLANDERS   DANIEL DEFOE

'I grew as impudent a Thief, and as dexterous as ever *Moll Cut-Purse* was'

Born and abandoned in Newgate Prison, Moll Flanders is forced to make her own way in life. She duly embarks on a career that includes husband-hunting, incest, bigamy, prostitution and pick-pocketing, until her crimes eventually catch up with her. One of the earliest and most vivid female narrators in the history of the English novel, Moll recounts her adventures with irresistible wit and candour – and enough guile that the reader is left uncertain whether she is ultimately a redeemed sinner or a successful opportunist.

Based on the first edition of 1722, this volume includes a chronology, notes on currency, and maps of London and Virginia in the late seventeenth century.

Edited with an introduction and notes by David Blewett

PENGUIN CLASSICS

AGNES GREY   ANNE BRONTË

'The name of governess, I soon found, was a mere mockery ... my pupils had no more notion of obedience than a wild, unbroken colt'

When her family becomes impoverished after a disastrous financial speculation, Agnes Grey determines to find work as a governess in order to contribute to their meagre income and assert her independence. But Agnes's enthusiasm is swiftly extinguished as she struggles first with the unmanageable Bloomfield children and then with the painful disdain of the haughty Murray family; the only kindness she receives comes from Mr Weston, the sober young curate. Drawing on her own experience, Anne Brontë's first novel offers a compelling personal perspective on the desperate position of unmarried, educated women for whom becoming a governess was the only respectable career open in Victorian society.

This edition also includes Charlotte Brontë's memoir of her sisters, the 'Biographical Notice of Ellis and Acton Bell'. Angeline Goreau examines Anne Brontë's complex relationship with her sisters and her unhappy career as a governess as influences in writing Agnes Grey.

'Amazingly modern ... Agnes Grey is a little masterpiece'
Victoria Glendinning, *Daily Telegraph*

Edited with an introduction and notes by Angeline Goreau

PENGUIN CLASSICS

THE PROFESSOR   CHARLOTTE BRONTË

'She was not handsome, she was not rich, she was not even
accomplished, yet she was my life's treasure; I must then be a man of
peculiar discernment'

Working as a professor in M Pelet's establishment in Brussels, William
Crimsworth meets the fascinating Directrice of the neighbouring school,
Mlle Zoräide Reuter and, recognizing her as an intellectual equal, becomes
powerfully attracted to her. Despite her betrothal to M Pelet, Mlle Reuter
will not release her hold over William, and she tries to stand in the way
of his finding love elsewhere. But new possibilities open up to him and he
is not to be so easily deterred. Published two years after the author's
death, *The Professor* draws on Charlotte Brontë's own professional and
personal experiences as a teacher in Brussels. Like *Jane Eyre* and *Villette*
it is the intimate first-person account of a life that brings extremes of
despair and joy.

In her introduction, Heather Glen examines the character of William in
the context of love of wealth and the importance of moral and social
propriety, and considers him as the model of a self-made man.

Edited with an introduction and notes by Heather Glen

PENGUIN CLASSICS

THE MOONSTONE   WILKIE COLLINS

'When you looked down into the stone, you looked into a yellow deep that drew your eyes into it so that they saw nothing else'

The Moonstone, a yellow diamond looted from an Indian temple and believed to bring bad luck to its owner, is bequeathed to Rachel Verinder on her eighteenth birthday. That very night the priceless stone is stolen again and when Sergeant Cuff is brought in to investigate the crime, he soon realizes that no one in Rachel's household is above suspicion. Hailed by T. S. Eliot as 'the first, the longest, and the best of modern English detective novels', *The Moonstone* is a marvellously taut and intricate tale of mystery, in which facts and memory can prove treacherous and not everyone is as they first appear.

Sandra Kemp's introduction examines *The Moonstone* as a work of Victorian sensation fiction and an early example of the detective genre, and discusses the technique of multiple narrators, the role of opium, and Collins's sources and autobiographical references.

'Enthralling and believable ... evokes in vivid language the spirit of a place' P. D. James, *Sunday Times*

Edited with an introduction and notes by Sandra Kemp

PENGUIN CLASSICS

CRANFORD
ELIZABETH GASKELL

'It is very pleasant dining with a bachelor ... I only hope it is not improper; so many pleasant things are!'

A portrait of the residents of an English country town in the mid-nineteenth century, *Cranford* relates the adventures of Miss Matty and Miss Deborah, two middle-aged spinster sisters striving to live with dignity in reduced circumstances. Through a series of vignettes, Elizabeth Gaskell portrays a community governed by old-fashioned habits and dominated by friendships between women. Her wry account of rural life is undercut, however, by tragedy in its depiction of such troubling events as Matty's bankruptcy, the violent death of Captain Brown and the unwitting cruelty of Peter Jenkyns. Written with acute observation, *Cranford* is by turns affectionate, moving and darkly satirical.

In her introduction, Patricia Ingham discusses *Cranford* in relation to Gaskell's own past and as a work of irony in the manner of Jane Austen. She also considers the implications of the novel as to class and empire. This edition also includes further reading, notes and an appendix on the significance of 'Fashion at Cranford'.

Edited with an introduction and notes by Patricia Ingham

PENGUIN CLASSICS

THE HISTORY OF TOM JONES
HENRY FIELDING

'He was indeed a thoughtless, giddy youth, with little sobriety in his manners, and less in his countenance'

A foundling of mysterious parentage brought up by Mr Allworthy on his country estate, Tom Jones is deeply in love with the seemingly unattainable Sophia Western, the beautiful daughter of the neighbouring squire – though he sometimes succumbs to the charms of the local girls. But when his amorous escapades earn the disapproval of his benefactor, Tom is banished to make his own fortune. Sophia, meanwhile, is determined to avoid an arranged marriage to Allworthy's scheming nephew and escapes from her rambunctious father to follow Tom to London. A vivid Hogarthian panorama of eighteenth-century life, spiced with danger and intrigue, bawdy exuberance and good-natured authorial interjections, *Tom Jones* (1749) is one of the greatest and most ambitious comic novels in English literature.

In his introduction to this new Penguin Classics edition, Thomas Keymer discusses narrative techniques and themes, the context of eighteenth-century fiction and satire, and the historical and political background of the Jacobite Rebellion. This volume also includes a chronology, further reading, notes, a glossary and an appendix on Fielding's revisions.

Edited by Thomas Keymer and Alice Wakely

With an introduction by Thomas Keymer

THE STORY OF PENGUIN CLASSICS

Before 1946 ...'Classics' are mainly the domain of academics and students, without readable editions for everyone else. This all changes when a little-known classicist, E. V. Rieu, presents Penguin founder Allen Lane with the translation of Homer's *Odyssey* that he has been working on and reading to his wife Nelly in his spare time.

1946 *The Odyssey* becomes the first Penguin Classic published, and promptly sells three million copies. Suddenly, classic books are no longer for the privileged few.

1950s Rieu, now series editor, turns to professional writers for the best modern, readable translations, including Dorothy L. Sayers's *Inferno* and Robert Graves's *The Twelve Caesars*, which revives the salacious original.

1960s The Classics are given the distinctive black jackets that have remained a constant throughout the series's various looks. Rieu retires in 1964, hailing the Penguin Classics list as 'the greatest educative force of the 20th century'.

1970s A new generation of translators arrives to swell the Penguin Classics ranks, and the list grows to encompass more philosophy, religion, science, history and politics.

1980s The Penguin American Library joins the Classics stable, with titles such as *The Last of the Mohicans* safeguarded. Penguin Classics now offers the most comprehensive library of world literature available.

1990s The launch of Penguin Audiobooks brings the classics to a listening audience for the first time, and in 1999 the launch of the Penguin Classics website takes them online to a larger global readership than ever before.

The 21st Century Penguin Classics are rejacketed for the first time in nearly twenty years. This world famous series now consists of more than 1300 titles, making the widest range of the best books ever written available to millions – and constantly redefining the meaning of what makes a 'classic'.

The Odyssey continues ...

The best books ever written

PENGUIN CLASSICS

SINCE 1946

Find out more at www.penguinclassics.com